RIPPLES OF DISSENT

RIPPLES OF DISSENT

WOMEN'S STORIES OF MARRIAGE IN THE 1890s

Edited by
BRIDGET BENNETT
University of Warwick

J. M. Dent & Sons London

First published in Great Britain in 1996 by
J. M. Dent, The Orion Publishing Group
5 Upper St Martin's Lane, London WC2H 9EA

Selection, introduction and other critical matter © J. M. Dent 1966

British Library cataloguing-in-publication data
is available upon request.

Typeset at The Spartan Press Ltd,
Lymington, Hants
Printed in England by
Butler & Tanner Ltd,
Frome & London

ISBN 0 460 87777 1

CONTENTS

NOTE ON THE EDITOR

BRIDGET BENNETT is a lecturer in the Department of English and Comparative Literary Studies at the University of Warwick. She works predominantly on British and American fiction of the late nineteenth and early twentieth centuries, and has written on, among others, Willa Cather and Charlotte Perkins Gilman. Her most recent book is on the American journalist and novelist Harold Frederic, which will appear in 1996. She is currently co-editing a collection of essays called *From Grub Street to the Ivory Tower*.

Special thanks to Gráinne Walshe and Sue Wiseman
for assistance, one way and another, with finding words;
to the many people who offered suggestions and gave practical
help, and to Sanju Velaní who often likes a mention and always
deserves one.

INTRODUCTION

'The bell rings, the guard locks the door, the train steams out, and as it passes the signal-box, a large well-kept hand, with a signet ring on the little finger, pulls down the blind on the window of an engaged carriage.' In a single sentence from 'Virgin Soil', George Egerton sets up a series of events which prefigure a young woman's sexual initiation at the hands of the brutal man whom she has just married. Each clause registers a new event which works towards the overall image of closure, of shutting out, of darkness. The bride of seventeen who, moments before, was weeping on her mother's shoulder, has passed from the visible realm of the narrative into the unspoken, even unspeakable or unwritable arena of marital sex, a world strictly censored and patrolled. The movement from the public performance of the wedding ceremony to the private one of the wedding night is ominously presaged. Her mother's silence and her inability to find words to speak of the sexual encounter which her daughter is shortly to experience (one which has been strenuously kept from her throughout her life) imply complicity.

The older woman's part in the system of flagrant abuse which, for Egerton, is characteristic of many marriages, forms one of the subjects of the story. Egerton sets out the drama of her narrative with uncomfortable skill. The progression from young unmarried woman to wife is charted with highly stylised symbolism: the locked door, the private carriage, the social privileging of relationships between men, the sounding of the bell, and the train; itself the site of so many erotic meetings and encounters in nineteenth-century fiction. As the heavy hand comes down and signals the new and disciplined privacy which conventionally characterises marital union, a range of questions is raised about how the institution of marriage is perceived at the turn of the century and how it is to be written, read, or understood. Is it a public institution or a private contract? What can be said about the manifestation of desire within the acceptable boundaries of the marriage contract? To what extent can female desire be contemplated or discussed in debates around marriage, and in what terms? What sort of language can women find to discuss their own agency either amongst themselves or with men, and how can they move between private debate and public pronouncement? In the stories of *Ripples of Dissent* women find voices to articulate these questions, to address these concerns, and to create new forms within which it may be possible to do so. In Egerton's 'Virgin Soil' the lowering of the blind is by no means the end: what the husband tries to censor, the wife will later reveal in full. The story's formal innovations are characteristic of many of the stories in this collection. It was such subversion of the conventions of nineteenth-century realism which also allowed women at the end of the century to voice their concerns, to express their dissent.

At the turn of the century marriage was being debated to an unprecedented degree both in Britain and in the United States, and was subject to new intellectual inquiry. Women at this period questioned at enormous length the possibilities open to them. Might marriage be reformed or must it be rejected altogether? How available were other sorts of sexual unions for women? One option open to women was to refuse marriage altogether until such time as it might be possible to have an equal and equitable relationship between the sexes. This argument was put by, amongst others, the American educator M. Carey Thomas, who in 1894 became the President of Bryn Mawr College. She wrote in 1881 to a male correspondent that, it 'is no woman's *duty* to marry; whether she be in love or not, it is her duty to consider true marriage, if you choose, a completion to a life but a completion which may come or not but will surely not come if she marry without love or if the man whom she love be in any way a hindrance to attaining the highest that she desires . . . In a transition state I think it would be quite often a *duty* and a pleasure not to marry.'[1] British women shared the belief that celibacy might be constituted as a political act, a way of criticising the sexual double standard and of protection against venereal infections. Margaret Harkness wrote to a friend that 'an unmarried woman living a true life is far nobler than a married woman', and Beatrice Webb noted in her diary that if numbers of intellectual women were to remain celibate, 'the special force of womanhood – motherly feeling – may be forced into public work'.[2] In each of these examples a high moral code is suggested – 'true marriage'; 'the highest that she deserves'; 'true life'; 'the special force of woman-hood': woman's body is represented as a sanctified site, one in which the future of the race is to be produced, and her sensibility is one which is innately refined, even spiritual, above that of men.

For some women the issue of marriage was one of reform rather than of rejection: sexual unions outside marriage – either lesbian or heterosexual – could not be substituted for a state ordained by God and set down by law. Marriage might be – should be – improved, but not abandoned. These, however, were topics which were up for debate, and a number of the woman writers repre-sented in this collection would argue, through their fiction, that this was not invariably the case. The question of women's desire was also widely contested. A number of the writers represented here, notably Kate Chopin, took the position that women's sexuality was not passive, nor was women's sexual desire minimal. Celibacy could not be an answer: instead women must find ways of allowing for sexual expression either within marriage or outside it.

Some women were more concerned with the question of collec-tive rights. In a letter to the New York *Tribune* in 1898, the American feminist Elizabeth Cady Stanton expressed outrage that women should be constrained by the legislative processes by which marriage was constituted, demanding, 'Shall women be denied the right of protest against laws in which she had no voice; laws which outrage the holiest affections of her nature; laws which transcend the limits of human legislation in a convention called for the express purpose of considering her wrongs?'[3] The British writer Mona Caird, whose 1894 novel *The Daughters of Danaus* epitomised for many the innovative and daring New Woman fiction, started a storm of protest with her two essays 'Ideal Marriage' and 'Marriage' in the *Westminster Review*. She argued that conventional marriage was a failure, that for women marriage was little more than a legalised form of slavery: women entered into it, very often, for financial reasons, and had their health ruined by frequent childbearing and by restrictions on their activities, their social responsibilities and their intellectual de-velopment. 'Dependence, in short, is the curse of our marriages, of our homes, and of our children, who are born of women who are not free – not free even to refuse to bear them', she wrote.[4]

Between August and September 1888 the *Daily Telegraph* printed twenty-seven thousand responses to the debate which her articles had stimulated, prompted by a further question which the paper raised, 'Is Marriage a Failure?' Yet as Judith Walkowitz has pointed out, the message which this flood of responses suggested was curiously mixed, due to the context in which it was received by its readership, since on the very pages in which the letters appeared another sexual drama of a terrifying kind was being reported – an account of the Whitechapel murders, or 'Jack the Ripper' murders as they became known. As she argues, the 'newspaper columns thus reveal a schizophrenic division of the sexual drama – the apparently petty disputes and squabbles of middle-class marriage were juxtaposed in apparent contrast to East End prostitution . . . the imaginative fantasies woven around the stories of the Ripper murders implicitly connect the two scenarios, and explicitly link the world of West End gender relations with the carnage of the East End'.[5] Gothic accounts of marriage as 'the horror', or as a form of murder or of living death, are represented in this collection; indeed deaths are not uncommon.

Campaigns for sexual purity and discussions about sexually transmitted diseases, the condition of prostitution and the age of consent, allowed women to speak about the relation between the sexes and to have a public voice in issues which had more traditionally been kept private. Some women advocated a more individualistic ethic. The infamous Victoria Woodhull, the first woman stockbroker on Wall Street and a self-declared proponent of 'free-love', made this point with characteristic acerbity: 'All this talk of women's rights is moonshine. Women have every right. They only have to exercise them. That's what we're doing.'[6] Polemical leaflets and articles about marriage abounded. In 1898 a book called *The Modern Marriage Market* appeared in Britain. It was a collection of essays which had already appeared in *The Lady's Realm* the previous year, and it was written by a surprisingly disparate group of women: the popular novelist Marie Corelli, Lady Jeune, Flora Annie Steel and the Countess of Malmesbury. What is interesting is the ways in which the very differing beliefs of these women reflect upon one another in the collection. Marie Corelli – appropriately for a romantic novelist – asserts the sacred nature of true love and expresses particular concern over the way in which young women are set up by their parents for marriage for financial reasons. She writes, 'A marriage is "arranged" as a matter of convenience or social interest; lawyers draft settlements and conclude the sale, – and a priest of the Most High God is called in to bless the bargain. But it is nevertheless a bargain, – a trafficking in human bodies and souls, as open and as shameless as any similar scene in Stamboul'.[7] Mercenary marriages, and marriages based primarily on financial exigency are common themes within these stories.

In 1897, the same year in which these articles first appeared in *The Lady's Realm*, Elizabeth Chapman commented that 'it has, for some time past, become difficult to take up a novel in which, openly or covertly, directly or indirectly, the institution of marriage is not either put upon its trial, or at any rate freely discussed and handled with as much or as little ceremony as though it were, say, a moot point of science or a minor question of politics. The once sacred, the once theoretically indissoluble life-tie between husband and wife has become, in short, an open question.'[8] Though her primary interest here is the novel, it is certainly also the case that in short fiction issues which increasingly concerned women – debates about the domestic sphere, about the world of work outside of the home, education, childbirth and contraception, the transmission of disease, suffrage, to name a few – were continuously being discussed and contested around the turn of the century by women and by men.

Though a great deal has been written about the New Woman novels of the 1890s, and of the representation of the Woman Question within this writing, the period following 1890 marked one of the high points of the development of the short story, a moment at which the dominance of the realist novel began to crumble and in its place a variety of experimental fictional forms emerged – some pre-Modernist, some proto-Modernist. A variety of determining factors, material as well as political, made this possible. One, particularly in Britain, was the decline in the cumbersome triple-decker novel, butt of much mordant humour. In 1884 one-hundred-and-ninety-three triple-decker novels were published: in 1897 only four appeared. Another related influence was the slackening of the dominance of the lending libraries, Mudie's and Smith's, and with this the loosening of the censorship with which they were credited. Another key factor in both Britain and the United States was the massive growth of the periodical press: *The Savoy*, *The Yellow Book*, *Harper's New Monthly*

Magazine and *The Idler* were just a few of the era's many journals regularly publishing fiction and bringing it to huge audiences. Periodicals were also changing as advertising became more sophisticated. By the turn of the century the revenue from adverts placed in the periodical press permitted the payment of considerable fees for pieces of short fiction. Indeed, even the boundaries between advertisements and literature were challenged as that advertisements seemed to move increasingly into the realm of fiction or of fictionality, occasionally by posing as literature, even parodying well-known pieces of literature at times. The American critic and novelist W. D. Howells, reviewing a book called *Good Advertising* (1896) in *Harper's Weekly*, invented a debate between himself and a friend about this new breed of person, the writer of advertising copy. His imaginary friend notes that 'some of those chaps make $15,000 or $20,000 by ad-smithing. They have put their art quite on a level with fiction pecuniarily.'[9] Just as the advertising industry was adjusting itself in order to take into account the new realities of late nineteenth-century capitalism, so writers of short fiction were accommodating themselves to the changing state of the literary market.

A dramatic change came about in the United States in 1891. The International Copyright Act of that year brought protection to the work of foreign nationals and meant that it was no longer profitable to indulge in copyright piracy. With the collapse of a previously lucrative market which had served American periodicals and magazines well, copy had to be looked for elsewhere. A new interest in American works was stimulated so, as Andrew Levy argues in *The Cultural Commerce of The American Short Story*, the 'new copyright agreement, when coupled with the growth within the American magazine industry, and the position of respectability occupied by the short story magazine aesthetics, catalyzed the explosion of national interest in the short story'.[10] The short story became profitable for magazine owners and publishers, and authors began to compete within a highly commercialised marketplace. The short story was a form which lent itself particularly to women writers: it made fewer demands on the time of women writers than the novel, and it could bring immediate cash to women writers who might be supporting themselves, and perhaps a family too, by their writing. For all of these reasons the short story, often

written by women, flourished at the turn of the century in Britain
and in the United States.

Women writers were interested in examining the ways in which
they and other women existed within the world in economic as
well as political terms. They were also particularly concerned with
showing the relationship between what woman read and the way
in which they lived their lives. Though this was not solely the
prerogative of women writers (Flaubert's Emma Bovary con-
structed her world through her reading to disastrous effect), for
radical women writers of polemical fiction it was important to
show that their female protagonists engaged with the world
around them in a critical and informed way. Certainly the writers
of New Woman fiction were explicit about the ways in which the
act of reading allowed middle-class women whose social status
was often shared by the protagonists of New Woman fiction to
engage with issues which their older female relatives found shocking or beyond their domain. An example of this in Ménie Muriel
Dowie's 1895 novel *Gallia* comes from the moment at which
Gallia's mother and aunt find that she is reading about the
Contagious Diseases Act in the newspapers. Though acts were
passed in 1864, 1866 and 1869, the campaigning against them
went on for much longer, and it was finally repealed in 1886.
Having expressed their shocked response to their discovery her
aunt tries to dissuade Gallia from becoming engaged with the
question since, she argues, as she has no political agency it is a
waste of her time to consider it. It is her mother, however, who
makes the most telling response: 'I think, dear, if you knew how
much phrases of that kind can hurt and distress other women who
have – who have striven to play their part of wife and mother
well, you would perhaps reserve them.'[11] Her quiet and resigned
comment demonstrates her belief in the power of passive feminine
'influence' within the domestic realm.

The writing in this collection is a refutation of silence and of
passivity. That is not to say that each of the stories has a radical
political agenda – far from it: instead they offer a range of
perspectives and investigations of courtship and engagement, of
the wedding ceremony itself, and of the aftermath. One of the
most difficult aspects of compiling an edition, beyond, that is, the
search for material itself, is the matter of how to justify certain

exclusions and how to accommodate certain texts. I have chosen to
compile a collection of pieces of short fiction at the turn of the
century and I have had to decide which years constitute this
particular period for the purposes of this work. The stories do not
necessarily reflect my own political positions or ideology. I do not
endorse many of the beliefs expressed in these stories. The reader
should approach them from a historical perspective and evaluate
them accordingly. Various stories which seemed tantalisingly
suitable have had to be left out since they did not fit my rough
chronology. A further problem was how to include the Anglo-
American dimension which enables the reader to trace trans-
Atlantic contiguities. Here, as elsewhere, I have not been very strict
with either myself or the final form of this work, instead allowing a
relative indulgence and a high degree of subjectivity to govern what
emerged from my researches. What unifies the stories is that they
were all written by women in English between 1890 and 1914, and
that they all meditate in some way upon, or provide a contribution
to, debates around the institution of marriage. Though the
majority of the stories are by British and American writers, there
are a few exceptions which I have justified owing to the fact that the
writers of these stories were in some way clearly associated with
Britain or America, living and/or publishing there for a period in
their lives. By making the collection chronological I hope to allow
for a degree of creativity on the part of the reader who can gather
and browse as she will, without having externally chosen
'groupings', beyond the chronological, imposed on her.

  The problem with such a collection is not where to begin, but
where to finish. There is a huge body of material to choose from,
and it makes any collection seem somewhat arbitrary. There are a
number of fine writers from Britain and America whose writing is
not represented here. What finally governed my choice was the
relative relation of the stories to each other: simply put, they
complemented each other and showed the great diversity and
richness of women's responses to marriage.

BRIDGET BENNETT

References

[1]Letter to Richard Cadbury, 10 February 1881, cited in Ruth Barnes
    Moynihan, Cynthia Russett, Laurence Crumpacker (eds.), *Second to*

None: A Documentary History of American Women, II (Lincoln & London: University of Nebraska Press, 1993) pp. 44–5.

[2] Cited in Elaine Showalter, *Sexual Anarchy: Gender and Culture at the Fin de Siècle* (London: Bloomsbury, (1990) 1991).

[3] Cited in Moynihan, et al (eds.), p. 13.

[4] Mona Caird, *The Morality of Marriage and Other Essays on the Status and Destiny of Women* (London: George Redway, 1897) p. 134.

[5] Judith R. Walkowitz, *City of Dreadful Delight: Narratives of Sexual Danger in Late-Victorian London* (London: Virago (1992) 1994) p. 168.

[6] Johanna Johnston, *Mrs Satan: The Incredible Saga of Victoria Woodhull* (London & Melbourne: Macmillan & Co. Ltd., 1967) p. 13.

[7] Marie Corelli et al., *The Modern Marriage Market* (London: Hutchinson & Co., 1898) p. 38.

[8] Elizabeth Rachel Chapman, *Marriage Questions in Modern Fiction, and Other Essays on Kindred Subjects* (London: John Lane, The Bodley Head, 1897) p. 10.

[9] Cited in Jackson Lears, *Fables of Abundance: A Cultural History of Advertising in America* (New York: Harper Collins, 1994). For a further account of consumerist desire in American culture at the turn of the century see also William Leach, *Land of Desire: Merchants, Power, and the Rise of a New American Culture* (New York: Vintage Books, 1993).

[10] See Andrew Levy, *The Cultural Commerce of the American Short Story* in Cambridge Studies in American Literature and Culture, (CUP 1993) pp. 30–34.

[11] Ménie Muriel Dowie, *Gallia*, edited by Helen Small (London: Everyman Paperbacks, 1995) pp. 34–5.

NOTE ON THE TEXTS

Amy Levy's *Wise in Her Generation* was first published in 1890. This, and other writings of Levy can be found in *The Complete Novels and Selected Writings of Amy Levy 1861–1889* edited by Melvyn New (Gainesville: University of Florida, 1993). Lucy Clifford's *On the Wane: A Sentimental Correspondence* appeared in *Love Letters of a Worldly Woman* (London: Edward Arnold, 1891). Mary Wilkins Freeman's *A New England Nun* was published, in 1891, in *A New England Nun and Other Stories* (New York: Harper, London: Osgood). E. Nesbit's *John Charrington's Wedding* first appeared in September 1891 in *Temple Bar*. Mary Belle Freeley's *A Ripple of Dissension and What Came of It* and *The Story of Eve* are both from *Fair to Look Upon* (Chicago: Morrill, Higgins and Co., 1892). They do not appear to have been published in England before now. *Mimi's Marriage* by Grace King appeared in *Balcony Stories* (New York: The Century Co., 1892). Olive Schreiner's *The Buddhist Priest's Wife* was written in 1892 and collected in 1923 in *Stories, Dreams and Allegories* (London: Unwin). Jane Barlow's *Between Two Lady Days* first appeared in her collection *Irish Idylls* (London: Hodder and Stoughton, 1893). *Elizabeth* by Margaret Deland appeared in 1893 in *Mr Tommy Dove and Other Stories* (New York: Houghton, Mifflin and Co.). Sarah Orne Jewett's *Miss Esther's Guest* was published in *A Native of Winby and Other Tales* (New York: Houghton, Mifflin and Co., 1893). *Virgin Soil* by George Egerton was collected in *Discords* (London: John Lane, 1894). Leila Macdonald's *Jeanne-Marie* first appeared in *The Yellow Book* in October 1894. Flora Annie Steel's *The Reformer's Wife* first appeared in 1894 in the October edition of *Macmillan's Magazine*. *The Prayer* by Violet Hunt was first published as *The Story of a Ghost* in *Chapman's Magazine of Fiction* in the Christmas number of December 1895. *The Pleasure-Pilgrim* by Ella D'Arcy was first published in *The Yellow Book* in April 1895. Kate

Douglas Wiggin's *Huldah the Prophetess* was first published in New York by Harper and Brothers in 1895. *Suggestion* by Ada Leverson was first published in *The Yellow Book* in April 1895. *A Correspondence* by Netta Syrett also first appeared in *The Yellow Book*, in October 1895. Willa Cather's *Tommy, the Unsentimental* first appeared in August 1896 in *The Home Monthly*. Ménie Muriel Dowie's *An Idyll in Millinery* was first published in *The Yellow Book* in July 1896. Kate Chopin's *The Storm* was written in 1898 but remained unpublished until 1969 when it appeared in Per Seyerstad's edition of Chopin's writing, *The Complete Works of Kate Chopin* (Baton Rouge: Louisiana State University). *The Story of a Wedding Tour* by Margaret Oliphant first appeared in 1898 in *A Widow's Tale and Other Stories* (Edinburgh: Blackwood's). Pauline E. Hopkins *Br'or Abr'm Jimson's Wedding* was first published in the *Colored American Magazine* in December 1901. Lady Gregory's *The Wedding of Maine Morgor* was published in *Cuchulain of Murthemine: The Story of the Men of the Red Branch of Ulster* (London: John Murray, 1902). Sara Jeanette Duncan's *A Mother in India* was first published in *The Pool in the Desert* in 1903 (New York: Appleton). Edith Wharton's *The Reckoning* was first published in 1904 in *The Descent of Man and Other Stories* (New York: Charles Scribner's Sons). Mary Austin's *The Fakir* appeared in 1909 in *Lost Borders*, a sequel to her 1903 *The Land of Little Rain* (New York and London: Harper and Brothers). Violet Jacob's *Providence and Colonel Dormer* appeared in a collection of 1910 called *The Fortune-Hunters and Other Stories* (London: John Murray). Charlotte Perkins Gilman's *If I Were a Man* was first published in *Physical Culture* in July 1914.

AMY LEVY

Wise in her Generation

I

It was a charming party at Mrs Westerleigh's; a good floor, a good band, and a respectable set of people. I wore my new gown from Russell and Allen's – no *débutante* foam of tulle or net, but a really handsome confection in white corded silk, the sort of thing which exactly suits my style, Nature never having cut me out for the part of *jeune fille*. We arrived a little late, but a great many people seemed to have room for my name on their programmes; indeed, throughout the evening I enjoyed the rather novel sensation of a ball-room success. Not that I set much value on such a bit of social gilt-gingerbread. All very well for boys and girls in their first season, but by no means fitted to satisfy the appetite of persons arriving at years of discretion.

The dancing had stopped when we got into the room, and I stood for a few moments in the doorway making up my book for the events of the night. Regy Walker was negotiating with me for the supper dances, when the Shands were announced. I looked up, without moving a hair, and saw them within a yard of me – Philip and Philip's wife.

The latter I observed to be slight and pale; not ugly, of course, for in these days even heiresses cannot afford to be ugly, but generally insignificant. But her maid, her tailor, and her corset-maker are evidently the best of their kind.

I don't know how long Regy Walker and I stood there adjusting our ball-cards; perhaps a minute, perhaps a hundred years. Then the room went round suddenly, and I found myself shaking hands with Philip.

Our eyes met; he smiled his wonderful smile. It might almost have been last year. But it can never be last year again.

Last year, Philip, you were a hard-working, ambitious young man of whom great things were already prophesied at the Bar; this year you are a person of importance – your fortune made, your position assured. Last year I was a one-idea'd young person in a white frock, who blushed and smiled with undisguised delight when her friend approached her; who had smiles and blushes for no one else; whose days were full of vague, delicious happiness; whose wakeful nights were sweeter than nights of dreams. This year I am a woman who knows her weakness, knows also her strength, and has had her experience.

It is the third day, and I have risen again.

Without knowledge of life there can be no true enjoyment of life. Life, I maintain, in the face of the sentimentalists, to be an acquired taste. For the educated palate there are all sorts of gustatory surprises – olives, caviare, a host of sauces – far more delicious than, if not quite so wholesome as, the roast meat and boiled pudding of domesticity. You were right, Philip; and I, who once believed myself your victim, crushed beneath the Juggernaut-car of your ambition – I was wrong.

Meanwhile, I have left us – Philip Shand and Virginia Warwick – shaking hands with one another, and smiling into one another's faces, with almost exaggerated amiability.

'Am I too late for a waltz?'

'There is only number eleven left.'

'A quadrille! I ask for bread, and you give me a stone.'

I wrote down his initials on my card, and he made off, smiling brilliantly.

I stood looking after him with a curious sense of unreality, divided between a desire to laugh aloud, and another – to go from the room, from the house, to some vague, impossible region of darkness and silence and solitude. At the same moment, I grew aware of a pair of wide-open grey eyes, fixed upon myself with unconventional intentness, from the distance. Their owner was a tall, fair, weedy young man, whose whole appearance was indefinably different from that of the surrounding people. It was not long before Mrs Westerleigh swept up to me with this unknown young man in her wake.

'Sir Guy Ormond – Miss Warwick.'

We both bowed, and he asked me for a dance, with a fervour quite disproportionate to the request.

'Some poor little waif of a swell!' was my reflection, as he wrote his name against the twelfth waltz – the only unclaimed dance on my card.

For it must be owned that we were that night a distinctly middle-class gathering, a great mixed mob of Londoners; no mere Belgravian birds of passage, but people whose interests and avocations lay well within the Great City.

'May I take you in to supper later on?' said Sir Guy earnestly.

'Yes, please,' I answered, giving him a glance almost as serious as his own. Certainly, there is no game so amusing as that which Philip taught me to play last year. At the opening of the eleventh dance Philip came up to me.

'You don't want to dance this thing?'

He lowered his voice to the old confidential pitch; but his manner was a shade less confident than of old. After all, why not? I hate quadrilles, and I like to talk with Philip.

'If you will allow me,' he said, as we strolled off to the conservatory, 'I will introduce you to my wife.'

And then I found myself bowing and smiling to a colourless person, who bowed and smiled in her turn, and announced her intention of calling on me at an early date.

A few minutes later I was in the conservatory, lounging in a delicious chair; a becoming pink lantern swung above my head. Opposite me, his chair drawn close to mine, sat a well-groomed gentleman in evening dress, with expressive eyes and a vivacious, intelligent face. A charming picture of manners, is it not?

Little by little I gave myself up to the pleasure of the moment, which, when all is said, was considerable.

He is not the Philip of last year, but he has the same eyes and the same voice. The Philip of last year never, indeed, existed, save in my imagination; but I have caught the trick of *bien-être* in the society of this person who looks like him; of basking in the glow of that radiant vitality, the warmth of that magnetic presence.

'May I take you in to supper?' said Philip presently.

'I have arranged to go in with Sir Guy Ormond.'

He looked at me curiously.

'The bloated aristocrat! But perhaps he is a friend of yours?'

'I was introduced to him tonight.'

'He's a good fellow; a little sentimental and dilettante, but you can afford to be sentimental on thirty thousand a year.'

Thirty thousand a year! Sir Guy was a person of more import-ance than I had imagined. I dropped my eyes to my fan, and Philip went on in his familiar, mocking fashion.

'Do you love blue-books? Are you devoted to poor-law reports?

What is your opinion of Toynbee Hall? And when, Miss Virginia Warwick, were you last at the People's Palace? By such paths lies the way to the royal favour.'

I looked up and met the glance, mocking and serious and curiously intent, of his brilliant eyes. At the same moment, someone brushed through the ferns and lounges to where we sat, and announced himself as my partner for the next waltz.

It was Sir Guy Ormond.

Philip rose at once, with an air of ostentatious magnanimity, a flourish of *fair play* in every line of him. The look in his eyes stung me. Was he insulting me, this polite person, bowing himself gracefully away? But after all, is there any deeper wrong, any crueller insult left for him to offer?

Let me write it down, once for all, that we must remain for ever unspoken, unexpressed.

If a man stabs you, or robs you, or injures your fair fame, do you take these things at his hands in silence? Even if he escape the world's punishment, do you smile upon him in the face of the world?

Idle questions, no doubt!

And I – I shall go on smiling at Philip to the end of the chapter!

2

I wonder, sometimes, that we do not go oftener to the bad, we girls of the well-to-do classes.

If you come to think of it, it is a curious ordeal we pass through at the very outset of our career. Take a girl in the schoolroom and see what her life is.

A dingy room, dowdy dresses, bread and butter, and governesses! In all the household there is, perhaps, no person of less importance than she. Then, one day, this creature, knowing nothing of the world, and less, if possible, of herself, is launched on the stream of fashionable or pseudo-fashionable life. At what has been hitherto her bedtime, she is arrayed gorgeously, whirled through a gas-lit city, and finally let loose in a crowded ballroom, there to sink or swim. There are lights, jewels, heavy scents, and dreamy, delicious music; it is all a whirl, a clatter, a profusion. And there are a great many people, gay, good-looking, well dressed. One person comes to her again and again. He is a great deal older than she, with all the assurance of strength and experience. Deferential and tyrannical, he entreats and commands at one and the same time. And he has a strange power of sympathy, a wonderful insight into her innocence; knows her better than herself, it seems, this charming, clever person. Everywhere he follows her about; with every look, with every tone, he says: '*I love you.*'

She does not know why she is so happy. All day long she dreams, dreams, or gossips of the night to come. If she thinks at all about it, she thinks prim thoughts such as have been instilled into her, and which have nothing to do with what she feels. The natural promptings of her modesty she mistakes for resistance to this unknown force, which is drawing her to itself as inevitably as the magnet draws the needle. With her little prudish defences, she believes herself equipped for any fray; she feels so strong, and, O God, she is so weak! One day a bolt falls from the clear sky; he is going to be married to a woman of fortune, of good connections; he is away in the country wooing his rich bride . . . Pshaw, what a rhodomontade! . . .*

All the girls, nearly, have gone through it; everyone knows how Carrie lost her looks after she came home from Cowes, and how Blanche fell off to a skeleton the year Fred Birch was married. Carrie looked blooming enough in the Park the other day in her new carriage; and Blanche is fatter than her husband, which is saying a great deal. Not go to the bad? But perhaps a good many of us *do* go after all, though the badness is not of a sort which demands the attention of philanthropists, such, for instance, as Sir Guy Ormond.

Sir Guy Ormond is very strong on all social questions. He is also an Agnostic, and a Socialist of an advanced type. He regards the baronetcy conferred on his father, a benevolent mill-owner at Darlington, in the light of a burden and an indignity.

How do I come by my facts? I gleaned them from no less a person than Sir Guy himself, in the course of two dances and a hasty supper.

The limpid fluency of that young man's discourse is something astonishing. However, he is quite intelligent, in a stupid way, and quite good. Not an atom of vice in his composition, I should say, and not an atom of humour.

Mrs Philip Shand called on me some days after the Westerleighs' party. She has that air of petulance, of protest, that

I have often noticed in very rich people. They have got into the way of expecting too much.

> You set a golden cage for happiness,
> And, lo, the uncertain creature flutters by
> To settle on your neighbour's hand, who has,
> Perhaps, no cage at all.

So much for the vanity of riches.

Mrs Philip was polite enough in her vague, dumb way, and hoped we should meet that night at the Roehamptons' dinner party. We did meet, and Philip was told off to take me in. I accepted the fact coolly enough, and he bore himself towards me with an air of ostentatious restraint; but finding it not so effective as he had, perhaps, supposed, he dropped into one of his moralising moods, which, to do him justice, are rare.

Philip has his faults, but he is not a bore; yet, like most of his sex, he is not without possibilities in that direction. 'In a civilisation like ours,' went on Philip, between his mouthfuls of *quenelle*,* 'there can be no middle course. You must go with the tide or drift into some stagnant backwater and rot. It's the old story of survival of the fittest.'

'Survival of the toughest,' I interposed flippantly; but he continued, 'If you want anything worth having, you must make for it and fight for it. If you don't get it for yourself, no one else will. Not that it is an unkind world. Quite the contrary. There is a great deal of kindness going about one way and another.'

'Exactly,' I answered, 'but the best of us can only be benevolent by fits and starts; our own pains and pleasures, like the poor, are always with us. Under the influence of a whim or a passion, people will do a great deal for one another. But for thorough-going, untiring support of one's own interest, there is, after all, no one like oneself.'

He looked at me, with an air of shocked and affectionate concern.

'Don't,' he said, 'don't! It doesn't do for a woman to talk like that!'

After dinner, Mrs Philip, evidently a dutiful wife, asked me to go with them next day to a private view at the Institute. I said yes without hesitation, and at the end of the evening Philip reminded me of the engagement. He had risen to say good night to me, and stood holding my hand, with no undue pressure, certainly, but not without a gentle reluctance to let it go.

I told you once, Philip, that I loved you, did I not? Not in words, it is true, but with perfect frankness, nevertheless. Perhaps, to put it very plainly, you think that I love you still.

But, indeed, you would be wrong.

Only, this thing I know: that life can hold no such moment in store for me as those bygone moments when my hand thrilled to yours; when our eyes flashed and lingered in mysterious meeting; when the air about us was tense with the unspoken and the unrevealed.

3

The Shands called for me at the appointed time, and I drove with them to the Institute, where the usual private-view crowd was assembled.

As we were going in, I was attracted by the sight of two people on a bench overlooking the staircase.

The long head, and straight, tow-coloured hair; the pale face, equine profile, and earnest manner were unmistakable; it did not take me half a second to recognise Sir Guy Ormond. I recognised his companion also; a discontented-looking woman, eccentrically dressed. It was Medora Grey, the poetess.

Poor, poor Medora! having enacted for a great many years, and entirely without success, the part of *jeune fille*, she has lately adopted that of *espirit fort* and no doubt Sir Guy (simple soul!) affords her ready appreciation.

Heaven save me from the laurels of third-rate female celebrity! Unless she happens to be Patti or Lady Burdett-Coutts, or Queen Elizabeth, there is only one way of success open to a woman: the way of marriage.

Sir Guy, unless my vanity be mistaken, looked as if he would very much like to join our party, but Medora had no intention of releasing him. No doubt she had schemes of bearing him back to Bedford Park, there to discuss bad cigarettes and questionable philanthropy in the shaded light of an aesthetic 'den'.

He *did* escape, however, a little later on, and joined us in the big room, when I soon found that he had quite as much to say about art as about philanthropy.

Philip's face began to display unmistakable signs of boredom and irritation, but, as for me, I listened and looked, put intelligent questions, and made brief but pertinent answers, which seemed to annoy Philip even more than the aesthetic discourse.

What, indeed, had become of Philip's magnanimity?

He fidgeted about me, changing from side to side, trying to attract my attention by various devices.

Presently Sir Guy and I strolled outside together, and stood leaning on the balustrade watching the people swarm up and down the great staircase.

Philip was soon at my elbow, wanting to know if I had had enough of it, in tones that admitted of but one reply. 'I am quite ready to go,' I said, and looked him full in the face with a sudden thrill of triumph and resolve.

Am I to witness yet further developments of that highly organised product, Mr Shand?

Having introduced me to my first experience, is he about to initiate me into further knowledge of life and character, as seen under conditions of highly artificial civilisation?

Highly artificial? The Dog and the Manger is an old-world story, adapted to quite a simple state of society – but I do myself too much honour!

Meanwhile, Sir Guy stood there pressing an invitation on the whole party of us for an At Home at Toynbee Hall. Men of his type and Philip's are like oil and vinegar; the invitation, and the acceptance with which, after some demur, it was met, are, I think, significant.

'That prig!' said Philip in the carriage, later on.

'Poor Sir Guy!' I laughed lightly. I was in good spirits. It was no polite fiction when I told my hostess that I had thoroughly enjoyed myself.

4

Sir Guy Ormond evidently admires me – so much so that a less experienced person might be inclined to jump at conclusions on the subject. But I know very well that a man does not go about the world with thirty thousand a year and a baronetcy without having some idea of his own value; and with all his high-flown theories, the son of the Darlington mill-owner has his share of shrewdness and caution. He is whimsical, too, and obstinate, like all men of his stamp; and having, moreover, such a passion for female society generally, must often, in all innocence, have roused un-founded hopes in the female breast particularly. Not that, accidental advantages apart, he is the sort of man that women naturally take to. Perhaps it is that he assumes towards them an attitude so few are capable of appreciating; he respects them.

As for me, I like him genuinely; he is such a good fellow; I wish sometimes that he were rather less so.

My room is full of blue-books, pamphlets, and philosophical treatises. *Sesame and Lilies* and Clifford's *Essays* are hobnobbing on the table; the *Bitter Cry of Outcast London* and a report of the Democratic Federation stand together on the shelf. This is an age of independence and side-saddles; but how often is woman doomed to ride pillion on a man's hobby-horse!

Philip stands by and notices everything with his quick eyes. And I – is it at the cost of dignity that I permit myself so much intimacy with Philip?

But Philip amuses me more than anyone I know; and I suppose that I amuse Philip – am sure of it, in fact – or he would have turned his back on me ages ago. But while I think of it, is it possible that in her mild, inarticulate fashion, Mrs Philip is beginning to hate me? This must be seen to at once. I have no intention of playing a losing game a second time with Philip. Indeed, I am acquiring such skill with games generally that Philip begins to respect me as he never respected me before. Sometimes I think he is a little afraid of me, and goes so far as to doubt if he has done the best for himself after all.

We should have been a well-matched pair; between us we might have moved the world!

5

In a world of surprises, there is perhaps nothing which astonishes us so much as our own feelings.

I have begun with a sententiousness worthy of Sir Guy himself, but my pinions refuse to sustain me at so giddy a height.

Let me, then, come down to facts.

The letter came on the 18th of June, by the first post. It is as well to be exact. I recognised the handwriting, and put it in my pocket unopened. When, in the privacy of my own room, I broke the seal, I found what I had half expected.

In eight closely written pages Sir Guy Ormond made me a formal offer of marriage.

Wordy, egotistical, pompous, it was, in the main, an honest and a generous letter.

I read it once, twice, then sat staring mechanically at myself in the glass opposite.

It was the moment of my triumph: I had won my game; it only remained for me to stretch out my hand and claim the stakes.

The reflection of my face caught my vision; its expression was scarcely one of triumph. And surely there must be some mistake in the calendar, some trick in the sand and quicksilver; I was not twenty, with smooth cheeks – I was a hundred years old, and wrinkled!

Still I sat there staring, a dull dismay, a stony incredulity taking possession of me.

For gradually it was brought home to me that by no possibility could I accept Sir Guy's offer.

I will take no undue credit to myself; I had no choice in the matter. I simply could not do it!

6

'Have you posted my letter, Célestine?'

'Yes, Mademoiselle. Shall I put out your gown?'

'I am not going out tonight, after all.'

Not to face Philip! Philip – this is the hardest part of all – who will think I have played my game and lost; who will undergo a mixed moment of disappointment and gratified pique as the state of the case dawns on him, then turn away with a shrug from a commonplace and uninteresting failure. These are mean thoughts! But have I ever pretended to magnanimity?

I am sorry for what I have just done – I shall be sorry for it all the days of my life!

A year hence, no doubt, I shall be capable not only of stalking, but also of killing my game; then, in all probability, there will be no game to kill.

I gave myself every chance. I waited a week; something stronger than myself withheld me from giving the answer I wished to give. I am defeated, a traitor to my own cause, having brought nothing but dishonour from the fray.

Let me open the window, and lean out to the stars.

Stars, you have often seen me weep, but tonight I have no tears to shed.

Something falls to the ground with a crash.

Only some books of Sir Guy's – the poor books he is so fond of, and writes his name in with a flourish.

(I am not sure that there are not some tears left, after all! Yet, can there be much pathos over a person with thirty thousand a year?)

Let me lean my forehead against the cool window-ledge, and hide my face from the stars.

Have I, too, been cruel? Have I also been the means of showing another human being the darker possibilities of his own soul?

Would it have been better, after all, to complete the wrong I had begun?

If I had loved you – but ah! my poor Sir Guy, that could never be, could never have been.

Here, with closed eyes and hidden face, and head bared to the night breeze, let me shut out thought.

The wind is soft and very sweet; there is no sound save the distant murmur of the Great City.

Black, black in its heart is the City; the blackness of man's heart is revealed in its huge, hideous struggle for existence.

Better be unfit and perish, than survive at such a cost.

'No, thank you, Célestine. I will shut the window, and I shall not want you again tonight.'

1890

LUCY CLIFFORD

On the Wane: A Sentimental Correspondence

(From *Love Letters of a Worldly Woman*.)

I

HE

St James Street, W.,
Monday, 23 June

MY DEAR AND PRECIOUS ONE, this is only a line to tell you that I shall come and dine with you and your mummy this evening, at the usual time. I have been thinking, my sweet, that we had much better be married soon. What is the good of waiting – beyond the winter anyway? We must make arrangements for the mummy, or why could she not come to us? I shall talk to you seriously about it tonight, so be prepared. I feel as if we can't go on living at different ends of London much longer; besides, what is the good of waiting?

No more time, dear, for I must post this at once. You had my long letter this morning. Yours was just like you. I think you are the greatest darling on earth, Gwen, – I have taken it very badly, you see, – and I have got something for you when I come that I think you will like. Till then be good and love me. Meet me down the lane if you can, like an angel – no, like yourself, which will be better.

YOUR DEVOTED
JIM

2

HE

Tuesday Night, 24 June

You were so very sweet last night, beloved; I do nothing but think of you. I do trust you, darling, absolutely, and if we must wait till Christmas, why, we must. But you will come to me then, won't you? and we will be the two happiest people on earth. I can't rest till I have seen you again. I have been thinking that if you met me tomorrow at four at the Finchley Road Station we could have a long walk, and drive back in a hansom in the cool of the evening in time for dinner. Shall we? If so, come in your big hat and the white dress, for that is how you look prettiest, you gypsy.

YOUR DEVOTED

JIM

3

SHE

Hampstead,
Wednesday Morning, June 25th

Only to say of course I will, darling. I will do anything you like. You looked so handsome last night that I was 'shocking' proud of you, as you would say. Mother says the sound of you in the house makes the whole place joyful. It does. I shall love a long walk – dear you, to think of it. I'll be there in the big hat and the white dress, according to the orders of His Majesty the King.

HIS VERY LOVING

GWEN

4

HE

(A MONTH LATER)

Wednesday, July 25th

DEAREST CHILD, sorry I could not come yesterday afternoon; it's an awful pull up that hill, and the day was so blazing hot that I confess I shirked it. You understand, don't you, darling? I'll come and dine on Friday anyway. My mother says you must go and stay with her this autumn. She is enjoying her month in town, I think. Goodbye, my child, no more time. I'm awfully vexed now I didn't charter a hansom yesterday to go up that blessed hill on the top of which it pleases you to live, or climb it on all fours, for I want to see you badly. I have been very busy, and naturally, while my mother is here, I have less time than usual.

YOUR LOVING

JIM

5

SHE

Wednesday night

Yes, old darling. I quite understand, and I'll count the hours till Friday. Of course I was disappointed yesterday, but I tried to console myself by thinking that you might have got sunstroke if you had come; and then in the evening, when I felt very downhearted, I read over a heap of your letters – I mean those you sent me in the winter, when you first loved me. They were so very loving that they made me quite happy again. Am I just the same to you? I don't know why I ask it; something makes me do so. Do you remember that night we walked up and down the garden till nearly twelve o'clock and talked of all manner of serious things? I often think of it. You said that when we were together we would work and read and try to understand the meaning of many things that seemed like lesson books in the wide world's school, and that now, in the holiday time, we did not want to think about. The lesson time would surely come, you said, so that we need not grudge ourselves our laughter and our joy. I remember that you said, too, that work was the most important thing in life, and I have been wondering if that is so. It seems rather a cold gospel. But perhaps you are right. Your love, for instance, will only make my happiness; but your work may help the whole world. Is that what you meant, darling? All this because of that happy night when you took my face between your hands and looked at me almost solemnly and said, 'This dear face is my life's history, thank God for that.' I love you so – oh, so much when I think of your voice – but I love you always.

GWEN

6

HE

Thursday morning

YOU DEAR SWEET, you are a most serious person, and a darling and a goose, and I long to kiss you; but look here, Gwennie, I can't come Friday either. Marsden insists on having half a dozen men to dine with him at the Club, and there must I be in the midst of them. Will Saturday do? Nice day Saturday, comes before Sunday, you know: best preparation in the world for it (seeing that I shall be made to go to church next morning and stay till the end of the sermon), will be seeing you the night before. I think I shall have to take a run to Clifton for a little bit next week, if so I shall miss your garden party, I fear; but we'll talk about this on Saturday.

YOURS EVER AND EVER AS YOU KNOW,

JIM

Work? Of course we must work. It is one's rent in the world, and honest folk must pay their way. Your work is to love me.

7

SHE

Thursday night

Yes, Jim dear, and I will always do it. Come on Saturday. I shall be miserable if you are not at our garden party, and fear I shall hardly have heart to go on with it. I am a selfish thing; but as you say will talk of it on Saturday.

YOUR LOVING

GWEN

8

HE
(A TELEGRAM)

Saturday, 7.30 p.m.

Awfully sorry. Relations turned up. Insist on my dining. Will come Monday.

JIM

9

SHE

Sunday, July 29th

Of course it could not be helped, dearest, yet when your telegram came I sat down and wept as devoutly as if I had been by the waters of Babylon. Relations are *exigeants*, I know, and you were quite right to go to them, yet I did so long for you; our little feast was ready, and I was ready; in the blue dress that you said I looked pretty in. I had pinned a rose on my shoulder, and wondered if you would pull it leaf by leaf away, – you did last time, do you remember? I shuddered while I thought of it. It was like – but I will not even write it. Oh, Jim dear, how well we can sometimes make ourselves shiver at the impossibilities! I know you love me, but the little things that have kept you away from me oftener than usual lately make me foolish and nervous; they are like thongs that threaten to become a whip, and would if you stayed away too long. But you won't? You know that I love you, as you do me, and that I am weaker and cannot bear the days apart as you can, you who have many things to fill your life, while I have only you to fill mine – only you, for whom I would die, and think death sweet if it did you even the least little good.

When I was ready last night I went out and walked up and down under the veranda, before the windows. I looked in at the drawing room and thought of how we would sit there on the little low sofa after dinner, watching the shadows that always seem to come stealing through the fir trees; and of how we would talk, as we always do, or of the days when we wondered and guessed about each other, and were afraid and hoped; or of how we would plan our future life and arrange the things we would some day do together. The dining-room window was open, and I looked in there, too, at our table spread, at the great roses in the bowl, and the candles ready for lighting. I thought of how you would sit at the head, as though you were master already, and of how, when we had nearly come to an end, dear Mother would rise, as she always does, and say, 'You will not mind if I go, dears? I am very tired;' and you would open the door and she would pass out, giving you a little smile as she went; and then you would come back and stoop and kiss me and say, 'My darling,' just as you always do, and each time seems like a first time. But you did not come, and did not come – and then there was a telegram. I know the quick, loud sound, the clangingness that only the telegraph boy puts into the bell, as well as I know your footstep. Sometimes my heart bounds to it; it leaps to heaven for a moment, for it means that you are coming; and sometimes it sinks. Oh, my darling, if you only knew how it almost stands still sometimes! – it did last night – for it means that you are not coming.

Jim, dear, I am a fool. I know you could not help it. But I love you dearly, and will all my life. I kiss the paper because your hands will touch it. Good night, my own.

GWEN

10

HE

Monday morning

YOU SWEET THING, your letter almost makes me ashamed of myself. You do love me, Gwen, and I am not half good enough for you. I wonder how I dared go in for a girl like you, or what I ever did to please God that He should give me a love like yours. I often think that you will be awfully disappointed when you get me every day of your life and find out what a commonplace beggar I am. You are certain to find that out anyhow. And yet, why should you? Does not Browning say:

> God be thanked, the meanest of His creatures,
> Boasts two soul sides, one to face the world with,
> One to show a woman when he loves her.

I don't suppose that I am the meanest of His creatures, but I am not as good as you, dear. There is a sort of looking-aheadness towards Heaven in you that is wholly lacking in me. I have felt very keenly lately, and wondered whether any vanity would let me stand being made the subject of your being disillusioned about mankind later on. There is one thing certain: whatever happens to us in the future, we have the memory of good love behind us; for I have loved you, Gwen dear; always remember that.

I will come up this evening, and we will have a happy time together. I think I must go to Clifton, after all. Mrs Seafield wants me to help them through with Tommy's coming of age. Awfully nice woman, Mrs Seafield, and one ought to encourage nice people by doing what they wish occasionally. Be good. Don't get low-spirited or entertain ghosts unawares, or do anything but love me till I come, and then I will tell you that I love you, which will be better than saying it here.

I think you ought to go away for a bit; you strike me, from your letters, as being a little strained and run down. It's all my fault, isn't it, dearest? For I prevented you from going to Italy last winter by making you be engaged to me; and then we didn't want to put the big distance between us. Till tonight.

YOUR LOVING
JIM

11

HE

(A TELEGRAM)

Clifton, August 3rd

No time to write. Garden party, etc., Friday. Letter tomorrow. Staying till Wednesday.

JIM

12

SHE

Tuesday, August 7th

DEAREST JIM, I have been hoping and hoping to hear from you. Is anything the matter, darling? Are you ill? Has a letter miscarried? Are you angry with me? I cannot believe that four whole days have passed without a word, and yet I know that I am foolish to worry myself, for this silence is probably due to some trivial accident. But you are all the wide world to me – you and my mother; and in these last days apart you seem to have tightened and tightened round my heart till I cannot even breathe without thinking of you, and the least little bit of fear about you makes me miserable.

I am very foolish, Jim, for on Monday night, after you had gone, I sat up till it was nearly daylight thinking over your words and looks. I fancied they had been different – that you had been different altogether lately. Perhaps it is only a calm setting in, a reaction after the wild love-making of the winter, when you seemed unable to live a single day without me. It could not be always like that; I knew it even at the time. Perhaps I fancy it all; write and tell me that I do. But I have felt since Monday as if only the ghost of your love remained to me. You didn't seem so glad to be with me; you did not look at me so often, and you broke off to talk of outside things just when I thought your heart was full of me and love of me.

Your mother came yesterday. She did not stay long. She did not ask me to go to her in the autumn. She said that she had heard from you, and my heart gave a throb of pain, knowing that I had not had a line. In her manner she seemed to divine that you had changed. I went upstairs after she had gone and prayed that if it were so I might never know it. But for my poor mummy I could have killed myself, so as to die in the midst of uncertainty that was torture, and yet joy compared to the knowledge that might come – the knowledge that your love had gone from me.

But tonight I am ashamed of all my foolishness, all my fears, and reproaching myself for doubting you; for I know that you love me – I do indeed. I live over all your words and looks. Do you remember that night by the pond – we stole out by the garden gate – when you said nothing could ever part us; that I was never, never to doubt you, no matter if you yourself had made me do so for the moment? You made me swear I never would. You looked down and said, 'My sweet wife,' and made me say, 'Yes, Jim, your wife' after you, because you wanted me to feel that the tie between us could never be broken. It is the memory of those words, of that night, that helps me through the misery and wicked doubting of you now. Come and beat me for the doubting with a thick, thick stick, and I will count each stroke as joy, and love you more and more for every one that falls. It is the memory of that night, too, that makes me send you this – that gives me courage to pour out all my heart to you. The days have passed for make-believes between us: I cannot pretend to you; I am yours, your own, and very own. Write me one line and make me happy again, and forgive me, or scold me, or do what you will, so that you love me – tell me that, and I shall be once more what I have been all these months, the happiest, most blessed girl in the whole wide world.

GWEN

13

HE

Wednesday, August 8th

DEAREST GWEN, what a sentimental child you are! I have been busy: tennis, dances, garden party, picnic, Tommy coming of age, and speeches – all sorts of things crowded into a week. No time for letter writing. It is very jolly here, and everything uncommonly well managed. Nice people in the neighbourhood; dinner party last night; took in Ethel Bertram – handsome girl, beautiful dark eyes, said to be worth a pile of money.

I think you ought to have more occupation, dear; you seem to be so dependent now on your affections and emotions; you want something more to fill your life. I wish you had a younger

companion than your mother – you must try and get one somehow. I am going on to Devonshire, on Thursday, for two or three
weeks, and shall, perhaps, stay here again for a day or two on my
way back. Don't fidget, dear child. No more time.

JIM

14

SHE

Thursday, 9th

Jim, darling, don't say I am sentimental – it sounds like a
reproach; but you know we always write each other foolish,
loving letters. I am glad you are having a good time. I suppose it
was very foolish of me to be unhappy, but it has been so odd to
find morning after morning going by and no sign from you. You
spoiled me at first by writing every day.

You didn't say you loved me in your note – tell me that you do
next time; but don't write till you want to do so. Be happy,
darling, and I will be happy too, in thinking of you.

GWEN

15

HE
(A TELEGRAM)

Horrabridge, S. Devon,
Friday, August 11th

Had letter yesterday. Will write soon. Here for some days.

JIM

16

SHE

Thursday, August 22d

Jim, dear, do send me a line. It is nearly a fortnight since I heard
from you, and for a long time your letters have been different,
they have indeed, though I have tried to disguise it from myself. I
cannot bear it any longer. Tell me what it all means, for it must
mean something. Speak out, I implore you. You are not afraid of
me, are you, darling? Your own loving

GWEN

17

HE

Horrabridge,
August 24th

It is strange how quickly a woman divines; and your heart has told you what I have not had the courage to say. Gwen, dear, I want to break it off, not because I do not think you what I have always thought you, or because I care for anyone else, but simply because I want to be free. Our engagement no longer gives me the pleasure it did; I look forward to marriage as a sort of bondage into which I do not want to enter. I am perfectly frank with you because I feel that in an important matter like this it is only right. Then, dear, you know my mother never approved of it; parents are prudent people, and she thought the whole business unwise. I struggled against her reasoning all I could, for I loved you, and thought of your face, and of how you loved me. But, Gwen dear, there is a good deal in what she says. You see you couldn't leave your mother; and we should have to be careful about money; for I am not a frugal beggar, and there are lots of difficulties. I ought to have thought of them before, but you were so sweet and good, a thousand times too good for me, that I could think of nothing but you. Say you forgive me, and believe that I have loved you, for I have, and you won't hold me to it, will you, Gwen? I know this will cost you a great deal, but you are a brave girl and will bear it; and don't reproach me – I could not bear your reproaches. I am a scoundrel and I know it, a ruffian, or I should love you beyond all things, as I ought.

J

18

SHE

August 25th

Hold you to it when you want to be free? I would not be so much of a cobweb. Thank God that in your letter you were able at least to say that you had loved me. Reproach you? Why should I? Men are different from women – it is not for women to judge them. Besides, I love you – I say it once more for this last time on earth – so much and so truly that I cannot be angry, much less reproachful. Go, and be happy, my darling. God bless you, and goodbye.

GWEN

19

He

(A MONTH LATER)

September 25th

I believe I ought to ask you for my letters back. Will you send them, or write and say that you have burned them? – which you prefer. Forgive me for troubling you.

  J. F.

P.S. I was so sorry to hear through the Markhams that you had been ill.

20

She

Hampstead,
September 27th

I send back your letters, and your ring, and other things. I ought to have sent them before, but I could not. I am glad you asked for them. Thank you, I am better; and tomorrow we start for Montreux, and stay there through the winter; perhaps much longer.

  Yours,
  G. W.

21

He

(A YEAR LATER)

London, July 30th

MY DEAR GWEN (forgive me, but I cannot bring myself to address you any more formally), I saw your dear mother's death in the paper, yesterday. You have not been out of my thoughts since. Perhaps I ought not to write to you, but I can't help telling you how grieved I am for all that you must be suffering. It seems so rough that you should be left alone in the world. I heard that your Aunt Mary was with you, and I hope that you may be going to live with her; but probably you are not able yet to think of your future.

  Of course I do not know if you are coming back to England

soon; but if not, and there is anything I could get or do for you over here, or anything I could do for you at any time, I can't tell you what a privilege I should think it. This is not time to say it, perhaps, but I respect no woman on earth as I do you, and I should think it the greatest honour to be of service to you. I dare not hope that you will send me any reply to this, still less that you ever think of me kindly. But do believe how true is my sympathy. Yours always,

    J. F.

22

SHE

Glion, August 5th

Thank you for your letter. Yes, my dear mother is gone; it seems so strange and still without her. I sit and stare into an empty world. Thank you; but there is nothing you can do for me. I always think of you kindly. Why should I not do so?

I am going to live with Aunt Mary. My mother arranged it all. We are not coming back to England yet; we stay here a little time, then go down to Montreux again for winter.

    YOURS,
    G. W.

23

HE
(SIX MONTHS LATER)

February 1st

I don't know how I am going to write to you; I have been longing to do it for months past and not daring.

It will be better to plunge at once. Gwennie, could you forgive me and take me back? I should not be mad enough to think it possible, but that I know you to be the dearest girl on earth, and the most constant. You did love me once, and though perhaps you will only laugh at my audacity, deep down in my heart something tells me that you care for me a little but still, or at least that you could care for me again. I remember you saying in one of your last letters that the time had passed for make-believes between us; and if, in spite of all, you have any feeling left for me, I know that you will tell me frankly and truly just as a less noble woman would hide it.

I have often wondered how I could throw away a love like yours. I must have been mad. I know now what it is, having once had it, to be without it. You are far more to me than you were in the old days – far more than any words can tell. I am always thinking of you – you are never out of my thoughts. Oh, my darling, forgive me and take me back! Longing for a word from you, yet hardly daring to hope – I am yours, loving you.

J.

24

SHE

February 3rd

Yes, I am just the same. I never loved anyone but you, and I have not left off loving you. I think I have known that you would come back to me. It feels like finding my way home, just when all the world was at an end. You do not know what anguish I have suffered and how I have tried to be brave; but without you, without my mother – O God! But now some light seems to be breaking through the darkness.

YOURS ONCE MORE, JIM, DEAR – MY JIM AGAIN.

GWEN

25

HE

February 5th

MY SWEET GWEN, MY OWN DEAR GIRL, I kissed your little letter and longed to kiss you. You are a million times too good for me, but you shall be happy this time if I can make you so. I can't believe that we are all right again. I should like to go down on my knees and ask you to forgive me for all I did, only I am such an impudent beggar that kneeling isn't much in my line.

And when shall we be married, my sweet? You had much better take possession of me as soon as possible – not that there is any fear of my going astray any more, but there's nothing to wait for, is there? When are you coming back from Montreux? Shall I come out and fetch you? I should like to – in fact I should rush off this very minute just to look at your dear face again, but that I am rather in awe of Aunt Mary – and I am rather in awe of you, too, my darling – and half afraid of seeing you for the first time. It is all too good to be true at least, it feels so just yet. I could get away for a whole fortnight in March, and I don't think I can go longer than that without seeing you. It is horrible to remember all the months in which we have been apart. Let us be together now, and forever, as soon as it is possible. We will be so happy, the fates won't know us.

YOUR HAPPY AND DEVOTED

JIM

26

SHE

February 12th

DEAR, your letter almost made me laugh – it was just like you.

It is very strange to sit down and write to you again and to know that all is right between us. I don't realise it yet; but I shall soon, I suppose. Now, I feel as if I were inside a dream, groping about, trying to find my way into the waking world and half fearing that there it would be different. But life has become a restful thing again; some of the aching loneliness seems to have been swept out of my heart – not all, for I miss my dear mother terribly, and keep longing to tell her about this; it chokes me to think she cannot hear, that, perhaps, she does not know.

My dear old Jim, how glad I am to come back to you and to be loved again! In my thoughts I listen to the sound of your laughter, and see your face, and hear your quick footstep. I shall laugh, too, presently, but now I am still too much crushed by the remembrance of the past months, as well as overcome by this great happiness to do anything but be very brave and silent. Soon I shall grow used to it, and shake my bells again. For some strange reason I don't want you to come yet. I am afraid of you, too, and yet I long to see and hear and know, not merely dream, as I half do still that you love me again, and that all the old life is going to begin once more. But come in March; Aunt Mary talks of going back to England in April.

We must not be married just yet, not till the summer is over, till the year is past – till I am your frivolous Gwennie again, instead of a grave person in a sober black gown. Dear Jim, I begin to think how wonderful it will be to be with you all my life, to do things for you, to fetch and carry and be useful. A woman's hands always long to be busy for those she loves; since Mother died mine have been idle – they are waiting for you. If I could only get rid of the tiredness that is still in my heart and soul – but I shall when I am with you. We will read and talk and think, and take long walks together – all this will make me strong again. We will begin when you come here – to this beautiful place. The snow is on the mountains white and thick, and the lake is blue. When the sun shines I wonder if heaven itself can be much better. Good night, dear Jim.

> YOUR
> GWEN

27

HE

February 15th

All right, my darling, I will come in March! I can hardly believe that I am going to see you again so soon; and oh, Gwennie, it is good to feel that you are mine again. You dear wifely thing, to plan how you will take care of me with your two sweet hands. I want you to have your ring back, my precious one; I shall bring it with me and put it on your finger.

I have been considering ways and means. Do you know that I am growing rich, and can give you many more luxuries and pretty frocks and things than I could have managed before? What do you say to a flat to begin with, somewhere on the right side of the park, not too far from the Club? My mother had one last year for a few months, and said it was much better and less trouble than a house.

Have you had a new photograph taken lately? I want to see if your face looks just the same, and what you have done with your dimple. I don't like to think of you in a black gown, my poor darling; you must try and put it off as soon as you can. I want to see you in the old blue one, and I would give anything to walk about with you once again in the garden at Hampstead. I often think of your face as it used to look under the trees, and of how we used to steal out in the dusk by the garden door, and over the heath and round by the pond. It is a thousand times better to think of than your Swiss mountains and blue lake out there. But I shall come and see those too, soon, and then I shan't be jealous of them any more. Tell me in your next letter that you love me, my darling (you didn't in your last), and that I am just the same to you as you are to me, only you are a hundred times more – more and more every day.

YOUR ADORING OLD

JIM

28

SHE

February 20th

MY DEAREST JIM, I am just the same, darling, and I love you; but I have not your wild spirits; that is all. The past year has sobered me down – only one year, as time is measured, but it has made me many long ones older.

I am glad you are growing rich; it shows that the world likes you. Yes, dear, we will have a flat if you like and where you like. It would be nice if we could get one somewhere away from noise and hurry. I long for a cosy room with bookshelves round it, and a library that will grow and grow, and prove that we have new books very often. I hope we shall do heaps of reading, for I have become quite studious; you will hardly know your frivolous sweetheart. But the walks by the lake or along the upper roads day after day, always alone amid the silences, have set me thinking. The world seems to have stretched out so far and to be so full of things it wants to tell us if we will but listen. I long to talk about them with you. We were young, and so much taken up with ourselves in the old days that we had little time to think of all that is most to us – after love.

You shall not scoff at this lovely place, you dear, bad person. I long to take you up to Les Avants, and over the way to Savoy, and to make you look towards the Rhone Valley – there at the head of the lake with the mountains on either side forming a gateway. I made a dozen romances about the far, far off in which the valley ends almost at the feet of Italy, till the other day, when I was sadly taken down by Uncle Alfred, who was here. I told him of all the mysteries and fairy stories that seemed to be lurking in the valley, and he laughed and said there was none there; it was only very long and very uninteresting, and might be described as Switzerland run to seed. I see it with such different eyes; but then they are not the eyes that are in my head. People say that Death is a sceneshifter; and so is every new experience. Experience has made all things look different to me; only those that are in my memory remain the same, all that I actually see and hear have changed.

Are you fond of the world, Jim, and do you think much about it? It seems such an absurd question, and yet it is not. I mean the world in itself. I have learned to see that it is very beautiful, and to feel so reverential when I think of all the human feet that have walked through it, and all the hands that have worked for it. I want to do my share of the work in it, too, if it be possible. I should like to make it something beautiful. A little while ago I read Mazzini; do you remember that he says we ought to regard the world as a workshop in which we have each to make something good or beautiful with the help of the others? I am not strong enough to do anything by myself, but if you and I together could ever do it, even the least little good, darling, it would be something to remember thankfully. We would count it as our tribute in return for each other's love, which it had given us. Sometimes I have thought that the world is like a great bank into which we put good and evil, joy and sorrow, for all the coming generations to draw upon. We won't leave them any evil or sorrow if we can help it, will we? I should never have done anything by myself save brood and dream; but now it seems as if a door is opening and we shall go through together to find a hundred things that we must do. I am so ambitious for you, Jim. I want you to do and be so much; and nothing achieved will ever seem enough or wholly satisfy me. I want you to climb the heavenly heights, my darling, not in the ordinary sense, but in work and deeds. Do you understand? Oh, how I pray that you do!

I am half ashamed to write all this to you. But so many things have crept into my heart and soul in these long months, and between the hours of sorrow and pain, and I do not want you to be a stranger among thoughts and longings I never expected to put into words. I wish I knew of the things that you think about, in the inner life that most of us live silently, and seldom speak of at all. We only can speak of them to the one person we love best, or to some strange being we may not even love, but that our soul seems to recognise as if it had found one it had known centuries before, or in some shadowy dreamland of which it could not give account. There are many walls of silences to break down between us, and many things on which we must build together before we know each other absolutely. Let us try to begin at once. Oh, Jim, don't laugh at me for writing all this! Remember I have only you in the wide world now. I love my mother still; I ache and long for her, but it is a different love from that which is given to the living – it is more like religion. I cannot hear her voice, or see her face; my hands cannot touch her: I have only you now in my human life. And it is a blessed rest, darling, to have your love again. I think I was dying of tiredness; but now I shall grow very strong – strong to love you, dear.

ALWAYS YOUR
GWEN

29

HE

February 25th

You are a dear, sweet, beloved child; but don't let us discuss heaven and earth and the musical glasses in our love letters – just yet at any rate. No doubt we shall come to it in time and double dummy too; but let us wait our turn. Tell me you love me again. I shall never get tired of hearing that; and in your next letter could you not say, 'I send you a kiss, Jim,' then I shall know it really is all right. I send you a thousand, just like Mary Jane the cook's young man.

I want to see you so much, you precious thing, that I am going to rush to you next week. Then we can go to Savoy and Les Avants and anywhere else you please. I shan't mind how long the walks are, or how lonely. You can bet we won't talk very big talk, but we'll be happier than any two people have been since Adam and Eve before they let the serpent in. I can't live any longer without seeing your dear face, and I think of starting on Tuesday. Shall I be welcome? – say, you gypsy. You will only just have time to send one more letter before I start; make it a nice one, my sweet.

YOUR DEVOTED
JIM

30

SHE

February 27th

DEAREST, you would have been welcome, but all our arrangements are suddenly altered. Aunt Mary has some important business, and we start for England tomorrow. We arrive on Wednesday morning. Isn't this good news, old dear? I am so glad, that I don't want to talk about anything but happiness now – not even of heaven and earth and the musical glasses. I am afraid of myself – of my two feet that will walk towards you, and my two eyes that will see you, and my ears that will hear you. I love you, and you know it. Goodbye till we meet. I will telegraph from Dover.

YOUR OWN
GWEN

P.S. Oh, but I can't, I am shy; and it's so long since—

3 1

(THREE WEEKS LATER)

Bryanston St, March 26th

DEAREST JIM, don't come this evening; there are so many things to look through; I must begin them indeed.

Thank you for your letter; you are very good to me, dear.

GWEN

3 2

HE

March 27th

Very well, my darling, I'll wait till tomorrow. Is anything the matter with you, sweet? It is odd, but since the first rush of meeting you have seemed so grave, and there is a little stately reserve that clings to you and makes me feel out in the cold. I cannot even guess of what you are thinking: before I always knew without your telling me. Don't be like that with me, dear one. Let us be just as we were in the old days. I love you ten times more than I used, and there is something sad in your face that makes me loathe myself for all the pain I once caused you. You have forgiven me, haven't you, my darling? I was a brute, but I know it; and I love you with all my heart.

YOUR DEVOTED
JIM

33
SHE

April 2nd

DEAREST JIM, I am sorry, but I can't go to the National Gallery-tomorrow. Aunt Mary wants me to help her a good deal just now. We think of going to Torquay for a little bit. This English wind is very cutting.

Thank you, dearie, for the magazines and the flowers. You are much too good to me; I often think that.

GWEN

34
HE

April 4th

MY DARLING, what is the matter? You are always making excuses now; don't you care about seeing me? Have I offended you? Send me one line. My love for you has grown through all the months you were away, but I can't help fearing that yours for me has waned.

JIM

35
SHE

April 6th

Yes, Jim dear, I care about seeing you, of course; but I have so many things to think about. Aunt Mary's cough is much worse, and we have decided to go off to Torquay at once. We shall be gone by the time you get this. I am so sorry not to have seen you again, but we shall be back in a fortnight if it is warmer. Oh, Jim dear, once more you are too good to me! Why have you sent me that packet?

YOUR GRATEFUL
GWEN

36

SHE

(A TELEGRAM)

April 8th

The address is Belle Vue, Torquay. Aunt Mary better: will write tomorrow.

37

HE

London, April 8th

GWEN, DEAR, this can't go on. Things are all wrong between us. I felt it even the first evening you came back. What is the matter? Do tell me, my darling. Is it anything that I have said or done? With greater love than words can tell,

YOUR MISERABLE OLD

JIM

38

SHE

(A TELEGRAM)

April 10th

Will write tomorrow. It is very difficult. Have been thinking day and night what to say, but you shall hear without fail tomorrow.

39

SHE

Torquay, April 11th

JIM, I am miserable too, more miserable than words can say. I want you to do for me what I did for you before – to set me free and let me go. I have struggled against it, tried, reasoned with myself, but all to no purpose. It is no use disguising the truth, cost you or me what it may. I am changed but I cannot tell why nor how, only that it is so. Dear Jim, forgive me, I entreat you, and let me go.

GWEN

40

He

London, April 12th

DEAREST, but there must be some meaning to this. Write and tell me what it is. You must care for me still, darling; you could not have been true to me all this time if you could change so easily. Write and tell me what has come over you. Perhaps it is something that I can explain away; I cannot bear to let you go. Speak out, I implore you, darling.

JIM

41

She

Torquay, April 13th

I do not know what has come over me. I do care for you, but I think it is simple affection or friendship that I feel – I am not in love any more. I did not know it at Montreux. Every day since we parted I had lived in the memory of your love. I thought I was just the same, and never dreamed of change till after we came back – then I found it out. All the life, all the reality, all the sunshine, seem to have gone out of my love for you. I used to feel my heart beat quick when you came; now it does not. I used to hear your footstep with a start of joy; it is nothing to me now; I listen to it curiously, or with a little dismay. I am not eager when you come, and cannot make myself so! I never go forward to meet you. Have you not noticed how I stand still on the hearth rug as you enter? Something holds me there with a sense of guilty coldness in my heart. Have you not felt the silence fall between us when we try to talk? We have nothing to say; and while we sit and stare at each other my soul seems to be far off, living another life. It is almost a relief when you go; yet I dread the tenderness of your goodbye. I used to think of home together as the dearest life; now I wonder now we should drag through the days. There are places I want to see, things I want to do, plans to think over, books to read, and between all these you seem to stand like a fate. It is my fault – all, all. You are just the same, but I am different; and I can't marry you, Jim; I can't indeed. I know the pain I am costing you; did I not suffer it through long, long months? But believe that I have tried to be true – tried and tried, dear. I did not dream till we met that only the ghost of the old love remained – the memory of it, the shadow; that the reality had slipped away; that pain had quenched it. I would give the wide world to be once again the girl who loved you, who was so merry and so happy, who used to walk about the Hampstead garden counting the minutes till you came. But it is no good. I am a woman, with only a remembrance of the girl, and I am altogether different. Forgive me, dear Jim; forgive me and let me go.

GWEN

42

HE

April 14th

MY DARLING, I can't do it; for God's sake don't throw me over, for I can't face it. It is all fancy, dear. You have been ill and strained and worried; you have been left too much alone; you have grown too introspective; wait, and it will all come right again. I love you more and more every day; and after all the months in which I loved you, and never dared to make a sign, you won't treat me like this? Think of the days we spent together long ago, and the plans we made. You are not going to chuck them all away? I would do anything on earth for you, and you shall have my whole life's devotion. Write and tell me that you will take it, my darling, and bear with me, and try to love me again. I can't let you go, Gwen. It's no good, I can't face it.

YOUR ADORING AND DEVOTED AND MISERABLE OLD
JIM

43

SHE

April 15th

But, Jim dear, you must – you must set me free. I can't go on; it is not that I am strained or morbid or too introspective, or anything of the sort, only this – I can't marry you, and I can't. Sorrow and loneliness have made me think, have opened my eyes wide, and I see that we are strangers inwardly, even while outwardly we are lovers. You loved me at Hampstead for my laughter, my love of you, my big hat, the shady garden, my gladness to be loved – for a hundred things that do not belong to the life that is mine now. So, too, I loved you back, because of your merry voice, your handsomeness, your love of me – because of the holiday time we made of life when we were together. But that time is over for ever and ever. You cannot give me back my laughter, happiness that almost frightened me; they are gone, they will never find their way to me again; and my love for you was bound up with them – it has gone, too. Sometimes my heart cries out, longing for its old feelings again, till I feel like Faust before he conjured Mephistopheles to him, save for his years – the actual years that time doles out; or like a Hindu for whom the time has come to vanish into the forest and dream. Only twenty-three, Jim, but youth has gone; you cannot have back the girl who laughed and loved you so – she does not exist; parting and silence killed her. It sounds like a reproach, but God knows it is not one. And no new feelings have grown up to take the place of the old ones that are dead. We are almost strangers, and I cannot reconcile myself to the thought of our being more than friends. I even shrink from you and shudder. Your laughter does not gladden me; your talk does not hold my senses any longer; and concerning the things of which I think most my lips of themselves refuse to speak.

The very ring on my finger frets and worries me. In the old days I used to kiss it, and wish it hurt me, that it burned or bit, so that I might feel through pain, as through all things, the joy of loving you. But now I turn and twist it round as a prisoner does his fetter, longing, yet afraid, as he is unable to shake it off, till you shall give me leave and set me free.

You can't marry me, Jim dear, feeling as I do now. It would be madness. It is of no use making our whole lives a failure, or a tragedy, because we have not the courage to face the pain of parting now. If I thought you would be happy with me I would hesitate, but we should neither of us be happy. And it is not as if this were a passing phase; I know that it is not. I live in another world from you now. I do not know if it is better or worse, only that it is different; it seems as if in the past months a hand was stretched out; I took it and went on, almost dazed – on and on while you stood still. I am going farther, and shall never return, but you will be in the world behind me. There may be happiness for me, and life and love once more; I do not know; but it will be far, far off, away from you. Between us all things have finished. I cannot turn and go back into the old year, the old love, the old life; I have passed them all by for good or ill. Oh, Jim, understand and let me go! forgive me all the pain I have cost you, and let me go.

GWEN

44

HE

April 15th

All right – go. I thought you the most constant girl on earth: that you loved me as I do you. Since it pleases you to play fast and loose with me, let it be so. My feelings, of course, are of no account weighed against your fancies. You have shaken all my faith in women; for I did believe in you, Gwen. Goodbye,

JIM

45

SHE
(A WEEK LATER)

April 22nd

I send back your letters and things once more – it is better to get it over. Return mine or burn them as you please. Aunt Mary cannot stand this English climate, and we start almost immediately for Italy; probably to live there altogether. I think it will be a relief to you to know this. I hope with all my heart that you will soon forget the pain I have given you, that all good things may come to you; and one day I hope that you will marry some one who will make you happy, and love you as I did long ago in the dear days at Hampstead.

GOODBYE,
GWEN

(1891)

MARY WILKINS FREEMAN

A New England Nun

It was late in the afternoon, and the light was waning. There was a difference in the look of the tree shadows out in the yard. Somewhere in the distance cows were lowing and a little bell was tinkling; now and then a farm-wagon tilted by, and the dust flew; some blue-shirted labourers with shovels over their shoulders plodded past; little swarms of flies were dancing up and down before the people's faces in the soft air. There seemed to be a gentle stir arising over everything for the mere sake of subsidence – a very premonition of rest and hush and night.

This soft diurnal commotion was over Louisa Ellis also. She had been peacefully sewing at her sitting-room window all the afternoon. Now she quilted her needle carefully into her work, which she folded precisely, and laid in a basket with her thimble and thread and scissors. Louisa Ellis could not remember that ever in her life she had mislaid one of these little feminine appurtenances, which had become, from long use and constant association, a very part of her personality.

Louisa tied a green apron round her waist, and got out a flat straw hat with a green ribbon. Then she went into the garden with a little blue crockery bowl, to pick some currants for her tea. After the currants were picked she sat on the back doorstep and stemmed them, collecting the stems carefully in her apron, and afterwards throwing them into the hen-coop. She looked sharply at the grass beside the step to see if any had fallen there.

Louisa was slow and still in her movements; it took her a long time to prepare her tea; but when ready it was set forth with as much grace as if she had been a veritable guest to her own self. The little square table stood exactly in the centre of the kitchen, and was covered with a starched linen cloth whose border pattern of flowers glistened. Louisa had a damask napkin on her tea-tray, where were arranged a cut glass tumbler full of teaspoons, a silver cream-pitcher, a china sugar-bowl, and one pink china cup and saucer.

Louisa used china every day – something which none of her neighbours did. They whispered about it among themselves. Their daily tables were laid with common crockery, their sets of best china stayed in the parlour closet, and Louisa Ellis was no richer nor better bred than they. Still she would use the china. She had for her supper a glass dish full of sugared currants, a plate of little cakes, and one of light white biscuits. Also a leaf or two of lettuce, which she cut up daintily. Louisa was very fond of lettuce, which she raised to perfection in her little garden. She ate quite heartily, though in a delicate, pecking way; it seemed almost surprising that any considerable bulk of the food should vanish.

After tea she filled a plate with nicely baked thin corn-cakes, and carried them out into the back yard.

'Cæsar!' she called. 'Cæsar! Cæsar!'

There was a little rush, and the clank of a chain, and a large yellow-and-white dog appeared at the door of his tiny hut, which was half hidden among the tall grasses and flowers. Louisa patted him and gave him the corn-cakes. Then she returned to the house and washed the tea-things, polishing the china carefully. The twilight had deepened; the chorus of the frogs floated in at the open window wonderfully loud and shrill, and once in a while a long sharp drone from a tree toad pierced it. Louisa took off her green gingham apron, disclosing a shorter one of pink and white print. She lighted her lamp, and sat down again with her sewing.

In about half an hour Joe Dagget came. She heard his heavy step on the walk, and rose and took off her pink and white apron. Under that was still another – white linen with a little cambric edging on the bottom; that was Louisa's company apron. She never wore it without her calico sewing apron over it unless she had a guest. She had barely folded the pink and white one with methodical haste and laid it in a table-drawer when the door opened and Joe Dagget entered.

He seemed to fill up the whole room. A little yellow canary that had been asleep in his green cage at the south window woke up and fluttered wildly, beating his little yellow wings against the wires. He always did so when Joe Dagget came into the room.

'Good evening,' said Louisa. She extended her hand with a kind of solemn cordiality.

'Good evening, Louisa,' returned the man, in a loud voice.

She placed a chair for him, and they sat facing each other, with the table between them. He sat bolt upright, toeing out his heavy feet squarely, glancing with a good-humoured uneasiness around the room. She sat gently erect, folding her slender hands in her white-linen lap.

'Been a pleasant day,' remarked Dagget.

'Real pleasant,' Louisa assented, softly. 'Have you been haying?' she asked, after a little while.

'Yes, I've been haying all day, down in the ten acre lot. Pretty hot work.'

'It must be.'

'Yes, it's pretty hot work in the sun.'

'Is your mother well today?'

'Yes, Mother's pretty well.'

'I suppose Lily Dyer's with her now?'

Dagget coloured. 'Yes, she's with her,' he answered, slowly.

He was not very young, but there was a boyish look about his large face. Louisa was not quite as old as he, her face was fairer and smoother, but she gave people the impression of being older.

'I suppose she's a good deal of help to your mother,' she said, further.

'I guess she is; I don't know how Mother'd get along without her,' said Dagget, with a sort of embarrassed warmth.

'She looks like a real capable girl. She's pretty looking too,' remarked Louisa.

'Yes, she is pretty fair looking.'

Presently Dagget began fingering the books on the table. There was a square red autograph album, and a Young Lady's Gift Book which had belonged to Louisa's mother. He took them up one after the other and opened them; then laid them down again, the album on the Gift Book.

Louisa kept eyeing them with mild uneasiness. Finally she rose and changed the position of the books, putting the album underneath. That was the way they had been arranged in the first place.

Dagget gave an awkward little laugh. 'Now what difference did it make which book was on top?' said he.

Louisa looked at him with a deprecating smile. 'I always keep them that way,' murmured she.

'You do beat everything,' said Dagget, trying to laugh again. His large face was flushed.

He remained about an hour longer, then rose to take leave. Going out, he stumbled over a rug, and trying to recover himself, hit Louisa's work-basket on the table, and knocked it on the floor.

He looked at Louisa, then at the rolling spools; he ducked himself awkwardly towards them, but she stopped him. 'Never mind,' said she. 'I'll pick them up after you're gone.'

She spoke with a mild stiffness. Either she was a little disturbed, or his nervousness affected her, and made her seem constrained in her effort to reassure him.

When Joe Dagget was outside he drew in the sweet evening air with a sigh, and felt much as an innocent and perfectly well-intentioned bear might after his exit from a china shop.

Louisa, on her part, felt much as the kind-hearted, long-suffering owner of the china shop might have done after the exit of the bear.

She tied on the pink, then the green apron, picked up all the scattered treasures and replaced them in her work-basket, and straightened the rug. Then she set the lamp on the floor, and began sharply examining the carpet. She even rubbed her fingers over it, and looked at them.

'He's tracked in a good deal of dust,' she murmured. 'I thought he must have.'

Louisa got a dustpan and brush, and swept Joe Dagget's track carefully.

If he could have known it, it would have increased his perplexity and uneasiness, although it would not have disturbed his loyalty in the least. He came twice a week to see Louisa Ellis, and every time, sitting there in her delicately sweet room, he felt as if surrounded by a hedge of lace. He was afraid to stir lest he should put a clumsy foot or hand through the fairy web, and he had always the consciousness that Louisa was watching fearfully lest he should.

Still the lace and Louisa commanded perforce his perfect respect and patience and loyalty. They were to be married in a month, after a singular courtship which had lasted for a matter of fifteen years. For fourteen out of the fifteen years the two had not once seen each other, and they had seldom exchanged letters. Joe had been all those years in Australia, where he had gone to make his fortune, and where he had stayed until he made it. He would have stayed fifty years if it had taken so long, and come home feeble and tottering, or never come home at all, to marry Louisa.

But the fortune had been made in the fourteen years, and he had come home now to marry the woman who had been patiently and unquestioningly waiting for him all that time.

Shortly after they were engaged he had announced to Louisa his determination to strike out into new fields, and secure a competency before they should be married. She had listened and assented with the sweet serenity which never failed her, not even when her lover set forth on that long and uncertain journey. Joe, buoyed up as he was by his sturdy determination, broke down a little at the last, but Louisa kissed him with a mild blush, and said goodbye.

'It won't be for long,' poor Joe had said, huskily; but it was for fourteen years.

In that length of time much had happened. Louisa's mother and brother had died, and she was all alone in the world. But greatest happening of all – a subtle happening which both were too simple to understand – Louisa's feet had turned into a path, smooth maybe under a calm, serene sky, but so straight and unswerving that it could only meet a check at her grave, and so narrow that there was no room for anyone at her side.

Louisa's first emotion when Joe Dagget came home (he had not apprised her of his coming) was consternation, although she would not admit it to herself, and he never dreamed of it. Fifteen years ago she had been in love with him – at least she considered herself to be. Just at that time, gently acquiescing with and falling into the natural drift of girlhood, she had seen marriage ahead as a reasonable feature and a probable desirability of life. She had listened with calm docility to her mother's views upon the subject. Her mother was remarkable for her cool sense and sweet, even temperament. She talked wisely to her daughter when Joe Dagget presented himself, and Louisa accepted him with no hesitation. He was the first lover she had ever had.

She had been faithful to him all these years. She had never dreamed of the possibility of marrying anyone else. Her life, especially for the last seven years, had been full of a pleasant peace, she had never felt discontented nor impatient over her lover's absence; still she had always looked forward to his return and their marriage as the inevitable conclusion of things. However, she had fallen into a way of placing it so far in the future that it was almost equal to placing it over the boundaries of another life.

When Joe came she had been expecting him, and expecting to be married for fourteen years, but she was as much surprised and taken aback as if she had never thought of it.

Joe's consternation came later. He eyed Louisa with an instant confirmation of his old admiration. She had changed but little. She still kept her pretty manner and soft grace, and was, he considered, every whit as attractive as ever. As for himself, his stent was done; he had turned his face away from fortune-seeking, and the old winds of romance whistled as loud and sweet as ever through his ears. All the song which he had been wont to hear in them was Louisa; he had for a long time a loyal belief that he heard it still, but finally it seemed to him that although the winds sang always that one song, it had another name. But for Louisa the wind had never more than murmured; now it had gone down, and everything was still. She listened for a little while with half-wistful attention; then she turned quietly away and went to work on her wedding clothes.

Joe had made some extensive and quite magnificent alterations in his house. It was the old homestead; the newly married couple would live there, for Joe could not desert his mother, who refused to leave her old home. So Louisa must leave hers. Every morning, rising and going about among her neat maidenly possessions, she felt as one looking her last upon the faces of dear friends. It was true that in a measure she could take them with her, but, robbed of her old environments, they would appear in such new guises that they would almost cease to be themselves. Then there were some peculiar features of her happy solitary life which she would probably be obliged to relinquish altogether. Sterner tasks than these graceful but half-needless ones would probably devolve upon her. There would be a large house to care for; there would be company to entertain; there would be Joe's rigorous and feeble old mother to wait upon; and it would be contrary to all thrifty village traditions for her to keep more than one servant. Louisa had a little still, and she used to occupy herself pleasantly in summer weather with distilling the sweet and aromatic essences from rose and peppermint and spearmint. By-and-by her still must be laid away. Her store of essences was already considerable, and there would be no time for her to distil for the mere pleasure of it. Then Joe's mother would think it foolishness; she had already hinted her opinion in the matter. Louisa dearly loved to sew a linen seam, not always for use, but for the simple, mild pleasure which she took in it. She would have been loath to confess how more than once she had ripped a seam for the mere delight of sewing it together again. Sitting at her window during long sweet afternoons, drawing her needle gently through the dainty fabric, she was peace itself. But there was small chance of such foolish comfort in the future. Joe's mother, domineering, shrewd old matron that she was even in her old age, and very likely even Joe himself, with his honest masculine rudeness, would laugh and frown down all these pretty but senseless old maiden ways.

Louisa had almost the enthusiasm of an artist over the mere order and cleanliness of her solitary home. She had throbs of genuine triumph at the sight of the window-panes which she had polished until they shone like jewels. She gloated gently over her orderly bureau drawers, with their exquisitely folded contents redolent with lavender and sweet clover and very purity. Could she be sure of the endurance of even this? She had visions, so startling that she half repudiated them as indelicate, of coarse masculine belongings strewn about in endless litter; of dust and disorder arising necessarily from a coarse masculine presence in the midst of all this delicate harmony.

Among her forebodings of disturbance, not the least was with regard to Cæsar. Cæsar was a veritable hermit of a dog. For the greater part of his life he had dwelt in his secluded hut, shut out from the society of his kind and all innocent canine joys. Never had Cæsar since his early youth watched at a woodchuck's hole; never had he known the delights of a stray bone at a neighbour's kitchen door. And it was all on account of a sin committed when hardly out of his puppyhood. No one knew the possible depth of remorse of which this mild-visaged, altogether innocent-looking old dog might be capable; but whether or not he had encountered remorse, he had encountered a full measure of righteous retribution. Old Cæsar seldom lifted up his voice in a growl or a bark; he was fat and sleepy; there were yellow rings which looked like spectacles around his dim old eyes; but there was a neighbour who bore on his hand the imprint of several of Cæsar's sharp white youthful teeth, and for that he had lived at the end of a chain, all alone in a little hut, for fourteen years. The neighbour, who was choleric and smarting with the pain of his wound, had demanded either Cæsar's death or complete ostracism. So Louisa's brother, to whom the dog had belonged, had built him his little kennel and tied him up. It was now fourteen years since, in a flood of youthful spirits, he had inflicted that memorable bite, and with the exception of short excursions, always at the end of the chain, under the strict guardianship of his master or Louisa, the old dog had remained a close prisoner. It is doubtful if, with his limited ambition, he took much pride in the fact, but it is certain that he was possessed of considerable cheap fame. He was regarded by all the children in the village and by many adults as a very monster of ferocity. St George's dragon could hardly have surpassed in evil repute Louisa Ellis's old yellow dog. Mothers charged their children with solemn emphasis not to go too near to him, and the children listened and believed greedily, with a fascinated appetite for terror, and ran by Louisa's house stealthily, with many sidelong and backward glances at the terrible dog. If perchance he sounded a hoarse bark, there was a panic. Wayfarers chancing into Louisa's yard eyed him with respect, and inquired if the chain were stout. Cæsar at large might have seemed an ordinary dog, and excited no comment whatever; chained, his reputation overshadowed him, so that he lost his own proper outlines and looked darkly vague and enormous. Joe Dagget, however, with his good-humoured sense and shrewdness, saw him as he was. He strode valiantly up to him and patted him on the head, in spite of Louisa's soft clamour of warning, and even attempted to set him loose. Louisa grew so alarmed that he desisted, but kept announcing his opinion in the matter quite forcibly at intervals. 'There ain't a better-natured dog in town,' he would say, 'and it's downright cruel to keep him tied up there. Some day I'm going to take him out.'

Louisa had very little hope that he would not, one of these days, when their interests and possessions should be more completely fused in one. She pictured to herself Cæsar on the rampage through the quiet and unguarded village. She saw innocent children bleeding in his path. She was herself very fond of the old dog, because he had belonged to her dead brother, and he was always very gentle with her; still she had great faith in his ferocity. She always warned people not to go too near him. She fed him an ascetic fare of corn-mush and cakes, and never fired his dangerous temper with heating and sanguinary diet of flesh and bones. Louisa looked at the old dog munching his simple fare, and thought of her approaching marriage and trembled. Still no anticipation of disorder and confusion in lieu of sweet peace and harmony, no forebodings of Cæsar on the rampage, no wild fluttering of her little yellow canary, were sufficient to turn her a hair's breadth. Joe Dagget had been fond of her and working for her all these years. It was not for her, whatever came to pass, to prove untrue and break his heart. She put the exquisite little stitches into her wedding garments, and the time went on until it was only a week before her wedding day. It was a Tuesday evening, and the wedding was to be a week from Wednesday.

There was a full moon that night. About nine o'clock Louisa strolled down the road a little way. There were harvest fields on either hand, bordered by low stone walls. Luxuriant clumps of bushes grew beside the wall, and trees – wild cherry and old apple trees – at intervals. Presently Louisa sat down on the wall and looked about her with mildly sorrowful reflectiveness. Tall shrubs of blueberry and meadowsweet, all woven together and tangled with blackberry vines and horse briers, shut her in on either side. She had a little clear space between them. Opposite her, on the other side of the road, was a spreading tree; the moon shone between its boughs, and the leaves twinkled like silver. The road was bespread with a beautiful shifting dapple of silver and shadow; the air was full of a mysterious sweetness. 'I wonder if it's wild grapes?' muttered Louisa. She sat there some time. She was just thinking of rising, when she heard footsteps and low voices, and remained quiet. It was a lonely place, and she felt a little timid. She thought she would keep still in the shadow and let the persons, whoever they might be, pass her.

But just before they reached her the voices ceased, and the footsteps. She understood that their owners had also found seats upon the stone wall. She was wondering if she could not steal away unobserved, when the voice broke the stillness. It was Joe Dagget's. She sat still and listened.

The voice was announced by a loud sigh, which was as familiar as itself. 'Well,' said Dagget, 'you've made up your mind, then, I suppose?'

'Yes,' returned another voice. 'I'm going day after tomorrow.'

'That's Lily Dyer,' thought Louisa to herself. The voice embodied itself in her mind. She saw a girl tall and full figured, with a firm, fair face, looking fairer and firmer in the moonlight, her strong yellow hair braided in a close knot. A girl full of a calm rustic strength and bloom, with a masterful way which might have beseemed a princess. Lily Dyer was a favourite with the village folk; she had just the qualities to arouse the admiration. She was good and handsome and smart. Louisa had often heard her praises sounded.

'Well,' said Joe Dagget, 'I ain't got a word to say.'

'I don't know what you could say,' returned Lily Dyer.

'Not a word to say,' repeated Joe, drawing out the words heavily. Then there was a silence. 'I ain't sorry,' he began at last, 'that that happened yesterday – that we kind of let on how we felt to each other. I guess it's just as well we knew. Of course I can't do anything any different. I'm going right on an' get married next week. I ain't going back on a woman that's waited for me fourteen years, an' break her heart.'

'If you should jilt her tomorrow, I wouldn't have you,' spoke up the girl, with sudden vehemence.

'Well, I ain't going to give you the chance,' said he, 'but I don't believe you would, either.'

'You'd see I wouldn't. Honour's honour, an' rights right. An' I'd never think anything of any man that went against 'em for me or any other girl. You'd find that out, Joe Dagget.'

'Well, you'll find out fast enough that I ain't going against 'em for you or any other girl,' returned he. Their voices sounded almost as if they were angry with each other. Louisa was listening eagerly.

'I'm sorry you feel as if you must go away,' said Joe, 'but I don't know but it's best.'

'Of course it's best. I hope you and I have got common sense.'

'Well, I suppose you're right.' Suddenly Joe's voice got an undertone of tenderness. 'Say, Lily,' said he, 'I'll get along well enough myself, but I can't bear to think – You don't suppose you're going to fret much over it?'

'I guess you'll find out I sha'n't fret much over a married man.'

'Well, I hope you won't – I hope you won't, Lily. God knows I do. And – I hope – one of these days – you'll – come across somebody else—'

'I don't see any reason why I shouldn't.' Suddenly her tone changed. She spoke in a sweet, clear voice, so loud that she could have been heard across the street. 'No, Joe Dagget,' said she, 'I'll never marry any other man as long as I live. I've got good sense, an' I ain't going to break my heart nor make a fool of myself; but I'm never going to be married, you can be sure of that. I ain't that sort of a girl to feel this way twice.'

Louisa heard an exclamation and a soft commotion behind the bushes; then Lily spoke again – the voice sounded as if she had risen. 'This must be put a stop to,' said she. 'We've stayed here long enough. I'm going home.'

Louisa sat there in a daze, listening to their retreating steps. After a while she got up and slunk softly home herself.

The next day she did her housework methodically; that was as much a matter of course as breathing; but she did not sew on her wedding clothes. She sat at her window and meditated. In the evening Joe came. Louisa Ellis had never known that she had any diplomacy in her, but when she came to look for it that night she found it, although meek of its kind, among her little feminine weapons. Even now she could hardly believe that she had heard aright, and that she would not do Joe a terrible injury should she break her troth-plight. She wanted to sound him without betraying too soon her own inclinations in the matter. She did it successfully, and they finally came to an understanding; but it was a difficult thing, for he was as afraid of betraying himself as she.

She never mentioned Lily Dyer. She simply said that while she had no cause of complaint against him, she had lived so long in one way that she shrank from making a change.

'Well, I never shrank, Louisa,' said Dagget. 'I'm going to be honest enough to say that I think maybe it's better this way; but if you'd wanted to keep on, I'd have stuck to you till my dying day. I hope you know that.'

'Yes, I do,' said she.

That night she and Joe parted more tenderly than they had done for a long time. Standing in the door, holding each other's hands, a last great wave of regretful memory swept over them.

'Well, this ain't the way we've thought it was all going to end, is it, Louisa?' said Joe.

She shook her head. There was a little quiver on her placid face.

'You let me know if there's ever anything I can do for you,' said he. 'I ain't ever going to forget you, Louisa.' Then he kissed her, and went down the path.

Louisa, all alone by herself that night, wept a little, she hardly knew why; but the next morning, on waking, she felt like a queen who, after fearing lest her domain be wrested away from her, sees it firmly insured in her possession.

Now the tall weeds and grasses might cluster around Cæsar's little hermit hut, the snow might fall on its roof year in and year out, but he never would go on a rampage through the unguarded village. Now the little canary might turn itself into a peaceful yellow ball night after night, and have no need to wake and flutter with wild terror against its bars. Louisa could sew linen seams, and distil roses, and dust and polish and fold away in lavender, as long as she listed. That afternoon she sat with her needle-work at the window and felt fairly steeped in peace. Lily Dyer, tall and erect and blooming, went past; but she felt no qualm. If Louisa Ellis had sold her birthright she did not know it, the taste of the pottage was so delicious, and had been her sole satisfaction for so long. Serenity and placid narrowness had become to her as the birthright itself. She gazed ahead through a long reach of future days strung together like pearls in a rosary, every one like the others, and all smooth and flawless and innocent, and her heart went up in thankfulness. Outside was the fervid summer afternoon; the air was filled with the sounds of the busy harvest of men and birds and bees; there were halloos, metallic claterrings, sweet calls, and long hummings. Louisa sat, prayerfully numbering her days, like an uncloistered nun.

(1891)

E. NESBIT

John Charrington's Wedding

No one ever thought that May Forster would marry John Charrington; but he thought differently, and things which John Charrington intended had a queer way of coming to pass. He asked her to marry him before he went up to Oxford. She laughed and refused him. He asked her again next time he came home. Again she laughed, tossed her dainty blonde head, and again refused. A third time he asked her; she said it was becoming a confirmed bad habit, and laughed at him more than ever.

John was not the only man who wanted to marry her: she was the belle of our village *coterie*, and we were all in love with her more or less; it was a sort of fashion, like heliotrope ties or Inverness capes. Therefore we were as much annoyed as surprised when John Charrington walked into our little local Club – we held it in a loft over the saddler's, I remember – and invited us all to his wedding.

'Your wedding?'

'You don't mean it?'

'Who's the happy fair? When's it to be?'

John Charrington filled his pipe and lighted it before he replied. Then he said:

'I'm sorry to deprive you fellows of your only joke – but Miss Forster and I are to be married in September.'

'You don't mean it?'

'He's got the mitten again, and it's turned his head.'

'No,' I said, rising, 'I see it's true. Lend me a pistol someone – or a first-class fare to the other end of Nowhere. Charrington has bewitched the only pretty girl in our twenty-mile radius. Was it mesmerism, or a love potion, Jack?'

'Neither, sir, but a gift you'll never have – perseverance – and the best luck a man ever had in this world.'

There was something in his voice that silenced me, and all chaff of the other fellows failed to draw him further.

The queer thing about it was that when we congratulated Miss

Forster, she blushed and smiled and dimpled, for all the world as though she were in love with him, and had been in love with him all the time. Upon my word, I think she had. Women are strange creatures.

We were all asked to the wedding. In Brixham everyone who was anybody knew everybody else who was anyone. My sisters were, I truly believe, more interested in the *trousseau* than the bride herself, and I was to be best man. The coming marriage was much canvassed at afternoon tea-tables, and at our little Club over the saddler's, and the question was always asked: 'Does she care for him?'

I used to ask that question myself in the early days of their engagement, but after a certain evening in August I never asked it again. I was coming home from the Club through the churchyard. Our church is on a thyme-grown hill, and the turf about it is so thick and soft that one's footsteps are noiseless.

I made no sound as I vaulted the low lichened wall, and threaded my way between the tombstones. It was at the same instant that I heard John Charrington's voice, and saw Her. May was sitting on a low flat gravestone, her face turned towards the full splendour of the western sun. Its expression ended, at once and for ever, any question of love for him; it was transfigured to a beauty I should not have believed possible, even to that beautiful little face.

John lay at her feet, and it was his voice that broke the stillness of the golden August evening.

'My dear, my dear, I believe I should come back from the dead if you wanted me!'

I coughed at once to indicate my presence, and passed on into the shadow fully enlightened.

The wedding was to be early in September. Two days before I had to run up to town on business. The train was late, of course, for we are on the South-Eastern, and as I stood grumbling with my watch in my hand, whom should I see but John Charrington and May Forster. They were walking up and down the unfrequented end of the platform, arm in arm, looking into each other's eyes, careless of the sympathetic interest of the porters.

Of course I knew better than to hesitate a moment before burying myself in the booking-office, and it was not till the train drew up at the platform, that I obtrusively passed the pair with my Gladstone, and took the corner in a first-class smoking carriage. I did this with as good an air of not seeing them as I could assume. I pride myself on my discretion, but if John were travelling alone I wanted his company. I had it.

'Hullo, old man,' came his cheery voice as he swung his bag into my carriage; 'here's luck. I was expecting a dull journey!'

'Where are you off to?' I asked, discretion still bidding me turn my eyes away, though I saw, without looking, that hers were red-rimmed.

'To old Branbridge's,' he answered, shutting the door and leaning out for a last word with his sweetheart.

'Oh, I wish you wouldn't go, John,' she was saying in a low, earnest voice. 'I feel certain something will happen.'

'Do you think I should let anything happen to keep me, and the day after tomorrow our wedding day?'

'Don't go,' she answered, with a pleading intensity which would have sent my Gladstone on to the platform and me after it. But she wasn't speaking to me. John Charrington was made differently; he rarely changed his opinions, never his resolutions.

He only stroked the little ungloved hands that lay on the carriage door.

'I must, May. The old boy's been awfully good to me, and now he's dying I must go and see him, but I shall come home in time for—' the rest of the parting was lost in a whisper and in the rattling lurch of the starting train.

'You're sure to come?' she spoke as the train moved.

'Nothing shall keep me,' he answered, and we steamed out. After he had seen the last of the little figure on the platform he leaned back in his corner and kept silence for a minute.

When he spoke it was to explain to me that his godfather, whose heir he was, lay dying at Peasmarsh Place, some fifty miles away, and had sent for John, and John had felt bound to go.

'I shall be surely back tomorrow,' he said, 'or, if not, the day after, in heaps of time. Thank Heaven, one hasn't to get up in the middle of the night to get married nowadays!'

'And suppose Mr Branbridge dies?'

'Alive or dead I mean to be married on Thursday!' John answered, lighting a cigar and unfolding *The Times*.

At Peasmarsh station we said goodbye, and he got out, and I saw him ride off. I went on to London, where I stayed the night.

When I got home the next afternoon, a very wet one, by the way, my sister greeted me with: 'Where's Mr Charrington?'

'Goodness knows,' I answered testily. Every man, since Cain, has resented that kind of question.

'I thought you might have heard from him,' she went on, 'as you're to give him away tomorrow.'

'Isn't he back?' I asked, for I had confidently expected to find him at home.

'No, Geoffrey,' my sister Fanny always had a way of jumping to conclusions, especially such conclusions as were least favourable to her fellow creatures, 'he has not returned, and, what is more, you may depend upon it he won't. You mark my words, there'll be no wedding tomorrow.'

My sister Fanny has a power of annoying me which no other human being possesses.

'You mark my words,' I retorted with asperity, 'you had better give up making such a thundering idiot of yourself. There'll be more wedding tomorrow than ever you'll take the first part in.' A prophecy which, by the way, came true.

But though I could snarl confidently to my sister, I did not feel so comfortable when late that night, I, standing on the doorstep of John's house, heard that he had not returned. I went home gloomily through the rain. Next morning brought a brilliant blue sky, gold sun, and all such softness of air and beauty of cloud as go to make up a perfect day. I woke with a vague feeling of having gone to bed anxious, and of being rather averse to facing that anxiety in the light of full wakefulness.

But with my shaving water came a note from John which relieved my mind and sent me up to the Forsters' with a light heart.

May was in the garden. I saw her blue gown through the hollyhocks as the lodge gates swung to behind me. So I did not go up to the house, but turned aside down the turfed path.

'He's written to you too,' she said, without preliminary greeting, when I reached her side.

'Yes, I'm to meet him at the station at three, and come straight on to the church.'

Her face looked pale, but there was a brightness in her eyes, and a tender quiver about the mouth that spoke of renewed happiness.

'Mr Branbridge begged him so to stay another night that he had not the heart to refuse,' she went on. 'He is so kind, but I wish he hadn't stayed.'

I was at the station at half-past two. I felt rather annoyed with

John. It seemed a sort of slight to the beautiful girl who loved him, that he should come as it were out of breath, and with the dust of travel upon him, to take her hand, which some of us would have given the best years of our lives to take.

But when the three o'clock train glided in, and glided out again having brought no passengers to our little station, I was more than annoyed. There was no other train for thirty-five minutes; I calculated that, with much hurry, we might just get to the church in time for the ceremony; but, oh, what a fool to miss that first train! What other man could have done it?

That thirty-five minutes seemed a year, as I wandered round the station reading the advertisements and the timetables, and the company's bye-laws, and getting more and more angry with John Charrington. This confidence in his own power of getting every-thing he wanted the minute he wanted it was leading him too far. I hate waiting. Everyone does, but I believe I hate it more than anyone else. The three thirty-five was late, of course.

I ground my pipe between my teeth and stamped with impati-ence as I watched the signals. Click. The signal went down. Five minutes later I flung myself into the carriage that I had brought for John.

'Drive to the church!' I said, as someone shut the door. 'Mr Charrington hasn't come by this train.'

Anxiety now replaced anger. What had become of the man? Could he have been taken suddenly ill? I had never known him have a day's illness in his life. And even so he might have telegraphed. Some awful accident must have happened to him. The thought that he had played her false never – no, not for a moment – entered my head. Yes, something terrible had happened to him, and on me lay the task of telling his bride. I almost wished the carriage would upset and break my head so that someone else might tell her, nor I, who – but that's nothing to do with this story.

It was five minutes to four as we drew up at the churchyard gate. A double row of eager onlookers lined the path from lychgate to porch. I sprang from the carriage and passed up between them. Our gardener had a good front place near the door. I stopped.

'Are they waiting still, Byles?' I asked, simply to gain time, for of course I knew they were by the waiting crowd's attentive attitude.

'Waiting, sir? No, no, sir; why, it must be over by now.'

'Over! Then Mr Charrington's come?'

'To the minute, sir; must have missed you somehow, and, I say, sir,' lowering his voice, 'I never see Mr John the least bit so afore, but my opinion is he's been drinking pretty free. His clothes was all dusty and his face like a sheet. I tell you I didn't like the looks of him at all, and the folks inside are saying all sorts of things. You'll see, something's gone very wrong with Mr John, and he's tried liquor. He looked like a ghost, and in he went with his eyes straight before him, with never a look or a word for none of us: him that was always such a gentleman!'

I had never heard Byles make so long a speech. The crowd in the churchyard were talking in whispers and getting ready rice and slippers to throw at the bride and bridegroom. The ringers were ready with their hands on the ropes to ring out the merry peal as the bride and bridegroom should come out.

A murmur from the church announced them; out they came. Byles was right. John Charrington did not look himself. There was dust on his coat, his hair was disarranged. He seemed to have been in some row, for there was a black mark above his eyebrow. He was deathly pale. But his pallor was not greater than that of the bride, who might have been carved in ivory – dress, veil, orange blossoms, face and all.

As they passed out the ringers stooped – there were six of them – and then, on the ears expecting the gay wedding peal, came the slow tolling of the passing bell.

A thrill of horror at so foolish a jest from the ringers passed through us all. But the ringers themselves dropped the ropes and fled like rabbits out into the sunlight. The bride shuddered, and grey shadows came about her mouth, but the bridegroom led her on down the path where the people stood with the handfuls of rice; but the handfuls were never thrown, and the wedding bells never rang. In vain the ringers were urged to remedy their mistake: they protested with many whispered expletives that they would see themselves further first.

In a hush like the hush in the chamber of death the bridal pair passed into their carriage and its door slammed behind them.

Then the tongues were loosed. A babel of anger, wonder, conjecture from the guests and the spectators.

'If I'd seen his condition, sir,' said old Forster to me as we drove off, 'I would have stretched him on the floor of the church, sir, by Heaven I would, before I'd have let him marry my daughter!'

Then he put his head out of the window.

'Drive like hell,' he cried to the coachman; 'don't spare the horses.'

He was obeyed. We passed the bride's carriage. I forbore to look at it, and old Forster turned his head away and swore. We reached home before it.

We stood in the hall doorway, in the blazing afternoon sun, and in about half a minute we heard wheels crunching the gravel. When the carriage stopped in front of the steps old Forster and I ran down.

'Great Heaven, the carriage is empty! And yet—'

I had the door open in a minute, and this is what I saw – No sign of John Charrington; and of May, his wife, only a huddled heap of white satin lying half on the floor of the carriage and half on the seat.

'I drove straight here, sir,' said the coachman, as the bride's father lifted her out, 'and I'll swear no one got out of the carriage.'

We carried her into the house in her bridal dress and drew back her veil. I saw her face. Shall I ever forget it? White, white and drawn with agony and horror, bearing such a look of terror as I have never seen since except in dreams. And her hair, her radiant blonde hair, I tell you it was white like snow.

As we stood, her father and I, half mad with the horror and mystery of it, a boy came up the avenue – a telegraph boy. They brought the orange envelope to me. I tore it open.

'Mr Charrington was thrown from the dogcart* on his way to the station at half-past one. Killed on the spot!'

And he was married to May Forster in our parish church at *half-past three*, in presence of half the parish.

'I shall be married, dead or alive!'

What had passed in that carriage on the homeward drive? No one knows – no one will ever know. Oh, May! oh, my dear!

Before a week was over they laid her beside her husband in our little churchyard on the thyme-covered hill – the churchyard where they had kept their love-trysts.

Thus was accomplished John Charrington's wedding.

(1893)

A Ripple of Dissension and What Came of It
(from *Fair to Look Upon*)

I was about to be married. My numerous charms and attractions had won the affections of a young man who was equally charming with myself.

We were sitting on a luxurious divan and he held my milk-white hand in his. I do not make that statement as a startling announcement of an unusual occurrence, but simply as a matter of fact.

We had been conversing about the culinary and domestic arrangements of our future home when matrimony had made us 'one flesh'; or, to use English, we had been wondering what under the canopy a good cooking stove would cost, when he asked suddenly and irrelevantly,

'And you will love me, always?'

'Of course,' said I, a little impatiently; for when one is deep in a mathematical problem such a question is a little annoying.

'And you will honour me always?' he next enquired.

'As long as you deserve to be honoured,' I replied, with the habitual good sense of my age and sex, mentally wondering if graniteware stewpans went with a cooking stove.

'And you will obey me?' he queried next, in a tone that plainly indicated that I'd have to. I left the mathematical problem for future solution and said, hesitatingly:

'Yes – if – I – can.'

'If you can?' he said, in sternly questioning tones; and a cloud no bigger than a man's hand appeared upon the heaven of our love.

'I don't believe a woman ever lived who ever obeyed anyone – God, angels, or men,' I cried.

'You are a traitor. You slander your sex,' he exclaimed, aghast.

'I deny the charge,' I replied, springing to my feet, with all the spirit of the above-mentioned age and sex. 'By that assertion I only add glory to their fame.'

He looked at me for a little while, too surprised to speak, and then said, in sarcastic tones, 'Consider our wedding postponed until you have had a little time to study your Bible. Good night.'

' "Study your Bible!" That is what everybody says when they want to prove any theory, creed, ism, or anything. I shall study my Bible diligently. Good night,' I replied, thinking it was not such very bad advice after all; and then I hummed a gay little tune for his benefit until I heard the hall door close.

And I have studied my Bible with the following result.

The Story of Eve

Away back when Adam was a young man – now I know that Adam is rather an ancient subject, but you need not elevate your eyebrows in scorn, for you will be ancient yourself some time – he found himself in Eden one day; he did not know why, but we do, don't we?

He was there because Eve was to come, and it was a foregone conclusion even in that early age that when she did appear she would want someone to hold her bouquet, open the door for her, button her gloves, tell her she was pretty and sweet and 'I never saw a woman like you before,' you know.

Her arrival was the greatest event the world has ever known, and the grandest preparations were made for it.

A blue sky arched gloriously over the earth, and sun, moon and stars flashed and circled into space, silvery rivers ran cool and slow through scented valleys, the trees threw cooling shadows on the fresh, damp grass, the birds sang in the rosy dawn, the flowers blushed in odourous silence and yet it was all incomplete; and Adam wandered restlessly around like a man who has lost his collar button.

But suddenly a great hush of expectancy fell upon the world. Not a bird fluttered its feathers, the flowers bowed their heads, the winds and the waters listening ceased their flowing and their blowing, the radiant moonshine mingled its light with the pale pink dawn and a million stars paled their eternal fires, as Eve, the first woman, stood in Eden.

And the world was young and beautiful. The first flush and bloom was on the mountains and the valleys, the birds were thrilled by the sweetness of their own songs, the waves broke into little murmurs of delight at their own liquid beauty, the stars of heaven and the unfading blue were above Adam's head – and yet he wasn't satisfied. Long he stood idly in the brightening dawn wondering why the days were so long and why there were so many of them, when suddenly out from the swinging vines and the swaying foliage Eve came forth.

And though there was a vacant look on her lovely face (for her baby soul had not yet awakened) Adam saw that her lips were red and her arm white and rounded and he whistled a soft, low whistle with a sort of 'O-won't-you-stop-a-moment?' cadence in the music, and Eve looked up; and I think at that moment he plucked a flower and offered it to her; and of course she did not understand it all, but Nature, not intelligence, asserted her power, and she reached out her hand and took the rose – and then for the first time in the world a woman blushed and smiled; and I suspect it was at that very moment that 'the morning stars first sang together'.

Woman has never been obedient. She has always had the germ of the ruler and autocrat in her soul. It was born when Eve first looked with longing eyes at the apple swinging in the sunlight.

While Adam was idly, lazily sunning himself in the garden was Eve contented to smell the fragrance of the violets and bask in the starlight of a new world? Oh no! She was quietly wandering around searching for the Serpent, and when she found him she smiled upon him and he thought the world grew brighter; then she laughed and his subjugation was complete; and then the naughty creature, without waiting for an introduction, led him to the famous apple tree, and standing on her tiptoes, reached up her hands and said with a soul-subduing little pout:

'See, I want that apple, but I can't reach it. Won't you please find a club and knock it off for me?' and she looked out of the corner of her eye and blushed divinely.

Now this Serpent represented, so it has always been believed, a very shrewd person. He saw that this woman had no garments, and that after she had eaten this fruit she would know better, and delight in clothes ever after. So he gave her the apple.

Almost instantly after she had eaten some, not because she particularly liked apples, or had any idea of their adaptability in the way of pies, sauce or cider, but because she wanted to 'be as gods knowing good and evil', as the Serpent said she would. Discontent with her wardrobe crept into her heart and ambition for something better sprang to life.

In the distance stood Adam. With a thrill of rapture she beheld him, her aroused soul flashed from her eyes and love was born, and she ran towards him through the flowers, pausing on the river's brink to rest, for weariness had touched her limbs.

She watched the waters running south out of the garden, and like one coming out of a dim, sweet twilight into a blaze of glory she looked and wondered 'why' it ran that way, and lo! Thought blossomed like a rose, and generosity laughed in the sunshine when she put the apple in Adam's hand; and Adam, with the only woman in the world beside him, and the first free lunch before him, forgot all about God and His commands and 'did eat', and the results proved that free lunches always did demoralise men – and always will. And modesty blushed rosy red when Adam put the apple to his lips, and invention and ingenuity, newborn, rushed to the rescue, and they gathered the fig leaves.

Then memory like a demon whispered in her ear: 'The day that ye eat thereof ye shall surely die.' She glanced at Adam and deadly fear chilled the joyous blood in her viens. Then she argued: 'He will be less angry with me, a woman, and His vengeance will fall less heavily on me than on the man to whom His command was given; and lo! Reason rose like a star on the waves of life, and shoulder to shoulder womanly devotion and heroism that fears neither God nor death in defense of its loved ones entered her soul, and she instructed Adam to say: "The woman tempted me," and deception trembled on her lips when she cried, "The serpent did tempt me," and the tears of regret and remorse watered the seeds of deception and they grew so luxuriously that women have always had that same way of getting out of scrapes ever since.

Yet to Eve belongs the honour of never having obeyed anyone – when it interfered with progress, advancement and intelligence – neither God, angels nor men.

The women of the nineteenth century make a profound salaam of admiration and respect to Eve, in whom they recognise the first courageous, undaunted poineer woman of the world

(1892)

GRACE KING

The Balcony

There is much of life passed on the balcony in a country where the summer unrolls in six moon-lengths, and where the nights have to come with a double endowment of vastness and splendour to compensate for the tedious, sun-parched days.

And in that country the women love to sit and talk together of summer nights, on balconies, in their vague, loose, white garments – men are not balcony sitters – with their sleeping children within easy hearing, the stars breaking the cool darkness, or the moon making a show of light – oh, such a discreet show of light! – through the vines. And the children inside, waking to go from one sleep into another, hear the low, soft mother-voices on the balcony, talking about this person and that, old times, old friends, old experiences; and it seems to them, hovering a moment in wakefulness, that there is no end of the world or time, or of the mother-knowledge; but, illimitable as it is, the mother-voices and the mother-love and protection fill it all – with their mother's hand in theirs, children are not afraid even of God – and they drift into slumber again, their little dreams taking all kinds of pretty reflections from the great unknown horizon outside, as their fragile soap-bubbles take on reflections from the sun and clouds.

Experiences, reminiscences, episodes, picked up as only women know how to pick them up from other women's lives – or other women's destinies, as they prefer to call them – and told as only women know how to relate them; what God has done or is doing with some other woman whom they have known – that is what interests women once embarked on their own lives – the embarkation takes place at marriage, or after the marriageable time – or, rather, that is what interests the women who sit of summer nights on balconies. For in those long-moon countries life is open and accessible, and romances seem to be furnished real and gratis, in order to save, in a languor-breeding climate, the ennui of reading and writing books. Each woman has a different way of picking up and relating her stories, as each one selects different pieces, and has a personal way of playing them on the piano.

Each story *is* different, or appears so to her; each has some unique and peculiar pathos in it. And so she dramatises and inflects it, trying to make the point visible to her apparent also to her hearers. Sometimes the pathos and interest to the hearers lie only in this – that the relater has observed it, and gathered it, and finds it worth telling. For do we not gather what we have not, and is not our own lacking our one motive? It may be so, for it often appears so.

And if a child inside be wakeful and precocious, it is not dreams alone that take on reflections from the balcony outside: through the half-open shutters the still, quiet eyes look across the dim forms on the balcony to the star-spangled or the moon-brightened heavens beyond; while memory makes stores for the future, and germs are sown, out of which the slow, clambering vine of thought issues, one day, to decorate or hide, as it may be, the structures or ruins of life.

Mimi's Marriage

This is how she told about it, sitting in her little room – her bridal chamber – not larger, really not larger than sufficed for the bed there, the armoire* here, the bureau opposite, and the washstand behind the door, the corners all touching. But a nice set of furniture, quite *comme il faut* – handsome, in fact – as a bride of good family should have. And she was dressed very prettily, too, in her long white *négligée* with plenty of lace and ruffles and blue ribbons – such as only the Creole girls can make, and brides, alas! wear – the pretty honeymoon costume that suggests, that suggests – well! to proceed. 'The poor little cat!' as one could not help calling her, so *migronne*, so blonde, with the pretty black eyes, and the rosebud of a mouth – whenever she closed it – a perfect kiss.

'But you know, Louise,' she said, beginning quite seriously at the beginning, 'Papa would never have consented, never, never – poor Papa! Indeed, I should never have asked him; it would only

have been one humiliation more for him, poor Papa! So it was
well he was dead, if it was God's will for it to be. Of course I had
my dreams, like everybody. I was so blonde, so blonde, and so
small; it seemed like a law I should marry a *brun*, a tall, handsome
brun, with a moustache and a fine baritone voice. That was how I
always arranged it, and – you will laugh – but a large, large house,
and numbers of servants, and a good cook, but a superlatively
good cuisine, and wine and all that, and long, trailing silk dresses,
and theatre every night, and voyages to Europe, and – well,
everything God had to give, in fact. You know, I get that from
Papa, wanting everything God has to give! Poor Papa! It seemed
to me I was to meet him at any time, my handsome *brun*. I used to
look for him positively on my way to school, and back home
again, and whenever I would think of him I would try and walk so
prettily, and look so pretty! *Mon Dieu!* I was not ten years old
yet! And afterwards it was only for that that I went into society.
What should girls go into society for otherwise but to meet their
brun or their blond? Do you think it is amusing, to economise and
economise, and sew and sew, just to go to a party to dance? No! I
assure you, I went into society only for that; and I do not believe
what girls say – they go into society only for that too.

'You know at school how we used to *tirer la bonne aventure.**
Well, every time he was not *brun, riche, avenant*, Jules, or Raoul,
or Guy, I simply would not accept it, but would go on drawing
until I obtained what I wanted. As I tell you, I thought it was my
destiny. And when I would try with a flower to see if he loved me
– *Il m'aime, un peu, beaucoup, passionément, pas du tout* – if it
were *pas du tout*, I would always throw the flower away, and
begin tearing off the leaves from another one immediately.
Passionément was what I wanted, and I always got it in the end.

'But Papa, poor Papa, he never knew anything of that, of
course. He would get furious when anyone would come to see me,
and sometimes, when he would take me in society, if I danced
with a 'nobody' – as he called no matter whom I danced with – he
would come up and take me away with such an air – such an air!
It would seem that Papa thought himself better than everybody in
the world. But it went worse and worse with Papa, not only in the
affairs of the world, but in health. Always thinner and thinner,
always a cough; in fact, you know, I am a little feeble-chested
myself, from Papa. And Clementine! Clementine with her children
– just think, Louise, eight! I thank God my Mama had only me, if

Papa's second wife had to have so many. And so naughty! I assure you, they were all devils; and no correction, no punishment, no education – but you know Clementine! I tell you, sometimes on account of those children I used to think myself in 'ell [making the Creole's attempt and failure to pronounce the h], and Clementine had no pride about them. If they had shoes, well; if they had not shoes, well also.

'"But Clementine!" I would expostulate, I would pray—

'"But do not be a fool, Mimi," she would say. "Am I God? Can I do miracles? Or must I humiliate your papa?"

'That was true. Poor Papa! It would have humiliated Papa. When he had money he gave; only it was a pity he had no money. As for what he observed, he thought it was Clementine's neglig-ence. For, it is true, Clementine had no order, no industry, in the best of fortune as in the worst. But to do her justice, it was not her fault this time, only she let him believe it, to save his pride; and Clementine, you know, has a genius for stories. I assure you, Louise, I was desperate. I prayed to God to help me, to advise me. I could not teach – I had no education; I could not go into a shop – that would be dishonouring Papa – and *enfin*, I was too pretty. 'And proclaim to the world,' Clementine would cry, 'that your papa does not make money for his family.' That was true. The world is so malicious. You know, Louise, sometimes it seems to me the world is glad to hear that a man cannot support his family; it compliments those who can. As if Papa had not intelligence, and honour, and honesty! But they do not count now as in old times, 'before the war'.

'And so, when I thought of that, I laughed and talked and played the thoughtless like Clementine, and made bills. We made bills – we had to – for everything; we could do that, you know, on our old name and family. But it is too long! I am sure it is too long and tiresome! What egotism on my part! Come, we will take a glass of anisette, and talk of something else – your trip, your family. No? no? You are only asking me out of politeness! You are so *aimable*, so kind. Well, if you are not *ennuyée* – in fact, I want to tell you. It was too long to write, and I detest a pen. To me there is no instrument of torture like a pen.

'Well, the lady next door, she was an American, and common, very common, according to Papa. In comparison to us she had no family whatever. Our little children were forbidden even to associate with her little children. I thought that was ridiculous –

not that I am a democrat, but I thought it ridiculous. But the children cared; they were so disobedient and they were always next door, and they always had something nice to eat over there. I sometimes thought Clementine used to encourage their disobedience, just for the good things they got to eat over there. But Papa was always making fun of them; you know what a sharp tongue he had. The gentleman was a clerk; and, according to Papa, the only true gentlemen in the world had family and a profession. We did not dare allow ourselves to think it, but Clementine and I knew that they, in fact, were in more comfortable circumstances than we.

'The lady, who also had a great number of children, sent one day, with all the discretion and delicacy possible, and asked me if I would be so kind as to – guess what, Louise! But only guess! But you never could! Well, to darn some of her children's stockings for her. It was God who inspired her, I am sure, on account of my praying so much to him. You will be shocked, Louise, when I tell you. It sounds like a sin, but I was not in despair when Papa died. It was a grief – yes, it seized the heart, but it was not despair. Men ought not to be subjected to the humiliation of life; they are not like women, you know. We are made to stand things; they have their pride – their *orgueil*, as we say in French – and that is the point of honour with some men. And Clementine and I, we could not have concealed it much longer. In fact, the truth was crying out everywhere, in the children, in the house, in our own persons, in our faces. The darning did not provide a superfluity, I guarantee you!

'Poor Papa! He caught cold. He was condemned from the first. And so all his fine qualities died; for he had fine qualities – they were too fine for this age, that was all. Yes; it was a kindness of God to take him before he found out. If it was to be, it was better. Just so with Clementine as with me. After the funeral – crack! everything went to pieces. We were at the four corners for the necessaries of life, and the bills came in – my dear, the bills that came in! What memories! what memories! Clementine and I exclaimed; there were some bills that we had completely forgotten about. The lady next door sent her brother over when Papa died. He sat up all night, that night, and he assisted us in all our arrangements. And he came in afterwards, every evening. If Papa had been there, there would have been a fine scene over it; he would have had to take the door, very likely. But now there was no one to make objections. And so when, as I say, we were at the four corners for the necessaries of life, he asked Clementine's permission to ask me to marry him.

'I give you my word, Louise, I had forgotten there was such a thing as marriage in the world for me! I had forgotten it as completely as the chronology of the Merovingian dynasty, alas! with all the other school things forgotten. And I do not believe Clementine remembered there was such a possibility in the world for me. *Mon Dieu!* when a girl is poor she may have all the beauty in the world – not that I had beauty, only a little prettiness. But you should have seen Clementine! She screamed for joy when she told me. Oh, there was but one answer according to her, and according to everybody she could consult, in her haste. They all said it was a dispensation of Providence in my favour. He was young, he was strong; he did not make a fortune, it was true, but he made a good living. And what an assistance to have a man in the family! – an assistance for Clementine and the children. But the principal thing, after all, was, he wanted to marry me. Nobody had ever wanted that before, my dear!

'Quick, quick, it was all arranged. All my friends did something for me. One made my *peignoirs** for me, one this, one that – *ma foi!* I did not recognise myself. One made all the toilet of the bureau, another of the bed, and we all sewed on the wedding dress together. And you should have seen Clementine, going out in all her great mourning, looking for a house, looking for a servant! But the wedding was private on account of poor Papa. But you know, Loulou, I had never time to think, except about Clementine and the children, and when I thought of all those poor little children, poor Papa's children, I said "Quick, quick," like the rest.

'It was the next day, the morning after the wedding, I had time to think. I was sitting here, just as you see me now, in my pretty new *négligée.* I had been looking at all the pretty presents I have shown you, and my trousseau, and my furniture – it is not bad, as you see – my dress, my veil, my ring, and – I do not know – I do not know – but, all of a sudden, from everywhere came the thought of my *brun*, my handsome *brun* with the moustache, and the *bonne aventure, riche, avenant*, the Jules, Raoul, Guy, and the flower leaves, and "*il m'aime, un peu, beaucoup, pas du tout*," *passionément*, and the way I expected to meet him walking to and from school, walking as if I were dancing the steps, and oh, my plans, my plans, my plans – silk dresses, theatre, voyages to

Europe, – and poor Papa, so fine, so tall, so aristocratic. I cannot
tell you how it all came; it seized my heart, and, *mon Dieu!* I cried
out, and I wept, I wept, I wept. How I wept! It pains me here now
to remember it. Hours, hours it lasted, until I had no tears in my
body, and I had to weep without them, with sobs and moans. But
this, I have always observed, is the time for reflection – after the
tears are all out. And I am sure God himself gave me my thoughts.
"Poor little Mimi!" I thougt, "*fi donc!* You are going to make a
fool of yourself now when it is all over, because why? It is God
who manages the world, and not you. You pray to God to help
you in your despair, and he has helped you. He has sent you a
good, kind husband who adores you; who asks only to be a
brother to your sisters and brothers, and son to Clementine; who
has given you more than you ever possessed in your life – but
because he did not come out of the *bonne aventure* – and who gets
a husband out of the *bonne aventure*? – and would your *brun*
have come to you in your misfortune?" I am sure God inspired
those thoughts in me.

'I tell you, I rose from that bed – naturally I had thrown myself
upon it. Quick I washed my face, I brushed my hair, and, you see
these bows of ribbons – look, here are the marks of the tears – I
turned them. *Hé*, Loulou, it occurs to me, that if you examined
the blue bows on a bride's *négligée*, you might always find tears
on the other side; for do they not all have to marry whom God
sends? and am I the only one who had dreams? It is the end of
dreams, marriage; and that is the good thing about it. God lets us
dream to keep us quiet, but he knows when to wake us up, I tell
you. The blue bows knew! And now, you see, I prefer my husband
to my *brun*; in fact, Loulou, I adore him, and I am furiously
jealous about him. And he is so good to Clementine and the poor
little children; and see his photograph – a blond, and not good
looking, and small!

'But poor Papa! If he had been alive, I am sure he never would
have agreed with God about my marriage.'

(1893)

OLIVE SCHREINER

The Buddhist Priest's Wife

Cover her up! How still it lies! You can see the outline under the white. You would think she was asleep. Let the sunshine come in; it loved it so. She that had travelled so far, in so many lands, and done so much and seen so much, how she must like rest now! Did she ever love anything absolutely, this woman whom so many men loved, and so many women; who gave so much sympathy and never asked for anything in return! Did she ever need a love she could not have? Was she never obliged to un-clasp her fingers from anything to which they clung? Was she really so strong as she looked? Did she never wake up in the night crying for that which she could not have? Were thought and travel enough for her? Did she go about for long days with a weight that crushed her to earth? Cover her up! I do not think she would have liked us to look at her. In one way she was alone all her life; she would have liked to be alone now! . . . Life must have been very beautiful to her, or she would not look so young now. Cover her up! Let us go!

Many years ago in a London room, up long flights of stairs, a fire burnt up in a grate. It showed the marks on the walls where pictures had been taken down, and the little blue flowers in the wallpaper and the blue felt carpet on the floor, and a woman sat by the fire in a chair at one side.

Presently the door opened, and the old woman came in who took care of the entrance hall downstairs.

'Do you not want anything tonight?' she said.

'No, I am only waiting for a visitor. When they have been, I shall go.'

'Have you got all your things taken away already?'

'Yes, only these I am leaving.'

The old woman went down again, but presently came up with a cup of tea in her hand.

'You must drink that; it's good for one. Nothing helps one like tea when one's been packing all day.'

The young woman at the fire did not thank her, but she ran her hand over the old woman's from the wrist to the fingers.

'I'll say goodbye to you when I go out.'

The woman poked the fire, put the last coals on, and went.

When she had gone the young one did not drink the tea, but drew her little silver cigarette case from her pocket and lighted a cigarette. For a while she sat smoking by the fire; then she stood up and walked the room.

When she had paced for a while she sat down again beside the fire. She threw the end of her cigarette away into the fire, and then began to walk again with her hands behind her. Then she went back to her seat and lit another cigarette, and paced again. Presently she sat down, and looked into the fire; she pressed the palms of her hands together, and then sat quietly staring into it.

Then there was a sound of feet on the stairs and someone knocked at the door.

She rose and threw the end into the fire and said without moving, 'Come in.'

The door opened and a man stood there in evening dress. He had a great-coat on, open in front.

'May I come in? I couldn't get rid of this downstairs; I didn't see where to leave it!' He took his coat off. 'How are you? This is a real bird's nest!'

She motioned to a chair.

'I hope you did not mind my asking you to come?'

'Oh no, I am delighted. I only found your note at my club twenty minutes ago.'

'So you really are going to India? How delightful! But what are you to do there? I think it was Grey told me six weeks ago you were going, but regarded it as one of those mythical stories which don't deserve credence. Yet I am sure I don't know! Why, nothing would surprise me.'

He looked at her in a half-amused, half-interested way.

'What a long time it is since we met! Six months, eight?'

'Seven,' she said.

'I really thought you were trying to avoid me. What have you been doing with yourself all this time?'

'Oh, been busy. Won't you have a cigarette?'

She held out the little case to him.

'Won't you take one yourself? I know you object to smoking with men, but you can make an exception in my case!'

'Thank you.' She lit her own and passed him the matches.

'But really what have you been doing with yourself all this time? You've entirely disappeared from civilised life. When I was down at the Grahams' in the spring, they said you were coming down there, and then at the last moment cried off. We were all quite disappointed. What is taking you to India now? Going to preach the doctrine of social and intellectual equality to the Hindu women and incite them to revolt? Marry some old Buddhist Priest, build a little cottage on the top of the Himalayas and live there, discuss philosophy and meditate? I believe that's what you'd like. I really shouldn't wonder if I heard you'd done it!'

She laughed and took out her cigarette case.

She smoked slowly.

'I've been here a long time, four years, and I want change. I was glad to see how well you succeeded in that election,' she said. 'You were much interested in it, were you not?'

'Oh, yes. We had a stiff fight. It tells in my favour, you know, though it was not exactly a personal matter. But it was a great worry.'

'Don't you think,' she said, 'you were wrong in sending that letter to the papers? It would have strengthened your position to have remained silent.'

'Yes, perhaps so; I think so now, but I did it under advice. However, we've won, so it's all right.' He leaned back in the chair.

'Are you pretty fit?'

'Oh, yes, pretty well; bored, you know. One doesn't know what all this working and striving is for sometimes.'

'Where are you going for your holiday this year?'

'Oh, Scotland, I suppose, I always do; the old quarters.'

'Why don't you go to Norway? It would be more change for you and rest you more. Did you get a book on sport in Norway?'

'Did you send it me? How kind of you! I read it with much interest. I was almost inclined to start off there and then. I suppose it is the kind of *vis inertiæ** that creeps over one as one grows older that sends one back to the old place. A change would be much better.'

'There's a list at the end of the book,' she said, 'of exactly the things one needs to take. I thought it would save trouble; you could just give it to your man, and let him get them all. Have you still got him?'

'Oh, yes. He's as faithful to me as a dog. I think nothing would induce him to leave me. He won't allow me to go out hunting since I sprained my foot last autumn. I have to do it surreptitiously. He thinks I can't keep my seat with a sprained ankle; but he's a very good fellow. Takes care of me like a mother.' He smoked quietly with the firelight glowing on his black coat. 'But what are you going to India for? Do you know anyone there?'

'No,' she said. 'I think it will be so splendid. I've always been a great deal interested in the East. It's a complex, interesting life.'

He turned and looked at her.

'Going to seek for more experience, you'll say, I suppose. I never knew a woman throw herself away as you do; a woman with your brilliant parts and attractions, to let the whole of life slip through your hands, and make nothing of it. You ought to be the most successful woman in London. Oh, yes; I know what you are going to say: 'You don't care.' That's just it; you don't. You are always going to get experience, going to get everything, and you never do. You are always going to write when you know enough, and you are never satisfied that you do. You ought to be making your two thousand a year, but you don't care. That's just it! Living, burying yourself here with a lot of old frumps. You will never do anything. You could have everything and you let it slip.'

'Oh, my life is very full,' she said. 'There are only two things that are absolute realities, love and knowledge, and you can't escape them.'

She had thrown her cigarette end away and was looking into the fire, smiling.

'I've let these rooms to a woman friend of mine.' She glanced round the room, smiling. 'She doesn't know I'm going to leave these things here for her. She'll like them because they were mine. The world's very beautiful, I think – delicious.'

'Oh, yes. But what do you do with it? What do you make of it? You ought to settle down and marry like other women, not go wandering about the world to India and China and Italy, and God knows where. You are simply making a mess of your life. You're always surrounding yourself with all sorts of extraordinary people. If I hear any man or woman is a great friend of yours, I always say: 'What's the matter? Lost his money? Lost his character? Got an incurable disease?' I believe the only way in which anyone becomes interesting to you is by having some complaint of mind or body. I believe you worship rags. To come and shut yourself up in a place like this away from everybody and everything! It's a mistake; it's idiotic, you know.'

'I'm very happy,' she said. 'You see,' she said, leaning forwards towards the fire with hands on her knees, 'what matters is that something should need you. It isn't a question of love. What's the use of being near a thing if other people could serve it as well as you can. If they could serve it better, it's pure selfishness. It's the need of one thing for another that makes the organic bond of union. You love mountains and horses, but they don't need you; so what's the use of saying anything about it! I suppose the most absolutely delicious thing in life is to feel a thing needs you, and to give at the moment it needs. Things that don't need you, you must love from a distance.'

'Oh, but a woman like you ought to marry, ought to have children. You go squandering yourself on every old beggar or forlorn female or escaped criminal you meet; it may be very nice for them, but it's a mistake from your point of view.'

He touched the ash gently with the tip of his little finger and let it fall.

'I intend to marry. It's a curious thing,' he said, resuming his pose with an elbow on one knee and his head bent forward on one side, so that she saw the brown hair with its close curls a little tinged with grey at the sides, 'that when a man reaches a certain age he wants to marry. He doesn't fall in love; it's not that he definitely plans anything; but he has a feeling that he ought to have a home and a wife and children. I suppose it is the same kind of feeling that makes a bird build nests at certain times of the year. It's not love, it's something else. When I was a young man I used to despise men for getting married; wondered what they did it for; they had everything to lose and nothing to gain. But when a man gets to be six-and-thirty his feeling changes. It's not love, passion, he wants; it's a home; it's a wife and children. He may have a house and servants; it isn't the same thing. I should have thought a woman would have felt it too.'

She was quiet for a minute, holding a cigarette between her fingers; then she said slowly:

'Yes, at times a woman has a curious longing to have a child, especially when she gets near to thirty or over it. It's something distinct from love for any definite person. But it's a thing one has to get over. For a woman, marriage is much more serious than for a man. She might pass her life without meeting a man whom she could possibly love, and, if she met him, it might not be right or possible. Marriage has become very complex now it has become so largely intellectual. Won't you have another?'

She held out the case to him. 'You can light it from mine.' She bent forward for him to light it.

'You are a man who ought to marry. You've no absorbing mental work with which the woman would interfere; it would complete you.' She sat back, smoking serenely.

'Yes,' he said, 'but life is too busy; I never find time to look for one, and I haven't a fancy for the pink-and-white prettiness so common and that some men like so. I need something else. If I am to have a wife I shall have to go to America to look for one.'

'Yes, an American would suit you best.'

'Yes,' he said, 'I don't want a woman to look after; she must be self-sustaining and she mustn't bore you. You know what I mean. Life is too full of cares to have a helpless child added to them.'

'Yes,' she said, standing up and leaning with her elbow against the fireplace. 'The kind of woman you want would be young and strong; she need not be excessively beautiful, but she must be attractive; she must have energy, but not too strongly marked an individuality; she must be largely neutral; she need not give you too passionate or too deep a devotion, but she must second you in a thoroughly rational manner. She must have the same aims and tastes that you have. No woman has the right to marry a man if she has to bend herself out of shape for him. She might wish to, but she could never be to him with all her passionate endeavour what the other woman could be to him without trying. Character will dominate over all and will come out at last.'

She looked down into the fire.

'When you marry you mustn't marry a woman who flatters you too much. It is always a sign of falseness somewhere. If a woman absolutely loves you as herself, she will criticise and understand you as herself. Two people who are to live through life together must be able to look into each other's eyes and speak the truth. That helps one through life. You would find many such women in America,' she said, 'women who would help you to succeed, who would not drag you down.'

'Yes, that's my idea. But how am I to obtain the ideal woman?'

'Go and look for her. Go to America instead of Scotland this year. It is perfectly right. A man has a right to look for what he needs. With a woman it is different. That's one of the radical differences between men and women.'

She looked downwards into the fire.

'It's a law of her nature and of sex relationship. There's nothing arbitrary or conventional about it any more than there is in her having to bear her child while the male does not. Intellectually we may both be alike. I suppose if fifty men and fifty women had to solve a mathematical problem, they would all do it in the same way; the more abstract and intellectual, the more alike we are. The nearer you approach to the personal and sexual, the more different we are. If I were to represent men's and women's natures,' she said, 'by a diagram, I would take two circular discs; the right side of each I should paint bright red; then I would shade the red away till in a spot on the left edge it became blue in the one and green in the other. That spot represents sex, and the nearer you come to it, the more the two discs differ in colour. Well then, if you turn them so that the red sides touch, they seem to be exactly alike, but if you turn them so that the green and blue paint form their point of contact, they will seem to be entirely unlike. That's why you notice the brutal, sensual men invariably believe women are entirely different from men, another species of creature; and very cultured, intellectual men sometimes believe we are exactly alike. You see, sex love in its substance may be the same in both of us; in the form of its expression it must differ. It is not man's fault; it is nature's. If a man loves a woman, he has a right to try to make her love him because he can do it openly, directly, without bending. There need be no subtlety, no indirectness. With a woman it's not so; she can take no love that is not laid openly, simply, at her feet. Nature ordains that she should never show what she feels; the woman who had told a man she loved him would have put between them a barrier once and for ever that could not be crossed; and if she subtly drew him towards her, using the woman's means – silence, finesse, the dropped handkerchief, the surprise visit, the gentle assertion she had not thought to see him when she had come a long way to meet him, then she would be damned; she would hold the love, but she would have desecrated it by subtlety; it would have no value. Therefore she must always go with her arms folded sexually; only the love which lays itself down at her feet and implores of her to accept it is love she can ever rightly take up. That is the true difference between a man and a woman. You may seek for love because you can do it openly; we cannot because we must do it subtly. A woman should always walk with her arms folded. Of course friendship is different. You are on a perfect equality with man then; you can ask him to come and see you as I asked you. That's the beauty of the intellect and intellectual life to a woman, that she drops her shackles a little; and that is why she shrinks from sex so. If she were dying perhaps, or doing something equal to death, she might . . . Death means so much more to a woman than a man; when you knew you were dying, to look round on the world and feel the bond of sex that has broken and crushed you all your life gone, nothing but the human left, no woman any more, to meet everything on perfectly even ground. There's no reason why you shouldn't go to America and look for a wife perfectly deliberately. You will have to tell no lies. Look till you find a woman that you absolutely love, that you have not the smallest doubt suits you apart from love, and then ask her to marry you. You must have children; the life of an old childless man is very sad.'

'Yes, I should like to have children. I often feel now, what is it all for, this work, this striving, and no one to leave it to? It's a blank, suppose I succeed . . .?'

'Suppose you get your title?'

'Yes, what is it all worth to me if I've no one to leave it to? That's my feeling. It's really very strange to be sitting and talking like this to you. But you are so different from other women. If all women were like you, all your theories of the equality of men and women would work. You're the only woman with whom I never realise that she is a woman.'

'Yes,' she said.

She stood looking down into the fire.

'How long will you stay in India?'

'Oh, I'm not coming back.'

'Not coming back! That's impossible. You will be breaking the hearts of half the people here if you don't. I never knew a woman who had such power of entrapping men's hearts as you have in spite of that philosophy of yours. I don't know,' he smiled, 'that I should not have fallen into the snare myself – three years ago I almost thought I should – if you hadn't always attacked me so incontinently and persistently on all and every point and on each and every occasion. A man doesn't like pain. A succession of slaps damps him. But it doesn't seem to have that effect on other men . . . There was that fellow down in the country when I was there last year, perfectly ridiculous. You know his name . . .' He moved his fingers to try and remember it – 'big, yellow moustache, a major, gone to the east coast of Africa now; the ladies unearthed it that he was always carrying about a photograph of yours in his pocket; and he used to take out little scraps of things you printed and show them to people mysteriously. He almost had a duel with a man one night after dinner because he mentioned you; he seemed to think there was something incongruous between your name and—'

'I do not like to talk of any man who has loved me,' she said. 'However small and poor his nature may be, he has given me his best. There is nothing ridiculous in love. I think a woman should feel that all the love men have given her which she has not been able to return is a kind of crown set up above her which she is always trying to grow tall enough to wear. I can't bear to think that all the love that has been given me has been wasted on something unworthy of it. Men have been very beautiful and greatly honoured me. I am grateful to them. If a man tells you he loves you,' she said, looking into the fire, 'with his breast uncovered before you for you to strike him if you will, the least you can do is to put out your hand and cover it up from other people's eyes. If I were a deer,' she said, 'and a stag got hurt following me, even though I could not have him for a companion, I would stand still and scrape the sand with my foot over the place where his blood had fallen; the rest of the herd should never know he had been hurt there following me. I would cover the blood up, if I were a deer,' she said, and then she was silent.

Presently she sat down in her chair and said, with her hand before her, 'Yet, you know, I have not the ordinary feeling about love. I think the one who is loved confers the benefit on the one who loves, it's been so great and beautiful that it should be loved. I think the man should be grateful to the woman or the woman to the man whom they have been able to love, whether they have been loved back or whether circumstances have divided them or not.' She stroked her knee softly with her hand.

'Well, really, I must go now.' He pulled out his watch. 'It's so fascinating sitting here talking that I could stay all night, but I've still two engagements.' He rose; she rose also and stood before him looking up at him for a moment.

'How well you look! I think you have found the secret of perpetual youth. You don't look a day older than when I first saw you just four years ago. You always look as if you were on fire and being burnt up, but you never are, you know.'

He looked down at her with a kind of amused face as one does at an interesting child or a big Newfoundland dog.

'When shall we see you back?'

'Oh, not at all!'

'Not at all! Oh, we must have you back; you belong here, you know. You'll get tired of your Buddhist and come back to us.'

'You didn't mind my asking you to come and say goodbye?' she said in a childish manner unlike her determinateness when she discussed anything impersonal. 'I wanted to say goodbye to everyone. If one hasn't said goodbye one feels restless and feels one would have to come back. If one has said goodbye to all one's friends, then one knows it is all ended.'

'Oh, this isn't a final farewell! You must come in ten years' time and we'll compare notes – you about your Buddhist Priest, I about my fair ideal American; and we'll see who succeeded best.'

She laughed.

'I shall always see your movements chronicled in the news-papers, so we shall not be quite sundered; and you will hear of me perhaps.'

'Yes, I hope you will be very successful.'

She was looking at him, with her eyes wide open, from head to foot. He turned to the chair where his coat hung.

'Can't I help you put it on?'

'Oh, no, thank you.'

He put it on.

'Button the throat,' she said, 'the room is warm.'

He turned to her in his great-coat and with his gloves. They were standing near the door.

'Well, goodbye. I hope you will have a very pleasant time.'

He stood looking down upon her, wrapped in his great-coat.

She put up one hand a little in the air. 'I want to ask you something,' she said quickly.

'Well, what is it?'

'Will you please kiss me?'

For a moment he looked down at her, then he bent over her.

In after years he could never tell certainly, but he always thought she put up her hand and rested it on the crown of his head, with a curious soft caress, something like a mother's touch when her child is asleep and she does not want to wake it. Then he looked round, and she was gone. The door had closed noiselessly. For a moment he stood motionless, then he walked to the fireplace and looked down into the fender at a little cigarette end lying there, then he walked quickly back to the door and opened it. The stairs were in darkness and silence. He rang the bell violently. The old woman came up. He asked her where the lady was. She said she had gone out, she had a cab waiting. He asked when she would be back. The old woman said, 'Not at all'; she had left. He asked where she had gone. The woman said she did not know; she had left orders that all her letters should be kept for six or eight months till she wrote and sent her address. He asked whether she had no idea where he might find her. The woman said no. He walked up to a space in the wall where a picture had hung and stood staring at it as though the picture were still hanging there. He drew his mouth as though he were emitting a long whistle, but no sound came. He gave the old woman ten shillings and went downstairs.

That was eight years ago.

How beautiful life must have been to it that it looks so young still!

(1892)

JANE BARLOW

Between Two Lady Days
(from *Irish Idylls*)

The Lady Day* in harvest, which fell six weeks or so after that
electrical July Sunday, was splendidly fine in Lisconnel, steeped
through and through with ripe August sunshine, and unruffled by
any restless breeze. Its serene beauty jarred upon Stacey Doyne's
mood, and, though she did not guess, helped to make the lag-foot
hours halt by more slowly and heavily. But she was keenlier alive to
a sense of aggravating circumstances when, at an early period of the
morning, it became evident that Mad Bell, seized by one of her
irresistible lyrical frenzies, had been driven to establish herself on a
sun-smitten bank near her door, whence her shrill singing resounded far and wide. What she sang loudest and longest was a
favourite ditty beginning:

> Before I was married, I used to dhrink tay,
> But since I am married, 'tis buttermilk-whey;
> Before I was married, I sat in the parlour,
> But since I am married, 'tis in the ash-corner.

A wish to escape beyond the range of that oft-repeated air led
Stacey to ramble away further than she otherwise would have done
over the heathery crests of the knockawn, where the sombre ruddy
bloom against the black peat-mould suggested the smouldering
and charring of half-extinguished embers, until at last she sat down
on a boulder between two sheltering clumps of broom and furze,*
which made her a low-roofed bower. Here Mad Bell was too far off
for the tune or words; only a faint skirl* came fitfully borne upon a
flagging breeze, scarcely 'a trace', as chemists say, upon the
surrounding atmosphere of stillness. Nothing else broke it either
with motion or sound, except when, ever and anon, a flight of little
wild birds got up suddenly in the distance, like a handful of dust
tossed into the air, and when a curlew cried plaintively across the

bog, a cunning tone-poet, who can set a whole landscape to melancholy in one quick chromatic phrase.

Stacey wanted, indeed, no external incitements to sadness, having at present ample grounds for it in her own situation and reflections. This radiant summer morning, with its arch of moteless sapphire and high tides of unstinted shining, should have ushered in her wedding day. It had all been arranged weeks ago – ages ago it seemed to her now – for the elder Dan's dissatisfaction with his son's choice had melted away rapidly and completely. In point of fact, on that very eventful Sunday evening, when the matter first came to light, the two O'Beirnes had on their homeward way met the Cross Priest posting up to Lisconnel in obedience to a tragical summons, and in the course of the explanations which ensued, the good-natured blacksmith betrayed himself into tacitly withdrawing any meditated opposition to the match.

'So, your Riverence, there's little signs of a buryin' over this business at all, at all,' said he, 'but I wouldn't say as much consarnin' a weddin'. Troth no I'd not. For to tell Your Riverence the truth, it's my belief that young gomeral there has a notion – himself and little Stacey Doyne – to be troublin' you, or Father Rooney – long life to him – one of these days. Och begorrah, that's the worth of the likes of them' – Dan privately thought that the three kingdoms would have been 'put to it' to produce the likes of his son – 'what better need you expec'?'

Father Carroll was humane enough to hear with relief that, after all, none of his parishioners had been burnt alive or blinded, and he naturally rejoiced at the abridgment of his long late ride. So he received the news more genially than usual, and as he turned his horse's willing head, he shook his whip handle jocularly at young Dan, saying, 'Indeed now, O'Beirne, I wouldn't put it past them, the pair of them. But if you're for setting up a wife, Dan, you'll have to be steady, and stick to your work, and mind what you're about. Clap on your blinkers, me lad, and keep the road straight before you, or you'll land more than yourself in the ditch.'

Dan, who looked very unwontedly sheepish, kicked a lump of turf in front of him further than his own shadow, which stretched a long way distortedly through the beams of the rising moon, as he answered, 'Och, sure me father wouldn't git his health if he didn't be talkin', so he wouldn't. Be the hoky, it's a won'erful man he is for romancin' intirely.'

After this, the current of the young couple's affairs, so far as they stood upon the choice of friends, was practically unimpeded; and their wooing undoubtedly deserved the benison* pronounced on those which are conducted with despatch. But the edict of destiny fulfils itself in many ways. At the time when young Dan entered into his engagement with Stacey Doyne, he had a prior one on hand, which his new tie did not dispose, or rather forbade, him to break. This was a journey all the way up to the county Antrim, where a friend of his held out prospects of a four weeks' job at a compressed peat manufactory, the manager of which found labour scarce in those harvesting days. Now young Dan O'Beirne being not only strong and stalwart, but endowed with an intuitive gift for understanding the 'quareness' of all sorts of machinery, Thomas McCrum, the northerner, who had himself got the promise of work up there, made no manner of doubt that so desirable a hand would find at all events temporary employment and a scale of remuneration which sounded prodigious in the ears of Lisconnel. Dan's contemplated marriage rendered the acquisition of a little ready money in a high degree expedient, if not absolutely necessary; for his father's philanthropy was of an humble personal kind, never known to enrich or in any way aggrandise the family in which it runs, and the O'Beirnes, despite forge and shebeen, were hardly better off than their struggling neightbours. Given a pound or two in hand for the purchase of 'a few odd sticks of things', and the rent of a cabin down below, Dan and Stacey could start housekeeping with light hearts; failing that, the match would be held imprudent even by people who entertained the most moderate views about marriage settlements. So Dan went off one morning, confident of returning with at least that sum a clear fortnight before Lady Day, which had been fixed for the wedding.

Stacey had plenty to distract her mind during his absence. There was the trousseau, for one thing. Her mother sold their pig prematurely, at somewhat of a sacrifice, that she might be able to buy a sufficiency of hideous strong brown wincey for a body and a skirt. These two articles of clothing are seldom simultaneously acquired in Lisconnel. And when, in the course of the negotiations at his shop in the Town, Mr Corr learned the purpose for which the stuff was required, he added gratis some yards of the stoutest grey holland in his stock to make Stacey a couple of large aprons – *praskeens*, she called them. Whereupon Lisconnel opined that Mr Corr always was a kind-hearted poor man. Then the wedding itself furnished a theme for endless planning and discussion, especially when Farmer Hilfirthy, down below, actually promised the loan of his jaunting-car* to meet the bridal party at Classon's Boreen,* halfway to the chapel. Stacey had never in her life been on a car or any other vehicle, and the prospect of the drive evidently heightened more than one would have imagined, her sense of the solemnity and importance of the whole ceremony.

Thus the days bustled on blithely enough, burnished up for her by the gleams of a happy hour which she knew came stealing towards her. Yet when it arrived, it proved to be the turning point whence all her fortunes began to wane through a twilight of doubt and despondency to an ever deepening despair. Dan did not reappear on the day when he was expected. Stacey, in her ignorance, felt not a little aggrieved at the delay, although she was quite sure that the next morning would bring him. Twelve hours seem a vast void of time, when you have already begun to count your intervening minutes one by one. But after two or three more days had trailed immeasurably by, she would have been humbly thankful for an assurance that she would see him again within a twelvemonth. So quickly may we learn to abate our claims upon good fortune.

It wanted just a week of the wedding day, when a man casually observed to Stacey's brother Matt, as they were hooding stooks* below at Hilfirthy's, that he had seen Dan O'Beirne going on board the Stranraer steamer up at Larne, shortly before he had himself returned to Lisconnel. The poor little bride-elect put a brave face on the matter when the news was communicated to her, and said cheerfully that Dan would be apt to be writing to explain the way of it. But in truth her heart sank down and down, and she felt a miserable conviction that no letter was coming. Soon, too, she knew – though they said, 'Shoo-whisht woman,' and broke off when she came near – how the neighbours were often standing in knots and saying it had a bad appearance, his slipping off out of the country that fashion, without a word to anybody; it looked like as if he had a notion of running away from the match. The sight of those shawled heads bobbing together over her fate chilled Stacey with despair at times, and at others stung her with a wrathful pang, under which she could almost have found it in her heart to break up their conclave violently, accusing them to their faces of telling lies and talking blathers and nonsense. But she always stopped short of any such strong measures, quailing before her consciousness that her life was being overcast by a great black cloud, in the coming on of which this gossips' gabble seemed merely a trivial fringe of shadow; and the one discourtesy she used was to shrink away from all occasions of discourse, either sitting mute in a retired recess of the dark cabin-room, or roaming off into the bog, where the solitude and silence toned down the brightness of the clear careless skies and made it more endurable.

In this way it came about that the blue-vaulted forenoon, which by rights should have seen her conversion into Mrs Daniel O'Beirne, was spent by Stacey in solitary forlornness, crouched among the sad-green furzes – 'mindin' th' ould goat' was how she described her occupation to her neighbours – and that a few hours later found her standing up uncomforted on the ridge, turning mournful grey eyes listlessly towards the rose and daffodil sunset, before she crept home through the gloaming, lit by no brighter hope than the prospect of sleepily forgetting her troubles until tomorrow. Days such as this came to her in a sequence. For amid the mellow sunshine of the late-summer weather, which was transmuting the grain-fields to roughened gold, and staining the brier-leaves with bronze and crimson, and bringing out the dim purplish bloom on all the wild dark berries – dewberries and frawns and sloes – and even finishing off the little grey lichen-cups with red sealing-wax rims, Stacey's hopes were shrivelling up and withering away. She did not really try to blind herself, whatever mien she would fain have confronted her world with. Each blank morning, and each cheerless evening, heard her paraphrase, 'Even here I will put off my hope and keep it no longer for my flatterer,' most piteous of vows, not oftener made than broken. After a few weeks had passed, she used to pray to her saints that she might not know of anybody going down to the Town, because she could not avoid the bitter moment of watching him return without letter or tidings.

Yet Stacey, sad as was her plight, should not monopolise our sympathy. Young Dan's unaccountable non-appearance flung a portentous shadow across his father's horizon. He was slower than the girl to take the alarm, his wider experience suggesting a larger variety of harmless contingencies; but when once fear got firm hold of him, it gripped him with a hardly less agonising rigour. If 'anythin' misfortnit had took and happint' his big handsome son, the light of his eyes had been put out; but if the

truth were that the lad had played a villain's trick on them, had
given the lie to his hand-promise, and run off from them, leaving
the girl to break her heart, why then old Dan was doubly bereft,
both of trust and hope. Moreover, his distress was complicated by
a feeling of compunction and responsibility towards Stacey and
her family, which made the sight of them painful to him, and still
forbade him to keep out of their way.

"Tisn't the lad's own fau't, that's sartin,' he said one late
November day, sitting on an old potatocreel by Mrs Doyne's fire.
'If I know the differ between porther* and potheen,* he'd no
more go for to do us a turn like that, except again his will, than
he'd reive the eyes out of his head. There's somethin' gone amiss
wid him that we haven't heard tell of.'

'True for you, Dan,' said Mrs Doyne, resignedly; 'I put it on
them ould steamboats meself. There's nothin' more dangerous.
Sure the on'y time I iver made free wid one of them, a matter of
twinty year back, away down at Lough Corrib, I came as nigh
losin' me life as you could think – set me fut over the edge of the
bit o' plank they'd laid down for the people to step on board by,
and in the black wather I'd ha' been on'y poor Mick grabbed a-
hould of me. And sure if Dan done such a thing, and he travellin'
the deep says, let alone a lough, what chanst 'ud he have but goin'
to the bottom? Or where's the use of the talk they keep of his
sendin' word in letters, and he all the while lyin' dhrownded dead
– the Lord have mercy on his sowl.'

'Och then, goodness guide you, Mrs Doyne, woman, but d'you
think the lad's a born nathural that he's not got the wit to step the
lenth of a bit of a gangway widout blundherin' overboard like an
ould blind horse? Troth, it's a quare thing if a young man can't
take a taste of divarsion for wunst in a way, but iverybody must
settle to murdher him behind his back.'

'Some of them do say 'twas that Maggie Farrelly he'd his mind
set on all the while, and he's took off out of this liefer than contint
himself wid anyone else. It's no credit to him to sarve us that way.
And the dacint lad he seemed, and the hape he thought of Stacey.
Bedad, he wouldn't have given her for his pick of the stars out of
the sky, if you were to believe him. I'd niver ha' supposed it of
him, so I wouldn't.'

'And it's great ould lies they were tellin', who iver tould you
that. Maggie Farrelly, bedad! Divil a hap'orth she was to him, let
alone he isn't the *slieveen* to be playin' fast and loose wid your

dacint little slip of a girl. It's little they've to do to be puttin' them bad stories on him, when he's overtook wid goodness can tell what ill-luck away from his own country.'

'Musha, man alive, isn't that what I was sayin' a minit ago? Dhrownded he mayn't be for sartin, but there's plinty more manners of desthruction in it – plinty. Sure the strongest iver stepped might be took suddint, like a candle-light in a puff of win' – the saints purtect us all. There was Peter Molloy of Glenish, as fine a young man as you'd see, at Mass one Sunday, and waked the next. A beautiful corp he made, and so 'ud poor Dan – onless it *was* dhrownin' after all, and no layin' out to be done on him.'

'Bad manners to it, woman, what talk have you of wakin' and burryin', and Maggie Farrelly? Cock her up! But it's true enough there do be girls will get round a man wid their slootherin', till he'll scarce know for a while what he's at; for a while just – it's past my belief that aught 'ud hould him long away from all of us here. I'm waitin' wid a job of plough-mendin' I have until he's back.'

'Och well, it's yourself knows the warld, Dan, and tubbe sure he might aisy enough git into bad company in them parts, and he'd ha' nobody to advise him agin it, or purvint them makin' a fool of him, the young bosthoon, wid nary a thraneen of sinse in his head.'

'Sinse is it? Bejabers Dan's got twyste the sinse of many a man double his age, and more to the back of that.'

'It's liker, then, somethin' disprit's after happenin' him – the crathur. But 'deed, and if the end of it was to ha' been his comin' home married to another girl, as some of them's supposin', it's as black a day for us 'twould—'

Here Stacey, to whom this balancing of probabilities had been as soothing as alternate stabs of ice and flame, stole forth from her dusky corner, and slipped out at the door. Her mother, however, just saw her vanish, and said dismayed, 'That was Stacey herself. Well now, I've a head, and so's a pin – I might ha' remembered she came in afore you did. We'd a right to ha' held our tongues.'

As Stacey emerged into the honey-coloured westering light, and began to saunter about aimlessly in the narrow grassy foot-tracks which threaded the shag of furze and heather on the slope behind her dwelling, she was descried by a group of neighbours who a little way off were watching Brian Kilfoyle cut scraws* from a green-swarded bank for the repair of his roof. When she guessed their observation, she made a feint of looking for bogberries, which were, as every one knew, no longer in season, and moved slowly off out of sight.

'There goes poor Stacey Doyne,' said Mrs Brian, 'moonin' along like some desolit ould crathur. It's a pity to see her.'

'I just wish I had the regulatin' of that young rip Dan O'Beirne,' said Mrs Quigley. 'I'd give him a goin' over he wouldn't be apt to forgit in one while.'

'Sure how can we tell he's to blame?' said Mrs Brian. 'Somethin's maybe gone agin' him. But any way, poor Stacey might as well put the thought of him out of her mind as soon as she can conthrive it. There's scarce a likeliness of his iver showin' his face agin in Lisconnel. We'll see that same wisp of cloud, that's after sailin' in behind the sun there, come sailin' back to us first – if you ask my opinion.'

'Och Stacey – Stacey Doyne – *she* wouldn't be over-long troubled frettin' after him, if she had but the chanst of e'er another one handy,' said Sally Sheridan, her words tumbling out thickly in a sudden spiteful flurry, as if they had been pent up unspoken for an irksome length of time. 'She'll niver want for a sweetheart, if it depinds on herself, though maybe she doesn't find them so aisy to pick up. I'm thinkin' 'twas herself done most of the coortin' for young O'Beirne; *he* was in no great hurry over the matter – at all evints he was in a greater one to be shut of her.'

'Just look here, me good girl,' said the widow McGurk, 'you've no call to be sayin' any such a thing now; none whatsomiver, even supposin' it was the truth you were tellin', instid of a black lie. Little Stacey Doyne's not the sort to be coortin' herself sweethearts; and she's no need, sorra a bit has she. For whativer may have come to him since, 'twas plain to be seen young Dan thought the warld hadn't her match, or anythin' fine enough for her in it.'

'And let me tell you, Sally Sheridan,' said Mrs Rafferty, 'that when a girl passes them kind of remarks, other people do be very apt to think she's judgin' accordin' to her own carryin's on, and it gives her an oncommon onplisant appearance.'

Miss Sally was in reality considerably disconcerted by the rebuke of her elders, who stood eyeing her severely from beneath their fluttering shawls, and who obviously had the sense of the company with them. However, she would not 'let on' that she minded, and strolled away, snatching at the bushes as she passed,

and humming a surly tune in a manner meant to indicate uncon-
cern.

'But it's a pity, so it is, about Stacey,' resumed Mrs Brian, 'you
can see be the look of her that she's just frettin' herself to
flitterjigs; and her poor mother was tellin' me yisterday that she'll
scarce open her lips from mornin' till night, but sits mopin' in the
corner, or sthreels off be herself on the bog. The poor woman's
fairly disthracted wid onaisiness, and I don't wonder at it. They
do say 'twas a disappointment of that sort gave Mad Bell's wits a
turn; and if Stacey was to go like her, deminted poor ould body,
bedad 'twould be a sorrowful sight, and fit to break the hearts of
them that rared her – Sakes and patience, Jim! keep from under
our feet, there's a good child. I was near waddlin' over you that
time like an ould duck.'

'Talkin' of Mad Bell,' said Mrs Rafferty, 'she's away wid herself
agin. Set off this mornin' afore it was light, so Big Anne tould
me. Sez she to Anne: "I'm afeard," sez she, "of them deep snow-
dhrifts out there on the bog." Goodness can tell what put snow in
the crathur's head. "Starvin' and perishin', starvin' and perishin',"
sez she, "'twill be wid yous here this winter, and I'm away to the
people where the ships is" – Galway belike. So off she wint.'

'Well now, that's a bad hearin', mark my words,' said Mrs
Quigley, looking scared; 'Mad Bell and folk like her do have
surprisin' notions about things, wheriver they git them. But
there's no great signs that I can see of a hard winter comin' on us –
would you say there was, Brian?'

'I dunno,' said Brian, trimming the edges of a symmetrical
smooth green sod; 'I perceived a couple of saygulls flyin' inland
this mornin', straight and steady – bad cess to them.'

'But Brian,' pursued Mrs Quigley, dropping her voice, 'have
you heard any talk lately about *Thim Ones*? For since young
Mick Ryan—'

'Och blathers,' said Brian.

'Whisht, whisht then,' said Mrs Brian, turning away hastily,
'the child's a-listenin'. Anyhow, I must be steppin' home.'

'And I,' said Mrs Quigley. 'Weary on it,' she observed
dejectedly, as they went down the road, 'maybe Stacey's as well
out of settin' up wid housekeepin' these times, if she knew but all.
Starvin's bad enough for yourself, but when it comes to the
childer – och wirra, that's starvin' wid heart-breakin' tacked on to
the end of it.'

Stacey, however, was as yet in no mood to take a philosophical view of the situation. She still carried her trouble in both hands, as we do with such things while they are new to us. Afterwards we generally stow them away in the pack which we keep on our shoulders, where they make their weight felt, it is true, but do not hinder us from going, more or less heavily, about our wonted avocations. And in mere course of time Stacey might so have disposed of hers, even if nothing had occurred to accelerate matters.

A day or two afterwards, she fell in with a crony of hers on one of her dismal bog-trottings. Jim Kilfoyle was a person who for some four years had been contemplating his world through a pair of very large and observant Irish-blue eyes, and drawing his own conclusions therefrom with an independence of thought which often gave the charm of originality to his theories. On the present occasion they had guided him to a spray of belated blackberries, which the vague November sunbeams had scarcely tinged even with the crudest red, but which he had no scruples about plucking in their rathest immaturity.

'Them berries are too green to be aitin', Jimmy,' Stacey remonstrated mildly; but he curtly replied, 'Here's two ones for yourself, and let me have a bit of food in paice.' So she prudently gave up the point.

When he had swallowed, with inexplicable satisfaction, the last hard knob of sour seeds, he sat staring at Stacey for some time, and then said meditatively: '*I* don't think you look anyways so like Mad Bell, Stacey.'

'Mercy be among us, Jim – like Mad Bell?' Stacey said, with a little laugh. At eighteen a pretty girl's vanity is perhaps the last peak to be submerged, and the first to reappear in any swelling tide of affliction, and a comparison between herself and the wizened little old cracked woman could not but strike her as grotesquely incongruous. 'Sure what at all should ail me to be lookin' like Mad Bell, poor ould crathur?'

'Me mother sez so, then,' said Jim, rather sternly, for he suspected a disabling of his judgement in Stacey's laugh. 'She and Mrs Quigley yisterday, when you were above on the hill. Sthreelin' about like Mad Bell, they said you were, and fit to break iverybody's heart.'

'Did they say – anythin' else, Jim?' said Stacey, with a catch in her voice, as if an icy gust had blown in her face and taken away her breath.

'Dunno,' said Jim, and either could not or would not supply any further information.

But what he had stated made her feel hot and cold. Hitherto, so far as her dreary preoccupation allowed her to consider external affairs, she had believed that she was keeping her miseries strictly to herself, and betraying to nobody how her world had been turned into a wilderness. And now she abruptly learned that her conduct had led her neighbours to suppose her going daft, an intolerable revelation, against which all her pride rose up in arms. It found an auxiliary in the feeling of self-reproach roused by Jim's reference to the breaking of everybody's heart. For she knew very well that 'everybody' in this connection could only mean her mother, towards whom she was conscious of having displayed during the past weeks a frank morosity and undisguised gloom. 'As cross as an ould weasel, and as conthráry as anythin' you could give a name to,' she called herself, in her awakening remorse. Under such circumstances, this demeanour, rightly interpreted, is often really tantamount to a friendly vote of confidence; yet it blackens in the retrospect when the memory, sensitised by the touch of conscience, is exposed to a new point of view. As Stacey sat silently beside the silent Jim, who had fallen to grubbing droves of scampering ants out of crevices in the bank with a little bit of twig, her thoughts turned upon troubles of which she was not the isolated victim; and when she presently got up and moved away, she said to herself: 'I'll slip home and be diggin' the pitaties for dinner.' The resolution sounds scarcely heroic, yet it nevertheless marks the place where Stacey, so to speak, faced about. A retreat in some disorder had been converted into a rally.

As if in confirmation of the saying that fortune favours the brave, Stacey soon happened upon a small scrap of comfort, which, flimsy as was its material, sometimes stood her in good stead. On that same afternoon, her half-instinctive groping about among her scanty resources for some object of distraction, ended in a determination to step out and ask Peg Sheridan for the loan of a skein of yarn, with which she might set herself up a piece of knitting. 'Peg's been oncommon good natured,' she reflected; 'she'll let me have it in a minit, if she's got e'er a thread.' But on her way to the Sheridans, Stacey was overtaken by old Ody Rafferty, who quitted his digging to shout that he hadn't seen her for a month of Sundays, and came shuffling down the potato-drill with uneludible nimbleness to intercept her at the dyke. She could not, without marked incivility, avoid stopping to speak, and when they had duly said, 'How's yourself this long while?' and, 'Finely, glory be to goodness,' Ody prevented her from passing on by catching a corner of her shawl.

'Stacey, me child, listen now to me,' he said; 'I was wantin' to tell you you've no call to be discouraged anyways about young Dan not comin' home.'

Stacey listened submissively. She was by this time acquainted with most of her neighbours' several theories as to her sweetheart's defection, and they were not on the whole consolatory.

'I'll tell you the way of it, Stacey,' he said, 'he's just took and enlisted. That's what he's after doin', and don't believe any one that sez anythin' differint. Sure, I've a right to know what I'm talkin' about, considerin' I've been well acquainted wid the lad from the time he was three feet high – that stands six-fut-two this day in his stockin' feet. It's many the mile we've thramped togither, himself, and meself, and misfortnit poor Jinny, and I know as well as I know me own name that he'd a great notion of soldierin'. Troth, I could ha' tould you that much iver since one day I saw him standin' lookin' after a milithry band that went by us down at Kilmacrone. And be the powers of smoke, he'll make a grand dragoon, Dan will; proud any regiment might be to git a hould of him. 'Twould do one's heart good to see him in his uniform – and so we will one of these fine days, for you may depind he's just schemin' to give us a quare ould surprise wid marchin' in on us in all his ilegance; and that's the raison why's he's niver said a word – just to take us unbeknownst. Not but what it may be a while first. I shouldn't wonder if Dan was apt to wait till he's got a bit of promotion. The idee I have in me own mind is that he'll likely put it off till he's riz to be a colour-seargint' – I fancy that Ody's own mind supposed this officer to derive his title from the peculiar gorgeousness of his accoutrements – 'and then he'll come back a sight to behould, he that wint off wid the daylight shinin' thro' the ould coat was on him like a fire blinkin' behind a gapped dyke. Och Stacey, it's the proud girl you'll be that day, jewel; that set up, you'll scarce have a word for one of the rest of us.'

'I'm sure I niver thought to mind him bein' raggetty like,' said Stacey piteously. 'And how'd he come home, seargint or no, if they're maybe sendin' him off to be kilt in the wars?'

'Is it kilt? Divil a much! Why, for one thing, I dunna believe there's e'er a war in it now, good or bad. I was spellin' over an ould *Cork 'Xaminer* a couple of days ago, and sorra a sign of a war could I see in it at all, no more than if the warld had took to wool-windin'. And another thing is, accordin' to what I'm informed, the throops these times don't iver get fightin' rightly at all, but just slinge about aisy miles off aich other, and let fly an odd cannon-ball or so now and agin to pacify whoiver it was sent them out. So it's a comical thing if an infant child, let alone a grown man, couldn't stand clear of that much widout puttin' himself greatly about. I tell you you needn't be vexin' your mind, Stacey, for as sure as me sowl's in me body it's enlisted Dan is, and steppin' home to Lisconnel he'll be afore we're any of us much oulder. He's the lad that 'ud niver go for to disremimber the ould people, and the ould place, let alone his bit of a *colleen dhu** — not if he was to become Head Commander-in-Gineral by land and say.'

Ody spoke with sincere conviction, and a wonted authoritativeness which did not fail to impress Stacey, and through many succeeding days she clung to the colour-sergeant hypothesis as desperately as if it had been a lifebuoy instead of a straw. In the long dark evenings, when it was too cold to lie down away from the fire on the puddly floor, and in the bleak mornings, when life waking up found Nought the answer persistently elicited by computations of happiness in prospect – a result which eighteen years old is prone to regard as a *reductio ad impossible* – Stacey sometimes shut out intrusive despairs with the help of Ody's glowing picture. Only it invariably happened that the martial figure, flaring and glittering along the bog-road, turned, before he came very near, into just Dan himself in his old scarecrow tatters, without any splendour or brilliancy at all. She had much need, in truth, of whatever cheering figments either faith or fancy could frame. For this winter was a pitiless season to Lisconnel and its inhabitants.

One December night they all shivered sorely in their lairs of heather and rags, as if the breath of a bitter frost were abroad. Still, in the morning no traces of such were visible, unless you noticed that the lingering brier and bracken leaves seemed suddenly to have been dipped in fierily vivid scarlet and orange. But when the potatoes for the next meal were gathered, faces lengthened and heads shook; for experienced eyes at once re-

cognised signs of a 'frost-blighting' that must entail a serious
shrinkage of estimated supplies. And soon after that they began to
draw omens from the flights of birds, flocks, mainly, of seagulls
small and great, who came swooping over the mirk of the bog,
lighting on it in patches of foam, scattered momently in a flickering of white wings as they fled on further inland. Herons, too,
passed, heavily and gloomily flapping and croaking; and long
trains of wild duck, scudding by like trails of smoke that knew
where it was going, till they dwindled into blurred pencil-marks
on the horizon. All these, if they did not exactly belong to 'the
nation of unfortunate and fatal birds', were watched coming and
going by foreboding eyes, as the harbingers of 'powerful severe
weather when they do be that plinty'.

And, sure enough, before Christmas there was deep snow. It
came wavering across the bogland on a north-west wind, and lay
strewn at first in handfuls, and then in armfuls, till at last a huge
lead-coloured cloud appeared to shatter itself sheer over Lisconnel
– 'Like as if,' to quote Pat Ryan, 'you were crumblin' a soft clod of
clay between your two hands;' and thenceforward all was one
blank of white, only broken here and there by the black mouth of
a bog-hole. Even these filled eventually, as the water in them froze
hard, and made of each a secret resting-place for the whirling
drifts, pitfalls into one of which the Quigley's fawn-coloured goat
floundered down, poor wretch, to her smothering death. For the
snow was accompanied by such a biting frost as seldom grips
Lisconnel, and the tiny dry flakes and granules seemed to be
ground fine and driven in tangible mists of stinging dust on the
wide-wailing storm.

'It's a good chanst we're gettin' to understand the sayin',
"When you see the snow like salt and male, your food and fire'll
be apt to fail,"' Brian Kilfoyle said one day, ruefully kicking at a
glittering powdery drift, which had sifted under the Doynes'
rickety door into their house, where he was talking to Stacey and
her mother. Brian, who is normally a big burly man, at that time
had assumed, in common with his neighbours, the aspect of an
incomplete structure, a framework with much filling out left to
do. 'It's siven weeks lyin' on us now sin' Christmas, and here's
Candlemas wid nary a sign of a change yit. But I'm glad to see you
houldin' up so well agin it, ma'am.'

'Och, indeed I'm keepin' iligant and grand, thank God,' said
Mrs Doyne, nervously fingering the largest hole in her frayed-out

apron. 'But as for Stacey there, the crathur, her face this minit isn't the breadth of the palm o' me hand; the two eyes of her'll prisintly be runnin' into one.'

Stacey shrank further into the background at the sound of her own name, and Brian Kilfoyle said: 'Ah, sure young things like her do be aisy perished – aye, and the ould people too. There's me poor mother, she and little Jim, since the bad turn he took a while ago, they don't seem to have an atom of warmth left in them. Scarce a wink they sleep of a night wid the could, though we do give them ivery rag we can conthrive. Our hearts are fairly broke wid them; for me mother, if we don't mind her, will be slippin' the wisp of an ould cloak off her on to one of the childer, and gittin' her death; and that Jim does be creepin' from one to the other like a lost dog at a fair, thryin' for a taste of heat somewheres, the misfortnit little spalpeen; its hands grabbin' you do be just dabs of ice. But divil a thraneen more have we got to put on them.'

There was a painful pause, and then Mrs Doyne said, apologetically, 'I wish to goodness gracious, Brian, I could offer you the loan of e'er an ould wrap, but indeed it's hard set we are, man, to keep the life from freezin' stiff in ourselves these times, wid the most we've got.'

'Tubbe sure, tubbe sure, ma'am,' Brian said, in hurried deprecation, 'how would you? Sure we must all shift for ourselves the best way we can, and we'll do right enough wunst this blamed black frost quits a hould.'

Brian had now carried out the purpose of his call, but he could not betray the fact by immediate departure, so he lingered gossiping in the doorway.

'Big Anne's sleepin' up at Widdy McGurk's these couple of nights back, did you hear tell?' he began. 'She got that scared and lonesome there be herself she couldn't abide it.'

For Mad Bell was, as we know, absent, and the Dummy had been some years dead.

'So they were sayin',' said Mrs Doyne. 'But look-a, Brian' – lowering her voice solemnly – 'div you know was there – anythin' special frightened her?'

'Well, yis,' he answered, in a reluctant sort of mumble, 'a fut goin' up and down along be her door, and nobody on the road; and somethin' that shook her latch and let a keen, and niver a breath of win' stirrin'. Lastewise that's the story she has. But just you tell me how many nights in the year there is widout a waft of win' goin' thro' it; and as for them bastes of goats, times and agin I've mistook a one of them pattin' by for somethin' in brogues. Howsome'er, what fairly terrified her was a voice that kep' callin', 'Anne, Big Anne,' imitatin' first one neighbour, and then another, and diff'rint in a manner from them all. She sez 'twas such hijeous clear moonlight she dursn't look out, and she lay in a could thrimble till the mornin', listenin' to a tappin' on the window – she'd stopped up the pane wid her ould saucepan-lid for 'fraid she might see somethin'. That was rattlin' belike.'

'Saints shield us around,' said Mrs Doyne, crossing herself, 'we'd be well off if there was nothin' worse than saucepans rattlin'. You've heard tell what happint young Mick Ryan about Holy Eve, when he'd a crib set for snipe be the river?'

Brian only said, 'Aye, aye,' uninvitingly, but she could not forego the recital.

'Just liftin' the basket he was, when he looked up, and if there wasn't *Wan of Thim* standin' on the opposite bank right fornint him, wid on'y the flow of the bit of sthrame between them – and *the Other* comin' jiggin' along over the strip of field, not a stone's throw off. Troth, poor Mick thought he couldn't git his heels out of it fast enough. I wonder he didn't lose his wits for good. When he fetched home, his people thought he was blind drunk – Och mercy, what at all's yon out there, Brian?' she interrupted herself, suddenly clutching him by the arm, and pointing through the open door. Far out upon the blanched waste something there was, moving dimly in the thickened light of the gloaming, but whether the form of man or beast, or of neither, could not be told. Brian, without speaking, went a step outside, and seemed to measure the distance which intervened between his own door and the place where he stood.

'It's just merely one of the goats trapesin' around,' he said.

Then he made a plunge, and rushed towards his cabin across the clogging snow, stumbling and tripping in a headlong haste, for which there was nothing apparent to account. Mrs Doyne banged and bolted the door behind him; and when, long afterwards, her two sons came home, they were obliged to kick and shake it for some time, with much strong language, uttered in unmistakably familiar tones, before courage enough was screwed up inside to give them admission.

On the next morning, Mrs Doyne, coming in with an icicle-fringed bucket, sustained another shock of a different kind. Stacey was sitting with folds of brown stuff spread about her, and with needle and thread in hand. It was the material got for her wedding gown, cut out by Biddy Ryan, who is 'quare and cute' about such things, and partially sewn together by Stacey's mother, before the day when the girl had passionately implored that it might be put away out of her sight, since when it had lain hidden underneath the dresser.

'I was considerin' the skirt would make a little sort o' frock like for the Kilfoyles' Jim,' Stacey said in explanation. ''Tis bad to be thinkin' of the bit of an imp perishin' all night. Then the lenth of grey holland 'ud make a petticoat might help to keep the life in ould Mrs Kilfoyle. I'd be sorry anythin' took her.' – The old woman had soothed Stacey's spirit by expressing confidence in the honesty of Dan. – 'And there'll be enough wincey left yit to ready up a body for your ugly ould self.'

'Och honey, but supposin' you might be wantin' it one of these days after all?' said Mrs Doyne unable to refrain from a protest against this implied abandonment of hope.

'Niver a want I'll want it,' said Stacey. 'He's dead and gone, mother jewel. 'Tis a sin to lave it lyin' up; there's a beautiful warmth in it. And I've set me mind on it oncommon.'

So Mrs Doyne assented, as she would to most things upon which Stacey with her great wistful eyes had set her mind; this acquiescence, however, not barring sundry bitter thoughts of a Dan hypothetically in the land of the living.

Stacey sewed hard all day, with horrible gobble-stitches it must be owned, for her education had been sadly neglected in many of its branches; besides which, the cold would scarcely let her hold the needle. By the time the daylight failed, she had finished two very quaint garments, whose cut would not bear criticism, but warm and stout of fabric. She felt impatient to convey them to the Kilfoyles; yet as she looked out over the gleaming snow, which had drawn all the light down out of the blank sky, some uncanny thoughts came before her mind so vividly that she shrank from traversing even those few roods of ground alone, and she determined to wait until her brothers came in. But as the evening wore on, and they did not arrive, she grew more and more fidgety. It would be a cruel pity to let Jim freeze through another whole night. His small cold hands seemed to keep dragging her towards the door, and at last she said to herself that she would chance it: maybe there wasn't a word of truth in them quare stories all the while; *she'd* niver seen aught. Watching her time, therefore, she stole out unobserved with her bundle into the moonlight.

She wished it had not been so bright. Just to run on blindly through dark shadows, which kept discreetly hidden whatever unchancy objects they might hold, would have seemed easier than to face that broad white glare, where anything dreadful would be seen so very plainly. The rush was made, however, without incident; and then Stacey sped out of the Kilfoyles' cabin almost as precipitately as she had sped into it, running away from the bewildered gratitude of its inhabitants, and the importunate memories and contrasts which this final disposition of her wedding gear did not fail to arouse.

But when she had gone only a few paces from their door, a sudden panic seized her. She was compelled by a sort of irresistible fascination to look fearfully round over the wilds that lay stark about and about her, as solitary as the unfathomed blue-black deeps, with their frost-burnished full moon and light-drowned start-flecks. Wafts of wind came murmuring from the far distance, here and there sweeping up a whirl of powdery flakes, as if someone lifted a corner of the great white sheet and let it fall again in a rumpled fold. The wind, of course, was full of sighs and voices, and shadows wavered and flitted on the snow. How could she tell what they might be? Suppose she should meet that strange little crying child, whom people said sometimes ran after them when they were late abroad on the bog? Or the limping old woman, who laughs in your face as she goes by? Terror whirled through Stacey's thoughts like an autumn gust among a drift of fallen leaves. She began to dart along as fast as the deep snow, a nightmare-like drag, would permit, and she kept her eyes fixed desperately on the track she trod in. Quite near her own door, however, she had to slacken her pace, because across her path stretched two furrow-shaped snow-drifts, into whose ungauged depths she dared not plunge her bare foot. And as she paused a moment irresolute, a voice close by spoke abruptly. 'You'll have to git over them,' it said, 'in standin' leps, as the Divil wint thro' Athlone.' Stacey did not scream or fly, for she knew the voice, and it was one which would have reassured her in the teeth of a North American blizzard, or the heart of a West Indian cyclone. 'So it's yourself, Dan,' she said.

Dan O'Beirne it was, a tall, gaunt, ragged figure, standing up blackly just beyond the sharp-cut shadow of the Doynes' cabin wall. 'Aye, 'tis so,' he said, with an anxious hurry in his manner. 'And are you thinking intirely too bad of me, Stacey, that I sted away so long? And you not hearin' a word, I'm tould, 'xcipt the letter I sint be Paddy Loughlin, the sthookawn,* that you niver got. Meself it is, sure enough, and pounds and pounds, and somethin' I stopped to get you up at Larne – on'y – there's the use of one hand mostly disthroyed on me, and I dunno, tellin' you the truth, if I'll iver walk any better than a trifle lame wid me left fut – just a trifle. Och, but, Stacey *asthore*,* maybe you'd liefer have nought to say to such an ould bosthoon of misery?'

'Sure it's all one,' said Stacey, 'why you sted away, since it's home you are agin; and the sorra a much I'd be mindin' if you hadn't a hand or a fut left on you at all, at all.' A speech whereof the first clause sounds rather poor-spirited, and the last distinctly unfeeling; but to which Dan took no exception.

He could give a more detailed account of himself, however, to less incurious friends, whom he told how, on finishing his engagement at the peat factory, a temptingly lucrative job had lured him over the straits to Scotland, whence he intended to return about Holy Eve, which change of plan he announced in a letter home, confided to one Paddy Loughlin, who proved an unreliable messenger. The truth is that Paddy 'cliver and clane' forgot his friend's letter in his own bustle about transmitting his earnings home in postal orders, and getting himself shipped back as a pauper to the most conveniently situated Union – a thrifty, if not strictly legitimate, mode of travelling occasionally adopted by itinerant harvest men. How, just before he should have started for home, he met with a bad accident while helping to rescue the factory foreman's son out of a whirl of jag-toothed wheels and hissing bands, 'like so many spider's webs all set a-goin' by the Divil', and had lain for a couple of months crippled in hospital, whence he had sent no word, 'lest they'd be fretted thinkin' he was took for death away from them all'.

'Oncommon kind people,' ran his account of his experiences there, 'and iverythin' done as agreeable as they could conthrive, barrin' that them doctors would be lookin' in of a mornin' and sayin' 'That leg had a right to come off to morra,' or 'He'll lose them two fingers, anyway,' as aisy and plisant as if the flesh wasn't creepin' on your bones to hear them. But sure they were intindin' no harm; it's the nature of them to keep choppin' and sawin'. The on'y wonder is that any one gits out of a place where they do be plinty, wid enough of his body left him to hould his sowl in.' Then how, recovering, unmulct after all of limb, he had straightway repaired home, bringing with him the 'pounds and pounds' presented to him by the grateful foreman, a suit of clothes much too good to think of wearing, and the promise of permanent employment at Sterry and Lawson's, whenever he chose to return.

Even so, Dan's homecoming could not be compared for external brilliancy with that of the colour sergeant. Indeed, after the first raptures of restoration had subsided, the elder Dan cast many a regretful glance at the halting gait and sling-suspended arm of his tall son; while Ody Rafferty sought to slur over the refutation of his own conjectures by insisting on the fact that, if the lad *had* took off to the most outrageous wars iver was, he'd more likely than not have come out of them with less destruction done on him than might be perceived now. Young Dan's native air seemed, however, to possess very salubrious qualities; and before he had been three weeks at home, his step began to regain its firmness, and strength and suppleness returned to his limp wrist and stiffened fingers. His cure was practically complete by the time that the black frost had broken, and the snow had vanished off the bog, leaving only its wraith on the frail-blossomed sloe-bushes, and the wedding day had come.

I met the bridal party proceeding towards the Town on Farmer Hilfirthy's loaned jaunting-car, and it struck me that I had never seen so many people at once on any vehicle. I caught a glimpse of Jim Kilfoyle in a queer brown frock sitting on the well, and just as they passed he was saying sternly, 'I' clare, Biddy Sheridan, if you don't lave houldin' me on, I'll let the greatest ould yell you iver heard, and terrify the horse.'

This was a morning in Easter week, and Lady Day in Spring too – a coincidence which led the widow McGurk to observe that you might meet as good fortune marrying on one Lady Day as another: a happy-go-lucky sentiment which Lisconnel appears disposed to adopt as a piece of local proverbial philosophy.

(1893)

MARGARET DELAND

Elizabeth

I

Mr Thomas Sayre had a very disagreeable moment when he learned that his mother had chosen to rent to an artist the top floor of her old house in Bulfinch Court.

'You had no business to let her do such a thing, without first telling me,' he said sharply to his sister. 'Mother only had to speak, and I'd have given her all the money she wanted.'

'But Mother never would speak, you know, Tom,' Elizabeth Sayre answered gently; 'and it scarcely seemed necessary, either, for you knew exactly how much her income was lessened when the bank failed.'

'Well, suppose I did? I didn't think – I mean, I didn't realise—' He paused. His sister did not reply, but her silence was significant. 'You ought to have reminded me,' he ended sullenly.

And indeed there was some excuse for his annoyance. He had come home on his first visit, after an absence of several years abroad, bringing with him his pretty daughter Fanny, and anxious to give his mother some of the overflowing satisfaction of his own life; and, as he told his wife afterwards, 'this lodger, this artist fellow, met me in the hall, and was going to do the honours of the house! A lodger showing me into my own home, if you please! Mother had not had my dispatch, and so was not looking for me.'

He had scarcely waited for his mother's kiss before he asked the meaning of the stranger's presence; and then he stored up the vials of his wrath, to pour them upon his sister's head, when, later in the evening, they should be alone.

'Well,' he said, after an uncomfortable pause, 'it's lucky I'm here now and can put a stop to it. How long has it been going on?'

'Mr Hamilton has been here four years—'

'He wouldn't be here four minutes,' Mr Sayre interposed viciously, 'if I could have my way. But I suppose I can't turn him out without some notice. Well, I'll arrange it. I'll see him the first thing in the morning. Oh, I'll be civil to him, Lizzie; you needn't be worried. Really, I don't blame the man, I blame *you*. My mother's house turned into a lodging house – it's outrageous to think that neither you nor aunt Susan wrote me about it!'

He glanced around the room with indignant pride. The suggestion of a lodger did seem out of place. And yet, could Mr Sayre have known it, the greater number of the houses on Bulfinch Court had gradually fallen to such cheap ends. They kept their dignity, however, in spite of their changed fortunes; and they had that air of accommodating themselves to circumstances with calm indifference, which is as characteristic of houses with a past as it is of people. Possibly these old residences not only endured, but were even a trifle amused at the changing human life which came and went through their wide halls, and below the carved white lintels of the front doors.

Admiral Bent's house, just opposite the Sayres', sheltered dapper young clerks now in its hall bedrooms; there were dressmakers on the ground floor, and some teachers two flights up. In the admiral's time, the manners and people were different, but possibly not so interesting. A little further down on that side of the Court was a house once made reverend by the name of 'parsonage'. When the clergyman died, his heirs let it to a pretty widow with two flaxen-haired children and a dog; and now the two or three old families left in the Court looked at the house doubtfully, and said they wished they knew something about the inmates; but none of them took the trouble to learn anything about them by calling. The heirs, however, found that in spite of rumours, the rent was paid promptly, so they had no reason to complain. The whole neighbourhood had run down. Mr Thomas Sayre pointed that out to his father a dozen years ago, but old Mr Sayre shook his white head.

'Your mother doesn't find fault,' he said.

Nor did she. Her husband found his happiness here; he loved every brick in the house, every tree on the sidewalk; the whole Court was full of small landmarks of association with his past; so, as he said, his wife found no fault – for his happiness was hers; the quiet of the forsaken old Court was a trial to her cheerful heart, and she did resent the behaviour of the children who came up out of the alley to play in the plot of grass in the middle of the square; they dropped orange skins about, and stared rudely at the

occasional passer-by, or followed in solemn and ecstatic proces-
sion the ubiquitous organ grinder in his daily tour up one side of
the Court and down the other. But William loved it all, and so,
she said to herself, 'it was of no consequence'. Afterward, when
William had been taken away from her, all these small
annoyances grew to have a certain beauty of their own; a deep
and tender sacredness, about which she spoke to her daughter,
and her husband's sister, Susan, with the simplicity of a child – a
characteristic which neither of her listeners shared, and scarcely
understood.

Her son understood her better; yet even he did not see that,
with all the frankness of a sweet old age, she would hesitate to tell
him that it had become necessary to take a lodger at No. 16. A
mother often feels that a child should have the intuitive knowledge which belongs to a parent, and it seemed to Mrs Sayre,
although she did not put it into words even to herself, that
Thomas, if he stopped to think, would be aware of her needs; but
of course, being his mother, she found immediate excuse that he
did not stop to think. She had been careful, during the four years
that Mr Hamilton had been an inmate of her house, to avoid
mentioning his name in her letters to her son; so now, on this, his
first visit home, as he walked up and down the sitting room,
scolding his sister to express his self-reproach, Mr Thomas Sayre
had many things to learn.

'Yes, it's outrageous, Lizzie, that neither you nor aunt Susan
wrote to me about it,' he repeated crossly. 'But I'll put an end to it,
now I've found it out for myself. I'll give the fellow notice
tomorrow!'

Elizabeth Sayre's face hardened. It was a delicate face, and fine;
with sensitive lips, and brown, calm eyes shining from under dark
brows; the straight, dark hair was parted in the middle, over a
tranquil forehead, and then brushed smoothly down behind her
ears; it was a face in which sweetness was hidden by determination, but the sweetness was there.

'No,' she said quietly. 'Mr Hamilton will remain here as long as
he wishes. Mother would be very sorry to have him go.'

'Her brother, his hands in his pockets, turned and looked at
her.

'Ah?' he said. The significance in his tone was unmistakable.
Elizabeth flushed like a rose, but she looked at him with clear,
direct eyes.

'*I* should be sorry to have him go, too. He is a very unhappy and lonely man, and if we can cheer him, and make his life brighter, we are glad to do it.'

'What is the matter with him?'

'He has lost his wife.'

'Oh!' Mr Sayre said blankly, but with a little irritation as well. He was mistaken, then; Lizzie was not 'interested'. 'Well, I can't help that,' he said. 'Widower or not, you can't expect me to let my mother come down to taking lodgers while I have plenty of money.'

'I should not have expected it.'

Thomas Sayre flushed angrily. 'Well, you've no right to re-proach me: you should have told me about it. As for this artist fellow, I suppose his wife died here, and mother had all the annoyance of that?'

'No, she did not die here,' his sister answered briefly, 'it was before he came here.'

'But he's been here four years!' cried Mr Sayre. Elizabeth looked at him with a puzzled frown. 'I mean, you said he was all broken up by his wife's death?'

'Well?'

'And she died four years ago!' He put his head back and laughed.

'Five years ago,' she corrected him; 'it was a year before he came here.'

'Five years?' He chuckled and slapped his thigh. 'My dear Lizzie, you are a great goose. I don't mean to imply that Mr Hamilton did not regret his wife properly, and all that sort of thing, but a man doesn't sit in dust and ashes for five years, you know. It's absurd to pretend he does, and give him house room as an expression of sympathy.'

'You don't know Mr Hamilton,' Elizabeth said. 'Dust and ashes may not be your idea of bereaved Love, Tom, but it is some people's; and perhaps if you had known his wife, even you might understand a grief lasting five years. She was a very lovely woman.'

'He has been comforted, though, since he has been here, has he?' Mr Sayre observed. ' "Even I" can understand that.'

He had begun to be good natured, as he found himself amused, but his sister turned upon him.

'No, and he never will be comforted! He will never care for

anyone else. Oh, how contemptible you are, Tom, how—' The indignant tears sprang to her eyes; 'Good night,' she said. 'I think we won't talk any longer. Of course he stays here. He leases the rooms by the year. I'll – I'll go upstairs now. Oh, *Tom!*'

She left him without trusting herself to look at him. Mr Sayre sat down, threw one leg over the arm of his chair, and whistled.

2

No. 16 Bulfinch Court was on the corner where Diamond Alley came over from the thoroughfare beyond to connect it with the world. The house had been painted white once, but was a dingy drab* now; the windows, set deep in the brick walls, had wide sills, upon which Mrs Sayre kept her flower pots and knitting basket, or where she could rest her book and her after-dinner cup of tea, with that happy disregard of order which tried the delicate precision of her daughter. There was a small yard in front of the house, enclosed by a high iron fence that looked like a row of black pikes, rusted here and there, or gray with matted cobwebs, and spotted with little white cocoons. The earth was hard and bare, except for a skim of green mould and occasional thin, wiry blades of grass; the continual shadow of a great ailantus tree which stood in one corner kept the yard faintly damp even in the hottest weather, and there was always the heavy scent of the strange blossoms, or else of the fallen leaves. Elizabeth tried to keep some pansies alive here in the summer, but they languished for want of sunshine.

On this still, hot August afternoon, the young woman looked as languid as her dark flowers. Her talk with her brother, the night before, and her shame that she had lost her temper, had been a pain that still showed itself in her face. Mr Sayre's indifference, too, to her repentance (for in the morning, when she asked his pardon, he only laughed, and said: 'Bless you, Lizzie, dear, that's all right. I was a bear; the fellow shall stay, if you think it wouldn't be the square thing to turn him out') – such indifference had pinched and chilled her, as a burly north wind might shut a flower. She knew intuitively that his change of purpose had something to do with that hint of Mr Hamilton's being 'comforted', which had so wounded her the night before in its slight to Love and Grief. Still, she felt the recoil of her own sharp words to her brother, as one unused to firearms feels the recoil of a shot, and her face betrayed the pain of self-reproach.

Thomas Sayre was out; he had taken his pretty Fanny and gone to make some calls on old friends, and now his mother was letting the moments of waiting for his return melt into a pleasant dream of her good son, her dear boy. The windows were open, and the noises of the alley came in. Elizabeth was moving about in the dusk, laying the table for tea. It was too hot for lights, and Mrs Sayre had put down her sewing and was sitting by the window, her active old hands folded in her lap. Once or twice she glanced at her daughter. Elizabeth's unfailing precision made this task of setting the table every evening a long one. Mrs Sayre lifted her hands at last with good-natured impatience.

'My dear, when you have a husband and children, you will really have to move about a little quicker. Dear me! when I was your age, I could have set ten tables in the time you've taken to set one!'

Elizabeth started, and blushed faintly.

'I didn't know you were in any hurry, Mother dear,' she said, and as she tried to make haste, one of the plates slipped through her fingers, striking another with that suspicious sound which tells of a nicked edge.

Mrs Sayre looked away, and tapped her fingers on the window sill.

'Oh, I am afraid I have chipped the willow plate!' Elizabeth said, with the sensitive quiver in her voice which always went to her mother's heart.

'Never mind, dearie,' she reassured her; 'it's no matter.'

Elizabeth sighed, and even frowned a little in the darkness; her mother's indifference was a continual trial to her. 'I ought not to have been so careless,' she said, with faint severity in her voice; and Mrs Sayre was silenced.

It was a relief to both of them when the third member of the household entered. Miss Susan Sayre was a tall, timid woman, older than Mrs Sayre, and yet, as is often the case with unmarried women, indefinitely younger than her sister-in-law; she had Elizabeth's exactness, but with it a deprecatory tremor that gave all her actions the effect of uncertainty. Many a time Mrs Sayre would hold her own dear old hands tight together, to keep from seizing some bit of work on which Miss Susan was toiling with laborious and painstaking clumsiness. 'It would be so much easier to do it myself,' she would think, although she hoped she would have the grace never to say so! 'Fussy,' she called her sister-in-law, sometimes, when she felt she must have the relief of speech. But she was glad to see her now, because of the disapproval of Elizabeth's silence.

She and 'Liz'beth did not seem to get along together, Mrs Sayre thought. Often enough, upon her knees, she had asked herself 'why?' searching her simple heart to find her own offense.

There is, perhaps, some psychical and uncomprehended reason why the truest confidences between mother and daughter are so difficult and so rare. Usually, a girl can speak of the deepest things in her life with greater ease to any one else than to her mother. Mrs Sayre felt her daughter's remoteness, but no one thought she did. Such generous, tender, healthy natures rarely think themselves of enough importance to use the phrase of the day, and say that 'they are not understood'. And yet it is very often the case; the more morbid souls about them are baffled by their very frankness and openness, and are really unable to understand them – and, too often, unable also to appreciate them.

Elizabeth, loving her mother with a curious intensity which spent itself in the subtleties of conscientious scruples, was as unaware of Mrs Sayre's longing for a more tender companionship as she was of her mother's ability to understand her – for, quite without confidences from Elizabeth, and in spite of 'not getting along', Mrs Sayre could read her daughter's nature with wonderful clearness, although she could not explain it in relation to her own. It would have been well for the daughter could the mother have boldly broken down the reserve between them, and confessed just what she read – confessed that she knew that the most vital interest in Elizabeth's life was Oliver Hamilton. She would have added to this that Lizzie did not know she was in love with Mr Hamilton. Here, however, would have been her first mistake: Elizabeth was perfectly aware that she loved him. Mrs Sayre made one other mistake, too: she said to herself, amused and good-natured and annoyed all together, that it was plain enough that Mr Hamilton was in love with 'Liz'beth. 'And there is no earthly reason why he shouldn't speak!' she reflected. But there was a reason, and an excellent reason, for Oliver Hamilton's silence: he did not know that he was in love with Elizabeth.

It was no wonder, though, that Mrs Sayre's penetration failed her here. How could she suppose that her daughter's one aim had been to keep the young man blind to any such possibility in himself as falling in love? She never imagined that Elizabeth was holding him rigidly to his ideal of the sacredness and eternity of love – an ideal which had sprung up out of his passionate grief when his wife died. That was five years ago. He had come then to Elizabeth, for she had been Alice's friend, that he might take that poor, empty, human comfort of talking of the past. He had told her all his grief, and his simple, hopeless conviction that his life was over; told it with that pathetic assertion of an undying sorrow with which human nature seeks to immortalise a moment.

Such loyalty seemed to Elizabeth so beautiful, that her reverence for it fed the flame of his devotion to his ideal, even as time began to stand between him and the substance of his grief. He did not know it – he could not, with Elizabeth's worshipping belief in it – but now, five years later, it was the memory of grief, not grief itself, which still darkened his life. It was a lonely life, save for Elizabeth's friendship: long days in his studio, dreaming over unfinished canvases, brooding upon anniversaries of which she reminded him; talking of an ideal love, in which he believed that he believed. And so, gradually, as his mind yielded to the pressure of her thought of him, and his life mirrored a loyalty which was hers, he began to be the embodiment of nobility to Elizabeth Sayre, and by and by the time had come when she said to herself, very simply, that she loved him; but she said, also, very proudly, that he would never love her. That 'never' was the very heart of her love for him.

Surely, the last person in the world to appreciate such a state of mind was Elizabeth's cheerful, simple-minded, sensible mother. And so she continued to hope and plan for this marriage which she so much desired, and to try by small hints to 'encourage' Oliver Hamilton. This hinting was, perhaps, the hardest thing which Elizabeth had to bear. Her silent endurance told of the smothered antagonism between mother and daughter, which each would have denied indignantly in herself, but was quite aware of in the other.

It had been a great relief to Mrs Sayre to confide her desires and impatience to her son. She had done it that very morning; which accounted for his change of mind in the matter of the objectionable lodger, when Elizabeth went to him with her apology for her quick words. With instant good nature, he had decided to further his mother's hopes. With this purpose in his mind, he had gone up to Mr Hamilton's studio that afternoon and looked at his sketches with far more helpful and discriminating criticism than Elizabeth, with her wondering praise, had ever given. Fanny went, too, hanging on her father's arm, shyly watching Mr Hamilton, or answering his occasional reference to herself in a half-frightened, schoolgirl fashion. She was certainly very pretty, Mr Hamilton thought.

'Pretty, and a dear child!' Mrs Sayre said, watching with the fondest pride, but with a curious jealousy, too, for her daughter's sake. Fanny was so gay and pretty, light-hearted and careless, she revealed Elizabeth's impossibilities.

'Not that I'd have Lizzie different,' she assured her sister-in-law, as they sat in the darkened parlour; while Elizabeth went to get another willow plate from the china closet – 'not that I'd have her different; only I would like to see her enjoy life a little more.'

I don't think 'Liz'beth is unhappy,' protested the old aunt, 'only she just doesn't show her happiness in the way we us to when we were girls.'

'*Girls*!' said Mrs Sayre. 'You really can't call Lizzie "girl", Susy. Why, I was married at her age, and had three children. Dear, dear, I wish the child was settled!'

'Oh, now, Jane,' remonstrated the other, mildly, 'I've always been happy, and there's no reason why 'Liz'beth shouldn't be, too, even if she doesn't marry. Indeed, it's better to be as I am than to be unhappily married; and that is possible, you know, Jane.'

'Not among nice people,' Mrs Sayre said, with decision. 'Not when people do their duty. And a poor husband's better than none. No woman's happy unless she's married. And then, to think here is poor, dear Oliver – well, well, I suppose the Lord knows best.'

'If you think so, sister, why don't you leave it in hands?' said Susan, piously. 'The Lord will provide, you know.'

'That's just it!' cried Mrs Sayre. 'He has provided, and she won't take his provision. And she's not as young as she was once, Susy, you can't deny that; little Fanny made me realise it. She's old enough herself to settle down, bless her heart! She's nineteen, isn't she? Here's 'Liz'beth,' she interrupted herself, as her daughter entered. 'She knows. How old is Fanny, 'Liz'beth – nineteen?'

'Eighteen, Mother. She is not nineteen until next month,' Elizabeth corrected her.

'Nonsense!' cried her mother; 'what difference does a week or two make? She's nineteen; and the first thing we know, she'll be getting married. I hope so, I'm sure. You needn't look shocked, my dear; I was eighteen when your blessed father married me. I believe in early marriages – anything to save a girl from being an old maid! And see here, Lizzie, I want Oliver Hamilton to see Fanny. I'm not a matchmaker, but there's no harm in Oliver's seeing Fanny.'

She looked at her daughter with something as much like malice as could come into her motherly face. Elizabeth smiled.

'But no good, either, if you mean that he might care for Fanny.'

'Oh, 'Liz'beth! 'Liz'beth! Where did you get your fancies?' cried the other. 'Not from me, surely. Lizzie, second marriages are the Lord's means of healing broken hearts. Oliver would be a thousand times better off with another wife, instead of brooding over his loss. Bless me, if I had died when I was a young woman, I would have made your dear father promise to get another wife as soon as he possibly could. I always used to say that my last words would be, "William, marry again!"'

'And you, mother,' Elizabeth inquired, smiling, 'you would have married again, if—'

'Not at all,' Mrs Sayre declared. 'That's quite different. It is the men who should remarry, not the women. It's a great misfortune when a man remains a widower. I wish you'd remember that, Lizzie.'

Elizabeth Sayre blushed with indignation, and made no reply. Mrs Sayre sighed. She was glad that Tom was at home for a little while. Tom was like her, she thought.

'Neither of us will ever be as good as Elizabeth,' she assured herself. And she seemed to find the assertion a comfort.

3

Mr Thomas Sayre knew the satisfaction of self-approval when he and his daughter turned their faces towards home. He had done his duty; he had made his visit, he had given himself the pleasure of adding to his mother's income, and now he could allow these dear people to drift into that pleasant background of his thoughts where he took his affection for them for granted. He congratulated himself, too, upon his kindness to his sister; he had done what he could to make Elizabeth happy; he had dropped a few hints to Mr Hamilton, even going so far as to refer, casually, to the time when Lizzie would marry somebody, and his mother would be left alone. 'Of course she'll marry one of these days. I only hope it will be some fellow who is worthy of her!' said Mr Sayre, feeling that he was very subtle, and that Hamilton must surely come to the point, pretty soon. Indeed, anxious to prove his friendliness, he had made the artist promise that when he came on to the academy with his picture, he would call upon him.

'Let us know when you're in town, Hamilton,' he said heartily. 'We'll be delighted to see you, and hear the latest news of Lizzie and the old people.'

And Mr Hamilton was glad to promise. He had enjoyed this visit. Thomas Sayre seemed like a breath of bracing mountain wind coming into his dreamy life; and Fanny gave him pleasure, too. Her fresh girlish laughter brightened all the old house, and her little foolish talk was as useless and as pleasant as the dancing sparkle of sunshine on deep, still water.

The night that Mr Sayre and his daughter went away, Oliver Hamilton came in to take Elizabeth to prayer meeting. This custom of going together every Wednesday evening to prayer meeting was very dear to both these people; there was no time when they talked so freely of Oliver's sacred past as when they came out into the solemn starlight, the last words of the benediction lingering in their reverent ears. That night, as they walked towards the church, Oliver began to speak of Alice almost immediately. 'How it brightened your mother and your aunt Susan, Elizabeth, to have your niece here! Do you know, she made me think of Alice, sometimes; there's a look—'

'Yes,' she answered thoughtfully, 'there is a look of Alice. And yet, dear little Fanny has not the earnestness in her face which made Alice the strength that she was to those who loved her. She was so strong. That is why she lives in your life still, Oliver.'

Oliver's quick appreciation of her words gratified her, as only the confirmation of an ideal can gratify one who loves. It brought a serious joy into her eyes, which he noticed as they sat side by side in the prayer meeting, singing from the same book, or standing together in prayer.

Oliver did not follow the service very closely. That merry glimpse of life which Mr Sayre's visit had given to No. 16 lingered in his thoughts. Ah, if Alice had only lived, how different his life would have been! How truly Elizabeth loved her, how truly she

understood her! What would he have done without Elizabeth? As
this thought came into his mind, another followed it, as the shadow
of a cloud chases the sunshine from an upland pasture: What
should he do without Elizabeth? 'When she marries' (Mr Sayre's
words suddenly sounded in his ears) – 'when she marries, what
shall I do?' The shock of the idea was almost physical. He turned
and looked at her; her face was bent a little, but he saw the pure line
of her cheek under the shadow of her chip hat, which was tied
beneath her chin with lavender ribbons. She wore a white crepe
shawl, embroidered above the deep, soft fringe with a running vine
of silk; her hands were clasped lightly in her lap; her gray alpaca
gown gleamed faintly in the light of the lamp on the wall above her.
Elizabeth marry? Impossible! But suppose she should? What
difference would it make to him? Would she not still be Alice's
friend – his friend? In this sudden confusion, his ideal seemed to
evade him. Did he – did he love Elizabeth?

He felt his face grow white. He had spiritually the sensation of a
man who wakes because he dreams that he is falling from a
height. Oliver Hamilton's eyes were opening to life and light and a
possibility. His grief was withdrawing, and withdrawing, and in
its place were pain and confusion and doubt.

Elizabeth, listening to the preacher, her head bending like a
flower on its stalk, was so calm and so remote that his reverence
for her was almost fear. When they rose to sing the last hymn, and
she missed his voice, she looked at him inquiringly, and, with an
effort, he followed mechanically the guidance he had known so
long. He tried to sing, but at first he was not aware of the words:

> Blest be the tie that binds
>   Our hearts in Christian love!
> The fellowship of kindred minds
>   Is like to that above.
>
> From sorrow, toil, and pain;
>   And sin we shall be free;
> And perfect love and friendship reign
>   Through all eternity!

Love, through all eternity!

'Do I love her?' he was asking himself, and the very question
seemed an affirmation.

'You didn't sing?' Elizabeth said, when they were alone under the stars.

'No,' he said shortly. She was startled at his tone, and looked at him anxiously, but without a question. (This habit of hers of waiting silently was, although she did not know it, a most insistent and inescapable question.) 'Elizabeth,' he said hoarsely, 'it has just come to me – I – Listen! What should I have done without you all these years? Do you – do you *understand*?'

It seemed to Elizabeth Sayre as though for one instant her heart stood still. But the pause between Oliver's words and her answer was scarcely noticeable.

'It has been a great privilege to me,' she said, with a breath as though her throat contracted; 'it is a great happiness to have helped you in any way. It is my love for Alice that has helped you.'

'*Alice!*'

Oliver made no answer. They walked on, Elizabeth knowing that her hand trembled on his arm, and feeling still that clutch upon her throat.

4

'Why, Lizzie, aren't you going to stop a minute? Aren't you going to sit down?'

Elizabeth stood on the threshold of the parlour, her hand on the door knob. Through her mother's words, she was listening to Oliver Hamilton's step as he went up to his studio. Mr Hamilton had left her at the front door, and gone at once to his rooms, instead of stopping as usual for a chat with Mrs Sayre. The rest of their walk home, after that word 'Alice,' had been full of forced and idle talk, which covered the shocked silence of their thoughts.

Mrs Sayre's voice now seemed to her daughter like a stone flung into a still pool, which shattered the silence, and let loose a clamorous repetition of this strange thing Oliver had said, or rather this terrible thing he had left unsaid. Elizabeth leaned against the door, holding the knob in a nervous grip.

'Come, child, sit down and tell us about the sermon,' Mrs Sayre commanded her, cheerily.

'No,' Elizabeth said, 'I only stopped to say good night. I – I am rather tired.'

'Why, what's happened to Oliver?' said Mrs Sayre. 'Why

doesn't he come in a minute? Have you and Elizabeth quarrelled, Oliver?' she called out goodnaturedly, thinking him still in the hall.

Elizabeth turned abruptly.

'Good night,' she said, and a moment later they heard her light step on the stairs.

Her mother and aunt looked at each other.

'I believe they *have* quarrelled, Susy. Why, she didn't kiss us good night,' said Mrs Sayre, in rather an awed voice.

Elizabeth, in the darkness of her bedroom, stood still in the middle of the floor, her fingers pressed hard upon her eyes, her heart beating so that she could hardly breathe. The white crepe shawl slipped from her shoulders, and fell like a curve of foam about her feet. The light from the street lamp, which flared in an iron bracket on the corner of No. 16, travelled across the worn carpet, and showed the spare, old-fashioned furnishing of the room; it struck a faint sparkle from the misty surface of the old mirror, and it gleamed along the edge of a little gilt photograph frame that was standing on the dressing table. Elizabeth, shivering a little, the soft colour deepening in her cheeks, and her eyelashes glittering with tears, saw the flickering gleam, and, with a sudden impulse, lifted the photograph, holding it close to her eyes and staring at it in the darkness. But the light from the lamp in the court was too faint to show the face. With an unsteady hand she struck a match and lit her candle. She had forgotten to take off her bonnet; she stood, the light flaring up into her face, looking with blurred eyes at Alice's picture. At last, with a long sigh, she kissed it gently and put it again on the table. Then she sat down on the edge of her bed, staring straight before her at the candle, burning steadily in the hot, still night; her hands were clasped tightly upon her knees.

It was long after that – it must have been nearly midnight – that Mrs Sayre heard a step in her bedroom, and said, with a start: 'What is it? Is that you, 'Liz'beth?'

'Yes, Mother dear. I – I wanted to kiss you. I wanted – you!'

Mrs Sayre gathered the slender figure down into her arms.

'Why, 'Liz'beth! Why, my precious child! Are you sick, my darling?'

'No, no,' she answered, a thrill of comfort in her voice; 'only I didn't kiss you good night. I oughtn't to have wakened you. Good night, Mother darling.'

'But, Lizzie,' said the tender old voice, 'something troubles you, my precious child. Did Oliver—' She felt the instant stiffening of the arms about her, and her daughter drew herself away.

'There's nothing the matter, Mother dear,' she said, her breathless voice quivering into calmness. 'You will go to sleep now, won't you? I ought not to have disturbed you.' And she had gone.

Mrs Sayre sighed. 'I wish I could learn not to speak about him,' she thought. 'Yet if she would only tell me!'

But nothing could have been more impossible. Alas for those natures that cannot give their sorrow to another! Elizabeth longed for sympathy and comfort, yet she knew not how to open her heart to receive it. Such natures suffer infinitely more than those happier souls whose pain rushes to their lips.

Elizabeth's struggle with herself had ended when she sought her mother; she knew what she must do. She said to herself with exultation that she loved Oliver with all her soul; loved him enough to help him to be true to himself. He had told her, oh, how often, in those earlier days, that to him marriage was for eternity as well as time; that Love, from its very nature, could not be untrue, and so there could be but one love in a life. 'If a second comes,' he used to say, 'either it is an impostor, or the first was; either the first marriage was not sacred, or the second will not be!' She remembered how she had heard him say once of a man who had suffered as he had suffered: 'No, his living is over; he can remember, but he cannot live again. If he dares to try, life will be ashes in his mouth!'

Should she let him try? Should she let him think that his love for Alice was not love, or his love for her was disloyalty to Alice? How plain, how easy, was the answer, just because she loved him!

5

The next morning Mrs Sayre looked at Elizabeth anxiously. It was evident that her daughter suffered, and she longed to find one weak spot in that armour of reserve where she might pour in the oil and wine of love. But Elizabeth's face had settled into the invincible calm which sympathy dare not touch. Indeed, her mother would even have wondered whether her suspicion, in that hurried kiss at midnight, had not been all wrong, had it not been for Mr Hamilton's manner.

Oliver Hamilton was too confused and dazed by his own possibilities to take thought of what his face or manner might betray. He said to himself that Elizabeth did not know what self-knowledge had leaped into his astounded brain in those brief words of his. But he would tell her; only, not today, – not today! He did not doubt that he loved her – at least he loved Love; but to love her gave the lie to five years' protestations!

Elizabeth made no effort to avoid him. She believed so firmly in his loyalty to the past – a loyalty so beautiful that it had kindled in her the very love which it denied – she believed so entirely in him and his love for the dead Alice, that she would not permit herself to doubt that his thought of her was only a fleeting fancy.

To avoid him was to confess a fear that it was more. So when, on Sunday afternoon, he suggested that they should go out and walk across the bridge and along the road that led over the marshes, she assented with pleasure – a pleasure in which, when they started, there was a thread of irritation, because she knew, as they walked down the Court, that her mother and aunt Susan were looking after them, and speculating as to whether Oliver was 'going to speak'. She was glad to turn into the first side street, and lose the consciousness of the eyes that were watching the back of her head. It was that sense of relief that made her draw a long breath, and Oliver instantly turned and looked at her with a solicitude in his eyes which was new.

'Are you tired?' he said gently.

'No,' she answered. She saw that the hour she had refused to think possible was coming, yet it should not come! 'Oh, Oliver,' she said hurriedly, 'I wish you would make a study of the marshes in September; there is no autumnal colouring so lovely as those stretches of bronze and red, with pools here and there that are like bits of the sky. Suppose we try to find just what you want, this afternoon, and then this week you can go to work. I wish you would really and seriously begin to work.'

'I want to, now, myself,' he said soberly. 'I have wasted too much time. Elizabeth, I have lived in a dream.'

'Yes,' she agreed, wondering whether the unsteadiness which she felt in her voice could be heard, 'I know you have. I have been thinking about it lately, and I wanted to say to you – I know you will forgive me for Alice's sake, if it seems a hard thing – I wanted to say to you that it seems to me you ought to make your grief an inspiration in your life, not a hindrance. It ought to mean achievement, not a dream, Oliver.'

He did not answer her, and when, a little later, he began to speak, it was of something else.

The walk across the marshes was towards the east; the city lay behind them, and the little tidal river, catching a faint glow on its darkening expanse, wandered on ahead, fading at last into the cold violet of the distant hills.

'Oh, this is what you ought to do,' Elizabeth said, as they paused a moment, and turned to look back at the town, whose windows flared with a sudden ruddy blaze. The house tops were black against the yellow sky; a cross upon a distant spire flashed, and then faded into the sunset. The sea stretched its fingers in among the marshes, and rifts of water shone blue with the faint upper sky, or fiercely red where the clouds along the west were mirrored. The salt grass had bronzed and bleached, and had a hundred rippling tints of dull purple or warmer russet. Some of it had been cut, and lay in sodden yellow swaths, and some had been gathered into haystacks, that stood here and there like little thatched domes. A group of boys were playing down by the water, and their black figures stood out clear against the amber sky; a tongue of flame from their bonfire leaped up, red and sharp, and lapsed again; and the lazy trail of white smoke, lying low along the marsh, brought to the two watchers the faint delicious scent of burning brush and drift.

'Oh, couldn't you do this?' Elizabeth said, breathless with the joy of colour. 'Oh, how wonderful the sky is!'

But Oliver, instead of planning for a picture, was staring into her face.

'Elizabeth,' he said, 'I want to tell you – something. When I said I wanted to begin to work, did you understand what I meant? My past, you know what it is to me, but – Oh, Elizabeth—'

She turned her eyes away from his, but she answered calmly: 'Yes, indeed, I do know what it is to you, Oliver; and it is your present, too – I know that. I know how real Alice is to you. It is she who makes your life now, just as she has made it in the past, and will make it in the future.'

He opened his lips to speak, but he had no words, only blank impatience at the impossibility of putting aside that sacred name;

and yet he was aware of a curious willingness to accept the check. He could not understand himself.

'Ought we not to go home?' Elizabeth was saying gently. 'See how grey the marshes are getting.'

He shivered.

'Yes, come.'

The walk home was very silent.

6

The yellow elm leaves were thick upon the ground in Bulfinch Court, when September, weary with its noon heats, held out an entreating hand to cool October. Mrs Sayre found it necessary to have a fire occasionally in the evening, and she could not understand why it was that Oliver Hamilton did not sometimes ask to join the little circle about the hearth.

'He used to, last autumn,' she complained. 'What's the matter, Lizzie – what does it mean?'

The anxious interest in her mother's face offended Elizabeth Sayre: 'Have you refused him?' it said. 'Have you had any disagreement?'

The indestructible tie between mother and daughter was sadly strained in those fading fall days. Elizabeth had withdrawn more and more into her own life; and she was too eager in her reticent living to know how cruelly she put her mother aside. The thought of Oliver Hamilton shut every other thought out. He loved her! Here was glory and sweetness, but pain and disappointment as well. His love for the dead Alice, his serene and lofty loyalty, in which Elizabeth had so rejoiced – where were they? Yet they should not cease! He must be true to his own ideal, she said to herself again and again; he must conquer this passing unfaith.

With this determination tingeing every action and word, absorbing every thought, it was no wonder Mrs Sayre felt shut out of her daughter's heart. Elizabeth lived, in those fall days, only to turn Oliver back to his own better life. In all her talks with him, as they went to prayer meeting or wandered through the picture galleries, or came home together from the library, there was this strange fencing and parrying. How many times, when she thought she saw the words trembling on his lips which would make him untrue to his best self, and bring her the sweetness of human love, had she turned his thoughts back to Alice! How many times, when the door to happiness had seemed about to open, had she closed it with that single word, 'Alice'!

Alice! Alice! The name rang in her ears; it seemed to her sometimes as though she hated Alice.

This suppressed excitement told upon her; her face grew paler, and there was a weary look in her eyes which her mother noted with anxiety. Mrs Sayre almost betrayed her satisfaction when, one evening late in September, Oliver told her that he was going to New York for a fortnight, and promised her to call upon her son while he was there. He told Elizabeth, gloomily, that he was glad to get away. Life was a miserable puzzle, he said, and he was going to forget it for a while if he could.

Her face brightened. 'I am so glad you are going!' she said. It was well that he should not see her for a time, she thought; he would have regained his old faith before he came back again.

The look of relief in her face did not escape him.

'She doesn't love me,' he said to himself. 'Well, I will not urge her, I will not trouble her; but our friendliness is over: it can never be the same again.'

Of course he was right. He was wakening to find himself still a man, although he had slept so long beneath his cloak of sorrow that he was yet half blind and dazed; and he knew that he and Elizabeth must be either more to each other, or less.

It would have been hard for him to say which was the stronger in his mind: his conviction that he was yet capable of love, or his shame that his love was capable of death. It was this confusion of shame and exultation and pain that made it easy for Elizabeth to check the words which came again and again to his lips. This sudden vanishing of the darkness of unreality left him groping in a blaze of light; he was full of bewilderment. He could not live as he had been living; he dared not think of Alice – it seemed as though his love for Elizabeth had masqueraded beneath the thought of Alice!

But Elizabeth felt a burden lifted when he went away.

'It will be all right when he comes back,' she said to herself; 'he does not know that I saw it, and he will forget it.' And so she fell into the old round of duties, and she and her mother came a little closer together, only jarring apart again when Mrs Sayre mentioned Oliver Hamilton in any way. But by the time his two weeks' absence had lengthened into three, and the fourth was just opening, Mrs Sayre had learned, she said to herself, to hold her tongue, and so she and her daughter came to know something like friendship, as well as the love which had always been theirs.

'But I would like to know what keeps Oliver,' she confided to her sister-in-law, as they sat beside the fire, in the Saturday evening dusk. ''Liz'beth won't let anybody see that she misses him, but she does.'

Susan shook her head doubtfully. 'I think Lizzie's glad he's gone. I can't say why, but that's how it seems to me.'

'Well, Susy,' interposed the other, with amiable contempt, 'you can't be expected to be a judge – *you*. But I, being married, understand such things. She misses him terribly, my dear. Well, I'm glad there's a letter from him tonight. I wish she'd come home and read it to us.'

Susan leaned forward and stirred the fire gently.

'I'm not married, Jane, I know,' she acknowledged humbly; 'but sometimes I think 'Liz'beth feels *proud* because Oliver's faithful to the deceased.'

Mrs Sayre took off her glasses and polished them quickly on her black silk apron. Her handsome black eyes snapped.

'Susy, if you weren't *born* an old maid, you never would have thought of anything so ridiculous!' She picked up the unopened letter from the table and looked at it longingly. 'Dear me! I wish I knew what was in it. It's thick enough to be an offer, and—'

She did not finish the sentence, for Elizabeth opened the sitting-room door. The faint glow of the fire dazzled her eyes, fresh from the rainy darkness of the streets, so that at first she did not notice the letter. Her mother, however, accustomed to the half-light, could see her daughter's face, and was troubled by its pallor.

There was a reason for it; a new pain had come to Elizabeth in her walk home. She had gone out early in the afternoon to visit a sick Sunday-school child; but, the call made, she had stood hesitating in the doorway of the tenement house. There was nothing of importance that she must do; there was no other visit which must be made. She might as well go home. But she was strangely restless; she did not want to go home. The thought of sitting by the fire, watching the rainy evening gather into darkness, while her mother and aunt Susan talked about Oliver, was unbearable. She had borne it often in the past, but then Oliver had been in the house; while they were speaking, she could listen for his step upon the stairs, or the sound of the studio door closing, and then the echo jarring through the empty halls. But how different it all was at No. 16 Bulfinch Court without him! All her life seemed bleak and useless, filled only with that gentle chatter over cups of tea by the fireside. No, she could not go home just yet. The rain beat against the houses on the opposite side of the street, and there was a gush and gurgle from the tin spout that carried the water from the gutters under the eaves. A sudden gust of wind twisted the loose folds of her umbrella into a wet spiral. She shook it and opened it, and then found herself plodding out into the rain.

She missed Oliver with a sort of sick pain about her heart which she did not understand. 'It's enough happiness to love him, even if he doesn't love me,' she assured herself, as she had done many times before, never doubting her own sincerity. Ever since she had recognised her love for him, she had been holding with all her might to this belief which human experience gives us the right at least to doubt – that the human heart can be satisfied to give love, when it receives none in return.

Elizabeth, walking aimlessly into the storm, feeding the hunger of her heart with this assertion, found herself at last on the road that led over the marshes.

The sky was low and dull; the grey rain was sweeping in from the sea, and through the sodden grass the winding fingers of water were blackened at the touch of the wind. The memory of the yellow August sunset came back to her, and Oliver's words; she bit her lip, and the landscape blurred as though with some sudden, driving mist.

It is hard enough at best to keep the exaltation of sacrifice in one's daily commonplace living; but when into that commonplace living creeps the suggestion that the sacrifice has been unnecessary, then a sick bewilderment falls upon the soul. This suggestion came now, suddenly, to Elizabeth Sayre. Perhaps she had made a terrible mistake! If Oliver loved her, whether he put it into words or not – if he *did*, was not the untruth to his ideal come? Would any hiding it from herself and him do away with the fact? Merely to keep him silent could not make him loyal to Alice.

Elizabeth caught her breath as one who sobs, and yet with a strange, sharp pang of joy. Oliver, by all those unuttered words, was hers!

But she would not allow herself to think such thoughts. Her mind was in a tumult; she doubted her own sincerity. She turned and began to walk back to town. She was very tired. Her dress was heavy with dampness, and her face wet with rain; her tears were hot upon her cheeks. No one noticed her in her long walk across the marshes; the occasional pedestrian cared only to shelter himself behind his umbrella, and did not look into the faces of young women foolish enough to be out in such a storm. When she got into town, it was quite dark; the street lamps gleamed with faint, quivering reflections along the wet pavements, and the people were pushing and jostling, in their haste to reach the cheerful shelter of their homes.

Elizabeth found herself thinking of the fireside and her mother's face. She was weary of herself; she wanted to escape from this strange triumph of defeat; for, at last, she knew, without reasoning about it, that she was going to accept the facts as they were – she was going to be happy, and let Oliver be happy. Joy had been hiding itself under the pain of the thought that Oliver might never regain the past. She knew now that she did not want him to regain it. *He loved her* – and she was glad.

She did not go into the sitting-room when she reached home; she was too wet, she said, standing in the doorway and smiling at her mother and aunt; tired, but with delicate colour deepening in her face, and with the rain still shining in her soft hair, all roughened by the wind and curling about her forehead. 'I'll go upstairs and put on some dry clothes, and then come down and set the tea-table,' she said; 'and I'm sorry I've been out so long, Mother dear.' There was a little burst of joyousness in her voice; yet all the while she was wondering whether a reaction would come, and she would find herself capable of taking up her sacrifice again. Then she saw the letter which her mother, in smiling silence, held up to her. Mrs Sayre's look turned her back into her old reserve; she would read her letter alone.

'I will be down in a moment and set the table,' she repeated, and, taking the letter, she slipped out into the chilly darkness of the hall and up to her bedroom.

It seemed to Mrs Sayre, waiting impatiently for news, that Elizabeth took a long time to read her letter. 'Liz'beth's like you, Susy,' she said, 'she can't hurry.' Indeed, the pause grew so long that Susan offered to go upstairs to see what detained 'Liz'beth. Susan was sensitive about her niece's slowness, because Mrs Sayre always pointed out in this connection Elizabeth's resemblance to her aunt. 'Do, Susy,' Mrs Sayre assented, 'and tell her we want to hear what Oliver says.' But Susan, when she returned, looked troubled, and did not bring any news of Oliver.

'Liz'beth's lying down. She says she has a headache. Dear me! I hope the child hasn't taken cold, Jane. Don't you think you'd better give her something hot to drink?'

Mrs Sayre's solicitude banished instantly all thought of Oliver. She went bustling up to her daughter's room, full of tender anxiety. But Elizabeth, lying white and still upon the bed, would only assure her, faintly, that she was tired; that her head ached; that there was nothing the matter with her; that she didn't want anything. 'Oh, nothing! *Nothing*! Only let me be alone, Mother, and – and perhaps I shall sleep. Oh, won't you *please* go?' Distressed and worried, there was nothing for Mrs Sayre to do but kiss her daughter, resting her soft old hand upon Elizabeth's forehead, and stroking her hair gently, with little murmuring sounds of love, and then slip out of the room, closing the door quietly behind her.

When she had gone, Elizabeth Sayre rose, with sudden, violent haste; she slipped the bolt of her door, and then fell upon her knees at her bedside.

Mrs Sayre knocked gently a few hours afterwards, but there was no answer, and she said to Susan that Elizabeth must be asleep, and sleep was the best thing for her; so she wouldn't disturb her by going in to see how she was. She meant to let her sleep in the morning, too, she told her sister-in-law. But when she went down to breakfast she found her daughter in the sitting-room. Elizabeth answered all her mother's inquiries, and kissed her gently, assuring her that she was quite well. A headache was of no consequence, she said; yet it made her absent-minded, and she did not talk very much. Breakfast was almost over, Mrs Sayre told her son afterwards, before Lizzie remembered the great piece of news, and said, with a sort of start:

'Mother, Mr Hamilton writes me to say that he is very happy. Fanny has promised to marry him. Tom is very much pleased, and I – I am so glad for dear little Fanny.'

(1893)

SARAH ORNE JEWETT

Miss Esther's Guest

I

Old Miss Porley put on her silk shawl, and arranged it carefully over her thin shoulders, and pinned it with a hand that shook a little as if she were much excited. She bent forward to examine the shawl in the mahogany-framed mirror, for there was a frayed and tender spot in the silk where she had pinned it so many years. The shawl was very old; it had been her mother's, and she disliked to wear it too often, but she never could make up her mind to go out into the street in summer, as some of her neighbours did, with nothing over her shoulders at all. Next she put on her bonnet and tried to set it straight, allowing for a wave in the looking-glass that made one side of her face appear much longer than the other; then she drew on a pair of well-darned silk gloves; one had a wide crack all the way up the back of the hand, but they were still neat and decent for everyday wear, if she were careful to keep her left hand under the edge of the shawl. She had discussed the propriety of drawing the ravelled silk together, but a thick seam would look very ugly, and there was something accidental about the crack.

Then, after hesitating a few moments, she took a small piece of folded white letter-paper from the table and went out of the house, locking the door and trying it, and stepped away bravely down the village street. Everybody said, 'How do you do, Miss Porley?' or 'Good mornin', Esther.' Every one in Daleham knew the good woman; she was one of the unchanging persons, always to be found in her place, and always pleased and friendly and ready to take an interest in old and young. She and her mother, who had early been left a widow, had been for many years the village tailoresses and makers of little boys' clothes. Mrs Porley had been dead three years, however, and her daughter 'Easter', as old friends called our heroine, had lived quite alone. She was made very sorrowful by her loneliness, but she never could be persuaded to take anybody to board: she could not bear to think of any one's taking her mother's place.

It was a warm summer morning, and Miss Porley had not very far to walk, but she was still more shaky and excited by the time she reached the First Church parsonage. She stood at the gate undecidedly, and, after she pushed it open a little way, she drew back again, and felt a curious beating at her heart and a general reluctance of mind and body. At that moment the minister's wife, a pleasant young woman with a smiling, eager face, looked out of the window and asked the tremulous visitor to come in. Miss Esther straightened herself and went briskly up the walk; she was very fond of the minister's wife, who had only been in Daleham a few months.

'Won't you take off your shawl?' asked Mrs Wayton affectionately; 'I have just been making gingerbread, and you shall have a piece as soon as it cools.'

'I don't know's I ought to stop,' answered Miss Esther, flushing quickly. 'I came on business; I won't keep you long.'

'Oh, please stay a little while,' urged the hostess. 'I'll take my sewing, if you don't mind; there are two or three things that I want to ask you about.'

'I've thought and flustered a sight over taking this step,' said good old Esther abruptly. 'I had to conquer a sight o' reluctance, I must say. I've got so used to livin' by myself that I shan't know how to consider another. But I see I ain't got common feelin' for others unless I can set my own comfort aside once in a while. I've brought you my name as one of those that will take one o' them city folks that needs a spell o' change. It come straight home to me how I should be feeling it by this time, if my lot had been cast in one o' them city garrets that the minister described so affecting. If 't hadn't been for kind consideration somewheres, Mother an' me might have sewed all them pleasant years away in the city that we enjoyed so in our own home, and our garding to step right out into when our sides set in to ache. And I ain't rich, but we was able to save a little something, and now I'm eatin' of it all up alone. It come to me I should like to have somebody take a taste out o' Mother's part. Now, don't you let 'em send me no rampin' boys like them Barnard's folks had come last year, that vexed dumb creatur's so; and I don't know how to cope with no kind o' menfolks or strange girls, but I should know how to do for a woman that's getting well along in years, an' has come to feel kind o' spent. P'raps we ain't no right to pick an' choose, but I should know best how to make that sort comfortable on 'count of doin' for Mother and studying what she preferred.'

Miss Esther rose with quaint formality and put the folded paper, on which she had neatly written her name and address, into Mrs Wayton's hand. Mrs Wayton rose soberly to receive it, and then they both sat down again.

'I'm sure that you will feel more than repaid for your kindness, dear Miss Esther,' said the minister's wife. 'I know one of the ladies who have charge of the arrangements for the Country Week, and I will explain as well as I can the kind of guest you have in mind. I quite envy her: I have often thought, when I was busy and tired, how much I should like to run along the street and make you a visit in your dear old-fashioned little house.'

'I should be more than pleased to have you, I'm sure,' said Miss Esther, startled into a bright smile and forgetting her anxiety. 'Come any day, and take me just as I am. We used to have a good deal o' company years ago, when there was a number o' Mother's folks still livin' over Ashfield way. Sure as we had a pile o' work on hand and was hurrying for dear life an' limb, a wagon-load would light down at the front gate to spend the day an' have an early tea. Mother never was one to get flustered same's I do 'bout everything. She was a lovely cook, and she'd fill 'em up an' cheer 'em, and git 'em off early as she could, an' then we'd be kind o' waked up an' spirited ourselves, and would set up late sewin' and talkin' the company over, an' I'd have things saved to tell her that had been said while she was out o' the room. I make such a towse over everything myself, but Mother was waked right up and felt pleased an' smart, if anything unexpected happened. I miss her more every year,' and Miss Esther gave a great sigh. 'I s'pose 't wa'n't reasonable to expect that I could have her to help me through with old age, but I'm a poor tool, alone.'

'Oh, no, you mustn't say that!' exclaimed the minister's wife. 'Why, nobody could get along without you. I wish I had come to Daleham in time to know your mother too.'

Miss Esther shook her head sadly. 'She would have set everything by you and Mr Wayton. Now I must be getting back in case I'm wanted, but you let 'em send me somebody right away, while my bush beans is so nice. An' if any o' your little boy's clothes wants repairin', just give 'em to me; 't will be a real pleasant thing

to set a few stitches. Or the minister's; ain't there something
needed for him?'

Mrs Wayton was about to say no, when she became conscious
of the pleading old face before her. 'I'm sure you are most kind,
dear friend,' she answered, 'and I do have a great deal to do. I'll
bring you two or three things tonight that are beyond my art, as I
go to evening meeting. Mr Wayton frayed out his best coat sleeve
yesterday, and I was disheartened, for we had counted upon his
not having a new one before the fall.'

''T would be mere play to me,' said Miss Esther, and presently
she went smiling down the street.

2

The Committee for the Country Week in a certain ward of Boston
were considering the long list of children, and mothers with
babies, and sewing-women, who were looking forward, some of
them for the first time in many years, to a country holiday. Some
were to go as guests to hospitable, generous farmhouses that
opened their doors willingly now and then to tired city people; for
some persons board could be paid.

The immediate arrangements of that time were settled at last,
except that Mrs Belton, the chairman, suddenly took a letter from
her pocket. 'I had almost forgotten this,' she said. 'It is another
place offered in dear quiet old Daleham. My friend, the minister's
wife there, writes me a word about it: "The applicant desires
especially an old person, being used to the care of an aged parent
and sure of her power of making such a one comfortable, and she
would like to have her guest come as soon as possible." My friend
asks me to choose a person of some refinement – 'one who would
appreciate the delicate simplicity and quaint ways of the hostess.'

Mrs Belton glanced hurriedly down the page. 'I believe that's
all,' she said. 'How about that nice old sewing-woman, Mrs
Connolly, in Bantry Street?'

'Oh, no!' someone entreated, looking up from her writing.
'Why isn't it just the place for my old Mr Rill, the dear old
Englishman who lives alone up four flights in Town Court and
has the bullfinch? He used to engrave seals, and his eyes gave out,
and he is so thrifty with his own bit of savings and an atom of a
pension. Someone pays his expenses to the country, and this

sounds like a place he would be sure to like. I've been watching for the right chance.'

'Take it, then,' said the busy chairman, and there was a little more writing and talking, and then the committee meeting was over which settled Miss Esther Porley's fate.

3

The journey to Daleham was a great experience to Mr Rill. He was a sensible old person, who knew well that he was getting stiffer and clumsier than need be in his garret, and that, as certain friends had said, a short time spent in the country would cheer and invigorate him. There had been occasional propositions that he should leave his garret altogether and go to the country to live, or at least to the suburbs of the city. He could not see things close at hand so well as he could take a wide outlook, and as his outlook from the one garret window was a still higher brick wall and many chimneys, he was losing a great deal that he might have had. But so long as he was expected to take an interest in the unseen and unknown he failed to accede to any plans about the country home, and declared that he was well enough in his high abode. He had lost a sister a few years before who had been his mainstay, but with his hands so well used to delicate work he had been less bungling in his simple household affairs than many another man might have been. But he was very lonely and was growing anxious; as he was rattled along in the train towards Daleham he held the chirping bullfinch's cage fast with both hands, and said to himself now and then, 'This may lead to something: the country air smells very good to me.'

The Daleham station was not very far out of the village, so that Miss Esther Porley put on her silk shawl and bonnet and everyday gloves just before four o'clock that afternoon, and went to meet her Country Week guest. Word had come the day before that the person for Miss Porley's would start two days in advance of the little company of children and helpless women, and since this message had come from the parsonage Miss Esther had worked diligently, late and early, to have her house in proper order. Whatever her mother had liked was thought of and provided. There were going to be rye shortcakes for tea, and there were some sprigs of thyme and sweet-balm in an old-fashioned wineglass on the keeping-room* table; mother always said they were so freshening. And Miss Esther had taken out a little shoulder-shawl and folded it over the arm of the rocking-chair by the window that looked out into the small garden where the London pride was in full bloom, and the morning glories had just begun to climb. Miss Esther was sixty-four herself, but still looked upon age as well in the distance.

She was always a prompt person, and had some minutes to wait at the station; then the time passed and the train was late. At last she saw the smoke far in the distance, and her heart began to sink. Perhaps she would not find it easy to get on with the old lady, and – well it was only for a week, and she had thought it right and best to take such a step, and now it would soon be over.

The train stopped, and there was no old lady at all.

Miss Esther had stood far back to get away from the smoke and roar – she was always as afraid of the cars as she could be – but as they moved away she took a few steps forward to scan the platform. There was no black bonnet with a worn lace veil, and no old lady with a burden of bundles; there were only the station master and two or three men, and an idle boy or two, and one clean-faced, bent old man with a bird-cage in one hand and an old carpet-bag in the other. She thought of the rye shortcakes for supper and all that she had done to make her small home pleasant, and her fire of excitement suddenly fell into ashes.

The old man with the bird-cage suddenly turned towards her. 'Can you direct me to Miss Esther Porley's?' said he.

'I can,' replied Miss Esther, looking at him with curiosity.

'I was directed to her house,' said the pleasant old fellow, 'by Mrs Belton, of the Country Week Committee. My eyesight is poor. I should be glad if anybody would help me to find the place.'

'You step this way with me, sir,' said Miss Esther. She was afraid that the men on the platform heard every word they said, but nobody took particular notice, and off they walked down the road together. Miss Esther was enraged with the Country Week Committee.

'*You* were sent to – Miss Porley's?' she asked grimly, turning to look at him.

'I was, indeed,' said Mr Rill.

'I am Miss Porley, and I expected an old lady,' she managed to say, and they both stopped and looked at each other with apprehension.

'I do declare!' faltered the old seal-cutter anxiously. 'What had I better do, ma'am? They most certain give me your name. Maybe you could recommend me somewheres else, an' I can get home tomorrow if 't ain't convenient.'

They were standing under a willow-tree in the shade; Mr Rill took off his heavy hat – it was a silk hat of bygone shape. A golden robin began to sing, high in the willow, and the old bullfinch twittered and chirped in the cage. Miss Esther heard some footsteps coming behind them along the road. She changed colour; she tried to remember that she was a woman of mature years and considerable experience.

''T ain't a mite o' matter, sir,' she said cheerfully. 'I guess you'll find everything comfortable for you,' and they turned, much relieved, and walked along together.

'That's Lawyer Barstow's house,' she said calmly, a minute afterward, 'the handsomest place in town, we think 't is,' and Mr Rill answered politely that Daleham was a pretty place; he had not been out of the city for so many years that everything looked beautiful as a picture.

4

Miss Porley rapidly recovered her composure, and bent her energies to the preparing of an early tea. She showed her guest to the snug bedroom under the low gambrel roof,* and when she apologised for his having to go upstairs, he begged her to re-member that it was nothing but a step to a man who was used to four long flights. They were both excited at finding a proper nail for the birdcage outside the window, though Miss Esther said that she should love to have the pretty bird downstairs where they could see it and hear it sing. She said to herself over and over that if she could have her long-lost brother come home from sea, she should like to have him look and behave as gentle and kind as Mr Rill. Somehow she found herself singing a cheerful hymn as she mixed and stirred the shortcakes. She could not help wishing that her mother were there to enjoy this surprise, but it did seem very odd, after so many years, to have a man in the house. It had not happened for fifteen years, at least, when they had entertained Deacon Sparks and wife, delegates from the neighbouring town of East Wilby to the County Conference.

The neighbours did not laugh at Miss Esther openly or cause her to blush with self-consciousness, however much they may have discussed the situation and smiled behind her back. She took the presence of her guest with delighted simplicity, and the country week was extended to a fortnight, and then to a month. At last, one day Miss Esther and Mr Rill were seen on their way to the railroad station, with a large bundle apiece beside the carpet-bag, though someone noticed that the bullfinch was left behind. Miss Esther came back alone, looking very woebegone and lonely, and if the truth must be known, she found her house too solitary. She looked into the woodhouse where there was a great store of kindlings, neatly piled, and her water pail was filled to the brim, her garden paths were clean of weeds and swept, and yet everywhere she looked it seemed more lonely than ever. She pinned on her shawl again and went along the street to the parsonage.

'My old lady's just gone,' she said to the minister's wife. 'I was so lonesome I could not stay in the house.'

'You found him a very pleasant visitor, didn't you, Miss Esther?' asked Mrs Wayton, laughing a little.

'I did so. He wa'n't like other men – kind and friendly and fatherly, and never stayed round when I was occupied, but entertained himself down street considerable, an' was as industrious as a bee, always asking me if there wa'n't something he could do about house. He and a sister some years older used to keep house together, and it was her long sickness used up what they'd saved, and yet he's got a little somethin', and there are friends he used to work for, jewellers, a big firm, that gives him somethin' regular. He's goin' to see' – and Miss Esther blushed crimson – 'he's goin' to see if they'd be willin' to pay it just the same if he come to reside in Daleham. He thinks the air agrees with him here.'

'Does he indeed?' inquired the minister's wife, with deep interest and a look of amusement.

'Yes 'm,' said Miss Esther simply, 'but don't you go an' say nothin' yet. I don't want folks to make a joke of it. Seems to me if he does feel to come back, and remains of the same mind he went away, we might be judicious to take the step—'

'Why, Miss Esther!' exclaimed the listener.

'Not till fall – not till fall,' said Miss Esther hastily. 'I ain't going to count on it too much anyway. I expect we could get along;

there's considerable goodness left in me, and you can always work better when you've got somebody beside yourself to work for. There, now I've told you I feel as if I was blown away in a gale.'

'Why, I don't know what to say at such a piece of news!' exclaimed Mrs Wayton again.

'I don't know's there's anything *to* say,' gravely answered Miss Esther. 'But I did laugh just now coming in the gate to think what a twitter I got into the day I fetched you that piece of paper.'

'Why, I must go right and tell Mr Wayton!' said the minister's wife.

'Oh, don't you, Mis' Wayton; no, no!' begged Miss Esther, looking quite coy and girlish. 'I really don't know's it's quite settled – it don't seem's if it could be. I'm going to hear from him in the course of a week. But I suppose *he* thinks it's settled; he's left the bird.'

(1893)

GEORGE EGERTON

Virgin Soil

The bridegroom is waiting in the hall; with a trifle of impatience he is tracing the pattern of the linoleum with the point of his umbrella. He curbs it and laughs, showing his strong white teeth at a remark of his best man; then compares the time by his hunter* with the clock on the stairs. He is florid, bright eyed, loose lipped, inclined to stoutness, but kept in good condition; his hair is crisp, curly, slightly grey; his ears peculiar, pointed at their tops like a faun's. He looks very big and well dressed, and, when he smiles, affable enough.

Upstairs a young girl, with the suns of seventeen summers on her brown head, is lying with her face hidden on her mother's shoulder; she is sobbing with great childish sobs, regardless of reddened eyes and the tears that have splashed on the silk of her grey, going-away gown.

The mother seems scarcely less disturbed than the girl. She is a fragile-looking woman with delicate fair skin, smoothly parted thin chestnut hair, dove-like eyes, and a monotonous piping voice. She is flushing painfully, making a strenuous effort to say something to the girl, something that is opposed to the whole instincts of her life.

She tries to speak, parts her lips only to close them again, and clasp her arms tighter round the girl's shoulders. At length she manages to say with trembling, uncertain pauses:

'You are married now, darling, and you must obey' – she lays a stress upon the word – 'your husband in all things – there are – there are things you should know – but – marriage is a serious thing, a sacred thing' – with desperation – 'you must believe that what your husband tells you is right – let him guide you – tell you—'

There is such acute distress in her usually unemotional voice that the girl looks up and scans her face – her blushing, quivering, faded face. Her eyes are startled, fawn-like eyes as her mother's, her skin too is delicately fair, but her mouth is firmer, her jaw squarer, and her piquant, irregular nose is full of character. She is slightly built, scarcely fully developed in her fresh youth.

'What is it that I do not know, Mother? What is it?' – with anxious impatience. 'There is something more – I have felt it all these last weeks in your and the others' looks – in his, in the very atmosphere – but why have you not told me before – I—' Her only answer is a gush of helpless tears from the mother, and a sharp rap at the door, and the bridegroom's voice, with an imperative note that it strikes the nervous girl is new to it, that makes her cling to her mother in a close, close embrace, drop her veil and go out to him.

She shakes hands with the best man, kisses the girlfriend who has acted as bridesmaid – the wedding has been a very quiet one – and steps into the carriage. The Irish cook throws an old shoe after them from the side door, but it hits the trunk of an elder-tree, and falls back on to the path, making that worthy woman cross herself and mutter of ill omens and bad luck to follow; for did not a magpie cross the path first thing this morning when she went to open the gate, and wasn't a red-haired woman the first creature she clapped eyes on as she looked down the road?

Half an hour later the carriage pulls up at the little station and the girl jumps out first; she is flushed, and her eyes stare helplessly as the eyes of a startled child, and she trembles with quick running shudders from head to foot. She clasps and unclasps her slender, grey-gloved hands so tightly that the stitching on the back of one bursts.

He has called to the station-master, and they go into the refreshment room together; the latter appears at the door and, beckoning to a porter, gives him an order.

She takes a long look at the familiar little place. They have lived there three years, and yet she seems to see it now for the first time; the rain drips, drips monotonously off the zinc roof, the smell of the dust is fresh, and the white pinks in the borders are beaten into the gravel.

Then the train runs in; a first-class carriage, marked 'engaged', is attached, and he comes for her; his hot breath smells of champagne, and it strikes her that his eyes are fearfully big and bright, and he offers her his arm with such a curious amused proprietary air that the girl shivers as she lays her hand in it.

The bell rings, the guard locks the door, the train steams out, and as it passes the signal-box, a large well-kept hand, with a signet ring on the little finger, pulls down the blind on the window of an engaged carriage.

Five years later, one afternoon on an autumn day, when the rain is falling like splashing tears on the rails, and the smell of the dust after rain fills the mild air with freshness, and the white chrysanthemums struggle to raise their heads from the gravel path into which the sharp shower has beaten them, the same woman, for there is no trace of girlhood in her twenty-two years, slips out of a first-class carriage; she has a dressing-bag in her hand.

She walks with her head down and a droop in her shoulders; her quickness of step is due rather to nervous haste than elasticity of frame. When she reaches the turn of the road, she pauses and looks at the little villa with the white curtains and gay tiled window-boxes. She can see the window of her old room; distinguish every shade in the changing leaves of the creeper climbing up the south wall; hear the canary's shrill note from where she stands.

Never once has she set foot in the peaceful little house with its air of genteel propriety since that eventful morning when she left it with him; she has always framed an excuse.

Now as she sees it a feeling of remorse fills her heart, and she thinks of the mother living out her quiet years, each day a replica of the one gone before, and her resolve weakens; she feels inclined to go back, but the waning sun flickers over the panes in the window of the room she occupied as a girl. She can recall how she used to run to the open window on summer mornings and lean out and draw in the dewy freshness and welcome the day, how she has stood on moonlight nights and danced with her bare white feet in the strip of moonlight, and let her fancies fly out into the silver night, a young girl's dreams of the beautiful, wonderful world that lay outside.

A hard dry sob rises in her throat at the memory of it, and the fleeting expression of softness on her face changes to a bitter disillusion.

She hurries on, with her eyes down, up the neat gravelled path, through the open door into the familiar sitting-room.

The piano is open with a hymn book on the stand; the grate is filled with fresh green ferns, a bowl of late roses perfume the room from the centre of the table. The mother is sitting in her easy chair, her hands folded across a big white Persian cat on her lap;

she is fast asleep. Some futile lace work, her thimble, and bright scissors are placed on a table near her.

Her face is placid, not a day older than that day five years ago. Her glossy hair is no greyer, her skin is clear, she smiles in her sleep. The smile rouses a sort of sudden fury in the breast of the woman standing in her dusty travelling cloak at the door, noting every detail in the room. She throws back her veil and goes over and looks at herself in the mirror over the polished chiffonnier* – scans herself pitilessly. Her skin is sallow with the dull sallowness of a fair skin in ill-health, and the fringe of her brown hair is so lacking in lustre that it affords no contrast. The look of fawn-like shyness has vanished from her eyes, they burn sombrefully and resentfully in their sunken orbits, there is a dragged look about the mouth; and the keynote of her face is a cynical disillusion. She looks from herself to the reflection of the mother, and then turning sharply with a suppressed exclamation goes over, and shaking the sleeping woman not too gently, says:

'Mother, wake up, I want to speak to you!'

The mother starts with frightened eyes, stares at the other woman as if doubting the evidence of her sight, smiles, then cowed by the unresponsive look in the other face, grows grave again, sits still and stares helplessly at her, finally bursting into tears with a 'Flo, my dear, Flo, is it really you?'

The girl jerks her head impatiently and says drily:

'Yes, that is self-evident. I am going on a long journey. I have something to say to you before I start! Why on earth are you crying?'

There is a note of surprised wonder in her voice mixed with impatience.

The older woman has had time to scan her face and the dormant motherhood in her is roused by its weary anguish. She is ill, she thinks, in trouble. She rises to her feet; it is characteristic of the habits of her life, with its studied regard for the observance of small proprieties, and distrust of servants as a class, that she goes over and closes the room door carefully.

This hollow-eyed, sullen women is so unlike the fresh girl who left her five years ago that she feels afraid. With the quiet selfishness that has characterised her life she has accepted the excuses her daughter has made to avoid coming home, as she has accepted the presents her son-in-law has sent her from time to time. She has found her a husband well-off in the world's goods, and there her responsibility ended. She approaches her hesitatingly; she feels she ought to kiss her, there is something unusual in such a meeting after so long an absence. It shocks her, it is so unlike the one she has pictured. She has often looked forward to it, often; to seeing Flo's new frocks, to hearing of her town life.

'Won't you take off your things? You will like to go to your room?'

She can hear how her own voice shakes; it is really inconsiderate of Flo to treat her in this strange way.

'We will have some tea,' she adds.

Her colour is coming and going, the lace at her wrist is fluttering. The daughter observes it with a kind of dull satisfaction, she is taking out her hat-pins carefully. She notices a portrait in a velvet case upon the mantelpiece; she walks over and looks at it intently. It is her father, the father who was killed in India in a hill skirmish when she was a little lint-locked maid barely up to his knee. She studies it with new eyes, trying to read what man he was, what soul he had, what part of him is in her, tries to find herself by reading him. Something in his face touches her strikes some underlying chord in her, and she grinds her teeth at a thought it rouses.

'She must be ill, she must be very ill,' says the mother, watching her, 'to think I daren't offer to kiss my own child!' She checks the tears that keep welling up, feeling that they may offend this woman who is so strangely unlike the girl who left her. The latter has turned from her scrutiny of the likeness and sweeps her with a cold criticising look as she turns towards the door, saying, 'I *should* like some tea. I will go upstairs and wash off the dust.'

Half an hour later the two women sit opposite one another in the pretty room. The younger one is leaning back in her chair watching the mother pour out the tea, following the graceful movements of the white, blue-veined hands amongst the tea things – she lets her wait on her; they have not spoken beyond a commonplace remark about the heat, the dust, the journey.

'How is Philip, is he well?' The mother ventures to ask with a feeling of trepidation, but it seems to her that she ought to ask about him.

'He is quite well, men of his type usually are; I may say he is particularly well just now, he has gone to Paris with a girl from the Alhambra!'

The older woman flushes painfully, and pauses with her cup

halfway to her lips and lets the tea run over unheeded on to her dainty silk apron.

'You are spilling your tea,' the girl adds with malicious enjoyment.

The woman gasps, 'Flo, but Flo, my dear, it is dreadful! What would your poor father have said! *No wonder* you look ill, dear, how shocking! Shall I – ask the vicar to – to remonstrate with him?—'

'My dear mother, what an extraordinary idea! These little trips have been my one solace. I assure you, I have always hailed them as lovely oases in the desert of matrimony, resting-places on the journey. My sole regret was their infrequency. That is very good tea, I suppose it is the cream.'

The older woman puts her cup on the tray and stares at her with frightened eyes and paled cheeks.

'I am afraid I don't understand you, Florence. I am old-fashioned' – with a little air of frigid propriety – 'I have always looked upon matrimony as a sacred thing. It is dreadful to hear you speak this way; you should have tried to save Philip – from – from such a shocking sin.'

The girl laughs, and the woman shivers as she hears her. She cries, 'I would never have thought it of Philip. My poor dear, I am afraid you must be very unhappy.

'Very,' with a grim smile, 'but it is over now, I have done with it. I am not going back.'

If a bomb had exploded in the quiet, pretty room the effect could hardly have been more startling than her almost cheerful statement. A big bee buzzes in and bangs against the lace of the older woman's cap and she never heeds it, then she almost screams:

'Florence, Florence, my dear, you can't mean to desert your husband! Oh, think of the disgrace, the scandal, what people will say, the' – with an uncertain quaver – 'the sin. You took a solemn vow, you know, and you are going to break it—'

'My dear mother, the ceremony had no meaning for me, I simply did not know what I was signing my name to, or what I was vowing to do. I might as well have signed my name to a document drawn up in Choctaw. I have no remorse, no prick of conscience at the step I am taking; my life must be my own. They say sorrow chastens, I don't believe it; it hardens, embitters; joy is like the sun, it coaxes all that is loveliest and sweetest in human nature. No, I am not going back.'

The older woman cries, wringing her hands helplessly: 'I can't understand it. You must be very miserable to dream of taking such a serious step.'

'As I told you, I am. It is a defect of my temperament. How many women really take the man nearest to them as seriously as I did! I think few. They finesse and flatter and wheedle and coax, but truth there is none. I couldn't do that, you see, and so I went to the wall. I don't blame them; it must be so, as long as marriage is based on such unequal terms, as long as man demands from a wife as a right, what he must sue from a mistress as a favour; until marriage becomes for many women a legal prostitution, a nightly degradation, a hateful yoke under which they age, mere bearers of children conceived in a sense of duty, not love. They bear them, birth them, nurse them, and begin again without choice in the matter, growing old, unlovely, with all joy of living swallowed in a senseless burden of reckless maternity, until their love, granted they started with that, the mystery, the crowning glory of their lives, is turned into a duty they submit to with distaste instead of a favour granted to a husband who must become a new lover to obtain it.'

'But men are different, Florence; you can't refuse a husband, you might cause him to commit sin.'

'Bosh, Mother, he is responsible for his own sins, we are not bound to dry-nurse his morality. Man is what we have made him, his very faults are of our making. No wife is bound to set aside the demands of her individual soul for the sake of imbecile obedience. I am going to have some more tea.'

The mother can only whimper:

'It is dreadful! I thought he made you such an excellent husband, his position too is so good, and he is so highly connected.'

'Yes, and it is as well to put the blame in the right quarter. Philip is as God made him, he is an animal with strong passions, and he avails himself of the latitude permitted him by the laws of society. Whatever of blame, whatever of sin, whatever of misery is in the whole matter rests *solely* and *entirely* with you, Mother' – the woman sits bolt upright – 'and with no one else – that is why I came here – to tell you that – I have promised myself over and over again that I would tell you. It is with you, and you alone the fault lies.'

There is so much of cold dislike in her voice that the other woman recoils and whimpers piteously:

'You must be ill, Florence, to say such wicked things. What have I done? I am sure I devoted myself to you from the time you were little; I refused' – dabbing her eyes with her cambric handkerchief – 'ever so many good offers. There was young Fortescue in the artillery, such a good-looking man, and such an elegant horseman, he was quite infatuated about me; and Jones, to be sure he was in business, but he was most attentive. Everyone said I was a devoted mother; I can't think what you mean, I—'

A smile of cynical amusement checks her.

'Perhaps not. Sit down, and I'll tell you.'

She shakes off the trembling hand, for the mother has risen and is standing next to her, and pushes her into a chair, and paces up and down the room. She is painfully thin, and drags her limbs as she walks.

'I say it is your fault, because you reared me a fool, an idiot, ignorant of everything I ought to have known, everything that concerned me and the life I was bound to lead as a wife; my physical needs, my coming passion, the very meaning of my sex, my wifehood and motherhood to follow. You gave me not one weapon in my hand to defend myself against the possible attacks of man at his worst. You sent me out to fight the biggest battle of a woman's life, the one in which she ought to know every turn of the game, with a white gauze' – she laughs derisively – 'of maiden purity as a shield.'

Her eyes blaze, and the woman in the chair watches her as one sees a frog watch a snake when it is put into its case.

'I was fourteen when I gave up the gooseberry-bush theory as the origin of humanity; and I cried myself ill with shame when I learnt what maternity meant, instead of waking with a sense of delicious wonder at the great mystery of it. You gave me to a man, nay more, you told me to obey him, to believe that whatever he said would be right, would be my duty; knowing that the meaning of marriage was a sealed book to me, that I had no real idea of what union with a man meant. You delivered me body and soul into his hands without preparing me in any way for the ordeal I was to go through. You sold me for a home, for clothes, for food; you played upon my ignorance, I won't say innocence, that is different. You told me, you and your sister, and your friend the vicar's wife, that it would be an anxiety off your mind if I were comfortably settled—'

'It is wicked of you to say such dreadful things!' the mother cries. 'And besides' – with a touch of asperity – 'you married him willingly, you seemed to like his attentions—'

'How like a woman! What a thorough woman you are, Mother! The good old-fashioned kitten with a claw in her paw! Yes, I married him willingly; I was not eighteen, I had known no men; was pleased that you were pleased – and, as you say, I liked his attentions. He had tact enough not to frighten me, and I had not the faintest conception of what marriage with him meant. I had an idea' – with a laugh – 'that the words of the minister settled the matter. Do you think that if I had realised how fearfully close the intimacy with him would have been that my whole soul would not have stood up in revolt, the whole woman in me cried out against such a degradation of myself?' Her words tremble with passion, and the woman who bore her feels as if she is being lashed by a whip. 'Would I not have shuddered at the thought of *him* in such a relationship? – and waited, waited until I found the man who would satisfy me, body and soul – to whom I would have gone without any false shame, of whom I would think with gladness as the father of a little child to come, for whom the white fire of love or passion, call it what you will, in my heart would have burned clearly and saved me from the feeling of loathing horror that has made my married life a nightmare to me – ay, made me a murderess in heart over and over again. This is not exaggeration. It has killed the sweetness in me, the pure thoughts of womanhood – has made me hate myself and *hate you*. Cry, Mother, if you will; you don't know how much you have to cry for – I have cried myself barren of tears. Cry over the girl you killed' – with a gust of passion – 'why didn't you strangle me as a baby? It would have been kinder; my life has been a hell, Mother – I felt it vaguely as I stood on the platform waiting, I remember the mad impulse I had to jump down under the engine as it came in, to escape from the dread that was chilling my soul. What have these years been? One long crucifixion, one long submittal to the desires of a man I bound myself to in ignorance of what it meant; every caress' – with a cry – 'has only been the first note of that. Look at me' – stretching out her arms – 'look at this wreck of my physical self. I wouldn't dare to show you the heart or the soul underneath. He has stood on his rights; but do you think, if I had known, that I would have given such insane obedience, from a mistaken sense of duty, as would lead to this? I have my rights too, and my duty to myself; if I had only recognised them in time.

'Sob away, Mother; I don't even feel for you – I have been burnt too badly to feel sorry for what will only be a tiny scar to you; I have all the long future to face with all the world against me. Nothing will induce me to go back. Better anything than that; food and clothes are poor equivalents for what I have had to suffer – I can get them at a cheaper rate. When he comes to look for me, give him that letter. He will tell you he has only been an uxorious husband, and that you reared me a fool. You can tell him too, if you like, that I loathe him, shiver at the touch of his lips, his breath, his hands; that my whole body revolts at his touch; that when he has turned and gone to sleep, I have watched him with such growing hatred that at times the temptation to kill him has been so strong that I have crept out of bed and walked the cold passage in my bare feet until I was too benumbed to feel anything; that I have counted the hours to his going away, and cried out with delight at the sight of the retreating carriage!'

'You are very hard, Flo. The Lord soften your heart! Perhaps' – with trepidation – 'if you had had a child—'

'Of his – that indeed would have been the last straw – no, Mother.'

There is such a peculiar expression of satisfaction over something – of some inner understanding, as a man has when he dwells on the successful accomplishment of a secret purpose – that the mother sobs quietly, wringing her hands.

'I did not know, Flo, I acted for the best. You are very hard on me!'

Later, when the bats are flitting across the moon, and the girl is asleep – she has thrown herself half-dressed on the narrow white bed of her girlhood, with her arms folded across her breast and her hands clenched – the mother steals into the room. She has been turning over the contents of an old desk; her marriage certificate, faded letters on foreign paper, and a bit of Flo's hair cut off each birthday, and a sprig of orange blossom she wore in her hair. She looks faded and grey in the silver light, and she stands and gazes at the haggard face in its weary sleep. The placid current of her life is disturbed, her heart is roused, something of her child's soul-agony has touched the sleeping depths of her nature. She feels as if scales have dropped from her eyes, as if the instincts and conventions of her life are toppling over, as if all the needs of protesting women of whom she has read with a vague displeasure have come home to her. She covers the girl tenderly, kisses her hair, and slips a little roll of notes into the dressing-bag on the table and steals out, with the tears running down her cheeks.

When the girl looks into her room as she steals by, when the morning light is slanting in, she sees her kneeling, her head, with its straggling grey hair bowed in tired sleep. It touches her. Life is too short, she thinks, to make anyone's hours bitter; she goes down and writes a few kind words in pencil and leaves them near her hand, and goes quickly out into the road.

The morning is grey and misty, with faint yellow stains in the east, and the west wind blows with a melancholy sough in it – the first whisper of the fall, the fall that turns the world of nature into a patient suffering from phthisis* – delicate season of decadence, when the loveliest scenes have a note of decay in their beauty; when a poisoned arrow pierces the marrow of insect and plant, and the leaves have a hectic flush and fall, fall and shrivel and curl in the night's cool; and the chrysanthemums, the 'goodbye summers' of the Irish peasants, have a sickly tinge in their white. It affects her, and she finds herself saying, 'Wither and die, wither and die, make compost for the loves of the spring, as the old drop out and make place for the new, who forget them, to be in their turn forgotten.' She hurries on, feeling that her autumn has come to her in her spring, and a little later she stands once more on the platform where she stood in the flush of her girlhood, and takes the train in the opposite direction.

(1894)

Jeanne-Marie

I

Jeanne-Marie lived alone in the white cottage at the far end of the village street.

It was a long narrow street of tall houses, stretching each side of the white shining road, for two hundred yards or more. A street that was cool and shadeful even in the shadeless summer days, when the sun burned most hotly, when the broad roads dazzled between their avenues of plane tree and poplar, and the mountains disappeared from the horizon in the blue haze of heat.

From her little garden Jeanne-Marie liked to look at the mountains each morning, and, when for two or three days following they were not to be seen, she would shake her head reproachfully, as at the failing of old friends.

'My boys, Jeanne-Marie is only thirty-seven,' Bourdet the innkeeper said to his companions, as they sat, one May afternoon, smoking under the chestnut trees in front of the café. They all looked up as he spoke, and watched Jeanne-Marie, as she walked slowly past them to her cottage.

'Bourdet has been paying court,' said Leguillon, the fat, redfaced butcher, with a chuckle, as he puffed at his long pipe. 'You see, he is anxious we should think her of an age suitable, before he tells us the betrothals are arranged.'

'For my part I should give many congratulations,' said the village postman and tobacconist, gruffly. 'Jeanne-Marie is worth any of our girls of the village, with their bright dresses and silly giggles.'

Bourdet laughed. 'You shall come to the wedding, my friends,' he said, with a wink and a nod of the head to the retreating figure, 'and since our friend Minaud there finds the girls so distasteful, he shall wait till our babies are old enough, and be betrothed to one of them.'

The postmaster laughed with the rest. 'But seriously,' he said,

'Bourdet will pardon me if I tell him our Jeanne-Marie is a good deal past the thirties.'

Laurent, the good-looking young farmer, who stood leaning against the tree round which their chairs were gathered, answered him gravely. 'Wait, *beau-père*, till you see her on Sunday coming from Mass on M. Bourdet's arm; the cap that hides the grey knot of hair at the back of the head is neat and bright – oh! so bright – pink or blue for choice, and if M. Bourdet chances to compliment the colour of the stockings – he is gay, you know, always – the yellow face turns rosy and all the wrinkles go.' And laughing maliciously at Bourdet, the young fellow turned away homewards.

Bourdet looked grave. "Tis your son-in-law that speaks like that, Minaud,' he said, 'otherwise I would say that in my day the young fellows found it better to amuse themselves with the young girls than to mock at the old ones.'

'You are right, my friend,' said Minaud. "Tis the regiment that taught Laurent this, and many other things. But it is a good boy, though with a sharp tongue. To these young ones it seems all foolishness to be an old girl.'

And the others nodded agreement.

So they sat, chatting, and drawing at their long pipes, while the afternoon sun gleamed on the little gardens and on the closed green shutters of the houses; and the slow, large oxen lumbered through the village street, their yoked heads pressed well down, and their tails flicking unceasingly at the swarm of flies.

Jeanne-Marie stood in her garden, blinking thoughtfully at the flowers, while she shaded her eyes with her hand. On her bare head the sparse brown hair was parted severely and neatly to each side, and the deep southern eyes looked steadily out of the tanned and wrinkled face. Her light cotton bodice fell away from the thin lines of her neck and shoulders, and her *sabots** clicked harshly as she moved about the garden.

'At least the good God has given me a fine crab-apple bloom this year,' Jeanne-Marie said, as she looked at the masses of rich blossom. On the wall the monthly roses were flowering thickly, and the Guelder roses bent their heads under the weight of their heavy bunches. 'In six days I shall have the peonies, and the white rose-bush in the corner is coming soon,' said Jeanne-Marie contentedly.

2

It was four and a half years ago that Jeanne-Marie had come to the white cottage next to the mill, with the communal school opposite. Till that autumn day, when a pair of stout oxen had brought her goods to the door, she had lived with her brother, who was *métayer** to M. François, the owner of the big villa a quarter of a mile beyond the village. Her father had been *métayer*, and when he died, his son Firman – a fine-looking young man, not long home from his service – had taken his place. So the change at the *métairie* had very little affected Jeanne-Marie.

But she missed her father sorely every day at midday, when she remembered that there was one less to cook for; that the tall, straight old figure would not come in at the door, and that the black pudding might remain uncooked for all Firman's noticing; and Jeanne-Marie would put the bouillon by the fire, and sit down and cry softly to herself.

They were very kind to her at the villa, and at night, when Firman was at the café, she would take the stockings and the linen and darn them in the kitchen, while she listened to the servants' talk, and suppressed her *patois* as much as possible, for they were from the North, and would not understand.

Two years after her father's death, Jeanne-Marie began to notice that Firman went no more to the café in the evening, and had always his shirt clean, and his best black smocked cape for the market in the town on Mondays, and for Mass on Sundays.

'It astonishes me,' she had said, when she was helping M. François' cook that day the château-folk had come to *déjeûner*, unexpectedly – for Jeanne-Marie's cooking was very good indeed –'because, you understand, that is not his way at all. Now, if it were Paul Puyoo or the young André, it would be quite ordinary; but with Firman, I doubt with him it is a different thing.'

And Anna had nodded her black head sagely over the *omelette aux fines herbes* as she answered, 'Jeanne-Marie, Firman wishes to marry; Jeanne-Marie, for my own part, I say it's that little fat blue-eyed Suzanne from the *métairie* on the hill.'

3

Suzanne looked very pretty the day she came home to Mr
François' *métairie*, leaning on her husband's arm; but Jeanne-
Marie was not there to see; she was sitting in the large chair in the
kitchen of the white cottage, and she was sobbing with her head in
her hands. 'And indeed the blessed Virgin herself must have
thought me crazy, to see me sitting sobbing there, with the house
in confusion, and not a thing to cook with in the kitchen,' she
said, shamefacedly, to Marthe Legrand from the mill, when she
came in, later, to help her. 'You should have remained,' Marthe
answered, nodding at her pityingly. 'You should have remained,
Jeanne-Marie; the old house is the old house, and the good God
never meant the wedding of the young ones to drive away the old
ones from the door.'

Jeanne-Marie drew in her breath at the words 'old ones'. 'But
the book says I am only thirty-four!' she told herself; and that
night she looked in the old Mass book, to be sure if it could be
true; and there was the date set down very clearly, in the
handwriting of Dubois, her father's oldest friend; for Jeanne-
Marie's father himself could neither read nor write – he was, as
he said with pride, of the old school, 'that kissed our sweethearts, and found that better than writing them long scribbles on
white paper, as the young ones do now; and thought a chat with
a friend on Sundays and holidays worth more than sitting
cramped up, reading the murders and the adulteries in the
newspapers'. So it was Dubois who wrote down the children's
births in the old Mass book. Yes, there they were. Catherine first
of all; poor Catherine, who was so bright and pretty, and died
that rainy winter when she was just twelve years old. Then
'*Jeanne-Marie, née le 28 Novembre 1854, à minuit,*' and added,
in the same handwriting, '*On nous raconte qu'à cette heure-là
nous étions en train de gagner une grande bataille en Russie!
Que ça lui porte bonheur!*' Eight years later: '*Jacques Firman, né
le 12 Fèvrier à midi.*' It all came back to Jeanne-Marie as she
read; that scene of his birth, when she was just eight years old.
She was sitting alone in the kitchen, crying, for they had told her
her mother was very ill, and had been ill all the night, and just as
the big clock was striking twelve she heard the voice of the
neighbour who had spent the night there, calling to her, '*Jeanne-
Marie, viens vite, ta mère veut te voir*'; and she had gone, timid

and hesitating, into the darkened room. The first thing she noticed was the large fire blazing on the open hearth – she had never known her father and mother have a fire before – and she wondered much whether it was being too cold that had made her mother ill, as it had little Catherine. She looked towards the bed and saw her mother lying there, her eyes closed, and very pale – so pale that Jeanne-Marie was frightened and ran towards her father; but he was smiling where he stood by the bed, and the child was reassured. She saw him stoop and kiss his wife on the forehead, and call her his '*bonne petite femme*', and taking Jeanne-Marie by the hand he showed her the *sage-femme** – the *sage-femme* who had come the night before to make her mother well – sitting near the fire with a white bundle in her arms, and thanked the good God aloud that he had sent him a fine boy at last. Old Dubois had come in gently, his béret in his hand, as Jeanne-Marie's father was speaking, and turning to the bed had reiterated emphatically, '*Tu as bien fait, chère dame, tu as bien fait.*'

Jeanne-Marie sat silently going over it all in her mind. '*Té,*' she murmured, 'how quickly they all go; the father, the mother, old Dubois, even Jeanne the *voisine*, is gone. I alone am left, and the good God knows if there will be any to cry for me when my turn comes to go.' She shut the old Mass book, and put it carefully back on the shelf, and she went to the old looking-glass and the tanned wrinkled face met its reflection very calmly and patiently. 'I think it was the hard work in the fields when I was young,' she said. 'Certainly Marthe was right. It is the face of an old woman, a face more worn than hers, though she is beyond forty and has borne so many children.'

4

Firman had urged his sister to stay on at the *métairie* after his marriage. 'You should not go, it is not natural,' he said one evening a few weeks before his wedding, while they were piling the small wood in the shed. 'The old house will not be the old house without you. Suzanne wishes it also. *Parbleu!* Is it the custom for the fathers to turn their sons out, when they marry? Then, why should I let the old sister go, now my time for marrying has come? Suzanne is a good girl and pretty, and has never even looked at any young fellow in the village – for I, as you know, am particular, and I like not the manners in some villages, where a girl's modesty is counted nothing – but blood is worth the most, *ma foi*, as the old father used to say; and badly must he think of me to see the old sister making room even for the little Suzanne.'

But Jeanne-Marie shook her head. 'I cannot well explain it, Firman,' she said. 'It's not that your Suzanne comes unwelcome to me – no, the good God knows it's not that – but it would be so strange. I should see the old mother's shadow, at the table where you sat, and in the bed where you lay. I might get foolish, and angry, Firman. So let me go, and, when the little ones come, I shall be their grandmother, and Suzanne will forgive me.'

That was four and a half years ago, and it was a very lonely four and a half years at the white cottage. Even the cooking, when it was for herself alone, became uninteresting, and the zest went out of it. Jeanne-Marie, in her loneliness, hungered for the animal life that had unconsciously formed a great part of her existence at the *métairie*. Every springtime she would sit, sometimes for hours, in her garden, watching the flocks of callow geese, as they wandered along the road in front of the mill, pecking at the ground as they went, and uttering all the time their little plaintive cries, that soothed her with its echo of the old home. When the boys in their bérets, with their long poles and their loud cries of 'guà, guà,' drove the cows and the oxen home from the fields at sunset, Jeanne-Marie would come out of her cottage, and watch the patient, sleek beasts, as they dawdled along. And she would think longingly of the evenings at the *métairie*, when she never missed going out to see the oxen, as they lay contentedly on their prickly bedding, moving their heavy jaws slowly up and down, too lazy even to look up as she entered.

Firman loved his oxen, for they were well trained and strong, and did good work; but Jeanne-Marie would have laughed in those days, had she been told she loved the animals of the farm. 'I remember,' she said to Marthe of the mill one day, 'how I said to the old father years ago: "When the children of M. François came to the *métairie*, it is – 'Oh, Jeanne-Marie, you will not kill that pretty little grey hen with the feathered legs,' and 'Oh! Jeanne-Marie, you must not drown so many kittens this time': but I say to them always: 'My children, the rich have their toys and have the time and money to make toys of their animals; but to us poor folk they are the useful creatures God has given us for food and work, and they are not playthings.'" So I said then; but now, ah, now Marthe, it is different. Do you remember how old Dubois forever quarrelled with young Baptiste, but when they wrote from the regiment to tell him the boy was dead of fever, during the great manœuvres, do you remember how the old father mourned, and lay on his bed for a whole day, fasting? So it always is, Marthe. The cow butts the calf with her horns, but when the calf is gone, the mother moans for it all the day.'

Firman was too busy with his farm and his new family ties to come much to see his sister, or to notice how rarely she came up to the *métairie* now. For Suzanne had never forgiven, and that was why Jeanne-Marie walked up so seldom to M. François's *métairie*.

Did not all the village say that it was Suzanne's doing that Firman's sister left the farm on his marriage? That Suzanne's jealousy had driven Jeanne-Marie away? And when this came to the ears of Firman's wife, and the old folks shook their heads in her presence over the strange doings of young couples nowadays, the relief that the dreaded division of supremacy with her husband's sister was spared her, was lost in anger against Jeanne-Marie, as the cause of this village scandal. The jealousy that she had always felt for the '*chère sœur*', whom Firman loved and respected, leapt up within her. 'People say he loves his sister, and that it is I who part them. They shall see – yes, they shall see.'

And bit by bit, with all a woman's subtle diplomacy, she drew her husband away from his sister's affection, until in a year or two their close intimacy had weakened to a gradually slackening friendship.

At night-time, when Firman's passionate southern nature lay under the thrall of his wife's beauty, she would whisper to him in her soft *patois*, 'Love me well, my husband, for I have only you to love; others are jealous of my happiness, and even Jeanne-Marie is envious of your wife, and of the babe that is to come.'

And the hot Spanish blood, that his mother had given him, would leap to Firman's face as he took her in his arms, and swore that all he loved, loved her; and those who angered her, he cared not for.

In the first year of their marriage, when Jeanne-Marie came almost every day, Suzanne would show her with pride all the changes and alterations in the old house. 'See here, my sister,' she said to her one day, only six months after the wedding, when she was taking her over the house, 'this room that was yours, we have dismantled for the time; did it not seem a pity to keep an unused room all furnished, for the sun to tarnish, and the damp to spoil?'

And Jeanne-Marie, as she looked round on the bare walls and the empty corners of the little room, where she and Catherine had slept together in the old days, answered quietly, 'Quite true, Suzanne, quite true. It would be a great pity.'

That night when she and Marthe sat together in the kitchen she told her of the incident.

'But, Jeanne-Marie,' Marthe interrupted eagerly, 'how was it you had left your furniture there, since it was yours?'

'How was it? But because little Catherine had slept in the old bed, and sat in the old chairs, and how could I take them away from the room?'

'Better that than let Suzanne break them up for firewood,' Marthe replied shortly.

When little Henri was born, a year after the marriage, Suzanne would not let Jeanne-Marie be at the *métairie*, and she sent Firman down beforehand to tell her that she feared the excitement of her presence. Jeanne-Marie knew she was disliked and distrusted, but this blow fell very heavily, though she raised her head proudly and looked her brother full in the face when he stammered out his wife's wishes.

'For the sake of our name, and what they will say in the village, I am sorry for this,' she said; and Firman went without a word.

But when he was gone Jeanne-Marie's pride broke down, and in the darkness of the evening she gathered her shawl round her, and crept up to the *métairie* door.

Hour after hour she sat there, not heeding the cold or the damp, her head buried in her hands, her body rocked backwards and forwards. 'I pray for Firman's child,' she muttered without ceasing. 'O dear Virgin! O blessed Virgin! I pray for my brother's child.' And when at length an infant's feeble cry pierced through the darkness, Jeanne-Marie rose and tottered home, saying to herself contentedly, 'The good God himself tells me that all is well.'

Perhaps the pangs of maternity quickened the capabilities for compassion in Suzanne's peasant mind. She sent for Jeanne-Marie two days later, and watched her with silent wonder, but without a sneer, as she knelt weeping and trembling before the small new bundle of humanity.

From that day little Henri was the idol of Jeanne-Marie's heart. All the sane instincts of wifehood and motherhood, shut up irrevocably within the prison of her maiden life, found vent in her devotion to her brother's child. The natural impulses, so long denied freedom, of whose existence and force she was not even aware, avenged their long suppression in this worship of Firman's boy.

To watch the growth of the childish being, the unveiling of his physical comeliness, and the gradual awakening of his perceptions, became the interest and fascination of her life. Every morning at eleven o'clock, when the cottage showed within the open door all white and shining after her energetic scrubbings, she would put on a clean bodice, and a fresh pink handkerchief for the little coil of hair at the back of her head, and sit ready and impatient, knitting away the time, till one o'clock struck, and she could start for the farm.

She would always arrive at the same hour, when the *métairie* dinner was finished, and Suzanne's fretful complaints: 'Jeanne-Marie, you are so proud, you will not come for the dinner or stay for the supper,' met only a smile and a deprecating shake of the head.

On her arrival, if Suzanne were in a good temper, she would surrender Henri to her, and Jeanne-Marie's hour of heaven reached her. If it were cold, she would sit in the kitchen, crooning snatches of old tunes, or chattering soft nothings in *patois* to the sleeping child. If fine, she would wander round the garden with him in her arms, sometimes as far as the road, where a chance passer's exclamation of '*Oh, le beau bébé!*' would flush her face with pleasure.

If Suzanne's temper chanced to be ruffled, if Firman had displeased her, or if the fitful jealousy that sprang up at times against her *belle-sœur*, happened to be roused, she would insist that little Henri was tired, and must not be moved; and Jeanne-Marie would sit for hours sadly watching the cot, in which the child lay, not daring to touch him or comfort him, even when he moaned and moved his arms restlessly in his sleep.

So her life went on till Henri was about a year old, when Suzanne's gradually increasing exasperation reached an ungovernable pitch. To her jealous imagination it had seemed for some time that the boy clung more to her sister than to her, and one day things reached a climax.

Jeanne-Marie had arrived with a toy bought for three sous from a travelling pedlar, and the child had screamed, and cried, because his mother, alleging that he was tired, refused to allow Jeanne-Marie to take him or show him the toy. The boy screamed louder and louder, and Jeanne-Marie sat, silent and troubled, in her corner. Even Firman, who was yoking his oxen in the yard, came in hurriedly, hearing the noise, and finding nothing wrong, pleaded with his wife. '*Mais, voyons, Suzanne*,' he began, persuasively, 'if *le petit* wants to see his toy, *la tante* may show it him, *n'est ce pas?*' And Suzanne, unable to bear it any longer, almost threw her child into Jeanne-Marie's lap, bursting out, 'Take him, then, and draw my baby's love from me, as you please. I want no child who hates his mother.' And sobbing loudly, she rushed out. Firman followed her, his hand-some face puckered with perplexity, and Jeanne-Marie and the baby were left alone. She bent low down over the deep Spanish eyes that were so like her own, and, while her tears dropped on his face, she held him to her feverishly. '*Adieu*,' she whispered, '*adieu, petit Henri. La tante* must not come to see him any more, and Henri must be a good boy and love his mother.' And with one long look at the child's eyes fixed on her so wonderingly, Jeanne-Marie rose softly and left the farm.

From that day started the great conflict between her love and her pride. Though, to her simple nature, the jealousy of a woman who seemed to her to have in abundance everything that made life worth living, was utterly incomprehensible, she said to herself over and over as she went home, that such a scene as that should never happen again. And as she lay in her narrow bed that night, and made her resolution for the future, she seemed to feel the very fibres of her heart break within her.

Firman came down next day to beg his sister to behave as if nothing had happened. 'You are pale and your face is all drawn, *chère sœur*,' he told her reproachfully, 'but you must not take the things like that. If poor Suzanne were herself and well, she would never have spoken as she did.' But Jeanne-Marie smiled at him.

'If I am pale, Firman, it is not for worrying over Suzanne. Tell her from me, I have been selfish all this time. I will not be so again. When she can spare the little Henri, she shall send him to play here with me, by Anna.' Anna was Suzanne's sixteen-year-old sister, who lived almost entirely at the *métairie* since her sister's marriage. 'And every Sunday afternoon I will come up, and will sit with him in the garden as I used to do. Tell this to Suzanne, with my love.'

And Firman told her; and mingled with the relief that Suzanne felt, that the face and figure which had become like a nightmare to her strained nerves, would appear only once a week at the farm, was gratitude that her sister had taken things so well. 'Anna shall take him every other day,' she observed to Firman, 'she shall see I am not jealous. It was the pain that took me suddenly yesterday, while you were speaking. For that matter, in the afternoon there is always much for me to do, and little Henri can very well go with Anna to the cottage.'

And no doubt she meant to keep her promise, but she was occupied mind and body with other things. The second baby would be born in a month, and in the afternoons, when she sat, languid and tired, she liked to have her sister Anna by her, and Henri playing by her side.

And after little Catherine was born, there was much for Anna to do. 'I could not well spare her if I would,' Suzanne would say to herself, 'what with two babies and me so long in getting on my feet this time.'

And Jeanne-Marie put on the clean white bodice every day before her dinner, and sat in the little garden with her eyes fixed on the turning in the white road that led to M. François's *métairie*, but it was not more than one day a week that Anna would come in sight, with little Henri in her arms. The other days Jeanne-Marie would sit, shading her eyes and watching, till long after the hour when she could expect them to appear.

At first, after the quarrel, she had believed in Suzanne's reiterated assurances that 'Anna would come every other day or so,' and many were the wasted afternoons of disappointment that she courted in her little garden. Sometimes she would rise to her feet, and a sudden impulse to go up to the farm, not a mile away, if only to kiss *le petit* and come home again, laid hold of her; but the memory of Suzanne's cold looks of surprise, and the 'Is anything wrong, Jeanne-Marie?' that would meet her, was sufficient to force her into her chair again with a little hopeless sigh.

'When the calf is gone, the mother mourns for it all the day,' Marthe said grimly, when she surprised her one day watching the white turning.

But Jeanne-Marie answered the miserably, 'Ah, but I never butt at my calf, and they have taken it from me all the same.'

There was great rejoicing in the cottage the day that Anna's white blouse and large green umbrella came in sight, and the three sat in the kitchen together: Anna eating smilingly the cakes and biscuits that grateful Jeanne-Marie made specially for her, and Henri crawling happily on the floor. 'He said "Maman" to Suzanne yesterday,' Anna would announce, as Jeanne-Marie hurried to meet her at the gate; or, 'Firman says he heard him say "*Menou*", when the white cat ran across the yard this morning.' And many were the attempts to induce Henri to make these utterances again. '*Je t'aime, je t'aime*,' Jeanne-Marie would murmur to him, as she kissed him again and again, and the little boy would look up at her with his dark eyes, and smile encouragingly.

All too quickly the time would go, and all too soon would come Anna's glance at the clock, and the dreaded words: 'Suzanne will make herself angry; we must go.'

And as Jeanne-Marie watched them disappear along the white road, the clouds of her loneliness would gather round her again.

The Sunday afternoons at the farm were looked forward to through all the week. There was little Catherine to admire, and in the summer days there was the orchard, where Henri loved to play, and where he and his aunt would sit together all the afternoon. If Suzanne were in a good temper, she would bring Catherine out in her arms, and the children would tumble about together in the long grass.

And so the time wore on, and as Henri grew in mind and body, and was able to prattle and run about the fields, Jeanne-Marie hungered for him with a love more absorbing than ever.

Two years had passed since Catherine's birth, and for the last year Anna would often bring her, when she came down to Jeanne-Marie's cottage. The one day a week had dropped gradually to every ten days; it was sometimes only every fortnight that one or both children would appear, and the days that little Henri came were marked white days on the simple calendar of Jeanne-Marie's heart.

5

Now, as Jeanne-Marie stood in her garden this hot May afternoon, and shaded her eyes, as she gazed at the broad white road, her face was troubled, and there was a drawn line of apprehension round the corners of her mouth. For lately Suzanne's jealous temper had flamed up again, and this alert jealously boded evil days for Jeanne-Marie.

Several times within the last two months, little Henri – now going on for four years old – had come toddling down to the cottage by himself, to his aunt's unbounded amazement and delight. 'Maman is at market,' he explained with dignity the first time, in answer to the wondering queries. 'Papa yoked the oxen to the big cart after dinner, and they went; Anna is talking all the afternoon to Pierre Puyoo in the road; and Henri was alone. So Henri came; Henri loves his aunt, and would like some biscuits.' Great was the content of that hour in the cottage, when Jeanne-Marie sat in the big armchair, and the boy prattled and ate his biscuits on her knee. Anna's hard young smile, that scorned emotion, was always *a gêne** to this harmony of old and young; also, there was no need to glance anxiously at the clock; for the oxen take two hours to get home from the market, and who leaves the town till late in the afternoon? 'Anna will miss *le petit*,' Jeanne-Marie suggested the first time; but he answered proudly: 'She will think *le petit* takes care of the geese in the meadow; do I not have charge of all the geese many afternoons? And when I am six years old, Papa has promised I may guard the cows, and bring them home to milk at sundown, as André Puyoo and Georges Vidal do, each day. Also, why cannot Henri come to see *la tante* when he likes?'

But nevertheless, the second and third occasions of these happy visits, always on market days, Jeanne-Marie became uneasy. Did Suzanne know of the boy's absences? Were those fitful jealousies she now displayed almost every Sunday, the result of her knowledge? And if she did not know, would there not be a burst of rage when she heard? Should Jeanne-Marie risk this joy by telling her of its existence, and asking her permission for its continuance? How well the hard tones of Suzanne's voice, framing each plausible objection, came to her mind, as she thought. No, she could not do it. Let the child come, and go on coming every market day, for as long as he could. She would say no word to encourage his keeping it secret from his mother; he would tell her one day, if he had not told her already, and then, if anger there was, surely the simple words, 'May not your child visit his aunt alone?' must bring peace again.

So Jeanne-Marie reasoned away her fears. But now, as she stood in her garden, her lips were trembling with anxiety.

Last Sunday she had been too ill to go up to the farm. A sudden agonising breathlessness, together with great dizziness, had forced her to bed, and Marthe's boy had gone up with the message. But neither that day nor the next, which was market day, nor any following day, had Suzanne, or Anna, or little Henri come to see her. And today was Saturday. And she realised wearily that tomorrow she could not get to the farm; she felt too ill and feeble. 'My heart aches,' she said to Marthe each day, 'my heart aches.'

The afternoon waned slowly, and the little group at the café increased in numbers, as the men sauntered through the village at sundown. The women stood at their doors, laughing and chatting with one another. M. le Curé passed down the street, smiling at the children. From the meadows came the cows and oxen, driven slowly along, their bells beating low harmonies as they went. The festive air of evening after a hot day touched all the tiny town. And Jeanne-Marie stood in her garden, waiting.

Suddenly, while she watched, her heart bounded within her, and a spasm of sudden pain drove the colour from her face, for she recognised the figure that was passing from the white turning into the broad road. Suzanne – Suzanne, who had not been near her cottage for a year – Suzanne, alone. She pressed her two hands under her left breast, and moved forward to the gate. She felt now she had known it for long. All the suspense of many days had given way to a dull certainty: little Henri was ill, was dying perhaps, and Suzanne had come with the news.

Jeanne-Marie had her hand on the latch to let her through; but she stood outside the gate, and said hoarsely, 'I will not come in.' Her face was flushed, there was no cap over her coil of brown hair, and she had on the dark dress she never wore except at the farm. All this Jeanne-Marie noticed mechanically, while that suffocating hurry at her heart seemed to eat away her energy and her power of speech.

But Suzanne was going to speak. The colour flamed into her face, and her teeth ground together, as if to force down the violence of her feeling, and then she spoke: 'Jeanne-Marie, you have done your work well. We knew you loved our boy. You were careful always to show us how far greater was your love for him than ours. And as you could not well turn him against me before my eyes, you waited – *ma foi*, how well you did it! – you waited till I was well away, and then, you taught him to sneak down to see you, and sneak home again before my return. *Mon Dieu!* it was a worthy son to us you wished to make of him. But it could not be, Jeanne-Marie. Your good God, you love so well, would not have it and so' – there came a sob in her voice that she choked down, and Jeanne-Marie's face went a shade greyer as she listened – 'it happened that I was long at the market last week, and you, knowing this would be so, because it was a big market, brought him home late, when the fever was springing from the marshes – it was Marguerite Vallée saw him and came and told me – and now these four days he has lain with fever, and the officier de santé tells us there grows something in his throat that may kill him in four days.'

The hard tones left her voice in the last phrase. A shadow of the love she persuaded herself she felt for Henri sprang up, and choked her anger. She forgot Jeanne-Marie for the moment, and saw only the little figure tossing with fever and delirium, and pity for her own sorrow filled her eyes with tears. She was surprised at the calm cruelty of her own words. Looking up curiously to see how her sister would take it, she started, for Jeanne-Marie's face seemed suddenly to have grown old and grey. She was struggling breathlessly to speak, and when her voice came, it sounded far off, and weak like the voice of a sick child.

'You know well that in your anger you have lied to me. Henri may be ill – and dying; it is not I who have made him so. You shall listen to me now, though I will not keep you here long; for the hand that struck my mother suddenly through the heart, struck me while you were speaking. You have kept me all these days in suspense, and now you have given the blow. Be satisfied, Suzanne.'

She paused, and the sound of her heavy breathing struck Suzanne's frightened senses like the knell of a doom.

'Listen to me. Henri came to me of his own will, and never did I persuade him or suggest to him to come. Never did he go home later than four o'clock; there was nothing done in secret; neither I, nor any in the village, thought it a crime he came to visit me. Often I have seen him keeping the geese in the long grass of the meadows at six, at seven o'clock. Seek the fever there – not on the village road before the sunset. As the good God hears me, never have I stood between that boy and his mother. Gradually you took from me every privilege my affection knew; but I said nothing. Ah, I loved him dearly; I was content to wait. But all that is over. If God grants me life – but He is good, and I think He knows my suffering all these years – I swear before Him your house shall be to me a house of strangers, Henri the child of strangers, and my brother's face unknown to me. Never shall my father's daughter hear again what I have heard from you today. All these years you have played upon my heart. You have watched the suffering; you have known how each word seemed so innocent, but stabbed so deep. You have seen your child wind himself round my heart, and every day, every hour, you have struggled to pluck him from me. Now, I tell you I tear your children from my heart; you have killed not only my body, but my love. Go, and leave me for ever, or by my father, I will curse you where you stand.'

She tottered forward, and with one horrified look at the agony of her menacing face, Suzanne turned and ran.

And Jeanne-Marie fell all her length on the garden soil.

6

The miller's boy saw her there, when he came past a few minutes later, and not daring to touch her, ran to the mill for help. Marthe and her husband came immediately and carried her into the cottage. At first, they thought she was dead, her face was so grey and sunken, but she came to herself, as they laid her on the bed, and shook her head faintly when Marthe suggested fetching the *officier de santé*.

As soon as she could speak she whispered, 'No, Marthe, it is the illness of the heart that killed my mother. The doctor told her she might have lived to be old, with much care, and if no great trouble or excitement had come to her; but, you see, I was much troubled just now, and so it has come earlier. Do not send for any doctor; he could but call it by the long name they called it when my mother died, and trouble one with vain touches and questions.'

So Marthe helped her to undress, and to get to bed quickly. The breathlessness and the pain had gone for a time, though she was very feeble, and could scarcely stand on her feet. But it was the grey look of her face that frightened Marthe, and her strained quietness. No questions could get out of her the story of the afternoon.

'Suzanne came to tell me little Henri was ill,' was all she would say; but Marthe only shook her head, and made her own deductions.

Jeanne-Marie would not hear of her staying with her for the night, and leaving her young children alone, and so it was settled the miller's boy should sleep below in the kitchen, and if Jeanne-Marie felt ill in the night, she would call to him, and he would fetch Marthe immediately.

Also, Marthe promised to call at the house of M. le Curé on her way home. He would be out late, since he had started only an hour ago to take the Host to old Groupé, who lay dying four kilometres away; but she would leave a message, and certainly, when he returned, however late, he would come round. It was nine o'clock before Marthe would leave, and even then she stopped reluctantly at the door, with a last look at the thin figure propped up on her pillows. 'Let me stay, Jeanne-Marie,' she said. 'You are so pale, and yet your eyes burn. I do not like to think of the long night and you sitting here.'

'It is easier than when I lie down, which brings the breathlessness. Do not worry yourself, Marthe, I shall sleep perhaps, and if I need anything, I have but to call to Jean below. Good night, and thank you, Marthe.'

The little house was very quiet. Jean had been asleep on his chair this hour past, and not a sound came from the slumbering village. There was no blind to the window of the bedroom, and Jeanne-Marie watched the moon, as it escaped slowly from the unwilling clouds, and threw its light on to the foot of the narrow bed.

For a long while she lay there, without moving, while through all her troubled, confused thoughts ran like an undercurrent the dull pain that wrenched at her heart. It seemed to take the coherency from her thinking, and to be the one unquiet factor in the calm that had come over her. She was surprised, herself, at this strange fatigue that had swept away even her suffering. She thought of little Henri and his illness without a pang. He seemed like some far-off person she had read about, or heard of, long ago.

She thought to herself, vaguely, that she must be dying, since she seemed to have lost all feeling.

Bit by bit, various little scenes between her and Henri came to her mind, with an extraordinary vividness. He was sitting on her knee in the cottage, and his clear child's voice rang like a bell in the silent room – so clearly, that Jeanne-Marie started, and wondered if she were light-headed or had been dreaming. Then the voice faded away, and she saw the cool, high grass of the orchard, and there was Henri laughing at her, and rolling among the flowers. How cool and fresh it looked; and Henri was asking her to come and play: '*Tante Jeanne-Marie, viens jouer avec ton petit. Tante Jeanne-Marie, tante Jeanne-Marie!*' She must throw herself on the grass with him – on the cool, waving grass. And she bent forward with outstretched arms; but the movement brought her to herself, and as she lay back on her pillows, suddenly the reality of suffering rushed back upon her, with the agonising sense of separation and of loss. Little Henri was dying; was dead perhaps; never to hear his voice, or feel his warm little arms round her neck. She could do nothing for him; he must die without her. 'Tante Jeanne-Marie! Tante Jeanne-Marie!' Was he calling her, from his feverish little bed? If he called, she must go to him, she could not lie here, this suffering was choking her. She must have air, and space to breathe in; this room was suffocating her. She must go to Henri. With a desperate effort she struggled to her feet, and stood supporting herself by the bedpost. The moon, that had hidden itself in the clouds, struggled out, the long, old-fashioned glass hanging on the wall opposite the bed became one streak of light, and Jeanne-Marie, gazing at herself, met the reflection of her own face, and knew that no power on earth could make her reach the farm where little Henri lay.

She stood, as if spellbound, marking the sunken look of the eyes, the grey-blue colour of the cheeks, the face that was the face of an old woman.

A sudden, fierce revolt against her starved life swept through her at the sight, and conquered even the physical pain raging at her heart. Still struggling for breath, she threw up her arms and tore the cotton nightgown from her shoulders, and stood there beating her breast with her hands.

'Oh, good God! good God! see here what I am. How old and shrunken before my time! Cursed be these breasts, that no child has ever suckled; cursed be this withered body, that no man has ever embraced. I could have loved, and lived long, and been made beautiful by happiness. Ah, why am I accursed? I die, unloved and neglected by my own people. No children's tears, no husband to close my eyes; old, worn out, before my time. A woman only in name – not wife, not mother. Despised and hideous before God and men – God and men.'

Her voice died away in a moan, her head fell forward on her breast, and she stumbled against the bed. For a long time she lay crouched there, insensible from mere exhaustion, until, just as the clocks were striking midnight, the door opened gently, and Marthe and M. le Curé came in. Jean, awakened by the sounds overhead, had run quickly for Marthe, and coming back together, they had met M. le Curé on his way.

They raised her gently, and laid her on the bed, and finding she still breathed, Marthe ran to fetch brandy, and the Curé knelt by the bed in prayer.

Presently, the eyes opened quietly, and M. le Curé saw her lips move. He bent over her, and whispered, 'You are troubled, Jeanne-Marie; you wish for the absolution?'

But her voice came back to her, and she said clearly, 'To die unloved, unmourned; a woman, but no wife; no mother.'

She closed her eyes again. There were noises singing in her head, louder and louder; but the pain at her heart had ceased. She was conscious only of a great loneliness, as if a curtain had risen, and shut her off from the room; and again the words came, whispered from her lips: 'A woman, accursed and wasted; no mother and no wife.'

But someone was speaking, speaking so loudly that the sounds in her head seemed to die away. She opened her eyes, and saw M. le Curé, where he knelt, with his eyes shining on her face, and heard his voice saying: 'And God said, "Blessed be the virgins above all women; give unto them the holy places; let them be exalted and praised by My church, before all men, and before Me. Worthy are they to sit at My feet – worthy are they above all women."'

A smile of infinite happiness and of supreme relief lit up Jeanne-Marie's face.

'Above all women,' she whispered. 'Above all women.'

And Jeanne-Marie bowed her head, and died.

(1894)

FLORA ANNIE STEEL

The Reformer's Wife

He was a dreamer of dreams, with the look in his large dark eyes which Botticelli put into the eyes of his Moses; that Moses in doublet and hose, whose figure, isolated from its surroundings, reminds one irresistibly of Christopher Columbus, or Vasco da Gama – of those, in fact, who dream of a Promised Land.

And this man dreamt as wild a dream as any. He hoped, before he died, to change the social customs of India.

He used to sit in my drawing-room, talking to me by the hour of the Prophet and his blessed Fátma – for he was a Mahommedan – and bewailing the sad degeneracy of these present days, when caste had crept into and defiled the Faith. I shall never forget the face of martyred enthusiasm with which he received my first invitation to dinner. He accepted it, as he would have accepted the stake, with fervour, and indeed to his ignorance the ordeal was supreme. However, he appeared punctual to the moment on the appointed day, and greatly relieved my mind by partaking twice of plum pudding, which he declared to be a surpassingly cool and most digestible form of nourishment, calculated to soothe both body and mind. Though this is hardly the character usually assigned to it, I did not contradict him, for not even his eager self-sacrifice had sufficed for the soup, the fish, or the joint, and he might otherwise have left the table in a starving condition. As it was, he firmly set aside my invitation to drink water after the meal was over, with the modest remark that he had not eaten enough to warrant the indulgence.

The event caused quite a stir in that faraway little town, set out among the ruins of a great city, on the high bank of one of the Punjab rivers; for the scene of this sketch lay out of the beaten track, beyond the reach of *babus** and barristers, patent-leather shoes and progress. Beyond the pale of civilisation altogether, among a quaint little colony of fighting Pathans who still pointed with pride to an old gate or two which had withstood siege after siege, in those old fighting days when the river had flowed beneath the walls of the city. Since then the water had ebbed seven miles to the south-east, taking with it the prestige of the stronghold, which only remained a picturesque survival; a cluster of four-storeyed purple-brick houses surrounded by an intermittent purple-brick wall, bastioned and loopholed. A formidable defence, while it lasted. But it had a trick of dissolving meekly into a sort of mud hedge, in order to gain the next stately fragment, or maybe to effect an alliance with one of the frowning gateways which had defied assault. This condition of things was a source of sincere delight to my Reformer Futteh Deen (Victory of Faith) who revelled in similes. It was typical of the irrational, illogical position of the inhabitants in regard to a thousand religious and social questions, and just as one brave man could break through these sham fortifications, so one resolute example would suffice to capture the citadel of prejudice, and plant the banner of abstract Truth on its topmost pinnacle.

For he dreamt excellently well, and as he sat declaiming his Persian and Arabic periods in the drawing-room with his eyes half-shut, like one in presence of some dazzling light, I used to feel as if something might indeed be done to make the Mill of God grind a little faster.

In the matter of dining out, indeed, it seemed as if he was right. For within a week of his desperate plunge, I received an invitation to break bread with the municipal committee in the upper storey of the Vice President's house. The request, which was emblazoned in gold, engrossed on silk paper in red and black, and enclosed in a brocade envelope, was signed by the eleven members and the Reformer, who, by the way, edited a ridiculous little magazine to which the committee subscribed a few rupees a month. Solely for the purpose of being able to send copies to their friends at Court, and show that they were in the van of progress. For a man must be that, who is patron of a 'Society for the General Good of All Men in All Countries'. I was, I confess it, surprised, even though a remark that now perhaps his Honour the Lieutenant-Governor would no longer suspect his slaves of disloyalty, showed me that philanthropy had begun at home. For the little colony bore a doubtful character, being largely leavened by the new Puritanism, which Government, for reasons best known to itself, chooses to confound with Wahabeeism.

The entertainment given on the roof amid starshine and

catherine-wheels proved a magnificent success, its great feature being an enormous plum pudding which I was gravely told had been prepared by my own cook. At what cost, I shudder to think; but the rascal's grinning face as he placed it on the table convinced me that he had seized the opportunity for some almost inconceivable extortion. But there was no regret in those twelve grave, bearded faces, as one by one they tasted and approved. All this happened long before a miserable, exotic imitation of an English vestry replaced the old patrician committees, and these men were representatives of the bluest blood in the neighbourhood, many of them descendants of those who in past times had held high offices of state, and had transmitted courtly manners to their children. So the epithets bestowed on the plum pudding were many-syllabled; but the consensus of opinion was indubitably towards its coolness, its digestibility, and its evident property of soothing the body and the mind. Again I did not deny it. How could I, out on the roof under the eternal stars, with those twelve foreign faces showing, for once, a common bond of union with the Feringhee? I should have felt like Judas Iscariot if I had struck the thirteenth chord of denial.

The Reformer made a speech afterwards, I remember, in which, being wonderfully well read, he alluded to love-feasts and sacraments, and a coming millennium, when all nations of the world should meet at one table, and – well! not exactly eat plum pudding together, but something very like it. Then we all shook hands, and a native musician played something on the *siringhi** which they informed me was 'God Save the Queen'. It may have been. I only know that the Reformer's thin face beamed with almost pitiful delight, as he told me triumphantly that this was only the beginning.

He was right. From that time forth the plum pudding feast became a recognised function. Not a week passed without one. Generally – for my gorge rose at the idea of my cook's extortion – in the summer-house in my garden, where I could have an excuse for providing the delicacy at my own expense. And I am bound to say that this increased intimacy bore other fruits than that contained in the pudding. For the matter of that it has continued to bear fruit, since I can truthfully date the beginning of my friendship for the people of India from the days when we ate plum pudding together under the starshine.

The Reformer was radiant. He formed himself and his eleven

into committees and sub-committees for every philanthropical object under the sun, and many an afternoon have I spent under the trees with my work watching one deputation after another retire behind the oleander hedge in order to permutate itself by deft rearrangement of members, secretaries, and vice presidents into some fresh body bent on the regeneration of mankind. For life was leisureful, lingering and lagging along in the little town where there was neither doctor nor parson, policeman nor canal officer, nor in fact any white face save my own and my husband's. Still we went far and fast in a cheerful, unreal sort of way. We started schools and debating societies, public libraries and technical art classes. Finally we met enthusiastically over an extra-sized plum pudding, and bound ourselves over to reduce the marriage expenditure of our daughters.

The Reformer grew more radiant than ever, and began in the drawing-room – where it appeared to me he hatched all his most daring schemes – to talk big about infant marriage, enforced widowhood, and the seclusion of women. The latter I considered to be the key to the whole position, and therefore I felt surprised at the evident reluctance with which he met my suggestion, that he should begin his struggle by bringing his wife to visit me. He had but one, although she was childless. This was partly, no doubt, in deference to his advanced theories; but also, at least so I judged from his conversation, because of his unbounded admiration for one who by his description was a pearl among women. In fact this unseen partner had from the first been held up to me as a refutation of all my strictures on the degradation of seclusion. So, to tell truth, I was quite anxious to see this paragon, and vexed at the constant ailments and absences which prevented our becoming acquainted. The more so because this shadow of hidden virtue fettered me in argument, for Futteh Deen was an eager patriot, full of enthusiasms for India and the Indians. Once the sham fortifications were scaled, he assured me that Hindustan, and above all its women, would come to the front and put their universe to shame. Yet, despite his successes, he looked haggard and anxious; at the time I thought it was too much progress and plum pudding combined, but afterwards I came to the conclusion that his conscience was ill at ease, even then.

So the heat grew apace. The fly-catchers came to dart among the *sirus* flowers and skim round the massive dome of the old tomb in which we lived. The melons began to ripen, first by ones and twos, then in thousands – gold, and green, and russet. The corners of the streets were piled with them, and every man, woman, and child carried a crescent moon of melon at which they munched contentedly all day long. Now, even with the future good of humanity in view, I could not believe in the safety of a mixed diet of melon and plum pudding, especially when cholera was flying about. Therefore, on the next committee-day I had a light and wholesome refection of sponge cakes and jelly prepared for the philanthropists. They partook of it courteously, but sparingly. It was, they said, super-excellent, but of too heating and stimulating a nature to be consumed in quantities. In vain I assured them that it could be digested by the most delicate stomach; that it was, in short, a recognised food for convalescents. This only confirmed them in their view, for, according to the *Yunâni* system, an invalid diet must be heating, strengthening, stimulating. Somehow in the middle of their upsidedown arguments I caught myself looking pitifully at the Reformer, and wondering at his temerity in tilting at the great mysterious mass of Eastern wisdom.

And that day, in deference to my Western zeal, he was to tilt wildly at the *zenâna** system.

His address fell flat, and for the first time I noticed a distinctly personal flavour in the discussion. Hitherto we had resolved and recorded gaily, as if we ourselves were disinterested spectators. However, the Vice President apologised for the general tone, with a side slash at exciting causes in the jelly and sponge cake, whereat the other ten wagged their heads sagely, remarking that it was marvellous, stupendous, to feel the blood running riot in their veins after those few mouthfuls. Verily such food partook of magic. Only the Reformer dissented, and ate a whole sponge cake defiantly.

Even so the final Resolution ran thus: 'That this committee views with alarm any attempt to force the natural growth of female freedom, which it holds to be strictly a matter for the individual wishes of the man.' Indeed it was with difficulty that I, as secretary, avoided the disgrace of having to record the spiteful rider, 'And that if any member wanted to unveil the ladies he could begin on his own wife.'

I was young then in knowledge of Eastern ways, and consequently indignant. The Reformer, on the other hand, was strangely humble, and tried afterwards to evade the major point by eating another sponge cake, and making a facetious remark about experiments and vile bodies; for he was a mine of quotations, especially from the Bible, which he used to wield to my great discomfiture.

But on the point at issue I knew he could scarcely go against his own convictions, so I pressed home his duty of taking the initiative. He agreed, gently. By and by, perhaps, when his wife was more fit for the ordeal. And it was natural, even the *mem-sahiba* must allow, for unaccustomed modesty to shrink. She was to the full as devoted as he to the good cause, but at the same time— Finally, the *mem-sahiba* must remember that women were women all over the world – even though occasionally one was to be found like the *mem-sahiba* capable of acting as secretary to innumerable committees without a blush. There was something so wistful in his eager blending of flattery and excuse that I yielded for the time, though determined in the end to carry my point.

With this purpose I reverted to plum puddings once more, and, I fear, to gross bribery of all kinds in the shape of private interviews and soft words. Finally I succeeded in getting half the members to consent to sending their wives to an after-dark at-home in my drawing-room, provided always that Mir Futteh Deen, the Reformer, would set a good example.

He looked troubled when I told him, and pointed out that the responsibility for success or failure now lay virtually with him, yet he did not deny it.

I took elaborate precautions to ensure the most modest seclusion on the appointed evening, even to sending my husband up a ladder to the gallery at the very top of the dome to smoke his after-dinner cigar. I remember thinking how odd it must have looked to him perched up there to see the twinkling lights of the distant city over the soft shadows of the *ferash* trees, and at his feet the glimmer of the white screens set up to form a conventional *zenán-khâna*.* But I waited in vain – in my best dress, by the way. No one came, though my *ayah* assured me that several jealously guarded *dhoolies** arrived at the garden gate and went away again when Mrs Futteh Deen never turned up.

I was virtuously indignant with the offender, and the next time he came to see me sent out a message that I was otherwise engaged. I felt a little remorseful at having done so, however, when, committee-day coming round, the Reformer was reported on the sick-list. And there he remained until after the first rain had fallen, bringing with it the real Indian spring – the spring full of roses and jasmines, of which the poets and the bul-buls sing. By this time the novelty had worn off philanthropy and plum pudding, so that often we had a difficulty in getting a quorum together to resolve anything; and I, personally, had begun to weary for the dazzled eyes and the eager voice so full of sanguine hope.

Therefore it gave me a pang to learn from the Vice President, who, being a Government official, was a model of punctuality, that in all posbability I should never hear or see either one or the other again. Futteh Deen was dying of the rapid decline which comes so often to the Indian student.

A recurrence of a vague remorse made me put my pride in my pocket and go unasked to the Reformer's house, but my decision came too late. He had died the morning of my visit, and I think I was glad of it.

For the paragon of beauty and virtue, of education and refinement, was a very ordinary woman, years older than my poor Reformer, marked with the small-pox, and blind of one eye. Then I understood.

(1903)

VIOLET HUNT

The Prayer

I

'*It is but giving over of a game, That must be lost.*' (Philaster)

'Come, Mrs Anne – come, my dear, you must not give way like this! You can't stand it – you really can't! Let Miss Kate take you away – now do!' urged the nurse, with her most motherly of intonations.

'Yes, Alice, Mrs Joyce is right. Come away – do come away – you are only making yourself ill. It is all over; you can do nothing! Oh, oh, do come away!' implored Mrs Arne's sister, shivering with excitement and nervousness.

A few moments ago Dr Graham had relinquished his hold on the pulse of Edward Arne with the hopeless movement of the eyebrows that meant – the end.

The nurse had made the little gesture of resignation that was possibly a matter of form with her. The young sister-in-law had hidden her face in her hands. The wife had screamed a scream that had turned them all hot and cold – and flung herself on the bed over her dead husband. There she lay; her cries were terrible, her sobs shook her whole body.

The three gazed at her pityingly, not knowing what to do next. The nurse, folding her hands, looked towards the doctor for directions, and the doctor drummed with his fingers on the bedpost. The young girl timidly stroked the shoulder that heaved and writhed under her touch.

'Go away! Go away!' her sister reiterated continually, in a voice hoarse with fatigue and passion.

'Leave her alone, Miss Kate,' whispered the nurse at last; 'she will work it off best herself, perhaps.'

She turned down the lamp as if to draw a veil over the scene. Mrs Arne raised herself on her elbow, showing a face stained with tears and purple with emotion.

'What! Not gone?' she said harshly. 'Go away, Kate, go away!
It is my house. I don't want you, I want no one – I want to speak
to my husband. Will you go away – all of you. Give me an hour,
half an hour – five minutes!'

She stretched out her arms imploringly to the doctor.

'Well . . .' said he, almost to himself.

He signed to the two women to withdraw, and followed them
out into the passage. 'Go and get something to eat,' he said
peremptorily, 'while you can. We shall have trouble with her
presently. I'll wait in the dressing-room.'

He glanced at the twisting figure on the bed, shrugged his
shoulders, and passed into the adjoining room, without, however,
closing the door of communication. Sitting down in an armchair
drawn up to the fire, he stretched himself and closed his eyes. The
professional aspects of the case of Edward Arne rose up before
him in all its interesting forms of complication . . .

It was just this professional attitude that Mrs Arne unconsciously
resented both in the doctor and in the nurse. Through all their
kindness she had realised and resented their scientific interest in
her husband, for to them he had been no more than a curious and
complicated case; and now that the blow had fallen, she regarded
them both in the light of executioners. Her one desire, expressed
with all the shameless sincerity of blind and thoughtless misery,
was to be free of their hateful presence and alone – alone with her
dead!

She was weary of the doctor's subdued manly tones – of the
nurse's commonplace motherliness, too habitually adapted to the
needs of all to be appreciated by the individual – of the childish
consolation of the young sister, who had never loved, never been
married, did not know what sorrow was! Their expressions of
sympathy struck her like blows, the touch of their hands on her
body, as they tried to raise her, stung her in every nerve.

With a sigh of relief she buried her head in the pillow, pressed
her body more closely against that of her husband, and lay
motionless.

Her sobs ceased.

The lamp went out with a gurgle. The fire leaped up, and died. She
raised her head and stared about her helplessly, then sinking
down again she put her lips to the ear of the dead man.

'Edward – dear Edward!' she whispered. 'Why have you left me? Darling, why have you left me? I can't stay behind – you know I can't. I am too young to be left. It is only a year since you married me. I never thought it was only for a year. "Till death us do part!" Yes, I know that's in it, but nobody ever thinks of that! I never thought of living without you! I meant to die with you . . .

'No – no – I can't die – I must not – till my baby is born. You will never see it. Don't you want to see it? Don't you? Oh, Edward, speak! Say something, darling, one word – one little word! Edward! Edward! are you there? Answer me for God's sake, answer me!

'Darling, I am so tired of waiting. Oh, think, dearest. There is so little time. They only gave me half an hour. In half an hour they will come and take you away from me – take you where I can't come to you – with all my love I can't come to you! I know the place – I saw it once. A great lonely place full of graves, and little stunted trees dripping with dirty London rain . . . and gas-lamps flaring all round . . . but quite, quite dark where the grave is . . . a long grey stone just like the rest. How could you stay there? – all alone – all alone – without me?

'Do you remember, Edward, what we once said – that whichever of us died first should come back to watch over the other, in the spirit? I promised you, and you promised me. What children we were! Death is not what we thought. It comforted us to say that then.

'Now, it's nothing – nothing – worse than nothing! I don't want your spirit – I can't see it – or feel it – I want you, you, your eyes that looked at me, your mouth that kissed me—'

She raised his arms and clasped them round her neck, and lay there very still, murmuring, 'Oh, hold me, hold me! Love me if you can. Am I hateful? This is me! These are your arms . . .'

The doctor in the next room moved in his chair. The noise awoke her from her dream of contentment, and she unwound the dead arm from her neck, and, holding it up by the wrist, considered it ruefully.

'Yes, I can put it round me, but I have to hold it there. It is quite cold – it doesn't care. Ah, my dear, you don't care! You are dead. I kiss you, but you don't kiss me. Edward! Edward! Oh, for heaven's sake kiss me once. Just once!

'No, no, that won't do – that's not enough! that's nothing! worse than nothing! I want you back, you, all you . . . What shall

I do? . . . I often pray . . . Oh, if there be a God in heaven, and if He ever answered a prayer, let Him answer mine – my only prayer. I'll never ask another – and give you back to me! As you were – as I loved you – as I adored you! He must listen. He must! My God, my God, he's mine – he's my husband, he's my lover – give him back to me!'

'Left alone for half an hour or more with the corpse! It's not right!'

The muttered expression of the nurse's revolted sense of professional decency came from the head of the staircase, where she had been waiting for the last few minutes. The doctor joined her.

'Hush, Mrs Joyce! I'll go to her now.'

The door creaked on its hinges as he gently pushed it open and went in.

'What's that? What's that?' screamed Mrs Arne. 'Doctor! Doctor! Don't touch me! Either I am dead or he is alive!'

'Do you want to kill yourself, Mrs Arne?' said Dr Graham, with calculated sternness, coming forward; 'come away!'

'Not dead! Not dead!' she murmured.

'He is dead, I assure you. Dead and cold an hour ago! Feel!' He took hold of her, as she lay face downwards, and in so doing he touched the dead man's cheek – it was not cold! Instinctively his finger sought a pulse.

'Stop! Wait!' he cried in his intense excitement. 'My dear Mrs Arne, control yourself!'

But Mrs Arne had fainted, and fallen heavily off the bed on the other side. Her sister, hastily summoned, attended to her, while the man they had all given over for dead was, with faint gasps and sighs and reluctant moans, pulled, as it were, hustled and dragged back over the threshold of life.

2

'Why do you always wear black, Alice?' asked Esther Graham. 'You are not in mourning that I know of.'

She was Dr Graham's only daughter and Mrs Arne's only friend. She sat with Mrs Arne in the dreary drawing-room of the house in Chelsea. She had come to tea. She was the only person who ever did come to tea there.

She was brusque, kind, and blunt, and had a talent for making inappropriate remarks. Six years ago Mrs Arne had been a widow for an hour! Her husband had succumbed to an apparently mortal illness, and for the space of an hour had lain dead. When suddenly and inexplicably he had revived from his trance, the shock, combined with six weeks' nursing, had nearly killed his wife. All this Esther had heard from her father. She herself had only come to know Mrs Arne after her child was born, and all the tragic circumstances of her husband's illness put aside, and it was hoped forgotten. And when her idle question received no answer from the pale absent woman who sat opposite, with listless lack-lustre eyes fixed on the green and blue flames dancing in the fire, she hoped it had passed unnoticed. She waited for five minutes for Mrs Arne to resume the conversation, then her natural impatience got the better of her.

'Do say something, Alice!' she implored.

'Esther, I beg your pardon!' said Mrs Arne. 'I was thinking.'

'What were you thinking of?'

'I don't know.'

'No, of course you don't. People who sit and stare into the fire never do think, really. They are only brooding and making themselves ill, and that is what you are doing. You mope, you take no interest in anything, you never go out – I am sure you have not been out of doors today?'

'No – yes – I believe not. It is so cold.'

'You are sure to feel the cold if you sit in the house all day, and sure to get ill! Just look at yourself!'

Mrs Arne rose and looked at herself in the Italian mirror over the chimney-piece. It reflected faithfully enough her even pallor, her dark hair and eyes, the sweeping length of her eyelashes, the sharp curves of her nostrils, and the delicate arch of her eyebrows, that formed a thin sharp black line, so clear as to seem almost unnatural.

'Yes, I do look ill,' she said with conviction.

'No wonder. You choose to bury yourself alive.'

'Sometimes I do feel as if I lived in a grave. I look up at the ceiling and fancy it is my coffin lid.'

'Don't please talk like that!' expostulated Miss Graham, pointing to Mrs Arne's little girl. 'If only for Dolly's sake, I think you should not give way to such morbid fancies. It isn't good for her to see you like this always.'

'Oh, Esther,' the other exclaimed, stung into something like vivacity, 'don't reproach me! I hope I am a good mother to my child!'

'Yes, dear, you are a model mother – and model wife too. Father says the way you look after your husband is something wonderful, but don't you think for your own sake you might try to be a little gayer? You encourage these moods, don't you? What is it? Is it the house?'

She glanced around her – at the high ceiling, at the heavy damask *portières*,* the tall cabinets of china, the dim oak panelling – it reminded her of a neglected museum. Her eye travelled into the farthest corners, where the faint filmy dusk was already gathering, lit only by the bewildering cross-lights of the glass panels of cabinet doors – to the tall narrow windows – then back again to the woman in her mourning dress, cowering by the fire. She said sharply – 'You should go out more.'

'I do not like to – leave my husband.'

'Oh, I know that he is delicate and all that, but still, does he never permit you to leave him? Does he never go out by himself?'

'Not often!'

'And you have no pets! It is very odd of you. I simply can't imagine a house without animals.'

'We did have a dog once,' answered Mrs Arne plaintively, 'but it howled so we had to give it away. It would not go near Edward . . . But please don't imagine that I am dull! I have my child.' She laid her hand on the flaxen head at her knee.

Miss Graham rose, frowning.

'Ah, you are too bad!' she exclaimed. 'You are like a widow exactly, with one child, stroking its orphan head and saying, "Poor fatherless darling."'

Voices were heard outside. Miss Graham stopped talking quite suddenly, and sought her veil and gloves on the mantelpiece.

'You need not go, Esther,' said Mrs Arne. 'It is only my husband.'

'Oh, but it is getting late,' said the other, crumpling up her gloves in her muff, and shuffling her feet nervously.

'Come!' said her hostess, with a bitter smile, 'put your gloves on properly – if you must go – but it is quite early still.'

'Please don't go, Miss Graham,' put in the child.

'I must. Go and meet your papa, like a good girl.'

'I don't want to.'

'You mustn't talk like that, Dolly,' said the doctor's daughter absently, still looking towards the door. Mrs Arne rose and fastened the clasps of the big fur cloak for her friend. The wife's white, sad, oppressed face came very close to the girl's cheerful one, as she murmured in a low voice –

'You don't like my husband, Esther? I can't help noticing it. Why don't you?'

'Nonsense!' retorted the other, with the emphasis of one who is repelling an overtrue accusation. 'I do, only—'

'Only what?'

'Well, dear, it is foolish of me, of course, but I am – a little afraid of him.'

'Afraid of Edward!' said his wife slowly. 'Why should you be?'

'Well, dear – you see – I – I suppose women can't help being a little afraid of their friends' husbands – they can spoil their friendships with their wives in a moment, if they choose to disapprove of them. I really must go! Goodbye, child; give me a kiss! Don't ring, Alice. Please don't! I can open the door for myself—'

'Why should you?' said Mrs Arne. 'Edward is in the hall; I heard him speaking to Foster.'

'No; he has gone into his study. Goodbye, you apathetic creature!' She gave Mrs Arne a brief kiss and dashed out of the room. The voices outside had ceased, and she had reasonable hopes of reaching the door without being intercepted by Mrs Arne's husband. But he met her on the stairs. Mrs Arne, listening intently from her seat by the fire, heard her exchange a few shy sentences with him, the sound of which died away as they went downstairs together. A few moments after, Edward Arne came into the room and dropped into the chair just vacated by his wife's visitor.

He crossed his legs and said nothing. Neither did she.

His nearness had the effect of making the woman look at once several years older. Where she was pale he was well coloured; the network of little filmy wrinkles that, on a close inspection, covered her face, had no parallel on his smooth skin. He was handsome; soft, well-groomed flakes of auburn hair lay over his forehead, and his steely blue eyes shone equably, a contrast to the sombre fire of hers, and the masses of dark crinkly hair that shaded her brow. The deep lines of permanent discontent furrowed that brow as she sat with her chin propped on her hands, and her elbows resting on her knees. Neither spoke. When the hands of the clock over Mrs Arne's head pointed to seven, the white-aproned figure of the nurse appeared in the doorway, and the little girl rose and kissed her mother very tenderly.

Mrs Arne's forehead contracted. Looking uneasily at her husband, she said to the child tentatively, yet boldly, as one grasps the nettle, 'Say good night to your father!'

The child obeyed, saying 'Good night' indifferently in her father's direction.

'Kiss him!'

'No, please – please not.'

Her mother looked down on her curiously, sadly . . .

'You are a naughty, spoilt child!' she said, but without conviction. 'Excuse her, Edward.'

He did not seem to have heard.

'Well, if you don't care—' said his wife bitterly. 'Come, child!' She caught the little girl by the hand and left the room.

At the door she half turned and looked fixedly at her husband. It was a strange ambiguous gaze; in it passion and dislike were strangely combined. Then she shivered and closed the door softly after her.

The man in the armchair sat with no perceptible change of attitude, his unspeculative eyes fixed on the fire, his hands clasped idly in front of him. The pose was obviously habitual. The servant brought lights and closed the shutters, drew the curtains, and made up the fire noisily, without, however, eliciting any reproof from his master.

Edward Arne was an ideal master, as far as Foster was concerned. He kept cases of cigars, but never smoked them, although the supply had often to be renewed. He did not care what he ate or drank, although he kept as good a cellar as most gentlemen – Foster knew that. He never interfered, he counted for nothing, he gave no trouble. Foster had no intention of ever leaving such an easy place. True, his master was not cordial; he very seldom addressed him or seemed to know whether he was there, but then neither did he grumble if the fire in the study was allowed to go out, or interfere with Foster's liberty in any way. He had a better place of it than Annette, Mrs Arne's maid, who would be called up in the middle of the night to bathe her mistress's forehead with eau-de-Cologne, or made to brush her long hair for hours together to soothe her. Naturally enough Foster and Annette compared notes as to their respective situations, and drew unflattering parallels between this capricious wife and model husband.

3

Miss Graham was not a demonstrative woman. On her return home she somewhat startled her father, as he sat by his study table, deeply interested in his diagnosis book, by the sudden violence of her embrace.

'Why this excitement?' he asked, smiling and turning round. He was a young-looking man for his age; his thin wiry figure and clear colour belied the evidence of his hair, tinged with grey, and the tired wrinkles that gave value to the acuteness and brilliancy of the eyes they surrounded.

'I don't know!' she replied. 'Only you are so nice and alive somehow. I always feel like this when I come back from seeing the Arnes.'

'Then don't go to see the Arnes.'

'I'm so fond of her, Father, and she will never come here to me, as you know. Or else nothing would induce me to enter her tomb of a house, and talk to that walking funeral of a husband of hers. I managed to get away today without having to shake hands with him. I always try to avoid it. But, Father, I do wish you would go and see Alice.'

'Is she ill?'

'Well, not exactly ill, I suppose, but her eyes make me quite uncomfortable, and she says such odd things! I don't know if it is you or the clergyman she wants, but she is all wrong somehow! She never goes out except to church; she never pays a call, or has anyone to call on her! Nobody ever asks the Arnes to dinner, and I'm sure I don't blame them – the sight of that man at one's table would spoil any party – and they never entertain. She is always alone. Day after day I go in and find her sitting over the fire, with that same brooding expression. I shouldn't be surprised in the least if she were to go mad some day. Father, what is it? What is the tragedy of the house? There is one, I am convinced. And yet, though I have been the intimate friend of that woman for years, I know no more about her than the man in the street.'

'She keeps her skeleton safe in the cupboard,' said Dr Graham. 'I respect her for that. And please don't talk nonsense about tragedies. Alice Arne is only morbid – the malady of the age. And she is a very religious woman.'

'I wonder if she complains of her odious husband to Mr Bligh. She is always going to his services.'

'Odious?'

'Yes, odious!' Miss Graham shuddered. 'I cannot stand him! I cannot bear the touch of his cold froggy hands, and the sight of his fishy eyes! That inane smile of his simply makes me shrivel up. Father, honestly, do you like him yourself?'

'My dear, I hardly know him! It is his wife I have known ever since she was a child, and I a boy at college. Her father was my tutor. I never knew her husband till six years ago, when she called me in to attend him in a very serious illness. I suppose she never speaks of it? No? A very odd affair. For the life of me I cannot tell how he managed to recover. You needn't tell people, for it affects my reputation, but I didn't save him! Indeed I have never been able to account for it. The man was given over for dead!'

'He might as well be dead for all the good he is,' said Esther scornfully. 'I have never heard him say more than a couple of sentences in my life.'

'Yet he was an exceedingly brilliant young man; one of the best men of his year at Oxford – a good deal run after – poor Alice was wild to marry him!'

'In love with that spiritless creature? He is like a house with someone dead in it, and all the blinds down!'

'Come, Esther, don't be morbid – not to say silly! You are very hard on the poor man! What's wrong with him? He is the ordinary, commonplace, cold-blooded specimen of humanity, a little stupid, a little selfish – people who have gone through a serious illness like that are apt to be – but on the whole, a good husband, a good father, a good citizen—'

'Yes, and his wife is afraid of him, and his child hates him!' exclaimed Esther.

'Nonsense!' said Dr Graham sharply. 'The child is spoilt. Only children are apt to be – and the mother wants a change or a tonic of some kind. I'll go and talk to her when I have time. Go along and dress. Have you forgotten that George Graham is coming to dinner?'

After she had gone the doctor made a note on the corner of his blotting-pad, 'Mem.: to go and see Mrs Arne,' and dismissed the subject of the memorandum entirely from his mind.

*

George Graham was the doctor's nephew, a tall, weedy, cumbrous young man, full of fads and fallacies, with a gentle manner that somehow inspired confidence. He was several years younger than Esther, who loved to listen to his semi-scientific, semi-romantic stories of things met with in the course of his profession. 'Oh, I come across very queer things!' he would say mysteriously. There's a queer little widow—!'

'Tell me about your little widow?' asked Esther that day after dinner, when, her father having gone back to his study, she and her cousin sat together as usual.

He laughed.

'You like to hear of my professional experiences? Well, she certainly interested me,' he said thoughtfully. 'She is an odd psychological study in her way. I wish I could come across her again.'

'Where did you come across her, and what is her name?'

'I don't know her name, I don't want to; she is not a personage to me, only a case. I hardly know her face even. I have never seen it except in the twilight. But I gathered that she lived somewhere in Chelsea, for she came out on to the Embankment with only a kind of lacy thing over her head; she can't live far off, I fancy.'

Esther became instantly attentive. 'Go on,' she said.

'It was three weeks ago,' said George Graham. 'I was coming along the Embankment about ten o'clock. I walked through that little grove, you know, just between Cheyne Walk and the river, and I heard in there someone sobbing very bitterly. I looked and saw a woman sitting on a seat, with her head in her hands, crying. I was most awfully sorry, of course, and I thought I could perhaps do something for her, get her a glass of water, or salts, or something. I took her for a woman of the people – it was quite dark, you know. So I asked her very politely if I could do anything for her, and then I noticed her hands – they were quite white and covered with diamonds.'

'You were sorry you spoke, I suppose,' said Esther.

'She raised her head and said – I believe she laughed – "Are you going to tell me to move on?"'

'She thought you were a policeman?'

'Probably – if she thought at all – but she was in a semi-dazed condition. I told her to wait till I came back, and dashed round the corner to the chemist's and bought a bottle of salts. She thanked

me, and made a little effort to rise and go away. She seemed very
weak. I told her I was a medical man, I started in and talked to
her.'

'And she to you?'

'Yes, quite straight. Don't you know that women always treat a
doctor as if he were one step removed from their father confessor
– not human – not in the same category as themselves? It is not
complimentary to one as a man, but one hears a good deal one
would not otherwise hear. She ended by telling me all about
herself – in a veiled way, of course. It soothed her – relieved her –
she seemed not to have had an outlet for years!'

'To a mere stranger!'

'To a doctor. And she did not know what she was saying half
the time. She was hysterical, of course. Heavens! what nonsense
she talked! She spoke of herself as a person somehow haunted,
cursed by some malign fate, a victim of some fearful spiritual
catastrophe, don't you know? I let her run on. She was convinced
of the reality of a sort of "doom" that she had fancied had
befallen her. It was quite pathetic. Then it got rather chilly – she
shivered – I suggested her going in. She shrank back; she said, "If
you only knew what a relief it is, how much less miserable I am
out here! I can breathe; I can live – it is my only glimpse of the
world that is alive – I live in a grave – oh, let me stay!" She seemed
positively afraid to go home.'

'Perhaps someone bullied her at home.'

'I suppose so, but then – she had no husband. He died, she told
me, years ago. She had adored him, she said—'

'Is she pretty?'

'Pretty! Well, I hardly noticed. Let me see! Oh, yes, I suppose
she was pretty – no, now I think of it, she would be too worn and
faded to be what you call pretty.'

Esther smiled.

'Well, we sat there together for quite an hour, then the clock of
Chelsea church struck eleven, and she got up and said
"Goodbye," holding her hand quite naturally, as if our meeting
and conversation had been nothing out of the common. There
was a sound like a dead leaf trailing across the walk and she was
gone.'

'Didn't you ask if you should see her again?'

'That would have been a mean advantage to take.'

'You might have offered to see her home.'

'I saw she did not mean me to.'

'She was a lady, you say,' pondered Esther. 'How was she dressed?'

'Oh, all right, like a lady – in black – mourning, I suppose. She has dark crinkly hair, and her eyebrows are very thin and arched – I noticed that in the dusk.'

'Does this photograph remind you of her?' asked Esther suddenly, taking him to the mantelpiece.

'Rather!'

'Alice! Oh, it couldn't be – she is not a widow, her husband is alive – has your friend any children?'

'Yes, one, she mentioned it.'

'How old?'

'Six years old, I think she said. She talks of the "responsibility of bringing up an orphan".'

'George, what time is it?' Esther asked suddenly.

'About nine o'clock.'

'Would you mind coming out with me?'

'I should like it. Where shall we go?'

'To St Adhelm's! It is close by here. There is a special late service tonight, and Mrs Arne is sure to be there.'

'Oh, Esther – curiosity!'

'No, not mere curiosity. Don't you see if it is my Mrs Arne who talked to you like this, it is very serious? I have thought her ill for a long time; but as ill as that—'

At St Adhelm's Church, Esther Graham pointed out a woman who was kneeling beside a pillar in an attitude of intense devotion and abandonment. She rose from her knees, and turned her rapt face up towards the pulpit whence the Reverend Ralph Bligh was holding his impassioned discourse. George Graham touched his cousin on the shoulder, and motioned to her to leave her place on the outermost rank of worshippers.

'That is the woman!' said he.

4

'Mem.: to go and see Mrs Arne.' The doctor came across this note in his blotting-pad one day six weeks later. His daughter was out of town. He had heard nothing of the Arnes since her departure. He had promised to go and see her. He was a little conscience-stricken. Yet another week elapsed before he found time to call upon the daughter of his old tutor.

At the corner of Tite Street he met Mrs Arne's husband, and stopped. A doctor's professional kindliness of manner is, or ought to be, independent of his personal likings and dislikings, and there was a pleasant cordiality about his greeting which should have provoked a corresponding fervour on the part of Edward Arne.

'How are you, Arne?' Graham said. 'I was on my way to call on your wife.'

'Ah – yes!' said Edward Arne, with the ascending inflection of polite acquiescence. A ray of blue from his eyes rested transitorily on the doctor's face, and in that short moment the latter noted its intolerable vacuity, and for the first time in his life he felt a sharp pang of sympathy for the wife of such a husband.

'I suppose you are off to your club? – er – good bye!' he wound up abruptly. With the best will in the world he somehow found it almost impossible to carry on a conversation with Edward Arne, who raised his hand to his hat-brim in token of salutation, smiled sweetly, and walked on.

'He really is extraordinarily good looking,' reflected the doctor, as he watched him down the street and safely over the crossing with a certain degree of solicitude for which he could not exactly account. 'And yet one feels one's vitality ebbing out at the finger-ends as one talks to him. I shall begin to believe in Esther's absurd fancies about him soon. Ah, there's the little girl!' he exclaimed, as he turned into Cheyne Walk and caught sight of her with her nurse, making violent demonstrations to attract his attention. 'She is alive, at any rate. How is your mother, Dolly?' he asked.

'Quite well, thank you,' was the child's reply. She added, 'She's crying. She sent me away because I looked at her. So I did. Her cheeks are quite red.'

'Run away – run away and play!' said the doctor nervously. He ascended the steps of the house, and rang the bell very gently and neatly.

'Not at—' began Foster, with the intonation of polite false-hood, but stopped on seeing the doctor, who, with his daughter, was a privileged person. 'Mrs Arne will see you, Sir.'

'Mrs Arne is not alone?' he said interrogatively.

'Yes, Sir, quite alone. I have just taken tea in.'

Dr Graham's doubts were prompted by the low murmur as of a voice, or voices, which came to him through the open door of the room at the head of the stairs. He paused and listened while Foster stood by, merely remarking, 'Mrs Arne do talk to herself sometimes, Sir.'

It was Mrs Arne's voice – the doctor recognised it now. It was not the voice of a sane or healthy woman. He at once mentally removed his visit from the category of a morning call, and prepared for a semi-professional inquiry.

'Don't announce me,' he said to Foster, and quietly entered the back drawing-room, which was separated by a heavy tapestry *portière* from the room where Mrs Arne sat, with an open book on the table before her, from which she had been apparently reading aloud. Her hands were now clasped tightly over her face, and when, presently, she removed them and began feverishly to turn page after page of her book, the crimson of her cheeks was seamed with white where her fingers had impressed themselves.

The doctor wondered if she saw him, for though her eyes were fixed in his direction, there was no apprehension in them. She went on reading, and it was the text, mingled with passionate interjection and fragmentary utterances, of the Burial Service that met his ears.

'"For as in Adam all die!" All die! It says all! For he must reign . . . The last enemy that shall be destroyed is Death. What shall they do if the dead rise not at all! . . . I die daily . . .! Daily! No, no, better get it over . . . dead and buried . . . out of sight, out of mind . . . under a stone. Dead men don't come back . . . Go on! Get it over. I want to hear the earth rattle on the coffin, and then I shall know it is done. "Flesh and blood cannot inherit!" Oh, what did I do? What have I done? Why did I wish it so fervently? Why did I pray for it so earnestly? God gave me my wish—'

'Alice! Alice!' groaned the doctor.

She looked up. '"When this corruptible shall have put on incorruption—" "Dust to dust, ashes to ashes, earth to earth—" Yes, that is it. "After death, though worms destroy this body—"'

She flung the book aside and sobbed.

'That is what I was afraid of. My God! My God! Down there – in the dark – for ever and ever and ever! I could not bear to think of it! My Edward! And so I interfered . . . and prayed . . . and prayed till . . . Oh! I am punished. Flesh and blood could not inherit! I kept him there – I would not let him go . . . I kept him . . . I prayed . . . I denied him Christian burial . . . Oh, how could I know . . .'

'Good heavens, Alice!' said Graham, coming sensibly forward. 'What does this mean? I have heard of schoolgirls going through the marriage service by themselves, but the burial service—'

He laid down his hat and went on severely, 'What have you to do with such things? Your child is flourishing – your husband alive and here—'

'And who kept him here?' interrupted Alice Arne fiercely, accepting the fact of his appearance without comment.

'You did,' he answered quickly, 'with your care and tenderness. I believe the warmth of your body, as you lay beside him for that half-hour, maintained the vital heat during that extraordinary suspension of the heart's action, which made us all give him up for dead. You were his best doctor, and brought him back to us.'

'Yes, it was I – it was I – you need not tell me it was I!'

'Come, be thankful!' he said cheerfully. 'Put that book away, and give me some tea, I'm very cold.'

'Oh, Dr Graham, how thoughtless of me!' said Mrs Arne, rallying at the slight imputation on her politeness he had purposely made. She tottered to the bell and rang it before he could anticipate her.

'Another cup,' she said quite calmly to Foster, who answered it. Then she sat down quivering all over with the suddenness of the constraint put upon her.

'Yes, sit down and tell me all about it,' said Dr Graham good-humouredly, at the same time observing her with the closeness he gave to difficult cases.

There is nothing to tell,' she said simply, shaking her head, and futilely altering the position of the teacups on the tray. 'It all happened years ago. Nothing can be done now. Will you have sugar?'

He drank his tea and made conversation. He talked to her of some Dante lectures he was attending; of some details connected with her child's kindergarten classes. These subjects did not interest her. There was a subject she wished to discuss, he could see that a question trembled on her tongue, and tried to lead up to it.

She introduced it herself, quite quietly, over a second cup. 'Sugar, Dr Graham? I forget. Dr Graham, tell me, do you believe that prayers – wicked unreasonable prayers – are granted?'

He helped himself to another slice of bread and butter before answering.

'Well,' he said slowly, 'it seems hard to believe that every fool who has a voice to pray with, and a brain where to conceive idiotic requests with, should be permitted to interfere with the economy of the universe. As a rule, if people were long-sighted enough to see the result of their petitions, I fancy very few of us would venture to interfere.'

Mrs Arne groaned.

She was a good Churchwoman, Graham knew, and he did not wish to sap her faith in any way, so he said no more, but inwardly wondered if a too rigid interpretation of some of the religious dogmas of the Vicar of St Adhelm's, her spiritual adviser, was not the clue to her distress. Then she put another question.

'Eh! What?' he said. 'Do I believe in ghosts? I will believe you if you will tell me you have seen one.'

'You know, Doctor,' she went on, 'I was always afraid of ghosts – of spirits – things unseen. I couldn't ever read about them. I could not bear the idea of some one in the room with me that I could not see. There was a text that always frightened me that hung up in my room: "Thou, God, seest me!" It frightened me when I was a child, whether I had been doing wrong or not. But now,' shuddering, 'I think there are worse things than ghosts.'

'Well, now, what sort of things?' he asked good-humouredly. 'Astral bodies—?'

She leaned forward and laid her hot hand on his.

'Oh, Doctor, tell me, if a spirit – without the body we know it by – is terrible, what of a body' – her voice sank to a whisper, 'a body – senseless – lonely – stranded on this earth – without a spirit?'

She was watching his face anxiously. He was divided between a morbid inclination to laugh and the feeling of intense discomfort provoked by this wretched scene. He longed to give the conversation a more cheerful turn, yet did not wish to offend her by changing it too abruptly.

'I have heard of people not being able to keep body and soul together,' he replied at last, 'but I am not aware that practically such a division of forces has ever been achieved. And if we could only accept the theory of the despiritualised body, what a number of antipathetic people now wandering about in the world it would account for!'

The piteous gaze of her eyes seemed to seek to ward off the blow of his misplaced jocularity. He left his seat and sat down on the couch beside her.

'Poor child! Poor girl! You are ill, you are over-excited. What is it? Tell me,' he asked her as tenderly as the father she had lost in early life might have done. Her head sank on his shoulder.

'Are you unhappy?' he asked her gently.

'Yes!'

'You are too much alone. Get your mother or your sister to come and stay with you.'

They won't come,' she wailed. They say the house is like a grave. Edward has made himself a study in the basement. It's an impossible room – but he has moved all his things in, and I can't – I won't go to him there . . .'

'You're wrong. For it's only a fad,' said Graham, 'he'll tire of it. And you must see more people somehow. It's a pity my daughter is away. Had you any visitors today?'

'Not a soul has crossed the threshold for eighteen days.'

'We must change all that,' said the doctor vaguely. 'Meantime you must cheer up. Why, you have no need to think of ghosts and graves – no need to be melancholy – you have your husband and your child—'

'I have my child – yes.'

The doctor took hold of Mrs Arne by the shoulder and held her a little away from him. He thought he had found the cause of her trouble – a more commonplace one than he had supposed.

'I have known you, Alice, since you were a child,' he said gravely. 'Answer me! You love your husband, don't you?'

'Yes.' It was as if she were answering futile prefatory questions in the witness-box. Yet he saw by the intense excitement in her eyes that he had come to the point she feared, and yet desired to bring forward.

'And he loves you?'

She was silent.

'Well, then, if you love each other, what more can you want? Why do you say you have only your child in that absurd way?'

She was still silent, and he gave her a little shake.

'Tell me, have you and he had any difference lately? Is there any – coldness – any – temporary estrangement between you?'

He was hardly prepared for the burst of foolish laughter that proceeded from the demure Mrs Arne as she rose and confronted him, all the blood in her body seeming for the moment to rush to her usually pale cheeks.

'Coldness! Temporary estrangement! If that were all! Oh, is

everyone blind but me? There is all the world between us! All the difference between this world and the next!'

She sat down again beside the doctor and whispered in his ear, and her words were like a breath of hot wind from some Gehenna of the soul.

'Oh, Doctor, I have borne it for six years, and I must speak. No other woman could bear what I have borne, and yet be alive! And I loved him so; you don't know how I loved him! That was it – that was my crime—'

'Crime?' repeated the doctor.

'Yes, crime! It was impious, don't you see? But I have been punished. Oh, Doctor, you don't know what my life is! Listen! Listen! I must tell you. To live with a— At first before I guessed when I used to put my arms round him, and he merely submitted – and then it dawned on me what I was kissing! It is enough to turn a living woman into stone – for I am living, though sometimes I forget it. Yes, I am a live woman, though I live in a grave. Think what it is! – to wonder every night if you will be alive in the morning, to lie down every night in an open grave – to smell death in every corner – every room – to breathe death – to touch it . . .'

The *portière* in front of the door shook, a hoopstick parted it, a round white-clad bundle supported on a pair of mottled red legs peeped in, pushing a hoop in front of her. The child made no noise. Mrs Arne seemed to have heard her, however. She slewed round violently as she sat on the sofa beside Dr Graham, leaving her hot hands clasped in his.

'You ask Dolly,' she exclaimed. 'She knows it, too – she feels it.'

'No, no, Alice, this won't do!' the doctor adjured her very low. Then he raised his voice and ordered the child from the room. He had managed to lift Mrs Arne's feet and laid her full length on the sofa by the time the maid reappeared. She had fainted.

He pulled down her eyelids and satisfied himself as to certain facts he had up till now dimly apprehended. When Mrs Arne's maid returned, he gave her mistress over to her care and proceeded to Edward Arne's new study in the basement.

'Morphia!' he muttered to himself, as he stumbled and faltered through gaslit passages, where furtive servants eyed him and scuttled to their burrows.

'What is he burying himself down here for?' he thought. 'Is it to get out of her way? They *are* a nervous pair of them!'

*

Arne was sunk in a large armchair drawn up before the fire. There was no other light, except a faint reflection from the gas-lamp in the road, striking down past the iron bars of the window that was sunk below the level of the street. The room was comfortless and empty, there was little furniture in it except a large bookcase at Arne's right hand and a table with a Tantalus on it standing some way off. There was a faded portrait in pastel of Alice Arne over the mantelpiece, and beside it, a poor pendant, a pen and ink sketch of the master of the house. They were quite discrepant, in size and medium, but they appeared to look at each other with the stolid attentiveness of newly married people.

'Seedy, Arne?' Graham said.

'Rather, today. Poke the fire for me, will you?'

'I've known you quite seven years,' said the doctor cheerfully, 'so I presume I can do that . . . There, now! . . . And I'll presume further—What have we got here?'

He took a small bottle smartly out of Edward Arne's fingers and raised his eyebrows. Edward Arne had rendered it up agreeably; he did not seem upset or annoyed.

'Morphia. It isn't a habit. I only got hold of the stuff yesterday – found it about the house. Alice was very jumpy all day, and communicated her nerves to me, I suppose. I've none as a rule, but do you know, Graham, I seem to be getting them – feel things a good deal more than I did, and want to talk about them.'

'What, are you growing soul?' said the doctor carelessly, lighting a cigarette.

'Heaven forbid!' Arne answered equably. 'I've done very well without it all these years. But I'm fond of old Alice, you know, in my own way. When I was a young man, I was quite different. I took things hardly and got excited about them. Yes, excited. I was wild about Alice, wild! Yes, by Jove! though she has forgotten all about it.'

'Not that, but still it's natural she should long for some little demonstration of affection now and then . . . and she'd be awfully distressed if she saw you fooling with a bottle of morphia! You know, Arne, after that narrow squeak you had of it six years ago, Alice and I have a good right to consider that your life belongs to us!'

Edward Arne settled in his chair and replied, rather fretfully, 'All very well, but you didn't manage to do the job thoroughly. You didn't turn me out lively enough to please Alice. She's annoyed because when I take her in my arms, I don't hold her tight enough. I'm too quiet, too languid! . . . Hang it all, Graham, I believe she'd like me to stand for Parliament! . . . Why can't she let me just go along my own way? Surely a man who's come through an illness like mine can be let off parlour tricks? All this worry – it culminated the other day when I said I wanted to colonise a room down here, and did, with a spurt that took it out of me horribly, – all this worry, I say, seeing her upset and so on, keeps me low, and so I feel as if I wanted to take drugs to soothe me.'

'Soothe!' said Graham. 'This stuff is more than soothing if you take enough of it. I'll send you something more like what you want, and I'll take this away, by your leave.'

'I really can't argue!' replied Arne . . . 'If you see Alice, tell her you find me fairly comfortable and don't put her off this room. I really like it best. She can come and see me here, I keep a good fire, tell her . . . I feel as if I wanted to sleep . . .' he added brusquely.

'You have been indulging already,' said Graham softly. Arne had begun to doze off. His cushion had sagged down, the doctor stooped to rearrange it, carelessly laying the little phial for the moment in a crease of the rug covering the man's knees.

Mrs Arne in her mourning dress was crossing the hall as he came to the top of the basement steps and pushed open the swing door. She was giving some orders to Foster, the butler, who disappeared as the doctor advanced.

'You're about again,' he said, 'good girl!'

'Too silly of me,' she said, 'to be hysterical! After all these years! One should be able to keep one's own counsel. But it is over now, I promise I will never speak of it again.'

'We frightened poor Dolly dreadfully. I had to order her out like a regiment of soldiers.'

'Yes, I know. I'm going to her now.'

On his suggestion that she should look in on her husband first she looked askance.

'Down there!'

'Yes, that's his fancy. Let him be. He is a good deal depressed about himself and you. He notices a great deal more than you think. He isn't quite as apathetic as you describe him to be . . . Come here!' He led her into the unlit dining-room a little way.

'You expect too much, my dear. You do really! You make too many demands on the vitality you saved.'

'What did one save him for?' she asked fiercely. She continued more quietly, 'I know. I am going to be different.'

'Not you,' said Graham fondly. He was very partial to Alice Arne in spite of her silliness. 'You'll worry about Edward till the end of the chapter. I know you. And' – he turned her round by the shoulder so that she fronted the light in the hall – 'you elusive thing, let me have a good look at you . . . Hum! Your eyes, they're a bit starey . . .'

He let her go again with a sigh of impotence. Something must be done . . . soon . . . he must think . . . He got hold of his coat and began to get into it . . .

Mrs Arne smiled, buttoned a button for him and then opened the front door, like a good hostess, a very little way. With a quick flirt of his hat he was gone, and she heard the clap of his brougham door and the order 'Home'.

'Been saying goodbye to that thief Graham?' said her husband gently, when she entered his room, her pale eyes staring a little, her thin hand busy at the front of her dress . . .

'Thief? Why? One moment! Where's your switch?'

She found it and turned on a blaze of light from which her husband seemed to shrink.

'Well, he carried off my drops. Afraid of my poisoning myself, I suppose?'

'Or acquiring the morphia habit,' said his wife in a dull level voice, 'as I have.'

She paused. He made no comment. Then, picking up the little phial Dr Graham had left in the crease of the rug, she spoke. 'You are the thief, Edward, as it happens, this is mine.'

'Is it? I found it knocking about: I didn't know it was yours. Well, will you give me some?'

'I will, if you like.'

Well, dear, decide. You know I am in your hands and Graham's. He was rubbing that into me today.'

'Poor lamb!' she said derisively. 'I'd not allow my doctor, or my wife either, to dictate to me whether I should put an end to myself, or not.'

'Ah, but you've got a spirit, you see!' Arne yawned. 'However, let me have a go at the stuff and then you put it on top of the wardrobe or a shelf, where I shall know it is, but never reach out to get it, I promise you.'

'No, you wouldn't reach out a hand to keep yourself alive, let alone kill yourself,' said she. 'That is you all over, Edward.'

'And don't you see that is why I did die,' he said, with earnestness unexpected by her. 'And then, unfortunately, you and Graham bustled up and wouldn't let Nature take its course . . . I rather wish you hadn't been so officious.'

'And let you stay dead,' said she carelessly. 'But at the time I cared for you so much that I should have had to kill myself, or commit suttee like a Bengali widow. Ah, well!'

She reached out for a glass half-full of water that stood on the low ledge of a bookcase close by the arm of his chair . . . 'Will this glass do? What's in it? Only water? How much morphia shall I give you? An overdose?'

'I don't care if you do, and that's a fact.'

'It was a joke, Edward,' she said piteously.

'No joke to me. This fag end of life I've clawed hold of doesn't interest me. And I'm bound to be interested in what I'm doing or I'm no good. I'm no earthly good now. I don't enjoy life, I've nothing to enjoy it with – in here –' he struck his breast. 'It's like a dull party one goes to by accident. All want to do is to get into a cab and go home.'

His wife stood over him with the half-full glass in one hand and the little bottle in the other. Her eyes dilated . . . her chest heaved . . .

'Edward!' she breathed. 'Was it all so useless?'

'Was what useless? Yes, as I was telling you, I go as one in a dream – a bad, bad dream, like the dreams I used to have when I overworked at college. I was brilliant, Alice, brilliant, do you hear? At some cost, I expect! Now I hate people – my fellow creatures. I've left them. They come and go, jostling me, and pushing me, on the pavements as I go along, avoiding them. Do you know where they should be, really, in relation to me?'

He rose a little in his seat – she stepped nervously aside, made as if to put down the bottle and the glass she was holding, then thought better of it and continued to extend them mechanically.

'They should be over my head. I've already left them and their petty nonsense of living. They mean nothing to me, no more than if they were ghosts walking. Or perhaps, it's I who am a ghost to them? . . . You don't understand it. It's because I suppose you have no imagination. You just know what you want and do your best to get it. You blurt out your blessed petition to your Deity and the idea that you're irrelevant never enters your head, soft, persistent, High Church thing that you are! . . .'

Alice Arne smiled, and balanced the objects she was holding. He motioned her to pour out the liquid from one to the other, but she took no heed; she was listening with all her ears. It was the nearest approach to the language of compliment, to anything in the way of loverlike personalities that she had heard fall from his lips since his illness. He went on, becoming as it were lukewarm to his subject—

'But the worst of it is that once break the cord that links you to humanity – it can't be mended. Man doesn't live by bread alone . . . or lives to disappoint you. What am I to you, without my own poor personality? . . . Don't stare so, Alice! I haven't talked so much or so intimately for ages, have I? Let me try and have it out . . . Are you in any sort of hurry?'

'No, Edward.'

'Pour that stuff out and have done . . . Well, Alice, it's a queer feeling, I tell you. One goes about with one's looks on the ground, like a man who eyes the bed he is going to lie down in, and longs for. Alice, the crust of the earth seems a barrier between me and my own place. I want to scratch the boardings with my nails and shriek something like this: "Let me get down to you all, there where I belong!" It's a horrible sensation, like a vampire reversed! . . .'

'Is that why you insisted on having this room in the basement?' she asked breathlessly.

'Yes, I can't bear being upstairs, somehow. Here, with these barred windows and stone-cold floors . . . I can see the people's feet walking above there in the street . . . one has some sort of illusion . . .'

'Oh!' She shivered and her eyes travelled like those of a caged creature round the bare room and fluttered when they rested on the sombre windows imperiously barred. She dropped her gaze to the stone flags that showed beyond the oasis of Turkey carpet on which Arne's chair stood . . . Then to the door, the door that she had closed on entering. It had heavy bolts, but they were not drawn against her, though by the look of her eyes it seemed she half imagined they were . . .

She made a step forward and moved her hands slightly. She

looked down on them and what they held . . . then changed the relative positions of the two objects and held the bottle over the glass . . .

'Yes, come along!' her husband said. 'Are you going to be all day giving it me?'

With a jerk, she poured the liquid out into a glass and handed it to him. She looked away – towards the door . . .

'Ah, your way of escape!' said he, following her eyes. Then he drank, painstakingly.

The empty bottle fell out of her hands. She wrung them, murmuring – 'Oh, if I had only known!'

'Known what? That I should go near to cursing you for bringing me back?'

He fixed his cold eyes on her, as the liquid passed slowly over his tongue . . .

'– Or that you would end by taking back the gift you gave?'

(1895)

ELLA D'ARCY

The Pleasure-Pilgrim

I

Campbell was on his way to Schloss Altenau, for a second quiet
season with his work. He had spent three profitable months there a
year ago, and he was hoping now for a repetition of that good
fortune. His thoughts outran the train; and long before his arrival
at the Hamelin railway station, he was enjoying his welcome by the
Ritterhausens, was revelling in the ease and comfort of the old
castle, and was contrasting the pleasures of his homecoming – for
he looked upon Schloss Altenau as a sort of temporary home – with
his recent cheerless experiences of lodging-houses in London,
hotels in Berlin, and strange indifferent faces everywhere. He
thought with especial satisfaction of the Maynes, and of the good
talks Mayne and he would have together, late at night, before the
great fire in the hall, after the rest of the household had gone to bed.
He blessed the adverse circumstances which had turned Schloss
Altenau into a boarding-house, and had reduced the Freiherr
Ritterhausen to eke out his shrunken revenues by the reception, as
paying guests, of English and American pleasure-pilgrims.

He rubbed the blurred window-pane with the fringed end of the
strap hanging from it, and, in the snow-covered landscape reeling
towards him, began to recognise objects that were familiar.
Hamelin could not be far off . . . In another ten minutes the train
came to a standstill.

He stepped down with a sense of relief from the overheated
atmosphere of his compartment into the cold bright February
afternoon, and saw through the open station doors one of the
Ritterhausen carriages awaiting him, with Gottlieb in his second-
best livery on the box. Gottlieb showed every reasonable consideration for the Baron's boarders, but had various methods of
marking his sense of the immense abyss separating them from the
family. The use of his second-best livery was one of these methods.

Nevertheless, he turned a friendly German eye up to Campbell, and in response to his cordial '*Guten Tag, Gottlieb. Wie geht's? Und die Herrschaften?*' expressed his pleasure at seeing the young man back again.

While Campbell stood at the top of the steps that led down to the carriage and the Platz, looking after the collection of his luggage and its bestowal by Gottlieb's side, he became aware of two persons, ladies, advancing towards him from the direction of the Wartsaal. It was surprising to see any one at any time in Hamelin station. It was still more surprising when one of these ladies addressed him by name.

'You are Mr Campbell, are you not?' she said. 'We have been waiting for you to go back in the carriage together. When we found this morning that there was only half an hour between your train and ours, I told the Baroness it would be perfectly absurd to send to the station twice. I hope you won't mind our company?'

The first impression Campbell received was of the magnificent apparel of the lady before him; it would have been noticeable in Paris or Vienna – it was extravagant here. Next, he perceived that the face beneath the upstanding feathers and the curving hat-brim was that of so very young a girl as to make the furs and velvets seem more incongruous still. But the sense of incongruity vanished with the intonation of her first phrase, which told him she was an American. He had no standards for American conduct. It was clear that the speaker and her companion were inmates of the Schloss.

He bowed, and murmured the pleasure he did not feel. A true Briton, he was intolerably shy; and his heart sank at the prospect of a three-mile drive with two strangers who evidently had the advantage of knowing all about him, while he was in ignorance of their very names. As he took his place opposite to them in the carriage, he unconsciously assumed a cold, blank stare, pulling nervously at his moustache, as was his habit in moments of discomposure. Had his companions been British also, the ordeal of the drive must have been a terrible one; but these young American ladies showed no sense of embarrassment whatever.

'We've just come back from Hanover,' said the girl who had already spoken to him. 'I go over once a week for a singing lesson, and my little sister comes along to take care of me.'

She turned a narrow, smiling glance from Campbell to her little sister, and then back to Campbell again. She had red hair, freckles on her nose, and the most singular eyes he had ever seen; slit-like eyes, set obliquely in her head, Chinese fashion.

'Yes, Lulie requires a great deal of taking care of,' assented the little sister sedately, though the way in which she said this seemed to imply something less simple than the words themselves. The speaker bore no resemblance to Lulie. She was smaller, thinner, paler. Her features were straight, a trifle peaked; her skin sallow; her hair of a nondescript brown. She was much less gorgeously dressed. There was even a suggestion of shabbiness in her attire, though sundry isolated details of it were handsome too. She was also much less young; or so, at any rate, Campbell began by pronouncing her. Yet presently he wavered. She had a face that defied you to fix her age. Campbell never fixed it to his own satisfaction, but veered in the course of that drive (as he was destined to do during the next few weeks) from point to point up and down the scale from eighteen to thirty-five. She wore a spotted veil, and beneath it a pince-nez, the lenses of which did something to temper the immense amount of humorous meaning which lurked in her gaze. When her pale prominent eyes met Campbell's, it seemed to the young man that they were full of eagerness to add something at his expense to the stores of information they had already garnered up. They chilled him with misgivings; there was more comfort to be found in her sister's shifting, red-brown glances.

'Hanover is a long way to go for lessons,' he observed, forcing himself to be conversational. 'I used to go there myself about once a week, when I first came to Schloss Altenau, for tobacco, or note-paper, or to get my hair cut. But later on I did without, or contented myself with what Hamelin, or even the village, could offer me.'

'Nannie and I,' said the young girl, 'meant to stay only a week at Altenau, on our way to Hanover, where we were going to pass the winter; but the castle is just too lovely for anything.' She raised her eyelids the least little bit as she looked at him, and such a warm and friendly gaze shot out, that Campbell was suddenly thrilled. Was she pretty, after all? He glanced at Nannie; she, at least, was indubitably plain. 'It's the very first time we've ever stayed in a castle,' Lulie went on; 'and we're going to remain right along now, until we go home in the spring. Just imagine living in a house with a real moat, and a drawbridge, and a Rittersaal, and suits of armour that have been actually worn in battle! And oh, that delightful iron collar and chain! You remember it, Mr Campbell? It hangs right close to the gateway on the courtyard side. And you know, in old days the Ritterhausens used it for the punishment of their serfs. There are horrible stories connected with it. Mr Mayne can tell you them. But just think of being chained up there like a dog! So wonderfully picturesque.'

'For the spectator perhaps,' said Campbell, smiling. 'I doubt if the victim appreciated the picturesque aspect of the case.'

With this Lulie disagreed. 'Oh, I think he must have been interested,' she said. 'It must have made him feel so absolutely part and parcel of the Middle Ages. I persuaded Mr Mayne to fix the collar round my neck the other day; and though it was very uncomfortable, and I had to stand on tiptoe, it seemed to me that all at once the courtyard was filled with knights in armour, and crusaders, and palmers, and things; and there were flags flying and trumpets sounding; and all the dead and gone Ritterhausens had come down from their picture frames, and were walking about in brocaded gowns and lace ruffles.'

'It seemed to require a good deal of persuasion to get Mr Mayne to unfix the collar again,' said the little sister. 'How at last did you manage it?'

But Lulie replied irrelevantly, 'And the Ritterhausens are such perfectly lovely people, aren't they, Mr Campbell? The old Baron is a perfect dear. He has such a grand manner. When he kisses my hand I feel nothing less than a princess. And the Baroness is such a funny, busy, delicious little round ball of a thing. And she's always playing bagatelle, isn't she? Or else cutting up skeins of wool for carpet-making.' She meditated a moment. 'Some people always *are* cutting things up in order to join them together again,' she announced, in her fresh drawling young voice.

'And some people cut things up, and leave other people to do the reparation,' commented the little sister, enigmatically.

And meantime the carriage had been rattling over the cobble-paved streets of the quaint medieval town, where the houses stand so near together that you may shake hands with your opposite neighbour; where allegorical figures, strange birds and beasts, are carved and painted over the windows and doors; and where to every distant sound you lean your ear to catch the fairy music of the Pied Piper, and at every street corner you look to see his tatterdemalion form* with the frolicking children at his heels.

Then the Weser bridge was crossed, beneath which the ice-floes jostled and ground themselves together, as they forced their way down the river; and the carriage was rolling smoothly along country roads, between vacant snow-decked fields.

Campbell's embarrassment began to wear off. Now that he was getting accustomed to the girls, he found neither of them awe-inspiring. The red-haired one had a simple childlike manner that was charming. Her strange little face, with its piquant irregularity of line, its warmth of colour, began to please him. What though her hair was red, the uncurled wisp which strayed across her white forehead was soft and alluring; he could see soft masses of it tucked up beneath her hat-brim as she turned her head. When she suddenly lifted her red-brown lashes, those queer eyes of hers had a velvety softness too. Decidedly, she struck him as being pretty – in a peculiar way. He felt an immense accession of interest in her. It seemed to him that he was the discoverer of her possibilities. He did not doubt that the rest of the world called her plain, or at least odd-looking. He, at first, had only seen the freckles on her nose, her oblique-set eyes. He wondered now what she thought of herself, how she appeared to Nannie. Probably as a very ordinary little girl; sisters stand too close to see each other's qualities. She was too young to have had much opportunity of hearing flattering truths from strangers; and, besides, the average stranger would see nothing in her to call for flattering truths. Her charm was something subtle, out of the common, in defiance of all known rules of beauty. Campbell saw superiority in himself for recognising it, for formulating it; and he was not displeased to be aware that it would always remain caviare to the multitude.

The carriage had driven through the squalid village of Dürrendorf, had passed the great Ritterhausen barns and farm buildings, on the tie-beams of which are carved Bible texts in old German; had turned in at the wide-open gates of Schloss Altenau, where Gottlieb always whipped up his horses to a fast trot. Full of feeling both for the pocket and the dignity of the Ritterhausens, he would not use up his beasts in unnecessary fast driving. But it was to the credit of the family that he should reach the Castle in fine style. And so he thundered across the drawbridge, and through the great archway pierced in the north wing, and over the stones of the cobbled courtyard, to pull up before the door of the hall, with much clattering of hoofs and a final elaborate whip-flourish.

2

'I'm jolly glad to have you back,' Mayne said, that same evening, when, the rest of the boarders having retired to their rooms, he and Campbell were lingering over the hall fire for a talk and smoke. 'I've missed you awfully, old chap, and the good times we used to have here. I've often meant to write to you, but you know how one shoves off letter-writing day after day, till at last one is too ashamed of one's indolence to write at all. But tell me – you had a pleasant drive from Hamelin? What do you think of our young ladies?'

'Those American girls? But they're charming,' said Campbell, with enthusiasm. 'The red-haired one is particularly charming.'

At this Mayne laughed so strangely that Campbell questioned him in surprise. 'Isn't she charming?'

'My dear chap,' Mayne told him, 'the red-haired one, as you call her, is the most remarkably charming young person I've ever met or read of. We've had a good many American girls here before now – you remember the good old Choate family, of course – they were here in your time, I think? – but we've never had anything like this Miss Lulie Thayer. She is something altogether unique.'

Campbell was struck with the name. 'Lulie – Lulie Thayer,' he repeated. 'How pretty it is!' And, full of his great discovery, he felt he must confide it to Mayne, at least. 'Do you know,' he went on, '*she* is really very pretty too? I didn't think so at first, but after a bit I discovered that she is positively quite pretty – in an odd sort of way.'

Mayne laughed again. 'Pretty, pretty!' he echoed in derision. 'Why, *lieber Gott im Himmel*, where are your eyes? Pretty! The girl is beautiful, gorgeously beautiful; every trait, every tint, is in complete, in absolute harmony with the whole. But the truth is, of course, we've all grown accustomed to the obvious, the common-place; to violent contrasts; blue eyes, black eyebrows, yellow hair; the things that shout for recognition. You speak of Miss Thayer's hair as red. What other colour would you have, with that warm, creamy skin? And then, what a red it is! It looks as though it had been steeped in red wine.'

'Ah, what a good description!' said Campbell, appreciatively. 'That's just it – steeped in red wine.'

'Though it's not so much her beauty,' Mayne continued. 'After all, one has met beautiful women before now. It's her wonderful generosity, her complaisance. She doesn't keep her good things to herself. She doesn't condemn you to admire from a distance.'

'How do you mean?' Campbell asked, surprised again.

'Why, she's the most egregious little flirt I've ever met. And yet, she's not exactly a flirt, either. I mean she doesn't flirt in the ordinary way. She doesn't talk much, or laugh, or apparently make the least claims on masculine attention. And so all the women like her. I don't believe there's one, except my wife, who has an inkling as to her true character. The Baroness, as you know, never observes anything. *Seigneur Dieu!* if she knew the things I could tell her about Miss Lulie! For I've had opportunities of studying her. You see, I'm a married man, and not in my first youth, and the looker-on generally gets the best view of the game. But you, who are young and charming and already famous – we've had your book here, by the by, and there's good stuff in it – you're going to have no end of pleasant experiences. I can see she means to add you to her ninety-and-nine other spoils; I saw it from the way she looked at you at dinner. She always begins with those velvety red-brown glances. She began that way with March and Prendergast and Willie Anson, and all the men we've had here since her arrival. The next thing she'll do will be to press your hand under the tablecloth.'

'Oh, come, Mayne, you're joking,' cried Campbell, a little brusquely. He thought such jokes in bad taste. He had a high ideal of Woman, an immense respect for her; he could not endure to hear her belittled, even in jest. 'Miss Thayer is refined and charming. No girl of her class would do such things.'

'But what is her class? Who knows anything about her? All we know is that she and her uncanny little friend – her little sister, as she calls her, though they're no more sisters than you and I are – they're not even related – all we know is, that she and Miss Dodge (that's the little sister's name) arrived here one memorable day last October from the Kronprinz Hotel at Waldeck-Pyrmont. By the by, it was the Choates, I believe, who told her of the castle – hotel acquaintances – you know how travelling Americans always cotton to each other. And we've picked up a few little auto- and biographical notes from her and Miss Dodge since. *Zum Beispiel*, she's got a rich father somewhere away back in Michigan, who supplies her with all the money she wants. And she's been travelling about since last May: Paris, Vienna, the Rhine,

Düsseldorf, and so on here. She must have had some rich experiences, by Jove, for she's done everything. Cycled in Paris: you should see her in her cycling costume, she wears it when the Baron takes her out shooting – she's an admirable shot by the way, an accomplishment learned, I suppose, from some American cowboy; then in Berlin she did a month's hospital nursing; and now she's studying the higher branches of the Terpsichorean art.* You know she was in Hanover today. Did she tell you what she went for?'

'To take a singing lesson,' said Campbell, remembering the reason she had given.

'A singing lesson! Do you sing with your legs? A dancing lesson, *mein lieber*. A dancing lesson from the ballet-master of the Hof Theatre. She could deposit a kiss on your forehead with her foot, I don't doubt. I must ask her if she can do the *grand écart* yet.' And when Campbell, in astonishment, wondered why on earth she should wish to learn such things, 'Oh, to extend her opportunities,' Mayne explained, 'and to acquire fresh sensations. She's an adventuress. Yes, an adventuress, but an end-of-the-century one. She doesn't travel for profit, but for pleasure. She has no desire to swindle her neighbour, but to amuse herself. And she's clever; she's read a good deal; she knows how to apply her reading to practical life. Thus, she's learned from Herrick not to be coy; and from Shakespeare that sweet-and-twenty is the time for kissing and being kissed. She honours her masters in the observance. She was not in the least abashed when, one day, I suddenly came upon her teaching that damned idiot, young Anson, two new ways of kissing.'

Campbell's impressions of the girl were readjusting themselves completely, but for the moment he was unconscious of the change. He only knew that he was partly angry, partly incredulous, and inclined to believe that Mayne was chaffing him.

'But Miss Dodge,' he objected, 'the little sister, she is older; old enough to look after her friend. Surely she could not allow a young girl placed in her charge to behave in such a way—'

'Oh, that little Dodge girl,' said Mayne contemptuously. 'Miss Thayer pays the whole shot, I understand, and Miss Dodge plays gooseberry, sheepdog, jackal, what you will. She finds her reward in the other's cast-off finery. The silk blouse she was wearing tonight, I've good reason for remembering, belonged to Miss Lulie. For, during a brief season, I must tell you, my young lady had the caprice to show attentions to your humble servant. I suppose my being a married man lent me a factitious fascination. But I didn't see it. That kind of girl doesn't appeal to me. So she employed Miss Dodge to do a little active canvassing. It was really too funny; I was coming in one day after a walk in the woods; my wife was trimming bonnets, or had neuralgia, or something. Anyhow, I was alone, and Miss Dodge contrived to waylay me in the middle of the courtyard. "Don't you find it vurry dull walking all by yourself?" she asked me; and then, blinking up in her strange little short-sighted way – she's really the weirdest little creature – "Why don't you make love to Lulie?" she said; "you'd find her vurry charming." It took me a minute or two to recover presence of mind enough to ask her whether Miss Thayer had commissioned her to tell me so. She looked at me with that cryptic smile of hers. "She'd like you to do so, I'm sure," she finally remarked, and pirouetted away. Though it didn't come off, owing to my bashfulness, it was then that Miss Dodge appropriated the silk "waist"; and Providence, taking pity on Miss Thayer's forced inactivity, sent along March, a young fellow reading for the army, with whom she had great doings. She fooled him to the top of his bent; sat on his knee; gave him a lock of her hair, which, having no scissors handy, she burned off with a cigarette taken from his mouth; and got him to offer her marriage. Then she turned round and laughed in his face, and took up with a Dr Weber, a cousin of the Baron's, under the other man's very eyes. You never saw anything like the unblushing coolness with which she would permit March to catch her in Weber's arms.'

'Come,' Campbell protested again, 'aren't you drawing it rather strong?'

'On the contrary, I'm drawing it mild, as you'll discover presently for yourself; and then you'll thank me for forewarning you. For she makes love – desperate love, mind you – to every man she meets. And goodness knows how many she hasn't met in the course of her career, which began presumably at the age of ten, in some "Amur'can" hotel or watering-place. Look at this.' Mayne fetched an alpenstock from a corner of the hall; it was decorated with a long succession of names, which, ribbon-like, were twisted round and round it, carved in the wood. 'Read them,' insisted Mayne, putting the stick in Campbell's hands. 'You'll see they're not the names of the peaks she has climbed, or the towns she has passed through; they're the names of the men she has fooled. And there's room for more; there's still a good deal of space, as you see. There's room for yours.'

Campbell glanced down the alpenstock – reading here a name, there an initial, or just a date – and jerked it impatiently from him on to a couch. He wished with all his heart that Mayne would stop, would talk of something else, would let him get away. The young girl had interested him so much; he had felt himself so drawn towards her; he had thought her so fresh, so innocent. But Mayne, on the contrary, was warming to his subject, was enchanted to have someone to listen to his stories, to discuss his theories, to share his cynical amusement.

'I don't think, mind you,' he said, 'that she is a bit interested herself in the men she flirts with. I don't think she gets any of the usual sensations from it, you know. My theory is, she does it for mere devilry, for a laugh. Or, and this is another theory, she is actuated by some idea of retribution. Perhaps some woman she was fond of – her mother even – who knows? – was badly treated at the hands of a man. Perhaps this girl has constituted herself the Nemesis for her sex, and goes about seeing how many masculine hearts she can break, by way of revenge. Or can it be that she is simply the newest development of the New Woman – she who in England preaches and bores you, and in America practises and pleases? Yes, I believe she's the American edition, and so new that she hasn't yet found her way into fiction. She's the pioneer of the army coming out of the West, that's going to destroy the existing scheme of things and rebuild it nearer to the heart's desire.'

'Oh, damn it all, Mayne,' cried Campbell, rising abruptly, 'why not say at once that she's a wanton, and have done with it? Who wants to hear your rotten theories?' And he lighted his candle without another word, and went off to bed.

3

It was four o'clock, and the Baron's boarders were drinking their afternoon coffee, drawn up in a semicircle round the hall fire. All but Campbell, who had carried his cup away to a side-table, and, with a book open beside him, appeared to be reading assiduously. In reality he could not follow a line of what he read; he could not keep his thoughts from Miss Thayer. What Mayne had told him was germinating in his mind. Knowing his friend as he did, he

could not on reflection doubt his word. In spite of much superficial cynicism, Mayne was incapable of speaking lightly of any
young girl without good cause. It now seemed to Campbell that,
instead of exaggerating the case, Mayne had probably under-
stated it. He asked himself with horror, what had this girl not
already known, seen, permitted? When now and again his eyes
travelled over perforce to where she sat, her red head leaning
against Miss Dodge's knee, and seeming to attract to, and concen-
trate upon itself all the glow of the fire, his forehead set itself in
frowns, and he returned to his book with an increased sense of
irritation.

'I'm just sizzling up, Nannie,' Miss Thayer presently complained, in her child-like, drawling little way. 'This fire is too hot
for anything.' She rose and shook straight her loose tea-gown, a
marvellous plush and lace garment created in Paris, which would
have accused a duchess of wilful extravagance. She stood smiling
round a moment, pulling on and off with her right hand a big
diamond ring which decorated the left. At the sound of her voice
Campbell had looked up, and his cold, unfriendly eyes encountered hers. He glanced rapidly past her, then back to his book. But
she, undeterred, with a charming sinuous movement and a frou-
frou of trailing silks, crossed over towards him. She slipped into
an empty chair next his.

'I'm going to do you the honour of sitting beside you, Mr
Campbell,' she said sweetly.

'It's an honour I've done nothing whatever to merit,' he
answered, without looking at her, and turned a page.

'The right retort,' she approved, 'but you might have said it a
little more cordially.'

'I don't feel cordial.'

'But why not? What has happened? Yesterday you were so
nice.'

'Ah, a good deal of water has run under the bridge since
yesterday.'

'But still the river remains as full,' she told him smiling, 'and
still the sky is as blue. The thermometer has even risen six
degrees.'

'What did you go into Hanover for yesterday?' Campbell
suddenly asked her.

She flashed him a comprehending glance from half-shut eyes. 'I
think men gossip a great deal more than women,' she observed,

'and they don't understand things either. They try to make all life suit their own preconceived theories. And why, after all, should I not wish to learn dancing thoroughly? There's no harm in that.'

'Only, why call it singing?' Campbell inquired.

Miss Thayer smiled. 'Truth is so uninteresting!' she said, and paused. 'Except in books. One likes it there. And I wanted to tell you, I think your books perfectly lovely. I know them, most all. I've read them away home. They're very much thought of in America. Only last night I was saying to Nannie how glad I am to have met you, for I think we're going to be great friends, aren't we, Mr Campbell? At least, I hope so, for you can do me so much good, if you will. Your books always make me feel real good; but you yourself can help me much more.'

She looked up at him with one of her warm, narrow red-brown glances, which yesterday would have thrilled his blood, and today merely stirred it to anger.

'You overestimate my abilities,' he said coldly; 'and, on the whole, I fear you will find writers a very disappointing race. You see, they put their best into their books. So not to disillusion you too rapidly' – he rose – 'will you excuse me? I have some work to do.' And he left her sitting there alone.

But he did no work when he got to his room. Whether Lulie Thayer was actually present or not, it seemed that her influence was equally disturbing to him. His mind was full of her: of her singular eyes, her quaint intonation, her sweet, seductive praise. Twenty-four hours ago such praise would have been delightful to him: what young author is proof against appreciation of his books? Now Campbell simply told himself that she laid the butter on too thick; that it was in some analogous manner she had flattered up March, Anson, and all the rest of the men that Mayne had spoken of. He supposed it was the first step in the process by which he was to be fooled, twisted round her finger, added to the list of victims who strewed her conquering path. He had a special fear of being fooled. For beneath a somewhat supercilious exterior, the dominant note of his character was timidity, distrust of his own merits; and he knew he was single-minded – one-idea'd almost – if he were to let himself go, to get to care very much for a woman, for such a girl as this girl, for instance, he would lose himself completely, be at her mercy absolutely. Fortunately, Mayne had let him know her character. He could feel nothing but dislike for her – disgust, even. And yet he was conscious how

pleasant it would be to believe in her innocence, in her candour.
For she was so adorably pretty; her flower-like beauty grew upon
him; her head, drooping a little on one side when she looked up,
was so like a flower bent by its own weight. The texture of her
cheeks, her lips, was delicious as the petals of a flower. He found
he could recall with perfect accuracy every detail of her appearance: the manner in which the red hair grew round her temples;
the way in which it was loosely and gracefully fastened up behind
with just a single tortoise-shell pin. He recollected the suspicion of
a dimple that shadowed itself in her cheek when she spoke, and
deepened into a delicious reality every time she smiled. He remembered her throat; her hands, of a beautiful whiteness, with
pink palms and pointed fingers. It was impossible to write. He
speculated long on the ring she wore on her engaged finger. He
mentioned this ring to Mayne the next time he saw him.

'Engaged? Very much so, I should say. Has got a *fiancé* in every
capital of Europe probably. But the ring-man is the *fiancé en titre*.
He writes to her by every mail, and is tremendously in love with
her. She shows me his letters. When she's had her fling, I suppose,
she'll go back and marry him. That's what these little American
girls do, I'm told: sow their wild oats here with us, and settle
down into *bonnes ménagères* over yonder. Meanwhile, are you
having any fun with her? Aha, she presses your hand? The
"gesegnete Mahlzeit" business after dinner is an excellent institution, isn't it? She'll tell you how much she loves you soon; that's
the next move in the game.'

But so far she had done neither of these things, for Campbell
gave her no opportunities. He was guarded in the extreme,
ungenial avoiding her even at the cost of civility. Sometimes he
was downright rude. That especially occurred when he felt himself inclined to yield to her advances. For she made him all sorts of
silent advances, speaking with her eyes, her sad little mouth, her
beseeching attitude. And then one evening she went further still. It
occurred after dinner in the little green drawing-room. The rest of
the company were gathered together in the big drawing-room
beyond. The small room has deep embrasures to the windows.
Each embrasure holds two old faded green velvet sofas in black
oaken frames, and an oaken oblong table stands between them.
Campbell had flung himself down on one of these sofas in the
corner nearest the window. Miss Thayer, passing through the
oom, saw him, and sat down opposite. She leaned her elbows on

the table, the laces of her sleeves falling away from her round white arms, and clasped her hands.

'Mr Campbell, tell me what have I done? How have I vexed you? You have hardly spoken two words to me all day. You always try to avoid me.' And when he began to utter evasive banalities, she stopped him with an imploring 'Ah, don't! I love you. You know I love you. I love you so much I can't bear you to put me off with mere phrases.'

Campbell admired the well-simulated passion in her voice, remembered Mayne's prediction, and laughed aloud.

'Oh, you may laugh,' she said, 'but I am serious. I love you, I love you with my whole soul.' She slipped round the end of the table, and came close beside him. His first impulse was to rise; then he resigned himself to stay. But it was not so much resignation that was required as self-mastery, cool-headedness. Her close proximity, her fragrance, those wonderful eye raised so beseechingly to his, made his heart beat.

'Why are you so cold?' she said. 'I love you so; can't you love me a little too?'

'My dear young lady,' said Campbell, gently repelling her, 'what do you take me for? A foolish boy like your friends Anson and March? What you are saying is monstrous, preposterous. Ten days ago you'd never even seen me.'

'What has length of time to do with it?' she said. 'I loved you at first sight.'

'I wonder,' he observed judicially, and again gently removed her hand from his, 'to how many men you have not already said the same thing.'

'I've never meant it before,' she said quite earnestly, and nestled closer to him, and kissed the breast of his coat, and held her mouth up towards his. But he kept his chin resolutely high, and looked over her head.

'How many men have you not already kissed ever since you've been here?'

'But there've not been many here to kiss!' she exclaimed naïvely.

'Well, there was March; you kissed him?'

'No, I'm quite sure I didn't.'

'And young Anson; what about him? Ah, you don't answer! And then the other fellow you don't answer! And then the other fellow – what's his name – Prendergast – you've kissed him?'

'But, after all, what is there in a kiss?' she cried ingenuously. 'It means nothing, absolutely nothing. Why, one has to kiss all sorts of people one doesn't care about.'

Campbell remembered how Mayne had said she had probably known strange kisses since the age of ten; and a wave of anger with her, of righteous indignation, rose within him.

'To me,' said he, 'to all right-thinking people, a young girl's kisses are something pure, something sacred, not to be offered indiscriminately to every fellow she meets. Ah, you don't know what you have lost! You have seen a fruit that has been handled, that has lost its bloom? You have seen primroses, spring flowers, gathered and thrown away in the dust? And who enjoys the one, or picks up the others? And this is what you remind me of – only you have deliberately, of your own perverse will, tarnished your beauty, and thrown away all the modesty, the reticence, the delicacy, which make a young girl so infinitely dear. You revolt me, you disgust me. I want nothing from you but to be let alone. Kindly take your hands away, and let me go.'

He shook her roughly off and got up, then felt a moment's curiosity to see how she would take the repulse.

Miss Thayer never blushed; had never, he imagined, in her life done so. No faintest trace of colour now stained the warm pallor of her rose-leaf skin; but her eyes filled up with tears. Two drops gathered on the under lashes, grew large, trembled an instant, and then rolled unchecked down her cheeks. Those tears somehow put him in the wrong, and he felt he had behaved brutally to her for the rest of the night.

He began to seek excuses for her: after all, she meant no harm; it was her upbringing, her *genre*; it was a *genre* he loathed; but perhaps he need not have spoken so harshly. He thought he would find a more friendly word for her next morning; and he loitered about the Mahlsaal, where the boarders come in to breakfast, as in an hotel, just when it suits them, till past eleven; but she did not come. Then, when he was almost tired of waiting, Miss Dodge put in an appearance, in a flannel wrapper, and her front hair twisted up in steel pins.

Campbell judged Miss Dodge with even more severity than he did Miss Thayer; there was nothing in this weird little creature's appearance to temper justice with mercy. It was with difficulty that he brought himself to inquire after her friend.

'Lulie is sick this morning,' she told him. 'I've come down to order her some broth. She couldn't sleep any last night, because of your unkindness to her. She's vurry, vurry unhappy about it.'

'Yes, I'm sorry for what I said. I had no right to speak so strongly, I suppose. But I spoke strongly because I feel strongly. However, there's no reason why my bad manners should make her unhappy.'

'Oh, yes, there's vurry good reason,' said Miss Dodge. 'She's vurry much in love with you.'

Campbell looked at the speaker long and earnestly to try and read her mind; but the prominent blinking eyes, the cryptic physiognomy, told him nothing.

'Look here,' he said brusquely, 'what's your object in trying to fool me like this? I know all about your friend. Mayne has told me. She has cried "Wolf" too often before to expect to be believed now.'

'But, after all,' argued Miss Dodge, blinking more than ever behind her glasses, 'the wolf did really come at last, you know; didn't he? Lulie is really in love this time. We've all made mistakes in our lives, haven't we? But that's no reason for not being right at last. And Lulie has cried herself sick.'

Campbell was a little shaken. He went and repeated the conversation to Mayne, who laughed derisively.

'Capital, capital!' he cried; 'excellently contrived. It quite supports my latest theory about our young friend. She's an actress, a born comédienne. She acts always, and to everyone: to you, to me, to the Ritterhausens, to the Dodge girl – even to herself when she is quite alone. And she has a great respect for her art; she'll carry out her rôle, *coûte que coûte*, to the bitter end. She chooses to pose as in love with you; you don't respond; the part now requires that she should sicken and pine. Consequently she takes to her bed, and sends her confidante to tell you so. Oh, it's colossal, it's *famos*.'

4

'If you can't really love me,' said Lulie Thayer – 'and I know I've been a bad girl and don't deserve that you should – at least, will you allow me to go on loving you?'

She walked by Campbell's side, through the solitary uncared-for park of Schloss Altenau. It was three weeks later in the year, and the spring feeling in the air stirred the blood. All round were signs and tokens of spring: in the busy gaiety of bird and insect life; in the purple flower-tufts which thickened the boughs of the ash-trees; in the young green things pushing up pointed heads from amidst last season's dead leaves and grasses. The snow-wreaths, that had for so long decorated the distant hills, were shrinking perceptibly away beneath the strong March sunshine.

There was every invitation to spend one's time out of doors, and Campbell passed long mornings in the park, or wandering through the woods and the surrounding villages. Miss Thayer often accompanied him. He never invited her to do so, but when she offered him her company, he could not, or at least did not, refuse it.

'May I love you? Say,' she entreated.

'"*Wenn ich Dich liebe, was geht's Dich an?*"' he quoted lightly. 'Oh, no, it's nothing to me, of course. Only don't expect me to believe you – that's all.'

This disbelief of his was the recurring decimal of their conversation. No matter on what subject they began, they always ended thus. And the more sceptical he showed himself, the more eager she became. She exhausted herself in endeavours to convince him.

They had reached the corner in the park where the road to the castle turns off at right angles from the road to Dürrendorf. The ground rises gently on the park-side to within three feet of the top of the boundary wall, although on the other side there is a drop of at least twenty feet. The broad wall-top makes a convenient seat. Campbell and the girl sat down on it. At his last words she wrung her hands together in her lap.

'But how can you disbelieve me,' she cried, 'when I tell you I love you, I adore you? When I swear it to you? And can't you see for yourself? Why, everyone at the Castle sees it.'

'Yes, you afford the Castle a good deal of unnecessary amusement. And that shows you don't understand what love really is. Real love is full of delicacy, of reticences, and would feel itself profaned if it became the jest of the servants' hall.'

'It's not so much my love for you, as your rejection of it, which has made me talked about.'

'Isn't it rather on account of the favours you've lavished on all my predecessors?'

She sprang to her feet, and walked up and down in agitation.

'But after all, surely, mistakes of that sort are not to be counted against us? I did really think I was in love with Mr March. Willie Anson doesn't count. He's an American too, and he understands things. Besides, he is only a boy. And how could I know I should love you before I had met you? And how can I help loving you now I have? You're so different from other men. You're good, you're honorable, you treat women with respect. Oh, I do love you so, I do love you! Ask Nannie if I don't.'

The way in which Campbell shrugged his shoulders clearly expressed the amount of reliance he would place on any testimony from Miss Dodge. He could not forget her 'Why don't you make love to Lulie?' addressed to a married man. Such a want of principle argued an equal want of truth.

Lulie seemed on the brink of weeping.

'I wish I were dead,' she struggled to say. 'Life's impossible if you won't believe me. I don't ask you any longer to love me. I know I've been a bad girl, and I don't deserve that you should; but if you won't believe that I love you I don't want to live any longer.'

Campbell confessed to himself that she acted admirably, but that the damnable iteration of the one idea became monotonous. He sought a change of subject. 'Look there,' he said, 'close by the wall, what's that jolly little blue flower? It's the first I've seen this year.'

He showed her where, at the base of the wall, a solitary blossom rose above a creeping stem and glossy dark green leaves.

Lulie, all smiles again, picked it with child-like pleasure. 'Oh, if that's the first you've seen,' she cried, 'you can take a wish. Only you mustn't speak until someone asks you a question.

She began to fasten it in his coat. 'It's just as blue as your eyes,' she said. 'You have such blue and boyish eyes, you know. Stop, stop, that's not a question,' and, seeing that he was about to speak, she laid her finger across his mouth. 'You'll spoil the charm.'

She stepped back, folded her arms, and seemed to dedicate herself to eternal silence, then relenting suddenly –

'Do you believe me?' she entreated.

'What's become of your ring?' Campbell answered beside the mark. He had noticed its absence from her finger while she had been fixing in the flower.

'Oh, my engagement's broken.'

Campbell asked how the *fiancé* would like that.

'Oh, he won't mind. He knows I only got engaged because he worried so. And it was always understood between us that I was to be free if I ever met anyone I liked better.'

Campbell asked her what sort of fellow this accommodating *fiancé* was.

'Oh, he's all right. And he's very good too. But he's not a bit clever, and don't let us talk about him. He makes me tired.'

'But you're wrong,' Campbell told her, 'to throw away a good, a sincere affection. If you really want to reform and turn over a new leaf, as you are always telling me you do, I should advise you to go home and marry him.'

'What, when I'm in love with you?' she cried reproachfully. 'Would that be right?'

'It's going to rain,' said Campbell. 'Didn't you feel a drop just then? And it's getting near lunch-time. Shall we go in?'

Their shortest way led through the little cemetery in which the departed Ritterhausens lay at peace in the shadow of their some-time home.

'When I die the Baron has promised I shall be buried here,' said Lulie pensively. 'Just here, next to his first wife. Don't you think it would be lovely to be buried in a beautiful, peaceful baronial graveyard, instead of in some horrid crowded city cemetery?'

Mayne met them as they entered the hall. He noticed the flower in his friend's coat. 'Ah, my dear chap, been treading the – periwinkle path of dalliance, I see? How many desirable young men have I not witnessed led down the same broad way by the same seductive lady! Always the same thing; nothing changes but the flower according to the season.'

When Campbell reached his room he took the poor periwinkle out of his coat, and threw it away into the stove.

And yet, had it not been for Mayne, Miss Thayer might have triumphed after all; might have convinced Campbell of her passion, or have added another victim to her long list. But Mayne had set himself as determinedly to spoil her game as she was bent on winning it. He had always the cynical word, the apt reminiscence ready, whenever he saw signs on Campbell's part of surrender. He was very fond of Campbell. He did not wish him to fall a prey to the wiles of this little American siren. He had watched her conduct in the past with a dozen different men; he genuinely believed she was only acting in the present.

Campbell, for his part, began to experience an ever-increasing exasperation in the girl's presence. Yet he did not avoid it; he could not well avoid it, she followed him about so persistently; but his speech would overflow with bitterness towards her. He would say the cruellest things; then, remembering them when alone, be ashamed of his brutalities. But nothing he said ever altered her sweetness of temper or weakened the tenacity of her purpose. His rebuffs made her beautiful eyes run over with tears, but the harshest of them never elicited the least sign of resentment. There would have been something touching as well as comic in this dog-like humility, which accepted everything as welcome at his hands, had he not been imbued with Mayne's conviction that it was all an admirable piece of acting. Or when for a moment he forgot the histrionic theory, then invariably there would come a chance word in her conversation which would fill him with cold rage. They would be talking of books, travels, sport, what not, and she would drop a reference to this man or to that. So-and-so had taken her to Bullier's, she had learned skating with this other; Duroy, the *prix de Rome* man, had painted her as Hebe; Franz Weber had tried to teach her German by means of Heine's poems. And he got glimpses of long vistas of amourettes played in every State in America, in every country of Europe, since the very beginning, when, as a mere child, elderly men, friends of her father's, had held her on their knee and fed her on sweetmeats and kisses. It was sickening to think of, it was pitiable. So much youth and beauty tarnished; the possibility for so much good thrown away. For if one could only blot out her record, forget it, accept her for what she chose to appear, a more endearing companion no man could desire.

5

It was a wet afternoon, the rain had set in at midday with a grey determination which gave no hopes of clearing. Nevertheless, Mayne had accompanied his wife and the Baroness into Hamelin. 'To take up a servant's character, and expostulate with a re-calcitrant dressmaker,' he explained to Campbell, and wondered what women would do to fill up their days were it not for the perennial crimes of dressmakers and domestic servants. He him-self was going to look in at the English Club; wouldn't Campbell come too? There was a fourth seat in the carriage. But Campbell was in no social mood; he felt his temper going all to pieces; a quarter of an hour of Mrs Mayne's society would have brought on an explosion. He thought he must be alone; and yet when he had read for half an hour in his room he wondered vaguely what Lulie was doing; he had not seen her since luncheon. She always gave him her society when he could very well dispense with it, but on a wet day like this, when a little conversation would be tolerable, of course she stayed away. Then there came down the long Rittersaal the tapping of high heels, and a well-known knock at his door. He went over and opened it; Miss Thayer, in the plush and lace tea-gown, fronted him serenely.

'Am I disturbing you?' she asked, and his mood was so capricious that, now she was standing there on his threshold, he thought he was annoyed at it. 'It's so dull,' she said, persuasively. 'Nannie's got a sick headache, and I daren't go downstairs, or the Baron will annex me to play Halma. He always wants to play Halma on wet days.'

'And what do you want to do?' said Campbell, leaning against the doorpost, and letting his eyes rest on the strange piquant face in its setting of red hair.

'To be with you, of course.'

'Well,' said he, coming out and closing the door, 'I'm at your service. What next?'

They strolled together through the room, and listened to the falling rain. The Rittersaal occupies all the space on the first floor that the hall and four drawing-rooms do below. Wooden pillars support the ceiling, dividing the apartment lengthwise into a nave and two aisles. Down the middle are long tables used for ceremonial banquets. Six windows look into the courtyard, and six out over the open country. The centre pane of each window is emblazoned with a Ritterhausen shield. Between the windows hang family portraits, and the sills are broad and low, and cushioned in faded velvet.

'How it rains!' said Lulie, stopping before one of the south windows. 'Why, you can't see anything for the rain, and there's no sound at all but the rain either. I like it. It makes me feel as though we had the whole world to ourselves.'

Then, 'Say, what would you like to do?' she asked him. 'Shall I fetch over my pistols, and we'll practise with them? You've no notion how well I can shoot. We couldn't hurt anything here, could we?'

Campbell thought they might practise there without inconvenience, and Lulie, bundling up the duchess tea-gown over one arm, danced off in very unduchess-like fashion to fetch the case.

It was a charming little box of cedar-wood and mother-o'-pearl, lined with violet velvet; and two tiny revolvers lay inside, hardly more than six inches long, with silver engraved handles.

'I won them in a bet,' she observed complacently, 'with the Hon. Billie Thornton. He's an Englishman, you know, the son of Lord Thornton. I knew him in Washington two years ago last fall. He bet I couldn't hit a three-cent piece at twenty yards, and I did. Aren't they perfectly sweet? Now, can't you contrive a target?'

Campbell went back to his room, drew out a rough diagram, and pasted it down on to a piece of cardboard. Then this was fixed up by means of a penknife driven into the wood of one of the pillars, and Campbell, with his walking-stick laid down six successive times, measured off the distance required, and set a chalk mark across the floor. Lulie took the first shot. She held the little weapon up at arm's length above her head, the first finger stretched out along the barrel; then, dropping her hand sharply so that the finger pointed straight at the butt, she pulled the trigger with the third. There was the sharp report, the tiny smoke film; and when Campbell went up to examine results, he found she had only missed the very centre by a quarter of an inch.

Lulie was exultant. 'I don't seem to have got out of practice any,' she remarked. 'I'm so glad, for I used to be a very good shot. It was Hiram P. Ladd who taught me. He's the crack shot of Montana. What! you don't know Hiram P.? Why, I should have supposed everyone must have heard of him. He had the next ranch to my Uncle Samuel's, where I used to go summers, and he made me do an hour's pistol practice every morning after bathing. It was he who taught me swimming too – in the river.'

'Damnation,' said Campbell under his breath, then shot in his turn, and shot wide. Lulie made another bull's-eye, and after that a white. She urged Campbell to continue, which he sullenly did, and again missed.

'You see I don't come up to your Hiram P. Ladd,' he remarked savagely, and put the pistol down, and walked over to the window. He stood with one foot on the cushioned seat, staring out at the rain, and pulling moodily at his moustache.

Lulie followed him, nestled up to him, lifted the hand that hung passive by his side, put it round her waist and held it there. Campbell, lost in thought, let it remain so for a second; then remembered how she had doubtless done this very same thing with other men in this very room. All her apparently spontaneous movements, he told himself, were but the oft-used pieces in the game she played so skilfully.

'Let go,' he said, and flung himself down on the window-seat, looking up at her with darkening eyes.

She, sitting meekly in the other corner, folded her offending hands in her lap.

'Do you know your eyes are not a bit nice when you're cross?' she said. 'They seem to become quite black.'

He maintained a discouraging silence.

She looked over at him meditatively.

'I never cared a bit for Hiram P., if that's what you mean,' she remarked presently.

'Do you suppose I care a button if you did?'

'Then why did you leave off shooting, and why won't you talk to me?'

He vouchsafed no reply.

Lulie spent some moments immersed in thought. Then she sighed deeply, and recommenced on a note of pensive regret: – 'Ah, if I'd only met you sooner in life, I should be a very different girl.'

The freshness which her quaint, drawling enunciation lent to this time-dishonoured formula made Campbell smile, till, remembering all its implications, his forehead set in frowns again.

Lulie continued her discourse. 'You see,' said she, 'I never had any one to teach me what was right. My mother died when I was quite a child, and my father has always let me do exactly as I pleased, so long as I didn't bother him. Then I've never had a home, but have always lived around in hotels and places: all winter in New York or Washington, and summers out at Longbranch or Saratoga. It's true we own a house in Detroit, on Lafayette Avenue, that we reckon as home, but we don't ever go there. It's a bad sort of life for a girl, isn't it?' she pleaded.

'Horrible,' he said mechanically. His mind was at work. The loose threads of his angers, his irritations, his desires, were knitting themselves together, weaving themselves into something overmastering and definite.

The young girl meanwhile was moving up towards him along the seat, for the effect which his sharpest rebuke produced on her never lasted more than four minutes. She now again possessed herself of his hand, and, holding it between her own, began to caress it in childlike fashion, pulling the fingers apart and closing them again, spreading it palm downwards on her lap, and laying her own little hand over it, to exemplify the differences between them. He let her be; he seemed unconscious of her proceedings.

'And then,' she continued, 'I've always known a lot of young fellows who've liked to take me round; and no one ever objected to my going with them, and so I went. And I enjoyed it, and there wasn't any harm in it, just kissing, and making believe, and nonsense. But I never really cared for one of them. I can see that now, when I compare them with you – when I compare what I felt for them with what I feel for you. Oh, I do love you so much,' she murmured: 'Don't you believe me?' She lifted his hand to her lips and covered it with kisses.

He pulled it roughly from her. 'I wish you'd give over such fool's play,' he told her, got up, walked to the table, came back again, stood looking at her with sombre eyes and dilating pupils.

'But I do love you,' she repeated, rising and advancing towards him.

'For God's sake, drop that damned rot,' he cried out with sudden fury. 'It wearies me, do you hear? It sickens me. Love, love, my God, what do you know about it? Why, if you really loved me, really loved any man – if you had any conception of what the passion of love is, how beautiful, how fine, how sacred – the mere idea that you could not come to your lover fresh, pure, untouched, as a young girl should, that you had been handled, fondled, and God knows what besides, by this man and the other – would fill you with such horror for yourself, with such supreme disgust, you would feel yourself so unworthy, so polluted . . . that . . . that . . . by God! you would take up that pistol there, and blow your brains out!'

Lulie seemed to find the idea quite entertaining. She picked the pistol up from where it lay in the window, examined it critically, with her pretty head drooping on one side, and then sent one of her long, red-brown caressing glances up towards him.

'And suppose I were to,' she asked lightly. 'Would you believe me then?'

'Oh . . . well . . . then, perhaps! If you showed sufficient decency to kill yourself, perhaps I might,' said he, with ironical laughter. His ebullition had relieved him; his nerves were calmed again. 'But nothing short of that would ever make me.'

With her little tragic air, which seemed to him so like a smile disguised, she raised the weapon to the bosom of her gown. There came a sudden, sharp crack, a tiny smoke-film. She stood an instant swaying slightly, smiling certainly, distinctly outlined against the background of rain-washed window, of grey falling rain, the top of her head cutting in two the Ritterhausen escutcheon. Then all at once there was nothing at all between him and the window; he saw

the coat of arms entire; but a motionless, inert heap of plush and
lace, and fallen wine-red hair, lay at his feet upon the floor.

'Child, child, what have you done?' he cried with anguish, and,
kneeling beside her, lifted her up, and looked into her face.

When from a distance of time and place Campbell was at last able
to look back with some degree of calmness on the catastrophe, the
element in it which stung him most keenly was this: he could
never convince himself that Lulie had really loved him after all.
And the only two persons who had known them both and the
circumstances of the case sufficiently well to have resolved his
doubts one way or the other, held diametrically opposite views.

'Well, listen, then, and I'll tell you how it was,' Miss Nannie
Dodge had said to him impressively, the day before he left Schloss
Altenau for ever. 'Lulie was tremendously, terribly in love with
you. And when she found that you wouldn't care about her, she
didn't want to live any more. As to the way in which it happened,
you don't need to reproach yourself for that. She'd have done it,
anyhow; if not then, why, later. But it's all the rest of your
conduct to her that was so mean, your cold, cruel, complacent
British unresponsiveness. I guess you'll never find another woman
to love you as Lulie did. She was just the darlingest, the sweetest,
the most loving girl in the world.'

Mayne, on the other hand, summed it up in this way: 'Of course,
old chap, it's horrible to think of; horrible, horrible, horrible! I
can't tell you how badly I feel about it. For she was a gorgeously
beautiful creature. That red hair of hers – Good Lord! You won't
come across such hair as that again in a lifetime. But, believe me,
she was only fooling with you. Once she had you in her hunting-
noose, once her buccaneering instincts satisfied, and she'd have
chucked you as she did all the rest. As to her death, I've got three
theories – no, two – for the first being that she compassed it in a
moment of genuine emotion, we may dismiss, I think, as quite
untenable. The second is, that it arose from pure misadventure.
You had both been shooting, hadn't you? Well, she took up the
pistol and pulled the trigger from mere mischief, to frighten you,
and quite forgetting one barrel was still loaded. And the third is, it
was just her histrionic sense of the fitness of things. The rôle she had
played so long and so well now demanded a sensational finale in the
centre of the stage. And it's the third theory I give the preference to.
She was the most consumate little actress I ever met.'

(1895)

KATE DOUGLAS WIGGIN

Huldah the Prophetess

'And they went unto Huldah the Prophetess and communed with her.'

Huldah Rumford came down the attic stairs two steps at a time.
Huldah was seventeen, which is a good thing; she was bewitchingly
pretty, which is a better thing; and she was in love, which is
probably the best thing of all, making due allowance, of course, for
the occasions in which it is the very worst thing that can happen to
anybody.

Mrs Rumford was frying doughnuts for breakfast. She was a
comfortable figure as she stood over the brimming 'spider'* with
her three-pronged fork poised in the air. She turned the yellow rings
in the hissing fat until they were nutbrown, then dropped them into
a bowl of sugar, from which they issued the most delicious
conspirators against the human stomach that can be found in the
catalogue of New England cookery.

The table was neatly laid near the screen door that opened from
the kitchen into the apple orchard. A pan of buttermilk biscuits as
large as saucers was sitting on the back of the stove, and half a
custard pie, left from the previous night's supper, occupied the
position of honour in front of Mrs Rumford's seat. If the pie had
been beefsteak, the doughnuts potatoes, and the saleratus* biscuits
leavened bread, the plot and the course of this tale might have been
different; but that is neither here nor there.

'Did you hear the rooster crowing on the doorstep, Mother?'
asked Huldah.

'Yes. I wondered if you heard him and would look out o' your
window to see where he was. And I can't seem to keep my dishcloth
in my hand this morning; if I've dropped it once I've dropped it a
dozen times: there's company coming, sure.'

'That rooster was crowin' on the fence last time I seen him, and
he's up there agin now,' said little Jimmy Rumford, with the most
offensive scepticism.

'What if he is?' asked Huldah, sharply. 'That means fair weather, and don't interfere with the sign of company coming: it makes it all the more certain.'

'I bet he ain't crowin' about Pitt Packard,' retorted Jimmy, with a large joy illuminating his sunburnt face. 'He ain't comin' home from Moderation this week; he's gone to work on the covered bridge there.'

Huldah's face fell. 'I'd ought to have known better than to turn my white skirt yesterday,' she sighed. 'I never knew it to fail bringing bad luck. I can't bear to have my clothes twisted all day, but every time I do get on a thing wrong side out and then turn it I vow I'll never do it again.'

'That's one o' the signs I haven't got so much confidence in,' said Mrs Rumford, skimming the cream from a pan of milk into the churn and putting the skimmed milk on the table. 'It don't come true with me more'n three times out o' five, but there's others that never fails. You jest hold on. Huldy; the dishcloth and the rooster knows as much 'bout what's goin' to happen as your white petticoat doos.'

'Jest about as much,' interpolated Jimmy, with his utterance somewhat choked by hot doughnut.

Huldah sat down at the table and made a pretence of eating something, but her heart was heavy within her. 'What are you churning for on Friday, Mother?' she asked.

'Why, I told you I was looking for strangers. It ain't Pitt Packard only that I expect; I believe the house is going to be choke-full o' company, and I'm gettin' ready for it. Yesterday mornin' I swept a black mark on the floor; in the afternoon I found two o' the settin'-room chairs standin' back to back, and my right hand kep' itchin' all day, so't I knew I was goin' to shake hands with somebody.'

'You told me 'twas the left hand,' said Jimmy.

'I never told you no such thing, Jimmy Rumford. Eat your breakfast, and don't contradict your mother, or I'll send you to bed quick's you finish eatin'. Don't you tell me what I said nor what I didn't say, for I won't have it. Do you hear me?'

'You did!' responded Jimmy, obstinately, preparing to dodge under the table in case of sudden necessity. 'You said your left hand itched, and it meant money comin', and you hoped Rube Hobson was goin' to pay you for the turkey he bought a year ago last Thanksgivin' time, so there!'

'So I did,' said the widow, reflectively. 'Come to think of it, so I did. It must 'a' been a Wednesday my right hand kep' itchin' so.'

'And comp'ny didn't come a Wednesday neither,' persevered Jimmy.

'Jimmy Rumford, if you don't behave yourself and speak when you're spoken to, and not before, you'll git a trouncin' that you'll remember consid'able of a spell afterwards.'

'I'm ready for it!' replied the youngster, darting into the shed and peeping back into the kitchen with a malignant smile. 'I dreamt o' Baldwin apples last night. 'Dream fruit out o' season, That's anger without reason.' I knew when I got up you'd get mad with me the first thing this morning, and I'm all prepared – when you ketch me!'

Both women gave a sigh of relief when the boy's flying figure disappeared around the corner of the barn. He was morally certain to be in mischief wherever he was, but if he was out of sight there was one point gained at least.

'Why do you care so dreadfully whether Pitt comes or not?' asked Mrs Rumford, now that quiet was restored. 'If he don't come today, then he'll come a Sunday; and if he don't come this Sunday, then he'll come the next one, so what's the odds? You and him didn't have a fallin' out last time he was home, did you?'

'Yes, if you must know it, we did.'

'Haven't you got any common sense, Huldy? Sakes alive! I thought when I married Daniel Rumford, if I could stand his temper it was nobody's business but my own. I didn't foresee that he had so much he could keep plenty for his own use and then have a lot left to hand down to his children, so't I should have to live in the house with it to the day of my death! Seems to me if I was a girl and lived in a village where men folks is as scarce as they be here, I'd be turrible careful to keep holt of a beau after I'd got him. What in the name o' goodness did you quarrel about?'

Huldah got up from the table and carried her plate and cup to the sink. She looked out of the window to conceal her embarrassment, and busied herself with preparations for the dish washing, so that she could talk with greater freedom.

'We've had words before this, plenty of times, but they didn't amount to anything. Pitt's good, and he's handsome, and he's smart; but he's awful dictatorial and fault-finding, and I just ain't going to eat too much humble pie before I'm married, for fear I won't have anything else to eat afterwards, and it ain't very fattening for a steady diet. And if there ever was a hateful old woman in the world it's his stepmother. I've heard of her saying mean things about our family every once in a while, but I wouldn't tell you for fear you'd flare up and say Pitt couldn't come to see me. She's tried to set him against me ever since we began to keep company together. She's never quite managed to do it, but she's succeeded well enough to keep me in continual trouble.'

'What's she got to say?' inquired Mrs Rumford, hotly. 'She never had a silk dress in the world till Eben Packard married her, and everybody knows her father was a horse doctor and mine was a reg'lar one!'

'She didn't say anything about fathers, but she did tell Almira Berry that no member of the church in good standing could believe in signs as you did and have hope of salvation. She said I was a chip off the old block, and had been raised like a heathen. It seems when I was over there on Sunday I refused to stand up and have my height measured against the wall, and I told 'em if you measured heights on Sunday you'd like as not die before the year was out. I didn't know then she had such a prejudice against signs, but since that time I've dragged 'em in every chance I got, just to spite her.'

'More fool you!' said her mother, beginning to move the dasher of the churn up and down with a steady motion. 'You might have waited until she was your mother-in-law before you began to spite her. The first thing you know you won't get any mother-in-law.'

'That's the only thing that would console me for losing Pitt!' exclaimed Huldah. 'If I can't marry him I don't have to live with her, that's one comfort! The last thing she did was to tell Aunt Hitty Tarbox she'd as lief have Pitt bring one of the original Salem witches into the house as one of the Daniel Rumford tribe.'

'The land sakes!' ejaculated the widow, giving a desperate and impassioned plunge to the churn dasher. 'Now I know why I dreamt of snakes and muddy water the night before she come here to the Ladies' Aid Club. Well, she's seventy, and she can't live forever; she can't take Eben Packard's money into the next world with her, either, and I guess if she could 'twould melt as soon as it got there.'

Huldah persevered with her confession, dropping an occasional tear in the dish water.

'Last time Pitt came here he said he should have three or four days' vacation the 12th of August, and he thought we'd better get married then. I was kind of shy, and the almanac was hanging alongside of the table, so I took it up and looked to see what day of the week the 12th fell on. "Oh, Pitt," I said, "we can't be married on a Friday, it's dreadful unlucky." He began to scold then, and said I didn't care anything about him if I wouldn't marry him when it was most convenient; and I said I would if 'twas any day but Friday; and he said that was all moonshine, and nobody but foolish old women believed in such nonsense; and I said there wasn't a girl in town that would marry him on a Friday; and he said there was; and I asked him to come right out and tell who he meant; and he said he didn't mean anybody in particular; and I said he did; and he said, well, Jennie Perkins would, on Friday or Sunday or wash day or any other day; and I said if I was a man I vow I wouldn't take a girl that was so anxious as all that; and he said he'd rather take one that was a little too anxious than one that wasn't anxious enough; and so we had it back and forth, till I got so mad I couldn't see the almanac. Then, just to show him I had more good reasons than one, I said, 'Besides, if we should be married on a Friday, we'd have to go away on a Saturday, and ten to one 'twould rain on our wedding trip.' 'Why would it rain Saturday more than any other day?' said he; and then I mistrusted I was getting into more trouble, but I was too mad to back out, and said I, 'It rains more Saturdays in the year than any other day;' and he said, 'Where'd you get that silly notion?' Then I said it wasn't any silly notion, it was gospel truth, and anybody that took notice of anything knew it was so; and he said he never heard of it in his life; and I said there was considerable many things that he'd never heard of that he'd be all the better for knowing; and he said he was like Josh Billings, he'd rather know a few things well than know so many things that wa'n't so.'

'You might have told him how we compared notes about rainy days at the Aid Club,' said her mother. 'You remember Hannah Sophia Palmer hadn't noticed it, but the minute you mentioned it she remembered how, when she was a child, she was always worryin' for fear she couldn't wear her new hat a Sunday, and it must have been because it was threatening weather a Saturday, and she was afraid it would keep up for Sunday. And the widow Buzzell said she always picked up her apples for pie baking on Friday, it was so apt to be dull or wet on a Saturday.'

'I told him all of that,' continued Huldah, 'and how old Mrs

Bascom said they had a literary society over to Edgewood that used to meet twice a month on Saturday afternoons, and it rained or snowed so often they had to change their meetings to a Wednesday. Then the first thing I knew Pitt stood up so straight he looked more than ten feet tall, and says he, 'If you don't marry me a Friday, Huldah Rumford, you don't marry me at all. You're nothing but a mass of superstition, and if you're so scared for fear it will rain on your wedding bonnet a Saturday, you can stay home under cover the rest of your life, for all I care. I'll wash the top buggy, put the umbrella under the seat, and take Jennie Perkins; she won't be afraid of a wetting so long as she gets it in good company.' "You're right," I said, "she won't, especially if the company's a man, for she'll be so dumfounded at getting one of 'em to sit beside her she won't notice if it rains pitchforks, and so far as I'm concerned she's welcome to my leavings!" Then he went out and slammed the kitchen door after him, but not so quick that I didn't get a good slam on the sitting-room door first.'

'He'll come back,' churned Mrs Rumford, philosophically. 'Jennie Perkins has got a pug nose, and a good-sized mole on one side of it. A mole on the nose is a sure sign of bad luck in love affairs, particularly if it's well to one side. He'll come back.'

But, as a matter of fact, the days went by, the maple trees turned red, and Pitt Packard did not come back to the Rumford farm. His comings and his goings were all known to Huldah. She knew that he took Jennie Perkins to the Sunday-school picnic, and escorted her home from evening meetings. She knew that old Mrs Packard had given her a garnet pin, a glass handkerchief box, and a wreath of hair flowers made from the intertwined tresses of the Packards and the Doolittles. If these symptoms could by any possibility be misinterpreted, there were various other details of an alarmingly corroborative character, culminating in the marriage of Pitt to Jennie on a certain Friday evening at eight o'clock. He not only married her on a Friday, but he drove her to Portland on a Saturday morning; and the Fates, who are never above taking a little extra trouble when they are dealing out misery, decreed that it should be one of the freshest, brightest, most golden mornings of the early autumn.

Pitt thought Portland preferable to Biddeford or Saco as a place to pass the brief honeymoon, if for no other reason than because the road thither lay past the Rumford house. But the Rumfords' blinds were tightly closed on the eventful Saturday, and an unnecessarily large placard hung ostentatiously on the front gate, announcing to passers-by that the family had gone to Old Orchard Beach, and would be home at sundown. This was a bitter blow to the bridegroom, for he had put down the back of the buggy with the intention of kissing the bride within full view of the Rumford windows. When he found it was of no use he abandoned the idea, as the operation never afforded him any especial pleasure. He asked Mrs Pitt if she preferred to go to the beach for her trip, but she decidedly favoured the gaieties of a metropolis. The excitement of passing the Rumford house having faded, Jennie's nose became so oppressive to Pitt that he finally changed places with her, explaining that he generally drove on the left side. He was more tranquil then, for her left profile was more pleasing, though for the life of him he could not help remembering Huldah's sweet outlines, the dimple in her chin, her kissable mouth, her delicate ear. Why, oh, why, had she inherited her father's temper and her mother's gift of prophecy, to say nothing of her grandfather's obstinacy and her grandmother's nimble tongue! All at once it dawned upon him that he might have jilted Huldah without marrying Jennie. It would, it is true, have been only a half-revenge; but his appetite for revenge was so dulled by satisfaction he thought he could have been perfectly comfortable with half the quantity, even if Huldah were not quite so uncomfortable as he wished her to be. He dismissed these base and disloyal sentiments, however, as bravely as he could, and kissed Jennie twice, in a little stretch of wood road that fell in opportunely with his mood of silent penitence.

About two o'clock clouds began to gather in the sky, and there was a muttering of thunder. Pitt endured all the signs of a shower with such fortitude as he could command, and did not put up the buggy top or unstrap the boot until the rain came down in good earnest.

'Who'd have suspicioned this kind of weather?' he growled, as he got the last strap into place and shook the water from his new straw hat.

'I was afraid of it, but I didn't like to speak out,' said Jennie, primly; 'they say it gen'ally does rain Saturdays.'

Meanwhile Huldah lay in the spare room at the back of the house and sobbed quietly. Mrs Rumford and the skeptical Jimmy had gone to Old Orchard, and Huldah had slipped out of the front door, tacked the obtrusive placard on the gatepost, and closed all the blinds in honour of the buried hopes that lay like a dead weight at the bottom of her heart.

She was a silly little thing, a vain little thing, and a spitfire to boot, but that did not prevent her suffering an appreciable amount, all that her nature would allow; and if it was not as much as a larger nature would have suffered, neither had she much philosophy or strength to bear it. The burden is fitted to the back as often as the back of the burden.

She frequently declared to herself afterwards that she should have had 'a fit of sickness' if it had not been for the thunderstorm that came up on that never-to-be-forgotten Saturday afternoon. She had waked that morning with a dull pain in her heart – a dull pain that had grown keener when she looked from her attic window and saw the sun shining clear in the sky. Not a cloud sullied the surface of that fair blue canopy on this day of the faithless Pitt's wedding journey. A sweet wind blew the tall feathers of the golden cock on the squire's barn till he stared the west directly in the eye. What a day to drive to Portland! She would have worn tan-coloured low shoes and brown open-work stockings (what ugly feet Jennie Perkins had!), a buff challis dress with little brown autumn leaves on it, a belt and sash of brown watered ribbon (Jennie had a waist like a flour barrel!), and a sailor hat with a bunch of yellow roses on one side – or would two brown quills, standing up coquettishly, have been more attractive? Then she would have taken a brown cloth shoulder cape, trimmed with rows upon rows of cream-coloured lace, and a brown parasol with an acorn of polished wood on the handle. Oh, what was the use of living when she could wear none of this bridal apparel, but must put on her old pink calico and go down to meet Jimmy's brotherly sneers? Was there ever such a cruelly sunshiny morning? A spot of flickering light danced and quivered on her blue wallpaper until she could bear it no longer, and pinned a towel over it. She sat down by the open window and leaned dejectedly on the sill, the prettiest picture of spiteful, unnecessary misery that the eye of mortal man ever rested upon, with her bright hair tumbling over her unbleached nightgown, and her little bare feet curled about the chair rounds like those of a disconsolate child. Nobody could have approved of or even sympathised with so trivial a creature, but plenty of people would have been so sorry for her they would have taken sensible, conscientious, unattractive Jennie Perkins out of Pitt Packard's buggy and substituted the heedless little Huldah, just for the pleasure of seeing her smile and blush. There was, however, no guardian imp to look after her ruined fortunes, and she went downstairs as usual to help about the breakfast, wondering to herself if there were any tragedies in life too terrible to be coexistent with three meals a day and the dishes washed after each one of them.

An infant hope stirred in her heart when she saw a red sparkle here and there on the sooty bottom of the teakettle, and it grew a little when her mother remarked that the dish water boiled away so fast and the cows lay down so much that she believed it would rain the next day. When, that same afternoon, the welcome shower came with scarce ten minutes' warning, Huldah could hardly believe her eyes and ears. She jumped from her couch of anguish and remorse like an excited kitten, darted out of the house unmindful of the lightning, drove the Jersey calf under cover, got the chickens into the coop, bolstered up the tomatoes so that the wind and rain would not blow the fruit from the heavily laden plants, opened the blinds, and closed the windows.

'It comes from the east,' she cried, dancing up and down in a glow of childish glee – 'it comes from the east, and it's blowing in on Jennie's side of the buggy!' She did not know that Pitt had changed places with his bride, and that his broad shoulder was shielding her from the 'angry airt'.

Then she flew into the kitchen and pinned up her blown hair in front of the cracked looking-glass, thinking with sympathetic tenderness how pretty she looked with her crown of chestnut tendrils tightened by the dampness, her round young cheeks crimsoned by the wind, and her still tearful eyes brightened by unchristian joy. She remembered with naughty satisfaction how rain invariably straightened Jennie Perkins' frizzes, and was glad, *glad*, that it did. Her angry passions were so beautifying that the radiant vision in the glass almost dazzled her. It made her very sorry for Pitt too. She hated to think that his ill temper and stubborn pride and obstinacy had lost him such a lovely creature as herself, and had forced him to waste his charms on so unappreciative and plain a person as Jennie Perkins. She remembered that Pitt had asked her to marry him coming home from the fair in a rain storm. If he meant anything he said on that occasion, he must be suffering pangs of regret today. Oh, how good, how sweet, how kind of it to rain and support her in what she had prophesied of Saturday weather!

All at once a healing thought popped into her head. 'I shall not live many years,' she reflected, 'not after losing Pitt, and having his mother crow over me, and that hateful Jennie Perkins, with the family hair wreath hanging over her sofa, and my wedding ring on her hand; but so long as I do live I will keep account of rainy Saturdays, and find a way to send the record to Pitt every New Year's day just to prove that I was right. Then I shall die young, and perhaps he will plant something on my grave, and water it with his tears; and perhaps he will put up a marble gravestone over me, unbeknownst to Jennie, and have an appropriate verse of Scripture carved on it, something like – 'SHE OPENETH HER MOUTH WITH WISDOM; AND IN HER TONGUE IS THE LAW OF KINDNESS.' I can see it as plain as if it was written. I hope they will make it come out even on the edges, and that he will think to have a white marble dove perched on the top, unless it costs too much.'

The years went on. Huldah surprised everybody by going away from home to get an education. She would have preferred marriage at that stage of her development, but to her mind there was no one worth marrying in Pleasant River save Pitt Packard, and, failing him, study would fill up the time as well as anything else.

The education forced a good many helpful ideas into pretty Huldah's somewhat empty pate, though it by no means cured her of all her superstitions. She continued to keep a record of Saturday weather, and it proved as interesting and harmless a hobby as the collecting of china or postage stamps.

In course of time Pitt Packard moved to Goshen, Indiana, where he made a comfortable fortune by the invention of an estimable pump, after which he was known by his full name of W. Pitt Fessenden Packard. In course of time the impish and incredulous Jimmy Rumford became James, and espoused the daughter of a wealthy Boston merchant. His social advancement was no surprise to Huldah and her mother, for, from the moment he had left home, they never dreamed of him save in conjunction with horned cattle, which is well known to signify unexampled prosperity.

In course of time, too, old Mrs Rumford was gathered to her fathers after a long illness, in which Huldah nursed her dutifully and well. Her death was not entirely unexpected, for Hannah Sophia Palmer observed spots like iron rust on her fingers, a dog howled every night under Almira Berry's window, and Huldah broke the kitchen looking-glass. No invalid could hope for re-

covery under these sinister circumstances, and Mrs Rumford
would have been the last woman in the world to fly in the face of
such unmistakable signs of death. It is even rumoured that when
she heard the crash of the glass in the kitchen she murmured
piously, 'Now lettest Thou Thy servant depart in peace,' and
expired within the hour.

Nineteen summers and winters had passed since Pitt Packard
drove 'her that was Jennie Perkins' to Portland on her wedding
trip. He had been a good and loyal husband; she had been a good
and faithful wife; and never once in the nineteen years had they so
much as touched the hem of the garment of happiness.

Huldah the Prophetess lived on in the old house alone. Time
would have gone slowly and drearily enough had it not been for
her ruling passion. If the first part of the week were fair, she was
hopeful that there was greater chance of rain or snow by Saturday; if it were rainy, she hoped there would be a long storm. She
kept an elaborate table showing the weather on every day of the
year. Fair Saturdays were printed in red ink, foul Saturdays in jet
black. The last days of December were generally spent in preparing a succinct statement from these daily entries. Then in the
month of January a neat document, presenting facts and figures,
but no word of personal comment or communication, was
addressed at first to Mr W. P. Packard, and of late years to W. Pitt
Fessenden Packard, and sent to Goshen, Indiana.

Mr Packard was a good and loyal husband, as I have said, but
there was certainly no disloyalty in the annual perusal of statist-
ical weather tables. That these tables though made out by one of
the weaker sex, were accurate and authentic, he had reason to
believe, because he kept a rigid account of the weather himself,
and compared Huldah's yearly record with his own. The weather
in Pleasant River did not, it is true, agree absolutely with the
weather in Goshen, but the similarity between Maine and Indiana
Saturdays was remarkable. The first five years of Pitt's married life
Huldah had the advantage, and the perusal of her tables afforded
Pitt little satisfaction, since it proved that her superstitions had
some apparent basis of reason. The next five years his turn came,
and the fair Saturdays predominated. He was not any happier,
however, on the whole, because, although he had the pleasure of
being right himself, he lost the pleasure of believing Huldah right.
So time went on, until Mrs Pitt died, and was buried under the

handsomest granite monument that could be purchased by the sale of pumps. For two years after this bereavement Huldah omitted sending her weather statistics to Mr Packard, thinking, with some truth, that it might seem too marked an attention from an attractive Maine spinster to a 'likely' Indiana widower.

Matters were in this state when Mr Packard alighted at the Edgewood station one bright day in August. He declined the offer of a drive, and soon found himself on the well-remembered road to Pleasant River. He had not trodden that dusty thoroughfare for many a year, and every tree and shrub and rock had a message for him, though he was a plain matter-of-fact maker of pumps. There was no old home to revisit, for his stepmother had died long ago, and Jennie had conscientiously removed the family wreath from the glass case and woven some of the departed lady's hair into the funereal garland. He walked with the brisk step of a man who knew what he wanted, but there was a kind of breathless suspense in his manner which showed that he was uncertain of getting it. He passed the Whippoorwill Mill, the bubbling spring, the old moss-covered watering trough, and then cut across the widow Buzzell's field straight to the Rumford farm. He kept rehearsing the subject matter of a certain speech he intended to make. He knew it by heart, having repeated it once a day for several months, but nobody realised better than he that he would forget every word of it the moment he saw Huldah – at least if the Huldah of today was anything like the Huldah of the olden time.

The house came in sight. It used to be painted white; it was drab now, and there was a bay window in the sitting room. There was a new pump in the old place, and, happy omen, he discovered it was one of his own manufacture. He made his way by sheer force of habit past the kitchen windows to the side door. That was where they had quarrelled mostly. He had a kind of sentiment about that side door. He paused a moment to hide his travelling bag under the grapevine that shaded the porch, and as he raised his hand to grasp the knocker the blood rushed to his face and his heart leaped into his throat.

Huldah stood near the window winding the old clock. In her right hand was a *Farmer's Almanac*. How well he knew the yellow cover! and how like to the Huldah of seventeen was the Huldah of thirty-six! It was incredible that the pangs of disappointed love could make so little inroad on a woman's charms. Rosy cheeks, plump figure, clear eyes, with a little more snap in them than was necessary for comfort, but not a whit too much for beauty; brown hair curling round her ears and temples – what an ornament to a certain house he knew in Goshen, Indiana!

She closed the wooden door of the clock, and, turning, took a generous bite from the side of a mellow August sweeting that lay on the table. At this rather inauspicious moment her eye caught Pitt's. The sight of her old lover drove all prudence and reserve from her mind, and she came to the door with such an intoxicating smile and such welcoming hands that he would have kissed her then and there even if he had not come to Pleasant River for that especial purpose. Of course he forgot the speech, but his gestures were convincing, and he mumbled a sufficient number of extracts from it to convince Huldah that he was in a proper frame of mind – this phrase meaning, to a woman, the one in which she can do anything she likes with a man.

They were too old, doubtless, to cry and laugh in each other's arms, and ask forgiveness for past follies, and regret the wasted years, and be thankful for present hope and life and love; but that is what they did, old as they were.

'I wouldn't have any business to ask you to marry such a dictatorial fool as I used to be, Huldah,' said Pitt, 'but I've got over considerable of my foolishness, and do say you will; say, too, you won't make me wait any longer, but marry me Sunday or Monday. This is Thursday, and I must be back in Goshen next week at this time. Will you, Huldah?'

Huldah blushed, but shook her head. She looked lovely when she blushed, and she hadn't lost the trick of it even at thirty-six.

'I know it's soon, but never mind getting ready. If you won't say Monday, make it Tuesday – do.'

She shook her head again.

'Wednesday, then? *Do* say Wednesday, Huldy dear!'

The same smile of gentle negation.

He dropped her hand disconsolately. 'Then I'll have to come back at Christmas time, I s'pose. It's just my busy season now, or I would stay right here on this doorstep till you was ready, for it seems to me as if I'd been waiting for you ever since I was born, and couldn't get you too soon.'

'Do you really want me to marry you so much, Pitt?'

'Never wanted anything so bad in my life.'

'Didn't you wonder I wasn't more surprised to see you today?'

'Nothing surprises me in women folks.'

'Well, it was because I've dreamed of a funeral three nights running. Do you know what that's a sign of?'

Pitt never winked an eyelash; he had learned his lesson. With a sigh of relief that his respected stepmother was out of hearing, he responded easily, 'I s'pose it's a sign somebody's dead or going to die.'

'No, it isn't; dreams go by contraries. It's a sign there's going to be a wedding.'

'I'm glad to know that much, but I wish while you was about it you'd have dreamed a little more and found out when the wedding was going to be.'

'I did; and if you weren't the stupidest man alive you could guess.'

'I know I'm slow-witted,' said Pitt, meekly, for he was in a mood to endure anything, 'but I've asked you to have me on every day there is except the one I'm afraid to name.'

'You know I've had plenty of offers.'

'Unless all the men folks are blind you must have had a thousand, Huldah.'

Huldah was distinctly pleased. As a matter of fact she had had only five; but five offers in the State of Maine implies a superhuman power of attraction not to be measured by the casual reader.

'Are you sorry you called me a mass of superstition?'

'I wish I'd been horsewhipped where I stood.'

'Very well, then. The first time you wouldn't marry me at all unless you could have me Friday, and of course I wouldn't take you Friday under those circumstances. Now you say you're glad and willing to marry me any day in the week, and so I'll choose Friday of my own accord. I'll marry you tomorrow, Pitt; and' – here she darted a roguishly sibylline glance at the clouds – 'I have a waterproof. Have you an umbrella for Saturday?'

Pitt took her at her word, you may be sure, and married her the next day, but I wish you could have seen it rain on Saturday! There never was such a storm in Pleasant River. The road to the Edgewood station was a raging flood; but though the bride and groom were drenched to the skin they didn't take cold; they were too happy. Love within is a beautiful counter-irritant.

Huldah didn't mind waiting a little matter of nineteen years so long as her maiden flag sank in a sea of triumph at the end; and it is but simple justice to an erring but attractive woman to remark that she never said 'I told you so' to her husband.

(1895)

ADA LEVERSON

Suggestion

If Lady Winthrop had not spoken of me as 'that intolerable, effeminate boy', she might have had some chance of marrying my father. She was a middle-aged widow; prosaic, fond of domineering, and an alarmingly excellent housekeeper; the serious work of her life was paying visits; in her lighter moments she collected autographs. She was highly suitable and altogether insupportable; and this unfortunate remark about me was, as people say, the last straw. Some encouragement from Father Lady Winthrop must, I think, have received; for she took to calling at odd hours, asking my sister Marjorie sudden abrupt questions, and being generally impossible. A tradition existed that her advice was of use to our father in his household, and when, last year, he married his daughter's schoolfriend, a beautiful girl of twenty, it surprised every one except Marjorie and myself.

The whole thing was done, in fact, by suggestion. I shall never forget that summer evening when Father first realised, with regard to Laura Egerton, the possible. He was giving a little dinner of eighteen people. *Through a mistake of Marjorie's* (my idea) Lady Winthrop did not receive her invitation till the very last minute. Of course she accepted – we knew she would – but unknowing that it was a dinner party, she came without putting on evening dress.

Nothing could be more trying to the average woman than such a *contretemps*; and Lady Winthrop was not one to rise, sublimely, and laughing, above the situation. I can see her now, in a plaid blouse and a vile temper, displaying herself, mentally and physically, to the utmost disadvantage, while Marjorie apologised the whole evening, in pale blue crêpe-de-chine; and Laura, in yellow, with mauve orchids, sat – an adorable contrast – on my father's other side, with a slightly conscious air that was perfectly fascinating. It is quite extraordinary what trifles have their little effect in these matters. *I* had sent Laura the orchids, anonymously; I could not help it if she chose to think they were from my father.

Also, I had hinted of his secret affection for her, and lent her Verlaine. I said I had found it in his study, turned down at her favourite page. Laura has, like myself, the artistic temperament; she is cultured, rather romantic, and in search of the *au-delà*. My father has at times – never to me – rather charming manners; also he is still handsome, with that look of having suffered that comes from enjoying oneself too much. That evening his really sham melancholy and apparently hollow gaiety were delightful for a son to witness, and appealed evidently to her heart. Yes, strange as it may seem, while the world said that pretty Miss Egerton married old Carington for his money, she was really in love, or thought herself in love, with our father. Poor girl! She little knew what an irritating, ill-tempered, absent-minded person he is in private life; and at times I have pangs of remorse.

A fortnight after the wedding, Father forgot he was married, and began again treating Laura with a sort of *distrait* gallantry as Marjorie's friend, or else ignoring her altogether. When, from time to time, he remembers she is his wife, he scolds her about the housekeeping in a fitful, perfunctory way, for he does not know that Marjorie does it still. Laura bears the rebukes like an angel; indeed, rather than take the slightest practical trouble she would prefer to listen to the strongest language in my father's vocabulary.

But she is sensitive; and when Father, speedily resuming his bachelor manners, recommended his visits to an old friend who lives in one of the little houses opposite the Oratory, she seemed quite vexed. Father is horribly careless, and Laura found a letter. They had a rather serious explanation, and for a little time after, Laura seemed depressed. She soon tried to rouse herself, and is at times cheerful enough with Marjorie and myself, but I fear she has had a disillusion. They never quarrel now, and I think we all three dislike Father about equally, though Laura never owns it, and is gracefully attentive to him in a gentle, filial sort of way.

We are fond of going to parties – not Father – and Laura is a very nice chaperone for Marjorie. They are both perfectly devoted to me. 'Cecil knows everything,' they are always saying, and they do nothing – not even choosing a hat – without asking my advice.

Since I left Eton I am supposed to be reading with a tutor, but as a matter of fact I have plenty of leisure; and am very glad to be of use to the girls, of whom I'm, by the way, quite proud. They are rather a sweet contrast; Marjorie has the sort of fresh rosy prettiness you see in the park and on the river. She is tall, and slim as a punt-pole, and if she were not very careful how she dresses, she would look like a drawing by Pilotelle in the *Lady's Pictorial*. She is practical and lively, she rides and drives and dances; skates, and goes to some mysterious haunt called *The Stores*, and is, in her own way, quite a modern English type.

Laura has that exotic beauty so much admired by Philistines: dreamy dark eyes, and a wonderful white complexion. She loves music and poetry and pictures and admiration in a lofty sort of way; she has a morbid fondness for mental gymnastics, and a dislike to physical exertion, and never takes any exercise except waving her hair. Sometimes she looks bored, and I have heard her sigh.

'Cissy,' Marjorie said, coming one day into my study, 'I want to speak to you about Laura.'

'Do you have pangs of conscience too?' I asked, lighting a cigarette.

'Dear, we took a great responsibility. Poor girl! Oh, couldn't we make Papa more—'

'Impossible,' I said, 'No one has any influence with him. He can't bear even me, though if he had a shade of decency he would dash away an unbidden tear every time I look at him with my mother's blue eyes.'

My poor mother was a great beauty, and I am supposed to be her living image.

'Laura has no object in life,' said Marjorie. 'I have, all girls have, I suppose. By the way, Cissy, I am quite sure Charlie Winthrop is serious.'

'How sweet of him! I am so glad. I got Father off my hands last season.'

'Must I really marry him, Cissy? He bores me.'

'What has that to do with it? Certainly you must. You are not a beauty, and I doubt your ever having a better chance.'

Marjorie rose and looked at herself in the long pier-glass that stands opposite my writing-table. I could not resist the temptation to go and stand beside her.

'I am just the style that is admired now,' said Marjorie, dispassionately.

'So am I,' I said reflectively. 'But *you* will soon be out of date.'

Everyone says I am strangely like my mother. Her face was of that pure and perfect oval one so seldom sees, with delicate

features, rosebud mouth, and soft flaxen hair. A blondness
without insipidity, for the dark-blue eyes are fringed with dark
lashes, and from their languorous depths looks out a soft
mockery. I have a curious ideal devotion to my mother; she died
when I was quite young – only two months old – and I often
spend hours thinking of her, as I gaze at myself in the mirror.

'Do come down from the clouds,' said Marjorie impatiently, for
I had sunk into a reverie. 'I came to ask you to think of something
to amuse Laura – to interest her.'

'We ought to make it up to her in some way. Haven't you tried
anything?'

'Only palmistry, and Mrs Wilkinson prophesied her all that she
detests, and depressed her dreadfully.'

'What do you think she really needs most?' I asked.

Our eyes met.

'Really, Cissy, you're too disgraceful,' said Marjorie. There was
a pause.

'And so I'm to accept Charlie?'

'What man do you like better?' I asked.

'I don't know what you mean,' said Marjorie, colouring.

'I thought Adrian Grant would have been more sympathetic to
Laura than to you. I have just had a note from him, asking me to
tea at his studio today.' I threw it to her. 'He says I'm to bring you
both. Would that amuse Laura?'

'Oh,' cried Marjorie, enchanted, 'of course we'll go. I wonder
what he thinks of me,' she added wistfully.

'He didn't say. He is going to send Laura his verses, "Hearts-
ease and Heliotrope".'

She sighed. Then she said, 'Father was complaining again today
of your laziness.'

'I, lazy! Why, I've been swinging the censer in Laura's boudoir
because she wants to encourage the religious temperament, and
I've designed your dress for the Clives' fancy ball.'

'Where's the design?'

'In my head. You're not to wear white; Miss Clive must wear
white.'

'I wonder you don't marry her,' said Marjorie, 'you admire her
so much.'

'I never marry. Besides, I know she's pretty, but that furtive
Slade-school manner of hers gets on my nerves. You don't know
how dreadfully I suffer from my nerves.'

She lingered a little, asking me what I advised her to choose for a birthday present for herself – an American organ, a black poodle, or an *édition de luxe* of Browning. I advised the last, as being least noisy. Then I told her I felt sure that in spite of her admiration for Adrian, she was far too good-natured to interfere with Laura's prospects. She said I was incorrigible, and left the room with a smile of resignation.

And I returned to my reading. On my last birthday – I was seventeen – my father – who has his gleams of dry humour – gave me *Robinson Crusoe*! I prefer Pierre Loti, and intend to have an onyx-paved bathroom, with soft apricot-coloured light shimmering through the blue-lined green curtains in my chambers, as soon as I get Margery married, and Laura more – settled down.

I met Adrian Grant first at a luncheon party at the Clives'. I seemed to amuse him. He came to see me, and became at once obviously enamoured of my stepmother. He is rather an impressionable impressionist, and a delightful creature, tall and graceful and beautiful, and altogether most interesting. Everyone admits he's fascinating; he is very popular and very much disliked. He is by way of being a painter. He has a little money of his own – enough for his telegrams, but not enough for his buttonholes – and nothing could be more incongruous than the idea of his marrying. I have never seen Marjorie so much attracted. But she is a good loyal girl, and will accept Charlie Winthrop, who is a dear person, good-natured and ridiculously rich – just the sort of man for a brother-in-law. It will annoy my old enemy Lady Winthrop – he is her nephew, and she wants him to marry that little Miss Clive. Dorothy Clive has her failings, but she could not – to do her justice – be happy with Charlie Winthrop.

Adrian's gorgeous studio gives one the complex impression of being at once the calm retreat of a medieval saint and the luxurious abode of a modern Pagan. One feels that everything could be done there, everything form praying to flirting – everything except painting. The tea party amused me, I was pretending to listen to a brown person who was talking absurd worn-out literary clichés – as that the New Humour is not funny, or that Bourget understood women, when I overheard this fragment of conversation.

'But don't you like Society?' Adrian was saying.

'I get rather tired of it. People are so much alike. They all say the same things,' said Laura.

'Of course they all say the same things to *you*,' murmured Adrian, as he affected to point out a rather curious old silver crucifix.

'That,' said Laura, 'is one of the things they say.'

About three weeks later I found myself dining alone with Adrian Grant, at one of the two restaurants in London. (The cooking is better at the other, this one is the more becoming.) I had lilies-of-the-valley in my button hole, Adrian was wearing a red carnation. Several people glanced at us. Of course he is very well known in Society. Also, I was looking rather nice, and I could not help hoping, while Adrian gazed rather absently over my head, that the shaded candles were staining to a richer rose the waking wonder of my face.

Adrian was charming of course, but he seemed worried and a little preoccupied, and drank a good deal of champagne.

Towards the end of dinner, he said – almost abruptly for him – 'Carington.'

'Cecil,' I interrupted. He smiled.

'Cissy . . . it seems an odd thing to say to you, but though you are so young, I think you know everything. I am sure you know everything. You know about me. I am in love. I am quite miserable. What on earth am I to do!' He drank more champagne. 'Tell me,' he said, 'what to do.' For a few minutes, while we listened to that interminable hackneyed *Intermezzo*, I reflected, asking myself by what strange phases I had risen to the extraordinary position of giving advice to Adrian on such a subject?

Laura was not happy with our father. From a selfish motive, Marjorie and I had practically arranged that monstrous marriage. That very day he had been disagreeable, asking me with a clumsy sarcasm to raise his allowance, so that he could afford my favourite cigarettes. If Adrian were free, Marjorie might refuse Charlie Winthrop. I don't want her to refuse him. Adrian has treated me as a friend. I like him – I like him enormously. I am quite devoted to him. And how can I rid myself of the feeling of responsibility, the sense that I owe some compensation to poor beautiful Laura?

We spoke of various matters. Just before we left the table, I said, with what seemed, but was not, irrelevance, 'Dear Adrian, Mrs Carington—'

'Go on, Cissy.'

'She is one of those who must be appealed to, at first, by her imagination. She married our father because she thought he was lonely and misunderstood.'

'*I* am lonely and misunderstood,' said Adrian, his eyes flashing with delight.

'Ah, not twice! She doesn't like that now.'

I finished my coffee slowly, and then I said, 'Go to the Clives' fancy-ball as Tristan.'

Adrian pressed my hand . . .

At the door of the restaurant we parted, and I drove home through the cool April night, wondering, wondering. Suddenly I thought of my mother – my beautiful sainted mother, who would have loved me, I am convinced, had she lived, with an extraordinary devotion. What would she have said to all this? What would she have thought? I know not why, but a mad reaction seized me. I felt recklessly conscientious. My father! After all, he was my father. I was possessed by passionate scruples. If I went back now to Adrian – if I went back and implored him, supplicated him never to see Laura again!

I felt I could persuade him. I have sufficient personal magnetism to do that, if I make up my mind. After one glance in the looking-glass, I put up my stick and stopped the hansom. I had taken a resolution. I told the man to drive to Adrian's rooms.

He turned round with a sharp jerk. In another second a brougham passed us – a swift little brougham that I knew. It slackened – it stopped – we passed it – I saw my father. He was getting out at one of the little houses opposite the Brompton Oratory.

'Turn round again,' I shouted to the cabman. And he drove me straight home.

(1895)

NETTA SYRETT

A Correspondence

I

'I think she is perfectly lovely,' Mrs Yeo exclaimed, enthusiastically.

She made a slight indicative movement towards the far corner of the drawing-room, where the folds of a white dress and the feathery edges of a fan were just visible from her corner of the sofa.

'Ah, I thought you would be surprised.'

Mrs Lockyer spoke in the proprietary tone of one who has discovered some priceless treasure and for the first time displays it to the gaze of the multitude.

'They are altogether an ideal couple, aren't they?' she continued. 'I always say *he* is quite ridiculously good looking – *too* handsome for a mere man!'

'They met in Rome, you say?'

'Yes, quite lately; only a few weeks ago, in fact, when the Armstrongs were travelling in Italy. He'd hardly known her a week before he proposed, and it's scarcely a fortnight now since the day they met – so her mother says. This is his last evening. He's going back tomorrow to Rome; he has some work to finish there, I understand. He's a sculptor, you know. Such a romantic occupation, isn't it? – and so *suitable*. He has such classical features himself – just like Apollo, or, well, *all* those Greeky-Roman people. To me he has the air of being the *least* little bit stand-off. What do you think? I daresay that's just my fancy though, for I hear he is quite charming, but alarmingly clever. He is more than ten years older than Miss Armstrong, they say, and *I* believe there's more difference than that even – don't you think so?' But Mrs Yeo's gaze had turned in the direction of the white dress again.

'She is very lovely,' she repeated, 'but I don't think she seems quite happy.'

The girl under discussion had risen from her seat and was

standing at the corner of the mantelpiece, one hand resting on the low shelf. From where Mrs Yeo was sitting she caught a glimpse of a very delicately tinted face; the light from a rose-shaded lamp above the girl's head fell softly on masses of rippling red-brown hair growing low on the forehead, and parted over the brows, Clytie fashion. Her long trailing gown fell in white folds to her feet.

Mrs Yeo was young and imaginative. Her friend's information about the sculptor fiancé had doubtless something to do with the fancifulness of the notion, yet, as she looked at the girl, her mind was full of vague ideas of Galatea,* the beautiful statue slowly awakening to this distressful life.

'Not happy?' echoed Mrs Lockyer. 'Oh, why not? She *ought* to be. It's a most desirable match in every way. Mr Margrave is well connected and rich, I believe; and' – this in a slightly lower key – 'between ourselves, the Armstrongs are not *particularly* well off. She's a very *quiet* girl, I think; not that I know much of her. She's so very young, you know, only just out, in fact. This is the first dinner they've given since her engagement, and—'

There was a sound of laughter and voices outside, and the usual little stir and flutter in the room as the men came in.

'Ah, he's speaking to her. How splendid they look together,' exclaimed Mrs Yeo, who was taking more than her usual interest in the engagement. The girl looked up with a quick start as the door opened, and hastily withdrew her foot from the fender, as though she had been guilty of some impropriety. She straightened herself, and hurriedly smoothed her dress, while her hand tightened mechanically on the fan she was holding.

A close observer might have thought the movement almost a shrinking one, and in the little fleeting smile with which she greeted her lover's approach, there was perhaps as much nervousness as pleasure.

She looked very young when she raised her eyes, which were clear blue, and at first sight, singularly childlike. But their expression was puzzling; it almost seemed – and Mrs Yeo was more interested than ever when she noticed this – as though a new nature was struggling in them tentatively, and in a half-frightened way, for life and utterance. It was this uncertain air about the girl altogether, which Mrs Yeo felt, and which appealed to her as pathetic. 'She wants someone to be *very* kind to her just now,' thought the tender-hearted little lady, as she watched the girl's face.

The man lingered a few moments beside her, leaning over the back of her chair, but at the first soft notes of a song, he turned towards the piano, and in the girl's attitude there was a faint suggestion of relief, though her eyes followed him rather wistfully.

The singer was a slim girl, with a somewhat striking face, and a cloud of dark wavy hair. She glanced up at Margrave with a smile of thanks, as he turned over a leaf for her, and when the song was ended he kept his place at her side. She did not move from the piano, but began to look over a pile of music as though searching for something.

There was a short silence.

'Cecily is lovelier than ever tonight,' she observed, abruptly.

Margrave smiled and glanced in the direction she was looking.

'Yes,' he assented. 'That Greek dress of hers is quite an inspiration.'

The girl – her name was Gretchen Verrol – bent to pick up a stray leaf before she replied. 'Thank you, don't trouble,' she said; then, 'You are praising *me* unawares,' she added.

'You designed it then?'

'And more, I made it, with these my proper hands,' with a little gesture.

'I honour you equally for your inventive and creative faculties,' he returned laughingly.

After a moment, with a sudden change of tone, 'Cecily is very fortunate in having you with her,' he said. 'You read with her, I think? She is very young,' and then he hesitated a little, 'I have seen so little of her, and scarcely ever alone, but I fancy she needs—' he paused.

'She is beautiful enough to need nothing besides,' Gretchen interlupted hastily. 'Why don't you go and talk to her now? She is by herself, and I'm not her governess quite, Mr Margrave,' she added.

A young man came up to the piano at the moment, and she held out a piece of music to him. 'Here is a song I know you sing, Mr Graham! Shall I play it for you?' she asked almost in the same breath.

Margrave looked at her a moment with an expression which was at first perplexed, and also a trifle disconcerted before he obediently went back to Cecily.

2

Five years' difference in the ages of two girls is not too much to admit the possibility of intimate friendship. Not that this was the term which could, with any appropriateness, describe the relation between Cecily and Gretchen Verrol, though they were constantly together, and though Gretchen, and all that she did, occupied, or at any rate till quite recently had occupied, nearly the whole of Cecily's mental horizon.

Gretchen Verrol was a distant cousin of Mrs Armstrong, for whom circumstances had rendered it unavoidable to do something in the way of help.

Most fortunately, both for herself and for the Armstrongs, it happened that Gretchen was clever and accomplished – 'the very companion we could have chosen for our dear Cecily,' as her mother frequently observed. This being the case, matters were easily arranged, and for a year previous to Cecily's engagement, Miss Verrol had lived with the Armstrongs, 'reading' with Cecily, helping her with her music, and generally 'forming her taste', as Mr Armstrong again frequently, if somewhat vaguely, remarked.

Mrs Armstrong was a slightly vague person altogether, but kindly natured and easygoing. Her one positive emotion being admiration for her young cousin, who soon held a very important, if not the most important, position in the household.

Whether her engagement had done anything towards lessening the exalted opinion of Gretchen which Cecily shared with her mother was a doubtful question.

'Do you like that Miss Verrol?' someone asked her once rather dubiously, and Cecily looked at her interrogator in a startled, half-awed fashion.

'She is so clever, you know,' she replied, irrelevantly as it seemed, glancing furtively behind her as she spoke.

Gretchen was still an object of as much wondering reverence to Cecily a year afterwards as she had been during the first week of their acquaintance, when Miss Verrol had already summed up her impressions of the latter, once and for all.

She practically knew Cecily, as she remarked to herself, after the first day, and at the end of the first week she proceeded to recapitulate and to get her by heart. An easy task! So easy that she had to sit and look at her with an air of critical wonder.

They were reading German. That is, Gretchen was. She had

been pronouncing the words with great distinctness, and Cecily, with laborious effort after imitation, had made strange weird sounds, unlike any language that was ever imagined, far less spoken. Presently Gretchen's voice stopped, and it was then that Cecily began to move restlessly, raising apprehensive eyes to those which her companion bent quietly upon her. The silence became a little oppressive; Cecily fidgeted, dropped her eyes, and began to pull the blotting-paper to pieces with nervous fingers. Gretchen laid a hand upon it, and quietly drew it away.

'It is no good for you to read this,' said Miss Verrol at last, calmly.

'No,' meekly assented Cecily.

'We've tried French – you don't seem to understand anything of that.'

'No,' she repeated hopelessly.

'Tell me – you don't really care for music, reading, poetry, pictures, do you?'

This was practically an assertion, though put in the form of a question. Cecily felt compelled to reply.

'No,' she acknowledged again, faintly.

Gretchen continued to look at her.

'It is very curious,' she remarked critically, as though she had come upon a totally new species and was interested.

Cecily suddenly dropped her fair head upon her arms, and burst into tears.

Miss Verrol waited silently till the storm was passed. There was a glass opposite, and she looked across at it as the girl raised her tear-stained face.

'It doesn't matter,' she said in the same critical tone. 'You are pretty enough to make it of no consequence. You even look pretty when you cry. Now, *I* look hideous.'

This was the first and only spoken allusion to Cecily's mental deficiencies that Gretchen ever made. The reading and music practising went on regularly as usual, and Cecily still persevered in her frantic attempts at the German accent. If there was the slightest trace of weariness in Gretchen's tone as she corrected her for the fourth or fifth time in one word, it was so faint as to be only just appreciable, and when at the end of the hour Cecily stole an apprehensive glance at her face, it was always calm and imperturbable.

'Now we will have the duet,' was what she usually said as she closed the book. Indeed, her patience during the hours devoted to 'mental culture' was altogether admirable, and if signs of Cecily's lack of intelligence had been otherwise wanting, they would have been supplied by the fact that, while humbly recognising the goodness and wisdom of Gretchen, and striving earnestly to be worthy of it, she would yet have found it a relief if the latter had *sometimes* lost her temper.

This absence of impatience or reproach paralysed her. Once when Gretchen had been called away in the middle of the duet, she sat vacantly staring at the keys for a moment.

All at once, with a sudden frantic movement, she half rose from her seat at the piano, a look of positive terror in her eyes.

'If only she would say something – *anything*! I can't *breathe* when she looks at me,' she panted breathlessly.

When Gretchen came back she was patiently practising a bar over and over again.

'Try it once more, Cecily,' Gretchen said, gazing straight before her out of the window. 'It isn't right.'

Mrs Armstrong found her cousin really invaluable. She was as clever with her fingers as with her brains, and when Cecily began to go out, she not only designed, but also made most of her charming gowns for evening wear.

She always helped her to dress for dances – dressed her, in fact – for Cecily generally stood quite passive to have her hair arranged, her flowers fastened in, or the folds of her gown artistically draped.

On these occasions Gretchen never failed to praise her beauty openly and with an air of impartial criticism, and then Cecily winced and trembled a little, but said nothing.

'I have a comfortable home, but I earn my living,' wrote Gretchen to a friend, when she had been with the Armstrongs about three months.

It was with real concern that a day or two after her daughter's engagement had been finally arranged Mrs Armstrong learnt that Gretchen was thinking of leaving her.

'Cecily will be broken hearted,' she exclaimed plaintively, 'and she won't be married just yet, you know. Besides, why should you go at all? I shall want you more than ever then.'

But Gretchen was firm.

'As long as I could be really of use to you, with Cecily, I did not feel myself dependent,' she explained. 'But now it will be different. No, Cousin Mary, that is only your kindness. I should not be happy in staying on.'

And Cousin Mary, though demurring, felt it selfish to stand in the way of the girl's prospects, especially as an acquaintance of hers, who was about to sail for New Zealand and wanted a governess, was overjoyed at securing such a charming person as Miss Verrol for her two girls.

'But I'm sure I don't know how to tell Cecily,' she lamented again and again. 'I don't know how she'll take it.'

Cecily took it with a start, and an expression not easy to read.

'But she's such a strange girl,' complained her mother, who was not given to analysis of character to any great extent.

3

Gretchen's departure had been finally arranged only the day before Margrave's return to Rome. He could hardly hope to finish the work he was engaged upon very speedily; it would probably be at least six months before he met Cecily again, and his complaint of having seen very little of her during his brief visit was by no means unfounded. It was difficult to tell how deeply the girl felt his absence. Perhaps her manner was even quieter and more subdued than usual, but that was the only noticeable difference in her behaviour. She very rarely mentioned his name.

There was a letter lying beside her plate on the breakfast table the morning after her lover's departure, and Gretchen, glancing across from her opposite seat, saw her quickly cover it with her hand, which she withdrew, a second after, in confusion. Her mother laughed.

'You are not going to read it now, then, Cecie?'

'No, Mother,' she replied, flushing hotly.

An hour or two later, Gretchen opened the door of Cecily's bedroom. She was preoccupied, and entered without knocking; indeed, she had taken the dress she had come for out of the wardrobe, and was leaving the room before she noticed that Cecily was there.

The girl sat in the corner of the window seat, trying to turn her head so as to hide that she was crying – an open letter lay on her lap.

Gretchen started. Instinctively her hand groped for the back of a chair she was passing; then she drew it away, and straightened herself.

'What is the matter, Cecily?' she asked – her voice sounded a little strained, but it was calm enough. 'You have not' – she paused – 'there is no bad news?'

Cecily's low sobs choked her voice. There was time for Gretchen to glance at her own face in the glass and to turn back to the light, before she replied.

'N – no,' she said at last, 'but—'

Gretchen crossed to her side. 'Won't you tell me?' she asked. There was a little tremble in her tone now. Cecily heard it, and looked up gratefully. Gretchen seemed sorry.

'I don't like to,' she murmured. 'You'll say – oh, it's too silly!' Her voice broke again in a half sob.

'Never mind. Tell me.'

'Only that – only – because – because I shall have to answer it.'

The confession broke from Cecily's lips hesitatingly, and then she laid one arm hopelessly against the window frame, and hid her wet eyes against it.

Gretchen did not speak for a minute.

'The letter, you mean?' she asked at length, quietly. 'Well – there is nothing so dreadful about that, is there?'

'Oh, yes, there is – yes, there *is* – for *me*!' wailed Cecily. 'You may read it.' She held out the letter, looking up at Gretchen despairingly. 'You'll see. He asks what I thought of some of those statues in Rome – and – and the pictures. And – I didn't think anything. Oh, Gretchen! I know I'm very stupid – but – I had no thoughts about them, except – I wondered why they kept broken statues in such grand places. But I can't tell him that, can I? Because people, clever people, think they are beautiful – without noses – or anything. And all that he says about the scenery – and you know what my spelling is like – and oh, Gretchen! Don't – don't smile like that!'

Cecily shrank back into the corner of the window seat, and covered her face with both hands. Perhaps she had never made such a long speech before – but Gretchen had seemed sorry.

There was quite a long silence. The crisp paper crackled as Miss Verroll turned the sheets; still Cecily did not look up.

'Well, do you want me to answer it for you?' The question was accompanied by a short laugh.

The girl's hands dropped from her face in a second, and her eyes sought Gretchen's inquiringly – incredulously.

'Gretchen – do you mean it? Would you? Not really?'

'Where is that silk gauze of yours?' asked Gretchen, crossing the room and stooping over a drawer.

'In that box,' replied Cecily, sighing – the chance of relief was gone then.

'You see,' pursued Gretchen, still turning over things in the drawer, 'it's not quite the same thing as doing your exercises.'

'No,' agreed Cecily, despondently. Then brightening, 'But, Gretchen – if you would – you are so clever. You know all about those statues – and the pictures – and the palaces. You could write about them.' She paused breathlessly.

'Oh, yes,' replied Miss Verrol carelessly. 'I daresay I could – I was considered good at composition – at school. Our relative positions would be somewhat reversed, wouldn't they? I should have to bring these exercises to you, for correction and amendment, and – naturally you are so much better up in the subject.'

Another pause.

'No, I really don't think I should dare to let you see my work. There would be so many faults.'

She had found the scarf now, and was busy smoothing out its creases.

'You have crushed this dreadfully,' she said, reproachfully.

'Oh, you don't think it's important enough to talk about,' cried Cecily desperately, 'but I can *never* do it alone. Can't you help me? I shouldn't want to see the letters you wrote, you know,' she assured her eagerly. 'So—'

Gretchen stopped short in the midst of shaking out the filmy folds.

'Not – you mean you would not want to see the letters *I* wrote to *your* lover?' she asked incredulously, fixing her eyes on the girl's face.

Cecily blushed painfully.

'No,' she hesitated. 'Not if you'd rather not. I know it is easier to do everything – if – if people are not watching you. And you will do all the important part, about the statues, beautifully, Gretchen. The only thing I could do would be to – to send my love.' Her voice faltered. 'Perhaps you wouldn't mind always putting that in, at the end, after the other things, you know?'

'Yes. What am I to say?'

'Just say' – the colour flamed in her cheeks again – 'I love you, Noel.' She turned her head away sharply, and looked out of the window.

Gretchen still stood beside her, motionless.

'Cecily,' she said at last, in a low voice, 'think – do you *really* want me to do this? I won't if you—'

'Yes,' she answered brokenly. 'If I could do it myself, of course I – I would rather – but I *can't*! And after all, it won't matter so very much, will it, Gretchen?' She turned to her like a child, imploring to be reassured by some wise and grown-up person. 'I shall *mean* all the things you say.'

'What about the handwriting?' asked Gretchen. Her voice sounded flat and wearied. 'Has he seen yours?'

'No. I have never written to him. There has been no occasion, you see, and he doesn't know yours.'

Miss Verrol went to the door. As she reached it, she paused with her hand on the lock.

'Remember, you wish it,' she said, turning her head over her shoulder to look at Cecily.

The girl rose from the window seat and came towards her. Her soft hair was all disordered, her cheeks were flushed, and her pretty blue eyes were still wet.

'Yes. You are very good to me, Gretchen,' she began timidly, putting out her arms. But Gretchen shrank away hastily.

'Mind – you will crumple this again,' she said.

4

Thus it happened that regularly every week a letter went to Rome, beginning, at Cecily's request (her own original contribution), 'My dearest Noel', and ending with 'your very loving Cecily'. The girl who wrote the letters sat up far into the night. Not that she was writing all the time. She read and reread sheets of close writing on thin foreign paper. Every time she came to an endearing word her colour came and went, and she drew in her breath quickly. To be accurate, the words of love were not many. The letters were perhaps a trifle wanting in colour for a lover. They were the letters of a clever, cultivated man, a little cold by nature. Perhaps *too* highly polished. But the reader did not criticise. She changed colour when she read 'my love'; she smiled triumphantly when he said how it gratified him to know that in their tastes and feelings they were so fully in sympathy. He had not been quite sure of this, he wrote – she had been so silent, so shy – and he had had to learn from her letters that he should have a wife as clever as she was beautiful. Once when she read words to this effect, Gretchen crumpled the paper fiercely in her hand, and sprang to her feet. With a smile of self-mockery, she went to the glass and deliberately studied herself. It reflected a little thin figure, with large, glittering eyes, irregular features, and a mass of rough, wavy hair. A somewhat striking apparition – picturesque, perhaps. But beautiful? A vision of Cecily's stately white love-liness swam before her eyes, and she turned away impatiently.

But the letter must be answered, and she sat down to her weekly task – a torture which she would not now forgo if Cecily begged it of her on her bended knees.

She knew that Cecily already repented of her request. Every time she handed Gretchen a letter from her lover, it was with a more reluctant action, a more wistful and appealing look.

She saw, but would not heed. Cecily had decided – the act was hers – let her abide by it!

In the meantime, every week she could write, with white lips and shaking hand, 'I love you, Noel.' Had not Cecily herself wished it?

'Madness! Of course, I know that,' she thought. 'But if I like to be mad just once before I go away to live out my dull, highly respectable life, who is there to hinder me? It's an inexpensive luxury. She'll tell him, of course, when they're married – though there'll be no occasion; he'll find it out quickly enough.' She smiled scornfully. 'But what does that matter? I shall be thousands of miles away by that time. I shall never know how he takes it, or what he thinks.' And then she sealed the letter.

Even then, though it was early morning, she sat a long time at the table, quite still, her face buried in her hands. When she looked up, it was drawn and haggard.

'And I've come to be a thing like this,' she whispered, with a slow self-scorn, 'about a man who has forgotten my existence. And – I am Gretchen Verrol!'

5

As time went on, drawing nearer to the expiration of the three months before her cousin's departure, Mrs Armstrong's lamentations became more and more frequent.

'Cecily, poor child, feels it dreadfully,' she repeated. 'She is really getting quite thin, and I think she looks ill, though her father says it's like my fidgetiness! But I don't care; she shall take a tonic in spite of what he says. I don't like the look of her at all sometimes. She has such a – I hardly know how to explain what I mean – such a curious, frightened expression. Have you noticed it? You know, Gretchen' (confidentially), 'in spite of a mother's natural feelings, and all that, I shall be glad to have her married. For my part, I don't approve of long engagements, but her father is so obstinate. The child feels unsettled, so of course she's miserable. I expect she misses Noel too, don't you? But she says so little, I hardly know *what* to think.'

There was no doubt that Cecily was growing thin. Her eyes were unnaturally large and bright; they had a wistful, troubled look, and lately she had taken to starting nervously when anyone spoke suddenly to her. Her mother talked of taking her away somewhere for change of air, as soon as Miss Verrol had gone.

'And I hope the voyage will do you good, too,' she added, looking at Gretchen critically. 'Do you know you are looking quite ill? Bless these young people, there's always something the matter with them now. I'm sure there never used to be, in *my* young days.'

The last day at the Armstrongs', after all her boxes were ready, Gretchen spent in paying farewell calls.

It was quite late in the afternoon before, the last goodbye said, and the last polite good wish for her happiness expressed, she found herself once more in front of the house she was so soon to leave. It was some moments before the door was opened in answer to her ring, and she stood on the top of the flight of steps and looked drearily up and down the street. It was a wet night – the pavements were all shining with rain, the gas-lamps were reflected waveringly in the puddles on the road. Only one person was in sight – a girl in a long shiny waterproof, picking her way carefully through the mud from one pavement to the other. The rain dripped steadily, drearily from the square portico overhead.

Gretchen shivered as she looked.

The door was opened and she stepped into the dazzle of the

brightly lighted hall, and began to take off her wet cloak. When the bright mist cleared, she saw that there was a portmanteau on the oak chest against the wall; a bundle of rugs lay beside it; from the drawing-room came a distant murmur of voices.

'Has anyone come, then, Price?' asked Gretchen, stopping at the last button of her waterproof.

'Yes, miss; Mr Margrave. He came unexpected, about two hours ago. I don't know why James hasn't taken up his things, I'm sure. I've told him to, times enough.' Gretchen put her cloak into the maid's hands and turned to the stairs.

'Will you have some tea, miss?'

'No, thank you,' she answered quietly.

Upstairs, the door of Cecily's room stood half-open. She was dressed for dinner already, and she stood before the fire, the tips of her fingers touching the mantelpiece, her forehead resting upon them.

Gretchen hesitated a moment, then went in. 'This is a delightful surprise for you, Cecily, isn't it?'

'Yes,' said Cecily starting. She had raised her head quickly when she heard Gretchen's step, but she did not turn round.

Gretchen stood looking at her with an indescribable expression.

'Why did he come?' she asked after a moment.

'He has been working too hard. The doctor said he was to rest a little, and take a holiday. So he made up his mind suddenly to come and see us. He wrote, but the letter hasn't come yet. We got a telegram just after you went out, about half an hour before he came.'

Something in her voice, though she had not listened to what she said, struck Gretchen as strange.

In spite of herself. 'You don't seem very glad, Cecily? You don't speak quite in the style of the orthodox engaged young lady,' she said, laughing a little as she drew nearer the fire.

'I am *not* engaged,' murmured Cecily.

'*What*!' Gretchen put her hand on the corner of the mantelpiece to steady herself. 'What are you saying? What do you mean?'

Cecily turned a pair of frightened eyes towards her. Gretchen was going to be angry. 'I – I have broken it off,' she whispered in a scared way.

'Since when?'

'Since he came here this afternoon.'

Gretchen broke into a shrill laugh. 'What a charming reception!' she cried.

Then she recovered herself. 'Tell me about it!' she exclaimed peremptorily.

Cecily glanced round the room despairingly, then at Gretchen, who had taken a low chair by the fire and was waiting with a pale face and that patient air she knew so well. There was no escape. 'May I shut the door?' she said meekly crossing the room, her white dress trailing, a tall stately figure in spite of her girlishness.

She came back to her place, but did not speak.

'Well?' said Gretchen.

'I don't know what you want me to tell you.'

'Why you broke it off.'

There was another long pause, then Cecily began to speak low and rapidly.

'I shall never make you understand,' she cried hopelessly. 'I didn't mean to do it, today. I – didn't even know that I had made up my mind to do it at all till just as I was going into the drawing-room to see him. Then I seemed to see that it was all no use.' Her voice sank to a whisper; she was trembling from head to foot.

'You musn't cry. You have to go down, remember,' Gretchen observed in even tones.

Cecily drew herself up, 'What more shall I tell you?' she cried passionately.

Gretchen had never heard this tone from her before; it startled her. She too rose, and they stood facing one another.

'Why do you ask me?' panted Cecily. 'You know – but if you like I will tell you. I don't mind now. Nothing matters now. I knew almost from the first that I could not marry him. He is so clever. And I – every moment I was afraid he would ask me something I didn't know. I didn't understand the way he talked. I didn't understand half of what he said to me. I should *never* have understood it,' she wailed. 'I was always afraid when he came to talk to me, and yet when he was away—' She checked herself. All the passion had died out of her tone now. 'If I hadn't known it before, his letters would have shown me. Oh, I did very wrong in asking you to write, Gretchen. I knew it, the first time he answered *your* letter, and praised what he thought I'd said.'

Gretchen suddenly caught her breath. 'You never—' she began.

'No, I was afraid to ask you not to go on with it when you'd been so kind, and taken so much trouble,' Cecily said. 'I see myself very plainly tonight. Just as though I was someone else – I see that besides – other things – I am a coward.'

Gretchen was silent.

'He would not listen at first.' It seemed that having begun her confession she *must* speak now, though the words came falteringly from her trembling lips. 'He said he didn't understand – he said there was no reason – I was playing with him. He spoke of my letters.' She paused.

'Well?' gasped Gretchen breathlessly.

'Then I thought at any rate I would not deceive him any longer – it was no good – so I told him you wrote them . . . Gretchen! *don't!* You – you frighten me!' she whispered hoarsely.

Gretchen had seized her by the wrist. Her eyes were burning in a face as white as death; they seemed to scorch the girl cowering down before her.

'*You little fool!*' she exclaimed, her hands dropping heavily at her sides. Each word stung like the sharp point of an icicle.

Cecily staggered back as though she had been struck.

It was out at last! This was what Gretchen had been feeling about her every minute for a whole year. The words expressed her whole attitude towards her; it was what Cecily had all the time dumbly wished, yet dreaded to hear her say. It was almost a relief – but she was dazed and confused – she did not yet understand what had forced the words, what had impelled Gretchen, at last, to give her spoken verdict. She still gazed at her, bewildered, hopeless.

'What did he think of me?' inquired Gretchen mockingly. Her tone was so careless and airy that Cecily half doubted for the moment whether she could have said those words in *that voice* a second before – then she looked again at her face, and knew that her ears had not deceived her.

She stood for a second with parted lips, and then a great fear crept up into her eyes, as she covered her face with both hands.

'Forgive me, Gretchen!' she murmured. 'You – you – know how stupid I am.'

It seemed a long time before Gretchen spoke. 'I shall not come down tonight,' she answered calmly. 'It might complicate matters perhaps. Say I have a headache, please. I shall arrange to go by the first train tomorrow. If you think you can invent any reason for this to Cousin Mary, it might be just as well. If not – it doesn't matter much.'

Cecily stood motionless till the door had opened, closed again, and the room was empty.

Then with a helpless movement, she sank down on the floor before the fire, her fair head buried in the cushions of the easy chair, to stifle her sobs.

'I can't think about Gretchen. I can't think about anyone but him,' she whispered to herself brokenly. 'What shall I do? I didn't make myself. It isn't fair. I should have been wretched if I'd ever been his wife. He would have been ashamed of me. And yet – yet!'

Presently she rose wearily; she poured out water and bathed her eyes, and then arranged her hair carefully before the glass.

In a few minutes, except that she was terribly pale, all traces of violent grief had vanished.

Yet to herself she looked so strange that she shuddered to see her own reflection in the glass, there was something about it that was so changed.

When she turned away, it seemed as though a mask had fallen upon a trembling living face. The gong sounded, and she went quietly downstairs. It was not till the next morning that her mother knew that the engagement was at an end.

Mrs Yeo had come up to town from her country house, on her usual spring visit, which was always devoted to shopping and incidental frivolties. She was at the theatre with her husband one evening. The house was full, and between the acts she leant forward on the red velvet cushion before her seat in the dress circle and inspected the stalls with a view to seeing how the hair was being worn this season, and whether the sleeves in the new dinner-dress she had ordered were *too* outrageous. The buzz of talk and the tuneful wail of the violins fell pleasantly on her ears, as she scanned the rows of backs for a possible acquaintance.

'There's a beautiful woman. In the second box – look,' her husband turned to her to say, lowering his glasses. 'Do you see? In white – next to a good-looking fellow with a priggish nose.'

'Why, it's Mrs Margrave!' she exclaimed in surprise, after a moment's scrutiny. 'Yes, isn't she *lovely*? And – yes, that wretched woman's there too,' she added with a change of tone.

'Mrs Margrave?' he repeated.

'Yes. You know, Jim. Cecily Armstrong. We dined at the Armstrongs' once, two or three years ago, don't you remember? I thought her beautiful then. Fancy seeing her here tonight. It must be quite two years since we met her. I wonder if she would recognise me?'

'She married that fellow, then? I had some idea it was all off?'

'So it was for a time. There was some mysterious fuss, don't you remember? But Mrs Armstrong worked it. Cecily always did what she was told. I don't believe the poor child was even consulted. Look!' she broke off to exclaim indignantly. 'He isn't paying her the smallest attention. He talks all the time to that horrid Miss Verrol. I *always* disliked her.'

Mrs Margrave was leaning back listlessly in her chair. Her fan lay upon her lap. She was apparently gazing straight before her, though her masses of rippling hair partly concealed her face from the Yeos.

'Who is she?'

'Why, you remember. That Miss Verrol who used to be Cecily's companion.'

'I thought she went to America, or New Zealand, or somewhere?'

'So she did, but Lady Fairfield had to come home when her father died, you know, and she brought Miss Verrol with her. I believe she's living in town with them now as governess, or secretary, or something; but she's always at the Margraves', I hear.' Mrs Yeo gave vent to an untranslatable little exclamation of disgust.

'But why?' asked her husband. He alluded to the ejaculation.

'My dear Jim! Can't you *see?* Look at them!'

The lights were lowered at the moment, and the curtain rose on the last act.

When it was over, and Mrs Yeo had collected her wraps, she turned to glance once more at the Margraves' box, but it was empty.

Down in the brightly lighted vestibule, however, when at length they reached it, she saw Cecily again.

She was standing a little out of the crush, beside one of the great doors. Her husband was wrapping a white cloak round Miss Verrol. She said something to him, with an upward glance as he did so, and they both laughed. Cecily, who stood patiently waiting at her side, shivered a little at the moment, yet Mrs Yeo fancied she did not feel the cold. As she passed her in the doorway, their eyes met.

For a moment there was no recognition in the long wistful gaze which Cecily unconsciously fixed upon her; then, all at once, she bent her head and smiled.

The crowd swept them apart, and in a few minutes Mrs Yeo was being whirled towards the Métropole in a hansom.

'You're very quiet,' her husband remarked presently. 'Didn't you enjoy the play?'

She put her hand on his, impulsively, and, as she turned to him, he saw there were tears in her eyes.

'You didn't notice her face, Jim, as we passed? I did. I shall never forget it. Poor girl! Poor child!'

(1895)

WILLA CATHER

Tommy the Unsentimental

'Your father says he has no business tact at all, and of course that's dreadfully unfortunate.'

'Business,' replied Tommy, 'he's a baby in business; he's good for nothing on earth but to keep his hair parted straight and wear that white carnation in his buttonhole. He has 'em sent down from Hastings twice a week as regularly as the mail comes, but the drafts he cashes lie in his safe until they are lost, or somebody finds them. I go up occasionally and send a package away for him myself. He'll answer your notes promptly enough, but his business letters – believe he destroys them unopened to shake the responsibility of answering them.'

'I am at a loss to see how you can have such patience with him, Tommy, in so many ways he is thoroughly reprehensible.'

'Well, a man's likeableness don't depend at all on his virtues or acquirements, nor a woman's either, unfortunately. You like them or you don't like them, and that's all there is to it. For the why of it you must appeal to a higher oracle than I. Jay is a likeable fellow, and that's his only and sole acquirement, but after all it's a rather happy one.'

'Yes, he certainly is that,' replied Miss Jessica, as she deliberately turned off the gas jet and proceeded to arrange her toilet articles. Tommy watched her closely and then turned away with a baffled expression.

Needless to say, Tommy was not a boy, although her keen grey eyes and wide forehead were scarcely girlish, and she had the lank figure of an active half-grown lad. Her real name was Theodosia, but during Thomas Shirley's frequent absences from the bank she had attended to his business and correspondence signing herself 'T. Shirley', until everyone in Southdown called her 'Tommy'. That blunt sort of familiarity is not unfrequent in the West, and is meant well enough. People rather expect some business ability in a girl there, and they respect it immensely. That, Tommy undoubtedly had, and if she had not, things would have gone at sixes and sevens in the Southdown National. For Thomas Shirley had big land interests in Wyoming that called him constantly away from home, and his cashier, little Jay Ellington Harper, was, in the local phrase, a weak brother in the bank. He was the son of a friend of old Shirley's, whose papa had sent him West, because he had made a sad mess of his college career, and had spent too much money and gone at too giddy a pace down East. Conditions changed the young gentleman's life, for it was simply impossible to live either prodigally or rapidly in Southdown, but they could not materially affect his mental habits or inclinations. He was made cashier of Shirley's bank because his father bought in half the stock, but Tommy did his work for him.

The relation between these two young people was peculiar; Harper was, in his way, very grateful to her for keeping him out of disgrace with her father, and showed it by a hundred little attentions which were new to her and much more agreeable than the work she did for him which was irksome. Tommy knew that she was immensely fond of him, and she knew at the same time that she was thoroughly foolish for being so. As she expressed it, she was not of his sort, and never would be. She did not often take pains to think, but when she did she saw matters pretty clearly, and she was of a peculiarly unfeminine mind that could not escape meeting and acknowledging a logical conclusion. But she went on liking Jay Ellington Harper, just the same. Now Harper was the only foolish man of Tommy's acquaintance. She knew plenty of active young businessmen and sturdy ranchers, such as one meets about live Western towns, and took no particular interest in them, probably just because they were practical and sensible and thoroughly of her own kind. She knew almost no women, because in those days there were few women in Southdown who were in any sense interesting, or interested in anything but babies and salads. Her best friends were her father's old business friends, elderly men who had seen a good deal of the world, and who were very proud and fond of Tommy. They recognised a sort of squareness and honesty of spirit in the girl that Jay Ellington Harper never discovered, or, if he did, knew too little of its rareness to value highly. Those old speculators and men of business had always felt a sort of responsibility for Tom Shirley's little girl, and had rather taken her mother's place, and been her advisers on many points upon which men seldom feel at liberty to address a girl. She was just one of them; she played whist and billiards with them, and made their cocktails for them, not scorning to take one herself occasionally. Indeed, Tommy's cocktails were things of fame in Southdown, and the professional compounders of drinks always bowed respectfully to her as though acknowledging a powerful rival.

Now all these things displeased and puzzled Jay Ellington Harper, and Tommy knew it full well, but clung to her old manner of living with a stubborn pertinacity, feeling somehow that to change would be both foolish and disloyal to the Old Boys. And as things went on, the seven Old Boys made greater demands upon her time than ever, for they were shrewd men, most of them, and had not lived fifty years in this world without learning a few things and unlearning many more. And while Tommy lived on in the blissful delusion that her role of indifference was perfectly played and without a flaw, they suspected how things were going and were perplexed as to the outcome. Still, their confidence was by no means shaken, and as Joe Elsworth said to Joe Sawyer one evening at billiards, 'I think we can pretty nearly depend on Tommy's good sense.'

They were too wise to say anything to Tommy, but they said just a word or two to Thomas Shirley, Sr, and combined to make things very unpleasant for Mr Jay Ellington Harper.

At length their relations with Harper became so strained that the young man felt it would be better for him to leave town, so his father started him in a little bank of his own up in Red Willow. Red Willow, however, was scarcely a safe distance, being only some twenty-five miles north, upon the Divide, and Tommy occasionally found excuse to run up on her wheel to straighten out the young man's business for him. So when she suddenly decided to go East to school for a year, Thomas, Sr, drew a sigh of great relief. But the seven Old Boys shook their heads; they did not like to see her gravitating towards the East; it was a sign of weakening, they said, and showed an inclination to experiment with another kind of life, Jay Ellington Harper's kind.

But to school Tommy went, and from all reports conducted herself in a most seemly manner; made no more cocktails, played no more billiards. She took rather her own way with the curriculum, but she distinguished herself in athletics, which in Southdown counted for vastly more than erudition.

Her evident joy on getting back to Southdown was appreciated by everyone. She went about shaking hands with everybody, her shrewd face, that was so like a clever wholesome boy's, held high with happiness. As she said to old Joe Elsworth one morning, when they were driving behind his stud through a little thicket of cottonwood scattered along the sun-parched bluffs,

'It's all very fine down East there, and the hills are great, but one gets mighty homesick for this sky, the old intense blue of it, you know. Down there the skies are all pale and smoky. And this wind, this hateful, dear, old everlasting wind that comes down like the sweep of cavalry and is never tamed or broken, O Joe, I used to get hungry for this wind! I couldn't sleep in that lifeless stillness down there.'

'How about the people, Tom?'

'O, they are fine enough folk, but we're not their sort, Joe, and never can be.'

'You realise that, do you, fully?'

'Quite fully enough, thank you, Joe.' She laughed rather dismally, and Joe cut his horse with the whip.

The only unsatisfactory thing about Tommy's return was that she brought with her a girl she had grown fond of at school, a dainty, white, languid bit of a thing, who used violet perfumes and carried a sunshade. The Old Boys said it was a bad sign when a rebellious girl like Tommy took to being sweet and gentle to one of her own sex, the worst sign in the world.

The new girl was no sooner in town than a new complication came about. There was no doubt of the impression she made on Jay Ellington Harper. She indisputably had all those little evidences of good breeding that were about the only things which could touch the timid, harassed young man who was so much out of his element. It was a very plain case on his part, and the souls of the seven were troubled within them. Said Joe Elsworth to the other Joe,

'The heart of the cad is gone out to the little muff, as is right and proper and in accordance with the eternal fitness of things. But there's the other girl who has the blindness that may not be cured, and she gets all the rub of it. It's no use. I can't help her, and I am going to run down to Kansas City for awhile. I can't stay here and see the abominable suffering of it.' He didn't go, however.

There was just one other person who understood the hopelessness of the situation quite as well as Joe, and that was Tommy. That is, she understood Harper's attitude. As to Miss Jessica's she was not quite so certain, for Miss Jessica, though pale and languid and addicted to sunshades was a maiden most discreet. Conversations on the subject usually ended without any further information as to Miss Jessica's feelings, and Tommy sometimes wondered if she were capable of having any at all.

At last the calamity which Tommy had long foretold descended upon Jay Ellington Harper. One morning she received a telegram from him begging her to intercede with her father; there was a run on his bank and he must have help before noon. It was then ten thirty, and the one sleepy little train that ran up to Red Willow daily had crawled out of the station an hour before. Thomas Shirley, Sr, was not at home.

'And it's a good thing for Jay Ellington he's not, he might be more stony hearted than I,' remarked Tommy, as she closed the ledger and turned to the terrified Miss Jessica. 'Of course we're his only chance, no one else would turn their hand over to help him. The train went an hour ago and he says it must be there by noon. It's the only bank in the town, so nothing can be done by telegraph. There is nothing left but to wheel for it. I may make it, and I may not. Jess, you scamper up to the house and get my wheel out, the tyre may need a little attention. I will be along in a minute.'

'O Theodosia, can't I go with you? I must go!'

'You go! O, yes, of course, if you want to. You know what you are getting into, though. It's twenty-five miles uppish grade and hilly, and only an hour and a quarter to do it in.'

'O, Theodosia, I can do anything now!' cried Miss Jessica, as she put up her sunshade and fled precipitately.

Tommy smiled as she began cramming bank notes into a canvas bag. 'Maybe you can, my dear, and maybe you can't.'

The road from Southdown to Red Willow is not by any means a favourite bicycle road; it is rough, hilly and climbs from the river bottoms up to the big Divide by a steady up grade, running white and hot through the scorched corn fields and grazing lands where the long-horned Texan cattle browse about in the old buffalo wallows. Miss Jessica soon found that with the peddling that had to be done there was little time left for emotion of any sort, or little sensibility for anything but the throbbing, dazzling heat that had to be endured. Down there in the valley the distant bluffs were vibrating and dancing with the heat, the cattle, completely overcome by it, had hidden under the shelving banks of the 'draws' and the prairie dogs had fled to the bottom of their holes that are said to reach to water. The whirr of the seventeen-year locust was the only thing that spoke of animation, and that ground on as if only animated and enlivened by the sickening, destroying heat. The sun was like hot brass, and the wind that blew up from the south was hotter still. But Tommy knew that wind was their only chance. Miss Jessica began to feel that unless she could stop and get some water she was not much longer for this vale of tears. She suggested this possibility to Tommy, but Tommy only shook her head, 'Take too much time,' and bent over her handle bars, never lifting her eyes from the road in front of her. It flashed upon Miss Jessica that Tommy was not only very unkind, but that she sat very badly on her wheel and looked aggressively masculine and professional when she bent her shoulders and pumped like that. But just then Miss Jessica found it harder than ever to breathe, and the bluffs across the river began doing serpentines and skirt dances, and more important and personal considerations occupied the young lady.

When they were fairly over the first half of the road, Tommy took out her watch. 'Have to hurry up, Jess, I can't wait for you.'

'O, Tommy, I can't,' panted Miss Jessica, dismounting and sitting down in a little heap by the roadside. 'You go on, Tommy, and tell him – tell him I hope it won't fail, and I'd do anything to save him.'

By this time the discreet Miss Jessica was reduced to tears, and Tommy nodded as she disappeared over the hill laughing to herself. 'Poor Jess, anything but the one thing he needs. Well, your kind have the best of it generally, but in little affairs of this sort my kind come out rather strongly. We're rather better at them than at dancing. It's only fair, one side shouldn't have all.'

Just at twelve o'clock, when Jay Ellington Harper, his collar crushed and wet about his throat, his eye glass dimmed with perspiration, his hair hanging damp over his forehead, and even the ends of his moustache dripping with moisture, was attempting to reason with a score of angry Bohemians, Tommy came quietly through the door, grip in hand. She went straight behind the grating, and standing screened in the bookkeeper's desk, handed the bag to Harper and turned to the spokesman of the Bohemians,

'What's all this business mean, Anton? Do you all come to bank at once nowadays?'

'We want 'a money, want 'a our money, he no got it, no give it,' bawled a big beery Bohemian.

'O, don't chaff 'em any longer, give 'em their money and get rid of 'em, I want to see you,' said Tommy carelessly, as she went into the consulting room.

When Harper entered half an hour later, after the rush was over, all that was left of his usual immaculate appearance was his eyeglass and the white flower in his buttonhole.

'This has been terrible!' he gasped. 'Miss Theodosia, I can never thank you.'

'No,' interrupted Tommy. 'You never can, and I don't want any thanks. It was rather a tight place, though, wasn't it? You looked like a ghost when I came in. What started them?'

'How should I know? They just came down like the wolf on the fold. It sounded like the approach of a ghost dance.'

'And of course you had no reserve? O, I always told you this would come, it was inevitable with your charming methods. By the way, Jess sends her regrets and says she would do anything to save you. She started out with me, but she has fallen by the wayside. O, don't be alarmed, she is not hurt, just winded. I left her all bunched up by the road like a little white rabbit. I think the lack of romance in the escapade did her up about as much as anything; she is essentially romantic. If we had been on fiery steeds bespattered with foam I think she would have made it, but a wheel hurt her dignity. I'll tend bank; you'd better get your wheel and go and look her up and comfort her. And as soon as it is convenient, Jay, I wish you'd marry her and be done with it. I want to get this thing off my mind.'

Jay Ellington Harper dropped into a chair and turned a shade whiter.

'Theodosia, what do you mean? Don't you remember what I said to you last fall, the night before you went to school? Don't you remember what I wrote you—'

Tommy sat down on the table beside him and looked seriously and frankly into his eyes.

'Now, see here, Jay Ellington, we have been playing a nice little game, and now it's time to quit. One must grow up sometime. You are horribly wrought up over Jess, and why deny it? She's your kind, and clean daft about you, so there is only one thing to do. That's all.'

Jay Ellington wiped his brow, and felt unequal to the situation.

Perhaps he really came nearer to being moved down to his stolid
little depths than he ever had before. His voice shook a good deal
and was very low as he answered her.

'You have been very good to me. I didn't believe any woman
could be at once so kind and clever. You almost made a man of
even me.'

'Well, I certainly didn't succeed. As to being good to you, that's
rather a break, you know; I am amiable, but I am only flesh and
blood after all. Since I have known you I have not been at all
good, in any sense of the word, and I suspect I have been anything
but clever. Now, take mercy upon Jess – and me – and go. Go on,
that ride is beginning to tell on me. Such things strain one's nerve.
Thank Heaven he's gone at last and had sense enough not to say
anything more. It was growing rather critical. As I told him I am
not at all super-human.'

After Jay Ellington Harper had bowed himself out, when
Tommy sat alone in the darkened office, watching the flapping
blinds, with the bank books before her, she noticed a white flower
on the floor. It was the one Jay Ellington Harper had worn in his
coat and had dropped in his nervous agitation. She picked it up
and stood holding it a moment, biting her lip. Then she dropped it
into the grate and turned away, shrugging her thin shoulders.

'They are awful idiots, half of them, and never think of anything beyond their dinner. But O, how we do like 'em!'

(1896)

ELLA D'ARCY

A Marriage

I

In the upstairs room of a City restaurant two young men were finishing their luncheon. They had taken the corner table by the window, and as it was past two o'clock the room was fairly empty. There being no one at either of the tables next them, they could talk at their ease.

West, the elder of the two, was just lighting a cigarette. The other, Catterson, who, in spite of a thin moustache, looked little more than a boy, had ordered a cup of black coffee. When even a younger man than he was at present, he had passed a couple of years in Paris, and he continued, by the manner in which he wore his hair, by his taste in neckties, and by his preferences in food and drink, to pay Frenchmen the sincerest flattery that was in his power.

But today he let the coffee stand before him untasted. His young forehead was pushed up into horizontal lines, his full-lipped mouth was slightly open with anxious, suspended breath. He gazed away, through the red velvet lounges, through the giltframed mirrors, to the distant object of his thought.

West, leaning back in his seat, emitting arabesques and spirals of brown-grey smoke, watched him with interest rather than with sympathy, and could not repress a smile when Catterson, coming abruptly out of dreamland, turned towards him, to say, 'You see, if it were only for the child's sake, I feel I ought to marry her, and the next may be a boy. I should like him to inherit the little property, small as it is. And I've no power to will it.'

His voice was half-decided, wholly interrogative, and West smiled. There had been a moment in all their conversations of the last six weeks, when some such remark from Catterson was sure to fall. Experience enabled West to anticipate its arrival, and he smiled to find his anticipation so accurately fulfilled.

'My dear chap, I see you're going to do it,' he answered, 'so it's useless for me to protest any more. But I'll just remind you of an old dictum, which, maybe, you'll respect, because it's in French: "*Ne faites jamais de votre maîtresse, votre femme.*"'

West spoke lightly, uttering the quotation just because it happened to flash through his mind; but all the same, it was a fixed idea of his, that if you married a girl of 'that sort', she was sure to discover, sooner or later, colossal vices; she was sure to kick over the traces, to take to drink, or to some other form of dissipation.

Catterson shrugged his shoulders, flushed, and frowned; then recovered his temper, and began again, stammeringly, tumultuously, his words tripping over one another in their haste. He always stammered a little in moments of emotion.

'But you d-don't know Nettie. She's not at all – s-she's quite different from what you think. Until she had the misfortune to meet with me, she was as good a girl as you could find.'

'No, I don't know her, I admit,' observed West, and smoked in silence.

'I have been thinking,' Catterson said presently, 'that I should like you to come down to see her. I should like you to make her acquaintance, because then I am sure you would agree I am right. I do want to have your support and approval, you know.'

West smiled again. It amused him to note the anxiety Catterson exhibited for his approval and support, yet he knew all the time that the young man was bent on marrying Nettie Hooper in spite of anything he could say.

But he understood the springs of the apparent contradiction. He understood Catterson fairly well, without being fond of him. They had been schoolmates. Chance lately, rather than choice on West's side, had again thrown them together; now the luncheon hour saw them in almost daily companionship. And, correcting his earlier impressions of the impulsive, sensitive, volatile little boy by these more recent ones, he read Catterson's as a weak, amiable, and affectionate nature; he saw him always anxious to stand well with his associates, to be liked and looked up to by his little world. To do as others do, was his ruling passion; what Brown, Jones, and Robinson might say of him, his first consideration. It was because at one time Robinson, Jones, and Brown had been represented for him by a circle of gay young Frenchmen that he had thought it incumbent upon him, when opportunity offered to tread in their footsteps. It was because he found his path set now within the respectable circles of British middle-class society, that his anomalous position was becoming a burden; that the double personality of married man and father in his riverside lodgings, of eligible bachelor in the drawing-rooms of Bayswater and Maida Vale, grew daily more intolerable to sustain. He could think of no easier way out of the dilemma than to make Nettie his wife, and let the news gradually leak out, that he had been married for the last two years.

Some of his arguments in favour of the marriage – and he required many arguments to outweigh his consciousness of the *mésalliance* – were that, for all practical purposes, he was as good as married already. He could never give Nettie up; he must always provide for her and the child as long as he lived. And his present mode of life was full of inconveniences. He was living at Teddington under an assumed name. At any moment one may be discovered, and an awkward situation may result.

These were some of his arguments. But then, too, he had developed the domestic affections to a surprising degree, and if his first passion for Nettie were somewhat assuaged, he had a much more tender feeling for her now than in the beginning. And he was devoted to his little daughter; a devotion which a few months ago he would have sworn he was incapable of feeling for any so uninteresting an animal as a baby. He reproached himself bitterly for having placed her at such a disadvantage in life as illegitimacy entails; he felt that he ought at least to give the expected child all the rights which a legal recognition can confer.

His chief argument, however, was that he had sinned, and that in marriage lay the only reparation; and let a man persuade himself that a certain course of action is the one righteous, the one honourable course to take – more particularly if it jumps with his own private inclinations – and nothing can deter him from it.

'Not even French proverbs,' laughed West into his beard.

'Come down and see her,' Catterson urged, and West, moved by a natural curiosity, as well as by a desire to oblige his friend, agreed to meet him that evening at Waterloo, that they might go down together.

His soul being eased through confession, Catterson regained at once the buoyant good spirits which were natural to him, but which, of late, secret anxieties and perturbation of mind had overshadowed completely. For when depressed he touched deeper depths of depression than his neighbour, in exact proportion to the unusual height and breadth of his gaiety in his moments of elation.

Now he enlivened the journey out from town, by cascades of exuberant talk, filling up the infrequent pauses with snatches of love-songs: the music-hall love-songs of the day.

Yet as the train approached Teddington, he fell into silence again. A new anxiety began to dominate him: the anxiety that West should be favourably impressed by Nettie Hooper. His manner became more nervous, his stammer increased; a red spot burned on either cheek. He could not keep his thoughts or his speech from the coming interview.

'She doesn't talk much,' he explained, as they walked along the summer sunset roads. 'She's very shy, but you mustn't on that account imagine she's not glad to see you. She's very much interested in you. She wants to meet you very much.'

'Of course she's not what's called a lady,' he began again, 'her people don't count at all. She, herself, wants to drop them. But you would never discover she wasn't one. She has a perfect accent, a perfect pronunciation. And she is so wonderfully modest and refined. I assure you, I've known very few real ladies to compare to her.'

He eulogised her economy, her good management. 'My money goes twice as far since she has had the spending of it. She's so clever, and you can't think how well she cooks. She has learned it from the old lady with whom we lodge. Mrs Baker is devoted to Nettie, would do anything for her, thinks there's no one like her in the world. And then she makes all her clothes, and is better dressed than any girl I see, although they only cost her a few shillings.'

He sang the praises of her sweetness, of her gentleness, of her domesticity. 'She's so absolutely unselfish; such a devoted mother to our little girl; and yet, she's scarcely more than a child herself. She won't be nineteen till next April.'

All which encomiums and dozens more wearied West's ear, without giving him any clear conception of their subject. He was thankful when Catterson suddenly broke off with, 'Here we are, this is Rose Cottage.'

West saw the usual creeper-covered, french-windowed, sham-romantic, and wholly dilapidated little villa, which realises the ideal of all young lovers for a first nest. To more prosaic minds it suggested earwigs and spiders in summer, loose tiles and burst pipes in winter, and general dampness and discomfort all the year round.

It stood separated from the road by a piece of front garden, in which the uncut grass waved fairy spearheads, and the unpruned bushes matted out so wide and thick, as to screen off completely the sitting-room from the passers-by.

The narrow gravel path leading up to the door was painted with mosses, the little trellis-work porch was giving way beneath the weight of vine-wood and rose-stem which lay heavy upon it; the virginia-creeper over the window-top swayed down to the ground in graceful diminishing tresses; the bedroom windows above blinked tiny eyes beneath heavy eyelids of greenery. An auctioneer would have described the place as a bijou bower of verdure, and West's sense of humour was tickled by the thoroughly conventional background it provided for the conventional *solitude à deux*.

Catterson rang that he might give notice of West's arrival, and a thin bell responded to his pull from the interior of the house. It was succeeded by the tapping of high heels along the oilcloth, the door opened, and a very little woman, in a dark woollen gown, stood within the threshold.

The nurse, the landlady, the servant, perhaps? West told himself that *this* could not be Nettie Hooper, this plain little creature, who was surely so much older than the girl Catterson had described.

But the next instant Catterson said, 'Nettie, this is my great friend, West,' and the little woman had given him a lifeless hand, while she welcomed him in curious, drawling tones.

'I'm so glad to see you. Jack is always talking about you. Do come in.'

He was certain she was plain, but he had no time to localise her plainness – to decide whether it lay in feature, complexion, or expression, for her back was towards him; he was following her into the sitting-room, and he looked down upon a dark head of hair, a meagre figure, a dowdy home-made gown.

'I hope you've got a good dinner for us,' Catterson began at once, stammering over every consonant. 'I don't know how West may be feeling, but I'm uncommonly hungry myself.'

'You didn't give me much time,' she answered. 'Your wire only came at four. I've got you some fish, and a steak.'

'And a salad? Good! Nettie's steaks are ripping, West, you'll see.'

'Oh, but Mrs Baker is going to cook the dinner tonight; I didn't think you'd wish me to leave you and Mr West, like that.'

During these not very illuminating remarks, West was revising his first impressions. He confessed that the girl had nice features, regular, well proportioned; that, though she lacked colour, her complexion was of a healthy paleness; that her expression could hardly be called disagreeable, for the difficulty lay in deciding whether she had any expression at all. All the same, she was plain; flat-chested, undeveloped, with clumsy feet and hands.

'You have a – quiet little place here,' he said to her to make conversation. He had been going to say 'a charming little place', but a glance round the dark, musty-smelling room was too much for his powers of unveracity.

'Yes, it's almost too quiet, while Jack is away. Don't you think, Mr West, I'm very good to stay here by myself all day long?'

She had the oddest voice, very drawling, measured, inanimate. It said nothing at all to the listener beyond the mere actual words.

'Come, you've got baby,' said Catterson, laughing, 'let alone Mrs Baker.'

'As though one's landlady and a baby of seventeen months were all the companionship one could require!' She laughed too.

She was almost pretty when she laughed, and West began to perceive that after all she might be no older than Catterson had said. She had the abundant crisp-growing hair, the irreproachable smoothness of skin found only in youth's company. Her eyes were really remarkable eyes, large, of a bluish-grey, clear as water, with the pupils very big.

Yes, she was exceedingly pretty. It took you some time to see it perhaps, but once you had seen it you wondered you could have overlooked it before. Yet West had no sooner admitted the fact than he began to qualify it. He said there was absolutely nothing in her face that appealed to your imagination; that such very limpid eyes go with a cold or a shallow nature, that such very large pupils denote either want of intelligence or want of strength.

And there was undeniably something common in her physiognomy, though at first he could not decide in which particular trait it lay. Was it in the cut of the nostril, the line of the mouth? No, he thought it was to be found, rather, in a certain unpleasing shininess of surface. Her cheek had less of the velvety texture of the peach, than the glaze of the white-heart cherry. The wings of the nose, its slightly aquiline bridge, reflected the light in little patches.

If her hair was unusually thick, it was coarse too, and of a uniform dark-brown colour. The front, cut short, seemed to rebel against the artificial curling to which it was subjected. Instead of lying on her forehead in rings as was no doubt intended, here was an undistinguishable fuzz, while there a straight mesh stood out defiantly.

She had pretty ears and execrably ugly hands, in the thick fingers of which, with squat nails broader than they were long, in the tough and wrinkled skin, the want of race of her ancestors was easily to be read. On the left hand she wore a plain gold ring.

So soon as the first fillip of greeting was spent, she became noticeable for her silences, had a way of letting every subject drop and expressed no opinions, or only those universal ones which every woman may express without danger of self-revelation. For instance, when West asked whether she cared for reading, she said she was passionately fond of it; but when pressed as to what she liked best to read, she mentioned, after considerable hesitation, *East Lynne* and *Shakespeare*.

As Catterson had said, there was no fault to find with her pronunciation or her accent; or what faults there were, were faults he himself was guilty of. West realised that she was quick in imitation, and, up to a certain point, receptive. She had carefully modelled her deportment on Catterson's, held her knife and fork, lifted her glass, and used her table napkin in precisely the same way he did. When, later on, West had occasion to see her handwriting he found it a curiously close copy of Catterson's own. Women, whose characters are still undeveloped, and whose writing therefore remains unformed, almost invariably do adopt, for a time, the handwriting of their lovers.

There was nothing in her manners or appearance to indicate her precise social origin, nor did West, by-the-by, ever learn anything definite concerning it. Catterson was very sensitive on the point, and only once made the vaguest, the most cursory reference to how he had met her.

Still less was there anything about Nettie Hooper to fit in with West's preconceived theories. As she sat there, placid, silent, quiet, he had to admit that as Catterson had said, she was not at all the sort of girl he had imagined her to be. And yet . . .

He made the above mental notes during the course of the dinner, while Catterson's nervousness gradually wore off, and his gaiety returned. His infatuation for Nettie led him, when in her presence, to the conviction that everyone else must be equally infatuated too.

The dining-room was small, and like the parlour looked out through a french window over a tangled slip of garden. The furniture consisted chiefly of Japanese fans, but there was also a round table, and at least three chairs. The arrangements, generally, were of a picnic character, and when Mrs Baker, a stout and loquacious old body, brought in the dishes, she stayed awhile to join in the conversation, addressing them all impartially as 'My dear', and Nettie in particular as 'My dear Life'.

But the meal, if simple, was satisfying, and Nettie herself left the table to make the coffee, as Catterson had taught her to do, in French fashion. He brought out from the *chiffonière* a bottle of green Chartreuse, and Nettie handed cigarettes and found an ashtray. She was full of ministering attentions.

While they smoked and talked, and she sat silent, her limpid eyes fixed mostly on Catterson, although every now and then, West knew they were turned upon him, wails were heard from upstairs.

'It's baby, poor little soul,' said Nettie, rising. 'Please, Jack, may I go and bring her down?'

She presently returned with a flannel-gowned infant in her arms. The child had just the same large, limpid, blue-grey eyes as the mother, with just the same look in them. She fixed West with the relentless, unswerving stare of childhood, and not all her father's blandishments could extract a smile.

Nettie, kissing the square-toed pink feet, addressed her as 'Blossom', and 'Dear little soul', then sat tranquilly nursing her, as a child might nurse a doll.

She had really many of a child's ways, and when Catterson, at the end of the evening, put on his hat to accompany West to the station, she asked in her long, plaintive drawl, 'May I come, too, Jack?' exactly as a child asks permission of parent or master. She put her head back again into the dining-room a moment after leaving it. 'What shall I put on, my cloak or my cape?' she said. 'And must I change my shoes?'

Catterson turned to West with a smile, which asked for congratulations. 'You see how docile she is, how gentle? And it's always the same. It's always my wishes that guide her. She never does anything without asking my opinion and advice. I don't know how a man could have a better wife. I know I should never find one to suit me better. But now you've seen her for yourself, you've come over to my opinion, I feel sure? You've got nothing further to urge against my marrying her, have you?'

West was saved the embarrassment of a reply by the reappearance of Nettie in outdoor things, and Catterson was too satisfied in his own mind with the effect she must have produced, to notice the omission.

He talked gaily on indifferent matters until the train moved out of the station, and West carried away with him a final vignette of the two young people standing close together beneath the glare of a gas-lamp, Catterson with an arm affectionately slipped through the girl's. His thin, handsome face was flushed with excitement and self-content. The demure little figure beside him, that did not reach up to his shoulder, in neat black coat and toque, stared across the platform up to West, from limpid, most curious eyes.

What the devil was the peculiarity of those eyes, he asked himself of impatiently? and hammered out the answer to the oscillations of the carriage, the vibration of the woodwork, the flicker of the lamp, as the train rumbled through the night and jerked up at flaring stations.

Beautiful as to shape and colour, beautiful in their fine dark lashes, in their thinly pencilled brows, these strange eyes seemed to look at you and ostentatiously to keep silence; to thrust you coldly back, to gaze through you and beyond you, as if with the set purpose of avoiding any explanation with your own.

It was this singularity which in the shock of first sight had repelled, which had shed over the face an illusory plainness, which had suggested age and experience, so that it had taken West an appreciable time to discover that Nettie Hooper was in reality quite young, and exceedingly pretty. But he had learned on a dozen previous occasions, that the first instantaneous, unbiased impression is the one to be trusted. Especially in so far as concerns the eyes. The eyes are very literally the windows of the soul.

2

Three years later, West and two men who don't come into this story at all, were spending the month of August up the river. An ill-advised proceeding, for the weather, so far, had proved deplorably wet, as the weather in August too often does, and of all sad places in wet weather, the river is incomparably the saddest.

But they had hired their boat, they had made their arrangements, dates were fixed, and places decided on. With the thoroughly British mental twist that to change your plans is to show inconsistency, and therefore weakness, West's companions were determined to carry these plans out to their prearranged end.

He scoffed at their mulishness, but submitted nevertheless, and following their example he rowed with bent head and set teeth through the continually falling rain, or sat, in their society during interminable hours waiting for it to cease, in an open boat beneath a dripping elm-tree. And as he gazed out over the leaden sheet of pock-marked water, he found amusement in telling himself that here at least was a typically national way of taking a holiday.

Nor, after all, did it always rain. There were occasional days of brilliant, if unstable sunshine, when the stream ran dimpling between its banks of sweet flag and loose-strife; when the sand-martins skimmed over the water with their pittering cry; when the dabchick, as the boat stole upon her, dived so suddenly, remained under for so long, and rose again so far off, that but for a knowledge of her habits, you would pronounce it a genuine case of bird suicide.

It was on one such a sunny, inspiriting Saturday, that a twenty mile pull from Maidenhead brought them by afternoon in sight of the picturesque old bridge at Sonning. Here, in Sonning, they were to pass the night and stay over till Monday. For here one of the men had an aunt, and he was under strict maternal orders to dine with her on Sunday.

There was the usual difference of opinion as to which of the two inns they should put up at, the White Hart being voted too noisy, the French Horn condemned as too swagger. But the question was settled by the White Hart, which you reach first on the Berkshire bank, proving full; they accordingly pulled round the mill-water on the right, to try their luck at the French Horn.

For those who do not know it, this may be described as one of the prettiest of riverside inns, a cosy-looking, two-storey house, with a wide verandah and a lawn sloping down to the water's edge. Beneath the trees on either side, tea was set out on wicker tea-tables, and each table had its encircling group of gay frocks and scarlet sunshades. It presented a Watteau-like picture of light and shadow and colour, the artistic value of which was increased by three conspicuous figures, which took the spectator's eye straight to the centre of the foreground.

A man, a girl, and a little child stood together, just above the wooden landing-steps, and a Canadian canoe, brilliant with newness and varnish, flaring with flame-coloured cushions, rocked gently on the water at their feet.

The young man held the painter in his hand; was dressed in immaculate white flannel, wore a pink and white striped shirt, and a waist-handkerchief of crimson silk.

The girl was the boating-girl of the stage. Where the rushes fringed the lawn you looked instinctively for footlights. The open-work silk stockings, the patent leather evening shoes, the silver belt compressing a waist of seventeen inches, were all so thoroughly theatrical. So was her costume of pale blue and white; so was the knot of broad ribbon fastening her sailor collar; so was the Jack Tar cap, with its blue and silver binding, set slightly on one side of her dark head. The child by her side was dressed in white embroidered muslin and a sun-bonnet.

'I say, West,' cried the man who steered, 'you who know all the actresses, tell us who's that little girl there, with the kid.'

West, who was sculling, turned his head.

'Oh, damn! It's Mrs Catterson,' he said, with the emphasis of a surprise, which is a disagreeable one.

Since the marriage, he had not seen very much of Nettie Catterson, although he was godfather to the boy. For one thing, it is difficult to see much of people who live in the suburbs; and though Catterson had moved twice, first from Teddington to Kingston, then from Kingston to Surbiton Hill, where he was now a householder, Surbiton remained equally out of West's way.

But there was another reason for his evasion of the constant invitations which Catterson pressed upon him in the City. It had not taken him long to perceive that he was far from being *persona grata* to Mrs Catterson. Whether this was to be accounted for by the average woman's inevitable jealousy of her husband's friends, whether it was she suspected his opposition to her marriage, or whether she could not forgive him for having known her while she was passing as Mrs Grey, he could not determine. Probably her dislike was compounded of all three reasons, with a preponderance, he thought, in favour of the last.

For with marriage, the possession of a semi-detatched villa at

Surbiton, and the entrance into such society as a visit from the clergyman's wife may open the door to, Nettie had become of an amazing conventionality, and surpassing Catterson himself in the matter of deference to Mrs Grundy, she seemed to have set herself the task of atoning for irregularity of conduct in the past, by the severest reprobation of all who erred in the present, and West's ribaldry in conversation, his light views on serious subjects, and his habitual desecration of the Sunday were themes for her constant animadversions and displeasure.

It was the rapid *résumé* of these, his demerits with Mrs Catterson, which had called forth his energetic 'Damn!'

At the same moment that he recognised her, Catterson recognised him, and sung out a welcome. The boat was brought alongside, and he was received by Nettie with a warmth which surprised him. His companions, with hasty cap-lifting, escaped across the lawn to get drinks at the bar, and secure beds for the night.

He looked after them with envy, and had to accept Nettie's invitation to tea.

'We were just quarrelling, Jack and I,' she said, 'where to have it. He wants to go down to Marlow, and I want it here. Now you've come, that settles it. We'll have it here.'

Catterson explained his reason: as Nettie wished to go out in the canoe again, they ought to go now while it was fine, as it was sure to rain later.

Nettie denied the possibility of rain with an asperity which informed West that he had arrived on the crest of a domestic disagreement, and he understood at once the cordiality of his reception.

She had developed none of the tempestuous views which his theories had required; on the contrary she appeared to be just the ordinary wife, with the ordinary contempt for her husband's foibles and wishes. She could talk of the trials of housekeeping and the iniquities of servants as to the manner born, and always imitative had lately given back the ideals of Surbiton with the fidelity of a mirror. But there were curious undercurrents beneath this surface smoothness, of which West now and then got an indication.

He renewed his acquaintance with Gladys, the little girl, who periodically forgot him, and asked after his godson. But the subject proved unfortunate.

Nettie's mouth took menacing lines. 'Cyril, I'm sorry to say, is a very naughty boy. I don't know what we're going to do with him, I'm sure.'

West couldn't help smiling. 'It's somewhat early days to despair of his ultimate improvement, perhaps? How old is he? Not three till December, I think?' He told himself that the open-hearted, sensitive, impulsive little fellow ought not to be very difficult to manage.

'He's old enough to be made to obey,' she said, with a glance at Catterson, which suggested some contentious background to the remark.

'Oh, well, one doesn't want to break the child's spirit,' Catterson protested.

'I think his spirit will have to be broken very soon,' asserted Nettie, 'if he goes on being as troublesome as he has been lately.'

Gladys, sitting by her mother's side, drank in everything that was said. She was now five years old, and a little miniature of Nettie. She turned her clear and stolid eyes from one to another.

'Cyril's a . . . naughty . . . little boy,' she observed in a piping drawl, a thin exaggeration of Nettie's own, and making impressive pauses between the words. 'He's never going to be tooked . . . up the river like me. Is he, Mother?'

'If you want to be a good little girl,' observed Catterson, 'you'll put your bread and jam into your mouth, instead of feeding your ear with it as you are doing at present.'

'Cyril don't have . . . no jam . . . for *his* tea,' she began again, "cos he's so naughty. He only has dry bread an'—'

'Come, come, don't talk so much, Gladys,' said her father impatiently, 'or perhaps you won't get "tooked" up the river again either.'

Nettie put an arm round her.

'Poor little soul! Mother'll take her up the river always, won't she? We don't mind what Papa says, do we?'

'Silly old Papa!' cried the child, throwing him one of Nettie's own looks. 'We don't mind what he says, we don't.'

All the same, when tea was over, and they prepared to make a start in the canoe, West their still somewhat unwilling guest, Catterson put his foot down and refused to take Gladys with them for various reasons. Four couldn't get into the canoe with safety or comfort; the child had been out all day, and had already complained of sickness from the constant swaying motion; but chiefly because it was undoubtedly going to rain. Nettie gave in with a bad grace, and the little girl was led off, roaring, by her maid.

Nettie had complained that the tea was cold, and that she could not drink it. She had insisted on Catterson having a second brew brought. Then when this came had pushed away her cup, and pronounced it as unpalatable as before. But no sooner were they some way down stream, than she said she was thirsty, and asked for ginger beer.

West remembered Catterson telling him long ago, how Nettie would suddenly wake up thirsty in the middle of the night, and how he would have to get up and go down to forage for something to quench her thirst. It had seemed to Catterson, in those days, very amusing, pathetic, and childlike, and he had told of it with evident relish and pride. But the little perversity which is so attractively provoking in the young girl, often comes to provoke without any attractiveness in the wife and mother.

Catterson turned the canoe when Nettie spoke, saying they had best go and get what she wanted at the White Hart, but West fancied he looked annoyed and slightly ashamed.

After this little episode, because of the ominous appearance of the sky, it was agreed to keep upstream towards the lock. But before they reached it the first great drops of rain were splashing into the water about them. The lock-keeper made them welcome. He and Catterson were old acquaintances. Having set out for them, and dusted down three Windsor chairs, he went to spread a tarpaulin over the canoe.

The darkness of the little room grew deeper every instant. Then came an illuminating flash followed by a shattering thunderpeal. The ear was filled with the impetuous downrush of the rain.

'There! Why wouldn't you let me bring Gladys?' cried Nettie. 'Poor little soul, she's so terrified of thunder, she'll scream herself into fits.'

'She's right enough with Annie,' said Catterson, somewhat too confidently.

Nettie replied that Annie was a perfect fool, more afraid of a storm than the child herself. 'Jack, you'll have to go back and comfort her. Jack, you *must* go!'

'My dear, in this rain!' he expostulated. 'How can you want me to do anything so mad?'

But Nettie had worked herself up into a paroxysm of maternal solicitude, of anguish of mind. West asked himself if it were entirely genuine, or partly a means of punishing Catterson for his self-assertion a while ago.

'Since you're so afraid of a little rain,' she concluded contemptuously, 'I'll go myself. I'm not going to let the child die in hysterics.'

She made a movement as though to leave the house. Catterson drew her back, and turning up the collar of his coat, went out. But before the canoe was fairly launched, West knew he must be wet to the skin. He stood and watched him paddling down against the closely serried, glittering lances of the rain, until lost in a haze of watery grey.

Then, for his life, he could not refrain from speaking. 'I think it's very unwise for Jack to get wet like that. It's not as though he were particularly strong. He comes of a delicate, short-lived family, as you probably know?'

But Nettie only stared silently before her as though she had not heard.

And there, in silence, they remained for another twenty minutes, while the rain flooded earth and river, and the thunder rumbled to and fro over the sky.

Nettie maintained an absolute silence, and West, leaning against the window-frame, beguiled the time in studying her with fleeting, inoffensive glances. He again noted the ugliness of her hands, to which, as they lay folded in her lap, the flashing of a half-hoop of fine diamonds, now worn above the wedding ring, carried first his attention. But when he raised his eyes to her small, pale face, he decided she was prettier than she used to be, more strikingly pretty at first sight. She had learned, perhaps, to bring out her better points. He thought she dressed her hair more becomingly; three years steady application of curling irons had at last induced it to lie in softer curls. Five years of married life had in no wise dimmed the transparency of her skin. Not a line recorded an emotion whether of pleasure or of pain. If she had lived through any psychic experiences, they had not left the faintest mark behind. And it was partly the immobility of countenance by which this smoothness of surface was maintained, which led West again to qualify his favourable verdict, just as he had done before.

He began to think that the predominant note in her character was coldness, heartlessness even. He remembered, not so long ago, hearing her relate as though it were a good story, how meeting old Mrs Baker one day in Kingston Market, she had passed her by with an unrecognising stare. Yet the old woman had been devoted to Nettie, as she herself used to boast; a certain feeling of gratitude, of kindliness might have been looked for in return.

But there must have been others, West told himself, to whom she owed a greater debt – the relations, or friends, who had brought her up, clothed her and fed her until the day she had met with Catterson. She never referred to these others, she never let slip the smallest allusion to her early life; she held her secrets with a tenacity which was really uncommon; but it was evident that she had turned her back on all who had ever befriended her with the same cold ease she had shown to Mrs Baker.

She was fond, apparently, of her little girl, but this particular affection was no contradiction to her general want of it; she saw in the child a reduplication of herself. For Gladys was the image of her mother, just as the little boy was Catterson over again; very nervous, sensitive, and eager for love and approval.

West mused over the curious want of sympathy Nettie had always displayed for the boy. It amounted almost to dislike. He had never been able to win her good word from the day of his birth, and his natural timidity was greatly augmented by her severe treatment. West was inclined to believe the reason to be a sort of jealousy for Gladys; that she resented the fact that Cyril was legitimate; that he would inherit under his grandfather's will while the little girl, the first born, the preferred child, could not.

Catterson had never alluded to the subject, but for all that, West knew that he was profoundly hurt by the difference Nettie made between the children. If he himself made any in his heart and West said it would be only natural if he loved Cyril most who adored his father and impulsively showed it, rather than Gladys who always coldly repulsed his overtures of affection, least in his conduct towards them he never let it appear. He even seemed to overlook Cyril a little, having learned by experience probably, what were the consequences of paying him too much attention. Cyrill was always left at home, while Gladys accompanied her parents everywhere.

Studying Nettie's physiognomy, tracing the lines of the mouth, the slightly backward drawn nostrils, the hard insensitive hands, West found himself rejoicing he did not stand in his poor little godson's shoes.

The storm was over, the sun was out again, and Nettie rising suggested they should go. They crossed over the top of the lockgates, picked their way between the puddles of the towing-path and so back over Sonning Bridge to the hotel.

Catterson was in his room changing his wet clothes, and Nettie went up to him. West found Gladys sitting in the verandah beside her nurse, tranquilly playing with a doll.

'Well, babe,' said he, in friendly tones, 'were you very much frightened by the thunder and lightning, just now?'

But she did not answer, she merely fixed her limpid eyes on his, thrusting him back with their coldly negative stare. Then ostentatiously, she reabsorbed herself in her game.

The next morning kept Catterson in bed with a bad cold and West, sooner than pass the day in the vicinity of Nettie, persuaded the nephew to abandon the aunt and the dinner, and both men into the extraordinary inconsistency of pushing on to Streatley.

3

One black morning in December, West remembered, for no reason at all, that it was the birthday of Cyril his godson. Cyril today entered on his fifth year, and West found himself making the usual 'damned silly reflections' on the flight of time. Dismissing these as stale and unprofitable, he began to wonder what present he could take the boy. He tried to remember what he himself had liked at the age of four, but he could recall nothing of that antediluvian period. He thought of a book, a paint-box, a white fur rabbit, but the delights of painting and reading were surely beyond Cyril's years, while the Bunny was perhaps too infantile. Finally, he set his face westward, trusting to find inspiration in the windows of the shops he passed. The heavenly smell of chocolate which greeted him at Buzard's made him decide on a big packet of bon-bons. He knew from previous experience with the Catterson children, that chocolates were sure to be appreciated.

The Cimmerian* morning had dragged its course through brown, orange, and yellow hours, to an afternoon of misty grey. But West nevertheless felt inclined for walking. As he crossed the park diagonally from the Marble Arch to Queen's Gate, his thoughts outran his steps, and were already with the Cattersons.

They had moved again, and now lived in South Kensington.

Nettie had become very intimate with a certain Mrs Reade, whose acquaintance she owed to a week spent in the same hotel. The two young women had struck up an effusive friendship, based on a similarity of taste in dress and amusement, Mrs Reade supplying the model for Nettie's faithful imitation. She copied her manners, she adopted her opinions and ideas. Mrs Reade had declared it was impossible to live so far out of town as Surbiton. The Cattersons therefore disposed of the lease of their house, and took one close to Mrs Reade's in Astwood Place.

Catterson had left his pretty suburban garden with the more reluctance that he disliked the Reades, considered the husband common, the wife loud, vulgar, bad style. But he had told West at the time, there was no price too high to pay for the purchase of domestic peace.

He was peaceably inclined by nature, but of late, any nervous energy which might have been contentiously employed was used up in fighting off the various trifling ailments that continuously beset him. He was always taking cold; now it was lumbago now a touch of congestion, now a touch of pleurisy. He spent half his days at home in the doctor's hands. Nettie made his bad health the ostensible reason for quitting Surbiton. The damp air rising from the river didn't suit him.

Town suited her, as she expressed it, 'down to the ground', and following in Mrs Reade's wake, she became one of the immense crowd of smartly-gowned nobodies, who, always talking as if they were somebodies, throng fashionable shops, cycle in the Park, and subscribe to Kensington Town Hall dances. It was far away from the days when she lived in lodgings at Teddington, made her own clothes, and cooked her own dinner.

Now she kept four maids, whom she was constantly changing. West seldom found the door opened by the same girl thrice.

Nettie was an exacting mistress, and had no indulgence for the class from which presumably she had sprung. Her servants were expected to show the perfection of angels, the capacity for work of machines, and the servility of slaves. And she was always detecting imperfections, laziness, or covert impertinence of manner or speech. Every six weeks or so there was a domestic crisis, and Mary or Jane left in tears, and without a character.

West could generally guess from the expression of Jane's or Mary's face how long she had been in Astwood Place. Disappointment, harrassment, and sullen discontent were the stages through which each new comer passed before reaching the tearful catastrophe.

From the serene appearance of the young person who today let him in, West judged she was but recently arrived. 'Mrs Catterson was out,' for which he was not sorry but 'the Master was at home,' which he had expected, having heard in the City that Catterson had not been at his office for some days.

He found him huddled up over the drawing-room fire, spreading out his thin hands to the blaze. Half lost in the depths of the armchair, sitting with rounded shoulders and sunken head, he seemed rather some little shrunken sexagenarian than a man still under thirty.

Gladys, with a picture-book open on her knee, sat on a stool against the fender. She did not move as West came in, but raising her eyes considered him, as was her wont, with a steadfast neutrality.

Catterson, turning, jumped up to greet him with something of his old buoyancy of manner; but the change which a few weeks had made in his face gave West a fresh shock. Nor could he disguise it sufficiently quickly – the painful impression.

'You think I'm looking ill, eh?' asserted Catterson, but with an eagerness which pleaded for a denial.

West lied instantly and heartily, but Catterson was not taken in.

'You think it's all UP with me, I see,' he said, returning to the chair, and his former attitude of dejection.

This was so exaggerated a statement of his thoughts that West tried absolute candour.

'I don't think you're looking very fit,' he said, 'but what you want is change. This dark, damp, beastly weather plays the deuce with us all. You should run down to Brighton for a few days. A man was telling me only last night that Brighton all this week has been just a blaze of sunshine.'

'Oh, Brighton!' Catterson repeated, hopelessly, 'I'm past that.' With the fingertip of one hand he kept probing and pressing the back of the other as it lay open upon his knee, searching for symptoms of the disease he most dreaded.

To change the channel of his thoughts, West turned to the little girl who still mutely envisaged him.

'Well, Gladys, have you forgotten, as usual, who I am?'

'No, I haven't ... you're Mithter Wetht,' she told him, the

piping drawl now complicated by a lisp, due to the fact that she had lost all her front teeth.

'Where's Sonny?' he asked her. 'I've got something for him,' and he put the packet of sweets down on the table by his elbow.

She reflected a moment as to who Sonny might be; then, 'Thyril's a naughty boy,' she said. 'He'th had a good . . . whipping . . . and hath been put to bed.'

'Oh poor old chap!' West exclaimed, ruefully. 'And on his birthday too. What has he done?'

But Gladys only repeated, 'He'th a . . . very . . . naughty boy,' in tones of dogmatic conviction. She seemed to detect the guest's sympathy with the culprit, and to resent it.

Voices and laughter were heard on the stairs. Nettie entered in her bonnet and furs, preceded by a big, overdressed woman, whom West easily identified as Mrs Reade. They had been shopping, and both were laden with small, draper's parcels.

Nettie did not seem pleased to find the drawing-room occupied. She gave West a limp hand without looking at him, which was one of her exasperating habits when put out, and then she attacked her husband for keeping up so big a fire. The heat of the room was intolerable, she said; it was enough to make anyone ill. She threw off her wraps with an exaggeration of relief, peevishly altered the position of a chair which West had pushed aside inadvertently, and began to move about the room, in the search, as he knew well, of some fresh grievance. Catterson followed her for a second or two with tragic eyes. Then he turned to the fire again. 'To me it seems very cold,' he murmured. 'I've not been warm all day.'

Mrs Reade declared he should take to 'byking'. That would warm him; there was nothing in the world like it. 'Indeed unless it maims you for life, it cures every evil that flesh is heir to.'

'But I suppose the chances are in favour of the maiming?' West asked her.

She laughed hilariously at this, and though she was certainly vulgar, as Catterson had complained, West couldn't help liking her. He always did like the women who laughed at his little jokes (Mrs Catterson never laughed at them). Besides, she was so obviously healthy and good-natured; handsome too, although you saw that in a few years, she would become too fat.

Nettie wondered why on earth Jack couldn't have had tea ready, pulled violently at the bell, and began to examine some patterns of silk she had brought home with her for the selection of an evening gown. Her lap was presently filled with little oblong pieces of black and coloured brocades.

'The green is exquisite, isn't it, Mimi?' she appealed to her friend. 'But do you think it would suit me? Wouldn't it make me look too pale? The heliotrope is sweet too, but then I had a gown last year almost that very shade. People would say I had only had it cleaned or turned. Perhaps, after all, I had better have black? I've not had a black frock for a long time, and it's always so smart-looking, isn't it?'

Mrs Reade thought that in Nettie's place she should choose the green, and have it made up with myrtle velvet and cream guipure. An animated discussion of dressmaking details began, during which the men sat, perforce, silent.

Gladys, meanwhile, had come over to the table on which the chocolates lay, where she stood, industriously picking open the paper.

Catterson presently caught sight of this.

'Gladys!' he exclaimed, with the sharp irritability of ill-health.

She had just popped a fat bon-bon into her mouth, and she remained petrified for a moment by so unaccustomed a thing as a rebuke. Then, for convenience sake, she took the sweet out again in her thumb and finger, and bust into sobs of anger and surprise.

Nettie was equally surprised and angry. 'What are you thinking of, Jack, frightening the poor child by shouting at her like that?'

'But did you see what she was doing, my dear, meddling with West's property?'

'Mr West shouldn't leave his sweets about on the table if he doesn't want the child to have them. Naturally, she thought they were for her.'

'Not at all. She knew they were for Cyril. She heard West say so.'

'After Cyril's behaviour to me this morning I certainly shall not allow him to have them. And I don't approve of sweets anyway. It ruins the children's teeth. I wish Mr West wouldn't bring them so often.'

This was sufficiently ungracious, and West's answer was sufficiently foolish. 'Perhaps you wish I wouldn't bring myself so often either?' said he.

'I've no doubt we could manage to get on just as well without you,' she retorted, and there were worlds of insult concentrated in the tone.

The only effectual answer would have been immediate departure, but consideration for Catterson held West hesitant. It is always because of their affection for the husband that the wife finds it so particularly easy, and perhaps so agreeable, to insult his friends. She offers them their choice between perpetual banishment and chunks of humble-pie.

Catterson put an end to the situation himself.

'Let's get away out of this, West,' he said, with flushed cheeks and shaking voice. 'Come down to my study.'

Here, the change of atmosphere brought on a fit of coughing, to which West listened with a *serrement de cœur*. In his mind's eye he saw Catterson again, vividly, as he had been a few years back; very gay and light hearted, full of pranks and tricks. Always restless, always talking, always in tip-top spirits; when he fell in love, finding expression for the emotion in the whistling and singing of appropriate love-ditties, the music-hall love-ditties of the day.

The foolish refrain of one of these recurred to West, ding-dong, pertinaciously at his ear:

> They know me well at the County Bank,
> Cash is better than fame or rank,
> Then hey go lucky! I'll marry me ducky,
> The Belle of the Rose and Crown.

And now Catterson, with pinched features, sunken eyes, and contracted chest, sat there pouring out a flood of bitterness against himself, life, and the gods for the granting of his prayer.

'You remember Nettie before I married her? Did she not appear the gentlest, the sweetest, the most docile girl in the world? Who would ever have imagined she could have learned to bully her husband and insult his friends like this?

'But the moment her position was assured she changed; changed completely. Why, look here, West, the very day we were married – you remember we went down to Brighton, and were married there – as we walked back along the King's Road, she stopped me before a shop and said, "You can just come in here and buy me some furs. Now I'm your wife you needn't suppose I'm going through another winter in my wretched little old coat of last year." It was her tone; the implication of what she had had to endure at my hands, before she had the right to command me. It was the first lifting of the veil on her true character.

'Perhaps if I had never married her – who knows? Women require to be kept under, to be afraid of you, to live in a condition of insecurity; to know their good fortune is dependent on their good conduct.

'I did the right thing? Yes . . . but we are told be not righteous overmuch; and there are some virtues which dig their own graves.'

He spoke in a disconnected manner; but his domestic misery was the string which threaded the different beads. Of West's interjected sympathy and well-meant efforts to turn his thoughts he took no heed.

'Marriage is the metamorphosis of women.' Where did I read that lately? It's odd but everything I now read relates to marriage. In every book I take up I find an emphatic warning against it. Why couldn't these have come in my way sooner? Why couldn't someone tell me?' Marriage is the metamorphosis of women – the Circe wand which changes back all these smiling, gentle, tractable little girls into their true forms.

'Oh, but after all, you say? . . . No, my wife does none of those things but she has made my life miserable, miserable . . . and that's enough for me. And if I were to try and explain how she does it, I daresay you would only laugh at me. For there's nothing tragic in the process. It's the thousand pin-pricks of daily life, the little oppositions, the little perversities, the faint sneers. At first you let them slip off again almost indifferently, but the slightest blow repeated upon the same place a thousand times draws blood at last.

'No, she doesn't care for me, and sometimes I almost think she hates the boy. Poor boy . . . it seems monstrous, incredible but I've caught her looking at him with a hardness, a coldness . . .'

He sat silent, looking wistfully away into space. West traced the beginning of a pleasanter train of ideas in the relaxed corners of his mouth, in the brightening of his sunken eyes.

'He's the dearest little chap, West! And so clever! Do you know, I believe he'll have the most extraordinarily logical and mathematical mind. He has begun to meditate already over what seems to him the arbitrariness of names. He wanted to know the other day, for instance, how a table had come to be called a table, why it wasn't called a chair, or anything else you like. And this morning, when we were talking, he and I, over the present I had given him, he posed me this problem: supposing two horses harnessed to a cart were galloping with it, just as fast as ever they could go, how much faster could ten horses gallop with it? Shows he thinks, eh? Not bad for a child of four?'

He began to forecast Cyril's career; he would put his name down at Harrow, because to Harrow he could get out to see him every week. He should have the advantages of Oxford or Cambridge, which Catterson had not had. He should enter one of the liberal professions, the Bar for choice.

And then his face clouded over again.

'But he shall never marry. He shall do anything else in life he pleases: but he shall never marry. For it's no matter how well a man may be born, it's no matter how fortunate he may be in life, if he's unfortunate in his marriage. And it seems to me, that one way or another, marriage spells ruin.'

He was back again in the unhappy present, and West felt his heart wrung. Yet there was no help to be given, no consolation possible. The one door of deliverance which stood open, was the one door which Catterson could not face, although his reluctant feet drew nearer to it every day.

But West had already observed that when life becomes impossible, when a man's strength is inadequate to the burdens imposed upon it, when the good he may yet accomplish is outweighed by the evils he may have to endure, then the door opens, the invisible hand beckons him through, and we know no further of his fate.

Though Catterson could not face it, and with an ominous spot burning on either cheek, tried to reabsorb himself again in plan for the future, West saw in it the only possible escape, and told himself it was better, even though it proved an eternal sleep, than what he daily had to endure.

The wife's cold heart, her little cruelties, her little meannesses all her narrowness, her emptiness of mind rose before him. What a hell upon earth to have to live in daily companionship with her, even if unrelated to her in any way! But for her husband she was the constant living reminder of his dead illusions. He could not look at her without seeing the poor, thin ghosts of his lost youth, of his shattered faith, hope, and happiness, gathered round her. Every indifference of hers, every neglect, must call up the memory of some warm protestation, of some dear attention in the past. And these were less hard to bear than the knowledge that those had never been genuine.

It is life as you anticipated it, brought still fresh and palpitating into contrast with the bleak reality, which is so intolerably hard to bear.

The contemplation of Catterson's position became so painful to West, that he felt he must get away even at the cost of brutality. He gave warmly the asked-for assurance to come again soon, and knew in his heart as he uttered it, that he would not soon find the courage to return.

In the hall he looked about him mechanically then let slip a hot and vigorous word on discovering he had left his hat up in the drawing-room and must go back.

The tea-table now stood by Nettie's elbow. She insisted that he should take a cup of tea, pressing it on him as a sort of peace offering, so that without actual rudeness he could not refuse. She was again gracious as far as she knew how to be. Possibly Mrs Reade, who studied the suavities of life, had been remonstrating with her.

Gladys lay on the hearthrug, her face in her hands, her elbows planted on the open book. The packet of sweets in a very knock-kneed and depleted condition stood beside her. She sucked a chocolate in her cheek, had kicked off her shoes, and drummed with her black-stockinged feet upon the floor.

West made a pretence of drinking his tea, but it was tepid, it was weak, and Nettie had put sugar into it without enquiring his tastes.

She and Mimi Reade were still discussing the patterns of the brocade.

'I do think the green perfectly sweet, Mimi,' she repeated, holding the scrap up at arm's length, so that the lamplight might slant over it 'and yet the black is a softer, richer silk, and would make up awfully well with jet trimmings, as you say. I don't know which I had better have.'

The two women turned and returned the problem, considered it again in all its bearings. They appeared to have forgotten West which was but natural, he had sat silent for so long. To himself, his brain seemed mesmerised by the vapidity of their talk, so that an imbecile point of interest grew up within it, as to which colour, eventually, Nettie would choose.

Meanwhile the study door opened, and Catterson's cough, which carried such poignant suggestions to West, was heard again upon the stairs. It seemed to speak suggestively to Nettie too.

'After all,' she said in her curious, drawling voice, 'it would be more prudent I suppose to decide on the black.'

(1898)

MÉNIE MURIEL DOWIE

An Idyll in Millinery

I

The actual reason why Liphook was there does not matter: he was there, and he was there for the second time within a fortnight, and on each occasion, as it happened, he was the only man in the place – the only man-customer in the place. A pale, shaven young Jew passed sometimes about the rooms, in the background.

Liphook could not stand still, the earliest sign of mental excitement, this; if he paused for a moment in front of one of the two console tables and glanced into the big mirror, it was only to turn the next second and make a step or two this way or that upon the spacious-sized, vicious-patterned Axminster carpet. His eye wandered, but not without a mark of resolution in its wandering – resolution not to wander persistently in one direction. First the partings in the curtains which ran before the windows seemed to attract him, and he glanced into the gay grove of millinery that blossomed before the hungry eyes of female passers-by in the street. Sometimes he looked through the archways that led upon each hand to further salons in which little groups of women, customers and saleswomen, were collected. Sometimes his eye rested upon the seven or eight unemployed shopladies who stood behind the curtains, like spiders, and looked with an almost malevolent contemptuousness upon the street starers who came not in to buy, but lingered long, and seemed to con the details of attractive models. More than once, a group in either of the rooms fascinated him for full a minute. One particularly, because its component parts declared themselves so quickly to his apprehension.

A young woman, with fringe carefully ordered to complete formlessness and fuzz, who now sat upon a chair and now rose to regard herself in a glass as she poised a confection of the *toque** breed upon her head. With her, a friend, older, of identical type, but less serious mien, whose face pringled into vivacious comment upon each venture; comment which of course Liphook could not overhear. With them both an elder lady; to whom the shop-woman, a person of clever *dégagé* manner and primrose hair, principally addressed herself; appealingly, confirmatively, rapturously, critically – according to her ideas upon the hat in question. In and out of their neighbourhood moved a middle-aged woman of French appearance, short necked, square shouldered, high busted, with a keen face of chamois leather colour and a head to which the black hair seemed to have been permanently glued – Madame Félise herself. When she threw a word into the momentous discussion the eyes of the party turned respectfully upon her; each woman hearkened. Even Liphook divined that the girl was buying her trousseau millinery; the older sister, or married friend, advising in crisp, humorous fashion, the elder lady controlling, deciding, voicing the great essential laws of order, obligation and convention; the shopwoman playing the pipes, the dulcimer, the sackbut, the tabor or the viol – Madame Félise the while commanding with invisible baton her intangible orchestra; directing distantly, but with ineludable authority, the very players upon the stage. At this moment She turned to him and his attention necessarily left the group. How did he find this? Did he care for the immense breadth in front? Everyone in Paris was doing it. Wasn't he on the whole a little bit sick of hydrangeas – everyone, positively everyone, had hydrangeas just now, and hydrangeas the size of cauliflowers. He made replies; he assumed a quiet interest, not too strong to be in character; he steered her away from the Parisian breadth in front, away from the hydrangeas, into a consideration of something that rose very originally at the back and had a *ruche* of watercresses to lie upon the hair, and three dahlias, and four distinct colours of tulle in aniline shades, one over the other, and an osprey, and a bird of Paradise, and a few paste ornaments; and a convincing degree of *chic* in its abandoned hideousness. Then he took a turn down the room towards the group aforesaid.

'It looks so *fearfully* married to have that tinsel crown, don't you know!' the elder sister or youthful matron was saying. 'I mean, it suggests dull calls, doesn't it? Dull people *always* have tinsel crowns, haven't you noticed? I don't want to influence you, but as I said before, I liked you in the Paris model.'

Every hat over which you conspicuously hover at Félise's, becomes, on the instant, a Paris model.

'So smart, Madam,' cut in the shoplady. 'And you can't have anything newer than that rustic brim in shot straw with just the little knot of gardenias at the side. Oh I *do* think it suits you!'

Liphook turned away. After all, he didn't want to hear what these poor, silly, feeble people were saying; he wanted to look . . .

'But Jim always likes me so much in pale blue, that I think—' began the girl.

'Why not have just a little tiny knot of forget-me nots *with* the gardenia. Oh, I'm shaw you'd like it.'

Thus flowed the oily current of the shoplady, reaching his ear as Liphook returned down the room. He could look again in the only direction that won his eyes and his thoughts; five minutes had been killed; there was time left him yet, for She had just been seized with the idea that something with a little more brim was really her style. After all, She craved no more than to be loose at Félise's, amid the spring models lit by a palely ardent town sun, and Harold's cheque-book looming in the comfortable shadow of his pocket.

At the back of each gilt and mirrored saloon was placed a work-table – in the manner of all hat shops – surrounded by chairs in which, mostly with their backs to the shops sat the girls who were making up millinery, their ages anywhere from sixteen to twenty-one. Seldom did the construction of a masterpiece appear to concern them, but they were spangling things; deftly turning loops into bows, curling feathers, binding ospreys into close sheaves; their heads all bent over their work, their neat aprons tied with tape bows at the back, their dull hair half-flowing and half-coiled – the inimitable manner of the London workgirl – their pale faces dimly perceived as they turned and whispered not too noisily: the whole thing recalling the soft, quietly murmurous groups of pigeons in the streets gathered about the scatterings of a cab-horse's nose-bag. Sometimes shopgirls with elaborately distorted hair came up and gave them disdainful-seeming orders, but the flock of sober little pigeons murmured and pecked at its work and ruffled no plumage of tan-colour or slate. And one of them, different from the others – how Liphook's eyes, in the brief looks he allowed himself, ate up the details of her guise. Dressed in something – dark-blue, it might have been – that fitted with a difference over her plump little figure; a fine and wide lawn collar spread over breast and shoulders; a smooth head, with no tags and ends upon the pale, yellow-tinted brow; a head as sleek and

as sweetly coloured as the coat of the cupboard-mouse; a face so
softly indented by its features, so fleckless, so *mat* in its flat tones,
so mignon in its delicate lack of prettiness as to be irresistible.
Lips, a dull greyish-pink, but tenderly curved at the pouting bow
and faithfully compressed at the dusk-downy corners – terribly
conscientious little lips that seemed as if never could they be
kissed to lighter humour. Eyes, with pale ash-coloured fringes,
neither long nor greatly curved, but so shy-shaped as ever eyes
were; eyes that could only be imagined by Liphook, and he was
sometimes of mind that they were that vaporous autumn blue;
and at other times that they were liquid, brook-coloured hazel.

But this was the maddest obsession that was riding him! A
London workgirl in a West End hat shop, a girl whose voice he
had never heard, near whom he had never, could never, come.
And Heaven forbid he should come near her; what did he want
with her? Before Heaven, and all these hats and mirrors, Viscount
Liphook could have sworn he wanted nothing of her. Yet he loved
her completely, desperately, exclusively. What name was there for
this feeling other than the name of love? Soiled with all ignoble
use, this name of love; though to do him justice, Liphook was not
greatly to blame in that matter. He was but little acquainted with
the word; he left it out of his *affaires de cœur*, and very properly,
for it did not enter into them. Still, his feeling for this girl, his
craving for the sound of her voice, his eye fascinated by her
smallest movement, his yearning for the sense of her nearer
presence – novel, inexplicable as this all was, might it not be love?
He stood there, quiet, inexpressive of face, in jealous hope of –
what next? And then She claimed his attention – in a whisper
which brought her head with its mahogany hair, and her face with
its ground-rice surface, close to his ear. She said:

'You don't mind five, eh? It's a model – and – don't you think it
becomes me? I do think this mushroom-coloured velvet and just
the three green orchids divine – and it's really very quiet!'

He assented, careful to look critically at the hat – a clever mass
of evilly imagined, ill-assorted absurdities. He had looked too
long at that work-table, at that figure, at that face – he dropped
into a chair – let his stick fall between his knees and cast his eyes
to the mirror-empanelled ceiling; there the heads, and feet of the
passers-by were seething grotesquely in a fashion that recalled the
Inferno of an old engraving.

Well, it would be time to look again soon – ah! She had risen;

thank goodness, not a tall woman – (She was five foot nine), small, and indolent of outline.

'I'll take it to the French milliner now, Madam, and she'll pin a pink rose in for you to see!'

It was a shop woman speaking to some customer, who with a hat in her hand, approached the work-table.

'If you please, Mam'zelle Mélanie,' she began, in a voice meant to impress the customer, 'would you pin in a rose for Madam to try? Madam thinks the pansy rather old-looking – etc., etc., etc.'

The French milliner; French, then! And what a dear innocent, young, crusty little face! What delicious surliness: the little brown bear that she was, growling and grumbling to do a favour. Well, bless that woman – and the pansy that looked old – he knew her name; enough to recognise her by, enough to address a note to her – and it should be a note! A note that would bring out a star in each grey eye – they were grey – after all. (The grey of a lingering, promising, but unbestowing twilight.) Reflecting, but unobservant, his glance left her face and focused the pale, fair, young Jew, who was seated, in frock-coat and hat, gloating over a pocket-book that had scraps of coloured silk and velvet pinned in it. He recalled his wandering senses.

'How much? Eight ten?'

'Well, I've taken a little black thing as well; it happens to be very reasonable. There, you don't mind?' Mrs Percival always went upon the principle of appearing to be careful of other people's money; she found she got more of it that way.

'My dear! – as long as you are pleased!' It was weeks since this tone had been possible to him. He scribbled a cheque and they got away.

'I know I've been an awful time, old boy,' said the mahogany-haired one, with rough good humour – the good humour of a vain woman whose vanity has been fed. 'Are you coming?'

'Er – no; in fact, I'm going out of town, I shan't see you for a bit – Oh, I wasn't very badly bored, thanks.'

She made no comment on his reply to her question; her coarsely pretty face hardly showed lines of relief, for it was not a mobile face, but she was pleased.

'Glad you didn't fret. I'd never dreamt you'd be so good about shopping. Yes, I'll take a cab. There is a call for 12.30, and I see it is nearly one now.'

He put her into a nice-looking hansom, lifted his hat and

watched her drive away. Then he turned and looked into the gaudy windows. His feelings were his own somehow, now that She had left him. He smiled; love warmed in him. Was the old pansy gone and the pink rose in its place? Had she pricked those creamy yellow fingers in the doing of it? No, she was too deft. Tired, flaccid little fingers! Was he never to think of anything or anyone again, except Mam'zelle Mélanie?

2

Now the mahogany-haired lady was not an actress: she was nothing so common as an actress; she belonged to a mysterious class, but little understood, even if clearly realised, by the public. It was not because she could not that she did not act; she had never tried to, there had been no question of capability – but she consented to appear at a famous West End burlesque theatre, to oblige the manager who was a personal friend of long standing. She 'went on' in the ballroom scene of a hoary but ever-popular 'musical comedy', because there was – not a part – but a pretty gown to be filled, and because she was surprisingly handsome, and of very fine figure, and filled that gown amazingly well. The two guineas a week that came her way at 'Treasury' went a certain distance in gloves and cab-fares, and the necessaries of life she had a different means of supplying. Let her position be understood: she was a very respectable person: there are degrees in respectability as in other things; there was no fear of vulgar unpleasantnesses with her and her admirers – if she had them. Mr John Holditch, the popular manager of several theatres, had a real regard for her. In private she called him 'Jock, old boy,' and he called her 'Mill' – because he recollected her *début*; but the public knew her as Miss Mildred Metcalf, and her lady comrades in the dressing-room as Mrs Percival, and it was generally admitted by all concerned that she was equally satisfactory under any of these styles. Oh, it will have been noticed and need not be insisted on, that Liphook called her 'my dear', and if it be not pushing the thing too far, I may add that her mother spoke of her as 'our Florrie'.

Liphook was a rich man whose occupation, when he was in town, was the dividing of days between the club, his rooms in Half Moon Street, his mother's house in Belgrave Square, and

Mrs Percival's abode in Manfield Gardens, Kensington. The only respect in which he differed from a thousand men of his class was, that he had visited the hat shop of Madame Félise, in the company of Mrs Percival, and had conceived a genuine passion for a little French milliner who sewed spangles on to snippets of nothingness at a table in the back of the shop.

The note had been written, had been answered. This answer, in fine, sloping, uneducated French handwriting, upon thin, lined, pink paper of the foreign character, had given Liphook a ridiculous amount of pleasure. The club waiters, his mother's butler, his man in Half Moon Street, these unimportant people chiefly noted the uncontrollable bubbles of happiness that floated to the surface of his impassive English face during the days that followed the arrival of that answer. He didn't think anything in particular about it; few men so open to the attractions of women as this incident proves him, think anything in particular at all, least of all, at so early a stage. He was not – for the sake of his judges it must be urged – meaning badly any more than he was definitely meaning well. He wasn't meaning at all. He cannot be blamed, either. The world is responsible for this sense of irresponsibility in men of the world – who are the world's sole making. Herein he was true to type; in so far as he did not think what the girl meant by her answer, type was supported by individual character. Liphook was not clever, and did not think much or with any success, on any subject. And if he had he wouldn't have hit the real reason; only experience would have told him that a French workgirl, from a love of pleasure and the national measure of shrewd practicality combined, never refuses the chance of a nice outing. She does not, like her English sister, drag her virtue into the question at all.

Never in his life, so it chanced, had Liphook gone forth to an interview in such a frame of mind as on the day he was to meet Mélanie outside the Argyll Baths in Great Marlboro' Street at ten minutes past seven. Apart from the intoxicating perfume that London seemed to breathe for him, and the gold motes that danced in the dull air, there was the unmistakable resistant pressure of the pavement against his feet (thus it seemed) which is seldom experienced twice in a lifetime; in the lifetime of such a man as Liphook, usually never. The Argyll Baths, Great Marlboro' Street: what a curious place for the child to have chosen, and she would be standing there, pretending to look into a shop window. Oh, of course, there were no shop windows to speak of in Great Marlboro' Street. (He had paced its whole length several times since the arrival of the pink glazed note). What would she say? What would she look like? Her eyes, drooped or raised frankly to his, for instance? That she would not greet him with bold, meaning smile and common phrase he knew – he felt. Dreaming and speculating, but wearing the calm leisured air of a gentleman walking from one point to another, he approached and – yes! there she was! A scoop-shaped hat rose above the cream-yellow brow; a big dotted veil was loosely – was wonderfully – bound about it; a little black cape covered the demure lawn collar; quite French *bottines** peeped below the dark-blue skirt. But – she was not alone, a man was with her. A man whom, even at some distance, he could discern to be unwelcome and unexpected, the pale fair young Jew in dapper frock-coat and extravagantly curved over-shiny hat. Loathsome-looking reptile he was, too, so thought Liphook as he turned abruptly with savage scrape of his veering foot upon the pavement, up Argyll Street. Perhaps she was getting rid of him; it was only nine minutes past seven, anyhow; perhaps he would be gone in a moment. Odious beast! In love with her, no doubt; how came it he had the wit to recognise her indescribable charm? (Liphook never paused to wonder how himself had recognised it, though this was, in the circumstances, even more remarkable.) Anyway, judging by that look he remembered, she would not be unequal to rebuffing unwelcome attention.

Liphook walked as far as Hengler's Circus and read the bills; the place was in occupation, it being early in March. He studied the bill from top to bottom, then he turned slowly and retraced his steps to the corner. Joy! she was there and alone. His pace quickened, his heart rose; his face, a handsome face, was strung to lines of pride, of passionate anticipation.

He had greeted her; he had heard her voice; so soft – dear Heaven! so soft – in reply; they had turned and were walking towards Soho, and he knew no word of what had passed.

'We will have a cab. You will give me the pleasure of dining with me. I have arranged it. Allow me.' Perhaps these were the first coherent words that he said. Then they drove along and he said inevitable, valueless things in quick order, conscious of the lovely interludes when her smooth tones, now wood-sweet, now with a harp-like thrilling *timbre* in them, again with the viol – or

was it the lute-note? – a sharp dulcidity that made answer in him
as certainly as the tuning-fork compels its octave from the rosewood board. The folds of the blue gown fell beside him; the
French pointed feet, miraculously short toed, rested on the atrocious straw mat of the wretched hansom his blindness had brought
him; the scoop-hat knocked the wicked reeking lamp in the centre
of the cab; the dotted veil, tied as only a French hand can tie a veil,
made more delectable the creams and twine-shades of the
monotonous-coloured kitten face. They drove, they arrived somewhere, they dined, and then of all things, they went into a church,
which being open and permitting organ music to exude from its
smut-blackened walls, seemed less like London than any place
they might have sought.

And it happened to be a Catholic church, and he – yes, he
actually followed the pretty ways of her, near the grease-smeared
pecten shell with its holy water, that stuck from a pillar: some
church oyster not uprooted from its ancient bed. And they sat on
prie-dieus, in the dim incense-savoured gloom; little unaspiring
lights seemed to be burning in dim places beyond, and sometimes
there were voices, and sometimes these ceased again and music
filled the dream-swept world in which Liphook was wrapped and
veiled away. And they talked – at least she talked, low murmurous recital about herself and her life, and every detail sunk and
expanded wondrously in the hot-bed of Liphook's abnormally
affected mind. The evening passed to night, and people stepped
about, and doors closed with a hollow warning sound that hinted
at the end of lovely things, and they went out and he left her at a
door which was the back entrance to Madame Félise's establishment; but he had rolled back a grey lisle-thread glove, and
gathered an inexpressibly precious memory from the touch of that
small hand that posed roses instead of pansies all the day.

And of course he was to see her again. He had heard all about
her. How a year since she had been fetched from Paris at the
instance of Goldenmuth. Goldenmuth was the fair young Jewish
man in the frock-coat and supremely curved hat. He was a
'relative' of Madame Félise, and travelled for her, in a certain sense,
in Paris. He had seen Mélanie in an obscure corner of the *Petit St
Thomas* when paying an airy visit to a lady in charge of some
department there. An idea had occurred to him. In three days he
arrived and made a proposition. He had conceived the plan of
transplanting this ideally French work-flower to the London shop,

and his plan had been a success. Her simple shrewd, much-defined little character clung to Mélanie in London, as in Paris; she had clever fingers, but beyond all, her appearance which Goldenmuth had the art to appreciate, soft but marked and unassailable by influence, told infinitely at that unobtrusive but conspicuous work-table.

Half mouse, half dove; never to be vulgarised, never to be destroyed.

Mélanie had a family, worthy *épicier* of Nantes, her father; her mother, his invaluable book-keeper. Her sister Hortense, cashier at the Restaurant des Trois Epeés; her sister Albertine, in the millinery like herself. Every detail delighted Liphook, every word of her rapid incorrect London English sank into his mind; in the extraordinarily narrow circumscribed life that Liphook had lived – that all the Liphooks of the world usually do live – little naïvely simple description of some quite different life is apt to sound surprisingly interesting, and if it comes from the lips of your Mélanie why . . .

But previous to the glazed pink note, if Liphook had crystallised any floating ideas he might have had as to the nature of the intimacy he expected, they would have tallied in no particular with the reality. In his first letter had been certain warmly worded sentences; at their first interview when he had interred two kisses below the lisle-thread glove, he had incoherrently murmured something lover-like. It had been too dark to see Mélanie's face at the moment; but when since, more than once, he had attempted similar avowals she had put her head on one side raised her face crinkled up the corners of the grey eyes, and twisted quite alarmingly the lilac-pink lips. So there wasn't much said about love or any such thing. After all, he could see her three or four times a week. On Sunday they often spent the whole day together; he could listen to her prattle; he was a silent fellow himself, having never learnt to talk and having nothing to talk about. He could in hansoms and quiet places, tuck her hand within his arm and beam affectionately into her face, and they grew always closer and closer to each other; as *camarades* still only as *camarades*. She never spoke of Goldenmuth except incidentally, and then very briefly; and Liphook, who had since seen the man with her in the street on two occasions, felt very unanxious to introduce the subject; after all he knew more than he wanted to about it, he said to himself. It was obvious enough. He had bought her two hats at

Félise's; he had begged to do as much, and she had advised him which he should purchase, and on evenings together she had looked ravishing beneath them. He knew many secrets of the hat trade; he knew and delightedly laughed over half a hundred fictions Mélanie exploded; he was in a fair way to become a man-milliner; even Goldenmuth could not have talked more trippingly of the concomitants of capotes.

One Sunday, when the sunniest of days had tempted them down the river, he came suddenly into the private room where they were to lunch and found her coquetting with her veil in front of a big ugly mirror; a mad sort of impulse took him, he gripped her arms to her side, nipped her easily off the floor, bent his head round the prickly fence of hat-brim and kissed her several times. She laughed with the low, fluent gurgle of water pushing through a narrow passage. She said nothing, she only laughed.

Somehow, it disorganised Liphook.

'Do you love me? Do you love me?' he asked rapidly, even roughly, in the only voice he could command, and he shook her a little.

She put her head on one side and made that same sweet crinkled-up kind of *moue moquante*, then she spread her palms out and shook them and laughed and ran away round the table. '*Est-ce que je sais, moi?*' she cried in French. Liphook didn't speak. Oh, he understood her all right but he was getting himself a little in hand first. A man like Liphook has none of the art of life; he can't do figure-skating among his emotions like your nervous, artistic-minded, intellectually trained man. After that one out-burst and the puzzlement that succeeded it, he was silent, until he remarked upon the waiter's slowness in bringing up luncheon. But he had one thing quite clear in his thick English head, through which the blood was still whizzing and singing. He wanted to kiss her again badly; he was going to kiss her again at the first opportunity.

But, of course, when he wasn't with her his mind varied in its reflections. For instance, he had come home one night from dining at Aldershot – farewell dinner to his Colonel it was – and he had actually caught himself saying 'I must get out of it,' meaning his affair with Mélanie. That was pretty early on, when it had still seemed, particularly after being in the society of worldly-wise friends who rarely, if ever, did anything foolish, much less emo-tional, that he was making an ass of himself, or was likely to if he didn't 'get out of it'. Now the thing had assumed a different aspect. He could not give her up; under no circumstances could he contemplate giving her up. Well then, why give her up? She was only a little thing in a hat shop, she would do very much better – yes, but, somehow he had a certain feeling about her, he couldn't – well, in point of fact, he loved her; hang it, he respected her; he'd sooner be kicked out of his Club than say one word to her that he'd mind a fellow saying to his sister.

Thus the Liphook of March, '95, argued with the Liphook of the past two and thirty years!

3

Liphook's position was awkward – all the other Liphooks in the world have said it was beastly awkward, supposing they could have another kind of man this little love story might not have been appropriate; occuring in the case of Liphook it was nothing less than melancholy. Not that he felt melancholy about it, no indeed; just sometimes, when he happened to think how it was all going to end, he had rather a bad moment, but thanks to his nature and training he did not think often.

Meantime, he had sent a diamond heart to Mrs Percival; there was more sentiment about a heart than a horse shoe; women looked at that kind of thing, and she would feel that he wasn't cooling off; so it had been a heart. That secured him several more weeks of freedom at any rate, and he wouldn't have the trouble of putting notes in the fire. For on receiving the diamond heart Mrs Percival behaved like a python after swallowing an antelope; she was torpid in satiety, and no sign came from her.

But one morning Liphook got home to Half Moon Street after his Turkish bath, and heard that a gentleman was waiting to see him.

'At least, hardly a gentleman, my lord. I didn't put him in the library,' explained the intuitive Sims.

Someone from his tailor's with so-called 'new' patterns, no doubt; well—

He walked straight into the room, never thinking, and he saw Goldenmuth. The man had an offensive orchid in his buttonhole. To say that Liphook was surprised is nothing; he was astounded, and too angry to call up any expression whatever to his face; he was rigid with rage. What in hell had Sims let the fellow in for? However, this was the last of Sims; Sims would go.

The oily little brute, with his odious hat in his hand, was speaking, was saying something about being fortunate in finding his lordship, etc.

'Be good enough to tell me your business with me,' said Liphook, with undisguised savagery. Though he had asked him to speak, he thought that when her name was mentioned he would have to choke him. His rival – by gad, this little Jew beggar was Liphook's rival. Goldenmuth hitched his sallow neck, as leathery as a turtle's, in his high, burnished collar, and took his pocket-book from his breast pocket – which meant that he was nervous, and forgot that he was not calling upon a 'wholesale buyer', to whom he would presently show a pattern. He pressed the book in both hands, and swayed forward on his toes – swayed into hurried speech.

'Being interested in a young lady whom your lordship has honoured with your attentions lately, I called to 'ave a little talk.' The man had an indescribable accent, a detestable fluency, a smile which nearly warranted you in poisoning him, a manner—! There was silence. Liphook waited; the snap with which he bit off four tough orange-coloured hairs from his moustache, sounded to him like the stroke of a hammer in the street.

Then an idea struck him. He put a question:

'What has it got to do with you?'

'I am interested—'

'So am I. But I fail to see why you should mix yourself up with my affairs.'

'Madame Félise feels—'

'What's she got to do with it?' Liphook tossed out his remarks with the nakedest brutality.

'The lady is in her employment and—'

'Look here, say what you've got to say, or go,' burst from Liphook, with the rough bark of passion. He had his hands behind his back; he was holding one with the other in the fear that they might get away from him, as it were. His face was still immobile, but the crooks of two veins between the temples and the eye corners stood up upon the skin; his impassive blue eyes harboured sullen hatred. He saw the whole thing. That old woman had sent her dirty messenger to corner him, to 'ask his intentions', to get him to give himself away, to make some promise. It was a kind of blackmail they had in view. The very idea of such creatures about Mélanie would have made him sick at another time; now he felt only disgust, and the rising obstinacy about committing himself at the unsavory instance of Goldenmuth. After all, they couldn't take Mélanie from him. She was free, she could go into another shop; he could marry . . . Stop – madness!

'Mademoiselle Mélanie is admitted to be most attractive – others have observed it—'

'You mean you have,' sneered Liphook, in the most ungentlemanly manner, it must be allowed.

'I must bring to the notice of your lordship,' said the Jew, with the deference of a man who knows he is getting his point, 'that so young as Mademoiselle is, and so innocent, she is not fitted to understand business questions; and her parents being at a distance it falls to Madame Félise and myself to see that – excuse me, my lord, but we know what London is – that her youth is not misled.'

'Who's misleading her youth?' Liphook burst out; and his schoolboy language detracted nothing from the energy with which he spoke. 'You can take my word here and now that she is in every respect as innocent as I found her. And now,' with a sudden reining in of his voice, 'we have had enough of this talk. If you are the lady's guardians you may reassure yourselves: I am no more to her than a friend. I have not sought to be any more.' Liphook moved in conclusion of the interview.

'Your lordship is very obliging, but I must point out that a young and ardent girl is likely, in the warmth of her affection, to be precipitate – that we would protect her from herself.'

'About this I have nothing to say, and will hear nothing,' exclaimed Liphook, hurriedly.

Goldenmuth used the national gesture: he bent his right elbow, turned his right hand palm upwards and shook it softly to and fro.

'Perhaps even I have noticed it. I am not insensible!'

Liphook had never heard a famous passage – he neither read nor looked at Shakespeare, so this remark merely incensed him. 'But,' went on the Jew, 'since she came to England – for I brought her – I have made myself her protector —'

'You're a liar!' said Liphook, who was a very literal person.

'Oh, my lord! I mean in the sense of being kind to her and looking after her, with Madame Félise's entire approval; so when I noticed the marked attentions of a gentleman like your lordship—'

'You're jealous,' put in Liphook, again quite inexcusably. But it would be impossible to over-estimate his contempt for this man. Belonging to the uneducated section of the upper class he was a man of the toughest prejudices on some points. One of these was that all Jews were mean, scurvy devils at bottom and that no kind of consideration need be shown them. Avoid them as you would a serpent; when you meet them, crush them as you would a serpent. He'd never put it into words, but that is actually what poor Liphook thought, or at any rate it was the dim idea on which he acted.

'Your lordship is making a mistake,' said Goldenmuth with a flush. 'I am not here in my own interest; I am here to act on behalf of the young lady.' Had the heavens fallen? In *her* interest? Then Mélanie? Never! As if a Thing like this could speak the truth!

'Who sent you?' Liphook always went to the point.

'Madame Félise and I talked it over and agreed that I should make it convenient to call. We have both a great regard for Mademoiselle; we feel a responsibility – a responsibility to her parents.'

What was all this about? Liphook was too bewildered to interrupt even.

'Naturally, we should like to see Mademoiselle in a position, an assured position for which she is every way suited.'

So it was as he thought. They wanted to rush a proposal. *Must* he chaffer with them at all?

'I can tell you that if I had anything to propose I should write it to the lady herself,' he said.

'We are not anxious to come between you. I may say I have enquired – my interest in Mademoiselle has led me to enquire – and Madame Félise and I think it would be in every way a suitable connection for her. Your lordship must feel that we regard her as no common girl; she deserves to be *lancée* in the right manner; a settlement – an establishment – some indication that the connection will be fairly permanent, or if not, that suit-able—'

'Is *that* what you are driving at, you dog, you?' cried Liphook, illuminated at length and boiling with passion. 'So you want to sell her to me and take your blasted commission? Get out of my house!' He grew suddenly quiet. It was an ominous change. 'Get out, this instant, before—'

Goldenmuth was gone, the street door banged.

'God! God!' breathed Liphook with his hand to his wet brow. 'What a hellish business!'

It was nine o'clock when Liphook came in that night. He did not know where he had been, he believed he had had something in the nature of dinner, but he could not have said exactly where he had had it.

Sims handed him a note.

He recognised a friend's hand and read the four lines it contained.

'When did Captain Throgmorton come, then?'

'Came in about three to 'alf past, my lord. He asked me if your lordship had any engagement tonight, and said he would wait at the Club till quarter past eight and that he should dine at the Blue Posts after that.'

'I see. Well,' he reflected a moment, 'Sims, pack my hunting things, have everything at St Pancras in time for the ten o'clock express, and,' he reflected again, 'Sims, I want you to take a note – no, never mind. That'll do.'

'V'ry good, my lord.'

Yes, he'd go. Jack Throgmorton was the most companionable man in the world – he was so silent. Liphook and he had been at Sandhurst together, they had joined the same regiment. Liphook had sent in his papers rather than stand the fag of India; Throgmorton had 'taken his twelve hundred' rather than stand the fag of anywhere. He was a big heavy fellow with a marked difficulty in breathing, also there was fifteen stone of him. His round eyes, like 'bulls'-eyes', the village children's best-loved goodies, stuck out of a face rased to an even red resentment. He had the hounds somewhere in Bedfordshire. His friends liked him enormously, so did his enemies. To say that he was stupid does not touch the fringe of a description of him. He had never had a thought of his own, nor an idea; all the same, in any Club quarrel, or in regard to a point of procedure, his was an opinion other men would willingly stand by. At this moment in his life, a blind instinct taught Liphook to seek such society; no one could be said to sum up more completely – perhaps because so unconsciously – the outlook of Liphook's world, which of late he had positively begun to forget. The thing was bred into Thromorton by sheer, persistent sticking to the strain, and it came out of him again mechanically, automatically, distilled through his dim brain a triple essence. The kind of man clever people have found it quite useless to run down, for it has been proved again and again that if he can only be propped up in the right place at the right moment, you'll never find his equal *in* that place. Altogether, a handsome share in 'the secret of England's greatness' belongs to him. The two men met on the platform beside a pile of kit-bags and suitcases, all with Viscount Liphook's name upon them in careful uniformity. Sims might have had the administration of an empire's affairs upon his mind, whereas he was merely chaperoning more boots and shirts than any one man has a right to possess.

'You didn't come last night,' said Captain Throgmorton, as though he had only just realised the fact. He prefaced the remark by his favourite ejaculation which, was 'Harr-rr' – he prefaced every remark with 'Harr-rr' – on a cold day it was not uninspiriting if accompanied by a sharp stroke of the palms; in April it was felt to be somewhat out of season. But Captain Throgmorton merely used it as a means of getting his breath and his voice under way. 'Pity,' he went on, without noticing Liphook's silence. 'Good bone.' This summed up the dinner with its famous marrowbones at the Blue Posts.

They got in. Each opened a *Morning Post*. Over the top of this fascinating sheet they flung friendly brevities from time to time.

'Shan't have more than a couple more days to rattle 'em about,' Captain Throgmorton remarked, after half an hour's silence, and a glance at the flying hedges.

Liphook began to come back into his world. After all it was a comfortable world. Yet had an angel for a time transfigured it, ah dear! how soft that angel's wings, if he might be folded within them . . . old world, dear, bad old world, you might roll by.

They were coming home from hunting next day. Each man bent ungainly in his saddle, their cords were splashed. The going had been heavy, and once it had been hot as well, but only for a while. Then they had hung about a lot, and though they found three times, they hadn't killed. Liphook was weary. When Throgmorton stuck his crop under his thigh, hung his reins on it, and lit a cigar, Liphook was looking up at the sky, where dolorous clouds of solid purple splotched a background of orange, flame-colour and rose. Throgmorton's peppermint eye rolled slowly round when it left his cigar-tip. He knew that when a man – that is, a man of Liphook's sort – is found staring at a thing like the sunset there is a screw loose somewhere.

'Wha' is it, Harold?' he said, on one side of his cigar.

Liphook made frank answer.

'What's she done then?'

'Oh, Lord, it isn't *her*.'

''Nother?' said Jack, without any show of surprise, and got his answer again.

'What sort?' This was very difficult, but Liphook shut his eyes and flew it.

'How old?'

'Twenty,' said Liphook, and felt a rapture rising. 'Jack, man,' he exclaimed, under the influence of the flame and rose, no doubt, 'what if I were to marry?'

Throgmorton was not, as has been indicated, a person of fine fibre. 'Do, and be done with 'em,' said he. And after all, as far as it went, it was sound enough advice.

'I mean marry her,' Liphook explained, and the explanation cost him a considerable expenditure of pluck.

An emotional man would have fallen off his horse – if the horse would have let him. Jack's horse never would have let him. Jack said nothing for a moment; his eye merely seemed to swell, then he put another question: 'Earl know about it?'

'By George, I should say not!'

'Harr-rr.'

That meant that the point would be resolved in the curiously composed brain of Captain Throgmorton, and by common consent not another word was said on the matter.

4

Two days had gone by. Liphook's comfortable sense of having acted wisely in coming out of town to think the thing over still supported him, ridiculous though it seems. For of course he was no more able to think anything over than a Hottentot. Thinking is not a natural process at all; savage men never knew of it, and many people think it quite as dangerous as it is unnatural. It has become fashionable to learn thinking, and some forms of education undertake to teach it; but Liphook had never gone through those forms of education. After all, to understand Liphook, one must admit that he approximated quite as nearly to the savage as to the civilised and thinking man, if not more nearly. His appetites and his habits were mainly savage, and had he lived in savage times he would not have been touched by a kind of love for which he was never intended, and his trouble would not have existed. However, he was as he was, and he was thinking things over; that is, he was waiting and listening for the most forceful of his instincts to make itself heard, and he had crept like a dumb unreasoning animal into the burrow of his kind, making one last effort to be of them. At the end of the week his loudest instinct was setting up a roar; there could be no mistaking it. He loved her. He could not part from her; he must get back to her; he must make her his and carry her off.

'Sorry to be leaving you, Jack,' he said one morning at the end of the week. They were standing looking out of the hall door together and it was raining. 'But I find I must go up this morning.'

Throgmorton rolled a glance at him, then armed him into the library and shut the door.

'What are you going to do?'

'Marry her.'

There was a silence. They stood there, the closest feeling of friendship between them, not saying a word.

'My dear Harold,' said Throgmorton at length, with much visible and more invisible effort. He put a hand heavily on Liphook's shoulder and blew hard in his mute emotion. Then he put his other hand on Liphook's other shoulder. Liphook kept his eyes down. He was richly conscious of all Jack was mutely saying. He felt the weight of every unspoken argument. The moment was a long one, but for both these slow-moving minds a very crowded moment.

'Come to the Big Horn Mountains with me,' Throgmorton remarked suddenly, '– and – and – har-rr write to her from there.'

He was proud of this suggestion; he knew the value of a really remote point to write from. It was always one of the first things to give your mind to, the choice of a geographically well-nigh inaccessible point to write from. First you found it, then you went to it, and when you got there, by Jove, you didn't need to write at all. Liphook smiled in impartial recognition of his friend's wisdom, but shook his head.

'Thanks,' he said. 'I've thought it all over' – he genuinely believed he had – 'and I'm going to marry her. Jack, old man, I love her like the very devil!'

In spite of the grotesqueness of the phrase, the spirit in it was worth having.

Throgmorton's hands came slowly off his friend's shoulders. He walked to the window, took out a very big handkerchief and dried his head. He seemed to look out at the dull rain battering on the gravel and digging yellow holes.

'I'll drive you to meet the 11.15,' he said at last and went out of the room.

Liphook put up his arms and drew a deep breath; it had been a stiff engagement. He felt tired. But no, not tired. Roll by, O bad old world – he has chosen the angel's wing!

Not one word had passed about Goldenmuth, Madame Félise, or the astounding interview; a man like Liphook can always hold his tongue, one of his greatest virtues. Besides, why should he ever think or breathe the names of those wretches again? Jack Throgmorton, in his splendid ignorance, would have been unable to throw light upon the real motive of these simple, practical French people. Liphook to his dying day would believe they had given proof of hideous iniquity, while in reality they were actuated by a very general belief of the *bourgeoise*, that to be 'established' with settlements, as the mistress of a viscount, is quite as good as becoming the wife of a grocer. They had been, perhaps, wicked, but innocently wicked; for they acted according to their belief, in the girl's best interest. Unfortunately they had had an impracticable Anglais to deal with and had had to submit to insult; in their first encounter, they had been worsted by British brute stupidity.

With a constant dull seething of impulses that quite possessed him, he got through the time that had to elapse before he could hear from her in reply to his short letter. He had done with thinking. A chance meeting with his father on the sunny side of Pall Mall one morning did not even disquiet him. His every faculty, every fibre was in thrall to his great passion. The rest of life seemed minute, unimportant, fatuous, a mass of trivial futilities.

There were two things in the world, and two only. There was Mélanie, and there was love. Ah, yes, and there was time!

Why did she not answer?

A note from the bonnet shop, re-enclosing his own, offered an explanation that entered like a frozen knife-blade into Liphook's heart. She had left. She was gone. Gone altogether, for good.

Absurd! Did they suppose they could – oh, a higher price was what they wanted. He'd go, by God he'd give it. Was he not going to marry her? He hurried to the hat shop. He dropped into the chair he had occupied when last in the shop, let his stick fall between his knees and stared before him into the mirrored walls. All the same tangled scene of passing people, customers, shop women and brilliant millinery was reflected in them; only the bright hats islanded and steady among this ugly fluctuation. Pools of fretful life, these circular mirrors; garish, discomfiting to gaze at, stirred surely by no angel unless the reflection of the mouse-maiden should ever cross their surfaces.

Fifteen minutes later he was standing gazing at the horrid clock and ornaments in ormolu that stood on the mantelpiece of the red velvet salon where he waited for Madame Félise.

She came. Her bow was admirable.

'I wrote to Mademoiselle, and my letter has been returned. The note says she has gone.' Liphook's schoolboy bluntness came out most when he was angry. 'Where has she gone? And why?'

'Aha! Little Mademoiselle! Yes, indeed, she has left us and how sorry we are! *Chère petite!* But what could we do? We would have kept her, but her parents—' A shrug and a smile punctuated the sentence.

'What about her parents?'

'They had arranged for her an alliance – what would you have? – we had to let her go. And the rezponsibility – after all—'

'What sort of an alliance?' The dog-like note was in his voice again.

'But – an alliance! I believe very good. A *charpentier* – a *charcutier*, I forget – but *bien solide!*'

'Do you mean you have sold her to some French—'

'Ah, my lord! how can you speak such things? Her parents are most rezpectable, she has always been most rezpectable – naturally we had more than once felt anxious here in London—'

'I wish to marry her,' said Liphook curtly, and he said it still, though he believed her to have been thrust upon a less reputable road. It was his last, his greatest triumph over his world. It fitted him nobly for the shelter of the angel's wing. He had learned the worst – and—

'I wish to marry her,' said Liphook.

'*Hélas!* But she is married!' shrieked Madame Félise in a mock agony of regret, but with surprise twinkling in her little black eyes.

'Married!' shouted Liphook. 'Impossible!'

'Ask Mr Goldenmuth, he was at the wedding.' Madame laughed, The true explanation of my lord's remarkable statement had just struck her. It was a *ruse*, an English *ruse*. She laughed very much, and it sounded and looked most unpleasant.

'His lordship was – a little unfriendly – a little too – too reserved – not to tell us, not even to tell Mademoiselle herself that he desired to *marry* her,' she said with villainous archness.

Liphook strode to the door. Yes, why, why had he not?

'I will find her, I know where her relatives live. If it is a lie, I'll make you sorry—'

'*Fi donc*, what a word! The ceremony at the *mairie* was on Thursday last.'

They were going downstairs and had to pass through the showrooms – quite near – ah, quite near – the table where the little grey and brown pigeons sat clustered, where the one ring-dove had sat too.

'It is sometimes the fate of a lover who thinks too long,' Madame was saying, with an air of much philosophy. 'But see now, if my lord would care to send a little souvenir' – Madame reached hastily to a model on a stand – '*comme cadeau de noce* here is something quite *exquis*!' She kissed the tips of her brown fingers – inimitably, it must be allowed. 'So simple, so young, so innocent – I could pose a little *nœud* of *myosotis*. Coming from my lord, it would be so delicate!'

Liphook was in a shop. There were people about. He was a lover, he was a fool, he was a gentleman.

'Er – thank you – not today,' he said; the air of the world he had repudiated came back to him. And a man like Liphook doesn't let you see when he is hit. That is the beauty of him. He knew it was true, but he would go to Paris; yes, though he knew it was true. He would not, could not see her. But he would go.

He stood a moment in the sun outside the shop, its windows like gardens behind him; its shop ladies like evil-eyed reptiles in these gardens. The carpets, the mirrors on the wall, the tables are at the back – and it was here he had first seen the tip and heard the flutter of an angel's wing!

'Lord Liphook,' said a voice, 'what an age . . .'

He turned and lifted his hat.

His world had claimed him.

(1896)

KATE CHOPIN

The Storm

I

The leaves were so still that even Bibi thought it was going to rain. Bobinôt, who was accustomed to converse on terms of perfect equality with his little son, called the child's attention to certain sombre clouds that were rolling with sinister intention from the west, accompanied by a sullen, threatening roar. They were at Friedheimer's store and decided to remain there till the storm had passed. They sat within the door on two empty kegs. Bibi was four years old and looked very wise.

'Mama'll be 'fraid, yes,' he suggested with blinking eyes.

'She'll shut the house. Maybe she got Sylvie helpin' her this evenin',' Bobinôt responded reassuringly.

'No; she ent got Sylvie. Sylvie was helpin' her yistiday,' piped Bibi.

Bobinôt arose and going across to the counter purchased a can of shrimps, of which Calixta was very fond. Then he returned to his perch on the keg and sat stolidly holding the can of shrimps while the storm burst. It shook the wooden store and seemed to be ripping great furrows in the distant field. Bibi laid his little hand on his father's knee and was not afraid.

2

Calixta, at home, felt no uneasiness for their safety. She sat at a side window sewing furiously on a sewing machine. She was greatly occupied and did not notice the approaching storm. But she felt very warm and often stopped to mop her face on which the perspiration gathered in beads. She unfastened her white sacque* at the throat. It began to grow dark, and suddenly realising the situation she got up hurriedly and went about closing windows and doors.

Out on the small front gallery she had hung Bobinôt's Sunday clothes to air and she hastened out to gather them before the rain fell. As she stepped outside, Alcée Laballière rode in at the gate. She had not seen him very often since her marriage, and never alone. She stood there with Bobinôt's coat in her hands, and the big raindrops began to fall. Alcée rode his horse under the shelter of a side projection where the chickens had huddled and there were plough and a harrow piled up in the corner.

'May I come and wait on your gallery till the storm is over, Calixta?' he asked.

'Come 'long in, M'sieur Alcée.'

His voice and her own startled her as if from a trance, and she seized Bobinôt's vest. Alcée, mounting to the porch, grabbed the trousers and snatched Bibi's braided jacket that was about to be carried away by a sudden gust of wind. He expressed an intention to remain outside, but it was soon apparent that he might as well have been out in the open: the water beat in upon the boards in driving sheets, and he went inside, closing the door after him. It was even necessary to put something beneath the door to keep the water out.

'My! what a rain! It's good two years sence it rain' like that,' exclaimed Calixta as she rolled up a piece of bagging and Alcée helped her to thrust it beneath the crack.

She was a little fuller of figure than five years before when she married; but she had lost nothing of her vivacity. Her blue eyes still retained their melting quality; and her yellow hair, dishevelled by the wind and rain, kinked more stubbornly than ever about her ears and temples.

The rain beat upon the low, shingled roof with a force and clatter that threatened to break an entrance and deluge them there. They were in the dining-room – the sitting-room – the general utility room. Adjoining was her bedroom, with Bibi's couch along side her own. The door stood open, and the room with its white, monumental bed, its closed shutters, looked dim and mysterious.

Alcée flung himself into a rocker and Calixta nervously began to gather up from the floor the lengths of a cotton sheet which she had been sewing.

'If this keeps up, *Dieu sait* if the levees goin' to stan' it!' she exclaimed.

'What have you got to do with the levees?'

'I got enough to do! An' there's Bobinôt with Bibi out in that storm – if he only didn't left Friedheimer's!'

'Let us hope, Calixta, that Bobinôt's got sense enough to come in out of a cyclone.'

She went and stood at the window with a greatly disturbed look on her face. She wiped the frame that was clouded with moisture. It was stiflingly hot. Alcée got up and joined her at the window, looking over her shoulder. The rain was coming down in sheets obscuring the view of far-off cabins and enveloping the distant wood in a grey mist. The playing of the lightning was incessant. A bolt struck a tall chinaberry tree at the edge of the field. It filled all visible space with a blinding glare and the crash seemed to invade the very boards they stood upon.

Calixta put her hands to her eyes, and with a cry, staggered backwards. Alcée's arm encircled her, and for an instant he drew her close and spasmodically to him.

'Bonté!' she cried, releasing herself from his encircling arm and retreating from the window. 'The house'll go next! If I only knew w'ere Bibi was!' She would not compose herself; she would not be seated. Alcée clasped her shoulders and looked into her face. The contact of her warm, palpitating body when he had unthinkingly drawn her into his arms, had aroused all the old-time infatuation and desire for her flesh.

'Calixta,' he said, 'don't be frightened. Nothing can happen. The house is too low to be struck, with so many tall trees standing about. There! aren't you going to be quiet? say, aren't you?' He pushed her hair back from her face that was warm and steaming. Her lips were as red and moist as pomegranate seed. Her white neck and a glimpse of her full, firm bosom disturbed him powerfully. As she glanced up at him the fear in her liquid blue eyes had given place to a drowsy gleam that unconsciously betrayed a sensuous desire. He looked down into her eyes and there was nothing for him to do but to gather her lips in a kiss. It reminded him of Assumption.

'Do you remember – in Assumption, Calixta?' he asked in a low voice broken by passion. Oh! she remembered; for in Assumption he had kissed her and kissed and kissed her; until his senses would well nigh fail, and to save her he would resort to a desperate flight. If she was not an immaculate dove in those days, she was still inviolate, a passionate creature whose very defencelessness had made her defence, against which his honour forbade him to prevail. Now – well, now – her lips seemed in a manner free to be tasted, as well as her round, white throat and her whiter breasts.

They did not heed the crashing torrents, and the roar of the elements made her laugh as she lay in his arms. She was a revelation in that dim, mysterious chamber; as white as the couch she lay upon. Her firm, elastic flesh that was knowing for the first time its birthright, was like a creamy lily that the sun invites to contribute its breath and perfume to the undying life of the world.

The generous abundance of her passion, without guile or trickery, was like a white flame which penetrated and found response in depths of his own sensuous nature that had never yet been reached.

When he touched her breasts they gave themselves up in quivering ecstasy, inviting his lips. Her mouth was a fountain of delight. And when he possessed her, they seemed to swoon together at the very borderland of life's mystery.

He stayed cushioned upon her, breathless, dazed, enervated, with his heart beating like a hammer upon her. With one hand she clasped his head, her lips lightly touching his forehead. The other hand stroked with a soothing rhythm his muscular shoulders.

The growl of the thunder was distant and passing away. The rain beat softly upon the shingles, inviting them to drowsiness and sleep. But they dared not yield.

The rain was over; and the sun was turning the glistening green world into a palace of gems. Calixta, on the gallery, watched Alcée ride away. He turned and smiled at her with a beaming face, and she lifted her pretty chin in the air and laughed aloud.

3

Bobinôt and Bibi, trudging home, stopped without at the cistern to make themselves presentable.

'My! Bibi, w'at will yo' mama say! You ought to be ashame'. You oughtn' put on those good pants. Look at 'em! An' that mud on yo' collar! How you got that mud on yo' collar, Bibi? I never saw such a boy!' Bibi was the picture of pathetic resignation. Bobinôt was the embodiment of serious solicitude as he strove to remove from his own person and his son's the signs of their tramp over heavy roads and through wet fields. He scraped the mud off Bibi's bare legs and feet with a stick and carefully removed all

traces from his heavy brogans. Then, prepared for the worst – the
meeting with an over-scrupulous housewife, they entered cauti-
ously at the back door.

Calixta was preparing supper. She had set the table and was
dripping coffee at the hearth. She sprang up as they came in.

'Oh, Bobinôt! You back! My! but I was uneasy. W'ere you been
during the rain? An' Bibi? He ain't wet? He ain't hurt?' She had
clasped Bibi and was kissing him effusively. Bobinôt's explanations and apologies which he had been composing all along the
way, died on his lips as Calixta felt him to see if he were dry, and
seemed to express nothing but satisfaction at their safe return.

'I brought you some shrimps, Calixta,' offered Bobinôt, hauling
the can from his ample side pocket and laying it on the table.

'Shrimps! Oh, Bobinôt! You too good fo' anything!' and she
gave him a smacking kiss on the cheek that resounded. *'J'vous
réponds*, we'll have a feas' tonight! Umph-umph!'

Bobinôt and Bibi began to relax and enjoy themselves, and when
the three seated themselves at table they laughed much and so loud
that anyone might have heard them as far away as Laballière's.

4

Alcée Laballière wrote to his wife, Clarisse, that night. It was a
loving letter, full of tender solicitude. He told her not to hurry
back, but if she and the babies liked it at Biloxi, to stay a month
longer. He was getting on nicely, and though he missed them, he
was willing to bear the separation a while longer – realising that
their health and pleasure were the first things to be considered.

5

As for Clarisse, she was charmed upon receiving her husband's
letter. She and the babies were doing well. The society was
agreeable; many of her old friends and acquaintances were at the
bay. And the first free breath since her marriage seemed to restore
the pleasant liberty of her maiden days. Devoted as she was to her
husband, their intimate conjugal life was something which she
was more than willing to forgo for a while.

So the storm passed and everyone was happy.

(1898)

MARGARET OLIPHANT

A Story of a Wedding Tour

They had been married exactly a week when this incident occurred.

It was not a love marriage. The man, indeed, had been universally described as 'very much in love', but the girl was not by anyone supposed to be in that desirable condition. She was a very lonely little girl, without parents, almost without relations. Her guardian was a man who had been engaged in business relations with her father, and who had accepted the charge of the little orphan as his duty. But neither he nor his wife had any love to expend upon her, and they did not feel that such visionary sentiments came within the line of duty. He was a very honourable man, and took charge of her small – very small – property with unimpeachable care.

If anything, he wronged himself rather than Janey, charging her nothing for the transfers which he made of her farthing's worth of stock from time to time, to get a scarcely appreciable rise of interest and income for her. The whole thing was scarcely appreciable, and to a large-handed man like Mr Midhurst, dealing with hundreds of thousands, it was almost ridiculous to give a moment's attention to what a few hundreds might produce. But he did so; and if there is any angel who has to do with trade affairs, I hope it was carefully put to his account to balance some of the occasions on which he was not perhaps so particular. Nor did Mrs Midhurst shrink from her duty in all substantial and real good offices to the girl. She, who spent hundreds at the dressmaker's every year on account of her many daughters, did not disdain to get Janey's serge frocks at a cheaper shop, and to have them made by an inexpensive work-woman, so that the girl should have the very utmost she could get for her poor little money.

Was not this real goodness, real honesty, and devotion to their duty? But to love a little thing like that with no real claim upon them, and nothing that could be called specially attractive about her, who could be expected to do it? They had plenty – almost more than enough – of children of their own. These children were big boys and girls, gradually growing, in relays, into manhood and womanhood, when this child came upon their hands. There was no room for her in the full and noisy house. When she was grown up most of the Midhurst children were married, but there was one son at home, who, in the well-known contradictiousness of young people – it being a very wrong and indeed, impossible thing – was quite capable of falling in love with Janey – and one daughter, with whom it was also possible that Janey might come into competition.

The young Midhursts were nice-looking young people enough, but Janey was very pretty. If Providence did but fully consider all the circumstances, it cannot but be felt that Providence would not carry out, as often is done, such ridiculous arrangements. Janey was very pretty. Could anything more inconvenient, more inappropriate, be conceived?

The poor little girl had, accordingly, spent most of her life at school, where she had, let it not be doubted, made many friendships and little loves; but these were broken up by holidays, by the returning home of the other pupils, while she stayed for ever at school: and not at one school, but several – for in his extreme conscientiousness her guardian desired to do her 'every justice', as he said, and prepare her fully for the life – probably that of a governess – which lay before her. Therefore, when she had become proficient in one part of her education she was carried on to another, with the highest devotion to her commercial value no doubt, but a sublime indifference to her little feelings. Thus, she had been in France for two years, and in Germany for two years, so as to be able to state that French and German acquired in these countries were among the list of her accomplishments. English, of course, was the foundation of all; and Janey had spent some time at a famous academy of music – her guardian adding something out of his own pocket to her scanty means, that she might be fully equipped for her profession. And then she was brought, I will not say home: Janey fondly said home, but she knew very well it did not mean home. And it was while Mrs Midhurst was actually writing out the advertisement for *The Times*, and the *Morning Post*, and the *Guardian*, which was to announce to all the world that a young lady desired an engagement as governess that her husband burst in with the extraordinary news that Mr Rosendale, who had chanced to travel with Janey from Flushing, on her return, and who had afterwards, by a still greater chance, met her when asked to lunch at the Midhursts', and stared very much at her, as they all remarked – had fallen in love with, and wanted to marry, this humble little girl.

'Fallen in love with Janey!' Mrs Midhurst cried. 'Fallen in love with you, Janey!' said Agnes Midhurst, with a little emphasis on the pronoun. He was not, indeed, quite good enough to have permitted himself the luxury of falling in love with Mr Midhurst's daughter, but he was an astonishing match for Janey. He was a man who was very well off: he could afford himself such a caprice as that. He was not handsome. He was a thickset little man, and did not dress or talk in perfect taste; but – in love! These two words made all the difference. Nobody had ever loved her, much less been 'in love' with her. Janey consented willingly enough for the magic of these two words. She felt that she was going to be like the best of women at last – to have someone who loved her, someone who was in love with her. He might not be '*joli, joli*', as they say in France. She might not feel any very strong impulse on her own part towards him; but if he was in love with her – in love! Romeo was no more than that with Juliet. The thought went to Janey's head. She married him quite willingly for the sake of this.

I am afraid that Janey, being young and shy, and strange, was a good deal frightened, horrified, and even revolted, by her first discoveries of what it meant to be in love. She had made tremendous discoveries in the course of a week. She had found out that Mr Rosendale, her husband, was in love with her beauty, but as indifferent to herself as any of the persons she had quitted to give herself to him. He did not care at all what she thought, how she felt, what she liked or disliked. He did not care even for her comfort, or that she should be pleased and happy, which, in the first moment even of such a union, and out of pure self-regard to make a woman more agreeable to himself, a man – even the most brutal – generally regards more or less. He was, perhaps, not aware that he did not regard it. He took it for granted that, being his wife, she would naturally be pleased with what pleased him, and his mind went no further than this.

Therefore, as far as Janey liked the things he liked, all went well enough. She had these, but no other. Her wishes were not consulted further nor did he know that he failed in any way towards her. He had little to say to her, except expressions of admiration. When he was not telling her that she was a little beauty, or admiring her pretty hair, her pretty eyes, the softness of her skin, and the smallness of her waist, he had nothing to say. He read his paper, disappearing behind it in the morning; he went to sleep after his midday meal (for the weather was warm); he played billiards in the evening in the hotels to which he took her on their wedding journey; or he overwhelmed her with caresses from which she shrank in disgust, almost in terror. That was all that being in love meant, she found; and to say that she was disappointed cruelly was to express in the very mildest way the dreadful downfall of all her expectations and hopes which happened to Janey before she had been seven days a wife. It is not disagreeable to be told that you are a little beauty, prettier than anyone else. Janey would have been very well pleased to put up with that; but to be petted like a little lapdog and then left as a lapdog is – to be quiet and not to trouble in the intervals of petting – was to the poor little girl, unaccustomed to love and athirst for it, who had hoped to be loved, and to find a companion to whom she would be truly dear, a disenchantment and disappointment which was almost more than flesh and blood could bear.

She was in the full bitterness of these discoveries when the strange incident occurred which was of so much importance in her life. They were travelling through France in one of those long night journeys to which we are all accustomed nowadays; and Janey, pale and tired, had been contemplating for some time the figure of her husband thrown back in the corner opposite, snoring complacently with his mouth open, and looking the worst that a middle-aged man can look in the utter abandonment of self-indulgence and rude comfort, when the train began to slacken its speed, and to prepare to enter one of those large stations which look so ghastly in the desertion of the night.

Rosendale jumped up instinctively, only half awake, as the train stopped. The other people in the carriage were leaving it, having attained the end of their journey, but he pushed through them and their baggage to get out, with the impatience which some men show at any pause of the kind, and determination to stretch their legs, or get something to drink, which mark the breaks in the journey. He did not even say anything to Janey as he forced his way out, but she was so familiar with his ways by this time that she took no notice. She did take notice, however, when, her fellow-passengers and their packages having all been cleared away, she suddenly became sensible that the train was getting slowly into motion again without any sign of her husband.

She thought she caught a glimpse of him strolling about on the opposite platform before she was quite sure of what was happening. And then there was a scurry of hurrying feet, a slamming of doors, and as she rose and ran to the window bewildered, she saw him, along with some other men, running at full speed, but quite hopelessly, to catch the train. The last she saw was his face, fully revealed by the light of the lamp, convulsed with rage and astonishment, evidently with a yell of denunciation on the lips. Janey trembled at the sight. There was that in him, too, though as yet in her submissiveness she had never called it forth, a temper as unrestrained as his love-making, and as little touched by any thought save that of his own gratification. Her first sensation was fright, a terror that she was in fault and was about to be crushed to pieces in his rage: and then Janey sank back in her corner, and a flood of feeling of quite another kind took possession of her breast.

Was it possible that she was alone? Was it possible that for the first time since that terrible moment of her marriage she was more safely by herself than any locked door or even watchful guardian could keep her, quite unapproachable in the isolation of the train? Alone!

'Safe!' Janey ventured to say to herself, clasping her hands together with a mingled sensation of excitement and terror and tremulous delight which words could not tell.

She did not know what to think at first. The sound of the train plunging along through the darkness, through the unknown country, filled her mind as if someone was talking to her. And she was fluttered by the strangeness of the incident and disturbed by alarms. There was a fearful joy in thus being alone, in having a few hours, perhaps a whole long tranquil night to herself: whatever came of it, that was always so much gained. But then she seemed to see him in the morning coming in upon her heated and angry. She has always felt that the moment would come when he would be angry, and more terrible to confront than any governess, or even principal of a ladies' college. He would come in furious, accusing her of being the cause of the accident, of doing something to set the train in motion; or else he would come in fatigued and dusty, claiming her services as if she were his valet – a thing which had, more or less, happened already and against which Janey's pride and her sense of what was fit had risen in arms. She thought of this for a little time with trouble, and of the difficulties she would have in arriving, and where she would go to, and what she would say. It was an absurd story to tell, not to his advantage, 'I lost my husband at Montbard.' How could she say it? The hotel people would think she was a deceiver. Perhaps they would not take her in. And how would he know where to find her when he arrived? He would feel that he had lost her, as much as she had lost him.

Just as this idea rose in her mind, like a new thing full of strange suggestions, the train began to shorten speed again, and presently stopped once more. She felt it to do so with a pang of horror. No doubt he had climbed up somewhere, at the end or upon the engine, and was now to be restored to his legitimate place, to fall upon her either in fondness or in rage, delighted to get back to her, or angry with her for leaving him behind: she did not know which would be the worst. Her heart began to beat with fright and anticipation. But to her great relief it was only the guard who came to the door. He wanted to know if madame was the lady whose husband had been left behind; and to offer a hundred apologies and explanations. One of those fools at Montbard had proclaimed twenty minutes' pause when there were but five. If he had but heard he would have put it right, but he was at the other end of the train. But madame must not be too much distressed; a few hours would put it all right.

'Then there is another train?' said Janey, her poor little head buzzing between excitement and relief.

'Not for some hours,' said the guard. 'Madame will understand that there is not more than one *rapide* in the middle of the night; but in the morning quite early there is the train omnibus. Oh, very early, at five o'clock. Before madame is ready for her dinner monsieur will be at her side.'

'Not till evening, then?' said Janey, with again a sudden acceleration of the movement of her heart.

The guard was desolated. 'Not before evening. But if madame will remain quietly in the carriage when the train arrives at the station, I will find the omnibus of the hotel for her – I will see to everything! Madame, no doubt, knows which hotel to go to?'

Janey, as a matter of fact, did not know. Her husband had told her none of the details of the journey; but she said with a quick breath of excitement, 'I will go to the one that is nearest, the one at the *gare*. There will be no need for any omnibus.'

'And the baggage? Madame has her ticket?'

'I have nothing,' cried Janey, 'except my travelling bag. You must explain that for me. But otherwise – otherwise, I think I can manage.'

'Madame speaks French so well,' the man said, with admiration. It was, indeed, a piece of good fortune that she had been made to acquire the language in the country: that she was not frightened to find herself in a foreign place, and surrounded by people speaking a strange tongue, as many a young English bride would have been. There was a moment of tremendous excitement and noise at the station while all was explained to a serious *chef de gare*, and a gesticulating band of porters and attendants, whose loud voices, as they all spoke together, would have frightened an ordinary English girl out of her wits. But Janey, in the strange excitement which had taken possession of her, and in her fortunate acquaintance with the language, stood still as a little rock amid all the confusion. 'I will wait at the hotel till my husband comes,' she said, taking out the travelling bag and her wraps, and maintaining a composure worthy of all admiration. Not a tear, not an outcry. How astonishing are these English, cried the little crowd, with that swift classification which the Frenchman loves.

Janey walked into the hotel with her little belongings, not knowing whether she was indeed walking upon her feet or floating upon wings. She was quite composed. But if anyone could only have seen the commotion within that youthful bosom! She locked the door of the little delightful solitary room in which she was placed. It was not delightful at all, but to Janey it was a haven of peace, as sweet, as secluded from everything alarming and terrible, as any bower. Not till evening could he by any possibility arrive – the man who had caused such a revolution in her life. She had some ten hours of divine quiet before her, of blessed solitude, of thought. She did not refuse to take the little meal that was brought to her, the breakfast of which she stood in need; and she was glad to be able to bathe her face, to take off her dusty dress, and put on the soft and fresh one, which, happily, had folded into very small space, and therefore could be put into her bag. Her head still buzzed with the strangeness of the position, yet began to settle a little. When she had made all these little arrangements she sat down to consider. Perhaps you will think there was very little to consider, nothing but how to wait till the next train brought him, which, after all, was not a very great thing to do. Appalling, perhaps, to a little inexperienced bride; but not to Janey, who had travelled alone so often, and knew the language, and all that.

But whoever had been able to look into Janey's mind would have seen that something more was there, – a very, very different thing from the question of how best to await his coming back. Oh, if he had loved her, Janey would have put up with many things! She would have schooled herself out of all her private repugnances; she would have been so grateful to him, so touched by the affection which nobody had ever bestowed upon her before! But he did not love her. He cared nothing about herself, Janey; did not even know her, or want to know her, or take into consideration her ways or her wishes. He was in love with her pretty face, her fresh little beauty, her power of pleasing him. If ever that power ceased, which it was sure to do, sooner or later, she would be to him less than nothing, the dreary little wife whom everybody has seen attached to a careless man: Janey felt that this was what was in store for her. She felt the horror of him, and his kind of loving, which had been such a miserable revelation to her. She felt the relief, the happiness, ah, the bliss, of having lost him for a moment, of being alone.

She took out her purse from her pocket, which was full of the change she had got in Paris of one of the ten pound notes which her guardian had given her when she left his house on her wedding morning. She took out the clumsy pocketbook, an old one, in which there were still nine ten pound notes. It was all her fortune, except a very, very small investment which brought her in some seven pounds a year. This was the remainder of another small investment which had been withdrawn in order to provide her with her simple trousseau, leaving this sum of a hundred pounds which her guardian had given her, advising her to place it at once for security in her husband's hands. Janey had not done this, she scarcely could tell why. She spread them on the table – the nine notes, the twelve napoleons of shining French money. A hundred pounds: she had still the twelve francs which made up the sum. She had spent nothing. There were even the few coppers over for the *agio*.* She spread them all out, and counted them from right to left, and again from left to right. Nine ten pound notes, twelve-and-a-half French napoleons – or louis, as people call them nowadays – making a hundred pounds. A hundred pounds is a large sum in the eyes of a girl. It may not be much to you and me, who know that it means only ten times ten pounds, and that ten pounds goes like the wind as soon as you begin to spend it. But to Janey! Why, she could live upon a hundred pounds for – certainly for two years: for two long delightful years, with nobody to trouble her, nobody to scold, nobody to interfere. Something mounted to her head like the fumes of wine. Everything began to buzz again, to turn round, to sweep her away as on a rapidly mounting current. She put back all the money in the pocketbook – her fortune, the great sum that made her independent; and she put back her things into the bag. A sudden energy of resolution seized her. She put on her hat again, and as she looked at herself in the glass encountered the vision of a little face which was new to her. It was not that of Janey, the little governess-pupil; it was not young Mrs Rosendale. It was full of life, and meaning, and energy, and strength. Who was it? Janey? Janey herself, the real woman, whom nobody had ever seen before.

It is astonishing how many things can be done in sudden excitement and passion which could not be possible under any other circumstances. Janey was by nature a shy girl and easily frightened, accustomed indeed to do many things for herself, and to move quietly without attracting observation through the midst of a crowd; but she had never taken any initiative, and since her marriage had been reduced to such a state of complete dependence on her husband's wishes and plans that she had not attempted the smallest step on her own impulse.

Now, however, she moved about with a quiet assurance and decision which astonished herself. She carried her few possessions back again to the railway station, leaving the small gold piece of ten francs to pay, and much overpay, her hour's shelter and entertainment at the hotel.

Nobody noticed her as she went through the bustle of the place and back to the crowded station, where a little leisurely local train was about starting – a slow train occupied by peasants and country folk, and which stopped at every station along the line. English people abound in that place at all hours, except at this particular moment, when the *rapide* going towards Italy had but newly left and the little country train was preparing in peace. Nobody seemed to notice Janey as she moved about with her bag on her arm. She took her ticket in her irreproachable French 'acquired in the country', which attracted no attention. She got into a second-class carriage in which there were already various country people, and especially a young mother with a baby, and its nurse in a white round cap with long streaming ribbons. Janey's heart went out to these people. She wondered if the young woman was happy, if her husband loved her, if it was not very sweet to have a child – a child must love you; it would not mind whether your cheeks were rosy or pale, whether you were pretty or not, whether you had accomplishments or languages acquired in the country.

Looking at this baby, Janey almost forgot that she was going out upon the world alone, and did not know where. It is a tremendous thing to do this, to separate from all the world you are acquainted with, to plunge into the unknown. Men do it often enough, though seldom without some clue, some link of connection with the past and way of return. Janey was about to cut herself off as by the Fury's shears from everything. She would never join her husband again. She would never fear her guardian again. She must drop out of sight like a stone into the sea. There was no longing love to search for her, no pardon to be offered, no one who would be heart-struck at the thought of the little girl lost and unhappy. Only anger would be excited by her running away, and a desire to punish, to shake her little fragile person to pieces, to make her suffer. She knew that if she did it at all, it must be final. But this did not overwhelm her. What troubled Janey a great deal more than the act of severance which she was about to accomplish, was the inevitable fib or fibs she must tell in order to account for her appearance in the unknown. She did not like to tell a fib, even a justifiable one. It was against all her traditions, against her nature. She felt that she could never do it anything but badly, never without exciting suspicions; and she must needs have some story, some way of accounting for herself.

This occupied her mind while the slow train crawled from station to station. It was the most friendly, idle, gossiping little train. It seemed to stop at the merest signal-box to have a talk, to drink as it were a social glass administered through that black hose, with a friend; it stopped wherever there were a few houses, it carried little parcels, it took up a leisurely passenger going next door, and the little electric bell went on tingling, and the guard cried 'En voiture!' and the little bugle sounded. Janey was amused by all these little sounds and sights, and the country all flooded with sunshine, and the flowers everwhere, though it was only March, and dark black weather when she had left home.

Left home! and she had no home now, anywhere, no place to take refuge in, nobody to write to, to appeal to, to tell if she was happy or unhappy. But Janey did not care! She felt a strange elation of ease and relief. All alone, but everybody smiling upon her, the young mother opposite beginning to chatter, the baby to crow to her, the nurse to smile and approve of the *bonne petite dame* who took so much notice of the child. Her head was swimming, but with pleasure, and the blessed sensation of freedom – pleasure tinctured with the exhilaration of escape, and the thrill of fright which added to the excitement. Yet at that moment she was certainly in no danger. He was toiling along, no doubt, fuming and perhaps swearing, on another slow train on the other side of Marseille. Janey laughed to herself a little guiltily at the thought.

And she had escaped! It was not her doing primarily. She might have gone on all her life till she had died, but for that accident which was none of her doing. It was destiny that had done it, fate. The cage door had been opened and the bird had flown away. And how nice it would be to settle down, with this little mother, just about her own age, for a neighbour, and to help to bring the baby up! The kind, sweet faces they all had, mother and baby and *bonne* all smiling upon her! When Janey looked out on the other side she saw the sea flashing in the sunshine, the red porphyry rocks reflecting themselves in the brilliant blue, and village after village perched upon a promontory or in the hollow of a bay. She had never in all her life before felt that sensation of blessedness, of being able to do what she liked, of having no one to call her to account. She did not know where she was going, but that was part of the pleasure. She did not want to know where she was going.

Then suddenly this sentiment changed, and she saw in a moment a place that smiled at her like the smiling of the mother and baby. It was one of those villages in a bay: a range of blue mountains threw forth a protecting arm into the sea to shield it: the roofs were red, the houses were white, they were all blazing in the sun. Soft olives and palms fringed the deep green of the pines that rolled back in waves of verdure over the country behind, and strayed down in groups and scattered files to the shore below. Oh, what a cheerful, delightsome place! And this was where the little group with the baby was preparing to get out. 'I will go too,' said Janey to herself, and her heart gave a little bound of pleasure. She was delighted to reach the place where she was going to stay – just as she had been delighted to go on in the little pottering train, not knowing where she was going, and not wishing to know.

This was how Janey settled herself on the day of her flight from the world. She scarcely knew what story it was she told to the young woman whose face had so charmed her, and whom she asked whether she would be likely to find lodgings anywhere, lodgings that would not be too expensive.

'My husband is – at sea,' Janey heard herself saying. She could scarcely tell what it was that put those words into her head.

'Oh, but yes,' the other young woman cried with rapture. Nothing was more easy to get than a lodging in St Honorat, which was beginning to try to be a winter resort, and was eager to attract strangers. Janey had dreamed of a cottage and a garden, but she was not dissatisfied when she found herself in a sun-bright room on the second floor of a tall white house facing the sea. It had a little balcony all to itself. The water rippled on the shore just over the road, the curve of the blue mountains was before her eyes.

I do not say that when she had settled down, when the thrill of movement was no longer in her brain, Janey was not without a shiver at the thought of what she had done. When the sun set, and that little chill which comes into the air of the south at the moment of its setting breathed a momentary cold about her, and when the woman of the house carefully closed the shutters and shut out the shining of the bay, and she was left alone with her candle, something sank in Janey's heart – something of the unreasonable elation, the fantastic happiness, of the day. She thought of 'Mr Rosendale' (she had never got so near her husband as to call him by any other name) arriving, of the fuss there would be about her and the inquiries.

Was it rash to have come to a place so near as this – within an hour or two of where he was? Was there a danger that someone might have seen her? That it might be found out that she had taken her ticket? But then she had taken her ticket for a place much further along the coast. She thought she could see him arrive all flaming with anger and eagerness, and the group that would gather round him, and how he would be betrayed by his bad French, and the rage he would get into! Again she laughed guiltily; but then got very grave again trying to count up all the chances – how some porter might have noticed and might betray her, how he might yet come down upon her furiously, to wreak upon her all the fury of his discomfiture. Janey knew by instinct that though it was in no way her fault, her husband would wreak his vengenance upon her even for being left behind by the train. She became desperate as she sat and thought it all over. It would be better for her to leap from the window, to throw herself into the sea, than to fall into his hands. There would be no forgiveness for her if he once laid hands upon her. Now that she had taken this desperate step, she must stand by it to the death.

Ten years had passed away since the time of that wedding tour.

Ten years! It is a very long time in a life. It makes a young man middle-aged, and a middle-aged man old. It takes away the bloom of youth, and the ignorance of the most inexperienced; and yet what a little while it is! – no more than a day when you look back upon it. The train from Marseille to Nice, which is called the *rapide*, goes every day, and most people one time or another have travelled by it.

One day last winter one of the passengers in this train, established very comfortably in the best corner of a sleeping carriage in which he had passed the night luxuriously, and from which he was now looking out upon the shining sea, the red rocks, the many bays and headlands of the coast, suddenly received such a shock and sensation as seldom occurs to any one. He was a man of middle-age and not of engaging aspect. His face was red, and his eyes were dull yet fiery. He had the air of a man who had indulged himself much and all his inclinations, had loved good living and all the joys of the flesh, had denied himself nothing – and was now paying the penalties. Such men, to tell the truth, are not at all unusual apparitions on that beautiful coast or in the train *rapide*. No doubt appearances are deceitful, and it is not always a bad man who bears that aspect or who pays those penalties: but in this case few people would have doubted.

His eyes were bloodshot, he had a scowl upon his brow, his foot was supported upon a cushion. He had a servant with him to whom he rarely spoke but with an insult. Not an agreeable man – and the life he was now leading, whatever it had been, was not an agreeable life. He was staring out the window upon the curves of the coast, sometimes putting up the collar of his fur coat over his ears, though it was a warm morning, and the sun had all the force of April. What he was thinking of it would be difficult to divine – perhaps of the good dinner that awaited him at Monte Carlo when he got there, perhaps of his good luck in being out of England when the east winds began to blow, perhaps of something

quite different – some recollection of his past. The *rapide* does not
stop at such small places as St Honorat, which indeed had not
succeeded in making itself a winter resort. It was still a very small
place. There were a few people on the platform when the train
rushed through. It seemed to pass like a whirlwind, yet notwith-
standing, in that moment two things happened. The gentleman in
the corner of the carriage started in his seat, and flung himself half
out of the window, with a sudden roar which lost itself in the tunnel
into which the train plunged. There was an awful minute in that
tunnel: for the servant thought his master had taken a fit, and there
was no light to see what convulsions he might have fallen into,
while at the same time he fought furiously against the man's efforts
to loose his wrappings and place him in a recumbent position,
exclaiming furiously all the time. He had not taken a fit, but when
the train emerged into the light he was as near to it as possible –
purple-red in his face, and shouting with rage and pain.

'Stop the train! stop the train!' he shouted. 'Do you hear, you
fool? stop the train! Ring the bell or whatever it is! Break the –
thing! Stop the train!'

'Sir, sir! If you will only be quiet, I will get your medicine in a
moment!'

'Medicine, indeed!' cried the master, indignantly, and every
furious name that he could think of mounted to his lips – fool,
idiot, ass, swine – there was no end to his epithets. 'I tell you I saw
her, I saw her!' he shouted. 'Stop the train! Stop the train!'

On the other hand, among the few insignificant persons,
peasants and others, who had been standing on the platform at St
Honorat when the *rapide* dashed past, there had been a woman
and child. The woman was not a peasant: she was very simply
dressed in black, with one of the small bonnets which were a few
years ago so distinctively English, and with an air which corre-
sponded to that simple coiffure. She was young, and yet had the
air of responsibility and motherhood which marks a woman who
is no longer in the first chapter of life. The child, a boy of nine or
ten, standing close by her side, had seized her hand just as the
train appeared impatiently to call her attention to something else;
but, by some strange spell of attraction or coincidence, her eyes
fixed upon that window out of which the gouty traveller was
looking. She saw him as he saw her, and fell back dragging the
boy with her as if she would have sunk into the ground. It was
only a moment and the *rapide* was gone, screaming and roaring

into the tunnel, making too much noise with the rush and sweep of its going to permit the shout of the passenger to be heard.

Ten years, ten long years, during which life had undergone so many changes! They all seemed to fly away in a moment, and the girl who had arrived at the little station of St Honorat alone, a fugitive, elated and intoxicated with her freedom, suddenly felt herself again the little Janey who had emancipated herself so strangely – though she had for a long time been frightened by every train that passed and every stranger who came near.

In the course of these long years all this had changed. Her baby had been born, her forlorn state had called forth great pity, great remark and criticism, in the village where she had found refuge – great censure also, for the fact of her marriage was not believed by everybody. But she was so lonely, so modest, and so friendly, that the poor little English stranger was soon forgiven. Perhaps her simple neighbours were glad to find that a prim Englishwoman, supposed to stand so fierce on her virtue, was in reality so fallible – or perhaps pity put all other sentiments out of court. She told her real story to the priest when the boy was baptised, and though he tried to persuade her to return to her husband, he only half believed in that husband, since the story was told not under any seal of confession. Janey never became absolutely one of his flock. She was a prim little Protestant in her heart, standing strong against the saints, but devoutly attending church, believing with simple religiousness that to go to church was better than not to go to church, whatever the rites might be, and reading her little English service steadily through all the prayers of the Mass, which she never learned to follow. But her boy was like the other children of St Honorat, and learned his catechism and said his lessons with the rest.

There were various things which she did to get a living, and got it very innocently and sufficiently, though in the humblest way. She taught English to the children of some of the richer people in the village, she taught them music. She had so much credit in this latter branch, that she often held the organ in church on a holiday and pleased everybody. Then she worked very well with her needle, and would help on an emergency at first for pure kindness, and then, as her faculties and her powers of service became known, for pay, with diligence and readiness. She found a niche in the little place which she filled perfectly, though only accident seemed to have made it for her. She had fifty pounds of her little fortune laid by for the boy. She had a share of a cottage in a garden

– not an English cottage indeed, but the upper floor of a two-storeyed French house; and she and her boy did much in the garden, cultivating prettinesses which do not commend themselves much to the villagers of St Honorat. Whether she ever regretted the step she had taken nobody ever knew. She might have been a lady with a larger house than any in St Honorat, and servants at her call. Perhaps she sometimes thought of that; perhaps she felt herself happier as she was. Sometimes, I think, she felt that if she had known the boy was coming she might have possessed her soul in patience, and borne even with Mr Rosendale. But then at the time the decisive step was taken she did not know.

She hurried home in a great fright, not knowing what to do, then calmed herself with the thought that even if he had recognised her, there were many chances against his following her, or at least finding her, with no clue, and after so many years. And then a dreadful panic seized her at the thought that he might take her boy from her. He had known nothing about the boy: but if he discovered that fact it would make a great difference. He could not compel Janey to return to him, but he could take the boy. When this occurred to her she started up again, having just sat down, and put on her bonnet and called the child.

'Are you going out again, Mother?' he cried.

'Yes, directly, directly: come, John, come, come!' she said putting his cap upon his head and seizing him by the hand. She led him straight to the presbytery, and asked for the *curé*, and went in to the good priest in great agitation, leaving the boy with his housekeeper.

'M. l'Abbé,' she said, with what the village called her English directness, 'I have just seen my husband go past in the train!'

'Not possible!' said M. l'Abbé, who only half believed there was a husband at all.

'And he saw me. He will come back, and I am afraid he will find me. I want you to do something for me.'

'With pleasure,' said the priest. 'I will come and meet Monsieur your husband, and I will explain—'

'That is not what I want you to do. I want you to let John stay with you, to keep him here till – till – He will want to take him away from me!' she cried.

'He will want to take you both away, *chère petite dame*. He has a right to do so.'

'No, no! But I do not ask you what is his right. I ask you to keep John safe, to keep him here – till the danger has passed away!'

The priest tried to reason, to entreat, to persuade her that a father, not to say a husband, had his rights. But Janey would hear no reason: had she heard reason either from herself or another, she would not have been at St Honorat now. And he gave at last a reluctant consent. There was perhaps no harm in it after all. If a man came to claim his rights, he would not certainly go away again without some appeal to the authorities – which was a thing it must come to sooner or later – if there was indeed a husband at all, and the story was true.

Janey then went back to her home. She thought she could await him there and defy him. 'I will not go with you,' she would say. 'I may be your wife, but I am not your slave. You have left me alone for ten years. I will not go with you now!' She repeated this to herself many times, but it did not subdue the commotion in her being. She went out again when it became too much for her, locking her door with a strange sense that she might never come back again. She walked along the sea shore, repeating these words to herself, and then she walked up and down the streets, and went into the church and made the round of it, passing all the altars and wondering if the saints did pay any attention to the poor women who were there, as always, telling St Joseph or the Blessed Mary all about it. She sank down in a dark corner, and said – 'Oh, my God! oh, my God!'

She could not tell Him about it in her agitation, with her heart beating so, but only call His attention, as the woman in the Bible touched the Redeemer's robe. And then she went out and walked up and down again. I cannot tell what drew her back to the station – what fascination, what dreadful spell. Before she knew what she was doing she found herself there, walking up and down, up and down.

As if she were waiting for someone! 'You have come to meet a friend?' someone said to her, with an air of suspicion. And she first nodded and then shook her head, but still continued in spite of herself to walk up and down. Then she said to herself that it was best so – that to get it over would be a great thing, now John was out of the way. He would be sure to find her sooner or later – far better to get it over! When the train came in, the slow local train, coming from the side of Italy, she drew herself back a little to watch. There was a great commotion when it drew up at the platform. A man got out and called all the loungers about to help to lift out a gentleman who was ill – who had had a bad attack in the train.

'Is there anywhere here we can take him to? Is there any decent hotel? Is there a room fit to put my master in?' he cried.

He was English with not much French at his command, and in

great distress. Janey, forgetting herself and her terrors, and strong in the relief of the moment that he whom she feared had not come, went up to offer her help. She answered the man's questions; she called the right people to help him; she summoned the *chef de gare* to make some provision for carrying the stricken man to the hotel.

'I will go with you,' she said to the servant, who felt as if an angel speaking English had suddenly come to his help. She stood by full of pity, as they lifted that great inert mass out of the carriage. Then she gave a great cry and fell back against the wall.

It was a dreadful sight the men said afterwards, enough to overcome the tender heart of any lady, especially of one so kind as Madame Jeanne. A huge man, helpless, unconscious, with a purple countenance, staring eyes, breathing so that you could hear him a mile off. No wonder that she covered her eyes with her hands not to see him; and then covered her ears with her hands not to hear him: but finally she hurried away to the hotel to prepare for him, and to call the doctor, that no time should be lost. Janey felt as if she was restored for the moment to life when there was something she could do. The questions were all postponed. She did not think of flight or concealment, or even of John at the presbytery. 'He is my husband,' she said, with awe in her heart.

This was how the train brought back to Janey the man whom the train had separated from her ten years before. The whole tragedy was of the railway, the noisy carriages, the snorting locomotives. He was taken to the hotel, but he never came to himself again, and died there next day, without being able to say what his object was, or why he had got out of the *rapide*, though unable to walk, and insisted on returning to St Honorat. It cost him his life; but then his life was not worth a day's purchase, all the doctors said, in the condition in which he was.

Friends had to be summoned, and men of business, and it was impossible but that Janey's secret should be made known. When she found herself and her son recognised, and that there could be no doubt that the boy was his father's heir, she was struck with a great horror which she never quite got over all her life. She had not blamed herself before, but now seemed to herself no less than the murderer of her husband: and could not forgive herself, nor get out of her eyes the face she had seen, nor out of her ears the dreadful sound of that labouring breath.

1898

PAULINE E. HOPKINS

Bro'r Abr'm Jimson's Wedding
A Christmas Story

It was a Sunday in early spring the first time that Caramel Johnson
dawned on the congregation of —— Church in a populous New
England City.

The Afro-Americans of that city are well-to-do, being of a frugal
nature, and considering it a lasting disgrace for any man among
them, desirous of social standing in the community, not to make
himself comfortable in this world's goods against the coming time,
when old age creeps on apace and renders him unfit for active
business.

Therefore the members of the said church had not waited to be
exhorted by reformers to own their unpretentious homes and small
farms outside the city limits, but they vied with each other in efforts
to accumulate a small competency urged thereto by a realization of
what pressing needs the future might bring, or that might have been
because of the constant example of white neighbours, and a due
respect for the dignity which *their* foresight had brought to the
superior race.

Of course, these small Vanderbilts and Astors of a darker hue
must have a place of worship in accord with their worldly prosperity,
and so it fell out that —— Church was the richest plum in the
ecclesiastical pudding, and greatly sought by scholarly divines as a
resting place for four years – the extent of the time limit allowed by
conference to the men who must be provided with suitable charges
according to the demands of their energy and scholarship.

The attendance was unusually large for morning service, and a
restless movement was noticeable all through the sermon. How
strange a thing is nature; the change of the seasons announces itself
in all humanity as well as in the trees and flowers, the grass, and in
the atmosphere. Something within us responds instantly to the
touch of kinship that dwells in all life.

The air, soft and balmy, laden with rich promise for the future,

came through the massive, half-open windows, stealing in refresh-
ing waves upon the congregation. The sunlight fell through the
coloured glass of the windows in prismatic hues, and dancing all
over the lofty star-gemmed ceiling, painted the hue of the broad
vault of heaven, creeping down in crinkling shadows to touch the
deep garnet cushions of the sacred desk, and the rich wood of the
altar with a hint of gold.

The offertory was ended. The silvery cadences of a rich soprano
voice still lingered on the air, 'O, Worship the Lord in the beauty
of holiness.' There was a suppressed feeling of expectation, but
not the faintest rustle as the minister rose in the pulpit, and after a
solemn pause, gave the usual invitation: 'If there is anyone in this
congregation desiring to unite with this church, either by letter or
on probation, please come forward to the altar.'

The words had not died upon his lips when a woman started
from her seat near the door and passed up the main aisle. There
was a sudden commotion on all sides. Many heads were turned –
it takes so little to interest a church audience. The girls in the choir
box leaned over the rail, nudged each other and giggled, while the
men said to one another, 'She's a stunner, and no mistake.'

The candidate for membership, meanwhile, had reached the
altar railing and stood before the man of God, to whom she had
handed her letter from a former Sabbath home, with head decor-
ously bowed as became the time and the holy place. There was no
denying the fact that she was a pretty girl; brown of skin, small of
feature, with an ever-lurking gleam of laughter in eyes coal black.
Her figure was slender and beautifully moulded, with a seductive
grace in the undulating walk and erect carriage. But the chief
charm of the sparkling dark face lay in its intelligence, and the
responsive play of facial expression which was enhanced by two
mischievous dimples pressed into the rounded cheeks by the
caressing fingers of the god of Love.

The minister whispered to the candidate, coughed, blew his
nose on his snowy clerical handkerchief, and, finally, turned to the
expectant congregation: 'Sister Chocolate Caramel Johnson—'

He was interrupted by a snicker and a suppressed laugh, again
from the choir box, and an audible whisper which sounded
distinctly throughout the quiet church –

'I'd get the Legislature to change that if it was mine, 'deed I
would!' then silence profound caused by the Reverend's stern
glance of reproval bent on the offenders in the choir box.

'Such levity will not be allowed among the members of the choir. If it occurs again, I shall ask the choir master for the names of the offenders and have their places taken by those more worthy to be gospel singers.'

Thereupon Mrs Tilly Anderson whispered to Mrs Nancy Tobias that, 'them choir gals is the mos' deceivines' hussies in the church, an' for my part, I'm glad the pastor called 'em down. That sister's too good lookin' for 'em, an' they'll be after her like er pack o' houn's, min' me, Sis' Tobias.'

Sister Tobias ducked her head in her lap and shook her fat sides in laughing appreciation of the sister's foresight.

Order being restored the minister proceeded:

'Sister Chocolate Caramel Johnson brings a letter to us from our sister church in Nashville, Tennessee. She has been a member in good standing for ten years, having been received into fellowship at ten years of age. She leaves them now, much to her regret, to pursue the study of music at one of the large conservatories in this city, and they recommend her to our love and care. You know the contents of the letter. All in favour of giving Sister Johnson the right hand of fellowship, please manifest the same by a rising vote.' The whole congregation rose.

'Contrary minded? None. The ayes have it. Be seated, friends. Sister Johnson, it gives me great pleasure to receive you into this church. I welcome you to its joys and sorrows. May God bless you, Brother Jimson?' (Brother Jimson stepped from his seat to the pastor's side.) 'I assign this sister to your class. Sister Johnson, this is Brother Jimson, your future spiritual teacher.'

Brother Jimson shook the hand of his new member, warmly, and she returned to her seat. The minister pronounced the benediction over the waiting congregation; the organ burst into richest melody. Slowly the crowd of worshippers dispersed.

Abraham Jimson had made his money as a janitor for the wealthy people of the city. He was a bachelor, and when reproved by some good Christian brother for still dwelling in single blessedness always offered as an excuse that he had been too busy to think of a wife, but that now he was 'well fixed', pecuniarily, he would begin to 'look over' his lady friends for a suitable companion.

He owned a house in the suburbs and a fine brick dwelling-house in the city proper. He was a trustee of prominence in the church, in fact, its 'solid man', and his opinion was sought and his advice acted upon by his associates on the Board. It was felt that any lady in the congregation would be proud to know herself his choice.

When Caramel Johnson received the right hand of fellowship, her aunt, the widow Maria Nash, was ahead in the race for the wealthy class-leader. It had been neck and neck for a while between her and Sister Viney Peters, but, finally it had settled down to Sister Maria with a hundred to one, among the sporting members of the Board, that she carried off the prize, for Sister Maria owned a house adjoining Brother Jimson's in the suburbs, and property counts these days.

Sister Nash had 'no idea' when she sent for her niece to come to B. that the latter would prove a rival; her son Andy was as good as engaged to Caramel. But it is always the unexpected that happens. Caramel came, and Brother Jimson had no eyes for the charms of other women after he had gazed into her coal-black orbs, and watched her dimples come and go.

Caramel decided to accept a position as housemaid in order to help defray the expenses of her tuition at the conservatory, and Brother Jimson interested himself so warmly in her behalf that she soon had a situation in the home of his richest patron where it was handy for him to chat with her about the business of the church, and the welfare of her soul, in general. Things progressed very smoothly until the fall, when one day Sister Maria had occasion to call, unexpectedly, on her niece and found Brother Jimson basking in her smiles while he enjoyed a sumptuous dinner of roast chicken and fixings.

To say that Sister Maria was 'set way back' would not accurately describe her feeling, but from that time Abraham Jimson knew that he had a secret foe in the Widow Nash.

Before many weeks had passed it was publicly known that Brother Jimson would lead Caramel Johnson to the altar 'come Christmas'. There was much sly speculation as to the 'widder's gittin' left', and how she took it from those who had cast hopeless glances towards the chief man of the church. Great preparations were set on foot for the wedding festivities. The bride's trousseau was a present from the groom and included a white satin wedding gown and a costly gold watch. The town house was refurnished and a trip to New York was in contemplation.

'Hump!' grunted Sister Nash when told the rumours. 'There's no fool like an ol' fool. Car'mel's a han'ful he'll fin', ef he gits her.'

'I reckon he'll git her all right, Sis' Nash,' laughed the neighbour, who had run in to talk over the news.

'I've said my word an' I ain't goin' change it, Sis'r. Min' me, I says, *ef he gits her*, an' I mean it.'

Andy Nash was also a member of Brother Jimson's class; he possessed, too, a strong sweet baritone voice which made him a great value to the choir. He was an immense success in the social life of the city, and had created sad havoc with the hearts of the coloured girls; he could have his pick of the best of them because of his graceful figure and fine easy manners. Until Caramel had been dazzled by the wealth of her elderly lover, she had considered herself fortunate as the lady of his choice.

It was Sunday, three weeks before the wedding that Andy resolved to have it out with Caramel.

'She's been hot an' she's been col', an' now she's luke warm, an' today ends it before this gent-man sleeps,' he told himself as he stood before the glass and tied his pale blue silk tie in a stunning knot, and settled his glossy tile at a becoming angle.

Brother Jimson's class was a popular one and had a large membership; the hour spent there was much enjoyed, even by visitors. Andy went into the vestry early, resolved to meet Caramel if possible. She was there, at the back of the room sitting alone on a settee. Andy immediately seated himself in the vacant place by her side. There were whispers and much head-shaking among the few early worshippers, all of whom knew the story of the young fellow's romance and his disappointment.

As he dropped into the seat beside her, Caramel turned her large eyes on him intently, speculatively, with a doubtful sort of curiosity suggested in her expression, as to how he took her flagrant desertion.

'Howdy, Car'mel?' was his greeting without a shade of resentment.

'I'm well; no need to ask how you are,' was the quick response. There was a mixture of cordiality and coquetry in her manner. Her eyes narrowed and glittered under lowered lids, as she gave him a long side-glance. How could she help showing her admiration for the supple young giant beside her? 'Surely,' she told herself, 'I'll have long time enough to git sick of old Rheumatics,' her pet name for her elderly lover.

'I ain't sick much,' was Andy surly reply.

He leaned his elbow on the back of the settee and gave his

recreant sweetheart a flaming glance of mingled love and hate,
oblivious to the presence of the assembled class members.

'You ain't over friendly these days, Car'mel, but I gits news of
your capers "roun" 'bout some of the members.'

'My – Yes?' she answered as she flashed her great eyes at him in
pretended surprise. He laughed a laugh not good to hear.

'Yes,' he drawled. Then he added with sudden energy, 'Are you
goin' to tie up to old Rheumatism sure 'nuff, come Chris'mas?'

'Come Chris'mas, Andy, I be. I hate to tell you but I have to do
it.'

He recoiled as from a blow. As for the girl, she found a keen
relish in the situation: it flattered her vanity.

'How comes it you've changed your mind, Car'mel, 'bout you
an' me? You've tol' me often that I was your first choice.'

'We – ell,' she drawled, glancing uneasily about her and avoiding her aunt's gaze, which she knew was bent upon her every
movement, 'I did reckon once I would. But a man with money
suits me best, an' you ain't got a cent.'

'No more have you. You ain't no better than other women to
work an' help a man along, is you?'

The colour flamed an instant in her face turning the dusky skin
to a deep, dull red.

'Andy Nash, you always was a fool, an' as ignerunt as a wil'
Injun. I mean to have a sure nuff brick house an' plenty of money.
That makes people respec' you. Why don' you quit bein' so
shifless and save your money? You ain't worth your salt.'

'Your head's turned with pianorer-playin' an' livin' up North.
Ef you'll turn *him* off an' come back home, I'll turn over a new
leaf. Car'mel,' his voice was soft and persuasive enough now.

She had risen to her feet; her eyes flashed, her face was full of
pride.

'I won't. I've quit likin' you, Andy Nash.'

'Are you in earnest?' he asked, also rising from his seat.

'Dead earnes'.'

'Then there's no more to be said.'

He spoke calmly, not raising his voice above a whisper. She
stared at him in surprise. Then he added as he swung on his heel
preparatory to leaving her: 'You ain't got him yet, my gal. But
remember, I'm waitin' for you when you need me.'

While this whispered conference was taking place in the back of
the vestry, Brother Jimson had entered, and many an anxious

glance he cast in the direction of the couple. Andy made his way slowly to his mother's side as Brother Jimson rose in his place to open the meeting. There was a commotion on all sides as the members rustled down on their knees for prayer.

Widow Nash whispered to her son as they knelt side by side, 'How did you make out, Andy?'

'Didn't make out at all, Mammy. She's as obstinate as a mule.'

'Well, then, there's only one thing mo' to do.'

Andy was unpleasant company for the remainder of the day. He sought, but found nothing to palliate Caramel's treachery. He had only surly, bitter words for his companions who ventured to address him, as the outward expression of inward tumult. The more he brooded over his wrongs the worse he felt. When he went to work on Monday morning he was feeling vicious. He had made up his mind to do something desperate. The wedding should not come off. He would be avenged.

Andy went about his work at the hotel in gloomy silence unlike his usual gay hilarity. It happened that all the female help at the great hostelry was white, and on that particular Monday morning was the duty of Bridget McCarthy's watch to clean the floors. Bridget was also not in the best of humours, for Pat McClosky, her special company, had gone to the priest's with her rival, Kate Connerton, on Sunday afternoon, and Bridget had not yet got over the effects of a strong rum punch taken to quiet her nerves after hearing the news.

Bridget had scrubbed a wide swathe of the marble floor when Andy came through with a rush order carried in scientific style high above his head, balanced on one hand. Intent upon satisfying the guest who was princely in his 'tips', Andy's unwary feet became entangled in the maelstrom of brooms, scrubbing-brushes and pails. In an instant the 'order' was sliding over the floor in a general mix-up.

To say Bridget was mad wouldn't do her state justice. She forgot herself and her surroundings and relieved her feelings in elegant Irish, ending a tirade of abuse by calling Andy a 'wall-eyed, bandy-legged nagur'.

Andy couldn't stand that from 'common, po' white trash', so calling all his science into play he struck out straight from the shoulder with his right, and brought her a swinging blow on the mouth, which seated her neatly in the five-gallon bowl of freshly made lobster salad which happened to be standing on the floor behind her.

There was a wail from the kitchen force that reached to every department. It being the busiest hour of the day when they served dinner, the dish-washers and scrubbers went on a strike against the 'nagur who struck Bridget McCarthy, the baste', mingled with cries of 'Lynch him!' Instantly the great basement floor was a battle ground. Every coloured man seized whatever was handiest and ranged himself by Andy's side, and stood ready to receive the onslaught of the Irish brigade. For the sake of peace, and sorely against his inclinations, the proprietor surrendered Andy to the police on a charge of assault and battery.

On Wednesday morning of that eventful week, Brother Jimson wended his way to his house in the suburbs to collect the rent. Unseen by the eye of man, he was wrestling with a problem that had shadowed his life for many years. No one on earth suspected him unless it might be the widow. Brother Jimson boasted of his consistent Christian life – rolled his piety like a sweet morsel beneath his tongue, and had deluded himself into thinking that *he* could do no sin. There were scoffers in the church who doubted the genuineness of his pretentions, and he believed that there was a movement on foot against his power led by Widow Nash.

Brother Jimson groaned in bitterness of spirit. His only fear was that he might be parted from Caramel. If he lost her he felt that all happiness in life was over for him, anxiety gave him a sickening feeling of unrest. He was tormented, too, by jealousy; and when he was called upon by Andy's anxious mother to rescue her son from the clutches of the law, he had promised her fair enough, but in reality resolved to do nothing but – tell the judge that Andy was a dangerous character whom it was best to quell by severity. The pastor and all the other influential members of the church were at court on Tuesday, but Brother Jimson was conspicuous by his absence.

Today Brother Jimson resolved to call on Sister Nash, and as he had heard nothing of the outcome of the trial, make cautious inquiries concerning that, and also sound her on the subject nearest his heart.

He opened the gate and walked down the side path to the back door. From within came the rhythmic sound of a rubbing-board. The brother knocked, and then cleared his throat with a preliminary cough.

'Come,' called a voice within. As the door swung open it revealed the spare form of the widow, who with sleeves rolled

above her elbows stood at the tub cutting her way through piles of
foaming suds.

'Mornin', Sis' Nash! How's all?'

'That you, Bro'r Jimson? How's yourself? Take a cheer an'
make yourself to home.'

'Cert'nly, Sis' Nash, don' care ef I do,' and the good brother
scanned the sister with an eagle eye. 'Yas'm I'm purty tol'rable
these days, thank God. Bleeg'd to you, Sister, I jes' will stop an'
res' myself befo' I repair myself back to the city.' He seated
himself in the most comfortable chair in the room, tilted it on the
two back legs against the wall, lit his pipe and with a grunt of
satisfaction settled back to watch the white rings of smoke curl
about his head.

'These are mighty ticklish times, Sister. How's you continue on
the journey? Is you strong in the faith?'

'I've got the faith, my brother, but I ain't on on mountaintop
this week. I'm way down in the valley; I'm jes' coaxin' the Lord to
keep me sweet,' and Sister Nash wiped the ends from her hands
and prodded the clothes in the boiler with the clothes-stick, added
fresh pieces and went on with her work.

'This is a worl' strewed with wrecks an' floatin' with tears. It's
the valley of tribulation. May your faith continue. I hear Jim
Jinkins has bought a farm up Taunton way.'

'Wan'ter know!'

'Doctor tells me Bro'r Waters is comin' after Chris-mus. They
do say as how he's stirrin' up things turrible; he's easin' his min'
on this lynchin' business, an' it's high time – high time.'

'Sho! Don' say so! What you reck'n he's goin tell us now,
Brother Jimson?'

'Suthin' 'stonishin', Sister. It'll stir the country from end to end.
Yes'm the Council is powerful strong as an organsation.'

'Sho! sho!' and the 'thrub, thrub' of the board could be heard a
mile away.

The conversation flagged. Evidently Widow Nash was not in a
talkative mood that morning. The brother was disappointed.

'Well, it's mighty comfort'ble here, but I mus' be goin'.'

'What's your hurry, Brother Jimson?'

'Business, Sister, business,' and the brother brought his chair
forward preparatory to rising. 'Where's Andy? How'd he come
out of that little difficulty?'

'Locked up.'

'You don' mean to say he's in jail?'

'Yes, he's in jail 'tell I git's his bail.'

'What might the sentence be, Sister?'

'Twenty dollars fine or six months at the Islan'.' There was silence for a moment, broken only by the 'thrub, thrub' of the washboard, while the smoke curled upward from Brother Jimson's pipe as he enjoyed a few last puffs.

'These are mighty ticklish times, Sister. Po' Andy, the way of the transgressor is hard.'

Sister Nash took her hands out of the tub and stood with arms akimbo, a statue of Justice carved in ebony. Her voice was like the trump of doom.

'Yes, an' men like you is the cause of it. You leadin' men with money an' chances don' do your duty. I arst you, I arst you fair, to go down to the jedge an' bail that po' chile out. Did you go? No, you hard-faced old devil, you lef him be there, an' I had to git the money from my white folks. Yes, an' I'm breakin' my back now, over that pile of clo's to pay that twenty dollars. Um! All the trouble comes to us women.'

'That's so, Sister; that's the livin' truth,' murmured Brother Jimson furtively watching the rising storm and wondering where the lightning of her speech would strike next.

'I tell you that it is our receiptfulness to each other is the reason we don't prosper an' God's a-punishin' us with fire an' with sward 'cause we's so jealous an' snaky to each other.'

'That's so, Sister; that's the livin' truth.'

'Yes, sir. A nigger's boun' to be a nigger 'tell the trump of doom. You kin skin him, but he's a nigger still. Broad-cloth, biled shirts an' money won' make him more or less, no, sir.'

'That's so, Sister; that's jes' so.'

'A nigger can't holp himself. White folks can run agin the law all the time an' they never gits caught, but a nigger! Every time he opens his mouth he puts his foot in it – got to hit that po' white trash gal in the mouth an' git jailed an' leave his po'r ol' mother to work her fingers to the secon' jint to get him out. Um!'

'These are mighty ticklish times, Sister. Man's boun' to sin; it's his nat'ral state. I hope this will teach Andy humility of the sperit.'

'A little humility'd be good for yourself, Abra'm Jimson.' Sister Nash ceased her sobs and set her teeth hard.

'Lord, Sister Nash, what compar'son is there 'twixt me an' a worthless nigger like Andy? My business is with the salt of the earth, an' so I have dwelt ever since I was consecrated.'

'Salt of the earth! But ef the salt have los' its saver how you goin' salt it ergin? No, sir, you cain't do it. It mus' be cas' out an' trodded under foot of men. That's who's goin' happen you Abe Jimson, hyar me? An' I'd like to trod on you with my foot, an' every ol' good fer nuthin' bag o' salt like you,' shouted Sister Nash. 'You're a snake in the grass. You done stole the boy's gal an' then try to git him sent to the Islan'. You cain't deny it, fer the jedge done tol' me all you said, you ol' rhinoceros-hided hypercrite. Salt of the earth! You!'

Brother Jimson regretted that Widow Nash had found him out. Slowly he turned, settling his hat on the back of his head.

'Good mornin', Sister Nash. I ain't no hard feelin's agains' you. I too near to the kingdom to let trifles jar me. My bowels of compassion yearns over you, Sister, a pilgrim an' a stranger in this unfriendly worl'.'

No answer from Sister Nash. Brother Jimson lingered.

'Good mornin', Sister Still no answer.

'I hope to see you at the weddin', Sister.'

'Keep on hopin', I'll be there. That gal's my own sister's chile. What in time she wants of a rheumatic ol' sap-head like you for, beats me. I wouldn't marry you for no money, myself, no, sir. It's my belief that you've done goophered her.'

'Yes, Sister, I've hearn tell of people refusin' befo' they was ask'd,' he retorted, giving her a sly look.

For answer the widow grabbed the clothes-stick and flung it at him in speechless rage.

'My, what a temper it's got,' remarked Brother Jimson soothingly as he dodged the shovel, the broom, the coal-hod and the stove-covers. But he sighed with relief as he turned into the street and caught the faint sound of the washboard now resumed.

To a New Englander the season of snow and ice with its clear biting atmosphere, is the ideal time for the great festival. Christmas morning dawned in royal splendour; the sun kissed the snowy streets and turned the icicles into brilliant stalactites. The bells rang a joyous call from every steeple, and soon the churches were crowded with eager worshippers – eager to hear again the oft-repeated, the wonderful story on which the heart of the whole Christian world feeds its faith and hope. Words of tender faith, marvellous in their simplicity fell from the lips of a world-renowned preacher, and touched the hearts of the listening multitude: 'The winter sunshine is not more bright and clear than the atmosphere of living joy, which stretching back between our eyes and that picture of Bethlehem, shows us its beauty in unstained freshness. And as we open once again those chapters of the gospel in which the ever fresh and living picture stands, there seems from year to year always to come some newer, brighter meaning into the words that tell the tale.

'St Matthew says that when Jesus was born in Bethlehem the wise men came from the East to Jerusalem. The East means man's search after God; Jerusalem means God's search after man. The East means the religion of the devout soul; Jerusalem means the religion of the merciful God. The East means Job's cry, "Oh, that I knew where I might find him!" Jerusalem means "Immanuel – God with us."'

Then the deep-toned organ joined the grand chorus of human voices in a fervent hymn of praise and thanksgiving:

> Lo! the Morning Star appeareth,
>   O'er the world His beams are cast;
> He the Alpha and Omega,
>   He, the Great, the First the Last!
> Hallelujah! hallelujah!
>   Let the heavenly portal ring!
> Christ is born, the Prince of glory!
> Christ the Lord, Messiah, King!

Everyone of the prominence in church circles had been bidden to the Jimson wedding. The presents were many and costly. Early after service on Christmas morning the vestry room was taken in hand by leading sisters to prepare the tables for the supper, for on account of the host of friends bidden to the feast, the reception was to be held in the vestry.

The tables groaned beneath their loads of turkey, salads, pies, puddings, cakes and fancy ices.

Yards and yards of evergreen wreaths encircled the granite pillars; the altar was banked with potted plants and cut flowers. It was a beautiful sight. The main aisle was roped off for the invited guests with white satin ribbons.

Brother Jimson's patrons were to be present in a body, and they had sent the bride a solid silver service, so magnificent that the sisters could only sigh with envy.

The ceremony was to take place at seven sharp. Long before

that hour the ushers in full evening dress were ready to receive the guests. Sister Maria Nash was among the first to arrive, and even the Queen of Sheba was not arrayed like unto her. At fifteen minutes before the hour, the organist began an elaborate instrumental performance. There was an expectant hush and much head-turning when the music changed to the familiar strains of the 'Wedding March'.

The minister took his place inside the railing ready to receive the party. The groom waited at the altar.

First came the ushers, then the maids of honour, then the flower girl – daughter of a prominent member – carrying a basket of flowers which she scattered before the bride, who was on the arm of the best man. In the bustle and confusion incident to the entrance of the wedding party no one noticed a group of strangers accompanied by Andy Nash enter and occupy seats near the door.

The service began. All was quiet. The pastor's words fell clearly upon the listening ears. He had reached the words: 'If any man can show just cause, etc.,' when like a thunder-clap came a voice from the back part of the house – an angry excited voice, and a woman of ponderous avoirdupois* advanced up the aisle.

'Hol' on that, pastor, hol' on! A man cain't have but one wife 'cause it's agin' the law. I'm Abe Jimson's lawful wife, an' hyars his six children – all boys – to pint out their daddy.' In an instant the assembly was in confusion.

'My soul,' exclaimed Viney Peters, 'the ol' serpent! An' to think how near I come to takin' up with him. I'm glad I ain't Car'mel.'

Sis'r Maria said nothing, but a smile of triumph lit up her countenance.

'Brother Jimson, is this true?' demanded the minister, sternly. But Abraham Jimson was past answering. His face was ashen, his teeth chattering, his hair standing on end. His shaking limbs refused to uphold his weight; he sank upon his knees on the steps of the altar.

But now a hand was laid upon his shoulder and Mrs Jimson hauled him upon his feet with a jerk.

'Abe Jimson, you know me. You run'd 'way from me up North fifteen year ago, an' you hid yourself like a groun' hog in a hole, but I've got you. There'll be no new wife in the Jimson family this week. I'm yer fus' wife and I'll be yer las' one. Git up hyar now, you mis'able sinner an' tell the pastor who I be.' Brother Jimson meekly obeyed the clarion voice. His sanctified air had vanished; his pride humbled into the dust.

'Pastor,' came in trembling tones from his quivering lips. 'These are mighty ticklish times.' He paused. A deep silence followed his words. 'I'm a weak-kneed, mis'able sinner. I have fallen under temptation. This is Ma' Jane, my wife, an' these hyar boys is my sons, God forgive me.'

The bride, who had been forgotten now, broke in:

'Abraham Jimson, you ought to be hung. I'm going to sue you for breach of promise.' It was a fatal remark. Mrs Jim son turned upon her.

'You will, will you? Sue him, will you? I'll make a choc'late Car'mel of you befo' I'm done with you, you 'ceitful hussy, hoodooin' hones' men from thar wives.'

She sprang upon the girl, tearing, biting, rendering. The satin gown and gossamer veil were reduced to rags. Caramel emitted a series of ear-splitting shrieks, but the biting and tearing went on. How it might have ended no one can tell if Andy had not sprang over the backs of the pews and grappled with the infuriated woman.

The excitement was intense. Men and women struggled to get out of the church. Some jumped from the windows and others crawled under the pews, where they were secure from violence. In the midst of the mêlée. Brother Jimson disappeared and was never seen again, and Mrs Jimson came into possession of his property by due process of law.

In the church Abraham Jimson's wedding and his fall from grace is still spoken of in eloquent whispers.

In the home of Mrs Andy Nash a motto adorns the parlour walls worked in scarlet wool and handsomely framed in gilt. The text reads: 'Ye are the salt of the earth; there is nothing hidden that shall not be revealed.'

(1901)

LADY GREGORY

The Wedding of Maine Morgor
(from *Cuchulain of Muirthemne*)

When Maine Morgor, the Very Dutiful, the son of Ailell and of
Maeve, set out for his wedding with Ferb, daughter of Gerg of Rath
Ini, in Ulster, he brought three troops of young men with him, and
fifty men in each troop, and this is the appearance that was on the
first two troops. Shining white shirts they had, striped with purple
down the sides; gold shields on their backs with borders of white
silver, with figures engraved on them, and with edges of white
bronze as sharp as knives. Great two-edged swords with silver hilts
at their belts; chains of white silver round their necks. And there
were neither helmets on their heads, or shoes on their feet.

And as to the third troop, the one Maine himself was in, there
were fifty reddish-brown horses in it, and fifty white horses with
red ears, with long manes and tails coloured purple, and bridles on
them, with a ball of red gold on the one side, and a ball of white
silver on the other side, and a gold or a silver bit to every one of
them. A collar of gold with bells from it on the neck of every horse,
and when the horses would be moving, the sound of these bells
would be as sweet as the strings of a harp when the player strikes it
with his hand. There was a chariot of white bronze ribbed with
gold and silver to every two of the horses; purple cushions sewed
with gold bound to every chariot; fifty fair slender young men in
these fifty chariots, and not one among them but was the son of a
king and a queen, and was a hero and a brave man of Connaught,
and they wearing purple cloaks about them, that had borders
ornamented with gold and silver, and a clasp of pure red gold to
every cloak; fine silk coats fastened with hooks of gold close to their
white bodies; fifty silver shields on their backs with gold rims
studded with carbuncles and other precious stones of every colour;
two candles of valour were the two shining spears on the hand of
every man of them; fifty rivets of bronze and of gold in every spear,
and if any man of them had a debt of a bushel of silver or gold, one
rivet from his spear would pay it. And there were precious stones

on their spears that would flame in the night like the rays of the sun. At their belts they had long, gold-hilted swords with silver sheaths; goads in their hands of white bronze with silver crooks. And as to the young men themselves, they were very handsome and stately, and large and shining; curled yellow hair on them, hanging down on their shoulders; proud, clear, blue eyes; their cheeks like the flowers of the woods in May, or like the foxglove of the mountains. There were seven greyhounds following Maine's chariot in chains of silver, and apples of gold on every chain. There were seven trumpeters with gold and silver trumpets, wearing clothes of many colours, and having all of them light yellow hair. And three Druids went in front of them, and they having bands of silver on their heads, and speckled cloaks on them, and carrying shields of bronze with ornaments of red copper. And there were three harpers with them, that had the appearance of kings.

It is like that they gathered at the royal house of Cruachan, and they went three times round the lawn before the house. And they said farewell to Maeve and to Ailell, and then they set out for Rath Ini.

'It is a fine setting out you are having,' said Bricriu, 'but maybe the coming back will not be so fine.'

'It is a journey that will be heard of in every place,' said Maine.

'I suppose,' said Bricriu, 'it is but a day visit you will make there, for you will hardly stop to feast through the night in a district that is under Conchubar.'

'I give my word,' said Maine, 'we will not turn back to Cruachan till we have feasted three days and three nights in Gerg's house.' He did not waste any more time talking, but set out on the journey.

When the messengers they sent before them came to Gerg's house at Rath Ini, the people there began to make all ready before them, and they laid down green-leaved birch branches and fresh green rushes in the house. Then Ferb sent her foster-sister, Find-choem, daughter of Erg, and bade her go a part of the way with the messengers, and bring her back word what appearance was on Maine and on his companions. She was not long away, and as soon as she came back she went with her report to the sunny parlour where Ferb was, and it is what she said: 'I never saw since Conchubar was in Emain, and I never will see till the end of life and time, a finer, or grander, or a more beautiful troop, than the troop that is coming now over the plain. It was the same as if I was in a sweet apple-garden, from the sweetness that came to me when the light wind passed over them and stirred their clothes.'

With that, the men of Connaught came to the dun, and the people within pressed upon one another to look at them. And the gates were set open, and their chariots unyoked, and baths of pure water were made ready for them. And then they were brought into the hall of heroes in the middle of the house, and they were given every sort of food and of drink that is to be found on the whole ridge of the world.

But as they were using the feast and making merry, there came a sudden blast of wind that shook the whole place, so that the hall they were in trembled, and the shields fell from their hooks, and the spears from their places, and the tables fell like leaves in an oak wood. All the young men were astonished, and Gerg asked Maine's Druids what meaning they could put on that blast. And Ollgaeth, Maine's chief Druid, said, 'I think it is no good sign for those who are come tonight to this wedding. A blast of wind,' he said, 'a sorrowful sound; it is the man that will conquer.

'A shield struck out of a white hand; the bodies of dead men laid under stones; a high stone over stiff bodies; the story is sorrowful!

'And if you will take my advice,' he said, 'you will quit this feast this very night.'

But he got a sharp rebuke from Maine for saying that, and Gerg said, 'There is no cause for any uneasiness, for the men of Ulster are not gathered at Emain at this time. And if they were itself,' he said, 'I and my two sons would be ready to go out and fight against Conchubar along with you.'

They hung up their arms then again, and gave no more heed to what the Druid had said.

Now on the morning of this very day, when Conchubar was lying in his sleep at Emain, he saw in a dream a beautiful woman coming to his bedside, and she having the appearance of a queen. Yellow plaited hair she had, and folds of silk over her white skin, and a cloak of green silk from her shoulders, and two sandals of white bronze between her soft feet and the ground. 'All good be with you, Conchubar,' she said.

'What is the reason of your coming?' said Conchubar.

'It is not long from this time,' she said, 'that Ulster will be attacked and will be robbed, and the Brown Bull of Cuailgne will

be driven away. And the son of the man that will do this thing,'
she said, 'Maine Morgor, son of Ailell and of Maeve, is coming
this very night to his wedding with Ferb, daughter of Gerg of Rath
Ini, and three times fifty young men with him. Rise up now,' she
said, 'there are but three times fifty men against you, and the
victory will be with you.'

Then Conchubar sprang up, and sent for Cathbad, the Druid,
and told him his vision. 'It is likely enough,' he said, 'that it is
meant to warn us against the men of Connaught. And you may be
sure,' he said, 'that if we stop here quietly, they will be doing their
robbery. And let me have the truth from you now, and tell me
what is best to do, for there is not the like of you among the
Druids.'

And Cathbad said, 'It is what your vision means, that many
men will get their death, and Maine of Connaught, he that is
above all disgrace, along with them; and he and his companions
will never go back again to beautiful Cruachan. But you yourself
will come back safe,' he said, 'with fame and victory.'

Then Conchubar set out, and there went with him Cathrach
Catuchenn, a queen with a great name, that had come to Emain
from the country of Spain for love of Cuchulain; and she went out
now with Conchubar's army. And there went with him as well,
the three outlaws of the race of the Fomor, Siabarcha, son of
Suilremar, and Berngal Brec, and Buri of the Rough Word. And
Facen, son of Dublongsech of the old stock of Ulster came, and
Fabric Fiacail from Great Asia, and Forais Fingalach from the Isle
of Man. So Conchubar set out, and three times fifty men with
him, but he brought none of the men of Ulster with him, but
himself and his chariot-driver Brod, and Imrinn the Druid, Cathbad's son. And none of them brought a servant with him, except
only Conchubar, but their shields on their backs, and their bright
green spears in their hands, and their heavy swords in their belts.
And if they were not many in number, the pride of their minds
was great.

When they were come within sight of Rath Ini, they saw a great
heavy cloud over it, the one end of it black and the middle red,
and the other end green. And Conchubar asked Imrinn the Druid,
'What is this cloud over the house a token of?'

'I know well,' said Imrinn, 'it is a sign there will be fighting
tonight, and the sorrow of death will be on the house like a cloud,
and it is for a young man the death darkness is made ready.'

Then Conchubar went on towards the dun, and just at that time the great vat that belonged to the house, and that got afterwards the name of the Ol Guala, was brought into the feasting hall, and it full of wine. But whoever went to draw it let the silver vessel fall into the vat, so that the wine flowed over the edges in three waves. 'My grief!' said Ollgaeth the Druid. 'It is not long before these vessels will be with strangers. He is not a happy son born of a mother that is in this house tonight.'

Then Conchubar came to the door, and the strangers that were with him gave their shout of attack around the dun, as their custom was. At that Gerg rose up, and his two sons with him, Conn Coscorach and Cobthach Cnesgel, and they took hold of their arms. And Gerg said to Maine, 'Let this be fought out now between us men of Ulster till you see which of us are the bravest. And we are all answerable for you, and it is best for you that we should fight together. But if we fall, then let you hold the place if you can.'

And then Gerg went out and his two sons along with him and their people. And they held the place, and fought Conchubar outside; and for a long time they did not let anyone go past them. And Gerg stood outside the door, and a hewing and cutting was aimed at him on every side, and five men of the Fomor fell by him, and Imrinn the Druid, along with them, and he cut his head off and brought it to the door with him.

Then Cathrach Catuchenn came between him and the door, and she made a sharp attack on him, and Gerg struck her head off, and brought it back with him into the house, for he had got a hard wound. And he threw the heads down before Maine, and he sat down on a bed, and gave a heavy sigh and asked for a drink. And then Conchubar and his people came up to the wall, and they were holding their shields over their heads with their left hands, and tearing down the wall with their right hands, till they were able to make their way through it.

Then Brod, Conchubar's chariot-driver, threw one of the spears he had in his hand into the house, and it went through Gerg's body, and through the body of Airisdech his servant that was behind him, so that the two of them fell together. And Conchubar attacked Gerg's people in the house, so that thirty of them fell, and he killed Conn, Gerg's son, by his own hand, and many of his own people got their death as well.

Then Nuagal, Gerg's wife, rose up, and she gave three great

angry cries of grief, and she took the head of her husband into her bosom. 'By my word,' she said, 'it is a fine servant's deed, Brod to have killed Gerg in his own house. But there are many,' she said, 'that will keen you, and as you have fallen on account of your daughter, many women shall have sorrow on account of you.' And she made this complaint: 'It is a good fight Gerg made, that is lying here now, the fair-haired champion with the red sword; he that was proud, openhanded, brave, wise, beautiful.

'Where is there a better hero than Gerg? Where is the man that has not anger on him. Where is the army that does not keen for your death?

'It is grief to me to see you on your bed of death, O beautiful fair-haired Gerg! It is a pity for me, you to be dead.

'Before you here in Rath Ini, and at Loch Ane and at Irard, and in the valleys of the south, there were many women that gave you their love.

'You were the friend of every army; everyone gave you full obedience; your friendly word was dear to everyone; surely it is you were the good adviser.

'It is great indeed your deeds were, it is stately your assemblies were; you were a king among great lords.

'Your house was great, it was well known, the house within which harm came to you; it was there Brod killed you in the hall of kings.

'It was a great harm and a great curse Brod put on us, he to kill a king of Ireland before his time; he has killed him; he has killed all of us along with him.'

Then Gerg's two sons said they would hold the place, and they were not without killing many in the fight. Then Maine could not hold in his strength any longer, and he went out to avenge his father-in-law. And his three times fifty companions rose up along with him, and it was not easy to stand against them. There was great pride in the mind, and great courage in the heart of every one of them, and there was great desire and longing on them to do high deeds.

And as to Maine, the king's son, he was stately, kind, mannerly, and although he was hardly out of his boyhood, he was braver in the fight than any other. He was gentle in the drinking-house, and he was hard in battle, and he was mindful of his enemies, and he was pitiful in wounding, and a spender of treasure, and a stone of anger, and a wave of justice; and he was the head in the gatherings of the three Connaughts, and their hand in spending, and their fitting king.

He thought it would be dishonour on him, ever to be overcome in equal fight by any men in the world, or the place to be taken that he was defending. And he went out and drove the Fomor away from the house, and it is not a hand of healing Maine had that time; and nine of the Fomor fell by his first attack. Then the outlaw of Great Asia, Fabric Fiacail, came up to the threshold, and began destroying the men before him, and no one stood against him till he came to the place where Maine was. And then they two set their shields one against the other, and they were fighting together till after midnight; and Fabric gave Maine three deep wounds, and when they were tired out with the fight, Maine struck off his head. Then Conchubar came, and thirty of Gerg's men were killed by him, and the two armies fell upon one another, and it is much that even the toes of their feet did not make an attack of their own. And the blood that was in the dun was as high as a man's knees, and in all the district round nothing could be heard but the striking of blows on shields, and the clinking of spears, and the clash of swords against one another, and the roar of beaten men.

And Maine, when he had overcome the Fomor, came where Facen, son of Dublongsech was, and they fought together a good while, and then Facen was killed. Then Maine and Cobthach were driven up into the house after their people were put down, and they held it bravely till morning, and no one was able to make a way in.

In this same night, the same woman that had brought news to Conchubar, went to where Maeve was lying in her sleep at Cruachan, and said to her, 'If you had the Druid sight, Maeve,' she said, 'you would not be in your sleep now.'

What has happened?' said Maeve.

'Conchubar is at this very moment,' said the strange woman, 'getting the upper hand of Maine, and he is on the point of putting him to death. Rise up now, and gather your men together,' she said, 'and go out and avenge him.'

With that Maeve wakened out of her sleep, and she called to Ailell and told him the vision, and told it to her people as well. 'There is no truth in it,' said Bricriu.

But when Fiannamail, the innkeeper's son at Cruachan, heard it he waited for no one and made no delay, but set out for the place where Maine was, for Maine was his foster-brother. And Maeve chose out seven hundred armed men, the best that were to be found in Cruachan at that time. And then Donall Dearg came, that was the best fighter in the province, and that was another of Maine's foster-brothers. And he set out in the same way, before the others, and thirty fighting men with him, and the name of every one of them was Donall. And then Maeve set out after them on her journey.

But as to Maine, he held the house till the bright rising of the sun on the morrow, and it was not pleasant rest this night brought to either side. When they could see each other by the light of day, each remembered the other to his hurt, and Conchubar began to rouse up his people. 'If it was the men of Ulster I had with me now,' he said, 'they would not be dragging on with this battle, the way the Fomor are doing.' When the Fomor heard that sharp reproach, their courage rose up in them, and they pressed on hard in the fight, and never left off till they were through the door of the house. The house they came into had a great name for grandeur, but it was bad work that was done in it now. There were a hundred tables of white silver in it, and three hundred of brass, and three hundred of white bronze. And there were thirty vessels with pure silver from Spain on their rims, and two hundred cowhorns ornamented with gold or silver, and thirty silver cups, and thirty brass cups, and on the walls there were hangings of white linen with wonderful figures worked on them.

Then the two armies met one another in the middle of the house; and a great many were killed there. And Cobthach, Gerg's son, after he had killed many of the Fomor, came to where Berngal Brec was hewing the heads off the men of Connaught, and they fought together, and Berngal was worsted in the end.

And as to Maine, he killed Buri of the Rough Word, and after that he went mad and raging through the house, and thirty other men fell by him. But when Conchubar saw the madness that was on Maine, he turned to him, and Maine waited for him, and they fought a long while, and Maine threw his casting spear so strong and straight, that it went through Conchubar's body; and while Conchubar was striving to draw out that spear, Maine wounded him with the long spear that was in his hand. Then Brod came to help Conchubar, and Maine gave him three heavy wounds, so that he was able to fight no more. But then Conchubar attacked him with blows on every side, until he laid him dead before him.

And after he had killed Maine, he began to attack the crowd about him, so that they fell, foot to foot, and neck to neck, all through the house. And at the end, there was not one of Maine's people left living; and of the three times fifty men that came with Conchubar, there was not one left living but himself and Brod, and if they were itself, they did not come whole out of it.

Then Conchubar drove Cogthach, Gerg's son, out of the house; and while he was following him over the plain, Ferb came with her foster-sister to the place where Maine was lying, and she cried and lamented over him, and she said, 'My grief! you are alone now, you that spent so many nights in company.' And she made this complaint: 'O young man, it is red your bed is! It is bad the signs were, and you coming into the house, a foretelling of tears to all your people.

'O son of Maeve! O branch of high honour! O son of Ailell who is not weak. It is a pity it is for my heart and my body, you to be lying there for ever!

'O young man, the best I ever saw; a rod of gold and you lying on the pillow; whenever you and an enemy met together, that was the last meeting there was between you.

'There is grief on me, you to be lying there, young man, son of Maeve; your face was ruddy, your hand was rough in battle; it is grief has been put into my heart that was waiting for you.

'It is seldom you were without arms up to this, until you were struck down, lying dead. The shining spear pierced you, the hard sword wounded you, till blood was dropping down on your cheeks.

'Och! What were you to me, and I not to have seen your death; my darling, my choice among men, he that was worth good treasure.

'He is my husband for all my days, great Maine, Ailell's son; I will die for the want of him, and he not able to come and care me.

'His purple cloak is grief to me, and himself lying there on the floor of the house, and his hand that was struck off after he fell, and his head in the hand of Conchubar.

'And his sword that was strong, heavy in striking, Conchubar has carried it far away; and his shield there where he fell, and he defending his people.

'He himself a hero, and no lie in it; it is he divided much riches; it is not a little thing he did to die like that, and he defending his people.

'The fair young man of Connaught to be lying there cold, and the best of his troop along with him; it is a pity for his people that died defending him; it is a pity for me, his unmarried wife.

'There is nothing I can do for you, Maine; it is on myself the hurt is come; my heart is broken with it, and I looking at you, Maine.'

Then Fiannamail, the innkeeper's son from Cruachan, came to the house, and Ferb saw him, and she said, 'Here is Fiannamail come to visit us, but whatever companions he has left at home, he will find none before him here.'

'That is rough news you are giving me, Ferb,' said Fiannamail, 'and indeed I am parted from my companions if it is they that are lying here,' he said.

'They are your companions indeed,' said Ferb. 'They overcame others, and now they are overcome themselves.'

And Fiannamail said, 'And Maine, is he living? My comrade, my dear friend, my prince at home!'

And Ferb said, 'It is bitter to me, you to ask this, for I know you did not think it was Maine's last bed you would find here.'

And then she told Fiannamail all that had happened. And Fiannamail said, 'When this news of the thing the people of Ulster have done goes out, they will be attacked in the west and in the east as long as there is a man living in Connaught.'

But Ferb said, 'There are not left of the army of Ulster but Conchubar himself and Brod his chariot-driver, and the both of them were wounded by Maine before Conchubar killed him at the last.'

Then Fiannamail went out to follow after Conchubar, to get satisfaction for Maine's death. And he met with Niall of the Fair Head, Conchubar's son, and a hundred men with him, and they looking for Conchubar; and for all they were so many, he fought a hot battle with them, till he fell dead.

And after he left Ferb, she was looking at the young men of Connaught, and she made this complaint: 'A pity it is, young men of Connaught, that there is not soft down in your pillows under you; you that took the defence and would not give it up. What troop was there better than yourselves, and now you are lying like a loosened thread.

'It is a heavy hand was laid on your eyes; you were given the sour drink of beaten men; your story is hard, it will be a cause of battles; it will be a foretelling of many tears.

'It is a pity there is no help for me to bring you, but only to be keening and crying over you; it would be better for me to go with you, and my ashes to be scattered abroad.

'You were the best of the armies of Ireland, young men of Connaught, and I keening you; many women will cry Och! Och! after your proud ways.

'It is proud you were coming into the house; it is not common men you had for your fathers. O beautiful young men of Connaught, it is a pity it is the way you are now!'

Then Donall Dearg came to the lawn before the dun. And Ferb's foster-sister saw him, and she said, 'It is a pity he was not here and Maine living, for he would have given him good help.'

And when Ferb heard he was there, she went out to him and she said, 'Well, Donall, hawk of valour, here is a thing for you to do, to avenge your foster-brother that has got his death.'

And it is what Donall said: 'If Maine has fallen, the man has fallen that was above all his companions, in courage, in wisdom, and in gentleness.'

And Ferb said, 'It is not the work of a hero, you to be sighing and keening and crying Ochone! But since Maine will not come back for that, it is better for you to go out against his enemies.'

And Donall said, 'I will go; I will destroy Conchubar, I will destroy his two sons in revenge for Maine.'

And Ferb said, 'If it had been yourself, Donall Dearg, that had got your death from the men of Ulster on account of me, the story of the great vengeance Maine did for it would be told in every place.'

Then Donall said, 'And as it is Maine Morgor himself has got his death, I will never go home westward so long as there is a man left living in Ulster.'

So Donall went out, and he had not long to wait till he saw a great troop coming towards him, and Feradach of the Long Hand, Conchubar's son, with them. And Donall and his men attacked them, but they were outnumbered, and all his men fell. And he himself wounded Feradach twice, but then his men came at him, and Feradach struck his head off, and let out his shout of victory, and his people shouted along with him.

And Ferb was gone into the house again, and she was looking at Maine. 'There is no good appearance on you now, the way you are, Maine,' she said, 'and my father got his death through you, and my father's son; but even so, I will die with the fret of losing you.' And it is what she said: 'There are many women and many young girls will be lonely after you, you to be the only one to fail them.

'It is beautiful you were up to this, proud and tall, going out with your young hounds to the hunting; it is spoiled your body is now, it is pale your hands are.

'It is bad the news is that will travel westward to Findabair of the Fair Eyebrows; the story of her brother that failed Ferb; it is not I that have not my fill of sorrow.'

Then Maeve and her men came up to where Conchubar was, and his two sons that had joined him, and they faced one another, and the fight began; and Maeve broke through the army of Ulster to get satisfaction for her son and for her people, and she killed Conchubar's two sons. But Conchubar stood out and faced her in spite of his wounds, and in spite of being tired out; for his hurts were healed by the greatness of his anger after his two sons being killed.

Then Maeve was driven back and lost the battle; and the Druids brought her away as was their custom; and Conchubar followed after them till they had passed Magh Ini. And then he turned back to spoil Gerg's dun, and he carried away with him all he could find of treasures; and he took away the great brass vat that was in the house, and brought it to Emain. And when it was filled with beer, all the province of Ulster used to drink from it; and it got the name of the Champion's Drinking Vat.

And Ferb died with grief for Maine, and Nuagal died with grief for her husband and for her two sons. And a grave was made for them, and a stone put over it, and their names were written in Ogham; and Rath Ini got the name of Duma Ferb, Ferb's Mound, after that.

And this was the first blood shed in Ulster on the account of the Brown Bull of Cuailgne.

(1902)

SARA JEANNETTE DUNCAN

A Mother in India

I

There were times when we had to go without puddings to pay
John's uniform bills, and always I did the facings myself with a
cloth-ball to save getting new ones. I would have polished his
sword, too, if I had been allowed; I adored his sword. And once, I
remember, we painted and varnished our own dog-cart, and very
smart it looked, to save fifty rupees. We had nothing but our pay –
John had his company when we were married, but what is that? –
and life was made up of small knowing economics, much more
amusing in recollection than in practice. We were sodden poor, and
that is a fact, poor and conscientious, which was worse. A big fat
spider of a money-lender came one day into the veranda – and
tempted us – we lived in a hut, but it had a veranda – and John
threatened to report him to the police. Poor when everybody else
had enough to live in the open-handed Indian fashion, that was
what made it so hard; we were alone in our sordid little ways.
When the expectation of Cecily came to us we made out to be
delighted, knowing that the whole station pitied us, and when
Cecily came herself, with a swamping burst of expense, we kept up
the pretence splendidly. She was peevish, poor little thing, and she
threatened convulsions from the beginning, but we both knew that
it was abnormal not to love her a great deal, more than life,
immediately and increasingly; and we applied ourselves honestly to
do it, with the thermometer at a hundred and two, and the nurse
leaving at the end of a fortnight because she discovered that I had
only six of everything for the table. To find out a husband's virtues,
you must marry a poor man. The regiment was under-officered as
usual, and John had to take parade at daylight quite three times a
week; but he walked up and down the veranda with Cecily
constantly till two in the morning, when a little coolness came. I
usually lay awake the rest of the night in fear that a scorpion would

drop from the ceiling on her. Nevertheless, we were of excellent mind towards Cecily; we were in such terror, not so much of failing in our duty towards her as towards the ideal standard of mankind. We were very anxious indeed not to come short. To be found too small for one's place in nature would have been odious. We would talk about her for an hour at a time, even when John's charger was threatening glanders and I could see his mind perpetually wandering to the stable. I would say to John that she had brought a new element into our lives – she had indeed! – and John would reply, 'I know what you mean,' and go on to prophesy that she would 'bind us together'. We didn't need binding together; we were more to each other, there in the desolation of that arid frontier outpost, than most husbands and wives; but it seemed a proper and hopeful thing to believe, so we believed it. Of course, the real experience would have come, we weren't monsters; but fate curtailed the opportunity. She was just five weeks old when the doctor told us that we must either pack her home immediately or lose her, and the very next day John went down with enteric.* So Cecily was sent to England with a sergeant's wife who had lost her twins, and I settled down under the direction of a native doctor, to fight for my husband's life, without ice or proper food, or sick-room comforts of any sort. Ah! Fort Samila, with the sun glaring up from the sand! – however, it is a long time ago now. I trusted the baby willingly to Mrs Berry and to Providence, and did not fret; my capacity for worry, I suppose, was completely absorbed. Mrs Berry's letter, describing the child's improvement on the voyage and safe arrival came, I remember, the day on which John was allowed his first solid mouthful; it had been a long siege. 'Poor little wretch!' he said when I read it aloud; and after that Cecily became an episode.

She had gone to my husband's people; it was the best arrangement. We were lucky that it was possible; so many children had to be sent to strangers and hirelings. Since an unfortunate infant must be brought into the world and set adrift, the haven of its grandmother and its Aunt Emma and its Aunt Alice certainly seemed providential. I had absolutely no cause for anxiety, as I often told people, wondering that I did not feel a little all the same. Nothing, I knew, could exceed the conscientious devotion of all three Farnham ladies to the child. She would appear upon their somewhat barren horizon as a new and interesting duty, and the small additional income she also represented would be almost nominal compensation for the care she would receive. They were excellent persons of the kind that talk about matins and vespers, and attend both. They helped little charities and gave little teas, and wrote little notes, and made deprecating allowance for the eccentricities of their titled or moneyed acquaintances. They were the subdued, smiling, unimaginatively dressed women on a small definite income that you meet at every rectory garden party in the country, a little snobbish, a little priggish, wholly conventional, but apart from these weaknesses, sound and simple and dignified, managing their two small servants with a display of the most exact traditions, and keeping a somewhat vague and belated but constant eye upon the doings of their country as chronicled in a biweekly paper. They were all immensely interested in royalty, and would read paragraphs aloud to each other about how the Princess Beatrice or the Princess Maud had opened a fancy bazaar, looking remarkably well in plain grey poplin trimmed with Irish lace – an industry which, as is well known, the Royal Family has set its heart on rehabilitating. Upon which Mrs Farnham's comment invariably would be, 'How thoughtful of them, dear!' and Alice would usually say, 'Well, if I were a princess, I should like something nicer than plain grey poplin.' Alice, being the youngest, was not always expected to think before she spoke. Alice painted in watercolours, but Emma was supposed to have the most common sense.

They took turns in writing to us with the greatest regularity about Cecily; only once, I think, did they miss the weekly mail, and that was when she threatened diphtheria and they thought we had better be kept in ignorance. The kind and affectionate terms of these letters never altered except with the facts they described – teething, creeping, measles, cheeks growing round and rosy, all were conveyed in the same smooth, pat, and proper phrases, so absolutely empty of any glimpse of the child's personality that after the first few months it was like reading about a somewhat uninteresting infant in a book. I was sure Cecily was not uninteresting, but her chroniclers were. We used to wade through the long, thin sheets and saw how much more satisfactory it would be when Cecily could write to us herself. Meanwhile we noted her weekly progress with much the feeling one would have about a faraway little bit of property that was giving no trouble and coming on exceedingly well. We would take possession of Cecily at our convenience; till then, it was gratifying to hear of our earned increment in dear little dimples and sweet little curls.

She was nearly four when I saw her again. We were home on three months' leave; John had just got his first brevet for doing something which he does not allow me to talk about in the Black Mountain country; and we were fearfully pleased with ourselves. I remember that excitement lasted well up to Port Said. As far as the Canal, Cecily was only one of the pleasures and interests we were going home to: John's majority was the thing that really gave savour to life. But the first faint line of Europe brought my child to my horizon; and all the rest of the way she kept her place, holding out her little arms to me, beckoning me on. Her four motherless years brought compunction to my heart and tears to my eyes; she should have all the compensation that could be. I suddenly realised how ready I was – how ready! – to have her back. I rebelled fiercely against John's decision that we must not take her with us on our return to the frontier; privately, I resolved to dispute it, and, if necessary, I saw myself abducting the child – my own child. My days and nights as the ship crept on were full of a long ache to possess her; the defrauded tenderness of the last four years rose up in me and sometimes caught at my throat. I could think and talk and dream of nothing else. John indulged me as much as was reasonable, and only once betrayed by a yawn that the subject was not for him endlessly absorbing. Then I cried and he apologised. 'You know,' he said, 'it isn't exactly the same thing. I'm not her mother.' At which I dried my tears and expanded, proud and pacified. I was her mother!

Then the rainy little station and Alice, all-embracing in a damp waterproof, and the drive in the fly, and John's mother at the gate and a necessary pause while I kissed John's mother. Dear thing, she wanted to hold our hands and look into our faces and tell us how little we had changed for all our hardships; and on the way to the house she actually stopped to point out some alterations in the flower borders. At last the drawing-room door and the smiling housemaid turning the handle and the unforgettable picture of a little girl, a little girl unlike anything we had imagined, starting bravely to trot across the room with the little speech that had been taught her. Halfway she came; I suppose our regards were too fixed, too absorbed, for there she stopped with a wail of terror at the strange faces, and ran straight back to the outstretched arms of her Aunt Emma. The most natural thing in the world, no doubt. I walked over to a chair opposite with my handbag and umbrella and sat down – a spectator, aloof and silent. Aunt

Emma fondled and quieted the child, apologising for her to me, coaxing her to look up, but the little figure still shook with sobs, hiding its face in the bosom that it knew. I smiled politely, like any other stranger, at Emma's deprecations, and sat impassive, looking at my alleged baby breaking her heart at the sight of her mother. It is not amusing even now to remember the anger that I felt. I did not touch her or speak to her; I simply sat observing my alien possession, in the frock I had not made and the sash I had not chosen, being coaxed and kissed and protected and petted by its Aunt Emma. Presently I asked to be taken to my room, and there I locked myself in for two atrocious hours. Just once my heart beat high, when a tiny knock came and a timid, docile little voice said that tea was ready. But I heard the rustle of a skirt, and guessed the directing angel in Aunt Emma, and responded, 'Thank you, dear, run away and say that I am coming,' with a pleasant visitor's inflection which I was able to sustain for the rest of the afternoon.

'She goes to bed at seven,' said Emma.

'Oh, does she?' said I. 'A very good hour, I should think.'

'She sleeps in my room,' said Mrs Farnham.

'We give her mutton broth very often, but seldom stock soup,' said Aunt Emma. 'Mamma thinks it is too stimulating.'

'Indeed?' said I, to all of it.

They took me up to see her in her crib, and pointed out, as she lay asleep, that though she had 'a general look' of me, her features were distinctively Farnham.

'Won't you kiss her?' asked Alice. 'You haven't kissed her yet, and she is used to so much affection.'

'I don't think I could take such an advantage of her,' I said.

They looked at each other, and Mrs Farnham said that I was plainly worn out. I mustn't sit up to prayers.

If I had been given anything like reasonable time I might have made a fight for it, but four weeks – it took a month each way in those days – was too absurdly little; I could do nothing. But I would not stay at Mamma's. It was more than I would ask of myself, that daily disappointment under the mask of gratified discovery, for long.

I spent an approving, unnatural week, in my farcical character, bridling my resentment and hiding my mortification with pretty phrases; and then I went up to town and drowned my sorrows in the summer sales. I took John with me. I may have been Cecily's mother in theory, but I was John's wife in fact.

We went back to the frontier, and the regiment saw a lot of service. That meant medals and fun for my husband, but economy and anxiety for me, though I managed to be allowed as close to the firing line as any woman.

Once the Colonel's wife and I, sitting in Fort Samila, actually heard the rifles of a punitive expedition cracking on the other side of the river – that was a bad moment. My man came in after fifteen hours' fighting, and went sound asleep, sitting before his food with his knife and fork in his hands. But service makes heavy demands besides those on your wife's nerves. We had saved two thousand rupees, I remember, against another run home, and it all went like powder, in the Mirzai expedition; and the run home diminished to a month in a boarding-house in the hills.

Meanwhile, however, we had begun to correspond with our daughter, in large round words of one syllable, behind which, of course, was plain the patient guiding hand of Aunt Emma. One could hear Aunt Emma suggesting what would be nice to say, trying to instil a little pale affection for the far-off papa and mamma. There was so little Cecily and so much Emma – of course, it could not be otherwise – that I used to take, I fear, but a perfunctory joy in these letters. When we went home again I stipulated absolutely that she was to write to us without any sort of supervision – the child was ten.

'But the spelling!' cried Aunt Emma, with lifted eyebrows.

'Her letters aren't exercises,' I was obliged to retort. 'She will do the best she can.'

We found her a docile little girl, with nice manners, a thoroughly unobjectionable child. I saw quite clearly that I could not have brought her up so well; indeed, there were moments when I fancied that Cecily, contrasting me with her aunts, wondered a little what my bringing up could have been like. With this reserve of criticism on Cecily's part, however, we got on very tolerably, largely because I found it impossible to assume any responsibility towards her, and in moments of doubt or discipline referred her to her aunts. We spent a pleasant summer with a little girl in the house whose interest in us was amusing, and whose outings it was gratifying to arrange; but when we went back, I had no desire to take her with us. I thought her very much better where she was.

Then came the period which is filled, in a subordinate degree, with Cecily's letters. I do not wish to claim more than I ought; they were not my only or even my principal interest in life. It was a long period; it lasted till she was twenty-one. John had had promotion in the meantime, and there was rather more money, but he had earned his second brevet with a bullet through one lung, and the doctors ordered our leave to be spent in South Africa. We had photographs, we knew she had grown tall and athletic and comely, and the letters were always very creditable. I had the unusual and qualified privilege of watching my daughter's development from ten to twenty-one, at a distance of four thousand miles, by means of the written word. I wrote myself as provocatively as possible; I sought for every string, but the vibration that came back across the seas to me was always other than the one I looked for, and sometimes there was none. Nevertheless, Mrs Farnham wrote me that Cecily very much valued my communications. Once when I had described an unusual excursion in a native state, I learned that she had read my letter aloud to the sewing circle. After that I abandoned description, and confined myself to such intimate personal details as no sewing circle could find amusing. The child's own letters were simply a mirror of the ideas of the Farnham ladies; that must have been so, it was not altogether my jaundiced eye. Alice and Emma and Grandmamma paraded the pages in turn. I very early gave up hope of discoveries in my daughter, though as much of the original as I could detect was satisfactorily simple and sturdy. I found little things to criticise, of course, tendencies to correct; and by return post I criticised and corrected, but the distance and the deliberation seemed to touch my maxims with a kind of arid frivolity, and sometimes I tore them up. One quick, warm-blooded scolding would have been worth a sheaf of them. My studied little phrases could only inoculate her with a dislike for me without protecting her from anything under the sun.

However, I found she didn't dislike me, when John and I went home at last to bring her out. She received me with just a hint of kindness, perhaps, but on the whole very well.

2

John was recalled, of course, before the end of our furlough, which knocked various things on the head; but that is the sort of thing one learned to take with philosophy in any lengthened term of Her Majesty's service. Besides, there is usually sugar for the pill; and in this case it was a Staff command bigger than anything we expected for at least five years to come. The excitement of it when it was explained to her gave Cecily a charming colour. She took a good deal of interest in the General, her papa; I think she had an idea that his distinction would alleviate the situation in India, however it might present itself. She accepted that prospective situation calmly; it had been placed before her all her life. There would always be a time when she should go and live with Papa and Mamma in India, and so long as she was of an age to receive the idea with rebel tears she was assured that Papa and Mamma would give her a pony. The pony was no longer added to the prospect; it was absorbed no doubt in the general list of attractions calculated to reconcile a young lady to a roof with which she had no practical acquaintance. At all events, when I feared the embarrassment and dismay of a pathetic parting with darling Grandmamma and the aunties, and the sweet cat and the dear vicar and all the other objects of affection, I found an agreeable unexpected philosophy.

I may add that while I anticipated such brokenhearted farewells I was quite prepared to take them easily. Time, I imagined, had brought philosophy to me also, equally agreeable and equally unexpected.

It was a Bombay ship, full of returning Anglo-Indians. I looked up and down the long saloon tables with a sense of relief and a solace; I was again among my own people. They belonged to Bengal and to Burma, to Madras and to the Punjab, but they were all my people. I could pick out a score that I knew in fact, and there were none that in imagination I didn't know. The look of wider seas and skies, the casual experienced glance, the touch of irony and of tolerance, how well I knew it and how well I liked it! Dear old England, sitting in our wake, seemed to hold by comparison a great many soft, unsophisticated people, immensely occupied about very particular trifles. How difficult it had been, all the summer, to be interested! These of my long acquaintance belonged to my country's Executive, acute, alert, with the marks of travail on them. Gladly I went in and out of the women's cabins and listened to the argot of the men; my own ruling, administering, soldiering little lot.

Cecily looked at them askance. To her the atmosphere was alien, and I perceived that gently and privately she registered objections. She cast a disapproving eye upon the wife of a Conservator of Forests, who scanned with interest a distant

funnel and laid a small wager that it belonged to the Messageries
Maritimes. She looked with a straightened lip at the crisply
stepping women who walked the deck in short and rather shabby
skirts with their hands in their jacket-pockets talking transfers
and promotions; and having got up at six to make a watercolour
sketch of the sunrise, she came to me in profound indignation to
say that she had met a man in his pyjamas; no doubt, poor
wretch, on his way to be shaved. I was unable to convince her that
he was not expected to visit the barber in all his clothes.

At the end of the third day she told me that she wished these
people wouldn't talk to her; she didn't like them. I had turned in
the hour we left the Channel and had not left my berth since, so
possibly I was not in the most amiable mood to receive a douche
of cold water. 'I must try to remember, dear,' I said, 'that you
have been brought up altogether in the society of pussies and
vicars and elderly ladies, and of course you miss them. But you
must have a little patience. I shall be up tomorrow, if this beastly
sea continues to go down; and then we will try to find somebody
suitable to introduce to you.'

'Thank you, Mamma,' said my daughter, without a ray of
suspicion. Then she added consideringly, 'Aunt Emma and Aunt
Alice do seem quite elderly ladies beside you, and yet you are
older than either of them, aren't you? I wonder how that is.'

It was so innocent, so admirable, that I laughed at my own
expense; while Cecily, doing her hair, considered me gravely. 'I
wish you would tell me why you laugh, Mamma,' quoth she. 'You
laugh so often.'

We had not to wait after all for my good offices of the next
morning. Cecily came down at ten o'clock that night quite happy
and excited; she had been talking to a bishop, such a dear bishop.
The bishop had been showing her his collection of photographs,
and she had promised to play the harmonium for him at the
eleven o'clock service in the morning. 'Bless me!' said I. 'Is it
Sunday?' It seemed she had got on very well indeed with the
bishop, who knew the married sister, at Tunbridge, of her very
greatest friend. Cecily herself did not know the married sister, but
that didn't matter – it was a link. The bishop was charming.
'Well, my love,' said I – I was teaching myself to use these forms of
address for fear she would feel an unkind lack of them, but it was
difficult – 'I am glad that somebody from my part of the world has
impressed you favourably at last. I wish we had more bishops.'

'Oh, but the bishop doesn't belong to your part of the world,' responded my daughter sleepily. 'He is travelling for his health.'

It was the most unexpected and delightful thing to be packed into one's chair next morning by Dacres Tottenham. As I emerged from the music saloon after breakfast – Cecily had stayed below to look over her hymns and consider with her bishop the possibility of the anthem – Dacres's face was the first I saw; it simply illuminated, for me, that portion of the deck. I noticed with pleasure the quick toss of the cigar overboard as he recognised and bore down upon me. We were immense friends; John liked him too. He was one of those people who make a tremendous difference; in all our three hundred passengers there could be no one like him, certainly no one whom I could be more glad to see. We plunged at once into immediate personal affairs, we would get at the heart of them later. He gave his vivid word to everything he had seen and done; we laughed and exclaimed and were silent in a concert of admirable understanding. We were still unravelling, still demanding and explaining when the ship's bell began to ring for church, and almost simultaneously Cecily advanced towards us. She had a proper Sunday hat on, with flowers under the brim, and a church-going frock; she wore gloves and clasped a prayer book. Most of the women who filed past to the summons of the bell were going down as they were, in cotton blouses and serge skirts, in tweed caps or anything, as to a kind of family prayers. I knew exactly how they would lean against the pillars of the saloon during the psalms. This young lady would be little less than a rebuke to them. I surveyed her approach; she positively walked as if it were Sunday.

'My dear,' I said, 'how *endimanchée* you look! The bishop will be very pleased with you. This gentleman is Mr Tottenham, who administers Her Majesty's pleasure in parts of India about Allahabad. My daughter, Dacres.' She was certainly looking very fresh, and her calm grey eyes had the repose in them that has never known itself to be disturbed about anything. I wondered whether she bowed so distantly also because it was Sunday, and then I remembered that Dacres was a young man, and that the Farnham ladies had probably taught her that it was right to be very distant with young men.

'It is almost eleven, Mamma.'

'Yes, dear. I see you are going to church.'

'Are you not coming, Mamma?'

I was well wrapped up in an extremely comfortable corner. I had *La Duchesse Bleue* uncut in my lap, and an agreeable person to talk to. I fear that in any case I should not have been inclined to attend the service, but there was something in my daughter's intonation that made me distinctly hostile to the idea. I am putting things down as they were, extenuating nothing.

'I think not, dear.'

'I've turned up two such nice seats.'

'Stay, Miss Farnham, and keep us in countenance,' said Dacres, with his charming smile. The smile displaced a look of discreet and amused observation. Dacres had an eye always for a situation, and this one was even newer to him than to me.

'No, no. She must run away and not bully her mamma,' I said. 'When she comes back we will see how much she remembers of the sermon,' and as the flat tinkle from the companion began to show signs of diminishing, Cecily, with one grieved glance, hastened down.

'You amazing lady!' said Dacres. 'A daughter – and such a tall daughter! I somehow never—'

'You knew we had one?'

'There was theory of that kind, I remember, about ten years ago. Since then – excuse me – I don't think you've mentioned her.'

'You talk as if she were a skeleton in the closet!'

'You *didn't* talk – as if she were.'

'I think she was, in a way, poor child. But the resurrection day hasn't confounded me as I deserved. She's a very good girl.'

'If you had asked me to pick out your daughter—'

'She would have been the last you would indicate! Quite so,' I said. 'She is like her father's people. I can't help that.'

'I shouldn't think you would if you could,' Dacres remarked absently; but the sea air, perhaps, enabled me to digest his thoughtlessness with a smile.

'No,' I said, 'I am just as well pleased. I think a resemblance to me would confuse me, often.'

There was a trace of scrutiny in Dacres's glance. 'Don't you find yourself in sympathy with her?' he asked.

'My dear boy, I have seen her just twice in twenty-one years! You see, I've always stuck to John.'

'But between mother and daughter – I may be old-fashioned, but I had an idea that there was an instinct that might be depended on.'

'I am depending on it,' I said, and let my eyes follow the little blue waves that chased past the handrail. 'We are making very good speed, aren't we? Thirty-five knots since last night at ten. Are you in the sweep?'

'I never bet on the way out – can't afford it. Am I old-fashioned?' he insisted.

'Probably. Men are very slow in changing their philosophy about women. I fancy their idea of the maternal relation is firmest fixed of all.'

'We see it a beatitude!' he cried.

'I know,' I said wearily, 'and you never modify the view.'

Dacres contemplated the portion of the deck that lay between us. His eyes were discreetly lowered, but I saw embarrassment and speculation and a hint of criticism in them.

'Tell me more about it,' said he.

'Oh, for heaven's sake don't be sympathetic!' I exclaimed. 'Lend me a little philosophy instead. There is nothing to tell. There she is and there I am, in the most intimate relation in the world, constituted when she is twenty-one and I am forty.' Dacres started slightly at the ominous word; so little do men realise that the women they like can ever pass out of the constated years of attraction. 'I find the young lady very tolerable, very creditable, very nice. I find the relation atrocious. There you have it. I would like to break the relation into pieces,' I went on recklessly, 'and throw it into the sea. Such things should be tempered to one. I should feel it much less if she occupied another cabin, and would consent to call me Elizabeth or Jane. It is not as if I had been her mother always. One grows fastidious at forty – new intimacies are only possible then on a basis of temperament—'

I paused; it seemed to me that I was making excuses, and I had not the least desire in the world to do that.

'How awfully rough on the girl!' said Dacres Tottenham.

'That consideration has also occurred to me,' I said candidly, 'though I have perhaps been even more struck by its converse.'

'You had no earthly business to be her mother,' said my friend, with irritation.

I shrugged my shoulders – what would you have done? – and opened *La Duchesse Bleue*.

3

Mrs Morgan, wife of a judge of the High Court of Bombay, and I sat amidships on the cool side in the Suez Canal. She was outlining 'Soiled Linen' in chain-stitch on a green canvas bag; I was admiring the Egyptian sands. 'How charming,' said I, 'is this solitary desert in the endless oasis we are compelled to cross!'

'Oasis in the desert, you mean,' said Mrs Morgan. 'I haven't noticed any, but I happened to look up this morning as I was putting on my stockings, and I saw through my porthole the most lovely mirage.'

I had been at school with Mrs Morgan more than twenty years agone, but she had come to the special enjoyment of the dignities of life while I still liked doing things. Mrs Morgan was the kind of person to make one realise how distressing a medium is middle age. Contemplating her precipitous lap, to which conventional attitudes were certainly more becoming, I crossed my own knees with energy, and once more resolved to be young until I was old.

'How perfectly delightful for you to be taking Cecily out!' said Mrs Morgan placidly.

'Isn't it?' I responded, watching the gliding sands.

'But she was born in sixty-nine – that makes her twenty-one. Quite time, I should say.'

'Oh, we couldn't put it off any longer. I mean – her father has such a horror of early débuts. He simply would not hear of her coming before.'

'Doesn't want her to marry in India, I daresay – the only one,' purred Mrs Morgan.

'Oh, I don't know. It isn't such a bad place. I was brought out there to marry, and I married. I've found it very satisfactory.'

'You always did say exactly what you thought, Helena,' said Mrs Morgan excusingly.

'I haven't much patience with people who bring their daughters out to give them the chance they never would have in England, and then go about devoutly hoping they won't marry in India,' I said. 'I shall be very pleased if Cecily does as well as your girls have done.'

'Mary in the Indian Civil and Jessie in the Imperial Service Troops,' sighed Mrs Morgan complacently. 'And both, my dear, within a year. It *was* a blow.'

'Oh, it must have been!' I said civilly.

There was no use in bandying words with Emily Morgan.

'There is nothing in the world like the satisfaction and pleasure one takes in one's daughters,' Mrs Morgan went on limpidly. 'And one can be in such *close* sympathy with one's girls. I have never regretted having no sons.'

'Dear me, yes. To watch oneself growing up again – call back the lovely April of one's prime, et cetera – to read every thought and anticipate every wish – there is no more golden privilege in life, dear Emily. Such a direct and natural avenue for affection, such a wide field for interest!'

I paused, lost in the volume of my admirable sentiments.

'How beautifully you talk, Helena! I wish I had the gift.'

'It doesn't mean very much,' I said truthfully.

'Oh, I think it's everything! And how companionable a girl is! I quite envy you, this season, having Cecily constantly with you and taking her about everywhere. Something quite new for you, isn't it?'

'Absolutely,' said I. 'I am looking forward to it immensely. But it is likely she will make her own friends, don't you think?' I added anxiously.

'Hardly the first season. My girls didn't. I was practically their only intimate for months. Don't be afraid; you won't be obliged to go shares in Cecily with anybody for a good long while,' added Mrs Morgan kindly. 'I know just how you feel about *that*.'

The muddy water of the Ditch chafed up from under us against its banks with a smell that enabled me to hide the emotions Mrs Morgan evoked behind my handkerchief. The pale desert was pictorial with the drifting, deepening purple shadows of clouds, and in the midst a blue glimmer of the Bitter Lakes, with a white sail on them. A little frantic Arab boy ran alongside keeping pace with the ship. Except for the smell, it was like a dream, we moved so quietly; on, gently on and on between the ridgy clay banks and the rows of piles. Peace was on the ship; you could hear what the Fourth in his white ducks said to the quartermaster in his blue denims; you could count the strokes of the electric bell in the wheelhouse; peace was on the ship as she pushed on, an ever-venturing, double-funnelled impertinence, through the sands of the ages. My eyes wandered along a plank-line in the deck till they were arrested by a petticoat I knew, when they returned of their own accord. I seemed to be always seeing that petticoat.

'I think,' resumed Mrs Morgan, whose glance had wandered in

the same direction, 'that Cecily is a very fine type of our English girls. With those dark grey eyes, a *little* prominent possibly, and that good colour – it's rather high now perhaps, but she will lose quite enough of it in India – and those regular features, she would make a splendid Britannia. Do you know, I fancy she must have a great deal of character. Has she?'

'Any amount. And all of it good,' I responded, with private dejection.

'No faults at all?' chaffed Mrs Morgan.

I shook my head. 'Nothing,' I said sadly, 'that I can put my finger on. But I hope to discover a few later. The sun may bring them out.'

'Like freckles. Well, you are a lucky woman. Mine had plenty, I assure you. Untidiness was no name for Jessie, and Mary – I'm *sorry* to say that Mary sometimes fibbed.'

'How lovable of her! Cecily's neatness is a painful example to me, and I don't believe she would tell a fib to save my life.'

'Tell me,' said Mrs Morgan, as the lunch-bell rang and she gathered her occupation into her work-basket, 'who is that talking to her?'

'Oh, an old friend,' I replied easily. 'Dacres Tottenham, a dear fellow, and most benevolent. He is trying on my behalf to reconcile her to the life she'll have to lead in India.'

'She won't need much reconciling, if she's like most girls,' observed Mrs Morgan, 'but he seems to be trying very hard.'

That was quite the way I took it – on my behalf – for several days. When people have understood you very adequately for ten years you do not expect them to boggle at any problem you may present at the end of the decade. I thought Dacres was moved by a fine sense of compassion. I thought that with his admirable perception he had put a finger on the little comedy of fruitfulness in my life that laughed so bitterly at the tragedy of the barren woman, and was attempting, by delicate manipulation, to make it easier. I really thought so. Then I observed that myself had preposterously deceived me, that it wasn't like that at all. When Mr Tottenham joined us, Cecily and me, I saw that he had listened more than he talked, with an ear specially cocked to register any small irony which might appear in my remarks to my daughter. Naturally he registered more than there were, to make up perhaps for dear Cecily's obviously not registering any. I could see, too, that he was suspicious of any flavour of kindness; finally, to avoid the strictures of his upper lip, which really, dear fellow, began to bore me, I talked exclusively about the distant sails and the Red Sea littoral. When he no longer joined us as we sat or walked together, I perceived that his hostility was fixed and his *parti pris*. He was brimful of compassion, but it was all for Cecily, none for the situation or for me. (She would have marvelled, placidly, why he pitied her. I am glad I can say that.) The primitive man in him rose up as Pope of nature and excommunicated me as a creature recusant to her functions. Then deliberately Dacres undertook an office of consolation; and I fell to wondering, while Mrs Morgan spoke her convictions plainly out, how far an impulse of reparation for a misfortune with which he had nothing to do might carry a man.

I began to watch the affair with an interest which even to me seemed queer. It was not detached, but it was semi-detached, and, of course, on the side for which I seem, in this history, to be perpetually apologising. With certain limitations it didn't matter an atom whom Cecily married. So that he was sound and decent, with reasonable prospects, her simple requirements and ours for her would be quite met. There was the ghost of a consolation in that; one needn't be anxious or exacting.

I could predict with a certain amount of confidence that in her first season she would probably receive three or four proposals, any one of which she might accept with as much propriety and satisfaction as any other one. For Cecily it was so simple; prearranged by nature like her digestion, one could not see any logical basis for difficulties. A nice upstanding sapper, a dashing Bengal Lancer – oh, I could think of half a dozen types that would answer excellently. She was the kind of young person, and that was the summing up of it, to marry a type and be typically happy. I hoped and expected that she would. But Dacres!

Dacres should exercise the greatest possible discretion. He was not a person who could throw the dice indifferently with fate. He could respond to so much, and he would inevitably, sooner or later, demand so much response! He was governed by a preposterously exacting temperament, and he wore his nerves outside. And what vision he had! How he explored the world he lived in and drew out of it all there was, all there was! I could see him in the years to come ranging alone the fields that were sweet and the horizons that lifted for him, and ever returning to pace the common dusty mortal road by the side of a purblind wife. On general principles, as a case to point at, it would be a conspicuous pity. Nor would it lack the aspect of a particular, a personal misfortune. Dacres was occupied in quite the natural normal degree with his charming self; he would pass his misery on, and who would deserve to escape it less than his mother-in-law?

I listened to Emily Morgan, who gleaned in the ship more information about Dacres Tottenham's people, pay, and prospects than I had ever acquired, and I kept an eye upon the pair which was, I flattered myself, quite maternal. I watched them without acute anxiety, deploring the threatening destiny, but hardly nearer to it than one is in the stalls to the stage. My moments of real concern for Dacres were mingled more with anger than with sorrow – it seemed inexcusable that he, with his infallible divining-rod for temperament, should be on the point of making such an ass of himself. Though I talk of the stage there was nothing at all dramatic to reward my attention, mine and Emily Morgan's. To my imagination, excited by its idea of what Dacres Tottenham's courtship ought to be, the attentions he paid to Cecily were most humdrum. He threw rings into buckets with her – she was good at that – and quoits upon the 'bull' board; he found her chair after the decks were swabbed in the morning and established her in it; he paced the deck with her at convenient times and seasons. They were humdrum, but they were constant and cumulative. Cecily took them with an even breath that perfectly matched. There was hardly anything, on her part, to note – a little discreet observation of his comings and goings, eyes scarcely lifted from her book, and later just a hint of proprietorship, as on the evening she came up to me on deck, our first night in the Indian Ocean. I was lying on my long chair looking at the thick, low stars and thinking it was a long time since I had seen John.

'Dearest Mamma, out here and nothing over your shoulders! You *are* imprudent. Where is your wrap? Mr Tottenham, will you please fetch Mamma's wrap for her?'

'If Mamma so instructs me,' he said audaciously.

'Do as Cecily tells you,' I laughed, and he went and did it, while I by the light of the quartermaster's lantern distinctly saw my daughter blush.

Another time, when Cecily came down to undress, she bent over me as I lay in the lower berth with unusual solicitude. I had been dozing, and I jumped.

'What is it, child?' I said. 'Is the ship on fire?'

'No, Mamma, the ship is not on fire. There is nothing wrong. I'm so sorry I startled you. But Mr Tottenham has been telling me all about what you did for the soldiers the time plague broke out in the lines at Mian-Mir. I think it was splendid, Mamma, and so does he.'

'Oh, *Lord*!' I groaned. 'Good night.'

4

It remained in my mind, that little thing that Dacres had taken the trouble to tell my daughter; I thought about it a good deal. It seemed to me the most serious and convincing circumstance that had yet offered itself to my consideration. Dacres was no longer content to bring solace and support to the more appealing figure of the situation; he must set to work, bless him! to improve the situation itself. He must try to induce Miss Farnham, by telling her everything he could remember to my credit, to think as well of her mother as possible, in spite of the strange and secret blows which that mother might be supposed to sit up at night to deliver to her. Cecily thought very well of me already; indeed, with private reservations as to my manners and – no, *not* my morals, I believe I exceeded her expectations of what a perfectly new and untrained mother would be likely to prove. It was my theory that she found me all she could understand me to be. The maternal virtues of the outside were certainly mine; I put them on with care every morning and wore them with patience all day. Dacres, I assured myself, must have allowed his preconception to lead him absurdly by the nose not to see that the girl was satisfied, that my impatience, my impotence, did not at all make her miserable. Evidently, however, he had created our relations differently; evidently he had set himself to their amelioration. There was portent in it; things seemed to be closing in. I bit off a quarter of an inch of wooden pen-handle in considering whether or not I should mention it in my letter to John, and decided that it would be better just perhaps to drop a hint. Though I could not expect John to receive it with any sort of perturbation. Men are different; he would probably think Tottenham well enough able to look after himself.

I had embarked on my letter, there at the end of a corner table of the saloon, when I saw Dacres saunter through. He wore a very conscious and elaborately purposeless air; and it jumped with my mood that he had nothing less than the crisis of his life in his pocket, and was looking for me. As he advanced towards me between the long tables doubt left me and alarm assailed me. 'I'm glad to find you in a quiet corner,' said he, seating himself, and confirmed my worst anticipations.

'I'm writing to John,' I said, and again applied myself to my pen-handle. It is a trick Cecily has since done her best in vain to cure me of.

'I am going to interrupt you,' he said. 'I have not had an opportunity of talking to you for some time.'

'I like that!' I exclaimed derisively.

'And I want to tell you that I am very much charmed with Cecily.'

'Well,' I said, 'I am not going to gratify you by saying anything against her.'

'You don't deserve her, you know.'

'I won't dispute that. But, if you don't mind – I'm not sure that I'll stand being abused, dear boy.'

'I quite see it isn't any use. Though one spoke with the tongues of men and of angels—'

'And had not charity,' I continued for him. 'Precisely. I won't go on, but your quotation is very apt.'

'I so bow down before her simplicity. It makes a wide and beautiful margin for the rest of her character. She is a girl Ruskin would have loved.'

'I wonder,' said I. 'He did seem fond of the simple type, didn't he?'

'Her mind is so clear, so transparent. The motive spring of everything she says and does is so direct. Don't you find you can most completely depend upon her?'

'Oh yes,' I said, 'certainly. I nearly always know what she is going to say before she says it, and under given circumstances I can tell precisely what she will do.'

'I fancy her sense of duty is very beautifully developed.'

'It is,' I said. 'There is hardly a day when I do not come in contact with it.'

'Well, that is surely a good thing. And I find that calm poise of hers very restful.'

'I would not have believed that so many virtues could reside in one young lady,' I said, taking refuge in flippancy, 'and to think that she should be my daughter!'

'As I believe you know, that seems to me rather a cruel stroke of destiny, Mrs Farnham.'

'Oh yes, I know! You have a constructive imagination, Dacres. You don't seem to see that the girl is protected by her limitations, like a tortoise. She lives within them quite secure and happy and content. How determined you are to be sorry for her!'

Mr Tottenham looked at the end of this lively exchange as though he sought for a polite way of conveying to me that I rather was the limited person. He looked as if he wished he could say things. The first of them would be, I saw, that he had quite a different conception of Cecily, that it was illuminated by many trifles, nuances of feeling and expression, which he had noticed in his talks with her whenever they had skirted the subject of her adoption by her mother. He knew her, he was longing to say, better than I did; when it would have been natural to reply that one could not hope to compete in such a direction with an intelligent young man, and we should at once have been upon delicate and difficult ground. So it was as well perhaps that he kept silence until he said, as he had come prepared to say, 'Well, I want to put that beyond a doubt – her happiness – if I'm good enough. I want her, please, and I only hope that she will be half as willing to come as you are likely to be to let her go.'

It was a shock when it came, plump, like that; and I was horrified to feel how completely every other consideration was lost for the instant in the immense relief that it prefigured. To be my whole complete self again, without the feeling that a fraction of me was masquerading about in Cecily! To be freed at once, or almost, from an exacting condition and an impossible ideal! 'Oh!' I exclaimed, and my eyes positively filled. 'You *are* good, Dacres, but I couldn't let you do that.'

His undisguised stare brought me back to a sense of the proportion of things. I saw that in the combination of influences that had brought Mr Tottenham to the point of proposing to marry my daughter consideration for me, if it had a place, would be fantastic. Inwardly I laughed at the egotism of raw nerves that had conjured it up, even for an instant, as a reason for gratitude. The situation was not so peculiar, not so interesting, as that. But I answered his stare with a smile; what I had said might very well stand.

'Do you imagine,' he said, seeing that I did not mean to amplify it, 'that I want to marry her out of any sort of *goodness*?'

'Benevolence is your weakness, Dacres.'

'I see. You think one's motive is to withdraw her from a relation which ought to be the most natural in the world, but which is, in her particular and painful case, the most equivocal.'

'Well, come,' I remonstrated. 'You have dropped one or two things, you know, in the heat of your indignation, not badly calculated to give one that idea. The eloquent statement you have just made, for instance – it carries all the patness of old conviction. How often have you rehearsed it?'

I am a fairly long-suffering person, but I began to feel a little annoyed with my would-be-son-in-law. If the relation were achieved it would give him no prescriptive right to bully me; and we were still in very early anticipation of that.

'Ah!' he said disarmingly. 'Don't let us quarrel. I'm sorry you think that; because it isn't likely to bring your favour to my project, and I want you friendly and helpful. Oh, confound it!' he exclaimed, with sudden temper. 'You ought to be. I don't understand this aloofness. I half suspect it's pose. You undervalue Cecily – well, you have no business to undervalue me. You know me better than anybody in the world. Now are you going to help me to marry your daughter?'

'I don't think so,' I said slowly, after a moment's silence, which he sat through like a mutinous schoolboy. 'I might tell you that I don't care a button whom you marry, but that would not be true. I do care more or less. As you say, I know you pretty well. I'd a little rather you didn't make a mess of it; and if you must I should distinctly prefer not to have the spectacle under my nose for the rest of my life. I can't hinder you, but I won't help you.'

'And what possesses you to imagine that in marrying Cecily I should make a mess of it? Shouldn't your first consideration be whether *she* would?'

'Perhaps it should, but, you see, it isn't. Cecily would be happy with anybody who made her comfortable. You would ask a good deal more than that, you know.'

Dacres, at this, took me up promptly. Life, he said, the heart of life, had particularly little to say to temperament. By the heart of life I suppose he meant married love. He explained that its roots asked other sustenance, and that it throve best of all on simple elemental goodness. So long as a man sought in women mere casual companionship, perhaps the most exquisite thing to be experienced was the stimulus of some spiritual feminine counterpart; but when he desired of one woman that she should be always and intimately with him, the background of his life, the mother of his children, he was better advised to avoid nerves and sensibilities, and try for the repose of the common – the uncommon – domestic virtues. Ah, he said, they were sweet, like lavender. (Already, I told him, he smelled the housekeeper's linen-chest.) But I did not interrupt him much; I couldn't, he was too absorbed. To temperamental pairing, he declared, the century owed its breed of decadents. I asked him if he had ever really recognised one; and he retorted that if he hadn't he didn't wish to make a beginning in his own family. In a quarter of an hour he repudiated the theories of a lifetime, a gratifying triumph for simple elemental goodness. Having denied the value of the subtler pretensions to charm in woman as you marry her, he went artlessly on to endow Cecily with as many of them as could possibly be desirable. He actually persuaded himself to say that it was lovely to see the reflections of life in her tranquil spirit; and when I looked at him incredulously he grew angry, and hinted that Cecily's sensitiveness to reflections and other things might be a trifle beyond her mother's ken. 'She responds instantly, intimately, to the beautiful everywhere,' he declared.

'Aren't the opportunities of life on board ship rather limited to demonstrate that?' I inquired. 'I know – you mean sunsets. Cecily is very fond of sunsets. She is always asking me to come and look at them.'

'I was thinking of last night's sunset,' he confessed. 'We looked at it together.'

'What did she say?' I asked idly.

'Nothing very much. That's just the point. Another girl would have raved and gushed.'

'Oh, well, Cecily never does that,' I responded. 'Nevertheless she is a very ordinary human instrument. I hope I shall have no temptation ten years hence to remind you that I warned you of her quality.'

'I wish, not in the least for my own profit, for I am well convinced already, but simply to win your cordiality and your approval – never did an unexceptional wooer receive such niggard encouragement! – I wish there were some sort of test for her quality. I would be proud to stand by it, and you would be convinced. I can't find words to describe my objection to your state of mind.'

The thing seemed to me to be a foregone conclusion. I saw it accomplished, with all its possibilities of disastrous commonplace. I saw all that I have here taken the trouble to foreshadow. So far as I was concerned, Dacres's burden would add itself to my philosophies, *voilà tout*. I should always be a little uncomfortable about it, because it had been taken from my back; but it would not be a matter for the wringing of hands. And yet – the hatefulness of the mistake! Dacres's bold talk of a test made no suggestion. Should my invention be more fertile? I thought of something.

'You have said nothing to her yet?' I asked.

'Nothing. I don't think she suspects for a moment. She treats me as if no such fell design were possible. I'm none too confident, you know,' he added, with a longer face.

'We go straight to Agra. Could you come to Agra?'

'Ideal!' he cried. 'The memory of Mumtaz! The garden of the Taj! I've always wanted to love under the same moon as Shah Jehan. How thoughtful of you!'

'You must spend a few days with us in Agra,' I continued. 'And as you say, it is the very place to shrine your happiness, if it comes to pass there.'

'Well, I am glad to have extracted a word of kindness from you at last,' said Dacres, as the stewards came to lay the table. 'But I wish,' he added regretfully, 'you could have thought of a test.'

5

Four days later we were in Agra. A time there was when the name would have been the key of dreams to me; now it stood for John's headquarters. I was rejoiced to think I would look again upon the Taj; and the prospect of living with it was a real enchantment; but I pondered most the kind of house that would be provided for the General Commanding the District, how many the dining-room would seat, and whether it would have a roof of thatch or of corrugated iron – I prayed against corrugated iron. I confess these my preoccupations. I was forty, and at forty the practical considerations of life hold their own even against domes of marble, world-renowned and set about with gardens where the bulbul sings to the rose. I smiled across the years at the raptures of my first vision of the place at twenty-one, just Cecily's age. Would I now sit under Arjamand's cypresses till two o'clock in the morning to see the wonder of her tomb at a particular angle of the moon? Would I climb one of her tall white ministering minarets to see anything whatever? I very greatly feared that I would not. Alas for the ageing of sentiment, of interest! Keep your touch with life and your seat in the saddle as long as you will, the world is no new toy at forty. But Cecily was twenty-one, Cecily who sat stolidly finishing her lunch while Dacres Tottenham talked about Akbar and his philosophy. 'The sort of man,' he said, 'that Carlyle might have smoked a pipe with.'

'But surely,' said Cecily reflectively, 'tobacco was not discovered in England then. Akbar came to the throne in 1526.'

'Nor Carlyle either for that matter,' I hastened to observe. 'Nevertheless, I think Mr Tottenham's proposition must stand.'

'Thanks, Mrs Farnham,' said Dacres. 'But imagine Miss Farnham's remembering Akbar's date! I'm sure you didn't!'

'Let us hope she doesn't know too much about him,' I cried gaily, 'or there will be nothing to tell!'

'Oh, really and truly very little!' said Cecily. 'But as soon as we heard Papa would be stationed here Aunt Emma made me read up about those old Moguls and people. I think I remember the dynasty. Babur, wasn't he the first? and then Humayon, and after him Akbar, and then Jehangir, and then Shah Jehan. But I've forgotten every date but Akbar's.'

She smiled her smile of brilliant health and even spirits as she made the damaging admission, and she was so good to look at, sitting there simple and wholesome and fresh, peeling her banana with her well-shaped fingers, that we swallowed the dynasty as it were whole, and smiled back upon her. John, I may say, was extremely pleased with Cecily; he said she was a very stisfactory human accomplishment. One would have thought, positively, the way he plumed himself over his handsome daughter, that he alone was responsible for her. But John, having received his family, straightaway set off with his staff on a tour of inspection, and thereby takes himself out of this history. I sometimes think that if he had stayed – but there has never been the lightest recrimination between us about it, and I am not going to hint one now.

'Did you read,' asked Dacres, 'what he and the Court poet wrote over the entrance gate to the big mosque at Fattehpur-Sikri? It's rather nice. "The world is a looking-glass, wherein the image has come and is gone – take as thine own nothing more than what thou lookest upon.'"

My daughter's thoughtful gaze was, of course, fixed upon the speaker, and in his own glance I saw a sudden ray of consciousness; but Cecily transferred her eyes to the opposite wall, deeply considering, and while Dacres and I smiled across the table, I saw that she had perceived no reason for blushing. It was a singularly narrow escape.

'No,' she said, 'I didn't. What a curious proverb for an emperor to make! He couldn't possibly have been able to see all his possessions at once.'

'If you have finished,' Dacres addressed her, 'do let me show you what your plain and immediate duty is to the garden. The garden waits for you – all the roses expectant—'

'Why, there isn't one!' cried Cecily, pinning on her hat. It was pleasing, and just a trifle pathetic, the way he hurried her out of the scope of any little dart; he would not have her even within range of amused observation. Would he continue, I wondered vaguely, as, with my elbows on the table, I tore into strips the lemon-leaf that floated in my finger-bowl – would he continue, through life, to shelter her from his other clever friends as now he attempted to shelter her from her mother? In that case he would have to domicile her, poor dear, behind the curtain, like the native ladies – a good price to pay for a protection of which, bless her heart! she would be all unaware. I had quite stopped bemoaning the affair; perhaps the comments of my husband, who treated it with broad approval and satisfaction, did something to soothe my sensibilities. At all events, I had gradually come to occupy a high fatalistic ground towards the pair. If it was written upon their foreheads that they should marry, the inscription was none of mine; and, of course, it was true, as John had indignantly stated, that Dacres might do very much worse. One's interest in Dacres Tottenham's problematical future had in no way diminished; but the young man was so positive, so full of intention, so disinclined to discussion – he had not reopened the subject since that morning in the saloon of the *Caledonia* – that one's feeling about it rather took the attenuated form of a shrug. I am afraid, too, that the pleasurable excitement of such an impending event had a little supervened; even at forty there is no disallowing the natural interests of one's sex. As I sat there pulling my lemon-leaf to pieces, I should not have been surprised or in the least put about if the two had returned radiant from the lawn to demand my blessing. As to the test of quality that I had obligingly invented for Dacres on the spur of the moment without his knowledge or connivance, it had some time ago faded into what he apprehended it to be – a mere idyllic opportunity, a charming background, a frame for his project, of prettier sentiment than the funnels and the handrails of a ship.

Mr Tottenham had ten days to spend with us. He knew the place well; it belonged to the province to whose service he was dedicated, and he claimed with impressive authority the privilege of showing it to Cecily by degrees – the Hall of Audience today, the Jessamine Tower tomorrow, the tomb of Akbar another, and the Deserted City yet another day. We arranged the expeditions in conference, Dacres insisting only upon the order of them, which I saw was to be cumulative, with the Taj at the very end, on the night precisely of the full of the moon, with a better chance of roses. I had no special views, but Cecily contributed some: that we should do the Hall of Audience in the morning, so as not to interfere with the club tennis in the afternoon, that we should bicycle to Akbar's tomb and take a cold luncheon – if we were sure there would be no snakes – to the Deserted City, to all of which Dacres gave loyal assent. I endorsed everything; I was the encouraging chorus, only stipulating that my number should be swelled from day to day by the addition of such persons as I should approve. Cecily, for instance, wanted to invite the Bakewells because we had come out in the same ship with them; but I could not endure the Bakewells, and it seemed to me that our having made the voyage with them was the best possible reason for declining to lay eyes on them for the rest of our natural lives. 'Mamma has such strong prejudices,' Cecily remarked, as she reluctantly gave up the idea; and I waited to see whether the graceless Tottenham would unmurmuringly take down the Bakewells. How stong must be the sentiment that turns a man into a boa-constrictor without a pang of transmigration! But no, this time he was faithful to the principles of his pre-Cecilian existence. 'They are rather Boojums,' he declared. 'You would think so, too, if you knew them better. It is that kind of excellent person that makes the real burden of India.' I could have patted him on the back.

Thanks to the rest of the chorus, which proved abundantly available, I was no immediate witness to Cecily's introduction to the glorious fragments which sustain in Agra the memory of the Moguls. I may as well say that I arranged with care that if anybody must be standing by when Dacres disclosed them, it should not be I. If

Cecily had squinted, I should have been sorry, but I would have found in it no personal humiliation. There were other imperfections of vision, however, for which I felt responsible and ashamed; and with Dacres, though the situation, Heaven knows, was none of my seeking, I had a little the feeling of a dealer who offers a defective *bibelot* to a connoisseur. My charming daughter – I was fifty times congratulated upon her appearance and her manners – had many excellent qualities and capacities which she never inherited from me; but she could see no more than the bulk, no further than the perspective; she could register exactly as much as a camera.

This was a curious thing, perhaps, to displease my maternal vanity, but it did. I had really rather she squinted, and when there was anything to look at I kept out of the way. I cannot tell precisely, therefore, what the incidents were that contributed to make Mr Tottenham, on our return from these expeditions, so thoughtful, with a thoughtfulness which increased, towards the end of them, to a positive gravity. This would disappear during dinner under the influence of food and drink. He would talk nightly with new enthusiasm and fresh hope – or did I imagine it? – of the loveliness he had arranged to reveal on the following day. If again my imagination did not lead me astray, I fancied this occurred later and later in the course of the meal as the week went on; as if his state required more stimulus as time progressed. One evening, when I expected it to flag altogether, I had a whim to order champagne and observe the effect; but I am glad to say that I reproved myself, and refrained.

Cecily, meanwhile, was conducting herself in a manner which left nothing to be desired. If, as I sometimes thought, she took Dacres very much for granted, she took him calmly for granted; she seemed a prey to none of those fluttering uncertainties, those suspended judgements and elaborate indifferences which translate themselves so plainly in a young lady receiving addresses. She turned herself out very freshly and very well; she was always ready for everything, and I am sure that no glance of Dacres Tottenham's found aught but direct and decorous response. His society on these occasions gave her solid pleasure; so did the drive and the lunch; the satisfactions were apparently upon the same plane. She was aware of the plum, if I may be permitted a brusque but irresistible simile; and with her mouth open, her eyes modestly closed, and her head in a convenient position, she waited, placidly, until it should fall in. The Farnham ladies would have been delighted with the result of their labours in the sweet reason

and eminent propriety of this attitude. Thinking of my idiotic
sufferings when John began to fix himself upon my horizon, I
pondered profoundly the power of nature in differentiation.

One evening, the last, I think, but one, I had occasion to go
to my daughter's room, and found her writing in her
commonplace-book. She had a commonplace-book, as well as a
Where Is It?, an engagement-book, an account-book, a diary, a
Daily Sunshine, and others with purposes too various to remember. 'Dearest mamma,' she said, as I was departing, 'there is only
one "P" in "opulence", isn't there?'

'Yes,' I replied, with my hand on the door handle, and added
curiously, for it was an odd word in Cecily's mouth, 'Why?'

She hardly hesitated. 'Oh,' she said, 'I am just writing down one
or two things Mr Tottenham said about Agra before I forget
them. They seemed so true.'

'He has a descriptive touch,' I remarked.

'I think he describes beautifully. Would you like to hear what
he said today?'

'I would,' I replied, sincerely.

'"Agra," ' read this astonishing young lady, '"is India's one pure
idyl. Elsewhere she offers other things, foolish opulence, tawdry
pageant, treachery of eunuchs and jealousies of harems, thefts of
kings' jewels and barbaric retributions; but they are actual,
visualised, or part of a past that shows to the backward glance
hardly more relief and vitality than a Persian painting' – I should
like to see a Persian painting – 'but here the immortal tombs and
pleasure-houses rise out of colour delicate and subtle; the vision
holds across three hundred years; the print of the court is still in
the dust of the city."'

'Did you really let him go on like that?' I exclaimed. 'It has the
licence of lecture!'

'I encouraged him to. Of course he didn't say it straight off. He
said it naturally; he stopped now and then to cough. I didn't
understand it all, but I think I have remembered every word.'

'You have a remarkable memory. I'm glad he stopped to cough.
Is there any more?'

'One little bit. "Here the Moguls wrought their passions into
marble, and held them up with great refrains from their religion,
and set them about with gardens; and here they stand in the
twilight of the glory of those kings and the noonday splendour of
their own."'

'How clever of you!' I exclaimed. 'How wonderfully clever of you to remember!'

'I had to ask him to repeat one or two sentences. He didn't like that. But this is nothing. I used to learn pages letter-perfect for Aunt Emma. She was very particular. I think it is worth preserving, don't you?'

'Dear Cecily,' I responded, 'you have a frugal mind.'

There was nothing else to respond. I could not tell her just how practical I thought her, or how pathetic her little book.

6

We drove together, after dinner, to the Taj. The moonlight lay in an empty splendour over the broad sandy road, with the acacias pricking up on each side of it and the gardens of the station bungalows stretching back into clusters of crisp shadows. It was an exquisite February night, very still. Nothing seemed abroad but two or three pariah dogs, upon vague and errant business, and the Executive Engineer going swiftly home from the club on his bicycle. Even the little shops of the bazaar were dark and empty; only here and there a light showed barred behind the carved balconies of the upper rooms, and there was hardly any tom-tomming. The last long slope of the road showed us the river curving to the left, through a silent white waste that stretched indefinitely into the moonlight on one side, and was crowned by Akbar's fort on the other. His long high line of turrets and battlements still guarded a hint of their evening rose, and dim and exquisite above them hovered the three dome-bubbles of the Pearl Mosque. It was a night of perfect illusion, and the illusion was mysterious, delicate, and faint. I sat silent as we rolled along, twenty years nearer to the original joy of things when John and I drove through the same old dream.

Dacres, too, seemed preoccupied; only Cecily was, as they say, herself. Cecily was really more than herself, she exhibited an unusual flow of spirits. She talked continually, she pointed out this and that, she asked who lived here and who lived there. At regular intervals of about four minutes she demanded if it wasn't simply too lovely. She sat straight up with her vigorous profile and her smart hat; and the silhouette of her personality sharply refused to mingle with the dust of any dynasty. She was a contrast, a protest; positively she was an indignity. 'Do lean back, dear child,' I exclaimed at last. 'You interfere with the landscape.'

She leaned back, but she went on interfering with it in terms of sincerest enthusiasm.

When we stopped at the great archway of entrance I begged to be left in the carriage. What else could one do, when the golden moment had come, but sit in the carriage and measure it? They climbed the broad stone steps together and passed under the lofty gravures into the garden, and I waited. I waited and remembered. I am not, as perhaps by this time is evident, a person of overwhelming sentiment, but I think the smile upon my lips was gentle. So plainly I could see, beyond the massive archway and across a score of years, all that they saw at that moment – Arjamand's garden, and the long straight tank of marble cleaving it full of sleeping water and the shadows of the marshalling cypresses; her wide dark garden of roses and of pomegranates, and at the end the Vision, marvellous, aerial, the soul of something – is it beauty? is it sorrow? – that great white pride of love in mourning such as only here in all the round of our little world lifts itself to the stars, the unpaintable, indescribable Taj Mahal. A gentle breath stole out with a scent of jessamine and such a memory! I closed my eyes and felt the warm luxury of a tear.

Thinking of the two in the garden, my mood was very kind, very conniving. How foolish after all were my cherry stone theories of taste and temperament before that uncalculating thing which sways a world and builds a Taj Mahal! Was it probable that Arjamand and her Emperor had loved fastidiously, and yet how they had loved! I wandered away into consideration of the blind forces which move the world, in which comely young persons like my daughter Cecily had such a place; I speculated vaguely upon the value of the subtler gifts of sympathy and insight which seemed indeed, at that enveloping moment, to be mere flowers strewn upon the tide of deeper emotions. The garden sent me a fragrance of roses; the moon sailed higher and picked out the little kiosks set along the wall. It was a charming, charming thing to wait, there at the portal of a silvered, scented garden, for an idyl to come forth.

When they reappeared, Dacres and my daughter, they came with casual steps and cheerful voices. They might have been a couple of tourists. The moolight fell full upon them on the platform under the arch. It showed Dacres measuring with his stick the length of the Sanscrit letters which declared the stately texts, and Cecily's expression of polite, perfunctory interest. They looked up at the height above them; they looked back at the vision behind. Then they sauntered towards the carriage, he offering a formal hand to help her down the uncertain steps, she gracefully accepting it.

'You – you have not been long,' said I. 'I hope you didn't hurry on my account.'

'Miss Farnham found the marble a little cold under foot,' replied Dacres, putting Miss Farnham in.

'You see,' explained Cecily, 'I stupidly forgot to change into thicker soles. I have only my slippers. But, Mamma, how lovely it is! Do let us come again in the daytime. I am dying to make a sketch of it.'

Mr Tottenham was to leave us on the following day. In the morning, after 'little breakfast', as we say in India, he sought me in the room I had set aside to be particularly my own.

Again I was writing to John, but this time I waited for precisely his interruption. I had got no further than 'My dearest husband', and my pen handle was a fringe.

'Another fine day,' I said, as if the old, old Indian joke could give him ease, poor man!

'Yes,' said he, 'we are having lovely weather.'

He had forgotten that it was a joke. Then he lapsed into silence while I renewed my attentions to my pen.

'I say,' he said at last, with so strained a look about his mouth that it was almost a contortion, 'I haven't done it, you know.'

'No,' I responded, cheerfully, 'and you're not going to. Is that it? Well!'

'Frankly—' said he.

'Dear me, yes! Anything else between you and me would be grotesque,' I interrupted, 'after all these years.'

'I don't think it would be a success,' he said, looking at me resolutely with his clear blue eyes, in which still lay, alas! the possibility of many delusions.

'No,' I said, 'I never did, you know. But the prospect had begun to impose upon me.'

'To say how right you were would seem, under the circumstances, the most hateful form of flattery.'

'Yes,' I said, 'I think I can dispense with your verbal endorsement.' I felt a little better. It was, of course, better that the connoisseur should have discovered the flaw before concluding the transaction; but although I had pointed it out myself I was not entirely pleased to have the article returend.

'I am infinitely ashamed that it should have taken me all these

days – day after day and each contributory – to discover what you
saw so easily and so completely.'

'You forget that I am her mother,' I could not resist the
temptation of saying.

'Oh, for God's sake don't jeer! Please be absolutely direct, and
tell me if you have reason to believe that to the extent of a
thought, of a breath – to any extent at all – she cares.'

He was, I could see, very deeply moved; he had not arrived at this
point without trouble and disorder not lightly to be put on or off.
Yet I did not hurry to his relief, I was still possessed by a vague
feeling of offence. I reflected that any mother would be, and I quite
plumed myself upon my annoyance. It was so satisfactory, when
one had a daughter, to know the sensations of even any mother.
Nor was it soothing to remember that the young man's whole
attitude towards Cecily had been based upon criticism of me, even
though he sat before me whipped with his own lash. His temerity
had been stupid and obstinate; I could not regret his punishment.

I kept him waiting long enough to think all this, and then I
replied, 'I have not the least means of knowing.'

I cannot say what he expected, but he squared his shoulders as
if he had received a blow and might receive another. Then he
looked at me with a flash of the old indignation. 'You are not near
enough to her for that!' he exclaimed.

'I am not near enough to her for that.'

Silence fell between us. A crow perched upon an opened
venetian and cawed lustily. For years afterwards I never heard a
crow caw without a sense of vain, distressing experience. Dacres
got up and began to walk about the room. I very soon put a stop
to that. 'I can't talk to a pendulum,' I said, but I could not
persuade him to sit down again.

'Candidly,' he said at length, 'do you think she would have me?'

'I regret to say that I think she would. But you would not dream
of asking her.'

'Why not? She is a dear girl,' he responded, inconsequently.

'You could not possibly stand it.'

Then Mr Tottenham delivered himself of this remarkable
phrase: 'I could stand it,' he said, 'as well as you can.'

There was far from being any joy in the irony with which I
regarded him and under which I saw him gather up his resolution
to go; nevertheless I did nothing to make it easy for him. I
refrained from imparting my private conviction that Cecily would

accept the first presentable substitute that appeared, although it was strong. I made no reference to my daughter's large fund of philosophy and small balance of sentiment. I did not even – though this was reprehensible – confess the test, the test of quality in these ten days with the marble archives of the Moguls, which I had almost wantonly suggested, which he had so unconsciously accepted, so disastrously applied. I gave him quite fifteen minutes of his bad quarter of an hour, and when it was over I wrote truthfully but furiously to John . . .

That was ten years ago. We have since attained the shades of retirement, and our daughter is still with us when she is not with Aunt Emma and Aunt Alice – Grandmamma has passed away. Mr Tottenham's dumb departure that day in February – it was the year John got his C.B. – was followed, I am thankful to say, by none of the symptoms of unrequited affection on Cecily's part. Not for ten minutes, so far as I was aware, was she the maid forlorn. I think her self-respect was too robust a character, thanks to the Misses Farnham. Still less, of course, had she any re- proaches to serve upon her mother, although for a long time I thought I detected – or was it my guilty conscience? – a spark of shrewdness in the glance she bent upon me when the talk was of Mr Tottenham and the probabilities of his return to Agra. So well did she sustain her experience, or so little did she feel it, that I believe the impression went abroad that Dacres had been sent disconsolate away. One astonishing conversation I had with her some six months later, which turned upon the point of a particu- larly desirable offer. She told me something then, without any sort of embarrassment, but quite lucidly and directly, that edified me much to hear. She said that while she was quite sure that Mr Tottenham thought of her only as a friend – she had never had the least reason for any other impression – he had done a service for which she could not thank him enough – in showing her what a husband might be. He had given her a standard; it might be high, but it was unalterable. She didn't know whether she could de- scribe it, but Mr Tottenham was different from the kind of man you seemed to meet in India. He had his own ways of looking at things, and he talked so well. He had given her an ideal, and she intended to profit by it. To know that men like Mr Tottenham existed, and to marry any other kind would be an act of folly which she did not intend to commit. No, Major the Hon. Hugh Taverel did not come near it – very far short, indeed! He had talked to her during the whole of dinner the night before about jackal-hunting with a bobbery pack – not at all an elevated mind. Yes, he might be a very good fellow, but as a companion for life she was sure he would not be at all suitable. She would wait.

And she has waited. I never thought she would, but she has. From time to time men have wished to take her from us, but the standard has been inexorable, and none of them has reached it. When Dacres married the charming American whom he caught like a butterfly upon her Eastern tour, Cecily sent them as a wedding present an alabaster model of the Taj, and I let her do it – the gift was so exquisitely appropriate. I suppose he never looks at it without being reminded that he didn't marry Miss Farnham, and I hope that he remembers that he owes it to Miss Farnham's mother. So much I think I might claim; it is really very little considering what it stands for. Cecily is permanently with us – I believe she considers herself an intimate. I am very reasonable about lending her to her aunts, but she takes no sort of advantage of my liberality; she says she knows her duty is at home. She is growing into a firm and solid English maiden lady, with a good colour and great decision of character. That she always had.

I point out to John, when she takes our crumpets away from us, that she gets it from him. I could never take away anybody's crumpets, merely because they were indigestible, least of all my own parents'. She has acquired a distinct affection for us, by some means best known to herself; but I should have no objection to that if she would not rearrange my bonnet-strings. That is a fond liberty to which I take exception; but it is one thing to take exception and another to express it.

Our daughter is with us, permanently with us. She declares that she intends to be the prop of our declining years; she makes the statement often, and always as if it were humorous. Nevertheless I sometimes notice a spirit of inquiry, a note of investigation in her encounters with the opposite sex that suggests an expectation not yet extinct that another and perhaps a more appreciative Dacres Tottenham may flash across her field of vision – alas, how improbable! Myself I can not imagine why she should wish it; I have grown in my old age into a perfect horror of cultivated young men; but if such a person should by a miracle at any time appear, I think it is extremely improbable that I will interfere on his behalf.

(1903)

EDITH WHARTON

The Reckoning

I

'The marriage law of the new dispensation will be: *Thou shalt not be unfaithful – to thyself.*'

A discreet murmur of approval filled the studio, and through the haze of cigarette smoke Mrs Clement Westall, as her husband descended from his improvised platform, saw him merged in a congratulatory group of ladies. Westall's informal talks on 'The New Ethics' had drawn about him an eager following of the mentally unemployed – those who, as he had once phrased it, liked to have their brain-food cut up for them. The talks had begun by accident. Westall's ideas were known to be 'advanced', but hitherto their advance had not been in the direction of publicity. He had been, in his wife's opinion, almost pusillanimously careful not to let his personal views endanger his professional standing. Of late, however, he had shown a puzzling tendency to dogmatise, to throw down the gauntlet, to flaunt his private code in the face of society; and the relation of the sexes being a topic always sure of an audience, a few admiring friends had persuaded him to give his after-dinner opinions a larger circulation by summing them up in a series of talks at the Van Sideren studio.

The Herbert Van Siderens were a couple who subsisted, socially, on the fact that they had a studio. Van Sideren's pictures were chiefly valuable as accessories to the *mise en scène* which differentiated his wife's 'afternoons' from the blighting functions held in long New York drawing-rooms, and permitted her to offer their friends whiskey and soda instead of tea. Mrs Van Sideren, for her part, was skilled in making the most of the kind of atmosphere which a layfigure and an easel create; and if at times she found the illusion hard to maintain, and lost courage to the extent of almost wishing that Herbert could paint, she promptly overcame such moments of weakness by calling in some fresh talent, some

extraneous re-enforcement of the 'artistic' impression. It was
in quest of such aid that she had seized on Westall, coaxing him,
somewhat to his wife's surprise, into a flattered participation in
her fraud. It was vaguely felt, in the Van Sideren circle, that all the
audacities were artistic, and that a teacher who pronounced
marriage immoral was somehow as distinguished as a painter
who depicted purple grass and a green sky. The Van Sideren set
were tired of the conventional colour scheme in art and conduct.

Julia Westall had long had her own views on the immorality of
marriage; she might indeed have claimed her husband as a
disciple. In the early days of their union she had secretly resented
his disinclination to proclaim himself a follower of the new creed;
had been inclined to tax him with moral cowardice, with a failure
to live up to the convictions for which their marriage was supposed to stand. That was in the first burst of propagandism,
when, womanlike, she wanted to turn her disobedience into a law.
Now she felt differently. She could hardly account for the change,
yet being a woman who never allowed her impulses to remain
unaccounted for, she tried to do so by saying that she did not care
to have the articles of her faith misinterpreted by the vulgar. In
this connection, she was beginning to think that almost everyone
was vulgar; certainly there were few to whom she would have
cared to intrust the defence of so esoteric a doctrine. And it was
precisely at this point that Westall, discarding his unspoken
principles, had chosen to descend from the heights of privacy, and
stand hawking his convictions at the street corner!

It was Una Van Sideren who, on this occasion, unconsciously
focused upon herself Mrs Westall's wandering resentment. In the
first place, the girl had no business to be there. It was 'horrid' –
Mrs Westall found herself slipping back into the old feminine
vocabulary – simply 'horrid' to think of a young girl's being
allowed to listen to such talk. The fact that Una smoked cigarettes
and sipped an occasional cocktail did not in the least tarnish a
certain radiant innocency which made her appear the victim,
rather than the accomplice, of her parents' vulgarities. Julia
Westall felt in a hot helpless way that something ought to be done
– that someone ought to speak to the girl's mother. And just then
Una glided up.

'Oh, Mrs Westall, how beautiful it was!' Una fixed her with
large limpid eyes. 'You believe it all, I suppose?' she asked with
seraphic gravity.

'All – what, my dear child?'

The girl shone on her. 'About the higher life – the freer expansion of the individual – the law of fidelity to one's self,' she glibly recited.

Mrs Westall, to her own wonder, blushed a deep and burning blush.

'My dear Una,' she said, 'you don't in the least understand what it's all about!'

Miss Van Sideren started, with a slowly answering blush. 'Don't *you*, then?' she murmured.

Mrs Westall laughed. 'Not always – or altogether! But I should like some tea, please.'

Una led her to the corner where innocent beverages were dispensed. As Julia received her cup she scrutinised the girl more carefully. It was not such a girlish face, after all – definite lines were forming under the rosy haze of youth. She reflected that Una must be six-and-twenty, and wondered why she had not married. A nice stock of ideas she would have as her dower! If *they* were to be a part of the modern girl's trousseau—

Mrs Westall caught herself up with a start. It was as though some one else had been speaking – a stranger who had borrowed her own voice: she felt herself the dupe of some fantastic mental ventriloquism. Concluding suddenly that the room was stifling and Una's tea too sweet, she set down her cup and looked about for Westall: to meet his eyes had long been her refuge from every uncertainty. She met them now, but only, as she felt, in transit; they included her parenthetically in a larger flight. She followed the flight, and it carried her to a corner to which Una had withdrawn – one of the palmy nooks to which Mrs Van Sideren attributed the success of her Saturdays. Westall, a moment later, had overtaken his look, and found a place at the girl's side. She bent forward, speaking eagerly; he leaned back, listening, with the depreciatory smile which acted as a filter to flattery, enabling him to swallow the strongest doses without apparent grossness of appetite. Julia winced at her own definition of the smile.

On the way home, in the deserted winter dusk, Westall surprised his wife by a sudden boyish pressure of her arm. 'Did I open their eyes a bit? Did I tell them what you wanted me to?' he asked gaily.

Almost unconsciously, she let her arm slip from his. 'What *I* wanted?'

'Why, haven't you – all this time?' She caught the honest wonder of his tone. 'I somehow fancied you'd rather blamed me for not talking more openly – before – You almost made me feel, at times, that I was sacrificing principles to expediency.'

She paused a moment over her reply, then she asked quietly, 'What made you decide not to – any longer?'

She felt again the vibration of a faint surprise. 'Why – the wish to please you!' he answered, almost too simply.

'I wish you would not go on, then,' she said abruptly.

He stopped in his quick walk, and she felt his stare through the darkness.

'Not go on—?'

'Call a hansom, please. I'm tired,' broke from her with a sudden rush of physical weariness.

Instantly his solicitude enveloped her. The room had been infernally hot – and then that confounded cigarette smoke – he had noticed once or twice that she looked pale – she mustn't come to another Saturday. She felt herself yielding, as she always did, to the warm influence of his concern for her, the feminine in her leaning on the man in him with a conscious intensity of abandonment. He put her in the hansom, and her hand stole into his in the darkness. A tear or two rose, and she let them fall. It was so delicious to cry over imaginary troubles!

That evening, after dinner, he surprised her by reverting to the subject of his talk. He combined a man's dislike of uncomfortable questions with an almost feminine skill in eluding them; and she knew that if he returned to the subject he must have some special reason for doing so.

'You seem not to have cared for what I said this afternoon. Did I put the case badly?'

'No – you put it very well.'

'Then what did you mean by saying that you would rather not have me go on with it?'

She glanced at him nervously, her ignorance of his intention deepening her sense of helplessness.

'I don't think I care to hear such things discussed in public.'

'I don't understand you,' he exclaimed. Again the feeling that his surprise was genuine gave an air of obliquity to her own attitude. She was not sure that she understood herself.

'Won't you explain?' he said with a tinge of impatience.

Her eyes wandered about the familiar drawing-room which had

been the scene of so many of their evening confidences. The shaded lamps, the quiet-coloured walls hung with mezzotints, the pale spring flowers scattered here and there in Venice glasses and bowls of old Sèvres, recalled, she hardly knew why, the apartment in which the evenings of her first marriage had been passed – a wilderness of rosewood and upholstery, with a picture of a Roman peasant above the mantelpiece, and a Greek slave in 'statuary marble' between the folding doors of the back drawing-room. It was a room with which she had never been able to establish any closer relation than that between a traveller and a railway station; and now, as she looked about at the surroundings which stood for her deepest affinities – the room for which she had left that other room – she was startled by the same sense of strangeness and unfamiliarity. The prints, the flowers, the subdued tones of the old porcelains, seemed to typify a superficial refinement which had no relation to the deeper significances of life.

Suddenly she heard her husband repeating his question.

'I don't know that I can explain,' she faltered.

He drew his armchair forward so that he faced her across the hearth. The light of a reading-lamp fell on his finely drawn face, which had a kind of surface-sensitiveness akin to the surface refinement of its setting.

'Is it that you no longer believe in our ideas?' he asked.

'In our ideas—?'

'The ideas I am trying to teach. The ideas you and I are supposed to stand for.' He paused a moment. 'The ideas on which our marriage was founded.'

The blood rushed to her face. He had his reasons, then – she was sure now that he had his reasons! In the ten years of their marriage, how often had either of them stopped to consider the ideas on which it was founded? How often does a man dig about the basement of his house to examine its foundation? The foundation is there, of course – the house rests on it – but one lives abovestairs and not in the cellar. It was she, indeed, who in the beginning had insisted on reviewing the situation now and then, on recapitulating the reasons which justified her course, on proclaiming, from time to time, her adherence to the religion of personal independence; but she had long ceased to feel the want of any such ideal standards, and had accepted her marriage as frankly and naturally as though it had been based on the primitive needs of the heart, and required no special sanction to explain or justify it.

'Of course I still believe in our ideas!' she exclaimed.

'Then I repeat that I don't understand. It was a part of your theory that the greatest publicity should be given to our view of marriage. Have you changed your mind in that respect?'

She hesitated. 'It depends on circumstances – on the public one is addressing. The set of people that the Van Siderens get about them don't care for the truth or falseness of a doctrine. They are attracted simply by its novelty.'

'And yet it was in just such a set of people that you and I met, and learned the truth from each other.'

'That was different.'

'In what way?'

'I was not a young girl, to begin with. It is perfectly unfitting that young girls should be present at – at such times – should hear such things discussed—'

'I thought you considered it one of the deepest social wrongs that such things never *are* discussed before young girls; but that is beside the point, for I don't remember seeing any young girl in my audience today—'

'Except Una Van Sideren!'

He turned slightly and pushed back the lamp at his elbow.

'Oh, Miss Van Sideren – naturally—'

'Why naturally?'

'The daughter of the house – would you have had her sent out with her governess?'

'If I had a daughter I should not allow such things to go on in my house!'

Westall, stroking his moustache, leaned back with a faint smile. 'I fancy Miss Van Sideren is quite capable of taking care of herself.'

'No girl knows how to take care of herself – till it's too late.'

'And yet you would deliberately deny her the surest means of self-denfence?'

'What do you call the surest means of self-defence?'

'Some preliminary knowledge of human nature in its relation to the marriage tie.'

She made an impatient gesture. 'How should you like to marry that kind of a girl?'

'Immensely – if she were my kind of girl in other respects.'

She took up the argument at another point.

'You are quite mistaken if you think such talk does not affect young girls. Una was in a state of the most absurd exaltation—' She broke off, wondering why she had spoken.

Westall reopened a magazine which he had laid aside at the beginning of their discussion. 'What you tell me is immensely flattering to my oratorical talent – but I fear you over-rate its effect. I can assure you that Miss Van Sideren doesn't have to have her thinking done for her. She's quite capable of doing it herself.'

'You seem very familiar with her mental processes!' flashed unguardedly from his wife.

He looked up quietly from the pages he was cutting.

'I should like to be,' he answered. 'She interests me.'

2

If there be a distinction in being misunderstood, it was one denied to Julia Westall when she left her first husband. Everyone was ready to excuse and even to defend her. The world she adorned agreed that John Arment was 'impossible', and hostesses gave a sign of relief at the thought that it would no longer be necessary to ask him to dine.

There had been no scandal connected with the divorce: neither side had accused the other of the offence euphemistically described as 'statutory'. The Arments had indeed been obliged to transfer their allegiance to a State which recognised desertion as a cause for divorce, and construed the term so liberally that the seeds of desertion were shown to exist in every union. Even Mrs Arment's second marriage did not make traditional morality stir in its sleep. It was known that she had not met her second husband till after she had parted from the first, and she had, moreover, replaced a rich man by a poor one. Though Clement Westall was acknowledged to be a rising lawyer, it was generally felt that his fortunes would not rise as rapidly as his reputation. The Westalls would probably always have to live quietly and go out to dinner in cabs. Could there be better evidence of Mrs Arment's complete disinterestedness?

If the reasoning by which her friends justified her course was somewhat cruder and less complex than her own elucidation of the matter, both explanations led to the same conclusion: John

Arment was impossible. The only difference was that, to his wife, his impossibility was something deeper than a social disqualification. She had once said, in ironical defence of her marriage, that it had at least preserved her from the necessity of sitting next to him at dinner; but she had not then realised at what cost the immunity was purchased. John Arment was impossible; but the sting of his impossibility lay in the fact that he made it impossible for those about him to be other than himself. By an unconscious process of elimination he had excluded from the world everything of which he did not feel a personal need: had become, as it were, a climate in which only his own requirements survived. This might seem to imply a deliberate selfishness; but there was nothing deliberate about Arment. He was as instinctive as an animal or a child. It was this childish element in his nature which sometimes for a moment unsettled his wife's estimate of him. Was it possible that he was simply undeveloped, that he had delayed, somewhat longer than is usual, the laborious process of growing up? He had the kind of sporadic shrewdness which causes it to be said of a dull man that he is 'no fool'; and it was this quality that his wife found most trying. Even to the naturalist it is annoying to have his deductions disturbed by some unforeseen aberrancy of form or function; and how much more so to the wife whose estimate of herself is inevitably bound up with her judgement of her husband!

Arment's shrewdness did not, indeed, imply any latent intellectual power; it suggested, rather, potentialities of feeling, of suffering, perhaps, in a blind rudimentary way, on which Julia's sensibilities naturally declined to linger. She so fully understood her own reasons for leaving him that she disliked to think they were not as comprehensible to her husband. She was haunted, in her analytic moments, by the look of perplexity, too inarticulate for words, with which he had acquiesced in her explanations.

These moments were rare with her, however. Her marriage had been too concrete a misery to be surveyed philosophically. If she had been unhappy for complex reasons, the unhappiness was as real as though it had been uncomplicated. Soul is more bruisable than flesh, and Julia was wounded in every fibre of her spirit. Her husband's personality seemed to be closing gradually in on her, obscuring the sky and cutting off the air, till she felt herself shut up among the decaying bodies of her starved hopes. A sense of having been decoyed by some world-old conspiracy into this bondage of body and soul filled her with despair. If marriage was the slow lifelong acquittal of a debt contracted in ignorance, then marriage was a crime against human nature. She, for one, would have no share in maintaining the pretence of which she had been a victim: the pretence that a man and a woman, forced into the narrowest of personal relations, must remain there till the end, though they may have outgrown the span of each other's natures as the mature tree outgrows the iron brace about the sapling.

It was in the first heat of her moral indignation that she had met Clement Westall. She had seen at once that he was 'interested', and had fought off the discovery, dreading any influence that should draw her back into the bondage of conventional relations. To ward off the peril she had, with an almost crude precipitancy, revealed her opinions to him. To her surprise, she found that he shared them. She was attracted by the frankness of a suitor who, while pressing his suit, admitted that he did not believe in marriage. Her worst audacities did not seem to surprise him: he had thought out all that she had felt, and they had reached the same conclusion. People grew at varying rates, and the yoke that was an easy fit for the one might soon become galling to the other. That was what divorce was for: the readjustment of personal relations. As soon as their necessarily transitive nature was recognised they would gain in dignity as well as in harmony. There would be no farther need of the ignoble concessions and connivances, the perpetual sacrifice of personal delicacy and moral pride, by means of which imperfect marriages were now held together. Each partner to the contract would be on his mettle, forced to live up to the highest standard of self-development, on pain of losing the other's respect and affection. The low nature could no longer drag the higher down, but must struggle to rise, or remain alone on its inferior level. The only necessary condition to a harmonious marriage was a frank recognition of this truth, and a solemn agreement between the contracting parties to keep faith with themselves, and not to live together for a moment after complete accord had ceased to exist between them. The new adultery was unfaithfulness to self.

It was, as Westall had just reminded her, on this understanding that they had married. The ceremony was an unimportant concession to social prejudice: now that the door of divorce stood open, no marriage need be an imprisonment, and the contract therefore no longer involved any diminution of self-respect. The nature of their attachment placed them so far beyond the reach of such contingencies that it was easy to discuss them with an open mind; and Julia's sense of security made her dwell with a tender insistence on Westall's promise to claim his release when he should cease to love her. The exchange of these vows seemed to make them, in a sense, champions of the new law, pioneers in the forbidden realm of individual freedom: they felt that they had somehow achieved beatitude without martyrdom.

This, as Julia now reviewed the past, she perceived to have been her theoretical attitude towards marriage. It was unconsciously, insidiously, that her ten years of happiness with Westall had developed another conception of the tie; a reversion, rather, to the old instinct of passionate dependency and possessorship that now made her blood revolt at the mere hint of change. Change? Renewal? Was that what they had called it, in their foolish jargon? Destruction, extermination rather – this rending of a myriad fibres interwoven with another's being! Another? But he was not other! He and she were one, one in the mystic sense which alone gave marriage its significance. The new law was not for them, but for the disunited creatures forced into a mockery of union. The gospel she had felt called on to proclaim had no bearing on her own case . . . She sent for the doctor and told him she was sure she needed a nerve tonic.

She took the nerve tonic diligently, but it failed to act as a sedative to her fears. She did not know what she feared; but that made her anxiety the more pervasive. Her husband had not reverted to the subject of his Saturday talks. He was unusually kind and considerate, with a softening of his quick manner, a touch of shyness in his consideration, that sickened her with new fears. She told herself that it was because she looked badly – because he knew about the doctor and the nerve tonic – that he showed this deference to her wishes, this eagerness to screen her from moral draughts; but the explanation simply cleared the way for fresh inferences.

The week passed slowly, vacantly, like a prolonged Sunday. On Saturday the morning post brought a note from Mrs Van Sideren. Would dear Julia ask Mr Westall to come half an hour earlier than usual, as there was to be some music after his 'talk'? Westall was just leaving for his office when his wife read the note. She opened the drawing-room door and called him back to deliver the message.

He glanced at the note and tossed it aside. 'What a bore! I shall have to cut my game of racquets. Well, I suppose it can't be helped. Will you write and say it's all right?'

Julia hesitated a moment, her hand stiffening on the chair-back against which she leaned.

'You mean to go on with these talks?' she asked.

'I – why not?' he returned; and this time it struck her that his surprise was not quite unfeigned. The perception helped her to find words.

'You said you had started them with the idea of pleasing me—'

'Well?'

'I told you last week that they didn't please me.'

'Last week? Oh—' He seemed to make an effort of memory. 'I thought you were nervous then; you sent for the doctor the next day.'

'It was not the doctor I needed; it was your assurance—'

'My assurance?'

Suddenly she felt the floor fail under her. She sank into the chair with a choking throat, her words, her reasons slipping away from her like straws down a whirling flood.

'Clement,' she cried, 'isn't it enough for you to know that I hate it?'

He turned to close the door behind them, then he walked towards her and sat down. 'What is it that you hate?' he asked gently.

She had made a desperate effort to rally her routed argument.

'I can't bear to have you speak as if – as if – our marriage – were like the other kind – the wrong kind. When I heard you there, the other afternoon, before all those inquisitive gossiping people, proclaiming that husbands and wives had a right to leave each other whenever they were tired – or had seen someone else—'

Westall sat motionless, his eyes fixed on a pattern of the carpet.

'You *have* ceased to take this view, then?' he said as she broke off. 'You no longer believe that husbands and wives *are* justified in separating – under such conditions?'

'Under such conditions?' she stammered. 'Yes – I still believe that – but how can we judge for others? What can we know of the circumstances—?'

He interrupted her. 'I thought it was a fundamental article of our creed that the special circumstances produced by marriage were not to interfere with the full assertion of individual liberty.'

He paused a moment. 'I thought that was your reason for leaving Arment.'

She flushed to the forehead. It was not like him to give a personal turn to the argument.

'It was my reason,' she said simply.

'Well, then – why do you refuse to recognise its validity now?'

'I don't – I don't – I only say that one can't judge for others.'

He made an impatient movement. 'This is mere hair-splitting. What you mean is that, the doctrine having served your purpose when you needed it, you now repudiate it.'

'Well,' she exclaimed, flushing again, 'what if I do? What does it matter to us?'

Westall rose from his chair. He was excessively pale, and stood before his wife with something of the formality of a stranger.

'It matters to me,' he said in a low voice, 'because I do *not* repudiate it.'

'Well?'

'And because I had intended to invoke it as—' He paused and drew his breath deeply. She sat silent, almost deafened by her heartbeats. 'As a complete justification of the course I am about to take.'

Julia remained motionless. 'What course is that?' she asked.

He cleared his throat. 'I mean to claim the fulfilment of your promise.'

For an instant the room wavered and darkened, then she recovered a torturing acuteness of vision. Every detail of her surroundings pressed upon her: the tick of the clock, the slant of sunlight on the wall, the hardness of the chair-arms that she grasped, were a separate wound to each sense.

'Mr promise—' she faltered.

'Your part of our mutual agreement to set each other free if one or the other should wish to be released.'

She was silent again. He waited a moment, shifting his position nervously; then he said, with a touch of irritability, 'You acknowledge the agreement?'

The question went through her like a shock. She lifted her head to it proudly. 'I acknowledge the agreement,' she said.

'And – you don't mean to repudiate it?'

A log on the hearth fell forward, and mechanically he advanced and pushed it back.

'No,' she answered slowly, 'I don't mean to repudiate it.'

There was a pause. He remained near the hearth, his elbow resting on the mantelshelf. Close to his hand stood a little cup of jade that he had given her on one of their wedding anniversaries. She wondered vaguely if he noticed it.

'You intend to leave me, then?' she said at length.

His gesture seemed to deprecate the crudeness of the allusion.

'To marry someone else?'

Again his eye and hand protested. She rose and stood before him.

'Why should you be afraid to tell me? Is it Una Van Sideren?'

He was silent.

'I wish you good luck,' she said.

3

She looked up, finding herself alone. She did not remember when or how he had left the room, or how long afterwards she had sat there. The fire still smouldered on the hearth, but the slant of sunlight had left the wall.

Her first conscious thought was that she had not broken her word, that she had fulfilled the very letter of their bargain. There had been no crying out, no vain appeal to the past, no attempt at temporising or evasion. She had marched straight up to the guns.

Now that it was over, she sickened to find herself alive. She looked about her, trying to recover her hold on reality. Her identity seemed to be slipping from her, as it disappears in a physical swoon. 'This is my room – this is my house,' she heard herself saying. Her room? Her house? She could almost hear the walls laugh back at her.

She stood up, weariness in every bone. The silence of the room frightened her. She remembered, now, having heard the front door close a long time ago: the sound suddenly re-echoed through her brain. Her husband must have left the house, then – her *husband*? She no longer knew in what terms to think: the simplest phrases had a poisoned edge. She sank back into her chair, overcome by a strange weakness. The clock struck ten – it was only ten o'clock! Suddenly she remembered that she had not ordered dinner . . . or were they dining out that evening? *Dinner – dining out* – the old meaningless phraseology pursued her! She must try to think of herself as she would think of someone else, a someone dissociated from all the familiar routine of the past, whose wants and habits must gradually be learned, as one might spy out the ways of a strange animal . . .

The clock struck another hour – eleven. She stood up again and walked to the door. She thought she would go upstairs to her room. *Her* room? Again the word derided her. She opened the door, crossed the narrow hall, and walked up the stairs. As she passed, she noticed Westall's sticks and umbrellas. A pair of his gloves lay on the hall table. The same stair carpet mounted between the same walls; the same old French print, in its narrow black frame, faced her on the landing. This visual continuity was intolerable. Within, a gaping chasm; without, the same untroubled and familiar surface. She must get away from it before she could attempt to think. But, once in her room, she sat down on the lounge, a stupor creeping over her.

Gradually her vision cleared. A great deal had happened in the interval – a wild marching and countermarching of emotions, arguments, ideas – a fury of insurgent impulses that fell back spent upon themselves. She had tried, at first, to rally, to organise these chaotic forces. There must be help somewhere, if only she could master the inner tumult. Life could not be broken off short like this, for a whim, a fancy; the law itself would side with her, would defend her. The law? What claim had she upon it? She was the prisoner of her own choice: she had been her own legislator, and she was the predestined victim of the code she had devised. But this was grotesque, intolerable – a mad mistake, for which she could not be held accountable! The law she had despised was still there, might still be invoked . . . invoked, but to what end? Could she ask it to chain Westall to her side? *She* had been allowed to go free when she claimed her freedom – should she show less magnanitmity than she had exacted? Magnanimity? The word lashed her with its irony – one does not strike and attitude when one is fighting for life! She would threaten, grovel, cajole . . . she would yield anything to keep her hold on happiness. Ah, but the difficulty lay deeper! The law could not help her – her own apostasy could not help her. She was the victim of the theries she renounced. It was as though some giant machine of her own making had caught her up in its wheels and was grinding her to atoms . . .

It was afternoon when she found herself out of doors. She walked with an aimless haste, fearing to meet familiar faces. The day was radiant, metallic: one of those searching American days so calculated to reveal the shortcomings of our street-cleaning and the excesses of our architecture. The streets looked bare and hideous; everything stared and glittered. She called a passing hansom, and gave Mrs Van Sideren's address. She did not know what had led up to the act, but she found herself suddenly resolved to speak, to cry out a warning. It was too late to save herself – but the girl might still be told. The hansom rattled up Fifth Avenue. She sat with her eyes fixed, avoiding recognition. At the Van Sideren's door she sprang out and rang the bell. Action had cleared her brain, and she felt calm and self-possessed. She knew now exactly what she meant to say.

The ladies were both out . . . the parlour maid stood waiting for a card. Julia, with a vague murmur, turned away from the door and lingered a moment on the sidewalk. Then she remembered that she had not paid the cab driver. She drew a dollar from her purse and handed it to him. He touched his hat and drove off, leaving her alone in the long empty street. She wandered away westward, towards strange thorough fares, where she was not likely to meet acquaintances. The feeling of aimlessness had returned. Once she found herself in the afternoon torrent of Broadway, swept past tawdry shops and flaming theatrical post-ers, with a succession of meaningless faces glinding by in the opposite direction . . .

A feeling of faintness reminded her that she had not eaten since morning. She turned into a side street of shabby houses, with rows of ash-barrels behind bent area railings. In a basement window she saw the sign *Ladies' Restaurant*. A pie and a dish of dough-nuts lay against the dusty pane like petrified food in an ethno-logical museum. She entered, and a young woman with a weak mouth and brazen eye cleared a table for her near the window. The table was covered with the red and white cotton cloth and adorned with a red and white cotton cloth and adorened with a bunch of celery in a thick tumbler and a salt-celler full of greyish lumpy salt. Julia ordered tea, and sat a long time waiting for it. She was glad to be away from the noise and confusion of the streets. The low-ceilinged room was empty, and two or three waitresses with thin pert faces lounged in the background staring at her and whispering together. At last the tea was brought in a discoloured metal teapot. Julia poured a cup and drank it hastily. It was black and bitter, but it flowed through her veins like an elixir. She was almost dizzy with exhilaration. Oh, how tired, how unutterably tired she had been!

She drank a second cup, blacker and bitterer, and now her mind was once more working clearly. She felt as vigorous, as decisive, as when she had stood on the Van Siderens' doorstep – but the wish to return there had subsided. She saw now the futility of such an attempt – the humiliation to which it might have exposed her . . . The pity of it was that she did not know what to do next. The short winter day was fading, and she realised that she could not remain much longer in the restaurant without attracting notice. She paid for her tea and went out into the street. The lamps were alight, and here and there a basement shop cast an oblong of gas-light across the fissured pavement. In the dusk there was something sinister about the aspect of the street, and she hastened back towards Fifth Avenue. She was not used to being out alone at that hour.

At the corner of Fifth Avenue she paused and stood watching the stream of carriages. At last a policeman caught sight of her and signed to her that he would take her across. She had not meant to cross the street, but she obeyed automatically, and presently found herself on the farther corner. There she paused again for a moment, but she fancied the policeman was watching her, and this sent her hastening down the nearest side street . . . After that she walked a long time, vaguely. Night had fallen, and now and then, through the windows of a passing carriage, she caught the expanse of an evening waistcoat or the shimmer of an opera cloak . . .

Suddenly she found herself in a familiar street. She stood still a moment, breathing quickly. She had turned the corner without noticing whither it led; but now, a few yards ahead of her, she saw the house in which she had once lived – her first husband's house. The blinds were drawn, and only a faint translucence marked the windows and the transom above the door. As she stood there she heard a step behind her, and a man walked by in the direction of the house. He walked slowly, with a heavy middle-aged gait, his head sunk a little between the shoulders, the red crease of his neck visible above the fur collar of his overcoat. He crossed the street, went up the steps of the house, drew forth a latchkey, and let himself in.

There was no one else in sight. Julia leaned for a long time against the area-rail at the corner, her eyes fixed on the front of the house. The feeling of physical weariness had returned, but the strong tea still throbbed in her veins and lit her brain with an unnatural clearness. Presently she heard another step draw near, and moving quickly away, she too crossed the street and mounted the steps of the house. The impulse which had carried her there prolonged itself in a quick pressure of the electric bell – then she felt suddenly weak and tremulous, and grasped the balustrade for support. The door opened and a young footman with a fresh inexperienced face stood on the threshold. Julia knew in an instant that he would admit her.

'I saw Mr Arment going in just now,' she said. 'Will you ask him to see me for a moment?'

The footman hesitated. 'I think Mr Arment has gone up to dress for dinner, madam.'

Julia advanced into the hall. 'I am sure he will see me – I will not detain him long,' she said. She spoke quietly, authoritatively, in the tone which a good servant does not mistake. The footman had his hand on the drawing-room door.

'I will tell him, madam. What name, please?'

Julia trembled: she had not thought of that. 'Merely say a lady,' she returned carelessly.

The footman wavered and she fancied herself lost, but at that instant the door opened from within and John Arment stepped into the hall. He drew back sharply as he saw her, his florid face turning sallow with the shock; then the blood poured back to it, swelling the veins on his temples and reddening the lobes of his thick ears.

It was long since Julia had seen him, and she was startled at the change in his appearance. He had thickened, coarsened, settled down into the enclosing flesh. But she noted this insensibly: her one conscious thought was that, now she was face to face with him, she must not let him escape till he had heard her. Every pulse in her body throbbed with the urgency of her message.

She went up to him as he drew back. 'I must speak to you,' she said.

Arment hesitated, red and stammering. Julia glanced at the footman, and her look acted as a warning. The instinctive shrinking from a 'scene' predominated over every other impulse, and Arment said slowly, 'Will you come this way?'

He followed her into the drawing-room and closed the door. Julia, as she advanced, was vaguely aware that the room at least

was unchanged: time had not mitigated its horrors. The contadina* still lurched from the chimney-breast, and the Greek slave
obstructed the threshold of the inner room. The place was alive
with memories: they started out from every fold of the yellow
satin curtains and glided between the angles of the rosewood
furniture. But while some subordinate agency was carrying these
impressions to her brain, her whole conscious effort was centred
in the act of dominating Arment's will. The fear that he would
refuse to hear her mounted like fever to her brain. She felt her
purpose melt before it, words and arguments running into each
other in the heat of her longing. For a moment her voice failed
her, and she imagined herself thrust out before she could speak;
but as she was struggling for a word Arment pushed a chair
forward, and said quietly: 'You are not well.'

The sound of his voice steadied her. It was neither kind nor
unkind – a voice that suspended judgement, rather, awaiting
unforseen developments. She supported herself against the back
of the chair and drew a deep breath.

'Shall I send for something?' he continued, with a cold embarrassed politeness.

Julia raised an entreating hand. 'No – no – thank you. I am
quite well.'

He paused midway towards the bell, and turned on her. 'Then
may I ask—?'

'Yes,' she interrupted him. 'I came here because I wanted to see
you. There is something I must tell you.'

Arment continued to scrutinise her. 'I am surprised at that,' he
said. 'I should have supposed that any communication you may
wish to make could have been made through our lawyers.'

'Our lawyers!' She burst into a little laugh. 'I don't think they
could help me – this time.'

Arment's face took on a barricaded look. 'If there is any
question of help – of course—'

It struck her, whimsically, that she had seen that look when
some shabby devil called with a subscription-book. Perhaps he
thought she wanted him to put his name down for so much in
sympathy – or even in money . . . The thought made her laugh
again. She saw his look change slowly to perplexity. All his facial
changes were slow, and she remembered, suddenly, how it had
once diverted her to shift that lumbering scenery with a word. For
the first time it struck her that she had been cruel. 'There *is* a

question of help,' she said in a softer key. 'You can help me, but only by listening. I want to tell you something . . .'

Arment's resistance was not yielding. 'Would it not be easier to – write?' he suggested.

She shook her head. 'There is no time to write . . . and it won't take long.' She raised her head and their eyes met. 'My husband has left me,' she said.

'Westall?' he stammered, reddening again.

'Yes. This morning. Just as I left you. Because he was tired of me.'

The words, uttered scarcely above a whisper, seemed to dilate to the limit of the room. Arment looked towards the door; then his embarrassed glance returned to Julia.

'I am very sorry,' he said awkwardly.

'Thank you,' she murmured.

'But I don't see—'

'No – but you will – in a moment. Won't you listen to me? Please!' Instinctively she had shifted her position, putting herself between him and the door. 'It happened this morning,' she went on in short breathless phrases. 'I never suspected anything – I thought we were – perfectly happy . . . Suddenly he told me he was tired of me . . . there is a girl he likes better . . . He has gone to her . . .' As she spoke, the lurking anguish rose upon her, possessing her once more to the exclusion of every other emotion. Her eyes ached, her throat swelled with it, and two painful tears ran down her face.

Arment's constraint was increasing visibly. 'This – this is very unfortunate,' he began. 'But I should say the law—'

'The law?' she echoed ironically. 'When he asks for his freedom?'

'You are not obliged to give it.'

'You were not obliged to give me mine – but you did.'

He made a protesting gesture.

'You saw that the law couldn't help you – didn't you?' she went on. 'That is what I see now. The law represents material rights – it can't go beyond. If we don't recognise an inner law . . . the obligation that love creates . . . being loved as well as loving . . . there is nothing to prevent our spreading ruin unhindered . . . is there?' She raised her head plaintively, with the look of bewildered child. 'That is what I see now . . . what I wanted to tell you. He leaves me because he's tired, but I was not tired; and I don't understand why he is. That's the dreadful part of it – the not understanding: I hadn't realised what it meant. But I've been thinking of it all day, and things have come back to me – things I hadn't noticed . . . when you and I . . .' She moved closer to him, and fixed her eyes on his with the gaze which tries to reach beyond words. 'I see now that *you* didn't understand, did you?'

Their eyes met in a sudden shock of comprehension: a veil seemed to be lifted between them. Arment's lip trembled.

'No,' he said, 'I didn't understand.'

She gave a little cry, almost of triumph. 'I knew it! I knew it! You wondered – you tried to tell me – but no words came. You saw your life falling in ruins . . . the world slipping from you . . . and you couldn't speak or move!'

She sank down on the chair against which she had been leaning. 'Now I know – now I know,' she repeated.

'I am very sorry for you,' she heard Arment stammer.

She looked up quickly. 'That's not what I came for. I don't want you to be sorry. I came to ask you to forgive me . . . for not understanding that *you* didn't understand . . . That's all I wanted to say.' She rose with a vague sense that the end had come, and put out a groping hand towards the door.

Arment stood motionless. She turned to him with a faint smile.

'You forgive me?'

'There is nothing to forgive.'

'Then you will shake hands for goodbye?' She felt his hand in hers: it was nerveless, reluctant.

'Goodbye,' she repeated. 'I understand now.'

She opened the door and passed out into the hall. As she did so, Arment took an impulsive step forward; but just then the footman, who was evidently alive to his obligations, advanced from the background to let her out. She heard Arment fall back. The footman threw open the door, and she found herself outside in the darkness.

(1904)

MARY AUSTIN

The Fakir

Whenever I come up to judgement, and am hard pushed to make good on my own account (as I expect to be), I shall mention the case of Netta Saybrick, for on the face of it, and by all the traditions in which I was bred, I behaved rather handsomely. I say on the face of it, for except in the matter of keeping my mouth shut afterwards, I am not so sure I had anything to do with the affair. It was one of those incidents that from some crest of sheer inexplicableness seems about to direct the imagination over vast tracts of human experience, only to fall away into a pit of its own digging, all fouled with weed and sand. But, by keeping memory and attention fixed on its pellucid instant as it mounted against the sun, I can still see the Figure shining through it as I saw it that day at Posada, with the glimmering rails of the P and S running out behind it, thin lines of light toward the bar of Heaven.

Up till that time Netta Saybrick had never liked me, though I never laid it to any other account than Netta's being naturally a little fool; afterwards she explained to me that it was because she thought I gave myself airs. The Saybricks lived in the third house from mine, around the corner, so that our back doors overlooked each other, and up till the coming of Dr Challoner there had never been anything in Netta's conduct that the most censorious of the villagers could remark upon. Nor afterwards for that matter. The Saybricks had been married four years, and the baby was about two. He was not an interesting child to anybody but his mother, and even Netta was sometimes thought to be not quite absorbed in him.

Saybrick was a miner, one of the best drillers in our district, and consequently away from home much of the time. Their house was rather larger than their needs, and Netta, to avoid loneliness more than for profit, let out a room or two. That was the way she happened to fall into the hands of the Fakir.

Franklin Challoner had begun by being a brilliant and promising student of medicine. I had known him when his natural gifts prophesied the unusual, but I had known him rather better than most, and I was not surprised to have him turn up five years later at Maverick as a Fakir.

It had begun in his being poor, and having to work his way through the medical college at the cost of endless pains and mortification to himself. Like most brilliant people, Challoner was sensitive and had an enormous egotism, and, what nearly always goes with it, the faculty of being horribly fascinating to women. It was thought very creditable of him to have put himself through college at his own charge, though in reality it proved a great social waste. I have a notion that the courage, endurance, and steadfastness which should have done Frank Challoner a lifetime was squeezed out of him by the stress of those over-worked, starved, mortifying years. His egotism made it important to his happiness to keep the centre of any stage, and this he could do in school by sheer brilliance of scholarship and the distinction of his struggles. But afterwards, when he had to establish himself without capital among strangers, he found himself impoverished of manliness. Always there was the compelling need of his temperament to stand well with people, and almost the only means of accomplishing it his poverty allowed was the dreadful facility with which he made himself master of women. I suppose this got his real ability discredited among his professional fellows. Between that and the sharp need of money, and the incredible appetite which people have for being fooled, somewhere in the Plateau of Fatigue between promise and accomplishment, Frank Challoner lost himself. Therefore, I was not surprised when he turned up finally at Maverick, lecturing on phrenology, and from the shape of their craniums advising country people of their proper careers at three dollars a sitting. He advertised to do various things in the way of medical practice that had a dubious sound.

It was court week when he came, and the only possible lodging to be found at Netta Saybrick's. Dr Challoner took the two front rooms as being best suited to his clients and himself, and I believe he did very well. I was not particularly pleased to see him, on account of having known him before, not wishing to prosecute the acquaintance; and about that time Indian George brought me word that a variety of redivivus long sought was blooming that year on a certain clayey tract over toward Waban. It was not supposed to flower oftener than once in seven years, and I was five days finding it. That was why I never knew what went on at Mrs Saybrick's. Nobody else did, apparently, for I never heard a breath of gossip, and *that* must have been Dr Challoner's concern, for I am sure Netta would never have known how to avoid it.

Netta was pretty, and Saybrick had been gone five months. Challoner had a thin, romantic face, and eyes – even I had to admit the compelling attracting of his eyes; and his hands were fine and white. Saybrick's hands were cracked, broken nailed, a driller's hands, and one of them was twisted from the time he was leaded, working on the Lucky Jim. If it came to that, though, Netta's husband might have been anything he pleased, and Challoner would still have had his way with her. He always did with women, as if to make up for not having it with the world. And the life at Maverick was deadly, appallingly dull. The stark houses, the rubbishy streets, the women who went about in them in calico wrappers,* the draggling speech of the men, the wide, shadowless table-lands, the hard, bright skies, and the days all of one pattern, that went so stilly by that you only knew it was afternoon when you smelled the fried cabbage Mrs Mulligan was cooking for supper.

At this distance I cannot say that I blamed Netta, am not sure of not being glad that she had her hour of the rose-red glow – *if* she had it. You are to bear in mind that all this time I was camping out in the creosote belt on the slope of Waban, and as to what had really happened neither Netta nor Challoner ever said a word. I keep saying things like this about Netta's being pretty and all, just as if I thought they had anything to do with it; truth is, the man had just a gift of taking souls, and I, even I, judicious and disapproving – but you shall hear.

At that time the stage from Maverick was a local affair going down to Posada, where passengers from the P and S booked for the Mojave line, returning after a wait of hours on the same day.

It happened that the morning I came back from Waban, Dr Challoner left Maverick. Being saddle weary, I had planned to send on the horses by Indian George, and take the stage where it crossed my trail an hour out from Posada, going home on it in the afternoon. I remember poking the botany-case under the front seat and turning round to be hit straight between the eyes, as it were, by Netta Saybrick and Dr Challoner. The doctor was wearing his usual air of romantic mystery; wearing it a little awry

– or perhaps it was only knowing the man that made me read the perturbation under it. But it was plain to see what Netta was about. Her hat was tilted by the jolting of the stage, while alkali dust lay heavy on the folds of her dress, and she never *would* wear hairpins enough; but there was that in every turn and posture, in every note of her flat, childish voice, that acknowledged the man beside her. Her excitement was almost febrile. It was part of Netta's unsophistication that she seemed not to know that she gave herself away, and the witness of it was that she had brought the baby.

You would not have believed that any woman would plan to run away with a man like Frank Challoner and take that great, heavy-headed, drooling child. But that is what Netta had done. I am not sure it was maternal instinct, either; she probably did not know what else to do with him. He had pale, protruding eyes and reddish hair, and every time he clawed at the doctor's sleeve I could see the man withhold a shudder.

I suppose it was my being in a manner confounded by this extraordinary situation that made it possible for Dr Challoner to renew his acquaintance with more warmth than the facts allowed. He fairly pitched himself into an intimacy of reminiscence, and it was partly to pay him for this, I suppose, and partly to gratify a natural curiosity, that made me so abrupt with him afterwards. I remember looking around, when we got down, at the little station where I must wait two hours for the return stage, at the seven unpainted pine cabins, at the eating-house, and the store, and the two saloons, in the instant hope of refuge, and then out across the alkali flat fringed with sparse, unwholesome pickleweed, and deciding that that would not do, and then turning round to take the situation by the throat, as it were. There was Netta, with that great child dragging on her arm and her hat still on one side, with a silly consciousness of Dr Challoner's movements, and he still trying for the jovial note of old acquaintances met by chance. In a moment more I had him around the corner of the station-house and out with my question.

'Dr Challoner, are you running away with Netta Saybrick?'

'Well, no,' trying to carry it jauntily. 'I think she is running away with me.' Then, all his pretension suddenly sagging on him like an empty cayaque: 'On my soul, I don't know what's got into the woman. I was as surprised as you were when she got on the stage with me' – on my continuing to look steadily at him – 'she was a pretty little thing . . . and the life is devilish dull there . . . I suppose I flirted a little' – blowing himself out, as it were, with an assumption of honesty – 'on my word, there was nothing more than that.'

Flirted! He called it that, but women do not take their babies and run away from home for the sake of a little flirting. The life was devilish dull – did he need to tell me that! And she was pretty – well, whatever had happened he was bound to tell me that it was nothing, and I was bound to behave as if I believed him.

'She will go back,' he began to say, looking bleak and drawn in the searching light. 'She must go back! She must!'

'Well, maybe you can persuade her,' said I, but I relented after that enough to take care of the baby while he and Netta went for a walk.

The whole mesa and the flat crawled with heat, and the steel rails ran on either side of them like thin tyres, as if the slagged track were the appointed way that Netta had chosen to walk. They went out as far as the section-house and back toward the deserted station till I could almost read their faces clear, and turned again, back and forth through the heat-fogged atmosphere like the figures in a dream. I could see this much from their postures, that Challoner was trying to hold to some consistent attitude which he had adopted, and Netta wasn't understanding it. I could see her throw out her hands in a gesture of abandonment, and then I saw her stand as if the Pit yawned under her feet. The baby slept on a station bench, and I kept the flies from him with a branch of pickleweed. I was out of it, smitten anew with the utter inutility of all the standards which were not bred of experience, but merely came down to me with the family teaspoons. Seen by the fierce desert light they looked like the spoons, thin and worn at the edges. I should have been ashamed to offer them to Netta Saybrick. It was this sense of detached helplessness toward the life at Maverick that Netta afterwards explained she and the other women sensed but misread in me. They couldn't account for it on any grounds except that I felt myself above them. And all the time I was sick with the strained, meticulous inadequacy of my own soul. I understood well enough, then, that the sense of personal virtue comes to most women through an intervening medium of sedulous social guardianship. It is only when they love that it reaches directly to the centre of consciousness, as if it were ultimately nothing more than the instinctive movement of right love to preserve itself by a voluntary seclusion. It was not her faithlessness to Saybrick that tormented Netta out there between the burning rails; it was going back to him that was the intolerable offence. Passion had come upon her like a flame-burst, heaven sent; she justified it on the grounds of its completeness, and lacked the sophistication for any other interpretation.

Challoner was a bad man, but he was not bad enough to reveal to Netta Saybrick the vulgar cheapness of his own relation to the incident. Besides, he hadn't time. In two hours the return stage for Maverick left the station, and he could never in that time get Netta Saybrick to realise the gulf between his situation and hers.

He came back to the station after a while on some pretext, and said, with his back to Netta, moving his lips with hardly any sound, 'She must go back on the stage. She must!' Then with a sudden setting of his jaws, 'You've got to help me.' He sat down beside me, and began to devote himself to the baby and the flies.

Netta stood out for a while expecting him, and then came and sat provisionally on the edge of the station platform, ready at the slightest hint of an opportunity to carry him away into the glimmering heat out toward the station-house, and resume the supremacy of her poor charms.

She was resenting my presence as an interference, and I believe always cherished a thought that but for the accident of my being there the incident might have turned out differently. I could see that Challoner's attitude, whatever it was, was beginning to make itself felt. She was looking years older, and yet somehow pitifully puzzled and young, as if the self of her had had a wound which her intelligence had failed to grasp. I could see, too, that Challoner had made up his mind to be quit of her, quietly if he could, but at any risk of a scene, still to be quit. And it was forty minutes till stage-time.

Challoner sat on the bare station bench with his arm out above the baby protectingly – it was a manner always effective – and began to talk about 'goodness', of all things in the world. Don't ask me what he said. It was the sort of talk many women would have called beautiful, and though it was mostly addressed to me, it was every word of it directed to Netta Saybrick's soul. Much of it went high and wide, but I could catch the pale reflection of it in her face like a miner guessing the sort of day it is from the glimmer of it on a puddle at the bottom of a shaft. In it Netta saw a pair of heroic figures renouncing a treasure they had found for the sake of the bitter goodness by which the world is saved. They had had the courage to take it while they could, but were much too exemplary to enjoy it at the cost of pain to any other heart. He started with the assumption that she meant to go back to Maverick, and recurred to it with a skilful and hypnotic insistence, painting upon her mind by large and general inference the picture of himself, helped greatly in his career by her noble renunciation of him. As a matter of fact, Saybrick, if his wife really had gone away with Dr Challoner, would have followed him up and shot him, I suppose, and no end of vulgar and disagreeable things might have come from the affair; but Challoner managed to keep it on so high a plane that even I never thought of them until long afterwards. And right here is where the uncertainty as to the part I really played begins. I can never make up my mind whether Challoner, from long practice in such affairs, had hit upon just the right note of extrication, or whether, cornered, he fell back desperately on the eternal rightness. And what was he, to know rightness at his need?

He was terribly in earnest, holding Netta's eyes with his own; his forehead sweated, hollows showed about his eyes, and the dreadful slackness of the corner of the mouth that comes of the whole mind being drawn away upon the object of attack to the neglect of its defences. He was so bent on getting Netta fixed in the idea that she must go back to Maverick that if she had not been a good deal of a fool she must have seen that he had given away the whole situation into my hands. I believed – I hope – I did the right thing, but I am not sure I could have helped taking the cue which was pressed upon me; he was as bad as they made them, but there I was lending my whole soul to the accomplishment of his purpose, which was, briefly, to get comfortably off from an occasion in which he had behaved very badly.

All this time Challoner kept a conscious attention on the stage stables far at the other end of the shadeless street. The moment he saw the driver come out of it with the horses, the man's soul fairly creaked with the release of tension. It released, too, an accession of that power of personal fascination for which he was remarkable.

Netta sat with her back to the street, and the beautiful solicitude with which he took up the baby at that moment, smoothed its dress and tied on its little cap, had no significance for her. It was not until she heard the rattle of the stage turning into the road that she stood up suddenly, alarmed. Challoner put the baby into my arms.

Did I tell you that all this time between me and this man there ran the inexplicable sense of being bonded together; the same suggestion of a superior and exclusive intimacy which ensnared poor Netta Saybrick no doubt, the absolute call of self and sex by which a man, past all reasonableness and belief, ranges a woman on his side. He was a Fakir, a common quack, a scoundrel if you will, but there was the call. I had answered it. I was under the impression, though not remembering what he said, when he had handed me that great lump of a child, that I had received a command to hold on to it, to get into the stage with it, and not to give it up on any consideration; and without saying anything, I had promised.

I do not know if it was the look that must have passed between us at that, or the squeal of the running-gear that shattered her dream, but I perceived on the instant that Netta had had a glimpse of where she stood. She saw herself for the moment a fallen woman, forsaken, despised. There was the Pit before her which Challoner's desertion and my knowledge of it had digged. She clutched once at her bosom and at her skirts as if already she heard the hiss of crawling shame. Then it was that Challoner turned toward her with the Look.

It rose in his face and streamed to her from his eyes as though it were the one thing in the world of a completeness equal to the anguish in her breast, as though, before it rested there, it had been through all the troubled intricacies of sin, and come upon the root of a superior fineness that every soul feels piteously to lie at the back of all its own affronting vagaries, brooding over it in a large, gentle way. It was the forgiveness – nay, the obliteration of offence – and the most Challoner could have known of forgiveness was his own great need of it. Out of that Look I could see the woman's soul rising rehabilitated, astonished, and on the instant, out there beyond the man and the woman, between the thin fiery lines of the rails, leading back to the horizon, the tall, robed Figure writing in the sand.

Oh, it was a hallucination, if you like, of the hour, the place, the perturbed mind, the dazzling glimmer of the alkali flat, of the incident of a sinful woman and a common fakir, faking an absolution that he might the more easily avoid an inconvenience, and I the tool made to see incredibly by some trick of suggestion how impossible it should be that any but the chief of sinners should understand forgiveness. But the Look continued to hold the moment in solution, while the woman climbed out of the Pit. I saw her put out her hand with the instinctive gesture of the sinking, and Challoner take it with the formality of farewell; and as the dust of the arriving stage billowed up between them, the Figure turned, fading, dissolving . . . but with the Look, consoling, obliterating . . . He too . . .!

'It was very good of you, Mrs Saybrick, to give me so much of a goodbye . . .' Challoner was saying as he put Netta into the stage; and then to me, 'You must take good care of her . . . goodbye.'

'Goodbye, Frank' – I had never called Dr Challoner by his name before. I did not like him well enough to call him by it at any time, but there was the Look; it had reached out and enwrapped me in a kind of rarefied intimacy of extenuation and understanding. He stood on the station platform staring steadily after us, and as long as we had sight of him in the thick, bitter dust, the Look held.

If this were a story merely, or a story of Franklin Challoner, it would end there. He never thought of us again, you may depend, except to thank his stars for getting so lightly off, and to go on in the security of his success to other episodes from which he returned as scatheless.

But I found out in a very few days that whether it was to take rank as an incident or an event in Netta Saybrick's life depended on whether or not I said anything about it. Nobody had taken any notice of her day's ride to Posada. Saybrick came home in about ten days and Netta seemed uncommonly glad to see him, as if in the preoccupation of his presence she found a solace for her fears.

But from the day of our return she had evinced an extraordinary liking for my company. She would be running in and out of the house at all hours, offering to help me with my sewing or to stir up a cake, kindly offices that had to be paid in kind; and if I slipped into the neighbours' on an errand, there a moment after would come Netta. Very soon it became clear to me that she was afraid of what I might tell. So long as she had me under her immediate eye she could be sure I was not taking away her character, but when I was not, she must have suffered horribly. I might have told, too, by the woman's code; she was really not respectable, and we made a great deal of that in Maverick. I might refuse to have anything to do with her and justified myself explaining why.

But Netta was not sure how much I knew, and could not risk betrayal by a plea. She had, too, the natural reticence of the villager, and though she must have been aching for news of Dr Challoner, touch of him, the very sound of his name, she rarely ever mentioned it, but grew strained and thinner; watching, watching.

If that incident was known, Netta would have been ostracised and Saybrick might have divorced her. And I was going dumb with amazement to discover that nothing had come of it, nothing *could* come of it so long as I kept still. It was a deadly sin, as I had been taught, as I believed – of damnable potentiality; and as long as nobody told it was as if it had never been, as if that look of Challoner's had really the power as it had the seeming of absolving her from all soil and stain.

I cannot now remember if I was ever tempted to tell on Netta Saybrick, but I know with the obsession of that look upon my soul I never did. And in the meantime, from being so much in each other's company, Netta and I became very good friends. That was why, a little more than a year afterwards, she chose to have me with her when her second child was born. In Maverick we did things for one another that in more sophisticated communities go to the service of paid attendants. That was the time when the suspicion that had lain at the bottom of Netta's shallow eyes whenever she looked at me went out of them for ever.

It was along about midnight and the worst yet to come. I sat holding Netta's hands, and beyond in the room where the lamp was, the doctor lifted Saybrick through his stressful hour with cribbage and toddy. I could see the gleam of the light on Saybrick's red, hairy hands, a driller's hands, and whenever a sound came from the inner room, the uneasy lift of his shoulders and the twitching of his lip; then the doctor pushed the whiskey over towards him and jovially dealt the cards anew.

Netta, tossing on her pillow, came into range with Saybrick's blunt profile outlined against the cheaply papered wall, and I suppose her husband's distress was good to her to see. She looked at him a long time quietly.

'Henry's a good man,' she said at last.

'Yes,' I said; and then she turned to me narrowly with the expiring spark of anxious cunning in her eyes.

'And I've been a good wife to him,' said she. It was half a challenge.

And I, trapped by the hour, became a fakir in my turn, called instantly on all my soul and answered – with the Look – 'Everybody knows that, Netta' – held on steadily until the spark went out. However I had done it I could not tell, but I saw the trouble go out of the woman's soul as the lids drooped, and with it out of my own heart the last of the virtuous resentment of the untempted. I had really forgiven her; how then was it possible for the sin to rise up and trouble her; more? Mind you, I grew up in a church that makes a great deal of the forgiveness of sins and signifies it by a tremendous particularity about behaviour, and the most I had learned of the efficient exercise of forgiveness was from the worst man I had ever known.

About an hour before dawn, when a wind began to stir, and out on the mesa the coyotes howled returning from the hunt, stooping to tuck the baby in her arms, I felt Netta's lips brush against my hand.

'You've been mighty good to me,' she said. Well – if I were pushed for it, I should think it worth mentioning – but I am not so sure.

(1909)

Providence and Colonel Dormer

Carborough is a small midland manufacturing town. It is hideous in winter and very little better in summer, and goodness only knows why I go on living in it. All the same, I *do* know. It is because of Theodora.

There seems to be a dull sameness in my reasons for doing things, for I settled in Carborough originally so as to be near Harsdown. Where my old friend Musgrave lived. But Musgrave is dead now, and his widow, to whom Harsdown was left for her lifetime, has since married a very offensive individual called Purefoy. Theodora is Musgrave's daughter by his first wife; for he, like that miserable snippet of feminity who survives him, married twice. (I suppose I am rather free with my epithets, but, after all, I am accountable to nobody, and I shall be seventy next birthday.) Musgrave was a good deal younger than I.

It was I who taught Theodora to ride. How I used to trot her out on a leading-rein in the old days at Harsdown, when she was a little creature with flying hair! Poor Tom Musgrave had a long time of ill-health before he died – the belated result of a wound he had brought back from Afghanistan – and he used to lie smoking and watching us from his long chair on the lawn, while the little girl and I galloped about the park on the other side of the sunk fence. How proud he was of her! How, in the name of fortune he could have . . . but these whys and wherefores are profitless, and I must go on to the main point.

I can't bear to think of the life that Theodora led after her stepmother remarried, and Major Middleton Purefoy came to swagger about in Tom's place – an undersized, red-faced man, with a bridge to his nose as thin and sharp as a knife-blade. I dined there soon after they came back from their wedding tour (Mrs Purefoy made it impossible for me to refuse), and I shall never forget him, nor the airs of possession that he gave himself at dinner. Theodora sat at the table like a stone image, her eyes on the tablecloth and her thick brows drawn into a line. She caught my hand suddenly, as I said good night to her in the hall at the end of the evening.

'Don't, my dear – don't,' I remember imploring her. 'There are things you must not say . . .'

(However, that's some little time ago now, and, as I said before, I must keep to the point.)

In the suburb of Carborough in which I live, there is a high old-fashioned house enclosed by a wall; it stands not far up the road, and the boughs of its beech trees send a pleasant shadow over the way. It is grey and severe looking, and it has belonged for generations to the Slaters, a family of mill-owners whose long connection with the place has almost landed them in the ranks of county society. Some of the county bigwigs know them, and some do not; and no one seems able to understand why old Slater, who is rich enough to do as he pleases about anything, has not bought or built himself a country place. But he seems to have no idea of doing so; perhaps he doesn't care to go far from his business; perhaps he likes the solid old mansion in which his father and his grandfather first saw the light.

Until a couple of years ago, when the events I am going to speak of happened, I had never had a glimpse inside those walls, unless I chanced to be passing when the gates opened to let someone out – old Slater on his way to his office; his wife, a plain, charitable woman, in her heavy landau; or Dick with his terrier. I was not acquainted with any member of this family of three; and the independence with which they pursued their way, seeking nothing of any man, and taking the world as they found it, raised a barrier as thick as their own garden wall between them and inquisitive strangers, while it increased the respect with which people spoke of them. Dick was the only one who came in for criticism, for some called him a 'lout'; principally, I suppose, because he has a dark, heavy face, and is strongly built. Theodora, who is nothing if not hasty, called him a 'lout' too.

Tom Musgrave had a purely business acquaintance with old Slater, and respected him as much as everyone else did, also he had invested a small sum in his mills; this money Theodora has inherited, and when, a few years ago, some new arrangements were made in the business, it became necessary for her, as a shareholder, to sign certain papers.

When it is a matter of business affairs, Theodora always comes to me – at least, she did in those days – for nothing would have induced her to consult Purefoy. Mrs Purefoy was as ignorant and unpractical as a woman can be, and any dealings with her would have meant interference from her husband, who dominated every detail of the establishment at Harsdown, like the beggar on horseback he was. So, one afternoon, when Theodora rode in to see me (as she did about twice a week), she asked me if she might interview old Slater at my house. Explanations were necessary, and he was to show her the documents himself. But, when the time came, he was called unexpectedly to London, and Dick, who had just returned from Cambridge and was in the business with his father, took his place. Old Slater was punctilious, and would no more have sent an underling to meet the young lady than he would have flown.

Theodora and I sat on for some time after Dick had gone, discussing our new acquaintance. As luncheon had been announced before his talk with her came to an end, I had asked him to stay for it. Personally he did not strike me as a 'lout', and I was a good deal interested to find that he had been in the Cambridge boat. Theodora liked him too.

'It's odd we should never have met him before,' she observed. 'I have seen his mother at garden parties often enough.'

'I fancy he works pretty hard,' said I, 'and he probably likes something more energetic after being shut up in the office. I loathe garden parties.'

'So do I, Uncle Charles,' she said (she always calls me Uncle Charles). 'We'll go to no more, shall we – you and I?'

She had slipped her arm through mine, and we were going down my front doorsteps, for her horse was waiting outside.

'Never,' said I. 'Come back soon, my dear.'

I watched her as she disappeared up the tree-bordered road. It was early spring, and the leafless twigs were like pencilling against the pure clearness of the declining afternoon. A blackbird, who was sitting on a bough, was trying his voice with a view to the future, and a little ring of purple crocuses had come up by my gate. Everything looked new and interesting, as it is apt suddenly to do when the earth is on the verge of reawakening; and Vanity, Theodora's horse, was shaking his head and sidling a little as he went along. Perhaps things looked interesting to him too.

I think, after myself, that Vanity was the creature Theodora loved best in the world. Poor Tom had given him to her only a month before his death. Also, he was three parts thoroughbred, had a mouth like silk, and the best manners in the world. He was a dark bay with black points.

Any pleasure she had in her life at home she owed to Vanity; and I owed a good deal to him too, for without him I should never have been able to see as much of her as I did. Mrs Purefoy hated me, and I abominated Purefoy, and certainly neither of them would have done anything towards facilitating our meetings. Besides which, there would probably have been no means of transport; for Purefoy, who seemed to have a genius for making economies with other people's money, had cut down the stable in the most drastic manner. His own steed was a tricycle. I suppose he felt safe on it.

Spring broke into summer and things jogged on in the usual way. Theodora came and went, and it struck me, as time passed by, that omnipresence, as a quality, seemed to be growing upon Dick Slater. Scarcely a day passed but I ran against him somewhere, and the proximity in which our respective houses stood appeared hardly to furnish a satisfactory explanation, considering the years we had lived within a stone's throw of each other without its happening once in a blue moon. The solution dawned upon me one afternoon, as I was going home rather later than usual from my walk, and saw him coming to meet me. Theodora was in front, riding slowly along the road towards my house. In a moment they had met, and, though she did not stop, it was easy to guess by Dick's face that that greeting had been the event of his day. He did not observe me till we passed each other in a few paces. Then he turned scarlet.

I was rather annoyed, but it was some time before I said anything to the girl. I knew that they had met a couple of times since their introduction in my house – once at a horse show, and once when they found themselves in the same railway carriage coming from London; and Theodora admitted that she very seldom came into Carborough without catching sight of him. All the same, I treated the matter as a huge joke, and chaffed her unmercifully about it. But one day the thunderbolt fell.

It was a soft autumn morning, and, as I had been fool enough to sit up the night before into the small hours, I had got up very late, and I was tying my tie when the parlour maid informed me from the other side of the door that Miss Musgrave was in the sitting-room. I hurried downstairs, wondering what could possibly have brought her at such an hour, and as I entered the room she ran to meet me like a hurricane.

'My dear child,' said I, 'what on earth is the matter?'

'Oh! Uncle Charles! Uncle Charles!' she cried. 'I have hardly slept a wink all night – I couldn't rest till I had come to tell you! Oh! you will be so angry – I have got into *such* a scrape, and you must get me out!'

'But what—'

'I didn't mean it,' she broke in, 'indeed, I never, *never* meant it! But he—'

'*He?*' I shouted. – 'Who? What is it? Have you had a row with Major Purefoy?'

'It was Mr Slater!' cried Theodora. 'Dick Slater! How could he? How could he? Oh, what a fool I have been!'

I was staggered.

I took her by the arm and forced her to sit down. She was on the verge of tears.

I got the story from her at last. I cannot give it in the incoherent torrent of her words, and I must do the best I can to put it into consecutive form. Looking back calmly now, I must admit that I was a good deal disturbed.

This is what had happened.

Behind the High Street of Carborough, and connected with it by a long, covered-in alley, there was a certain tumbledown colony of houses called 'Gask's Row', which was inhabited (it is gone now) by a few families of the very poorest class. A faint scent of cabbages pervaded it, emanating from over the battered wooden palings, for the spot was the site of an old market garden which had been sold for building purposes during the early commercial growth of the town, and the walls of the surrounding houses seemed to stare down in contempt on this forlorn remnant of a less ambitious era. A thriving publican named Gask was the owner of the place.

Among the dwellers in Gask's Row was an old widow-woman, whose crippled son precariously supported both her and himself by basket-making. Theodora had been interested in the pair for some time, and often, when she had come to see me, she would ride on into the High Street, and having left Vanity at the stables of the Crown Hotel, disappear down Gask's Alley to visit her friends; and once or twice – so I discovered afterwards – she had come face to face with Dick as she emerged again, and he had fetched her horse and put her into the saddle.

Well, on the previous day she had knocked at the window's

door to find a dismal scene awaiting her. It was the usual story. The old woman's rent was long overdue, and Gask had sent the day before to tell her that if it was not forthcoming in twenty-four hours he would put her and her son into the street. There was one and twopence in the house, and the debt amounted to nearly four pounds.

Theodora had not been to the cottage for some time, and it is probable that, had she gone there every day, she would have heard nothing of their trouble from either mother or son. At four o'clock Gask's man was to return.

The girl put her hand in her pocket. The little she found there was not worth counting, and, at that moment, she owed every penny of her quarter's money; for Vanity's keep ran away with a good deal of it, as Major Purefoy saw to it that he was not groomed for nothing. She was dismayed. The widow sat, with her hands clasped on her knee, waiting for the inevitable as best she might, and Jim, her son, was collecting their trumpery possessions into a heap. It was past a quarter to three and Gask's man might come at any minute, he said. The cripple listened for his step with trepidation, for the man was a rough customer, and there had been rough times with him on the previous day. He entreated Theodora to go. There was no good in her staying.

She rushed out of the house blinded by her own tears, and, coming up the alley, she met Gask's man, very drunk.

Her heart smote her as she saw his condition and thought of those two poor creatures waiting for him in the cottage.

'Go back!' she exclaimed. 'It is not time yet!'

For answer he thrust heavily past her.

'Stop! Stop!' she called after him, between her sobs.

But he took no heed. She turned away in despair, and halfway up the dark passage she nearly ran into Dick Slater's arms.

'What is it? Oh, what has that brute been saying to you?' cried he, as his eyes fell upon her face. 'I saw him turn in here, and I came because I was afraid you might meet him.'

She was struggling with her tears.

'What has he done? What has he done?' reiterated the young man angrily. 'Let me go after him – I'll teach him to frighten you like that!'

'No, no – you don't understand!' cried Theodora, clinging to his arm. 'It's not that – it's nothing to do with me!'

And then she poured out the whole story.

Dick is a much more excitable man than he looks, and he was head over heels in love, and maddened, no doubt, by her touch. And her distress, I suppose, must have been the last straw.

'Don't, don't be so unhappy,' he burst out, as she ended, 'and for Heaven's sake don't cry. Don't you know that I would do anything in the whole world for you? Only let me help them, and let me do it for your sake! I will make everything right, if you will only love me a little; there is nothing on this earth I will not do. Say that I may.'

At this moment a sound fell upon Theodora's ear. It was the town clock in the High Street striking four. She lost her head utterly.

'Oh, yes, yes – anything! If you will only go!' she cried. 'Oh, please, please, stop him before it's too late – now – at once! Go, and I will stay here till you come back. Oh, thank goodness you are here!'

'Go and wait for me at the Library,' said Dick very quietly. 'I will settle everything and bring your horse to you there.'

And, with that, he disappeared down the squalid alley.

It is to be hoped that Jim and his mother slept peacefully that night in their hovel; but Theodora, in her bed at Harsdown, was in a very different plight. Dick had returned to her some time later, and, though he made no allusion to what had passed between them in Gask's Alley, and had merely told her that all was made straight with the landlord, she had recognised vividly that he had not forgotten it, and, as he put her on Vanity's back, there came over her the realisation of what she had done. He did not so much as speak of their next meeting – so she told me afterwards – but, for all that, she recognised what she had let herself in for. Out of her own mouth she had condemned herself, and he had every right to hold her to her words. The idea was terrific.

It makes me laugh now, to look back and see myself and Theodora sitting, one at either side of my untouched breakfast-table, with the eggs and bacon growing cold between us. But I did not laugh then. I was very angry with Dick, and angry with her, too.

I made her drink some coffee, and, when breakfast was done, we went into my study.

'I suppose I shall have to write to him,' I said, as I lit my pipe.

We sat down to concoct the letter. Theodora was humble and

penitent enough to disarm an ogre, but I was not going to be mollified. I was very stern with her.

'I really don't know *what* I said to him, Uncle Charles,' protested she, as I interrogated her, pen in hand. 'I was in such a state of mind that I hardly knew what I was doing. If you had only seen that horrible drunken fellow, Uncle Charles, you would understand – I know you would. I don't even remember whether I promised anything. I only know that he said he'd do it for my sake, and I begged him to help. It's all too dreadful!' wailed Theodora, looking at me with miserable, beautiful eyes. I suppose she looked at Dick like that.

We had got no further when Maria, the parlour maid, brought in a note for her. I had never seen the handwriting before, but, all the same, we both knew by instinct that it came from the house up the road. She read it, and then passed it to me.

Dear Miss Musgrave [it began],
I know you are at Colonel Dormer's, so I am sending this over by hand. I am writing to tell you that I see now how badly I behaved yesterday, and to ask your forgiveness for it. I have no excuse to offer for letting my feelings run away with me as I did, and taking such unpardonable advantage of your distress. But I only spoke the truth, and I am not going to take back one word of it. What I want to assure you is that anything you said in your agitation shall be as if it had never been spoken. If you will do me one kindness, to show that you have forgiven me, you will let me help that woman permanently.
I am,
Very truly yours,
R. SLATER.

'Well,' began Theodora, when I had finished reading, 'what do you think of it, Uncle Charles?'

'What do I think of it?' said I. 'There's only one thing to think of it. The boy's a gentleman. All the same, the next time you meet him, you had better remember that he's a man too!'

But there was no next time for several months to come, for winter was soon upon us, and Theodora went away to pay a couple of visits. I met Dick occasionally when I was out, and, when I did, I made a point of speaking to him. Once I asked him to luncheon, and I was certain that he guessed how much I knew by the steady way in which his eyes met mine when Theodora's name was mentioned. 'I don't care if you *do* know,' they said. I must say I liked him.

It was when Theodora came back from her visits that a thing

happened which put the affair of Dick Slater into the background. I was reading one afternoon by the fire when she walked in, rather to my surprise, for, though I knew she was due back at Harsdown that day, I did not expect her to look in so soon. She wore a long coat, and a little leather bag was in her hand.

'Why, you've come straight from the station,' I remarked, as I noticed it.

She shook her head, and looked at me rather strangely; and my mind went back to that other time when she had suddenly rushed in.

'Tell me,' was all I could say. 'Surely it's not Dick Slater this time!'

'No,' she answered, 'it's worse. I'm never going home again.'

I stared.

'But, my dear child, what are you going to do?' I exclaimed. 'What in Heaven's name—'

'I'm coming here,' she announced. 'Uncle Charles, you must take me in – you will, won't you? If not, of course I can go to the Crown—'

'Don't talk nonsense about the Crown,' I said sharply. 'Really, Theodora, you are too silly.'

It seemed she had arrived at home before luncheon, and, when that meal was over, she was told that Major Purefoy would be glad to speak to her in the smoking-room. It was not often he desired her company, and she opened the door, with an apprehension of coming trouble. The fellow was sitting at his writing-table with a little pile of money and notes before him. He plunged into his subject at once. There were great retrenchments necessary at Harsdown, he said; he and his wife had been looking very carefully into things since she went away, and they had come to the decision that expenses must be cut down yet further in the stable. They meant to keep no more horses; nothing but a pony to draw the mowing-machine and go in the message-cart.

Theodora told me that the suspicion of what he had done had entered her mind with his first words, and that his nervousness as he approached the point was not needed to make her sure of what was coming. She knew that when she went to the stables she would find Vanity's box empty. She stood looking at him, dumb, as he finished his speech.

'But,' he concluded, 'as you paid for his keep and his share of my groom's attention (though nothing towards his actual stabling), I have decided that it is right to give you the whole of the price he fetched from the dealer. Here it is.'

And he pushed the pile of notes and sovereigns towards her.

'You have sold my horse!' cried she, 'You have sold my father's last present to me! How dared you do such a thing?'

'I have given you my reasons,' said Major Purefoy.

And Theodora gathered the whole heap of money into her hand and threw it in his face.

'Never, never, *never* will I go back!' she said, throwing out her hands. 'You needn't ask me, Uncle Charles.'

'My dear, I'm not going to,' said I.

And so Theodora and I set up house together.

It's an ill wind that blows nobody good, and my age gave me the advantage of being able to offer her a home. We were extremely happy too – at least, I know I was – and all went well until the biting days of March set in, and I took to my bed and lay at death's door with double pneumonia.

I was nearly sixty-seven, and at sixty-seven pneumonia is no joke; but, nevertheless, Theodora and a hospital nurse managed between them to drag me from that uncomfortable spot on the borderland of the next world back into my old place in this one. And the experience, as I recovered by slow steps, brought me up short against a fact which both she and I seemed to have over-looked; and I realised that my fag-end of a life was indeed a frail thing to stand between a highly impulsive and very good-looking young woman and the world. She had cut herself adrift from the Purefoys, and, though she had a good many friends, there was not one relation who could be expected to give her a home when my time should come. Her mother had been an only child; Tom Musgrave's one sister was married to an Australian, and his surviving brother – the man to inherit Harsdown after Mrs Purefoy's death – was a bachelor, who spent his life in exploring Africa.

The thought of all this sat on my conscience like a load and got between me and my rest at night; I had abetted the girl in leaving her home, and, instead of it, I had provided her with a makeshift. Her high spirit, her very moderate means, her rashness, her beauty, her generous heart – all these stood round me like a row of accusers, like so many possibilities of destruction. She was only twenty-six; old enough, perhaps, to take care of herself . . . perhaps not . . .

When I had got so far, I had a relapse, and Theodora and the nurse fell to again in their uphill fight with the enemy. Then, having weighed many things over and over again in my mind, I took my final resolution; and on the very first day on which my two dragons consented to leave me alone, I induced them both to go out for a walk. Then I sent for Dick Slater.

We sat together for nearly an hour, he and I. Perhaps I did an unwarrantable thing; perhaps I was clumsy, perhaps I was too outspoken. All the same, it did not seem to offend Dick. He sat straight and stiff in his chair over against mine, like a schoolboy being lectured, and with that rather disconcerting way he has of looking straight into one's eyes. He said but little, but it was pretty easy to see what he felt. I gave him some fatherly advice, and I told him the story of Vanity. I wished Purefoy had been in the room to see him, though it would hardly have been a safe place for the little red-faced man.

'I can never thank you enough, sir,' said Dick, as he took up his hat.

'It isn't a matter of thanks,' I rejoined, 'it's a matter of transferring my responsibilities.'

'Call it what you like,' he answered, 'so long as the result's the same.'

When I heard Theodora's step in the hall, I felt like a traitor, and when she found out that he had been with me she was furious.

'It was simply shameful of Maria to let him in,' she exclaimed, 'and I shall tell her so.'

I sat still, and prayed that Maria would not give me away.

But Maria is Maria (which is high praise), and the nurse said that the visitor had done me good – as, indeed, he had – so Theodora's wrath melted: for it was no feeling against the young man which worried her, but her fears for me. She had spoken to him once or twice since the autumn, for she had felt – and rightly, I thought – that absolute avoidance of him would be undignified after his letter. She did not want him to think she was afraid of him.

As I grew stronger, my anxieties faded a little, and, reflecting on what I had done when in their grip, I told myself that, in spite of my age, I was as rash as Theodora herself. The part I had pledged myself to play struck me as a much more difficult one than I had bargained for, and it was with a feeling not much short of dismay

that I attacked my companion one evening after dinner. The nurse
had gone and we were settling into our old ways again.

'Don't you think, my dear,' I began – and to my guilty mind my
voice seemed to vibrate with hypocrisy – 'that we might ask
young Slater to dine one day? Maria has told me how good he was
in coming to inquire for me when I was ill. You don't dislike him,
do you – I mean, not to that extent?'

'I don't dislike him at all,' said she.

'And you aren't afraid of him, surely, Theodora?'

'Afraid of him? Heavens, no!'

She tossed her head.

'Ask him tomorrow, if you like,' she said, with her chin in the air.
I did, and he came. After dinner I fell asleep.

At eleven o'clock I woke. A few minutes earlier Dick had taken
his leave; he would not disturb Colonel Dormer, he said, and he
only hoped he had not tired him. As a matter of fact, I *was* rather
tired, because keeping in one position with one's eyes shut for any
length of time in a strain. When I opened them, Theodora was
standing with her foot on the fender, gazing into the fire. She
would have looked like a white statue if her face had not been a
little flushed. She made Dick's excuses; she had let him out
quietly, so as not to awake me, she said.

I expressed shame for my rudeness, but she was not attentive.
Suddenly she faced round on me.

'Do you know where Vanity is?' she asked.

By this time I really was rather sleepy, and, I suppose, off my
guard.

'I know,' I murmured, 'I heard.'

'*What?*' cried she.

'That dealer was buying for Slater – I heard it ever so long ago,'
I exclaimed, terrified back into my wits. (Heaven forgive me for
the lie!)

We went upstairs in silence.

A couple of days later a note came for me:

Dear Col. Dormer,
I was telling Miss Musgrave the other night that I have got her horse. So far, I
have kept him out at Barnes's Inn Farm, but now he is here. There is a lot of
business at the office this week and I cannot use him for the next few days. Do
you think she would care for a ride? If so, a line to me will bring him at any
hour she likes. May I have an answer?
    Very truly yours,
                                            R. SLATER.

Evidently I was not the only subtle person to be reckoned with.

Theodora was looking at me with sparkling eyes.

'Do you think I might?' she asked breathlessly.

She rode next day, and the day after, and the day after that; and on the last occasion Dick came to fetch the horse himself; his groom was busy, it appeared. As he led Vanity up a side road to the house behind the walls, he kissed the beast's neck. I know that because an acquaintance of mine was looking out of a back window and saw him do it. The acquaintance was an old lady who was a member of the Society for the Prevention of Cruelty to Animals, and she was much touched by the incident.

'And I always thought he was such a lout,' she added irrelevantly, when she told me.

Evidently that old idea was to die hard.

After this, we saw a good deal of him. What happened to his business in those days I can't imagine and have never asked; but I fancy now that old Slater was in the secret, and gave his son his head.

But the climax did not come until May brought the warm weather which was health to me; and I was going up my front doorsteps one evening, when the door opened, and Dick came rushing out. I caught him by the sleeve. There was that in his expression which made me hurry into the sitting-room. Theodora was there alone; but she did not look as if she had been alone along.

'Did you meet him?' she said, coming up to me. 'I have promised to marry him. Oh, Uncle Charles, you *don't know* how good he is!'

I really could not help smiling; for I had known it perhaps longer than she had. But it would have been too ungenerous to say so then.

And that is two years ago, and I am smiling still.

For we did not do so badly for Theodora – Providence and I.

(1910)

CHARLOTTE PERKINS GILMAN

If I Were a Man

'If I were a man . . .' that was what pretty little Mollie Mathewson always said when Gerald would not do what she wanted him to – which was seldom.

That was what she said this bright morning, with a stamp of her little high-heeled slipper, just because he had made a fuss about that bill, the long one with the 'account rendered', which she had forgotten to give him the first time and been afraid to the second – and now he had taken it from the postman himself.

Mollie was 'true to type'. She was a beautiful instance of what is reverentially called 'a true woman'. Little of course – no true woman may be big. Pretty, of course – no true woman could possibly be plain. Whimsical, capricious, charming, changeable, devoted to pretty clothes and always 'wearing them well', as the esoteric phrase has it. (This does not refer to the clothes – they do not wear well in the least – but to some special grace of putting them on and carrying them about, granted to but few, it appears.)

She was also a loving wife and a devoted mother possessed of 'the social gift' and the love of 'society' that goes with it, and, with all these was fond and proud of her home and managed it as capably as – well, as most women do.

If ever there was a true woman it was Mollie Mathewson, yet she was wishing heart and soul she was a man.

And all of a sudden she was!

She was Gerald, walking down the path so erect and square shouldered, in a hurry for his morning train, as usual, and, it must be confessed, in something of a temper.

Her own words were ringing in her ears – not only the 'last word', but several that had gone before, and she was holding her lips tight shut, not to say something she would be sorry for. But instead of acquiescence in the position taken by that angry little figure on the veranda, what she felt was a sort of superior pride, a sympathy as with weakness, a feeling that 'I must be gentle with her', in spite of the temper.

A man! Really a man – with only enough subconscious memory of herself remaining to make her recognise the differences.

At first there was a funny sense of size and weight and extra thickness, the feet and hands seemed strangely large, and her long, straight, free legs swung forward at a gait that made her feel as if on stilts.

This presently passed, and in its place, growing all day, wherever she went, came a new and delightful feeling of being *the right size*.

Everything fitted now. Her back snugly against the seat-back, her feet comfortably on the floor. Her feet? . . . His feet! She studied them carefully. Never before, since her early school days, had she felt such freedom and comfort as to feet – they were firm and solid on the ground when she walked; quick, springy, safe – as when, moved by an unrecognisable impulse, she had run after, caught, and swung aboard the car.

Another impulse fished in a convenient pocket for change – instantly, automatically, bringing forth a nickel for the conductor and a penny for the newsboy.

These pockets came as a revelation. Of course she had known they were there, had counted them, made fun of them, mended them, even envied them; but she never had dreamed of how it *felt* to have pockets.

Behind her newspaper she let her consciousness, that odd mingled consciousness, rove from pocket to pocket, realising the armoured assurance of having all those things at hand, instantly get-at-able, ready to meet emergencies. The cigar case gave her a warm feeling of comfort – it was full; the firmly held fountain pen, safe unless she stood on her head; the keys, pencils, letters, documents, notebook, chequebook, bill folder – all at once, with a deep rushing sense of power and pride, she felt what she had never felt before in all her life – the possession of money, of her own earned money – hers to give or to withhold, not to beg for, tease for, wheedle for – hers.

That bill – why, if it had come to her – to him, that is – he would have paid it as a matter of course, and never mentioned it – to her.

Then, being he, sitting there so easily and firmly with his money in his pockets, she wakened to his life long consciousness about money. Boyhood – its desires and dreams, ambitions. Young manhood – working tremendously for the wherewithal to make a home – for her. The present years with all their net of cares and hopes and dangers; the present moment when he needed every cent for special plans of great importance, and this bill, long overdue and demanding payment, meant an amount of inconvenience wholly unnecessary if it had been given him when it first came; also, the man's keen dislike of that 'account rendered'.

'Women have no business sense!' she found herself saying. 'And all that money just for hats – idiotic, useless, ugly things!'

With that she began to see the hats of the women in the car as she had never seen hats before. The men's seemed normal, dignified, becoming, with enough variety for personal taste, and with distinction in style and in age, such as she had never noticed before. But the women's—

With the eyes of a man and the brain of a man; with the memory of a whole lifetime of free action wherein the hat close-fitting on cropped hair, had been no handicap; she now perceived the hats of women.

The massed fluffed hair was at once attractive and foolish, and on that hair, at every angle, in all colours, tipped, twisted, tortured into every crooked shape, made of any substance chance might offer, perched the formless objects. Then, on their formlessness the trimmings – these squirts of stiff feathers, these violent outstanding bows of glistening ribbon, these swaying, projecting masses of plumage which tormented the faces of bystanders.

Never in all her life had she imagined that this idolised millinery could look, to those who paid for it, like the decorations of an insane monkey.

And yet, when there came into the car a little woman, as foolish as any, but pretty and sweet-looking, up rose Gerald Mathewson and gave her his seat. And, later, when there came in a handsome red-cheeked girl, whose hat was wilder, more violent in colour and eccentric in shape than any other – when she stood nearby and her soft curling plumes swept his cheek once and again – he felt a sense of sudden pleasure at the intimate tickling touch – and she, deep down within, felt such a wave of shame as might well drown a thousand hats for ever.

When he took his train, his seat in the smoking car, she had a new surprise. All about him were the other men, commuters too and many of them friends of his.

To her they would have been distinguished as 'Mary Wade's husband', 'the man Belle Grant is engaged to', 'that rich Mr Shopworth', or 'that pleasant Mr Beale'. And they would all have lifted their hats to her, bowed, made polite conversation if near enough – especially Mr Beale.

Now came the feeling of open-eyed acquaintance of knowing men – as they were. The mere amount of this knowledge was a surprise to her – the whole background of talk from boyhood up, the gossip of barber shop and club, the conversation of morning and evening hours on trains, the knowledge of political affiliation, of business standing and prospects, of character – in a light she had never known before.

They came and talked to Gerald, one and another. He seemed quite popular. And as they talked, with this new memory and new understanding, an understanding which seemed to include all these men's minds, there poured in on the submerged consciousness beneath a new, a startling knowledge – what men really think of women.

Good, average, American men were there; married men for the most part, and happy – as happiness goes in general. In the minds of each and all there seemed to be a two-storey department, quite apart from the rest of their ideas, a separate place where they kept their thoughts and feelings about women.

In the upper half were the tenderest emotions, the most exquisite ideals, the sweetest memories, all lovely sentiments as to 'home' and 'mother', all delicate admiring adjectives, a sort of sanctuary, where a veiled statue, blindly adored, shared place with beloved yet commonplace experiences.

In the lower half – here that buried consciousness woke to keen distress – they kept quite another assortment of ideas. Here, even in this clean-minded husband of hers, was the memory of stories told at men's dinners, of worse ones overheard in street or car, of base traditions, coarse epithets, gross experiences – known, though not shared.

And all these in the department 'woman', while in the rest of the mind – here was new knowledge indeed.

The world opened before her. Not the world she had been reared in – where Home had covered all the map, almost, and the rest had been 'foreign', or 'unexplored country', but the world as it was – man's world, as made, lived in, and seen, by men.

It was dizzying. To see the houses that fled so fast across the car window, in terms of builders' bills, or of some technical insight into materials and methods; to see a passing village with lamentable knowledge of who 'owned it' and of how its Boss was rapidly aspiring in state power, or of how that kind of paving was a failure; to see shops, not as mere exhibitions of desirable objects, but as business ventures, many mere sinking ships, some promising a profitable voyage – this new world bewildered her.

She – as Gerald – had already forgotten about that bill, over which she – as Mollie – was still crying at home. Gerald was 'talking business' with this man, 'talking politics' with that, and now sympathising with the carefully withheld troubles of a neighbour.

Mollie had always sympathised with the neighbour's wife before.

She began to struggle violently with this large dominant masculine consciousness. She remembered with sudden clearness things she had read, lectures she had heard, and resented with increasing intensity this serene masculine preoccupation with the male point of view.

Mr Miles, the little fussy man who lived on the other side of the street, was talking now. He had a large complacent wife; Mollie had never liked her much, but had always thought him rather nice – he was so punctilious in small courtesies.

And here he was talking to Gerald – such talk!

'Had to come in here,' he said. 'Gave my seat to a dame who was bound to have it. There's nothing they won't get when they make up their minds to it – eh?'

'No fear!' said the big man in the next seat. 'They haven't much mind to make up, you know – and if they do, they'll change it.'

'The real danger,' began the Rev. Alfred Smythe, the new Episcopal clergyman, a thin, nervous, tall man with a face several centuries behind the times, 'is that they will overstep the limits of their God-appointed sphere.'

'Their natural limits ought to hold 'em, I think,' said cheerful Dr Jones. 'You can't get around physiology, I tell you.'

'I've never seen any limits, myself, not to what they want, anyhow,' said Mr Miles. 'Merely a rich husband and a fine house and no end of bonnets and dresses, and the latest thing in motors, and a few diamonds – and so on. Keeps us pretty busy.'

There was a tired grey man across the aisle. He had a very nice wife, always beautifully dressed, and three unmarried daughters, also beautifully dressed, – Mollie knew them. She knew he worked hard, too, and she looked at him now a little anxiously.

But he smiled cheerfully.

'Do you good, Miles,' he said. 'What else would a man work for? A good woman is about the best thing on earth.'

'And a bad one's the worst, that's sure,' responded Miles.

'She's a pretty weak sister, viewed professionally,' Dr Jones averred with solemnity.

The Rev. Alfred Smythe added, 'She brought evil into the world.'

Gerald Mathewson sat up straight. Something was stirring in him which he did not recognise – yet could not resist.

'Seems to me we all talk like Noah,' he suggested drily. 'Or the ancient Hindu scriptures. Women have their limitations, but so do we, God knows. Haven't we known girls in school and college just as smart as we were?'

'They cannot play our games,' coldly replied the clergyman.

Gerald measured his meagre proportions with a practised eye.

'I never was particularly good at football myself,' he modestly admitted, 'but I've known women who could outlast a man in all-round endurance. Besides – life isn't spent in athletics!'

This was sadly true. They all looked down the aisle where a heavy ill-dressed man with a bad complexion sat alone. He had held the top of the columns once, with headlines and photographs. Now he earned less than any of them.

'It's time we woke up,' pursued Gerald, still inwardly urged to unfamiliar speech. 'Women are pretty much *people*, seems to me. I know they dress like fools – but who's to blame for that? We invent all those idiotic hats of theirs, and design their crazy fashions, and, what's more, if a woman is courageous enough to wear common-sense clothes – and shoes – which of us wants to dance with her?

'Yes, we blame them for grafting on us, but are we willing to let our wives work? We are not. It hurts our pride, that's all. We are always criticizing them for making mercenary marriages, but what do we call a girl who marries a chump with no money? Just a poor fool, that's all. And they know it.

'As for Mother Eve – I wasn't there and can't deny the story, but I will say this. If she brought evil into the world, we men have had the lion's share of keeping it going ever since – how about that?'

They drew into the city, and all day long in his business, Gerald was vaguely conscious of new views, strange feelings, and the submerged Mollie learned and learned.

(1914)

NOTES

AMY LEVY
Wise in Her Generation

p.5 a rhodomontade: a brag or a boast.
p.6 quenelle: finely chopped, highly seasoned meatballs.

E. NESBIT
John Carrington's Wedding

p.55 dogcart: a two-wheeled horse drawn cart.

GRACE KING
The Balcony

p.61 armoire: a closet or cupboard.
p.62 tirer la bonne aventure: to play a popular fortune-telling game. One participant would ask questions about their future life and pick numbers which they hoped would give them the answers that they desired. The other participant would read the answers which related to those numbers, and so arrive at the first person's 'real' future.
p.65 peignoir: a loose dressing gown, worn by a woman.

OLIVE SCHRIENER
The Buddhist Priest's Wife

p.69 vis inertiae: force of inertia.

JANE BARLOW
Between Lady Days

p.78 Lady Day: 25 March, Annunciation Day.
p.78 furze: gorse.
p.78 skirl: a shrill cry.
p.80 benison: blessing.

p.81 jaunting-car: a low-set, two-wheeled open with side seats.

p.81 boreen: a small road or track.

p.81 hooding stooks: covering stooks; a stook is a stack of sheaves, set up in a field.

p.82 porther: stout.

p.82 potcheen: distilled illicit liquor, made from potatoes.

p.84 scraws: thin sods.

p.90 colleen dhu: a dark-haired girl.

p.96 sthookawn: literally stupid – hence an idiot or clown.

p.96 asthore: a term of endearment.

MARGARET DELAND
Elizabeth

p.102 drab: a dull grey or brown colour.

SARAH ORNE JEWITT
Miss Esther's Guest

p.126 keeping-room: sitting-room or parlour.

p.127 gambrel roof: a mansard roof; one in which the lower part of the roof is steeper than the upper part.

GEORGE EGERTON
Virgin Soil

p.132 hunter: a pocket watch enclosed within and protected by metal casing.

p.133 chiffonnier: an ornamental cabinet.

p.140 phthisis: a disease of the throat and lungs; often a tubercular illness.

LEILA MACDONALD
Jeanne-Marie

p.142 sabots: wooden shoes.

p.143 métayer: a farmer who pays rent with a fixed portion of crops.

p.145 sage-femme: a midwife.

p.153 was always a gêne: was always embarrassed by it.

FLORA ANNIE STEEL
The Reformer's wife

p.160 babus: a term used both for a scholarly or learned man and, in a derogatory sense, for an Indian clerk who wrote in English.

p.162 siringhi: a stringed instrument.

p.164 zenâna: system of separating the sexes and enclosing women in secluded quarters.

p.165 zenán-khâna: a carriage for women.

p.165 dhoolies: covered litters.

VIOLET HUNT
The Prayer

p.172 portières: curtains hung over doors or door frames.

ELLA D'ARCY
The Pleasure-Pilgrim

p.195 tatterdemalion form: a ragamuffin or a person dressed in ragged clothing.

p.199 the Terpsichorean art: dancing.

KATE DOUGLAS WIGGIN
Huldah the Prophetess

p.217 spider: a frying pan, usually one with feet.

p.217 saleratus: sodium bicarbonate used in baking powder; a leavening agent.

NETTA SYRETT
A Correspondence

p.239 Galatea: a sea nymph who was the daughter of Nerus and Doris.

ELLA D'ARCY
A Marriage

p.279 Cimmerian: a word suggesting dense darkness.

MÉNIE MURIEL DOWIE
An Idyll in Millinery

p.288 toque: a kind of bonnet or cap, often a small and close-fitting one usually without a brim or with a very narrow brim.

p.295 bottines: half-boots or buskins.

KATE CHOPIN
The Storm

p.310 sacque: a loose jacket.

MARGARET OLIPHANT
A Story of a Wedding Tour

p.322 agio: money-changing, or a percentage charged for changing money.

PAULINE E. HOPKINS
Bro'r Abr'm Jimson's Wedding

p.345 avoirdupois: a measurement of weight; weight.

SARA JEANNETTE DUNCAN
A Mother in India

p.360 enteric: enteric fever; typhoid.

EDITH WHARTON
The Reckoning

p.410 contadina: peasant girl.

MARY AUSTIN
The Fakir

p.415 wrapper: a loose outer garment, worn by women.

BIOGRAPHICAL NOTES

MARY AUSTIN (1864–1934) was born in Carlinville, Illinois, and attended Blackburn College where she studied mathematics and science. Having moved to California with her mother in 1888 she married there in 1891. The marriage was not a success and she left her husband and moved to a community of artists. In 1911 she moved to New York, and after an illness moved to Santa Fe in Mexico where she eventually died. With the publication in 1903 of *The Land of Little Rain* it was clear that Austin was helping to create a pioneering regional writing of the Southwest. Significantly, her work was sympathetic to the situation of Native Americans. Other writing includes *The Arrowmaker* (1911); *A Woman of Genius* (1912); *The Ford* (1917); *The Young Woman* (1918); *No. 26 Jayne Street* (1920); *The American Rhythm* (1923); *Everyman's Genius* (1925); *Experiences Facing Death* (1931); *Starry Adventure* (1931); and *Earth Horizons* (1932).

JANE BARLOW (1857–1917) was born in Clontarf, Co. Dublin. She was educated at home. When she was eight her family moved to Raheny where she lived for the rest of her life. In the 1880s she began to publish poetry under the pseudonym of Owen Balair and in 1883 one of her pieces of short fiction appeared in the *Cornhill* magazine. But it was with the success of her collections of short stories *Walled Out* (1886) and *Bogland Studies* (1892) that her name was made as a writer deeply interested in Irish life and capturing an Irish voice, though her phonetic rendering of dialect (admired by some) was often condemned. In 1893 she published *Irish Idylls*. Her novels include *From the East Unto the West* (1898); *Foundings of Fortunes* (1902); *A Strange Land* (1908); *Flaws* (1911) and *In Mio's Youth* (1917).

WILLA CATHER (1873–1947) was born in Virginia and at the age of nine moved with her family to Red Cloud, Nebraska. She studied at the University of Nebraska, Lincoln, and after graduating worked as a journalist, notably in New York where she edited *McClure's Magazine*. Her most significant relationships were with women, firstly Isabelle

McClung and then Edith Lewis, who were her companions for many years. She was a prolific writer of journalism, fiction and literary criticism, and she also produced some poetry. Her writing includes *The Troll Garden* (1905); *O Pioneers!* (1913); *The Song of the Lark* (1915); *My Ántonia* (1918); *One of Ours* (1922) for which she was awarded a Pulitzer prize; *The Professor's House* (1925); and *Sapphira and the Slave Girl* (1940).

KATE CHOPIN (1851–1904) was born in St Louis, Missouri, and though she lived in New Orleans and Cloutierville for a period during her married life, she returned to St Louis in 1884, two years after her husband's death, and died there of a cerebral haemorrhage. By 1889 she had started publishing her writing, and though her first novel *At Fault* appeared in 1890, it was with her collections of stories *Bayou Folk* (1894) and *A Night in Acadie* (1897) that she received enthusiastic acclaim. *The Storm* was written in 1898 but Chopin did not attempt to find a publisher for it, due to its frank treatment of sex and female desire. It remained unpublished until 1969. In 1899 *The Awakening* appeared, Chopin's most famous, and controversial, piece of writing. The hostile response to the novel contributed to the rejection in 1900 of her collection *A Vocation and a Voice*.

(SOPHIA) LUCY CLIFFORD (1849–1929) was born in the West Indies and moved to England where she married a professor of applied mathematics. In 1879, after only four years of married life, he died leaving her with two children. She began to write to support her family and *Anyhow Stories* appeared in 1882, followed by *Mrs Keith's Crime* (1885) which appeared anonymously; *Love Letters of a Worldly Woman* (1891); *Aunt Anne* (1892); *A Wild Proxy* (1893); *A Flash of Summer* (1894); *A Woman Alone* (1901); and a number of other novels, as well as several plays which include *The Likeness of the Light* (1900) and *A Long Duel* (1901).

ELLA D'ARCY (1857–1939) was born in London and educated both in Germany and France. She wrote a number of stories which first appeared in periodicals (particularly *The Yellow Book* of which she was assistant editor) and were collected as *Monochromes* (1895) and *Modern Instances* (1898). In 1898 she published a novel, *The Bishop's Dilemma*. In 1924 her translation of *Ariel* by André Maurois appeared. She also wrote a biography of Rimbaud which was never published. She never married, and she died in Kent.

MARGARET DELAND (1857–1945) was born in Pennsylvania where

most of her works are based. She was a prolific writer, and her most famous work is *John Ward, Preacher* (1887). Other writing includes *The Old Garden and Other Verses* (1886); *Sidney* (1890); *The Story of a Child* (1892); *Mr Tommy Dove and Other Stories* (1893); *Philip and His Wife* (1894); *The Awakening of Helen Richie* (1906); *The Iron Woman* (1911); *The Hands of Esau* (1914); and *Captain Archer's Daughter* (1932). Towards the end of her life she published her recollections from her childhood as *If this be I, as I suppose it be* (1935).

MÉNIE MURIEL DOWIE (1867–1945) was born in Liverpool. She was educated there and in Germany and France. In 1890 she travelled alone in the Carpathians and the following year published *A Girl in the Karpathians*. In the same year she married her first husband and travelled with him to the Balkans and to Egypt. Later she would piece together her observations for her fiction. In 1893 she edited a collection of four biographies called *Women Adventurers*. *Gallia*, her most famous novel, and one of the most influential and scandalous New Woman novels, was published in 1895. This was followed in 1897 by a collection of stories, *Some Whims of Fate*, and later by two novels which draw upon her travels, *The Crook of the Bough* (1898) and *Love and His Mask* (1901). *Things About Our Neighbourhood* appeared in 1903, the year in which she divorced, remarried, and gave up writing. She died in Arizona.

SARA JEANETTE DUNCAN (1862–1922) was born in Brantford, Ontario. For a while she worked as a teacher, and then later was a journalist with the Toronto *Globe* and Montreal *Star*. Her first book, dedicated to the British matron 'Mrs Grundy' was called *A Social Departure: How Orthodocia and I Went Round the World by Ourselves* and was followed in 1891, the year of her marriage, by *An American Girl in London*. After her marriage she moved to Calcutta where her husband worked. While there she wrote editorials for the Indian *Daily News*. The protagonist of her 1891 novel reappeared in 1898 in *A Voyage of Consolation*. Her novels of life in colonial India include *The Simple Adventures of a Memsahib* (1893); *His Honour and a Lady* (1896) and *The Burnt Offering* (1909). She also wrote *A Daughter of Today* (1894); *Those Delightful Americans* (1902); *The Imperialist* (1904); *Cousin Cinderella: A Canadian Girl in London* (1908); *The Consort* (1912); and *His Royal Happiness* (1914). She died in Surrey.

GEORGE EGERTON (Mary Chavelita Dunne) (1859–1945) was born in

Melbourne, but though she lived in Australia, New Zealand, Chile, the United States, Ireland and Norway, she made her reputation in England and died there, in Sussex. She eloped with a married man in 1888 and lived with him in Norway (though she left him rapidly and eventually married twice more) where she learned Norwegian. She began writing the extraordinary short fiction which appeared first in periodicals (which include *The Yellow Book*) and was eventually published as *Keynotes* (1893); *Discords* (1894); *Symphonies* (1897); and *Fantasies* (1898). Her reputation is based upon the first two of these collections and her publisher John Lane, who was also the publisher of *The Yellow Book*, established a series called *Keynotes* (whose contibutors included Ella D'Arcy). Her later writing, which included plays, a translation of Knut Hamsun's *Hunger* which appeared in 1899, short fiction, and adaptations, never lived up to her seminal short fiction of the 1890s, and has received little attention.

MARY BELLE FREELEY was an American writer who appears to have published only a single book, the collection *Fair to Look Upon*, a series of feminist reworkings of the Bible, which was published in Chicago in 1892. Her work lightheartedly anticipates the 1895 publication of *The Woman's Bible*, edited by Elizabeth Cady Stanton. The collection of vignettes appears never to have been published in England and nothing is known of her life.

MARY E. WILKINS FREEMAN (1852–1930) was born in Randolph, Massachusetts. She was the only one of her siblings to reach adulthood. After the death of both her parents she moved into the women-dominated family home of her childhood friend Mary John Wales where she lived in contentment for two decades. She married in 1902 and moved to Metuchen, New Jersey with her husband. The marriage was not a success and in 1922 the couple were formally separated. She died in Metuchen. Freeman was widely recognised for her achievements and won the William Dean Howells gold medal for fiction as well as membership of the National Institute of Arts and Letters. She is most celebrated for her earlier collections of short fiction, and particularly for her representation of women's lives and relationships. Her writing includes the collections *A Humble Romance and Other Stories* (1887) and *A New England Nun and Other Stories* (1891); and the novels *Jane Field* (1893) and *Pembroke* (1894), as well as the play *Giles Corey, Yeoman* (1893) about the Salem witch trials.

CHARLOTTE PERKINS GILMAN (1860–1935) was born in Hartford,

Connecticut. She was a great-niece of Harriet Beecher Stowe which was a source of enormous pride to her. Gilman was a hugely productive writer of fiction and non-fiction as well as poetry; she was a feminist theorist and journalist and, somewhat notoriously, a holder of eugenicist views. Her first marriage was unsuccessful and she moved to California and eventually divorced her husband in 1892. On his remarriage to her best friend she sent her daughter to live with them, an arrangement which caused scandal. She had already been writing for some time, and she continued with speaking tours and lectures, campaigning and writing throughout her life. She married a cousin in 1900 and seems to have enjoyed a happy relationship with him until his death a year before her suicide. Recent feminist scholarship has also investigated the significance of her passionate friendship with Martha Luther. Her most celebrated piece of writing is *The Yellow Wallpaper* (1892), and her *Women and Economics* (1898) confirmed her status as an important feminist social commentator. For many years she edited (and contributed almost all the articles for) *The Forerunner* in which much of her fiction first appeared. Her Utopian novel *Herland* (1915) and its follow-up *With Her in Ourland* (1916) dramatise many of her political positions.

LADY (AUGUSTA) GREGORY (1852–1932) was born, and died, in County Galway. She is best known for her involvement with the Celtic Revival, and was a co-director of the Abbey Theatre along with W. B. Yeats and J. M. Synge. In 1880 she married an Irish nationalist MP who was considerably older than her and the marriage ended with his death in 1892. His autobiography, put together by her, was published two years later and she then began to collect and translate Irish folk legends which included *Cuchulain of Muirthemine* (1902); *Poets and Dreamers* (1902); and *Visions and Beliefs in the West of Ireland* (1920). She learned Gaelic in order to carry out this project. She also wrote a number of one-act plays, a collection of which were published in 1907. Later plays include *The Golden Apple* (1916); *The Dragon* (1920); and *A Story Brought by Brigit* (1924).

PAULINE E. HOPKINS (1859–1930) was born in Portland, Maine, but spent most of her life in Boston, where she eventually died. She wrote two musical dramas, both of which were performed, *Colored Aristocracy* (1877) and *Slave's Escape; or the Underground Railroad* (1879). She worked as a stenographer to support herself, for it was not until 1900 that she published her work. *Contending Forces: A Romance Illustrative of Negro Life North and South*, her first novel, was published by the Colored Cooperative Publishing Company. Her next three novels, *Hagar's Daughter* (published under the pseudonym of Sarah A. Allen); *Of One Blood*; and *Winona*; as well as several pieces of short fiction and a number of non-fiction prose, appeared in the *Colored American Magazine* which the firm also published.

VIOLET HUNT (1866–1942) was born in Durham to a liberal intellectual family. Her father was Alfred William Hunt and her mother Margaret Raine Hunt. She studied at Kensington Art School and did not begin her writing career until she was in her late twenties. In 1908 she began contributing to the *English Review* which had been founded by Ford Madox Hueffer, as he then was. She became increasingly involved in the journal and began a long relationship with him. She wrote a considerable amount of short fiction and several collections appeared, including *Tales of the Uneasy* (1911); and *More Tales of the Uneasy* (1925). Novels include *A Hard Woman* (1895); *The Way of Marriage* (1896); *Unkisst, Unkind!* (1897); The *Celebrity at Home* (1904) and *The Celebrity's Daughter* (1913). She died in London.

VIOLET JACOB (1863–1946) was born in Montrose, Scotland. She wrote a number of novels and some short fiction, but is better known as a poet. Works include *The Sheep-Stealers* (1902); *The Infant Moralist* (1903) (with Helena Mariota Carnegie) which she illustrated too; *The Interloper* (1904); *The Golden Heart and Other Fairy Stories* (1904); *The History of Aythan Waring* (1908); *Irresolute Catherine* (1908); *Stories Told by the Miller* (1909); *The Fortune Hunters and Other Stories* (1910); *Flemington* (1911); *Bonnie Joann and Other Poems* (1921); *The Good Child's Year Book* (1927) which she also illustrated; *The Northern Lights and Other Poems* (1927); *The Lairds of Dun* (1931) and *The Scottish Poems of Violet Jacob* (1944). In 1977 the manuscripts of several pieces of fiction were discovered and these have since been published. She died in Kirriemuir, Angus.

SARAH ORNE JEWETT (1849–1909) was born in South Berwick, New England. She contributed to many magazines and was widely known for her writing of New England life which, though realist, is thematically experimentalist, as recent critics have argued. Her work includes *Deephaven* (1877); *A Country Doctor* (1884); *A White Heron* (1886); *The Country of the Pointed Firs* (1896); and *The Tory Lover* (1901). She never married, but in later life lived with Annie Adams Fields, the essayist and biographer, in a 'Boston marriage'.

GRACE KING (1851–1932) was born in New Orleans to an English-speaking Protestant family and, though not herself Creole, was educated amongst French-speaking Catholic Creoles. At the New Orleans Cotton Centennial she gave a talk titled 'The Heroines of Fiction' and shortly after this, as a result of a chance meeting with the magazine editor Richard Watson Gilder, she wrote 'Monsieur Mott' as a response to George W. Cable's portrayal of Creole life, which she had criticised. The story appeared in the *New Princeton Review* in 1886. Her short stories began to appear in periodicals at this time, and collections include *Tales of Time and Place* (1892) and *Balcony Stories* (1892). She wrote a number of historical works which include *Jean Baptiste Le Moyne, Sieur de Bienville* (1892); *A History of Louisiana* (1893) (a collaborative textbook); *New Orleans: The Place and the People* (1895); *His Men in the Land of Florida* (1898) and *Creole Families of New Orleans* (1921). Her novels include *The Pleasant Ways of St Médard* (1916) and *La Dame de St Hermine* (1924). A posthumous memoir appeared in 1932, *Memories of a Southern Woman of Letters*. She died in New Orleans.

ADA LEVERSON (1862–1933) was born in London, and was educated at home, becoming familiar with English, German and French literature as well as the classics. Though her early work was primarily short fiction and other short pieces, she also published a number of novels. Her output began in *Punch* and other periodicals, including *The Yellow Book*. Oscar Wilde called her the 'Sphinx', a name which has stuck. After her separation from her husband in 1902 she turned to writing novels and produced six between 1907 and 1916, including *The Twelfth Hour* (1907); *Love's Shadow* (1908); *The Limit* (1911) and *Love at Second Sight* (1916). Her last work was *Letters to the Sphinx from Oscar Wilde, with Reminiscences of the Author* (1930.) She died in London.

AMY LEVY (1861–1889) was born in London. She attended Newnham College, Cambridge, becoming the first Jewish woman to matriculate. Her first volume of poetry, *Xantippe and Other Verse*, appeared in 1881 while she was still a student. Yet it was in 1888 with the publication, and controversy surrounding her novel of Jewish life, *Reuben Sachs*, that her reputation was established. Other publications include *A Minor Poet and Other Verses* (1884); two novels, *The Romance of a Shop* (1888) and *Miss Meredith* (1889); and the posthumously published *A London Plane Tree and Other Verse* (1889). She committed suicide in 1889.

LEILA MACDONALD is reputed to be descended from Flora Macdonald. She married Hubert Crackanthorpe, the short-story writer, in 1893, and their brief married life became the subject of sensationalism and gossip after his suicide in the Seine. The little that is known about her comes from details of this relationship. She was primarily a poet, and her work appeared in *The Yellow Book*. Her collection *A Wanderer and Other Poems* was published in 1904.

E. NESBIT (1858–1924) was born in London. She is probably best known for her children's fiction which includes *The Psammead or Five Children and It* (1902); *The Phoenix and the Carpet* (1904); *The Story of the Amulet* (1906); *The Railway Children* (1906); *The Enchanted Castle* (1907); and *The Magic City* (1910); yet she also wrote poetry and novels and short fiction for adults as well as a number of plays. Nesbit was an active socialist and was one of the founding members of the Fabian Society (she named one of her children Fabian and used the pseudonym Fabian Bland for a collaborative piece with her first husband Hubert Bland). Nesbit married her first husband while seven months pregnant and had several affairs during the marriage, as he did. His lover Alice Hoatson lived with the couple, and her two children by Bland were passed off as Nesbit's. Her collections of poetry include *Lays and Legends* (1886); *Leaves of Life* (1888); *A Pomander of Verse* (1895); and *Ballads and Lyrics of Socialism* (1908). Her fiction includes the collection *Grim Tales and Something Wrong* (1893); as well as *The Prophet's Mantle* (1895) (as Fabian Bland); *Homespun* (1896); *The Secret of Kyrieals* (1899) and *The Lark* (1922).

MARGARET OLIPHANT (1828–1897) was born in Scotland. She was educated at home and then in Liverpool. She began to write and publish early, establishing a pattern of productivity which would last throughout her life. After her marriage in 1852, she moved to London, but was widowed seven years later and turned to writing with a greater seriousness than ever in order to support her family. Among her many works are over one hundred novels which include *Passages in the Life of Mrs Margaret Maitland* (1849); *Caleb Field* (1851); *The Greatest Heiress in England* (1879); *Hester* (1883); *Kirsteen* (1890) and *Sir Robert's Fortune* (1895). Her biographies include a *Life of Edward Irving* (1862). Critical and non-fiction work includes a *Literary History of England* (1882) and *The Victorian Age of English Literature* (1892), as well as *Annals of a Publishing House* (1897) (she was associated with *Blackwood's Magazine* and the firm of the same name for some years). Her autobiography appeared in 1899.

OLIVE SCHREINER (1855–1920) was born in Wittbergen, Basutoland, of mixed German and English parentage. She came to London in 1881, carying with her the manuscript of her most celebrated work *The Story of an African Farm* which was published in 1883 under the pseudonym Ralph Iron. In 1889 she returned to South Africa. *Dreams*, a collection of allegories, appeared in 1890, and another collection, *Dream Life and Real Life* two years later. A political allegory *Trooper Peter Hacket of Mashonaland* was published in 1897. In 1911 *Woman and Labour* was published. She lived in England between 1913 and 1920 leaving her estranged husband in South Africa. He came to England briefly that year and they returned to South Africa together. She died in Cape Town. *From Man to Man*, the long novel which she had worked on for many years, appeared in 1926. Her husband edited her letters and wrote a biography after her death.

FLORA ANNIE STEEL (1847–1929) was born in Harrow-on-the-Hill. After her marriage she left England and moved to India in 1868. There she became particularly interested in the situation of Indian women and founded a school for Indian girls in Kasur in 1884. When she left India five years later she estimated that 20,000 had been educated there. After her return from India in 1889 she wrote a significant amount of fiction, which includes *On the Face of the Waters* (1896). She also collected Punjabi folk tales which were published in 1894 as *Tales of the Punjab*. She was a keen supporter of women's rights, and a suffragist. Her writing includes *The Complete Indian Housekeeper and Cook* (1890) (with G. Gardiner) which was reprinted many times; *The Adventures of Akbar* (1913); *India* (1900); *Mahabharata: A Tale of Indian Heroes* (1923); *The Curse of Eve* (1923) which advocates birth control for women; *English Fairy Tales* (1918); *Indian Scene* (1933); and *A Book of Mortals* (1905).

NETTA SYRETT (Christina Middleton) (1865–1943) wrote several plays for children as well as thirty novels. Her writing includes *Nobody's Fault* (1896); *The Garden of Delight* (1905) which she also illustrated; *The Fairy Doll* (1906); *The Child of Promise* (1907); *Anne Page* (1908); *The Endless Journey and Other Stories* (1912); *Barbara of the Thorn* (1913); *Rose Cottingham Married* (1916); *Robin Goodfellow and Other Fairy Plays for Children* (1918); *Strange Marriage* (1930); *Angel Unawares* (1936); and '. . . *As Dreams Are Made On*' (1938). In 1939 her autobiography *The Sheltering Tree* appeared.

EDITH WHARTON (1862–1937) was born in New York. Her first published work was the privately printed *Verses* (1878) and her first collection of short stories, *The Greater Inclination*, was published in 1899, followed by *The Descent of Man and Other Stories* (1904). In 1905 *The House of Mirth* was published, and in 1911 the bleak New England novel *Ethan Frome* appeared. She also wrote criticism such as *The Writing of Fiction* (1925) and on household aesthetics in her collaborative book *The Great Decoration of Houses* (1897). Her many novels include *The Reef* (1912); *The Custom of the Country* (1913); *Summer* (1917); *The Age of Innocence* (1920) for which she won a Pulitzer prize; *A Backward Glance* (1934) for which she won another; and *The Buccaneers* (1938). She was elected both to the National Institute of Arts and Letters and the American Academy of Arts and Letters. She died in France.

KATE DOUGLAS WIGGIN (1856–1923) was born in Philadelphia. She moved to San Franscisco to work in one of the United States' first kindergartens between 1878 and 1884. She is best known as an author of children's books such as *The Bird's Christmas Carol* (1887); *Patsy* (1889); *Rebecca of Sunnybrook Farm* (1903); *The Story of Mother Carey's Chickens* (1911) which was later dramatised. She wrote a number of works on the theory of education, and did a large amount of editorial work. She wrote an autobiography, *My Garden of Memory* (1923), in order to raise funds for a kindergarten.

SUGGESTIONS FOR FURTHER READING

There is a huge body of writing which might, broadly speaking, be relevant to this collection of short fiction. The following list is not intended to be anything other than a brief and personal set of suggestions.

Elizabeth Ammons, *Conflicting Stories: American Women Writers at the Turn into the Twentieth Century* (OUP, 1992). Each chapter of Ammon's timely and political book deals with a different writer or grouping of writers enabling her to read a number of neglected woman writers with and against more celebrated writers, Gertrude Stein with Mary Austin for instance, or Jessie Fauset with Edith Wharton or Willa Cather with Humishuna. A major reappraisal of women's writing in the United States at the turn of the century which reads against the canon.

Gail Cunningham, *The New Woman and the Victorian Novel* (London: Macmillan, 1978). Though this is now somewhat dated it remains a very profitable source.

Kate Flint, *The Woman Reader, 1837–1914* (Oxford: Clarendon Press, 1993). Wide-ranging account of the relation between women and reading. Part IV is particularly pertinent to this collection.

Shirley Foster, *Victorian Women's Fiction: Marriage, Freedom and the Individual* (New Jersey: Barnes & Noble, 1985). Though Foster's focus is on the period just prior to that which this collection encompasses, and her focus is primarily on the novel, this documents women's responses to marriage in this earlier period and is useful background reading.

Pat Jalland, *Women, Marriage and Politics, 1860–1914* (Oxford: Clarendon Press, 1986). Fascinating detail of issues of women's health – particularly pregnancy and childbirth – finance, courtship, and single women, together with many case histories which provide a counterpart to fiction about women and marriage.

Terry Lovell, *Consuming Fiction* (London: Verso, 1987). See indexed references to 'New Woman' writing.

Jane Eldridge Miller, *Rebel Women: Feminism, Modernism and the Edwardian Novel* (London: Virago Press, 1994). Miller's primary interest is in the position of women and writing in Britain in a period more often associated with male writers such as E. M. Forster and D. H. Lawrence than with women like May Sinclair, Ada Leverson and Violet Hunt. This is not a book exclusively concerned with women's writing, but it is a welcome antidote to some of what has been written on the period, and an useful addition to current scholarship on the 1890s.

Lyn Pykett, *The 'Improper' Feminine* (London: Routledge, 1992). Again, see indexed references.

Elaine Showalter, *Sexual Anarchy: Gender and Culture at the* Fin de Siècle (London: Bloomsbury (1990) 1991). Too famous, perhaps, to need much introduction and too influential to be left out. Showalter's work is both accessible and scholarly.

Claudia Tate, *Domestic Allegories of Political Desire: The Black Heroine's Text at the Turn of the Century* (OUP, 1992). Another important rereading and redefining of the period, challenging assumptions and adding new voices to debates about the turn of the century.

Judith R. Walkowitz, *City of Dreadful Delight: Narratives of Sexual Danger in Late-Victorian London* (London: Virago (1992) 1994). A fascinating and sophisticated work of cultural history. Chapter five, on the Men and Women's Club is particularly useful in relation to this collection.

ACKNOWLEDGEMENTS

The editor and the publishers wish to thank the following for permission to use copyright material:

Mrs J. Pearson on behalf of the Estate of Flora Annie Steel for 'The Reformer's Wife', 1903;

Random House, Inc for Charlotte Perkins Gilman, 'If I Were A Man' from *The Charlotte Perkins Gilman Reader*, pp. 32–7;

Colin Smythe Ltd on behalf of the Estate of Lady Gregory for 'The Wedding of Maine Morgor' from *Cuchulain of Muirthemne*, 1902;

The University of Nebraska Press for Willa Cather, 'Tommy the Unsentimental' as edited in *Willa Cather's Collected Short Fiction*, 1892–1912, ed. Virginia Faulkner. Copyright © 1965, 1970 by the University of Nebraska Press. Copyright © renewed 1993 by the University of Nebraska Press.

Every effort has been made to trace all the copyright holders but if any have been inadvertently overlooked the publishers will be pleased to make the necessary arrangement at the first opportunity.